No Clue
at the Inn

KATE KINGSBURY

BERKLEY PRIME CRIME, NEW YORK

THE BERKLEY PUBLISHING GROUP
Published by the Penguin Group
Penguin Group (USA) Inc.
375 Hudson Street, New York, New York 10014, USA

Penguin Group (Canada), 90 Eglinton Avenue East, Suite 700, Toronto, Ontario M4P 2Y3, Canada
(a division of Pearson Penguin Canada Inc.)
Penguin Books Ltd., 80 Strand, London WC2R 0RL, England
Penguin Group Ireland, 25 St. Stephen's Green, Dublin 2, Ireland (a division of Penguin Books Ltd.)
Penguin Group (Australia), 250 Camberwell Road, Camberwell, Victoria 3124, Australia
(a division of Pearson Australia Group Pty. Ltd.)
Penguin Books India Pvt. Ltd., 11 Community Centre, Panchsheel Park, New Delhi—110 017, India
Penguin Group (NZ), Cnr. Airborne and Rosedale Roads, Albany, Auckland 1310, New Zealand
(a division of Pearson New Zealand Ltd.)
Penguin Books (South Africa) (Pty.) Ltd., 24 Sturdee Avenue, Rosebank, Johannesburg 2196,
South Africa

Penguin Books Ltd., Registered Offices: 80 Strand, London WC2R 0RL, England

This is a work of fiction. Names, characters, places, and incidents either are the product of the author's
imagination or are used fictitiously, and any resemblance to actual persons, living or dead, business
establishments, events, or locales is entirely coincidental. The publisher does not have any control over
and does not assume any responsibility for author or third-party websites or their content.

NO CLUE AT THE INN

A Berkley Prime Crime Book / published by arrangement with the author

PRINTING HISTORY
Berkley Prime Crime trade edition / November 2003
Berkley Prime Crime mass-market edition / November 2005

Copyright © 2003 by Doreen Roberts Hight.
Cover art by Dan Craig.
Cover design by Judith Murello.

ISBN: 0-425-19849-9

BERKLEY® PRIME CRIME
Berkley Prime Crime Books are published by The Berkley Publishing Group,
a division of Penguin Group (USA) Inc.,
375 Hudson Street, New York, New York 10014.
The name BERKLEY PRIME CRIME and the BERKLEY PRIME CRIME design
are trademarks belonging to Penguin Group (USA) Inc.

PRINTED IN THE UNITED STATES OF AMERICA

10 9 8 7 6 5 4 3 2 1

Praise for
the Pennyfoot Hotel and Manor House
mysteries of Kate Kingsbury . . .

"A charming cast of characters." —*The Literary Times*

"Sitting Marsh and its array of small-town citizens are realistically and humorously depicted."

—*The Mystery Reader*

"Likable characters, period details, and a puzzle that kept me guessing until the end . . . Very enjoyable."

—*Mystery News*

"Delightful and charming." —*Painted Rock Reviews*

"Always most enjoyable." —*I Love a Mystery*

"Well-drawn characters." —*Publishers Weekly*

"Full of humor, suspense, adventure and touches of romance . . . delightful." —*Rendezvous*

"A fun-to-read historical mystery." —*Midwest Book Review*

"Trust me, you will not be disappointed . . . Ms. Kingsbury has created a memorable series with delightful characters that can be enjoyed over and over again."

—*Myshelf.com*

"Sublime . . . Fascinating mid-twentieth-century mystery."

—*BookBrowser*

Visit Kate Kingsbury's website at
www.doreenrobertshight.com

Manor House Mysteries by Kate Kingsbury

A BICYCLE BUILT FOR MURDER
DEATH IS IN THE AIR
FOR WHOM DEATH TOLLS
DIG DEEP FOR MURDER
PAINT BY MURDER
BERRIED ALIVE
FIRE WHEN READY

Pennyfoot Hotel Mysteries by Kate Kingsbury

ROOM WITH A CLUE
DO NOT DISTURB
SERVICE FOR TWO
EAT, DRINK, AND BE BURIED
CHECK-OUT TIME
GROUNDS FOR MURDER
PAY THE PIPER
CHIVALRY IS DEAD
RING FOR TOMB SERVICE
DEATH WITH RESERVATIONS
DYING ROOM ONLY
MAID TO MURDER
NO CLUE AT THE INN

ACKNOWLEDGMENTS

My grateful thanks to my wonderful, dedicated editor, Cindy Hwang, for all the times you've come through for me. Bless you.

To my husband, Bill, for your unfailing support and understanding. You are, indeed, the wind beneath my wings.

To Anne Wraight, in Canterbury, England, for all the incredible books, magazines, and brochures that give me so much pleasure and so much information. I'm truly grateful.

CHAPTER
❧ 1 ❧

"I simply cannot believe we are almost at the end of 1912. How time does fly." Cecily Sinclair Baxter waited for a response from her husband, who sat at the opposite end of the breakfast table, hidden behind the pages of the *London Times*.

When he didn't answer, she picked up the envelope from the embossed silver platter and carefully slit it open with a slim ivory letter opener. The letter was addressed to both Mr. and Mrs. Hugh Baxter, and normally she allowed her husband to take care of such matters. Since Baxter was engrossed in his newspaper, however, she felt justified in taking matters into her own hands.

In any case, she was most curious to know why the cousin of her previous husband had gone to the trouble of penning a letter to her, instead of ringing her on the telephone.

She was rather proud of the fact that her house, situated just yards from the common in the fashionable London suburb of Wimbledon, was one of the few to boast a telephone. It had taken weeks of arguing with the telephone company, but finally, thanks to Baxter having set up his business as a personal financial advisor right there in their home, the coveted line had been set up.

The problem now was that none of her personal friends had a telephone with which to ring her. Unless they used the public system, of course, which was terribly inconvenient and somewhat demeaning. Edward Sandringham, on the other hand, had access to a telephone right there at the Pennyfoot Hotel. With a sigh, she corrected herself. It wasn't a hotel now. Edward had turned it into some kind of motoring club. Thank heavens he'd at least kept the name of Pennyfoot.

She unfolded the single sheet of paper, noticing at once the crest embedded at the top of the page. A large scrolled *P* entwined with double *C*. Pennyfoot Country Club. She had to admit, the name did hold rather a ring to it.

Quickly she scanned the first few lines, then uttered an audible gasp that prompted Baxter to lower the pages of his precious newspaper.

"Is something wrong?"

"No . . . well, yes . . . that is . . ."

The pages rattled as Baxter laid them down on the table. "What *is* it, my dear? Not Michael, I hope? Andrew?"

Cecily stared at him, her heart beginning to thump with alarming irregularity. "No, no, not the boys. As far as I know, that is. I haven't heard from either one of them in absolutely ages. You'd think they'd have the time to jot down a few words to their mother now and then, wouldn't you?"

Baxter narrowed his light gray eyes. "The letter?"

"So sorry, darling. You know how distracted I get when it comes to my two sons." Cecily smiled fondly at her husband. They had been married less than two years, yet at times it seemed to her as if they had been married forever. On the other hand, every detail of their wedding, so soon after the death of Edward VII, was still as vivid in her mind as if it had all happened mere days ago.

Baxter's eyes crinkled at the edges. "Yes, I do know how easily you are distracted, my love. But I am on pins and needles with apprehension, wondering what startling news could possibly be contained in that letter that is causing it to tremble in your hands."

Cecily took a steadying breath. "Perhaps I should read it to you."

"I think that is an excellent idea."

"I'll get straight to the important part."

"Please do."

She wrinkled her nose at him, then began reading. "'I have been called away on urgent business to South Africa, where I shall be spending several weeks. Unfortunately this means I shall be absent from the club during the Christmas Season. I recently lost my manager, and I haven't been able to find another one as yet. I hesitate to ask, but I was wondering if you both would consent to manage things at the Pennyfoot for me while I'm away.'"
She looked up, studying her husband's face in an effort to gauge his thoughts.

He said nothing at first, but raised his hand and smoothed it over his dark hair.

She absently noted that the gray wings at his temples had widened somewhat since they'd left Badgers End. Her heart skipped with excitement. They had not returned to the Pennyfoot since then. It would be so marvelous to go back there for a short while, and relive all the wonderful memories.

Baxter, however, seemed less enthusiastic about the news. "Spend Christmas at the Pennyfoot . . . *working?*"

"Oh, come now. It will be fun!" Cecily leaned forward, determined now to take Edward up on his offer. "We can have a reunion! We'll invite Mrs. Chubb and Gertie down from Scotland. It's been so long since we saw our godchildren. Goodness, the twins must be so big now. How I'd love to see James and Lilly again!" She clasped her hands and gazed appealingly into her husband's handsome face.

"But, my dear, think of the work involved. You must remember how tiring it was when you owned the Pennyfoot. You worked such dreadfully long hours for weeks . . . no, months on end."

"So did you. I really don't think I could have kept up with it all if you hadn't been my manager." Cecily breathed a sigh. "Those were wonderful days."

"Viewed from a distance, I suppose they do seem that way. I'm not so sure, however, that I would enjoy being at the beck and call of everyone again. In any case, managing a country club, I imagine, must be quite different from managing a hotel. We don't have the experience—"

"Piffle!" Cecily straightened her back. "What can be so different? People stay there, they eat there, they are entertained there, and they go home. We can hire Madeline to help with the Christmas decorations, and we can put on a pantomime. I'm quite sure Phoebe would love to help with that. I wonder if the members of her dance team are still living in Badgers End. It will be so good to see them all again. I've missed everyone so much. Oh, there's so much to think about! I shall start making notes this very minute."

It was Baxter's turn to utter a deep sigh. "I can see you've made up your mind about this. Does Edward say exactly when he would want us down there?"

Cecily quickly read through the rest of the letter. "No, he doesn't. I shall have to ring him. He says he wrote the letter rather than using the telephone because he wanted to give us time to think it over." She looked up again. "But it will be Christmas in another month. We simply have to decide right away."

Baxter picked up his teaspoon and stirred his tea, even though Cecily knew quite well he had stirred it earlier. She watched him anxiously, prepared to argue against every one of his objections.

"Why don't I give the chap a ring," Baxter said at last. "I'll find out exactly what the duties would entail. Then we can make a final decision."

Cecily let out her breath. "Then you'll ring him today? He's very likely anxious to hear our answer."

The spoon chinked against the bone china as he laid it in the saucer. "I promise I'll ring him just as soon as I get into my office." He glanced at the pendulum clock ticking away on the wall. "Which I must do right now if I'm to get any work done this morning." He rose, bringing Cecily to her feet as well. "I will see your later, then?"

Cecily swept around the table and raised her chin for

his kiss. "Please don't bury yourself in there for too long. You know how involved you become in your work."

"I won't." He dropped a light kiss on her mouth. "I'll join you for the midday meal."

"You won't forget to ring Edward?"

"First thing, I swear."

"Thank you, darling." She watched him leave the room, then wandered to the window that overlooked the street. The light clip-clop of horses' hooves echoed across the pavement as a carriage swept by, while two ladies wearing warm coats and decorative hats hovered on the curb.

A thick, damp fog hung dismally in the air, almost obliterating the row of elegant houses opposite her. The clammy London fog was so different from the light sea mists of Badgers End.

Sometimes days would pass by before she saw the sun, whereas the ocean mists of Southeast England would dissipate as soon as the sun had warmed the sky, no matter the time of year.

How she missed the sweeping bay with its bobbing fishing boats—the white cliffs rising high above, topped by the cool green grass of Putney Downs.

When she closed her eyes, she could see so clearly the sparkling white walls of the Pennyfoot Hotel, with its roof garden nestled among the chimney pots, dominating the majestic Esplanade with its grandeur.

She missed the rose garden and the bowling greens. She missed the picturesque church and the vicarage. But most of all she missed her good friends—Phoebe Carter-Holmes, with her fussy little ways and her determination to keep up appearances at all costs, and the gentle, sometimes mysterious, Madeline Pengrath, with her strange healing powers and her uncanny ability to see beyond the boundaries confining mere mortals.

The ache in her throat was almost unbearable, and she turned away from the window in an effort to dismiss the bittersweet memories from her mind. At that moment the door across the room was flung open, and Baxter charged in, his face reddened by his obvious agitation.

"I'm sorry, Cecily, but we will *not* be working at the Pennyfoot Country Club during the Christmas Season."

Dismay held her rigid. "Why ever not? I don't understand. It can't be that difficult? Surely Edward can——"

"Forgive me for interrupting, my dear, but I'm quite sure you will agree with me when I tell you what Sandringham has just told me."

A feeling of foreboding, such as she hadn't felt since her adventurous days at the Pennyfoot, chilled her. "What is it? What's happened?"

"Sandringham said in his letter that he'd recently lost his manager?"

"Yes, I believe he did. But what——"

"He didn't say *where* he'd lost him, I presume?"

"No, just that he hadn't had time to find anyone else, but——"

"Well, I can tell you where he lost him." Baxter sank down heavily on his chair then, apparently realizing that his wife was still standing, shot up again. "The poor blighter drowned in an abandoned well."

"A well?" Cecily frowned. "What well?"

"According to Sandringham, it was on vacant farmland

that was waiting to be sold. The chap was wandering around there and *supposedly* fell in."

Something in Baxter's tone of voice worried Cecily. She sat down, thus allowing her husband to do likewise. "Supposedly? Are you suggesting it wasn't an accident?"

Baxter dismissed the question with a jerk of his hand. "I don't know what to think. Sandringham seemed to think there was something odd about it. He said the chap was known to have one too many down the pub at times, but he wasn't a habitual drunkard. No one seems to know why the poor blighter was wandering around a deserted farm in the first place. It wasn't as if he had money to buy the place. All very suspicious if you ask me."

"What do the constables have to say about it?"

"Well, you know what Northcott is like. Ignoring the whole thing, as usual. Sandringham wanted him to notify the inspector, but Northcott told him there wasn't any evidence of foul play. Didn't satisfy Sandringham, though. He said he knew the chap rather well. Said he didn't think he was the sort to poke around a place like that on his own, much less careless enough to fall into a well."

Cecily felt a familiar tingling in her ears. It had been a long time, but she remembered well the tantalizing urge to delve into a mysterious situation and search for answers. That urge had landed her in more trouble than she cared to admit, but oh, how she missed the excitement of the hunt and the tremendous satisfaction of cornering the prey.

"You can wipe that bemused expression from your face," Baxter said, somewhat shortly. "I know what you're thinking and the answer is an irrevocable no. We are not going down to Badgers End this Christmas. I won't have you risking your life, not to mention mine, in yet another reckless escapade. If this manager chap has met with a violent end by someone else's hand, then the constabulary can take care of it. And that's the end of it."

Cecily stiffened her spine. "I think not, my dear husband. This is as much my decision as yours, and at the very least, we can discuss it."

Baxter's face, when he so desired, could be as cold and as impervious as an iceberg. "May I remind you that you are my wife, and as such, I have a responsibility for your health and well-being."

"You may remind me all you like," Cecily said evenly. "Nevertheless, you are very well aware of the contempt with which I hold such old-fashioned notions. I am your wife, undoubtedly, but I am also your partner. My wishes are every bit as important as yours. I was under the impression we had agreed upon that before our wedding."

"You agreed. I simply neglected to raise an objection."

"Because you knew very well I would not have married you had you done so."

Baxter's features relaxed just a little bit. "Perhaps so. Very well then, I shall rephrase my words. I'm far too fond of you to allow you to risk bodily harm in the pursuit of what could possibly turn out to be another of your pesky investigations. Not to mention the risk of inciting the wrath of Police Inspector Cranshaw, who no doubt is under the blissful, if sadly mistaken, assumption that you had left your nefarious past behind you forever."

Cecily allowed him to finish, then folded her hands and regarded him with her brows drawn together. "You know, Bax, sometimes I think I liked you better when you were a man of few words."

After a long moment, Baxter's mouth twitched into a reluctant smile. "Indubitably, my dear madam."

"The fact remains, Edward is in dire need of someone to take care of the Pennyfoot while he is away. You and I share a vast amount of experience and knowledge that is simply going to waste right now. It would be criminal to refuse Edward the benefit of our administration, particularly since he hasn't been able to find anyone to replace his manager. You know as well as I do how crucial the Christmas Season is to a hotel in a place like Badgers End. He cannot simply close the place down. It would likely ruin him."

"It's not a hotel. It's a country club."

"I'd prefer it, dearest, if you didn't split hairs."

"It's not exactly splitting hairs. One has to be a member to stay at a country club, and members are bound by certain rules and regulations. We shall have to learn those rules and see that our patrons abide by them."

"You always did enjoy flaunting your authority. You'll be in your element."

Conflicting expressions flitted across his face, and taking advantage of his indecision, Cecily pressed her argument home. "Besides," she added quietly, "you know very well that James would never forgive us."

It was a low blow, and one that she knew would strike home. Baxter owed his life to her dead husband, and vice versa. As he lay dying, James had thought enough of his friend to extract a promise from Baxter to take care of his wife in the event of his death.

Baxter had fulfilled that promise with loyalty, integrity, and commitment. The sole uncertainty he had confessed to on the eve of their wedding was that James might not approve of their marriage.

Cecily had settled his doubts on that score. Now she waited, holding her breath, wondering if the memory of James could still influence the decisions of this resolute and beloved man who had taken her as his wife.

It seemed a long time before Baxter answered her. The clock ticked loudly in the otherwise silent room, while outside a dog barked at a passing horse and carriage, and the faint roar of a motor car—a sound Cecily would never get used to—signaled yet another roadhog about to invade the fashionable street.

Finally, Baxter heaved a sigh, rose from his chair, and moved to her side. He reached for her hand and brought it to his lips, before murmuring, "You make it difficult for me to refuse. If I agree to this, however, I must ask two things."

She eyed him warily. "And they are?"

"First, since I am well aware it is futile to forbid you to poke your nose into what doesn't concern you, I must insist that you swear you will not take a step in any direction without informing me of your intentions."

She nodded in relief. "Done. And the second?"

"That at all times, while in public, you call me by my given name, Hugh. I refuse to answer to Baxter. It gives one the impression I'm still your underling."

She could feel her grin stretching her mouth. "I have a confession to make. Even while I was the owner of the Pennyfoot, and you were my manager, never once did I ever think of you as my underling. I was always in awe of you."

Baxter grunted, though she could tell he was pleased. "Then, my dear madam, you had a remarkable way of concealing your reverence." He bent down and brushed her lips with his. "You will call me Hugh?"

"I will call you anything you want, as long as we are together again at the Pennyfoot Hotel."

"The Pennyfoot Country Club."

Cecily sighed. "Very well, but it will always be a hotel to me, no matter what changes Edward may have wrought." She caught his hand and clung to it. "Oh, Bax, think of it. Badgers End at Christmastime. It always was my favorite time of the year there."

His eyes mirrored his concern. "You have missed it that much?"

She pressed his hand to her cheek. "I can be happy anywhere with you, you must know that. But Badgers End is special. It's where we fell in love. It will always be my favorite place to be with you."

He squeezed her hand, then let it go. "I can only hope, my love, that we are not making a mistake. It will be difficult enough after all this time to fall back into the managing duties of a large establishment. But if there is a potential crime complicating matters, I dread to think what might happen."

"You always did worry too much." Cecily rose from her chair. "There could be nothing more to this man's death than a simple accident."

"And if it's not an accident?"

She smiled blithely at him. "Then, dear Hugh, I imagine we will be reliving more than our managerial duties."

"And that," Baxter said heavily, "is exactly what worries me."

CHAPTER

❧ 2 ❧

Ten days later, Cecily alighted from the carriage, her heart too full to speak as she gazed at the impressive facade of the Pennyfoot Country Club. She noticed at once that the front entrance had been refurbished, the new double doors making the approach to the hotel even grander.

Memories crowded her mind—faces, voices, laughter, and tears. Visions of elegant women in magnificent gowns floating across the sprung floor of the vast ballroom while musicians filled the air with stirring melodies. Memories of nimble waiters weaving between tables bearing trays loaded with sumptuous meals.

In its heyday the Pennyfoot had been the most renowned hotel on the southeast coast. His Majesty Edward VII had stayed there many times, and the celebrated composer,

Jerome Kern, had paid them a visit from America, though no one had known who he was until much later. Aristocrats, gamblers . . . even smugglers . . . had been signed into the guest books, and more than one philanderer had whiled away a weekend in pleasurable pursuit of a comely maiden.

Cecily's eyes misted as she remembered Gertie, her chief housemaid, enormous in her pregnancy, heaving huge pots of water to the stove, while frail little Doris stoked the coals. She could picture Mrs. Chubb, the belligerent housekeeper, arms folded across her bountiful bosom, face smudged with flour, glaring at Michel, the French chef, whose accent disappeared with a full glass of excellent brandy. How she missed them all.

"Hope you had a pleasant journey on the way down from the Smoke, m'm."

Cecily tucked her hands inside her muff, and smiled at the eager young man who had met them at the railway station and driven them with such gusto down her beloved Esplanade. "Yes, thank you. Raymond? Is that your name?"

The young man nodded, his dark eyes narrowed against the stiff, salty breeze from the sea. "Yes, m'm. I'm the stable manager, though now it's horses *and* motor cars. Raymond Stebbings at your service." He touched the brim of his cap. "Welcome back to Badgers End, Mrs. Baxter."

"Thank you, Raymond. It's very good to be back." She took a deep, cleansing breath of the fresh sea air and let it out on a sigh. Although thick clouds had turned the water a dark gray, the ocean seemed fairly calm, with only a few white flecks of foam here and there.

How clearly she remembered the sharp smell of salty brine, the fierce chill of the wind on her cheeks, the mournful cries of hungry seagulls wheeling above the gentle waves. Caught up in nostalgia, she was speechless again.

Baxter moved to her side. "I, for one, Raymond, will feel a good deal more welcome once we are enclosed inside the warm walls of this establishment instead of freezing out here on the oceanfront."

Raymond gave him a smart salute. "Sorry, sir. If you'll come this way, I'll take you into the club. I'll see to your luggage later."

Baxter nodded and, grasping Cecily's arm, followed the lithe young man up the sparkling steps of the Pennyfoot to the enormous double doors, upon which hung a pair of lush holly wreaths, trimmed with red and gold velvet ribbon.

Raymond opened the door with a sweeping gesture that narrowly missed knocking Cecily off her feet. Baxter clicked his tongue in annoyance, but Cecily hurried into the foyer, anxious to see what changes Edward had made to the interior.

To her immense satisfaction, everything looked much the same, though the blue Axminster had been replaced by plush gold and green carpeting that just about covered the entire floor of the foyer and swept grandly up the curving staircase.

The grandfather clock still stood in the corner, partially obscured by a small Christmas tree. The long desk where the guests were registered seemed to have been unaltered by Edward's renovations.

In front of the desk, a tall, boney-faced woman in a

black afternoon dress and frilly white apron stood between two nervous-looking housemaids.

Raymond stood back, allowing Cecily and Baxter to approach, and the woman bustled forward, dipping a slight curtsey as she reached them.

"Mr. and Mrs. Baxter, in the absence of Mr. Sandringham, who regrets he was unable to wait for your arrival, it is my extreme pleasure to welcome you to the Pennyfoot Country Club. My name is Miss Bunkle, I'm the Pennyfoot's housekeeper, and I'd like to introduce two of our housemaids, Jeanette and Moira." She beckoned with a sharp movement of her hand. "Come forward, girls."

In their navy blue ankle-length dresses and white aprons, the two maids looked somewhat alike. Both of them seemed impossibly thin, with dark hair scraped back from their scrubbed faces. The difference was in the eyes. Jeanette's confident brown eyes sparkled with mischief, while those of the younger girl, Moira, were lighter gold in appearance and clouded with anxiety, as if she were terrified she would make a mistake.

Both maids darted forward and dropped a curtsey, muttering, "Good morning, madam. Good morning, sir."

"Should you require a personal maid," Miss Bunkle said, "Jeanette will be most happy to oblige."

"Thank you, Miss Bunkle, but I doubt that will be necessary." Cecily gave the maid an encouraging smile.

Jeanette seemed disappointed, while Miss Bunkle appeared a trifle put out. "Very well, madam," she said, her expression suggesting that Cecily had made a grave error in declining a personal maid.

Cecily turned her attention to the housekeeper, noting

with some surprise the knitting needle securing the tight bun on top of her head. Apparently Miss Bunkle was not one to observe traditional costume. "My husband and I are happy to be back in the Pennyfoot Hot . . . Country Club. As soon as we are settled, we'll schedule a meeting and familiarize ourselves with our duties."

"Very well, madam." Miss Bunkle flicked her fingers at Jeanette. "Take Mr. and Mrs. Baxter to their suite and see that they have everything they need. Then I'll see you in the kitchen. Raymond, fetch the luggage and bring it up to the suite right away."

"Right ho!" Raymond winked at Moira, earning a frown from Miss Bunkle, before disappearing through the front doors.

Jeanette headed for the stairs and Cecily followed, conscious of Miss Bunkle's sharp gaze on their backs as she and Baxter ascended to the first floor.

"You'll be in Mr. Sandringham's suite," Jeanette explained as she led them down the hallway to what used to be Cecily's rooms. "He's done it up a bit since you was here, m'm. Got it all posh, he has."

She paused at the door, unlocked it, and pushed it open. Cecily walked in, her eyes widening at the sight that met her eyes. The wall between the sitting room and the room next door had been removed, doubling the space. Sleek settees and armchairs replaced her Queen Anne furniture, and the chaise longue had been relegated to the bedroom, where, much to her astonishment, a private and quite modern water closet had been installed.

"Oh, my." She clutched her throat at the sight of

gleaming brass fixtures above a marble basin, and a footed tub that looked big enough to hold two people. "I've never seen anything quite like this."

Baxter, staring over her shoulder, seemed dumbfounded.

"Only one like it on this part of the coast, m'm," Jeanette informed her. "Even the hotels in Wellercombe don't have private WCs like this."

"I say," Baxter murmured, "Sandringham certainly does well for himself."

Cecily dropped her muff on the bed. "This is all very nice. Tell me, Jeanette. How do you like working at the Pennyfoot Country Club?"

Jeanette seemed surprised at the question. "I like it very well, m'm. Miss Bunkle can be a bit of an old biddy at times, and Frenchie gets on my nerves with his banging and shouting, but—"

Baxter frowned. "Frenchie?"

"Yes, sir. Frenchie. The chef."

Cecily hid a smile. "She's referring to Michel," she said solemnly.

"Oh, good Lord. I'd forgotten he was still here."

"Well, he's still in the kitchen," Jeanette said with a smirk, "but I wouldn't say he's all there, if you get my meaning. Especially when he's been at the brandy."

Cecily saw Baxter's frown of disapproval and hurriedly asked, "What about the manager, Mr. Wrotham? Was he a good man to work for?"

Jeanette shook her head, while Cecily did her best to ignore Baxter's raised eyebrows. "No one liked him, m'm. Least, no one as I know. Had a big opinion of himself, he did. Talked to everyone like dirt. Like he was better'n anybody else. You'd have thought he owned the place the way he carried on sometimes. I'm not surprised someone done him in."

Baxter cleared his throat. "Quite, quite. Well, run along now, girl. Mrs. Baxter will let you know if she needs you later on."

"Yes, sir." Jeanette bobbed an untidy curtsey and hurried out, pulling the door closed behind her.

Baxter muttered an oath under his breath. "That girl is entirely too familiar. Miss Bunkle will have to keep her in her place."

Cecily sank onto the bed and began easing off her elbow-length gloves. "I rather think we'll have to get used to some relaxation of customs. Things are changing so rapidly it's difficult to keep up with them."

"The world may be changing," Baxter said firmly, "but manners are not. As long as we are in charge of this establishment, I insist that the staff treat everyone with the proper decorum. Just as they did when we were here. It hasn't been that long since we left, and I refuse to allow the integrity and the reputation of the Pennyfoot Hotel to be besmirched by impertinent staff. I don't care who they are."

Cecily smiled as she watched him pace back and forth, his hands behind his back. "Bax, darling, as you yourself pointed out so adamantly, this is no longer our Pennyfoot Hotel. It's Edward's country club. Whether we like it or not, things have changed."

"That doesn't mean we have to put up with insubordinate staff. I certainly don't intend to, and I sincerely hope that you will not stand for it, either. Not only is the Pennyfoot's reputation at stake, but ours, as well. If Edward has allowed the standards to deteriorate, then it will be in everyone's best interests to restore some sense of decorum." He paused in front of her, a scowl marring his handsome features. "And you promised you wouldn't call me Bax."

She rose. "Only when we are not alone. Calm down, dearest, it's not like you to become so agitated over something so trivial."

He started to say something, but she laid her fingers on his mouth. "Jeanette reminds me of Gertie when she first started at the Pennyfoot. You must remember how sullen and rebellious she was? Always cursing and complaining?"

To her relief a smile tugged at his lips. "I remember only too well. I despaired of her ever losing that stubborn insolence."

Cecily laughed. "To be perfectly honest with you, I don't think she ever did. She just tempered it somewhat when she was in our presence."

Baxter folded his arms around her. "No doubt you are right. I wonder if life is treating her well. And Mrs. Chubb, for that matter."

Cecily pulled back to look up at his face. "Well, we shall very soon find out. I've invited them all as guests for the Christmas Season and they have accepted. Gertie, Ross and the twins, and Mrs. Chubb. They should arrive tomorrow."

Baxter did his best to look unaffected by the news, but his eyes gleamed with pleasure. "Why didn't you tell me?"

"I did mention it, actually. You weren't listening to me. It will make our duties here much more pleasant when we're surrounded by old friends."

"I'm sure they will be ecstatic to find themselves

guests in the very establishment where they once waited on people. A refreshing turnabout of events, I would say."

Cecily hugged him. "Then you are pleased?"

He dropped a kiss on her nose. "I am pleased, my love. This was a good idea."

"Then you'll be even more happy to know that Samuel, Doris, and Daisy will also be here, though Doris might be a little late in arriving since she has theater engagements."

"Well, you have been busy." He moved away from her, and wandered over to the windows that overlooked the grounds. "Our former staff—all back as guests. It will be good to see everyone again. Though I hope they arrive soon. It looks as if it might snow."

She went to stand beside him. "Everything appears to be much the same out there."

"Yes, though the lawns seem a little ragged, and the topiaries need trimming."

Cecily sighed. "They never did do as well after poor John Thimble died. I wonder if the roof garden is still there. We need to take a tour of the place as soon as we've talked to Miss Bunkle."

Baxter sniffed. "Odd sort of woman, didn't you think? Looks like a good meal would do her good, and did you see that knitting needle stuck in her hair?"

"Yes, I did wonder about that myself." Cecily went back to the dressing table and sat down in front of the huge mirror. "I'll have to ask her what she thought of the late manager, Barry Wrotham."

"I was hoping you'd wait a day or two before concerning yourself about him."

"I'd intended to wait until tomorrow, at least." Cecily began pulling the long pins from her hat. "But that was before Jeanette uttered that interesting comment about someone having 'done him in,' to use her quaint expression."

Baxter groaned. "I might have known you'd pounce on that. I shouldn't have to warn you about taking the word of a housemaid as fact."

"Quite right, darling. But since Edward, also, was under the impression that Barry Wrotham's death was not an accident, it does raise some questions, don't you think?"

"Questions that, no doubt, you will do your utmost to have answered," Baxter said dryly.

Cecily smiled. "As you would say, indubitably."

He came and stood behind her, looking gravely at her reflection in the mirror. "You promised me you would not do anything impulsive without consulting me."

She gazed at his image, marveling yet again at the circumstances that had granted her a second fulfilling love in her life. "I promised, my love, and I shall do my best to keep that promise."

"I wonder why that doesn't ease my mind."

"Because you are such a worrier." She removed her hat, then rose and moved into his arms again. "I am not about to do anything that would jeopardize my life right now. I'm far too happy. Besides, I would imagine that in a day or two we shall learn quite a bit about the Pennyfoot's previous manager without any real effort on my part."

"I am happy to hear that."

"Besides, it's Christmas. Church bells, Christmas carolers, sleigh rides, candles on the Christmas trees . . . how can one be preoccupied with dark thoughts at such a joyous season of festivities?" She moved away from him. "I had messages sent to Phoebe and Madeline, informing them that we would be arriving today. I'm anxious to meet them again. I want to ask them if they'll assist me with the decorations and the pantomime."

"You plan to present a pantomime?" Baxter shook his head in wry amusement. You have a little over two weeks left before Christmas Day."

"All the more reason to begin preparations right away. I have decided to try our hand at *Aladdin*. I heard that Doris performed in the pantomime last year, so she can play Aladdin and she will be a tremendous help. If she gets here on time, that is."

"I trust you're not asking Phoebe to use that infernal dance troupe in your pantomime."

"It wouldn't be a Pennyfoot presentation without them."

"Of course. The tradition must go on. Even if it spells disaster."

She laughed. "I have to admit, poor Phoebe had her share of disasters. Fortune tended to work against her at every turn. I can only hope—" She broke off as a sharp tap sounded on the door.

"It's about time," Baxter muttered as he strode through the door into the sitting room. "I was wondering what that dratted lad had done with our luggage."

There was a pause while Baxter opened the door then, from the sitting room, Cecily heard Jeanette's clear voice announce, "I've brought some tea and scones, Mr. Baxter. Miss Bunkle says Mrs. Baxter must be dying for a cuppa."

Cecily hurried into the room as Jeanette carried the

heavy tray over to a low table in front of a settee. "How thoughtful of Miss Bunkle," she murmured, seating herself on the green sateen couch. "Thank you, Jeanette."

"Yes, m'm." The young girl turned to Baxter. "Raymond said to tell you that your luggage will be up in a short while. We've just had eight toffs arrive and he had to take care of them. He said to say he's sorry for the delay."

Baxter nodded, his expression clearly stating his displeasure.

Jeanette reached for the teapot, but Cecily raised her hand. "Thank you, but I can manage. I'm sure you have quite enough to do with guests arriving."

"Yes, m'm, that we do. All eight of them arrived at once, they did. Toffs from London with their wives. Raymond says the men are belchers from Lincoln's Inn, whatever that means."

"Not belchers," Baxter said shortly. "Benchers. They are barristers, the governing body of the Inns of the Court."

Jeanette appeared unimpressed. "Oh, well, anyway, the ladies are all dressed up really fancy—"

"Since everyone is far too busy to attend to our luggage," Baxter said, sounding pompous now, "perhaps your presence downstairs might be helpful."

Jeanette gave him a cheerful grin. "Yes, sir. I'm on my way." She scurried over to the door, then apparently remembering she'd omitted a curtsey, turned and dipped her knees. "Oh, I nearly forgot, m'm. Miss Bunkle said you had a visitor. Since you'd only just arrived and everything, she asked the lady to come back tomorrow."

Cecily uttered a small gasp of disappointment at the thought of missing one of her friends. "Oh, who was it, do you know? Mrs. Carter-Holmes? No, she's Fortescue now, of course. Or was it Miss Pengrath, perhaps?"

Jeanette shook her head. "Neither, m'm. It were Mr. Wrotham's widow. Said it was urgent she speak to you. Miss Bunkle said to tell you she'd be back tomorrow afternoon."

"Thank you, Jeanette." Cecily waited until the girl had closed the door behind her before turning to Baxter. "Well, what do you suppose the widow of Edward's manager would want to talk to me about?"

"I hesitate to speculate." Baxter raised his chin and closed his eyes. "I can guarantee, however, that she's not coming to welcome us to her dead husband's position."

"My thoughts exactly," Cecily answered with a great deal of satisfaction. "It seems as if we shall learn more about the late Barry Wrotham than I anticipated. I can hardly wait."

CHAPTER
❧ 3 ❧

The meeting with Miss Bunkle and her staff went very well. Cecily was relieved to discover she hadn't forgotten any of the intricacies of managing a hotel, and according to Miss Bunkle's reports, there didn't seem that much difference in the general day-to-day procedures involved. A country club, as she had already pointed out to Baxter, really wasn't that much different from a hotel after all.

Baxter visibly relaxed as the meeting progressed. He seemed to approve of Miss Bunkle, in spite of her odd hair ornament. When he complimented the housekeeper on her firm control of the staff, the woman actually blushed, much to Cecily's amusement. It would seem that marriage had not robbed Baxter of any of his suave charm.

She said as much to him later, as they stood at the wall

of the roof garden looking down on the cove below. With his hair ruffled by the blustery wind blowing directly off the ocean, he seemed younger and more carefree than she'd seen him in many months.

This little interlude would be so good for both of them, she thought, as Baxter turned to face her with a quizzical expression.

"Charm? I wasn't attempting to charm the lady. I was simply trying to establish a working relationship. I have the impression that Miss Bunkle can be a bit of an old battleship when it comes to rules and regulations."

"A trait that I'm quite sure has earned your utmost admiration."

He tilted his head. "You're not just the tiniest bit jealous, by any chance?"

She laughed out loud. "Of course I am, darling. You happen to be an uncommonly handsome man."

"Who happens to be married to a very beautiful lady."

"You see? You can't help being charming. Even to your wife."

For answer he placed an arm about her shoulders and pulled her close. "So what do you think about the new rules? Not too confining, on the whole?"

"I thought most of them unnecessary. Particularly that ridiculous one about women being barred from the lounge bar and the card rooms."

"Ah, yes." Baxter heaved a heavy sigh. "I had a feeling you would raise some objections to that one. At least we can be thankful that since we are now a country club, the card rooms are no longer illegal. We do have to remember, however, that the new rules are tradition and have to be observed."

"They should be done away with, if you ask me. Positively Victorian. This will set the Women's Movement back five years. I find it utterly appalling that a man cannot take his wife into certain rooms of an establishment where they are both residing. Rooms into which, I might add, two years ago women were at least tolerated. It simply doesn't make sense."

"I do hope you are not going to make an issue of this, my love." Baxter tightened his hold on her shoulders. "We must remember that rules are set for a reason, and as temporary administrators, we have no right to question them."

"We might not have the right to change them," Cecily said crisply, "but I'll defend to my death the right to question them."

"Yes, I thought you might."

She shivered as a fresh gust of wind buffeted her body. "That wind is rather keen, don't you think? I had forgotten how cold it can be up here in the winter. I much preferred the summer, when we could linger in the warm breeze. I used to enjoy the scent of roses while we watched the fishing boats come home."

"Then we shall return to our suite." Baxter guided her toward the narrow door that led to the stairway. "I'm nursing the small hope that Raymond has by now delivered our luggage, and I can change into something a little more fitting for my position."

She eyed him as he paused to allow her to proceed him through the door. His best charcoal gray suit, worn with a light gray waistcoat and starched white shirt, fitted him perfectly. His silk gray and white striped tie was knotted precisely, and with perhaps the exception of his hair, which remained ruffled despite his repeated attempts to smooth it down with his hand, he looked regal enough to be presented at the royal court without raising an eyebrow.

"You look quite dapper, my love," she informed him as she raised the hem of her skirt to clear the doorstep. "I think the patrons of the Pennyfoot Country Club are fortunate to have such a debonair fellow taking care of their needs."

She had her back to him, and couldn't see his frown, though she heard it in his voice. "My instincts tell me that this abundance of compliments is leading up to something I don't care to hear."

"I can't imagine what that could be." She waited until they had descended the first flight of stairs before adding, "Unless, of course, you object to my plan to pay a visit to Dr. Prestwick later this week."

His groan echoed down the stairwell as they turned the corner. "I knew it. I suppose it's too much to hope that the chap has found a wife? I rather thought he was interested in Madeline Pengrath when we left Badgers End."

"I thought so, too." Cecily reached the bottom of the stairs and waited for her husband to join her. "I'll have to ask Madeline about that. I do hope she and Phoebe manage to visit soon."

Baxter started to answer, then stopped short at the sight of Raymond standing in front of their suite, surrounded by several bags and two large trunks.

"Oh, there you are, m'm," the young man exclaimed when he caught sight of Cecily. "I was just about to send one of the maids to look for you. I didn't want to leave your luggage out here in the hallway."

Baxter strode forward and unlocked the door for him.

"Just drop them in the sitting room. I'll take care of them later."

"Yes, sir. Thank you, sir." Raymond struggled in with the heavy load, placing the baggage neatly side by side on the thick carpet.

"Here." Baxter handed him a folded note, but Raymond shook his head.

"That's all right, sir. I don't take nothing from the staff, especially the guv'nor. Mr. Wrotham never gave me nothing, and I don't expect it from you, neither. Wouldn't be right."

Watching the surprise on her husband's face, Cecily knew the young man had made a favorable impression. Pouncing on the opportunity, she said carefully, "I understand Mr. Wrotham was a very efficient manager."

Raymond's grin faded. "I s'pose you could say that, m'm. He was always barking orders, if that's what you mean."

"I'm sure you must all miss him very much. It must have been such a shock to hear about his accident. Such a tragic death." Cecily deliberately ignored the warning gleam in Baxter's eyes and kept her gaze fixed firmly on Raymond's face.

Raymond appeared to be concentrating on lining up the luggage. "I don't know about missing him, m'm. It were a shock to find him like that, I can tell you."

Cecily caught her breath. "*You* found him? I didn't know that."

"Yes, m'm. Mr. Sandringham sent me out looking for him. I saw his bicycle leaning against the fence of that farm and I went in to look for him." Raymond wiped his forehead with the back of his hand. "I don't know what made me look in the well. Just a feeling, I s'pose. Anyway, I sort of glanced in as I passed and I saw something floating around down there. When I looked proper-like, I could tell it was a man. Gave me a really bad turn, it did."

"I can quite imagine. So what did you do next?"

"I flew out of there and rushed back here to tell Mr. Sandringham. He rang for the constable. P.C. Northcott came up right away."

"Did you see anything unusual lying around the well when you found Mr. Wrotham?"

"No, m'm. Not that I can recall, anyhow." He straightened his back. "Everyone's really happy that you and Mr. Baxter are taking over, m'm. We weren't that fond of Mr. Wrotham, if you know what I mean. Bit of a bully, he was. Always swearing at the girls, and giving them a swipe with the back of his hand if they didn't mind straightaway. No one really liked him, except for Miss Bunkle, but then she didn't have to put up with his temper the way we did. To tell you the truth, I'm not really surprised he ended up in a bad way. I could see it coming, I could."

Baxter loudly cleared his throat. "Yes, well, that will be all, Raymond. Thank you. I can manage from here."

"Did the constable question all the staff?" Cecily persisted, at the risk of incurring Baxter's disapproval.

Raymond shook his head. "Nah, m'm, they didn't. P.C. Northcott, well, he's a bit of a duffer, ain't he. Said as how it were an accident, so there were no need to bother everyone with a bunch of questions."

"But you don't seem to think it was an accident," Cecily prompted.

Raymond looked uncomfortable. "It's not my place to say, m'm, but if you want the truth, there ain't that many people what do think it were an accident. Except for the bobbies. And no one's going to tell them any different, are they."

"Yes, well, that will be all, Raymond." Baxter strode to the door and opened it, looking pointedly at the young man until he disappeared. After closing the door, rather firmly in Cecily's opinion, he gave her one of his reproachful scowls. "Without any real effort on your part, I think you said."

She sent him a mischievous grin. "Did I? How very impractical of me." She sidled up to him. "Darling, how am I going to find out anything if I don't ask a few questions now and then?"

He was about to answer when a light tap on the door cut off his words. With a muttered exclamation, he opened it to reveal Moira standing in the doorway. Upon glancing at his face, the maid jumped backward as if she'd touched a hot stove, then stood there, apparently having forgotten why she was there.

Baxter, never having been one for patience with the staff, barked at her, "Well, girl, speak up! What is it?"

Cecily clicked her tongue and hurried forward. Gently ushering Baxter aside, she smiled at the terrified girl. "Moira, isn't it?"

The girl nodded, her eyes wide with apprehension.

"Did you have a message for me?"

The maid nodded again.

Baxter grunted, rolled his eyes at the ceiling, and much to Cecily's relief, backed away from the door.

Cecily tried again. "Did Miss Bunkle send you?"

This time the maid shook her head. Her mouth opened and closed, then she managed to stammer, "There's two ladies to see you, m'm."

"Did they leave their names?"

Moira looked stricken for a moment, then mumbled, "Mrs. Fortescue was one of them. Can't remember the other one. Sorry, m'm. I'm new here and things get sort of muddled in me 'ead sometimes."

"Is that a fact," Baxter muttered dryly.

Ignoring him, Cecily said quietly, "Please show the ladies up here, Moira, and then bring us a decanter of sherry, and some sliced apples with a variety of cheeses. Oh, and some cream crackers."

"Yes, m'm." The girl dipped her knees and rushed off.

Cecily closed the door and turned to regard her husband. "Bax, darling, you really should curb that sharp edge to your tongue when addressing the staff. You'll intimidate those poor girls."

"It appears that some of them need intimidating."

"That's as may be, but we don't want them taking fright and giving in their notice right before Christmas."

"From what I've heard, Wrotham was far more threatening than I could ever be. If they could put up with him, I have every confidence they will learn to abide my thoroughly charming nature. Debonair, didn't you say?"

She grinned at him. "*Touché*. Now, unless you want to listen to a lot of girlish gossip, might I suggest that you take this time to reacquaint yourself with your office while I greet Phoebe and, I presume, Madeline. Though I have to admit, I'm rather surprised to hear that the two of them arrived together. They never could be within a yard of each other without squabbling."

"Perhaps marriage to the colonel had mellowed the good lady." Baxter picked up a heavy trunk by its two handles and staggered into the boudoir with it. Raising his voice, he called back to her, "I just can't imagine those two living together. Can you imagine our ridiculously fussy Phoebe putting up with that befuddled fool? I don't think he's ever strung two complete sentences together, and when he does manage it, he doesn't make any blasted sense."

Cecily also raised her voice to answer him. "It's understandable, I suppose. The poor man had such dreadful experiences in the Boer War, it's not surprising he's a little strange in the head."

"Strange?" Baxter emerged from the boudoir, his voice still loud. "Fortescue is more than a little strange. He's positively *insane*."

At that precise moment a light tap on the door announced the presence of visitors.

Cecily gasped, her hand flying to her mouth. "Do you think they heard?" she whispered urgently.

Baxter shrugged. "I'd say it's a trifle too late to worry about it now. Though I do suggest you open the door before your guests think you are ignoring them."

"Heavens!" Cecily flew to the door and flung it wide. There in front of her stood her two dearest friends in the whole world.

Phoebe's outfit, as usual, was impeccable, from the huge flower-bedecked brim of her hat to the elegant elbow-length gloves and the pearl-buttoned shoes peeking out from under the hem of her gray, heavy silk tea gown. A dainty parasol swung from her arm, and in the other she cradled a round tin of chocolate-covered biscuits—one of Cecily's very favorite treats.

By contrast, Madeline looked more like a woodland sprite, conjured up from the depths of the green forest. A crown of mistletoe covered her long, dark, flowing hair, and beneath her serviceable coat her soft muslin dress floated around her toes, which had been tucked into shoes that appeared too large for her dainty feet. She thrust a small delicate bouquet of tea roses at Cecily, who exclaimed in delight.

"Roses? At this time of the year?"

"From Porter's greenhouse. I ordered them especially." She flung her arms about Cecily, putting the delicate blooms in extreme danger of being crushed. "You look wonderful, Cecily. Marriage agrees with you."

She peered past Cecily's shoulder to where Baxter was still struggling with the luggage. "I'm happy to see you are taking such good care of my good friend, Baxter."

Baxter mumbled something and carried the last of the bags into the boudoir.

Not to be outdone, Phoebe stepped forward and kissed the air on each side of Cecily's face. "How absolutely divine you look, Cecily, dearest. I have missed you so much. This is going to be a magnificent Christmas Season now that you are back in Badgers End. Here. For you and Mr. Baxter. An early gift."

Cecily took the tin of biscuits with a gasp of pleasure. "How thoughtful of you, Phoebe. Thank you both so much. The two of you look absolutely breathtaking. How wonderful it is to see you both again."

"Rather than intrude upon this somewhat cloying mutual admiration society," Baxter announced as he emerged from the boudoir, "I'll take my leave and allow you ladies to chatter to your heart's content."

Phoebe fluttered her eyelashes at him. "I do hope we're not chasing you out, Mr. Baxter."

Baxter allowed her a brief glance. "Not at all. I have work to do. Please excuse me, ladies."

Madeline waited until he'd opened the door, then said sweetly, "Should you find yourself in need of a potion while you are here, Baxter, I'll be happy to oblige. Free of charge, of course."

Baxter paused, and Cecily held her breath. There were those in the village who swore by Madeline's potions. There were even men who insisted that their virility in certain private matters was greatly enhanced by the strange concoctions of herbs and wildflowers. Baxter was well aware of this, though he was adamant in his disbelief that such powers as those attributed to Madeline actually existed. Nonetheless Cecily waited, half expecting him to make some derisive comment to offend her friend.

After a second or two, he said gruffly, "Thank you, Miss Pengrath, but I assure you, I have no need for such debatable assistance. You may ask my wife should you be in any doubt of that."

He closed the door firmly behind him, while Phoebe's shocked gasp was drowned out by Madeline's gurgling laugh. In a voice that always reminded Cecily of the wind in the bulrushes on Deep Willow Pond, she murmured, "You are a fortunate woman, Cecily. There goes a real man."

"Really, Madeline," Phoebe said crossly. "Have you no shame? What possesses you to talk so unbecomingly in front of a gentleman?"

"Perhaps if you had been half as bold, Phoebe dear," Madeline answered, "you might have landed yourself a gentleman instead of that buffoon with whom you are sadly saddled."

Phoebe drew herself up another inch and glared at the other woman. "That buffoon, as you so crudely call him, is a prince in every way. He treats me in the manner to which ladies such as I have been accustomed, and he is delightful and entertaining company. At least he had the chivalry to ask for my hand in marriage. Perhaps, if you had been more of a lady and less of a hussy, you might have held the interest of a certain doctor, instead of losing him to that simpering fool, Winifred Chesterton."

Glimpsing the light of battle in Madeline's eyes, Cecily hurried to intervene. "How is Dr. Prestwick these days? I intend to visit him later this week. I do hope he's well?"

"Quite well," Madeline said shortly.

Phoebe's skirts rustled as she settled herself on the sateen couch. "He's doing very well," she said a trifle smugly. "His waiting room is constantly packed with patients, whether they are legitimate or not. Most of them are women, of course. Our handsome doctor always did have a way with the women."

Cecily, who had once been the object of the good doctor's affections, knew only too well how utterly devastating Dr. Kevin Prestwick's appeal could be to a vulnerable woman. She glanced at Madeline, who seemed unaffected by Phoebe's barbs as she floated across the floor in the direction of a comfortable royal blue armchair.

Seating herself, Madeline said blithely, "Dr. Prestwick bestows his good nature on everyone, man or woman. It's not his fault if some misguided ladies misinterpret a good bedside manner for something inappropriate."

Phoebe tittered behind a delicate gloved hand. "I don't think Winifred Chesterton is misinterpreting anything, judging by the way he was looking at her as she hung on his arm the other morning."

"That's a matter of opinion." Madeline's beautiful eyes narrowed. "I happen to know that Kevin is not in the least interested in that woman. He has said as much to me. He does, after all, spend most of his spare time with me, not with Winifred Chesterton."

"Yes," Phoebe allowed. "I suppose he does. Then again, since he has yet to ask for your hand in marriage, one has to wonder if his intentions are honorable. It's a pity you have no father to question the doctor's purpose in pursuing a relationship with you."

Madeline's lips curved in the smile that always made Cecily nervous. "Phoebe, dear, I do believe that the doctor's purposes are none of your business. Perhaps you should keep a still tongue, lest you wake up one morning to find it transformed into that of a viper."

Phoebe pulled a lace-trimmed handkerchief from her sleeve and fluttered it in front of her face. "I was merely concerned for your welfare, Madeline. There's no need to become vindictive. Perhaps you should save your doubtful threats for Winifred, since she appears to be intent on ensnaring your prospective suitor."

"Don't think I haven't considered the prospect," Madeline said darkly.

Deciding that it was time to change the subject, Cecily said hastily, "Did either of you make the acquaintance of Mr. Barry Wrotham, by any chance?"

Madeline made a face. "Yes, he came to me about a month ago, looking for some of my potions. Quite an unpleasant man. I could sense a dark shadow hanging over him, even then. I thought about warning him, but his attitude was so offensive, I decided to let fate have its way." She looked directly into Cecily's eyes, and her voice changed to a low tone that Cecily knew well. "It wasn't an accident, you know," she said softly. "Someone pushed Mr. Wrotham down that well. Someone extremely dangerous. I have to warn you, Cecily. The shadow hangs over you, as well. Be very careful, for whoever killed Barry Wrotham could very well make you his next victim."

CHAPTER

❦ 4 ❦

Cecily was well used to her friend's dire warnings. Madeline's remarkable penchant for foreseeing the future was legendary, if somewhat unreliable. She had succeeded enough times, however, to give Cecily a decided chill at her words.

In an effort to lighten the moment, she uttered a breezy laugh. "Now, Madeline, what makes you think I have any intention of concerning myself with the death of a man whom I've never met."

The odd light still gleamed in Madeline's eyes. "Not only will you involve yourself," she said softly, "you will place yourself in grave danger. Please, my friend, beware of those who wish you harm. It could well be your undoing this time."

"Really, Madeline," Phoebe muttered. "You are positively macabre. Enough of this silly game."

Fortunately, at that moment a tap on the door announced the arrival of the cheese and sherry. The disruption managed to diffuse the somber atmosphere in the room, though Cecily could not quite rid herself of a vague sense of foreboding. She was thankful when the conversation turned to the upcoming Christmas Season.

"You really do need to do something more imaginative with the decorations," Madeline declared after sipping at her sherry. She placed the slim glass on the table in front of her. "The holly wreaths on the front doors are a nice touch, but the tree in the foyer is pitiable. I hope you have a larger tree in the library?"

"I haven't looked yet," Cecily admitted. "Hugh and I went up to the roof garden and then talked to Miss Bunkle in her room, but other than that, I haven't seen much of the hotel since I arrived."

Madeline looked surprised. "You call your husband Hugh now?"

"Only in company," Cecily confessed. "I gave him my promise. I must admit, it does sound rather demeaning to call him Baxter in front of everyone. It's not as if he's in my employ anymore. We are equal partners now."

Madeline nodded her approval.

"I thought the tree was very nice," Phoebe observed, having successfully ignored the exchange.

"Naturally you would think so." Madeline reached for the cheese knife and cut herself a square of Gorgonzola. "Judging from the meager decorations in the church, your taste is sadly lacking in the Christmas spirit."

She waved the knife at Cecily. "The Pennyfoot always

looked so wonderful at Christmastime. There used to be garlands of holly and gigantic red ribbons adorning the bannisters of the staircase. Those lovely handmade ornaments you used to have on the trees in the foyer and library. Candles to light in the evening, and enormous swaths of ribbons and velvets in red and green sweeping across the ballroom. Huge bunches of mistletoe everywhere."

"I wondered when we were coming to that," Phoebe muttered nastily. "In my opinion, any woman who walks around with mistletoe in her hair is begging to be ravished."

"Really," Madeline murmured. "What an utterly delicious thought."

"As a matter of fact," Cecily said firmly, "I was intending to ask if you would be willing to see to the decorations for us, Madeline. I'm sure they are in storage somewhere in the hotel . . . I mean club."

"I'd be delighted." She grinned at Phoebe. "You can help if you promise me faithfully you will not complain every five minutes."

"Actually, Phoebe," Cecily said before that lady could deliver the retort hovering on her tight lips, "I was rather hoping that you might be willing to put together a pantomime for us. Since the men will be off on their traditional hunt for pheasant on Boxing Day, I thought it would be nice to entertain the ladies with their special event. Though no doubt the gentlemen will join them. Everyone seems to love a pantomime at Christmastime. I know it's terribly short notice, of course, but—"

"Oh, I'd adore to help!" Phoebe clapped her hands in delight. "It's been simply *ages* since I've organized anything more challenging that a christening at the church. Algie is such a bore when it comes to events. He simply refuses to allow me to put on a revue at the church hall. He keeps insisting it's immoral, no matter how much I try to explain that everything would be in good taste."

"I would imagine your habit of creating disasters has more to do with his reluctance," Madeline said. "I still haven't forgotten the fiasco of the lost python, or the time a member of your dance team did her best to stab one of the guests through the heart."

Phoebe visibly bristled. "It wasn't the girl's fault. Her foot slipped during the sword dance. Accidents happen in the best of productions. Even on the London stages, so I've been told."

Cecily loudly cleared her throat. "Well, I'm sure things will work out beautifully for the pantomime. I suggest we all meet at Dolly's Teashop the day after tomorrow to discuss the plans. I can't wait to sink my teeth into one of Dolly's exquisite Banbury cakes."

The ladies readily agreed and, accepting the hint, rose to take their leave. Cecily offered to show them around the newly renovated Pennyfoot before they left, then accompanied them as far as the main doors before heading toward the narrow hallway to her husband's office.

As she approached the staircase, she saw a couple descending to the foyer. It wasn't often she was struck by a woman's beauty, but the lovely creature on the arm of the distinguished-looking gentleman was the sort of woman who would attract attention everywhere she went.

Instead of a hat, she wore a band of cream velvet fastened with a white silk camellia around a mound of luxurious dark brown curls atop her head.

Cecily's mouth positively watered at the sight of the woman's exquisite gown. It was the color of champagne,

composed of panels of Swiss eyelet embroidery, which
were divided by tiny insertions of gorgeous French Val
lace. Her Gibson collar accentuated the woman's long,
slim neck as she swept down the stairs with the air of one
accustomed to grandeur and the services accorded by it.

Guessing that these were two of the "toffs" Jeanette
was talking about, Cecily hurried forward to greet the
pair as they reached the bottom of the staircase.

"Welcome to the Pennyfoot Country Club," she said as
the couple paused in front of her. "May I introduce
myself? I'm Cecily Baxter, the present manager of this
establishment. If I or any of my staff can be of any service
to you, please don't hesitate to ask."

The gentleman raised his eyebrows, looking down at
her as if she were a vagrant who had wandered in off the
street. "A woman manager? How very droll."

"Temporary manager, actually," Cecily corrected,
deciding that she didn't like the man. "My husband and I
are helping out the owner of the Pennyfoot, Edward Sandringham, who happens to be my cousin. As a matter of
fact, I sold the hotel to him two years ago."

If she'd hoped to impress him, she was disappointed.
"Really," the gentleman answered, sounding bored.
"Well, I am Sir John Gilroy, K.C. Permit me to introduce
my wife, Lady Lucille."

Cecily smiled at the woman. "I'm delighted to make
your acquaintance, your ladyship."

"*Merci.*" Lady Lucille stared at a spot slightly above
Cecily's head. "It is our very great pleasure to return to
the club. I can only hope that the service is as impeccable
as always."

Even without the thick French accent, Cecily would

have guessed the lady's origin. She positively breathed Paris. "We shall do our best," she said, a little miffed at the suggestion that the new management might not come up to snuff. "This is not your first visit to the Pennyfoot Country Club, I assume."

"On the contrary. We come here quite often," Sir John said, answering for her. "In fact, we were here quite recently for the hunting season."

"Then you should enjoy the pheasant hunt on Boxing Day."

"I'm looking forward to it."

"Ah, there you are, John, old boy." The voice boomed down the staircase, startling Lady Lucille to the point of bringing a flush to her cheeks.

Cecily watched the portly gentleman rapidly descend, one hand on the bannister, the other clasping the arm of a scowling woman who was doing her best to keep up with him without tripping over the hem of her ruffled satin skirt.

"Evening, Lionel," Gilroy muttered.

The newcomer seemingly ignored him, his avid gaze instead devouring the delectable Lady Lucille. "Thought we'd join you for supper, old chap," he said a trifle breathlessly as he reached the bottom of the steps.

Gilroy nodded. "This is Mrs. Baxter, the new manager of the club. Mrs. Baxter, may I present Lionel Fitzhammer, K.C., and his wife, Barbara."

Fitzhammer held out his hand and Cecily reluctantly put hers into it, doing her very best not to visibly recoil when the scarlet-cheeked gentleman pressed his rubbery lips against her fingers.

"Charmed, I'm sure," she muttered, and withdrew her hand rather smartly.

"Have you met the others yet?" Lionel asked, standing close enough to Lucille that his wife was forced to hover in the background. "They should be down shortly. Though Percy's a bit of a slowcoach. He'll probably be late to the table. He usually is."

"No, I haven't met the rest of your party yet." Cecily tried to sound fascinated. "I understand that all four of you gentlemen are members of the King's Council."

"You are correct," Fitzhammer said, his gaze once more fastened greedily on Lucille. "Percy Chatsworth, K.C., and his wife, Amelia, and Roger Peebles, K.C., with his wife, Gretchen. We are all Masters of the Bench, here to enjoy the Christmas Season in this excellent establishment."

"Then we shall do our best to make your stay a memorable one. We are honored to have you all as our guests." Cecily met the wary gaze of Barbara Fitzhammer and smiled at her. Although the woman's lackluster brown hair and pleasant looks were vastly overshadowed by those of the flamboyant Lucille, her eyes were cornflower blue and quite beautiful.

"Jolly good," her husband muttered. "The Pennyfoot has always been one of our favorite places to stay, wouldn't you say, John?"

"Quite, quite." Gilroy pulled a fob watch from the pocket of his waistcoat and flipped open the lid. "I suppose we should make our way to the dining room."

"Oh, please, don't let me detain you." Cecily backed out of the way to allow them to pass. "I trust you will enjoy your evening meal."

"Bound to, madam," Fitzhammer boomed. "What with that excellent French chef of yours. Can't beat the French for knowing how to tickle a man's palate, eh, what?"

He gave Gilroy a sly dig with his elbow, his gaze riveted on Lady Lucille's face. The lady lifted her chin in a haughty gesture of contempt, yet her glance slid sideways at her husband, as if concerned the comment would offend him.

Sir John, however, merely grasped his wife's elbow, muttered his excuses, and steered her down the hallway, leaving a trail of expensive perfume behind. Fitzhammer barely took the time to bid Cecily good evening before charging after them with his unfortunate spouse in tow.

Left alone, Cecily breathed a sigh. It had been a long day and she was hungry. All she could think about now was retiring for the evening and enjoying a quiet meal alone with her husband in their suite. After spending two years in the quiet peace of her London town house, she found the bustle and noise of the club to be oppressive. It would take some time to accustom herself to all the upheaval again.

Feeling just a little depressed, for whatever reason she couldn't be sure, she made her way down the hallway to Baxter's office. Tomorrow would be another day. Her pulse quickened at the remembrance that she had an appointment with Wrotham's widow in the morning. She could hardly wait to find out what it was the late manager's wife had to tell her that was apparently so urgent.

If there was one thing that was clear after her discussions with Raymond and Jeanette, it was that quite a few people believed Wrotham's death was not an accident. She couldn't help wondering if Wrotham's widow shared that belief and, if so, might perhaps shed some light on what really happened. In any case, the meeting should prove to be quite interesting.

*   *   *

The following morning, Cecily arose feeling somewhat lethargic, thanks to a restless night in a strange bed. Baxter, apparently, had no trouble sleeping, and in fact, his snoring had been part of Cecily's problem—a fact she kept to herself. In the past Baxter had emphatically denied that he snored, and she had given up trying to convince him otherwise.

After a light breakfast of poached eggs and haddock in their suite, Baxter announced he had work to do. He kissed his wife and left, leaving Cecily to wait for the arrival of Barry Wrotham's widow.

Emily Wrotham arrived midmorning, just as Cecily returned from inspecting the accommodations for Mrs. Chubb, Gertie, and her family. Jeanette ushered the woman into Cecily's suite, and waited for her to remove her navy blue coat, which reminded Cecily of a military uniform with its large buttons on the shoulders.

Underneath, Emily Wrotham wore a serviceable skirt and a plain white shirtwaist relieved only by tiny rows of tucking down the front. Although she was young in appearance, her shoulders were bowed, as if she were too weary to raise her head.

Reminding herself that the poor woman had recently lost her husband, Cecily invited her to sit, and ordered Jeanette to have coffee and currant buns brought up to the room.

"I am so sorry to hear of your loss," Cecily murmured as the widow seated herself on the very edge of the couch. "It must have been a dreadful shock for you."

"Dreadful." Emily's thin voice wavered, and she sought in her sleeve for a large white handkerchief. After dabbing at her eyes, she said tearfully, "The police constable insists that Barry's death was an accident." She gulped, cleared her throat, loudly blew her nose, then added, "They are mistaken, Mrs. Baxter. Someone pushed my Barry down that well. I'm quite sure of it."

Cecily lowered herself onto the comfortable armchair. "That's a rather serious statement, Mrs. Wrotham. What makes you so certain that the constables are mistaken?"

Emily blew her nose again, with more delicacy this time. "Barry hadn't been himself for quite some time before that day. I knew something was wrong, but every time I asked him about it, he insisted all was well. In the end he got quite cross with me for asking him about it. So I had to give up asking. Then, on the day he . . . he . . . died, Sunday it was, he told me he would be working all afternoon here at the club. Stocking the wine cellar, he told me. I was upset because it was his afternoon off, but he said it couldn't wait and he had to take care of it right away."

She paused, and Cecily waited a moment or two before prompting, "But you found out he wasn't stocking the wine cellar?"

Emily Wrotham nodded her head. "He'd been giving me that story about working late so many times, he must have forgotten he'd used the one about the wine cellar just two weeks before. I knew he wouldn't have to restock it that quickly, so I came here to see for myself."

"And he wasn't here."

"No, he wasn't." Emily's pale gray eyes filled with tears again. "I thought he was with another woman. I'd had my suspicions for a long time. Working at a place like this, he was bound to meet a hussy or two. I suppose I was expecting it in a way. He'd grown tired of me a long time ago. I could tell." A sob escaped, and she quickly smothered it with her crumpled handkerchief.

"I'm so sorry, Mrs. Wrotham." Anger burned in Cecily's breast when she saw the misery etched on Emily's once pretty face. Any sympathy she might have had for Barry Wrotham's ignoble fate was immediately erased. In her opinion, men who cheated on their wives ought to be horse-whipped. The pain and misery they caused while indulging in their selfish whims could not be measured.

"In any case," Emily said, still fighting tears, "I was really angry. I wanted him caught with whoever he was with, to bring shame on her and to put an end to it. So I told Mr. Sandringham that Barry was missing. I told him he'd never come home and I was afraid something had happened to him. I could tell Mr. Sandringham didn't care that much, but he knew I was worried about Barry, so he sent Raymond out to see if he could find him."

"Ah, yes. Raymond told me about finding your husband's body."

Another sob escaped her lips. "Yes, well, Raymond saw his bicycle leaning against the fence and went in to the farm to look for him. He found him . . . floating . . . in the well." This time her sobs overcame her.

Cecily was thankful to hear Jeanette's light tap on the door, thus giving Emily a chance to compose herself while she took charge of the refreshments.

After serving both women with a steaming cup of cof-fee and a buttered bun, Jeanette left the room, though not without raising a questioning eyebrow at Cecily as she passed by her chair.

Cecily pretended not to notice. That young maid's curiosity would no doubt get her into trouble one day, she thought, as she took a sip of her coffee.

Within a few moments, Emily Wrotham appeared composed enough to continue her story. "What puzzles me," she told Cecily, "is why my husband was on that farm in the first place. The land is being offered for sale, I understand, but Barry had no money to buy a place like that, and in any case, he's no farmer. I can't imagine what he'd be doing, wandering around an abandoned farm all alone."

"Perhaps, if your suspicions about another woman are justified, your husband might have intended to meet someone there."

Emily nodded her agreement. "That's what I think. It's the only answer, really. I think someone lured him there in order to kill him. And it's my thinking that perhaps the husband or suitor of whomever my husband was dallying with had a hand in it. Why else would someone want to kill a man like my Barry? He wasn't perfect, by any means, but he never harmed anyone in his entire life." Her words ended on a burst of weeping that took some time to dissolve.

Cecily let the woman cry, understanding that she needed to indulge in her grief. While she waited for Emily to control her sobs, she thought about what she'd heard. There was a ring of plausibility to the widow's words, though she had to admit that until now she hadn't thought about there being another woman involved. It would seem there was much more to Barry Wrotham than she'd realized.

When the widow seemed to have found her composure again, Cecily asked gently, "Have you spoken to the constable about your suspicions?"

"Oh, no." Emily dabbed at her pink nose. "I couldn't, Mrs. Baxter. For one thing, I don't know for sure that Barry was seeing someone else. I wouldn't want that sort of thing spread all over town if it isn't true. I have my children to consider. It's bad enough they lost their father. I don't want them thinking ill of him if I'm wrong about him."

"I see." Cecily's heart went out to this poor woman who had been left to raise her children alone. "Then why have you come to me?"

Emily leaned forward, her eyes glittering, her voice a low, fierce whisper. "I do believe, Mrs. Baxter, that the answer to it all lies somewhere right here, at the Pennyfoot Country Club. Someone either staying here or working here knows something, I'll stake my life on it. I want to know the truth. If someone did kill my husband, I want to know who it is and I want him punished. No one should be free to take a life without paying for it. I can't rest easy until I know the truth and see that justice is done."

"You do know that if your suspicions prove to be correct, then people will eventually be aware that your husband was being unfaithful to you."

Emily raised her small pointed chin. "If it's the truth, then I'll tell the children myself. I can't stay here anyway without Barry. I'll be taking the children back to London for Christmas, and we won't be coming back. We'll be living with my parents. I just can't leave until I know what really happened to him. I asked Mr. Sandringham to help me, but he was too busy getting ready for his trip. He told me to talk to you. He said you were very good at that sort of thing."

Cecily leaned back in her chair. So that was why Edward had told Baxter he thought there was something odd about Wrotham's death. Dear Edward. Had he mentioned the fact that Barry's widow suspected foul play, Baxter would have adamantly refused to put a foot in Badgers End.

"I really can't promise anything," she said, reaching for her currant bun. "But I'll certainly look into it, if you like. Is there anything else you can tell me? Did your husband ever mention another woman by name? Or even a man's name you didn't recognize?"

"No, nothing. It was just a feeling I had, really. I know that's not much help, but believe me, Mrs. Baxter, when your husband is straying, somehow you can tell. Just little things. Like the way he avoided looking me in the eyes when he left for work."

She uttered a shuddering sigh. "He used to talk about his job all the time at first, then he got so he didn't want to talk about it at all. He was always in a hurry to get out of the house. Sometimes he didn't even bother to kiss me goodbye. He never used to be like that." She looked down at her hands, twisting the handkerchief around her fingers. "As I said, just little things."

"Well, I'll do my best to find out what I can." Cecily rose to her feet, and Emily followed suit, tucking her damp handkerchief back into her sleeve.

"I am much obliged, Mrs. Baxter. I know I can trust you to be discreet."

"Of course." Cecily tugged on the bell rope to summon a maid. "Though I have to warn you again, the truth will most likely come out in the end."

"If it *is* the truth. Then so be it."

Moira arrived a few minutes later to help the widow on with her coat, then escorted her out the door. After they'd left, Cecily wandered to the window to cast a wary eye on the darkening sky.

The clouds looked heavy and gray, and dried leaves drifted and swirled across the manicured lawn. It would seem that Baxter had been right in his prediction, for even as she watched, scattered snowflakes began to dance in the wind.

Mrs. Chubb and Gertie would be arriving soon. She could only hope that their stay would be uneventful. Much as she had missed the excitement of chasing after criminals, she had to admit, nothing would spoil Christmas more than the ugliness of murder once more invading the walls of the Pennyfoot.

CHAPTER
✿ 5 ✿

Gertie and her family arrived that afternoon in a flurry of excited greetings, hugs, and tears. The snow had begun falling quite heavily, coating the Esplanade and the roof of the Pennyfoot like a soft white coverlet.

Holding a hand of each twin, Cecily lead the party inside the warm foyer of the Pennyfoot, marveling at how big the children had grown. Their excitement at the sight of the Christmas tree was so infectious Cecily rashly promised them they could help Madeline decorate it.

"You'll be bloody sorry you did that, m'm," Gertie said, removing the tartan wool scarf she'd wrapped around her hat. "If I know these two, they'll have the bleeding tree upside down before you can blink."

"Gertie," Mrs. Chubb said sharply. "You promised. Not in front of the children."

"Sorry." Gertie grinned happily at Cecily. "I promised I wouldn't use them words. I'm getting better at it, but now and again they slip out." She stopped short, staring at her feet. "Crikey, look at this carpet. Must have cost a bleeding fortune."

Mrs. Chubb rolled her eyes and groaned, while Cecily laughed. "It is such a joy to see you all again," she said. "You have no idea how much I've missed you. Especially my godchildren." She beamed down at the twins, who were staring wide-eyed at the sweeping staircase as if they'd never seen one before.

"Are we going up there?" Lillian asked, pointing a chubby finger at the stairs.

"What have I told you about pointing, girl," Mrs. Chubb said sharply.

"It's rude," James said loudly. He gave his sister a shove. "Lilly's rude . . . Lilly's rude . . . Lilly's rude."

Gertie raised her hand. "Shut up, you two, or I'll box your bleeding ears."

The twins dived behind Cecily and clung to her skirt.

"I'm sure she doesn't mean it," Cecily said, laughing.

"Be the death of me, they will," Gertie said darkly. "I never thought——" She broke off, staring at Miss Bunkle, who was making her way across the foyer toward them. "Blimey, who the heck's that? Does she know she's got a knitting needle stuck in 'er hair?"

When the housekeeper reached them, Cecily hastily made the introductions. "Mrs. Chubb used to be the housekeeper here," she informed Miss Bunkle. "And Mrs. McBride was our chief housemaid."

"Really." Miss Bunkle sniffed, and looked down her nose at the twins. "And I suppose these were footmen?"

No doubt it was supposed to be a joke, but Gertie's chin shot up. "If you must know, these children were born right here in this hotel," she said, emphatically sounding her aitches. "That was in the good old days, when this *was* a posh hotel, not a bleeding country club for roadhogs."

"Gertie!" Mrs. Chubb gave her a horrified glare. "Mind your manners."

Miss Bunkle seemed unaffected by Gertie's scathing comments, dismissing them with a haughty toss of her head. "Your rooms are ready," she said, "if you care to follow Jeanette." She gestured at the maid hovering at the base of the staircase. "I'll have Raymond bring up your luggage as soon as possible."

"Blimey," Gertie murmured. "I never thought I'd end up being waited on at the Pennyfoot. It don't seem right, some'ow."

"I know what you mean." Mrs. Chubb slipped her hands out of her muff and glanced in the direction of the kitchen stairs. "I feel as I should be going downstairs, not up them."

"I'm sure you'll soon get used to it." Cecily beamed at them both. "Come on, I'll show you to your rooms myself." She smiled at Miss Bunkle. "There's no need for Jeanette to go up with us."

Miss Bunkle dipped her head. "Very well, Mrs. Baxter." She raised her hand. "Come along, Jeanette."

The maid scuttled forward, giving Gertie a curious stare as she drew close. "Did you really used to be the chief housemaid here?" she asked in a loud whisper.

Gertie grinned. "You bet your bleeding boots I did. I was

bloody good at me job, too. Best housemaid around, you just ask madam, here. Why, I could tell you stories—"

"Jeanette, stop bothering the guests and get down below stairs," Miss Bunkle ordered, raising her voice just enough to sound assertive.

Jeanette scurried off toward the kitchen stairs, while Gertie watched her go, an almost wistful expression on her face. "I dunno," she said softly, "but them days seemed so simple then. Nothing to worry about except getting the tables laid proper and the meals served."

Mrs. Chubb huffed out her breath. "And the ovens stoked with coals, the grates blackened every day, the floors washed, the sinks cleaned, the laundry done, the carpets swept, the beds made, the furniture dusted, the silver polished—"

"Heavens!" Cecily laughed. "You're making me feel tired, Mrs. Chubb."

"Me, too." Gertie dug an elbow in the stout lady's ribs. "Come on, Chubby, get up to your room before you feel tempted to go down there and start bleeding ordering everyone about."

Mrs. Chubb wagged a finger in Gertie's face. "I told you not to call me that."

"Oops!" Gertie grinned at Cecily. "Got a blinking memory like a sieve, I do."

Muttering under her breath, Mrs. Chubb grabbed each twin by the hand and headed for the staircase.

"Don't take any notice of us, m'm," Gertie said as she followed behind with Cecily. "Me and Mrs. Chubb get along really well. A lot different from the old days when she used to box me ears for talking back to her. She's more like me mum now. Still tries to tell me what to do, but she knows I'm old enough not to care."

Cecily sighed. "It's hard to think that things have changed so much when everything looks so familiar."

"It do, indeed, m'm." Gertie looked earnestly at her. "I wanted to say, m'm, it's really, really nice of you to invite us like this. As guests, I mean. Though I have to admit, it do feel strange."

"I hope not too strange for you to enjoy your visit. Since you are my guests, I think we can dispense with you referring to me as 'm'm' while you are here."

"Oh, no, m'm, I couldn't." Gertie gave her head an emphatic shake. "It wouldn't seem right. Me and Mrs. Chubb talked about that on the way down on the train. We both agreed we couldn't stop addressing you the way we've always been used to, that's all. I hope you don't mind."

"Of course not. You must do whatever makes you the most comfortable." Cecily smiled at the sight of the twins dragging Mrs. Chubb up the stairs. "I just want everyone to enjoy the Christmas Season."

"I'm sure we will, m'm. Is Michel still here?"

"Yes, he is. And delighted at the thought of seeing everyone again."

"Go on with you, m'm." Gertie lifted her skirts as she began to climb the stairs. "I bet he didn't bleeding tell you that."

Cecily laughed. "No, he didn't. He made some vague comments about his peace being shattered and the reputation of the country club being forever sullied. But I could tell he was excited at the news."

"Hope he's got a good supply of brandy. He's going to

need it with all of us around. What about the twins, Daisy and Doris? Are they coming?"

"Daisy will be arriving with Samuel tomorrow. Doris won't be here until later. She has a theatrical engagement to finish before she can leave London."

"I can't wait to see them again." Gertie heaved a sigh. "I really miss them. Daisy especially. She was always so good at taking care of me own twins. I wonder if they'll remember her." Gertie hugged herself in her excitement. "This is going to be the best bleeding Christmas ever."

"What about Ross? When will he be arriving? I was hoping he'd come down with you."

"So was I." Gertie paused for breath at the first landing. Mrs. Chubb and the twins had already disappeared around the curve of the next flight of stairs. "To tell you the truth, m'm, his business ain't doing that well. Not much call for gardeners in Scotland nowadays. Most people take care of their own, and those what don't buy their vegetables from the greengrocers. He doesn't say much, but I know he worries about it. He stayed behind to finish up with the customers he's got for Christmas stuff, but I don't know what he's going to do after that."

"I'm sorry to hear that," Cecily murmured. "It must be a worry for you."

"It's his health I'm worried about, m'm." Gertie began climbing the second flight of stairs. "Got this awful cough, he has. Reminds me of when Ethel got ill with hers. I'll be glad if he does give up the gardening. The weather in Scotland is bleeding shocking in the winter. It's blinking cold enough to freeze the—"

She broke off as a man and a woman appeared on the stairs above her on their way down.

The woman's hair, visible beneath the upswept brim of her hat, was an exquisite shade of auburn, and her pale skin seemed colorless in comparison. She wore a fashionable suit of dark gray, with a silver soutache braid trimming the coat and the hem of the gored skirt. Her gloved hand clung to the bannisters as she paused to allow Cecily and Gertie to pass.

Her companion was dark in complexion, as if he had spent a good many weeks in the glare of the sun. His comely features were perfectly arranged on his face, and he gave both of them an engaging smile as they passed by him, then continued on down the stairs with the elegant woman.

"Flippin' 'eck," Gertie said when they were out of earshot. "Now there's a good-looking chap. Bet that suit cost a bob or two."

"I think the gentleman must be one of the Benchers staying here," Cecily said as they reached the next landing. "I met the other two and their wives last night, but there are two more I haven't met as yet."

"Benchers?" Gertie looked puzzled. "I'm not sure I know what you mean."

"They are barristers," Cecily explained. "The highest ranked of the judicial office. They sit on the Bench at the Inns of Court. Most prestigious position. Some members of the royal family have been Royal Benchers, including Prince Albert and King George the Fifth, I do believe."

"Blimey," Gertie said, sounding impressed, though it was obvious by her expression she didn't have the slightest idea what Cecily was talking about. "Right posh toffs, then. I reckon the country club doesn't do that bad after all."

At least she had that right, Cecily reflected as she joined Mrs. Chubb and the impatient twins on the landing.

The next few minutes were spent getting everyone settled. Then Cecily left them alone to relax after their long journey and went down to the kitchen to order up a tray of refreshments.

Mrs. Chubb had elected to keep the twins with her in her room, so that Gertie and Ross could have some privacy, an arrangement of which Cecily heartily approved. Having completed her mission in the kitchen, she then went in search of her husband. It had been far too long since she'd had a word alone with Baxter. She had forgotten how much time could be taken up with the business of managing a hotel. Country club. Try as she might, she could not think of the Pennyfoot as anything but a hotel. And she probably never would.

"She don't look like no housemaid to me," Jeanette said as she lifted a cauldron of hot water from the stove. "I ask you, what's a housemaid and a housekeeper doing staying as guests at the very hotel what they worked at once? Don't make any sense, do it."

Moira shrugged, her fingers busy peeling the shell from a hard-boiled egg. "It's not our place to say, is it."

Jeanette dumped the water into the sink and carried the empty pot back to the stove. "Oh, don't be such a ninny. Who's going to know if we talk about them?" She nodded her head in the direction of the ceiling. "I wish I could be a spider on the wall in some of those boudoirs. I reckon I'd see enough to make me eyes bulge out."

Moira's cheeks flamed, and she lowered her chin. "It's none of our business what goes on upstairs."

Jeanette stomped back to the sink and began slipping soiled dinner plates into the water. "Maybe not, but I reckon I could tell you a thing or two that would shock the living daylights out of you."

Moira raised her chin. "Like what?"

Jeanette grinned. "See? I knew you were just as nosy as me. What if I was to tell you I knew something about Rotten Wrotham that no one else knew?"

Moira's eyes grew wide with apprehension. "What do you mean?"

"Can't tell you, can I. But I can tell you this, them toffs upstairs aren't all that blinking perfect, neither. You'd be shocked if you knew what I know."

Moira went back to shelling her eggs. "I don't believe you know anything. You're just making it up to sound big, that's all."

"Am I then?" Jeanette swished the dishes in the hot water and stacked them onto the draining board. "Well, I wouldn't be too sure. You know the really handsome one? The one with the dark curly hair and the suntan? His wife is the one with all that red hair?"

"You mean Mr. Peebles?"

"Yeah, that's his name. Roger Peebles. Well, he's no angel, that's for sure."

"Go on!" Moira's eyes gleamed with excitement. "Did he make a grab at you?"

"Maybe he did and maybe he didn't." Now that she

had Moira's full attention, Jeanette was thoroughly enjoying herself. "All I can tell you is, there's a lot more to him than meets the eye."

"You got a crush on him, then?"

Jeanette wiped her hands on her apron and glanced over her shoulder at her friend. "So what if I have?"

"You'd better not let your Wally know that." Moira looked worried. "You know what a temper Wally's got. He's likely to do something bad to Mr. Peebles if he thinks he's after you."

"He wouldn't have no say in it." Jeanette grabbed a dishcloth in one hand and a wet plate in the other. "He's only me blinking boyfriend, not me husband."

"Don't matter." Moira carried the broken shells over to the oven and opened the door. A blast of hot air erupted from the searing red coals inside as she threw the shells into the furnace, sending sizzling golden sparks dancing up the chimney. "Wally thinks you belong to him, and he won't take kindly to another man mucking about with his girlfriend."

"Here, I never said he—"

Jeanette snapped her mouth shut as Miss Bunkle sailed into the kitchen, flapping her apron in front of her face to cool it off. "Great heavens it's hot in here. Did someone forget to close the door on the oven again?"

"No, Miss Bunkle." Moira scraped her hands down the front of her apron. "I've just been burning the egg shells, that's all."

"Well, get that door shut, girl, before we lose all the heat out of that stove. Michel will be here at any minute to start the evening meal. He won't be too happy if his oven's gone cold."

"Yes, Miss Bunkle." Moira slammed the heavy door shut and returned to the table, where the newly skinned eggs waited to be chopped.

Jeanette went on drying the dishes, her mind conjuring up a vision of Mr. Peebles chasing her around the bedroom, and her running slow enough for him to catch her.

The next morning Baxter seemed anxious to get back to his accounts, which according to him, had been badly mismanaged. He seemed in a sour mood, and barely acknowledged Cecily's reminder that she was meeting Phoebe and Madeline later that morning at Dolly's Teashop. Which, she told herself, gave her justification for neglecting to tell him that she planned to pay Dr. Prestwick a visit on the way. There was no sense in aggravating his temper. She would simply tell him about it later, when he'd recovered from whatever was displeasing him.

After giving him a loving kiss on the cheek, she left him to his work. Raymond was waiting for her outside when she emerged into the cold, clean sea air, and she was glad of her black marabou stole snuggled warmly around her shoulders as she settled down in the carriage.

Raymond had suggested they use one of the motor cars, but Cecily had declined. It was difficult enough getting used to the noise of the dratted things. She just hated the thought of riding in one. Although Baxter had hinted more than once that he would like to own a motor car, so far when he'd brought up the subject, she'd managed to steer the conversation to another topic.

Sooner or later, she knew she would have to accept the fact that this was the modern mode of transportation. But right now, she was determined to enjoy the steady jogging of the carriage wheels, and the soothing clip-clop of horses' hooves on the snow-dusted street.

The Esplanade always looked so deserted in the winter. Stretching in a graceful curve along the seafront, with only a low barrier of railings separating the street from the smooth golden beach, it seemed to be mourning the warm summer days when the tiny shops were bustling with customers and children with kites soaring behind them raced across the sands.

Right now the dismal row of shops huddled behind ugly boards that sheltered the windows from the winter storms. Few people braved the seafront in winter, and those who did hurried to their destinations, rather than dawdle and browse as they did in the height of the season.

The brisk tattoo of the horses' hooves kept up a steady pace as they turned up the hill into the town. Cecily's pulse quickened, her gaze eager to settle on fondly remembered places. Saint Bartholomew's, where the vicar, Phoebe's son, Algie, conducted his services in his stuttering, stammering manner that sent most of his parishioners into a doze before he was halfway through.

Cecily smiled, wondering how Algie was tolerating his new stepfather. Colonel Fortescue had been a regular guest at the Pennyfoot Hotel before he married Phoebe. Although most people held the opinion that the colonel's mind had been severely diminished by his earth-shattering experiences in the Boer War, a view that Cecily reluctantly shared, apparently the colonel had been astute enough to propose marriage to Phoebe Carter-Holmes. No doubt in the secure knowledge that the lady would take great pains in taking care of him as efficiently and as selflessly as she did her bumbling son.

Cecily was looking forward to hearing more about Phoebe's union with the bizarre retired soldier. But first, her meeting with Dr. Prestwick demanded her attention.

As they reached the High Street, she was overjoyed to find that here the spirit of Christmas prevailed with a vengeance. Huge boughs of berry-laden holly and fir adorned just about every shop front in the High Street. Paper chains in red, green, yellow, and blue, cut into delicate and intricate patterns, graced windows full of seasonal fare. Rows of plucked ducks and geese hung by their feet in Abbitsons the Butchers, while Harris the Drapers had clothed its mannequins in swathes of red and green velvet.

By the time they reached the doctor's house, Cecily was thoroughly imbued with the spirit of the season. She was relieved to note that the usual row of carriages had not yet arrived when Raymond reined in the horses in front of the neat front garden. She had deliberately left early, hoping to arrive before the office opened. By the looks of things, she had succeeded.

After asking Raymond to wait, she rapped on the front door, her heart leaping with expectation at the thought of seeing the handsome doctor again. She had refrained from her customary habit of sending a calling card in the hopes of surprising him. She wanted to catch him off guard, so to speak. He was more likely to tell her what she wanted to know if he was unprepared for her visit.

She was most anxious to know exactly what Dr. Prestwick's opinion was of the death of Barry Wrotham. No doubt the good doctor would be hesitant to tell her anything at first, but in the past she'd been able to persuade him otherwise. She could only hope that she was still able to do so. So far, all she had were vague suspicions and theories.

Nothing substantial upon which to base an investigation that, if she didn't take care, could very well lead her into a great deal of trouble.

She needed the doctor's complete cooperation. And if she was to solve this case before Mrs. Wrotham left for London, she needed it now.

CHAPTER
❀ 6 ❀

The front door of Dr. Prestwick's house opened abruptly to reveal a gray-haired woman wearing a cap and apron, her lined faced creased in a frown. "The doctor's not ready yet to receive patients," she said crisply, and started to close the door.

"Oh, I'm not a patient," Cecily called out. "I'm an old friend of the doctor's, here to pay him a short visit."

The woman peered around the door with a suspicious look on her face. "Do you have an appointment, madam?"

"Well, no," Cecily admitted. "But I'm quite sure if you tell the doctor that Mrs. Baxter is here to see him . . . no, wait. Perhaps you'd better tell him Cecily Sinclair."

The housekeeper's expression darkened. "Perhaps you

should come back later," she said. "*After* you have made an appointment."

Right on the heels of her words came another voice, smooth and mellow, yet filled with surprise. "Cecily? It can't be." The housekeeper disappeared and the door was thrown wide.

The man who stood on the doorstep stared at Cecily as if she'd materialized out of thin air. "Good Lord. It is. I'd heard you were coming down to Badgers End, but I had no idea you were already here."

Cecily laughed up at him. "Kevin! You don't look a day older."

"And neither do you, my dear." He held out his hand. "In fact, if anything, you look younger. Do come in. This is such a pleasant surprise. At least, I hope it is." His piercing blue eyes narrowed. "You're not here as a patient, I trust?"

Putting her hand in his, Cecily allowed him to escort her into the narrow hallway. The familiar smell of disinfectant and furniture polish brought back so many memories. She looked about her, noticing at once that the walls of the waiting room had been papered with an embossed design of milkmaids and cows in shades of cream and brown. Rather pleasing, especially when one had to sit and wait with nothing better to look at.

"I'm quite well," she told Prestwick, in a delayed answer to his question. "I happened to be coming into town today to meet with Phoebe and Madeline, and I thought I'd take the opportunity to stop by and visit with you awhile."

At the mention of Madeline, she thought she saw a shadow cross the doctor's face.

"Ah, yes. Madeline. How is she? I haven't seen her in quite a few days."

"Really?" Cecily followed him into his office and took the chair he offered. "Then you must not have had much time to spare lately."

Prestwick's expression was evasive. "Do I detect a note of disapproval in that remark?"

Cecily laughed. "It's not my place to pass judgment on you. It's just that I thought you and Madeline . . . well, you know."

"Do I?" Prestwick shuffled some papers on the desk in front of him, his expression carefully bland. "Madeline and I are good friends, that's all. I enjoy her company. I trust she enjoys mine."

"I'm quite certain of that." Cecily hesitated, then added recklessly, "She cares about you a great deal. I do hope you don't do anything that will bring her pain. She's had a hard life. She deserves some happiness."

Prestwick's eyebrow twitched. "I have no wish to hurt anyone, Cecily. But I'm sure you didn't come here to talk about Madeline."

Accepting his effort to change the subject, she said brightly, "No, of course I didn't."

"I didn't think so." Prestwick tilted his chair back and crossed his slender hands across his chest. "If I were to wager a bet, I'd say you're here to inquire about the recent death of one of our citizens, are you not?"

Cecily did her best to look offended. "Why, Kevin, whatever do you mean? I stopped by to visit with an old friend, that's all."

He bowed his head. "Then I misjudged you, my dear. Please accept my apologies."

"Of course."

"So you have no interest at all in the death of the late manager of the Pennyfoot Country Club."

She tilted her head to one side. "Should I?"

He threw back his head, and a roar of laughter erupted from his throat. "Cecily, Cecily, Cecily. You are as transparent as a pane of glass. How can you sit there and tell me you're not gasping to know every single detail of Barry Wrotham's premature demise?"

She grinned happily at him. "Well, I must admit, my curiosity is somewhat piqued. After all, there does seem to be strange circumstances surrounding the accident. If it was an accident."

Prestwick shook his head, his mouth still curved in amusement. "You will never change, my dear, I'm happy to say. But I'm afraid this time you will be disappointed. There is no murderer lurking about Badgers End. I'm afraid you will have to curb your investigative instincts for a while. Barry Wrotham's death, sinister as it may appear, was an accident, pure and simple."

"May I ask how you arrived at that conclusion?"

Prestwick shrugged. "I don't see why not. There were no marks on the body indicating foul play. Death was by drowning. Wrotham was a regular visitor at the George and Dragon, and more than once left there with more in his belly than he could handle."

"You're saying he was intoxicated and fell into the well?"

"That's the official verdict, yes. P.C. Northcott ruled it as accidental and I signed the death warrant. Wrotham was buried a week or so ago."

"Do you have any idea of the time he died?"

Prestwick's eyes narrowed. "Cecily, if you know something I don't, perhaps you should tell me now. It could save us both a good deal of trouble later on."

Cecily folded her hands in her lap. "I don't know any more than you do, which is why I'm asking the questions. I simply want to settle things in my mind, nothing more."

Prestwick picked up a pencil and tapped it on the desk before answering. "As far as I could tell, Wrotham had been dead less than two hours before he was found."

"On Sunday afternoon?"

"Yes. Several people saw him in the George and Dragon at midday. It was his habit to stop there on his way home, since Sunday was his half-day off."

"Did anyone mention that he'd had too much to drink, or that he appeared to be intoxicated when he left?"

"Not as far as I know. As I said, there was no investigation."

"And no one has questioned why Barry Wrotham should be wandering around an abandoned farm all alone on a Sunday afternoon? He must have known it was deserted . . . how long has it been since the owner left?"

"At least a year, so I believe." Looking serious now, Prestwick leaned forward. "If you want my advice, Cecily, let things be. There's no reason to suppose this is anything but an accident, and if you start poking around and asking questions, you're likely to raise the wrath of a few people, including our good friend Inspector Cranshaw. I doubt if he'll have much patience with you, after all the trouble you caused him in the past."

Cecily raised her chin. "I solved more than one case for

the inspector and P.C. Northcott. More often than not by asking questions and using my brains to sift out the truth. He should be thanking me, not condemning me."

Prestwick's lips twitched. "I doubt that will happen. But in this case, you are looking for something that isn't there. Tell me the truth now, isn't this just a case of you having missed all the excitement of tracking down villains? Aren't you trying just a little too hard to make a mountain out of an anthill?"

"I thought that was molehill."

"I like anthill better. Never could stand moles. They can do more damage to a garden in one night than a midwinter hailstorm."

Aware that he was deliberately changing the subject again, Cecily gave in. "Very well, Kevin, if you are so certain this unfortunate event was an accident, I suppose I must accept it. But it was very nice to see you again. You must join us for dinner at the Pennyfoot soon." She rose from her chair, and straightened her hat with both hands. "I should take my leave before you are deluged with patients all clamoring for your attention."

Prestwick jumped up and hurried around the desk to her side. "It was a very great pleasure to see you, Cecily. I trust your husband is well?"

"Very well, thank you." Cecily moved to the door and waited for him to open it. "I hope we shall see you again soon?"

"Just as soon as I can find the time." He opened the door for her and stood back to let her pass. "I mean it, Cecily. Forget about Wrotham's death and just enjoy the Christmas Season. I'm sure you have more than enough to worry about with all the responsibilities of taking care of the Pennyfoot guests."

"I do indeed." She smiled up at him. "Thank you, Kevin. I'll remember you to Madeline. I'll be meeting with her in a few minutes."

Prestwick tightened his lips ever so slightly. "Please, give her my regards."

Outside in the cruel bite of the wind, Cecily hurried down the path to where Raymond waited with the carriage. The horses stamped with impatience, steam drifting from their nostrils as they tossed their heads.

"Straight to Dolly's Teashop, Raymond," she told him, and tugged her stole more securely around her shoulders. She was looking forward immensely to Dolly's warm tearoom, a very hot cup of tea, and a warm, luscious Banbury cake.

For the time being she would try to forget about Barry Wrotham's bizarre death, though she had no intention of giving up on it. Too many people had their suspicions about the accident. In any case, she was a great believer in hunches, and this time the tingling in her bones was so acute she could feel her flesh creep.

There was something else bothering her at that moment, however. Something that demanded her immediate attention. There was no doubt in her mind that all was not well between Dr. Prestwick and her dear friend Madeline. And right then that was more important to her than the death of a man whom apparently no one liked.

Arriving at Dolly's Teashop, Cecily paused in front of the square-paned window and gazed in admiration at the magnificent Christmas cakes on display. The center one was raised above the others, and had been painstakingly decorated in glittering white royal icing. Tiny silver sugar beads nestled in the thick white swirls circling the top and bottom, and red and green sprinkles dusted the smooth shell pattern around the edges. Miniature sprigs of holly had been piped at intervals in the border, and a green paper sleeve wrapped around the sides of the cake. It made Cecily's mouth water just looking at it.

The familiar tinkle of the bell as she opened the door warmed her instantly. She was pleased to see nothing had changed. The familiar fragrance of newly baked bread blended with the exotic aroma of ginger and nutmeg, every bit as heavenly as she remembered.

The china jugs and vases shared space with boughs of fir and mistletoe on the wide mantelpiece, the decorative plates still balanced on the picture rail, and the large copper coal scuttle stood guard in the hearth as always. Even the polished brass fender with the dent in the right-hand corner had not been replaced, much to her delight.

The room was crowded, as usual, and the air hummed with lowered voices and the occasional titter of laughter. To Cecily's delight, Madeline and Phoebe were already seated at their favorite table close to the fireplace, where enormous flames leapt and sputtered up the wide chimney.

Phoebe's face was partially hidden beneath the brim of her hat, which tilted at an alarming angle, threatening to dislodge the mound of fruit and feathers adorning it. Madeline, as usual, was hatless, and gloveless, and as always, the target of many disdainful stares which she blithely ignored.

Madeline's presence in the village had always been clouded with controversy. Most people were afraid of her, intimidated by tales of her mystic powers, which were mostly embroidered with half-truths. There was no doubt Madeline was capable of some things that defied explanation and, at times, had unsettled Cecily quite considerably. It was doubtful, however, if Madeline had half the capacity attributed to her . . . magical or otherwise.

Nevertheless, her reputation exceeded her abilities, and most people tended to avoid her whenever possible, unless desperate enough to brave her cottage in search of a potion to cure their ills.

Apparently blissfully unaware of the sensation she caused, Madeline waved vigorously at the sight of Cecily, while tapping Phoebe smartly on the arm to get her attention.

Cecily was halfway across the room, threading her way delicately between the tables, when a strident voice rang out, easily overwhelming the quiet voices around her.

"Mrs. Sinclair! I don't believe it! Whatever brings you back here?"

Cecily smiled at the woman lumbering toward her, her massive bosom narrowly missing the heads of her customers as she squeezed by them. "Dolly! How lovely to see you again!"

"Well, this is a surprise." Dolly's florid face was wreathed in smiles as she held out her two chubby hands and grasped Cecily's. "Let me look at you. Well, looks as if the Smoke hasn't done you any harm, that's for sure."

"Not at all." Cecily withdrew her hands and edged over to the table where Phoebe and Madeline were waiting. "And I see the teashop is still doing a wonderful business."

"Aye, that it is, thank the good Lord. How's that handsome manager of yours? No, wait. He's your husband now, isn't he." Dolly's rolls of fat jiggled as she uttered a deep belly laugh. "Can't call you Mrs. Sinclair now, can I. It's going to take some getting used to, remembering to call you Mrs. Baxter and that's a fact."

"It took a great deal of time before I was used to it." Cecily wiggled her gloved fingers at Phoebe and Madeline and sat down on the empty chair. "I do hope you still make those sublime Banbury cakes, Dolly. I've had the taste in my mouth for them ever since I arose this morning."

"That I do, Mrs. Sinclair. Oops!" Dolly's double chin wobbled as her hearty laugh rang out again. "There I go again. Mrs. Baxter, it is. I'll remember eventually. I'll send Letty in with the cakes right away. These ladies wanted to wait until you arrived." She wagged a thick finger at Madeline. "Shame on you for not telling me it was Mrs. Sinclair you were waiting for."

Madeline shrugged. "We thought you would enjoy the surprise."

"You mean Mrs. Baxter." Phoebe snickered behind her hand. "You should have seen your face, Dolly. You looked as if you'd seen a ghost."

"I thought I had for a moment." Dolly clamped her pudgy fingers down on Cecily's unsuspecting shoulder. "Come back here to live, have you?"

"Oh, no." Cecily smiled with genuine regret. "We're just here for the Christmas Season. Baxter and I are helping out at the Pennyfoot until Edward finds another manager."

"Ah, yes, after that poor bugger fell down the well. Serves him right, that's what I say. Never had a good word to say to anybody. That's what you get for drinking on an empty belly. Should have been looking where he was going. Pity, that it is." She shifted her huge body around and pointed it in the direction of the kitchen. "Hope you enjoy your tea and buns, ladies. Come and see me again, Mrs. Sin . . . Baxter, before you leave. And bring that nice-looking husband of yours with you the next time."

Phoebe simpered as Dolly strode off, bumping chairs with her hips as she went. "Can you imagine Baxter in here sipping tea and nibbling on Dolly's pastries?"

"He'd far rather be at the George and Dragon enjoying a pint of ale." Cecily glanced at Madeline. "I've just had a nice visit with Dr. Kevin Prestwick. He asked to be remembered to you."

A faint pink hue crept over Madeline's alabaster cheeks. "Thank you," she murmured.

Phoebe pounced immediately. "You haven't seen him lately? Didn't you tell us that he spent every moment of his spare time with you?"

Wishing she hadn't mentioned it, Cecily hurried to change the subject. "What is the colonel doing with his time while you are enjoying Dolly's delectable baking?"

Ignoring her, Phoebe leaned toward Madeline, her eyes probing the other woman's face. "He's seeing that hussy, Winifred Chesterton, isn't he."

Madeline's expression froze. "I haven't the slightest idea whom Dr. Prestwick is seeing, nor do I care."

"I knew it!" Phoebe sat back with a look of triumph. "I saw them together just the other day."

Giving Phoebe a reproachful frown, Cecily laid her

hand on Madeline's arm. "I'm so sorry, Madeline. I had no idea."

Madeline lifted her shoulders. "I just didn't want to talk about it. That's why I didn't tell you. The doctor and I had a disagreement. I haven't seen him in quite some time."

"I'm so sorry to hear that. He didn't say anything . . ." Cecily let her voice trail off, not knowing quite what to say.

Even Phoebe had the grace to look contrite. "I'm sorry, too, Madeline. If I'd known this was serious, I would never—"

"It's quite all right," Madeline said, interrupting her. "Kevin has never made me any promises and I didn't expect anything from him."

"But you wanted to marry him," Phoebe said with her usual lack of tact.

"Phoebe—" Cecily began in protest, but Madeline raised her hand.

"No, she's quite right. I was rather hoping. It just didn't happen, that's all."

"What happened?" Cecily asked, abandoning all efforts to mind her own business. "When I left Badgers End, I was so sure you and Kevin were becoming close."

Madeline gave her a brave smile. "It wasn't meant to be, that's all. We have such differing views. He won't accept my methods of curing ills, and I can't accept his rigid beliefs."

"You argued about medicine?"

"Yes, we did. There are so many kinds of herbal medicine, some of which have been successfully used for centuries.

Kevin dismisses anything that hasn't been invented in a laboratory, and won't even consider that nature has its own powers of healing. Even though he is fully aware that a great deal of modern medicine is synthetic re-creations of plants. After a while, the arguments became tiresome. One day I attempted to treat his headache with a potion of herbs and he was quite insulting. I just couldn't fight him anymore."

"I find that most distressing," Phoebe said, dabbing at actual tears in her eyes with her lace-edged handkerchief. "How sad that two people with the same magnificent purpose, to heal the poorly, can be so contrary in their ways to go about it. It's a great shame that you cannot find some kind of compromise, so that the ill can benefit from both means of treatment."

Once in a while, Cecily thought, smiling at her friend, Phoebe had a way of putting her finger right to the heart of the problem. "Phoebe's right," she said, laying her fingers on Madeline's arm. "Both you and Kevin have a wealth of knowledge and experience that could be a tremendous benefit to everyone if only you could find a way to share and accept each other's beliefs."

Madeline's lovely face creased in a frown. "Perhaps you should talk to Kevin. He's the one who's being stubborn. He just won't listen to reason and I am tired of talking to deaf ears. As far as I'm concerned, we will do better apart." She gazed out of the window, saying brightly, "I wonder if we shall have a white Christmas this year."

Cecily heard the slight break in her voice, and her heart ached for Madeline. Sensing that she had said more than enough at the risk of upsetting her friend, however, she accepted the change of subject and glanced in the direction of the kitchen. "Now where on earth is that girl with my Banbury cakes?" she murmured. "I'm positively starving."

CHAPTER
❀ 7 ❀

An hour or so later Cecily bade her two friends farewell and once more approached the carriage that Raymond had brought back shortly before the appointed time.

Instead of returning directly to the Pennyfoot, however, on an impulse she asked Raymond to drive her out to the abandoned farm where Barry Wrotham had met his untimely end. It had occurred to her, while listening to Madeline and Phoebe bicker about the arrangements for the pantomime, that as long as there had been no investigation into the accident, it was quite unlikely that a thorough search had been conducted.

"Tell me," she asked Raymond as he helped her into the carriage, "has anyone bothered to look around the abandoned farmhouse?"

"You mean the one where Wrotham died? Not as far as I know, m'm." Raymond waited while she settled herself on the creaking leather seat. "Don't s'pose the bobbies saw any need to muck about out there, seeing as how they all swear it were an accident."

"No, I don't suppose so." Cecily looked him straight in the eye. "I wonder if the house is securely locked."

Raymond's eyes brightened with the light of adventure. He pretended to consider the matter, stroking his chin in a purely theatrical gesture. "Hmmm. Well, I reckon there's only one way to find out, m'm."

Cecily beamed. "Exactly what I was thinking, Raymond. If we are to do a little snooping, however, there's one thing I must ask of you."

Raymond grinned. "I won't say nuffing to nobody, m'm. Though I daresay nobody would be surprised. After all, everyone's heard plenty of tales in the village about how you chased after murderers and whatnot when you was owner of the Pennyfoot. Almost got done in yourself now and then, so the stories go."

"Really." Cecily tucked her hands in her muff. "Well, don't believe everything you hear, Raymond. Village tales have a way of growing out of proportion when passed from one eager tongue to another."

"Yes, m'm. But don't you worry. Me lips are sealed." He tightened his lips and drew his thumb across them. "On me honor."

"Thank you, Raymond. I'm sure I can trust you to keep your word." She settled back to enjoy the ride.

The road they took wound up the cliffs to cross Putney Downs, giving Cecily a wonderful view of the bay.

Though the heavy clouds had turned the sea a dull gray and a thin mist hung over the water, the entire sweep of the Esplanade as well as the tiny cottages lining the cove were plainly visible. Not at all like the dense fog of London that obscured anything farther than ten yards away.

She didn't miss the city at all, Cecily realized as she watched the warm walls of the George and Dragon appear through the haze at the foot of the hill. She was perfectly content to be back in her beloved Badgers End, where the peace and quiet of the countryside was undisturbed by the infuriating honking of horns and the constant explosions and ugly black smoke of the motor cars.

About a mile and a half from the pub, Raymond steered the horses onto a gravel road, where they jogged for a few more yards before coming to a halt in front of wide wooden gates. Raymond hopped down and pushed open the gates, then climbed back to urge the horses through before climbing back down to close the gates behind them.

Now they were on a rutted track than ran alongside a harvested cornfield. The cold weather had hardened the earth, and the wheels bumped and bounced as they made their way to another pair of gates, where Raymond went through the procedure of opening and shutting them once more. At last they arrived at a courtyard in front of what appeared to be stables, and the horses clattered to a halt.

Cecily climbed down from the carriage, shivering in the cutting breeze that chilled her bones. She followed Raymond around the side of the stables, picking her way carefully between the deep ruts dug by centuries of wagon wheels.

Raymond led her through another gate and up a winding garden path, lined with straggly weeds and long, unmown grass. The windows of the rambling farmhouse blinked ominously through their shrouds of dust, and a loose drainpipe rattled in the wind.

The heavy front door refused to budge when Raymond tried the handle. "Looks like it's locked tight, m'm," he said, his expression taut with anticipation.

"Well then, I suppose we shall just have to find another way in," Cecily said calmly.

Raymond's eyes lit up with delight. "Yes, m'm. That we shall." He stood back and studied the front of the house. "Can't see no broken windows or nothing. You just hang on here, m'm, and I'll take a quick gander around the back."

He disappeared, and Cecily huddled in the doorway in a vain attempt to escape the cold bite of the wind. The entire place appeared to be utterly deserted. A dilapidated broken-down wagon with one wheel missing sat in the courtyard, and several broken barrels lay on their side nearby. One of the doors to the stable must have lost its latch, since it swung dismally back and forth in the wind, its hinges groaning in protest.

Overhead, seagulls wheeled in search of food, their endless cries echoing across the rooftop of the decaying farmhouse. It was a mournful sound and tugged at Cecily's heart. A family had lived and thrived here once, until the encroaching industrial revolution had taken its toll on the farmers, robbing so many of their livelihoods.

She was a staunch advocate of modern technology and the benefits it could bring. As she had argued with Baxter many times, sacrifices had to be made in the pursuit of progress. But there were times when it saddened her to think how much a modern society had cost in traditions and customs that had been an essential part of life for centuries. How unfortunate that in the interests of improving one way of life, another was forced to disappear.

A faint tinkle of glass somewhere in the distance interrupted her thoughts. She stepped out from the doorway, looking anxiously from right to left. It wouldn't do for her to be caught intruding on someone's property uninvited.

It only occurred to her at that moment that in her anxiety to search the farmhouse, she had broken her promise to Baxter. He would be most displeased with her if he knew she had ventured into forbidden territory without notifying him first.

To her relief, nothing moved but the leaves and a stray piece of paper tossed along the ground by the wind. Her curiosity aroused, she was about to go after it when the handle on the door rattled and the hinges squealed as it slowly opened inward.

Raymond's face peered out at her, one cheek smeared with dirt. "Funny thing, m'm," he murmured as he stepped back to let her in. "I was leaning me elbow against one of the windows and it sort of caved in."

"Goodness." Cecily peered at his elbow. "You didn't hurt yourself, I hope."

"No, m'm. You see, I was holding me coat over me elbow at the time."

"Yes, I do see." She straightened. "You must have leaned rather hard, Raymond."

He grinned with pride. "Yes, m'm. Reckon I did."

"Well, it can't be helped." She nodded her approval. "Thank you, Raymond."

"My pleasure, m'm." He turned and waved his hand at the darkened hallway. "Don't seem to be much in here, though. No furniture or nothing."

"Well, I suppose it won't cost us anything to look." Cecily moved down the hallway and peered into what once must have been the parlor. The room was quite empty, with just a small stove standing forlorn on one corner. Trying not to imagine a family huddled around its warmth, she turned her back on the desolate room.

"I think I'll take a look in the upstairs rooms, Raymond. Perhaps you should stay down here and keep an eye on the courtyard, just in case we should have a surprise visitor."

Raymond pulled his cap from his head and touched his forehead with it. "Right you are, m'm. I'll whistle if I see anybody."

"A good idea. Please do." She started up the narrow staircase, each one squeaking as she stepped on it. The dark clouds outside allowed little light to filter through the grimy windows, and she made her way carefully down the upstairs hallway, wary of stepping on a loose board in the gloom and turning her ankle.

She reached the door of the first room and peered inside. It was completely bare, and abandoning it, she moved on to the next room.

Stepping inside, she looked cautiously around. The bedroom was quite large, with a huge window overlooking the fields at the back of the house. She could see nothing in there but a rolled-up blanket against one wall and a tattered magazine lying next to it. The musty smell wrinkled her nose, and she could see her breath form in front of her face as she moved cautiously across the room.

The magazine bearing the previous month's date had a picture of the very latest fashion in outerwear on the cover. As she bent closer to peer at it, the floor popped loudly beneath her feet, making her jump. Her heart, galvanized by the unexpected sound, pounded with an urgency that made her uncomfortable.

Taking a last look around, she was about to leave when she spied something outside the window. An enterprising robin had built a nest on the broad windowsill. She smiled, imagining the tiny eggs hatching and each fledgling balanced precariously on the very edge of the carefully constructed nest, awaiting its first fluttering leap into the air.

She turned away from the window and was about to retreat from the room when she spied a tiny glint of light in front of the rolled-up blanket. She hurried toward it and crouched down, tilting her head this way and that to catch the sparkle again. Then she saw it. Half-hidden beneath the woolen blanket, a long pin lay caught between the floorboards.

In her attempt to pry it loose, Cecily thrust the blanket aside. As she did so, something fell out and rolled noisily across the floor, scaring her half to death. A long-necked bottle smacked against the opposite wall and lay still.

Leaving it for the moment, Cecily returned to her task.

At last she pulled the pin from its resting place and examined it. No wonder it had sparkled in the light. It was a gold hat pin, adorned with a large diamond at one end. A very expensive hat pin. Certainly not the kind one would expect a farmer's wife to possess.

Her excitement rising, Cecily shook out the blanket. The quality of the material was excellent, and it appeared to have had little use. Hardly any dust rose from it, suggesting that it had recently been left there. Clearly not a year ago, when presumably the owners had left, according to Kevin.

Finding nothing more in the folds of the blanket, Cecily rolled it up again and left it where she had found it. The label on the bottle declared its contents to have been an excellent cognac. Again, not something one would normally find in a farmer's house.

Unless this particular farmer had been unusually wealthy, and that seemed unlikely judging by the general state of the house and the broken-down wagon outside, then it would seem that Emily Wrotham's suspicions could very well be right.

Her husband might well have been indulging in an illicit liaison when he visited the farm that day. If so, it was quite possible that a rival for the lady's affections had rid himself of his opponent. A just end, perhaps, but an illegal one, nevertheless.

Cecily rose to her feet. She had promised the grieving widow to find out the truth. She wasn't at all certain that Emily Wrotham would welcome evidence that bore out her suspicions.

After placing the bottle back behind the blanket,

Cecily pinned the hat pin onto her bodice and covered it with her stole. Then she made her way down the creaking staircase to the hallway below.

Raymond emerged from the parlor as she reached the foot of the stairs. "Find anything, m'm?"

"Nothing of interest." She nodded at the rooms down the hall. "I'll just take a hasty peek down here."

"Very well, m'm. I'll wait on the doorstep if you don't mind. The smell in here is getting up me nose."

She could sympathize with him. The unpleasant odor of damp and mildew was much stronger downstairs. "Of course. I shan't be more than a minute or two." She hurried down the hallway and into each room, not really surprised to find nothing but more dust and cobwebs. Barry Wrotham had chosen well . . . a large, fairly comfortable room, certainly less damp, at the back of the house, hidden from prying eyes of anyone who might wander into the courtyard.

That's if it *were* Barry Wrotham, she reminded herself. It could have been anyone dallying with some dolly in an abandoned house. But then, why else would a man lie to his wife and visit a deserted farm, with seemingly no interest in buying it? It would seem that the Pennyfoot's ex-manager was hiding something, and another woman would appear to be the most likely answer.

Nevertheless, past experience had taught her never to jump to conclusions, and until she had absolute proof, she would have to keep her deductions to herself for the time being.

Raymond stood waiting for when she stepped out onto the porch, his face pinched with cold. She could actually hear his teeth chattering as he handed her back into the carriage. "Straight home," she told him, "and when you get back, you may tell Michel I ordered a glass of brandy for you. It will help warm your insides."

Raymond touched the peak of his cap. "Thank you, m'm. Much obliged." He clambered up onto his seat and gave the impatient horses their reins. The carriage bumped and swayed across the rutted ground, crunched down the gravel path, and then they were off down the coast road to the Pennyfoot.

The midday meal had already been served when Cecily arrived back at the club. Miss Bunkle was in the foyer and gave Cecily a disapproving frown as she hurried through the front door.

"Mr. Baxter has been asking for you, madam," she said. "He sounded quite concerned. I told him Raymond had gone to fetch you from the teashop more than an hour ago. I've been expecting him back long before this."

"Thank you, Miss Bunkle," Cecily said brightly. "Please don't blame Raymond. It was my fault. I detained him. I'll have a word with Mr. Baxter right away."

"Thank you, madam." Miss Bunkle bowed her head, then glided away across the floor, her back as stiff as a ship's mast.

Cecily pulled a face. The woman performed her duties admirably, by all accounts, but Cecily much preferred the sometimes muddled, befuddled, but always well-meaning methods of Altheda Chubb. Life had been so much more fun in the old days at the Pennyfoot.

Aware that her disgruntled mood was due more to her imminent confrontation with her husband than any discord with Miss Bunkle, Cecily headed for Baxter's office.

He rose immediately as she entered after the briefest of taps on the door. Rounding the desk with an alacrity that surprised her, he grasped her by the arms and looked keenly into her face.

"Cecily, are you all right? Where the devil have you been? I've been half out of my mind with worry, imagining all sorts of dire calamities. What happened to you? Miss Bunkle said Raymond had left over an hour ago to fetch you back. What took you so long?"

She laughed up at him. "Dearest, if you would just stop firing questions at me, I'll do my best to explain."

He pulled her close and gave her a brief hug before letting her go. "Sit down, and tell me where you have spent the better part of this day."

She sat, wondering how she would find the words to explain why she had broken her word to him. "I don't suppose you have anything to eat in here?" She gave him her most appealing smile. "I'm quite cold and extremely hungry."

"I'm not surprised. You missed the midday meal." He reached for the bell rope and tugged on it. "I'll have the kitchen bring something for you."

"Thank you, darling. You are so incredibly thoughtful. I really don't know what I would do without you. I am such a fortunate woman."

His eyes narrowed in suspicion. "That sounds ominous."

She gave him an innocent stare. "What does, dearest?"

"All those expansive compliments. I fear you are leading up to something."

"Well, really." She managed a light laugh. "Can't a woman compliment her husband without risk of being accused of insincerity?"

"Oh, I don't doubt that you are sincere. It's your choice of time to compliment me that gives me reason to question your motive."

A sharp tap on the door saved her from answering. She waited while Baxter gave Jeannette his order, and tried not to notice the girl's curious glance directed at her as she turned to leave.

The door closed behind her, and Cecily braced herself for Baxter's inevitable inquisition.

"All right," he said. "While we are waiting for your meal to arrive, perhaps you can enlighten me as to why you have been missing for the last several hours."

"I did tell you I was meeting Phoebe and Madeline for elevenses, did I not?"

"You did." Baxter returned to his chair and sat down, his hands folded across his chest. "But upon inquiring as to your whereabouts, I was informed that you had left here shortly after ten o'clock. Which meant you would have arrived in the town at twenty past ten. It is now—" He pulled his watch from his waistcoat pocket and examined it, then snapped it shut and replaced it in his pocket. "—a quarter past two. I hardly think it took you four hours to consume one or two of Dolly's buns and a cup of tea."

"Banbury cakes, actually."

His eyes narrowed. "Cecily, please tell me what are you keeping from me."

Although his attitude irked her, she could hardly ignore the warning in his voice. "Oh, very well. I took the opportunity to call on Dr. Prestwick before I went to the teashop. I wanted to ask him a few questions, that's all."

"I thought as much." His voice was perfectly calm, but a pink patch on each side of his face made Cecily uneasy. "Why didn't you mention to me that you intended to see him?"

"I meant to, but you charged off to the office with no more than a faint peck on my cheek, and didn't give me time to tell you anything."

"So you thought you'd punish me by sneaking off to see an ex-suitor of yours."

She stared at him, her resentment fading. "Why, Hugh darling, I do believe you are jealous."

He drummed his fingers on the table. "Do I have reason to be?"

She burst out laughing. "Of course not. You know very well how much I adore you. No man could ever live up to you. I simply wanted to ask Kevin some questions about Barry Wrotham's accident. I swear."

To her immense relief, his stern features relaxed. "I see. So you do agree Wrotham's death was an accident, then."

"I didn't say that."

"No, you didn't." He sighed. "I don't know why I live in such hopes."

She laughed. "Come now, darling. We agreed that I should look into this, did we not?"

"We also agreed that you would not conduct an investigation without informing me about it first."

"You are quite right. I'm sorry. But you really were in rather a hurry this morning."

"Very well. I'll accept that."

"Good." She took a deep breath. "Then I hope you'll

also accept the fact that I acted purely on impulse when I left the teashop and went to search the farmhouse where Barry Wrotham died."

His expression worried her. Perhaps this time she had gone too far. She closed her eyes and waited for the inevitable explosion.

CHAPTER

❧ 8 ❧

A deep flush consumed Baxter's cheeks. He half rose from his chair, then sat down again. "You did *what?*"

"I just thought I'd have a quick look around," Cecily said hurriedly. "No one was there and Raymond accompanied me so I was perfectly safe."

"That's not the point, is it." His disapproving gaze seemed to pierce her heart. "We specifically agreed—"

"You're right, darling. I'm most terribly sorry. But I really didn't see any danger in it."

"You never do. What about the time you visited a certain dentist without telling me why you were going? You didn't see any danger in that, either. I almost lost you that time."

"Well, yes, I do admit, that was rather a mistake."

Baxter muttered an oath under his breath and buried his forehead in his hands. "Cecily, what is the point of promising me something if you don't intend to keep it? I thought I could trust you."

"And you can, darling. Really. You know how I am. I get an idea in my head, and before I know it, I've popped off to take care of it."

"You will very likely pop right off this earth if you cannot control your wickedly impulsive streak." He lifted his head. "What do I have to do to make you understand that I am responsible for your welfare, and by breaking your promise to me, you are making my task terribly difficult, if not downright impossible?"

Cecily bent her head and tried to sound suitably contrite. "I do understand, Hugh, really I do. I swear it won't happen again." She laid a hand against her breast. "Upon my heart, I swear."

He was prevented from answering by the arrival of Jeanette bearing a tray loaded with cold chicken and ham, wedges of cheddar cheese, slices of apples and pears, pickled onions, and crusty bread. The meal was accompanied by a jug of cider and two glasses. The maid waited for Baxter to clear a space on his desk before laying down the tray.

Baxter sat in silence until she'd left the room, then filled both glasses with cider, one of which he offered Cecily. "This should help warm you. You still look pinched with cold."

"I am." She took the glass and sipped the golden liquid. "I told poor Raymond to ask Michel for a brandy. He was chilled to the bone."

"No wonder Michel has ordered such a large supply of

brandy. It's bad enough he drinks the stuff all day long, but if he's giving it to the staff as well, we shall soon see our profits disappearing in a haze of alcohol."

Cecily wrinkled her nose at him. "He had to order extra brandy for the Christmas puddings. He told me he would begin steaming them this week. Besides, Raymond had to wait quite some time in the cold air for me. I thought he well deserved a brandy."

"Raymond is young. His body can adapt much more efficiently than yours."

"Are you suggesting I am old?"

"I wouldn't dare."

"Good. I would hope that you are far too much of a gentleman to remind me that I am older than you."

"Are you? I'd quite forgotten that."

She beamed at him. "Darling Hugh. You always know exactly the right thing to say. No wonder Miss Bunkle gazes at you with such adoration in her eyes."

His contemptuous snort delighted her. She reached for a wedge of cheese and a hunk of bread. "This is so much fun. Like picnicking, only more comfortable. I never did see the enjoyment in sitting in a field tormented by ants and bees."

Baxter munched on a slice of apple before replying. "I remember quite well that you used to adore sitting in a field with me."

"Ah, yes, well . . . I wasn't thinking about the ants and the bees then."

"Am I to take it that the bloom has gone off the romance now?"

She grinned happily at him. "Nothing could ever take

the bloom from my passion for you, my love. But you must admit, this is so much more cozy than sharing your meal with a herd of curious cows."

"Indubitably."

"By the way, you seem to be enjoying my lunch. Did you not eat in the dining room?"

"I didn't have much of an appetite. I hate dining alone. I did far too much of it in my life."

"I'm sorry, darling. From now on I'll make every effort to be here at mealtimes. Now let me tell you about our plans for the pantomime. Which reminds me, we need to order a large tree for the library."

Baxter munched in companionable silence while she divided her time between elaborating on her conversation with Madeline and Phoebe and avidly devouring the delectable offerings on the tray.

After a while, Baxter leaned back with a satisfied sigh. "Well, did you find anything at the farmhouse to justify your visit?"

She struggled with her conscience for several seconds before finally blurting out, "I found a hat pin. That's all. Oh, and an empty bottle of cognac."

He sighed. "Well, I hope you're satisfied. If the constables couldn't find anything to indicate a murder had been committed, I'm sure you won't find anything either."

"Perhaps, but I don't intend to give up just yet." She dabbed at the corners of her mouth with her serviette. "After all, I promised Emily Wrotham I would find out why her husband lied about working on his afternoon off when he was actually wandering around an abandoned farm for no apparent reason."

Baxter's eyes turned rather bleak. "Why is it you have

no trouble keeping your promises to everyone except me?"

She rose at once and hurried to his side. After placing a kiss on his cheek, she murmured, "Because, my darling, sometimes you extract promises from me that are miserably challenging to keep."

"Only because I care about your safety. I would be lost without you."

"And I you. So please don't fret so much. I'm really quite good at taking care of myself."

"I'll remind you of those words the next time you find yourself in dire peril."

"Piffle. I learned my lesson long ago. I watch my step with the utmost vigilance now."

"As you have demonstrated today."

She straightened. "There are times, Baxter, when I'm quite tempted to poke a finger in your eye."

To her immense satisfaction, he laughed out loud. "There, you see? You are still playing with fire."

"Then perhaps I'd better leave before I'm burned."

"Well, before you go, I have some news for you. Samuel and Daisy arrived earlier."

"Bax! Why on earth didn't you tell me before!" Cecily glanced at the pendulum clock on the wall behind him. "How long ago? Where are they now?"

"I didn't tell you because I didn't want you flying out of here without putting some food in your stomach. Besides, I believe they have taken our godchildren for a walk along the beach with Mrs. Chubb and Gertie."

"In this weather?" Cecily hurried to the door. "I do trust they wrapped up those babies warmly enough. That wind is so bitter."

"I imagine Gertie knows how to take care of her children by now."

She looked back at him. "We are talking about *Gertie*."

"Ah, yes. I see what you mean." He smiled. "Perhaps you should go after them and make sure all is well."

"Exactly what I had in mind." She blew him a kiss. "Until later, my love."

"Very well, and please, do try to stay out of trouble."

If she hadn't felt so guilty about breaking her promise to him, she would have made some sharp retort. There were times when Baxter made her feel as inadequate as a juvenile. On the other hand, it was rather comforting to know he worried about her so.

She left him frowning over his ledgers, and went in search of her special guests. After checking with the desk clerk to make sure the party hadn't yet returned, she made for the front doors.

The clouds had thinned when she stepped outside again, and patches of blue sky promised a clear, cold evening with the nip of frost in the air.

Apart from the holly wreaths on the hotel doors, there was little to indicate the festive season as Cecily made her way down the Esplanade. Yet the very essence of Christmas was in the air, so prevalent, yet also elusive and impossible to define. It was more a feeling, she decided. An air of expectancy, as if everyone knew something very special was forthcoming, and the whole world was full of excited anticipation.

The dusting of snow had melted, leaving a sparkling dry pavement to walk on. Guessing that her visitors had headed toward the town, Cecily hurried in that direction, and it wasn't long before she spied the straggling group in the distance.

The twins hopped excitedly from one side of the pavement to the other, while Mrs. Chubb did her best to restrain them from darting out into the street. Gertie and Daisy appeared to be deep in conversation, while Samuel, who looked exactly the same as he had the last time Cecily had seen him, gazed out to sea as he lagged behind the rest of the group.

Mrs. Chubb saw Cecily first, and lifted her gloved hand in greeting. The twins rushed headlong toward her, and Cecily leaned down to catch them both in her arms. She gave the two wriggling bodies a hug, then let them go, envying them their abundance of energy.

Daisy dipped a curtsey as she reached her and Samuel pulled off his cap. "It's lovely to see you, madam," Daisy said, her dark eyes alight with excitement in her pretty face. "I can't tell you how good it is to be back in Badgers End."

"Yeah," Samuel agreed. "I forgot how good it smells down here. A lot different than the Smoke. You can breathe deep without choking."

Cecily laughed. "How wonderful to see you all. Just like old times. All we need now are Doris and Ross to complete our reunion."

"Doris will be down by the end of the week, m'm," Daisy said, grabbing hold of James, who seemed intent on climbing over the railing to the beach.

"I want to dig in the sand!" James howled in protest.

"Me, too. Me, too!" Lillian jumped up and down, dislodging the bright red tam-o'-shanter from her head.

"They're tired," Mrs. Chubb said. "All this excitement is wearing them out."

"When's Father Christmas coming?" James demanded, dragging his boots as Daisy pulled him along.

"He don't come to naughty boys and girls," Daisy told him sternly. "So you'd better be good."

"Don't want to be good." James dug in his heels, jerking Daisy to a halt.

"Come 'ere," Gertie said, taking his hand. "If you don't behave, I'll tell your papa what a bad boy you are when he gets here."

The threat had the desired effect, and the twins allowed themselves to be led by the hand once more.

"Let's all go back to the hotel," Cecily suggested, "and we'll have tea and crumpets in the library by the fire."

Gertie fanned herself with an imaginary fan. "Blimey! Fancy me taking tea and crumpets with madam in the library. I never would have imagined it in the old days."

Cecily laughed. "Well, don't tell anyone, but according to the rules, which are ridiculously strict, none of us are supposed to be in the library unless we have membership in the club. Then again, some rules are just begging to be broken."

Mrs. Chubb looked worried. "We don't want to get anyone into trouble. Perhaps we should have tea in the kitchen instead. After all, that's where we're used to having it."

"Nonsense," Cecily said briskly. "As long as I am managing the hotel, I'll entertain my guests where I please. Now come along, everyone. It's really getting quite cold out here."

"Looks like snow again," Samuel observed, his gaze on the clouds gathering over the turbulent ocean.

"Well, I hope it waits until my better half gets down here." Gertie made a grab for Lillian's hand. "I don't want him stuck on the train halfway between here and Edinburgh."

"Or Doris on the way down from London for that matter." Cecily smiled at Samuel. "I'm sure you must be anxious for her to arrive. I'm really looking forward to seeing her myself. I want to ask her to help us with the Christmas pantomime. Do you think she'll agree?"

Samuel shrugged. "I reckon she will. That's all she ever thinks about these days, is her singing. Never has time for me no more."

"Samuel's just about given up on Doris, m'm," Daisy put in. "Can't say as I blame him. He never sees her anymore. She's always busy with the theater."

"And her admirers. Lined up at the stage door, they are. I don't get a look-in these days."

"I'm sorry to hear that," Cecily said in dismay. "I always thought that you and Doris were meant for each other."

Samuel gave her a trace of a grin. "Ah well, I'll survive. Lots more fish in the sea, so they say."

Disturbed by the news, Cecily led the group back to the Pennyfoot. First Madeline and Kevin, now Doris and Samuel. They had all seemed so happy with each other just a short two years ago. She was so fond of them all, it was sad to see them break apart. It would seem that everything was changing after all.

She'd taken a special interest in Doris and Daisy ever since the girls had arrived at the Pennyfoot, looking far too young and fragile for the heavy work of a scullery maid. At first it had been impossible to tell them apart—but it soon became obvious that Daisy was by far the stronger and couldn't sing a note in tune, while her more delicate twin had the voice of an angel.

Cecily had been happy for Doris's success on the stage,

but she could only hope that the child hadn't sacrificed her future happiness to follow her dream.

By that evening the delectable aroma of Michel's Christmas puddings permeated the entire first floor of the Pennyfoot. The fragrance of nutmeg, lemon rind, and allspice even reached to the second floor, causing Cecily to pause with her nose sniffing the air as she emerged from her suite behind Baxter.

"Now it really smells like Christmas," she said, with a long sigh of satisfaction. "I just hope Michel remembered to put in the silver threepenny pieces. I can hardly wait for the dinner on Christmas Day. No matter how much goose and rib roast I eat, the second Michel carries in that pudding flaming in brandy, I'm hungry all over again."

Baxter gave her a fond smile. "Is there ever a time when you're not hungry? For a woman of your pleasing figure, you have a remarkable appetite and a capacity to satisfy it without any of it settling on your waistline."

She raised her eyebrows at him. "I'm not sure if you've just paid me a compliment or handed me an insult."

He placed an affectionate arm about her shoulders. "I would never have the audacity to insult you, my love."

"Or the courage."

He sighed. "That, too. I have no doubt as to who would fare the worst."

"I'm happy that you recognize the folly of such a hazardous venture."

He was about to answer when the sound of voices raised in harmony interrupted her. "Listen," she said, lifting her hand to her ear. "It sounds as if our carol singers have arrived."

"It does, indeed." He offered her his arm and together

they descended the curving staircase to the first floor.

Ten or so carol singers stood formed in a semicircle in the foyer, while the beautiful refrain of "O Little Town of Bethlehem" echoed down the hallway.

Standing in the corner watching them, one hand possessively grasping his wife's elbow, Sir John Gilroy looked impressive in black coattails and a white bow tie. At his side, Lady Lucille was magnificent in pearl pink satin, the ostrich feathers in her hair matching exactly the shade of her gown.

Lionel Fitzhammer hovered just a little too close to her, while she quite obviously ignored him. Lionel's wife, Barbara, seemed to fade into the background as usual.

Catching sight of the couple she and Gertie had passed on the stairs, Cecily nudged Baxter's arm. "You haven't met our distinguished guests as yet. I think we should go over there so that I can introduce you."

Baxter cast a glance across the room. "I wasn't aware you had met them."

"I haven't met them all. But since they are all standing over there together, I think this would be a good time." Without giving him any time to argue, she skirted the carolers and headed for the group, who seemed on the point of leaving as she approached.

She greeted Sir John and his wife, then introduced Baxter to them. Sir John, in turn, introduced the Fitzhammers. The handsome gentleman from the stairs and his wife proved to be Roger Peebles and his wife, Gretchen, leaving the fourth couple, older than the rest by a good ten years, Cecily judged, to be Percy and Amelia Chatsworth. After exchanging some pleasantries, the group bade them good night and made their way to the front doors. As they had left, Cecily glimpsed snow falling thick and fast, covering the roofs of a row of shiny motor cars lined up outside. No doubt the Benchers were seeking more excitement than the Pennyfoot offered that evening. She really needed to start working on the pantomime.

"They seem pleasant enough," Baxter remarked, just as the carolers began a rousing chorus of "God Rest Ye Merry Gentlemen."

"I suppose so, though I can't say I care for the way Mr. Fitzhammer leers at Lady Lucille."

Baxter stared at her in amusement. "You wish he paid a little more attention to you, perhaps?"

"Great heavens, no." Cecily shook her head in disgust. "I simply fail to see why the man can't be satisfied with the woman he married. It's obvious he ignores poor Mrs. Fitzhammer. If I were her, I'd be fluttering my eyelashes at the handsome Roger Peebles. That would give Lionel something to think about."

"And what about Peebles's wife? Don't you think she'd mind if Mrs. Fitzhammer ogled her husband?"

Cecily shrugged. "Mrs. Peebles appears quite able to take care of herself. I think the person who is made most uncomfortable is Lady Lucille. She pretends indifference, but I think she's wary of her husband's wrath over Fitzhammer's lechery."

"If you ask me, Gilroy seems unaware of anything amiss." Baxter gave her arm a little shake. "I think you are making far too much of all this. The four men are obviously good friends, and their wives seem happy enough. You have quite enough on your mind without concerning yourself about the private affairs of our guests."

She smiled at him. "You're quite right. Let us enjoy

this beautiful singing, and when they are finished, we'll take them down to the kitchen to enjoy some hot cocoa and shortbread. I asked Miss Bunkle to order some in. It's a shame Mrs. Chubb is no longer the housekeeper. She made excellent shortbread. Michel is a wonderful chef but he can't make pastries as well as Mrs. Chubb."

"Perhaps we should hire a pastry chef," Baxter suggested.

"It's worth considering, I suppose." Cecily sighed, thinking of the days when she could enjoy her ex-housekeeper's fluffy cream slices and chocolate eclairs.

By the time the carolers had ended their recital, the foyer had become quite crowded with onlookers. Cecily spied Miss Bunkle at the head of the kitchen stairs and made her way over there with Baxter close behind her.

"I have invited the singers to the kitchen," Cecily told the housekeeper when she'd reached her. "I thought they might enjoy some hot cocoa and shortbread."

"Very well, madam. I'll see to it." Miss Bunkle peered at Cecily's chest. "It's none of my business, madam, but are you aware you have a hat pin lodged in your bodice? It doesn't look too secure. It wouldn't do to lose it."

Cecily glanced down at the hat pin, which had worked itself loose from the folds of her shirtwaist. She had quite forgotten she'd pinned it there. Until now it had been hidden under a pleat. "Oh, thank you, Miss Bunkle. You're quite right. I should hate to lose it." She could sense Baxter's intense gaze on her as she fastened the pin securely once more.

"Funny thing, madam," Miss Bunkle said, staring at the pin. "One of our guests asked me not too long ago if I had a hat pin she could borrow since she'd mislaid hers. I thought she might have dropped it somewhere here in the club. You didn't happen to find that one, did you?"

Cecily looked her straight in the eye. "I can assure you, Miss Bunkle, this pin was not lost in the Pennyfoot."

Miss Bunkle nodded. "Excuse me for asking, madam. I was just wondering, that's all."

"That's quite all right, Miss Bunkle. Please see that our carolers have their fill of refreshments." She turned to leave, then paused, looking back at the housekeeper. "By the way, do you happen to remember the name of the guest who mislaid the hat pin?"

She hoped that she was the only one to hear Baxter's sharp intake of breath.

"I remember very well," Miss Bunkle said, looking smug. "She's here tonight. It was Sir John Gilroy's wife, Lady Lucille."

CHAPTER

❊ 9 ❊

"It has to be mere coincidence, of course," Baxter said as he accompanied Cecily down the hallway. "I seriously doubt that the wife of a Master of the Bench would be visiting a farmhouse in this remote village. Especially since the house has been empty for a good many months. What would be her purpose?"

"What, indeed?" Cecily murmured. "Unless she had an assignation with someone there."

"Are you suggesting that Lady Lucille was meeting a lover?" Baxter demanded, obviously put out by the very idea.

"Not at all," Cecily said innocently. "As you say, it was simply a coincidence. Lady Lucille lost a hat pin. I found one. It doesn't mean it's the same one."

"But you intend to ask her about it anyway," said Baxter, a little desperately.

"Well, there is something I'd like to look at first." She paused in front of Baxter's office. "I'd like to have a peek at the ledgers."

Baxter frowned. "May I ask why?"

"Certainly." She glanced down the hallway to make sure they were alone. "I noticed there was a fairly new register on the counter this morning. I assume you have the previous one in the safe?"

"Yes, I do. Jeannette brought it into me last night."

"Good." She looked pointedly at the lock. "You do have the key, I hope?"

"Of course." He drew a ring of keys from his pocket and fitted one into the lock. "You still haven't told me why you want to examine the register."

"I'm curious, that's all. I would just like to know when the Gilroys' previous visit took place."

He paused, one hand holding the door closed. "Cecily, I don't think I like this. I hope you're not imagining—"

"I'm not imagining anything, darling. I simply want to look. There's no harm in that, is there?"

He sighed and pushed the door open. "I suppose not. But I have that nasty feeling again that this is going to lead us right into trouble."

"Piffle. You worry far too much about things that might never happen."

She waited impatiently for him to retrieve the ledger from the safe. He laid it on the desk for her, and she opened it, flipping feverishly through the pages until she found what she wanted—the scrawled signature of Sir John Gilroy. Underneath, one below the other, lay the signatures of the other three Benchers. Apparently all four were accustomed to visiting the Pennyfoot together.

Cecily pointed to Gilroy's signature and slid her finger across the line, uttering a soft exclamation of triumph as she did so.

"What is it?" Baxter asked, leaning forward to peer over her shoulder at the page.

"Look at this." Cecily tapped the spot with her finger. "They were all here three weeks ago. The same time that Barry Wrotham met with his accident."

Baxter straightened. "That doesn't mean they had anything to do with it. Cecily, I must emphatically warn you. These people are extremely influential. They are Barristers-at-Law, for heaven's sake. The governing body of the Inns of Court. Think what it would mean if you even suggested they might be involved in something as ugly as murder. Not only would their reputation suffer, they could bring the entire world down on our heads. It could even mean the end of the Pennyfoot if they chose."

"You are dashing far ahead of me," Cecily said, closing the ledger with a snap. "I'm not going to rush up to them and accuse one of them of murdering Mr. Wrotham."

"Thank heavens." Baxter took out his handkerchief and dabbed his brow. "For a moment I thought—"

"Not without proof, that is."

Baxter's groan was heart-wrenching. "Cecily, for pity's sake. This time I beg you not to pursue this line of thinking. It can only lead to disaster for all of us."

"Not if I can prove that one of them is guilty." She laid her hands on her husband's shoulders and pushed him gently down on his chair. "Just hear me out and then tell me what you think about my theory."

Once more he groaned, lifting his hands in a gesture of defeat. "Very well. But I have to admit to a certain amount of skepticism."

"That's all right. I just want to voice my ideas, to get them set straight in my mind." She seated herself opposite him and folded her hands in her lap. "Supposing Lady Lucille were engaged in a liaison with one of the other Benchers. Since they are all staying at the Pennyfoot, she could hardly conduct that kind of relationship here in the club."

"It would be rather difficult, I agree."

"Quite. So, her lover discovers the abandoned farmhouse. The perfect place for a tryst. Wrotham suspects what is going on and follows them. A Peeping Tom, so to speak. Emily Wrotham thinks her husband was cheating on her, but I think Barry Wrotham might have become enthralled with watching the lovers. Perhaps this romance has been going on for some time. So, Wrotham spies on the happy couple, and then gets caught. Perhaps he threatens to tell all. The lover has to silence him. So he pushes our nosy manager down the well. It would be impossible for Wrotham to climb out, and no one is going to hear his cries for help. No one except his murderer, of course."

"And Lady Lucille," Baxter reminded her.

"She might not have known what happened." Cecily frowned. "Though she certainly would have guessed when Wrotham's body was found."

"Surely she would have told her husband about her suspicions?"

"Not if she'd been engaged in an entanglement with one of his associates. It certainly would explain that nervous little glance she's always directing at him."

Baxter shook his head. "All this is pure conjecture, of course. You have no proof that the pin you found in the farmhouse belongs to Lady Lucille. After all, you mentioned that Emily Wrotham suspected her husband of betraying her with another woman. The pin could belong to Wrotham's unknown paramour."

Cecily withdrew the pin from her bodice and twisted it around in the glow of the gas lamps. "I sincerely doubt it. This pin belongs to a lady of wealth. Look at how the diamond sparkles in the light. Wrotham was a man of modest means. No one with whom he would associate would ever be able to afford something like this."

"Well, until you know for certain to whom the pin belongs, it is dangerous to speculate. I must insist that you proceed with the utmost caution. If you are correct in your assumptions, whoever the culprit may be, he will go to great lengths to keep his secret. He has a great deal to lose."

"Indeed he does," Cecily murmured, fastening the pin to her bodice once more. "But Wrotham lost his life. If someone killed him, then he should pay for it."

"Agreed. I would just prefer that someone else hand him the bill. I don't suppose you would consider talking to P.C. Northcott about your suspicions?"

Her glance of contempt was enough.

He sighed, and ran a hand over his hair to smooth it down. "Very well, but I am holding you to your promise, Cecily. I must warn you, if you violate my trust again, I shan't answer for the consequences."

"Don't worry, darling. I shall consult you before my every move. For instance, at the very first opportunity, I intend to show the pin to Lady Lucille, tell her Miss Bunkle mentioned she'd lost one, and ask her if this one belongs to her. She might not know where she lost it and will claim it. After all, it *is* a most expensive pin."

"She could deny it belongs to her."

"True."

"That's if it is hers, of course."

Cecily smiled. "If not, then I shall have to rethink my theory."

"And I shall be vastly relieved."

She rose, and held out her arms to her husband. "I think it's time we retired for the night. I'm weary, and we have a long day tomorrow."

He had risen with her, and moved around the desk to accept her hug. "You will take care, my love?"

"Of course." She drew back to look at him. "Did you order my Christmas tree for the library?"

"I did indeed." He dropped a kiss on her nose. "It will be here tomorrow."

"That's wonderful. Madeline will be here to begin the decorating, and Phoebe has promised to stop by with Colonel Fortescue."

Baxter lifted his chin and groaned. "As if we don't have enough bedlam to confuse us. It's been two years since we last saw the inimitable colonel. His brain must be even more addled by now."

"Not according to Phoebe." Cecily laughed. "I must admit, I'm amazed at how well that marriage seems to be working. Those two people are well suited to each other. They each bring something to the marriage that the other needs. And that is how a successful marriage should be."

He tilted his head on one side and gave her a quizzical look. "Is that how you see us?"

"Of course. You give me strength and stability. I give you enthusiasm and drama in your life."

He grimaced. "Sometimes a little too much drama."

"Ah, my love, admit it. Excitement adds a little spice to life."

"You are all the excitement I need. I can manage very well without your adventures to enhance it."

Her protest was smothered by his kiss. Which, in her opinion, was a very satisfying ending to an interesting day.

It was late in the following day when Cecily found the opportunity to speak to Lady Lucille alone. Ross had arrived that morning, having spent the night in nearby Wellercombe. Thanks to the heavy snowfall, he'd been prevented from reaching the Pennyfoot when he'd arrived at the train station.

Gertie was overjoyed to see him earlier than she'd expected, and the twins raced up and down the stairs in their excitement, convinced that now Papa was there, Father Christmas would arrive any minute.

In desperation, after the midday meal, Gertie and Daisy had left Ross to rest in his room while they took the children outside to build a snowman. Mrs. Chubb had asked to be driven into town, since she was anxious to visit with some of her old friends.

Samuel, meanwhile, had requested permission to examine the six motor cars belonging to the Pennyfoot. Much to Cecily's surprise, he'd explained that he was in training to be an automobile mechanic, and generously offered his services free as practice in overhauling the vehicles.

Baxter had seemed somewhat reluctant, but uttered no objections when Cecily accepted Samuel's offer. Baxter had retired to his office shortly after, leaving Cecily to pursue her quest, though not before extracting one more promise from her to watch her step.

As luck would have it, that afternoon the four Benchers had chosen to visit the card rooms where, according to Jeannette, they were engaged in a fiercely competitive game of baccarat.

"You should see 'em, m'm," she confided, having met Cecily in the hallway after returning from the card room, where she had been serving the four men the Pennyfoot's best scotch. "Money flying everywhere. I never saw betting go so fast. Look!" She pulled three silver florins from her pocket. "They gave me this, just for pouring them drinks."

Thankfully remembering that gambling was legal now that the Pennyfoot was a club, Cecily reminded Jeannette that gossip about the guests was strictly forbidden. "The Pennyfoot has always had a reputation for keeping silent about what goes on between these walls," she told the excited young girl. "I wouldn't want that trust violated. Our guests depend on us to respect their privacy."

"Oh, I respect it, all right, m'm. I'm very good at keeping me mouth shut about what goes on here." She glanced over her shoulder as if making sure no one could overhear her, then in a conspiratorial whisper added, "You wouldn't believe half of the goings-on I see, and that's a fact."

Well aware of what many of the "goings-on" entailed, Cecily hustled the girl back to the kitchen, again reminding her that it was none of their business.

In the days when the Pennyfoot had been a hotel, the illegal card rooms, hidden below in the wine cellar, had been bustling with notables. The boudoirs were notorious for entertaining the lewd assignations of various members of the aristocracy and the upper crust of London. Although the card rooms were no longer an embarrassment, the boudoirs had apparently lost none of their former notoriety.

The list of guests named Smith, Jones, or Brown was endless. In fact, as Cecily was well aware, it had become so common for such names to be used to conceal one's true identity, that persons with the legitimate name of Smith made up another one so as not to be suspected of philandering.

She was on her way to the library to inspect the new Christmas tree when she encountered Lady Lucille who, it seemed, was heading in the same direction.

The lady seemed disinclined to talk, making it clear she felt it beneath her station to be caught conversing with the hired help. Cecily had to remind herself that she was no longer the owner of the Pennyfoot, and was therefore relegated to the realm of the employed. Bearing that in mind, she was overly solicitous when she addressed the woman.

"I wonder if I might have a word with you, your ladyship," she said as she stood back to allow Lucille to enter the library ahead of her. "I have something that might be of importance to you."

Lucille looked at her with the expression of one who seriously doubted that such an lowly being could have anything to say that would be remotely worthy of her time. "And what might that be?"

Following her into the library, Cecily caught sight of the Christmas tree in the corner of the spacious room. She had no time to dwell on it now, however. Thankful to see they were alone in the room, she carefully removed the pin from the pocket of her skirt. "Miss Bunkle informed me that you had mislaid a hat pin when you were here last. I found this one and wondered if it might belong to you." She held the pin up to the light, so that the diamond glittered as it spun in her fingers. "It's awfully pretty. I'm quite sure anyone would hate to lose something as appealing as this."

She had been watching Lucille's face carefully as she spoke. The other woman's eyes had widened just a fraction, and she blinked rapidly as she raised a delicate hand to her throat. "It is indeed *très magnifique*, Madame Baxter. It is not mine, however. I found my missing hat pin later. I did not lose it after all."

"Well, how fortunate for you." Cecily replaced the pin in her pocket. "I shall have to ask the other ladies if the pin belongs to them. I was thinking perhaps it had been stolen, since I found it in rather an unusual place. It was on the floor of a bedroom in an abandoned farmhouse."

Lucille's eyelashes fluttered again and a slight flush spread over her cheeks. "Is that so." She'd managed to put a great deal of disgust into those words, obviously hoping to imply she wouldn't be caught dead in a farmhouse. Abandoned or not. She turned away, and moved toward the bookcases, indicating that the conversation was over.

Cecily was not that easily dismissed, however. She followed Lucille to the racks of books. "Strangely enough, it was the same farm where poor Mr. Wrotham met his end."

Lady Lucille kept on moving down the shelves, but Cecily noticed that the woman's hand shook quite visibly as she reached for a book.

Pressing home her point, Cecily said quietly, "One has

to wonder if Mr. Wrotham wandered into a situation he wasn't supposed to see. Two lovers enjoying a secluded hideaway, perhaps. Having witnessed a scene that could cause a great deal of trouble for the pair involved, it could well have become necessary to make sure Mr. Wrotham did not pass on his discovery to anyone else. After all, when one is in a position of eminence, one can sometimes be forced to go to extraordinary lengths to protect one's image, wouldn't you say?"

Lady Lucille spun on her heel so sharply a hairpin slipped from her tightly bound hair and bounced off her shoulder. "Madame Baxter, I have not the least idea what your babbling means. I have many excellent works of fiction from which I can choose right here on these shelves. I have no interest at all in your stories. If you will excuse me, I should like to examine these shelves without you here to bother me."

Cecily lowered her gaze before the other woman saw the resentment smoldering there. "My apologies, Lady Lucille. I shall go in search of the other ladies and ask them if the pin belongs to any of them. I'm sorry to have disturbed you."

She headed to the door, and had reached it when Lady Lucille said sharply, *"Attende, s'il vous plaît!"*

Cecily turned, waiting expectantly as Lady Lucille moved toward her, her hand outstretched.

"The pin. Give it to me," she said, obviously making an effort to sound more amicable. "I will ask my companions if it belongs to any of them. I am quite sure you have enough to do with the work of running such an excellent establishment, *non?* I will be happy to relieve you of an extra burden."

Cecily smiled. "That is most kind of you, your lady-ship. But I couldn't possibly trouble you with any of my duties. Enjoy your reading. Good day."

Just before she escaped through the door, she glimpsed Lady Lucille's narrowed eyes, and the expression in them sent a nasty chill down her back. There was no doubt in her mind that, given enough reason, the elegant lady could be a formidable foe.

What also seemed apparent, Cecily reflected as she hurried down the hallway, was that Lady Lucille was vastly disturbed by the discovery of the pin and where it was found. Either the pin did, indeed, belong to her, or she knew who was the owner.

What's more, Cecily was convinced her theory was on the right track. It seemed highly possible that one of the ladies was engaged in an illicit alliance with one of the Benchers, and that Wrotham found out about it. It also seemed feasible to assume that Lady Lucille was the lady involved, since she had mislaid her hat pin when she was visiting the Pennyfoot the same week Wrotham died. Which left one large question looming in Cecily's mind: Which of the Benchers would be foolish enough to dally with Sir John Gilroy's wife?

She broached the question to Baxter when she joined him in his office a short while later.

Her husband seemed distracted, and was rather short with her. "You are assuming all this, Cecily. You don't have an ounce of justification for your suspicions. It's no wonder Inspector Cranshaw becomes so incensed when you inter-fere in his investigations."

"Inspector Cranshaw is a fool," Cecily said mildly. "He wouldn't leave a dunderhead like P.C. Northcott in charge if he had any brains. Here we have a situation fraught with unanswered questions and ominous possibilities, and Northcott is ignoring the whole thing."

"Well, while I have to agree with your assessment of the police constable, have you considered at all the possibility that you are simply overreacting to an unfortunate circumstance simply because there is an element of mystery about it?"

Cecily leaned two hands on his desk. "Baxter, dear, I love you dearly, but sometimes you can be deliberately obtuse. Wrotham's body was found floating in a well on abandoned farmland where he had no good reason to be, several yards from a farmhouse that is supposed to have been uninhabited for at least a year, yet the magazine I found there was dated just a month ago, and a very expensive diamond pin, which no farmer's wife would ever be able to afford, was found lying next to a fine, pure wool blanket that showed no sign of wear. Not only that, I'm convinced that Lucille was lying when she denied the pin was hers. If that doesn't add up to ominous possibilities, then you are right, I am overreacting."

Baxter blinked. "Well, when you put it like that . . ."

"Thank you. I'm pleased that you see my point. Now, as I said before you so loudly voiced your skepticism, which one of the Benchers would you suppose would risk his career to spend an afternoon with Lucille in a deserted farmhouse?"

"If it were Lucille who had been there, her lover could be anyone. It doesn't necessarily have to be one of her husband's associates, does it?"

"No, but it seems the most likely answer. If it were someone else entirely, why meet him here with so many witnesses about? Why not meet him in London, which after all, has a great many more places to offer seclusion and a great deal more comfortable at that. No, I think that Lucille and her lover took the opportunity where they could, when they could seize the moment to slip off together without being missed. Or perhaps the whole affair exploded into passion for the first time while they were here at the Penny-foot together, and their assignation was purely on impulse."

"Well, we all know where impulses tend to lead us, don't we."

She wrinkled her nose at him. "Come now, Bax. If you had to choose one, which Bencher would you select for Lady Lucille's lover?"

"I haven't the slightest idea. By the way, did you happen to notice if the Christmas tree had arrived in the library?"

"Yes, it has. I caught a glimpse of it but I didn't have time to examine it closely. Don't change the subject. I really would like to know your opinion. It's important to me."

Baxter leaned back in his chair, a perplexed frown marring his face. "Oh, very well. Though I can't say that I've paid much attention to the group. That handsome chap, I suppose. The one with the flame-haired wife."

"Ah, you managed to pay some attention, I see." She grinned at his expression of discomfort. "It's all right, I'm teasing. Roger Peebles is certainly a possibility. The sort of man a woman like Lucille would enjoy conquering. Then there's Fitzhammer, who is obviously infatuated with the lovely Lucille. Though I do believe she regards him with contempt. I wonder—" She broke off as a sharp tap sounded on the door.

After a short pause, during which Baxter raised his eyebrows at her in question, he called out, "You may come in!"

The door opened and Miss Bunkle's head appeared in the gap, the knitting needle in her hair scraping against the doorjamb. "Oh, I'm sorry to disturb you, sir . . . madam. I thought you'd be alone. That is . . ."

"Come in, Miss Bunkle," Baxter said impatiently. "You're not interrupting anything important." He ignored Cecily's meaningful look of indignation at his comment. "Is there something that needs my attention?"

"Yes, sir." Miss Bunkle edged into the room and stood wringing her hands for a moment before bursting out, "It's my pearls, Mr. Baxter. I'm afraid they've been stolen. There's a thief somewhere in the Pennyfoot and I believe it's one of the staff."

CHAPTER

❦ 10 ❦

It had taken quite a while to calm down the normally unflappable Miss Bunkle. After questioning her closely about where she had last seen her pearls, Cecily had promised to look into the matter. As she remarked to Baxter after Miss Bunkle had left, it wouldn't do to bring in the constable until they had at least attempted to solve the problem themselves. The last thing the Pennyfoot needed was for word to get out that a thief was loose in the building.

Much disturbed by the latest turn of events, Cecily began questioning the staff. Jeannette and Moira seemed vastly upset at the thought they might be accused of stealing the pearls, and Cecily had to assure them that she was simply exploring all avenues before calling in the constables.

Jeannette, especially, was quite beside herself. "No one's never called me a thief before," she declared, her cheeks red with indignation. "I never stole nothing in me life. I swear I didn't."

"No one is accusing you," Cecily told her, "or anyone else for that matter. We must ask everyone if they have seen or heard anything that might help us find the pearls."

"I reckon the old biddy lost 'em," Jeannette said, nodding her head at the parlor, where Miss Bunkle was fortunately out of earshot. "What's an old bird like her doing with pearls anyway? They'd look pretty daft strung around her scraggy neck."

"They were a family heirloom and of great sentimental value to Miss Bunkle. It isn't up to you to question why she has them, Jeannette. The point is, we need everyone to keep their eyes and ears open, just in case you should see or hear something that might help us find the pearls. If they are not found soon, we shall have to call in the constables."

"Yes, m'm." The girl stared down at her shoes, her bottom lip jutting at a stubborn angle. "All I know is, I didn't steal them."

Sighing, Cecily left the kitchen and made her way up the stairs to the first floor. It pained her to think that a trusted member of the staff had committed theft on the premises. The staff of the Pennyfoot had always been treated well, with generous pay and free time.

According to Baxter, Edward had been even more charitable than she had, thanks to the thriving business he had worked hard to build. To discover a miscreant among the carefully chosen workers saddened her as much as if it had been a member of her own family.

Deep in thought, she came close to colliding with the tall figure who had stepped out from the card room in front of her in the narrow hallway. She recognized Sir John Gilroy, and the handsome Roger Peebles hovering right behind him, as well as the older Bencher, Percy Chatsworth. Fitzhammer, the lecherous one as Cecily had dubbed him, apparently was still engrossed in a card game.

Cecily greeted the three men and added, "If you should happen to be looking for Lady Lucille, Sir John, I left her in the library about an hour ago."

Gilroy nodded, his expression somewhat forbidding. "Thank you, Mrs. Baxter. I believe she planned to take a book back to our suite. She has more than likely returned there by now."

He was about to move on when the impulse struck her. She pulled the hat pin from her pocket and held it up to the light so all three men could plainly see it. "I found this hat pin yesterday. I was wondering if any of you gentlemen recognized it as belonging to your wife."

Gilroy stared at her as if she'd committed a sin by mentioning the pin, while Chatsworth merely looked bored. Peebles, on the other hand, frowned at the pin as though he were trying to remember where he'd seen it before.

When none of them answered her, Cecily turned to Gilroy. "I understand your wife mislaid one during a previous visit, Sir John. Would you care to take a closer look, just in case it should belong to her?"

Rather impatiently he reached out and took it from her, squinting at it in the dim light of the corridor. Finally, he muttered brusquely, "I believe this might belong to my wife. I gave her one like it as an anniversary gift. I had no idea she had mislaid it. She'll be most relieved to have it returned to her. I'm very much obliged to you, Mrs. Baxter."

Elated at having her suspicions confirmed, Cecily beamed. "Not at all, Sir John. I'm happy to have been of service."

He stared back at her, his expression stony, as if a shutter had closed over his face.

Somewhat unnerved, she glanced back at Roger Peebles, and was intrigued to find him now watching Sir John with a furtive expression in his eyes. He seemed ill at ease, and fidgeted with his watch chain as if anxious to be somewhere else.

She watched the men move off down the hallway, wondering how Lucille was going to explain why she hadn't told her husband about the loss of his valuable gift, and what he would say if he learned where Cecily had found it.

She could at least be certain that it was Lucille who had been meeting someone in the farmhouse. If the pin had been stolen, like Miss Bunkle's pearls, or even found in the hotel and taken to the farmhouse by someone else, there would have been no need for Lucille to lie about the pin belonging to her.

Cecily uttered a heavy sigh. On the other hand, she was no closer to learning with whom the lady had taken such risks. Or if, indeed, the clandestine couple had anything to do with Barry Wrotham's death. Baxter was right. She had no proof that any of her theories were the right ones.

She had no time to ponder further at that moment, as a

commotion at the front door suggested visitors had arrived. She recognized the strident voice at once and hurried forward to greet the newcomers.

Phoebe stood just inside the closed doors, her hand on the arm of a stout gentleman whose red face beneath the elegant top hat he wore contrasted sharply with his frost white whiskers. The colonel was talking loudly and with a great deal of agitation, brandishing his free arm as if staving off imaginary assailants and completely ignoring the quiet pleas of his wife.

Cecily crossed the foyer at top speed, conscious of the stares of several people standing at the reception counter. "Phoebe! And Colonel Fortescue! What a pleasure it is to see you both again."

The colonel mercifully stopped bellowing, his watery, bloodshot eyes staring at her as if she had sprouted horns. "Cecily? Is that you? Good Lord, old bean, what the devil are you doing in this den of iniquity? Have you no blasted shame? What? What?"

Phoebe sent her a look of apology. "He thinks he's in a house of ill repute," she whispered from behind her gloved hand.

Cecily raised her eyebrows. "What on earth gave him that idea?"

"We passed a group of young ladies running down the steps outside. They were unescorted by gentlemen, and seemingly in high spirits. They called out to us, wishing us a happy Christmas, and I'm afraid that dear Freddie thought they were offering their services."

"Damn disgusting if you ask me," the colonel boomed. "Can't think why my wife would bring me here." He leaned over Phoebe, his eyelids flapping up and down in agitation. "Unless you're trying to get rid of me, what? What? Heaven knows what ghastly things happen to the poor blighters who get lured into this obscene harem."

"Oh, don't be such a dunce, Freddie," Phoebe said crossly. "This is a country club, and a very respectable establishment. Surely you remember the time when Cecily owned the Pennyfoot Hotel?"

The colonel blinked at Cecily. "The Pennyfoot Hotel. Why, by George, of course I remember! Jolly good show, old girl. Nice to be back in the old Pennyfoot. So where's Baxter then, the old goat? What have you done with him? Hope you haven't sent him packing, what? What?"

Aware of the odd glances being directed at them, Cecily said hurriedly, "Baxter is in the office. I'm sure he will be pleased to see you. You remember where it is, don't you?"

"Right ho, old bean. Think I'll toddle off for a quick snifter in the bar. Tell the governor to join me in there when he's ready."

"You're not toddling anywhere without me, Freddie," Phoebe said crisply. "In any case, the bar is not where it used to be. The drawing room is no longer there, either. You'll never find your way on your own."

"I'm afraid you won't be able to go in the bar with him," Cecily said. "Club rules, I'm sorry to say. No women allowed in the bar. Not even me."

"Whose rules are they?" Phoebe demanded. "Not that peculiar woman with a knitting needle stuck in her head?"

"I say, old fruit, bit painful what?" The colonel twisted

the end of his mustache with a flourish. "Reminds me of the time I had an arrow shot right through my bloody pith helmet. Did I ever tell you—"

"A hundred times," Phoebe said rudely. She turned to Cecily. "Is Madeline here yet? I really need to talk to her about the backdrops for the pantomime. Are we meeting in the library?"

"I suppose we could," Cecily murmured. "Although it's not as private as it used to be. Perhaps it would be better to have our meeting in my suite. At least we have no fear of being disturbed there."

"Good idea. I'll take Freddie to the bar and he can wait there for me."

The colonel's eyes lit up. "I say, jolly good idea, old bean."

"And you are to have no more than two glasses," she told him sternly.

"Oh, right, of course, old fruit. Anything you say."

"Then that's settled." Cecily glanced at the grandfather clock ticking away in the corner of the foyer. "I have one small errand to run, but it won't take me more than a minute or so. I'll meet you in my suite." She handed Phoebe the key. "I shan't be long."

She left Phoebe to explain to the colonel why the bar had been moved since he was last there. The last thing she heard him bellow before she passed out of earshot was an explosive, "Well, I never heard such blasted stuff and nonsense. Tell them to put the damn thing back where it belongs!"

Reaching the library door, Cecily turned the handle and entered the quiet room. She was thankful to see that Lady Lucille had left, and that no one else disturbed the peace of what used to be her favorite room in the hotel.

She wanted to take a closer look at the towering Christmas tree that she'd spotted earlier by the French windows. She was pleased to see that it was just as magnificent as her first impression of it.

The fragrance of it filled the room, and the thick branches laden with pine needles swooped down to the floor in perfect symmetry, leaving no unsightly gaps to be filled. The woodsman had done a fine job. Madeline would have a fine time decorating such a grand specimen.

Well content with the tree, Cecily wandered over to the fireplace. The portrait of James Sinclair, her late husband, had once hung on the wall overlooking the long Jacobean table where she had conducted so many committee meetings.

Now the portrait had been replaced by a turbulent seascape, and the Jacobean table with its constant vase of roses had been banished in favor of more armchairs and trestle tables.

Still, the memories could not be destroyed. It had been here in this room where she had once shared a cigar now and then with Baxter, and it had been here in this room where she had received her first inkling that his concern for her was something more than just a promise to her late husband.

She turned from the fireplace and gazed at the warm paneled walls and the shelves crammed with books that reached from the floor to the lofty ceiling. This was still her favorite room. Because it held so many wonderful memories. And because the spirit of everything that had mattered in her life still hovered within its walls.

She, Madeline, and Phoebe had spent so many pleasant hours discussing the frequent events that were held at the hotel to entertain the guests. Balls and tea dances, with

Phoebe's sometimes bizarre presentations on the stage, were an integral part of the hotel's routine.

The tableaux, dances, plays, and even a magician were some of the most memorable events Phoebe had presided over, with the help of her inept, argumentative dance troupe, who invariably managed to bring disaster to the entertainment in some strange manner or other.

Much as Phoebe lamented each calamity, Cecily was of the private opinion that the guests actually adored the chaos that ensued, and would have been vastly disappointed had the performance been anything less than a catastrophe.

The door opened abruptly, shattering her thoughts. Jeanette stood in the doorway, and she dropped a curtsey when she caught sight of Cecily. "Begging your pardon, m'm, but Miss Bunkle sent me to tell you that the last of your special guests has arrived."

"Doris is here?" Cecily hurried to the door. "How wonderful. Where is she?"

"Raymond took her up to her room, m'm." Jeanette waited for Cecily to exit the room, then closed the door and followed her up the hallway. "Is it true she's on the stage, m'm?"

"Doris is a professional performer, yes."

"In London?"

"Yes." Cecily paused. "Jeanette, I'd prefer that the guests didn't know that about Doris. I don't want her pestered by stage-struck admirers. I don't know who told you . . ."

"Samuel told Moira and she told me." Jeanette looked worried. "I haven't told no one else, m'm. Honest I haven't. I—"

Her sentence was cut off by a hefty sneeze that echoed up the wide staircase. Smothering her nose in a large white handkerchief, Jeanette ducked another curtsey and rushed off for the kitchen.

Cecily watched her go with a frown. The girl seemed unnecessarily agitated. This business of the stolen pearls must be making the staff uneasy. She would have to abandon her efforts to find out what happened to Wrotham for the time being and concentrate on searching for Miss Bunkle's pearls.

Sighing, she made for the stairs. She was looking forward to seeing Doris again. The young girl had been one of her favorites. It wasn't until she'd reached the first landing that she remembered Phoebe, who was no doubt waiting for her in her suite at this very moment. Her reunion with Doris would have to wait after all.

She found both Phoebe and Madeline ensconced in her living room engaged in a heated argument over where to hang the mistletoe.

"It would be inviting serious embarrassment to hang mistletoe in the main hallway," Phoebe asserted, wagging her finger at Madeline to emphasize her point. "It is too dark and too narrow to pass a person without coming within reach. Heaven knows what liberties some of these gentlemen might take at such an enticing opportunity."

Madeline rolled her eyes at the ceiling. "Just listen to her. As if a simple sprig of mistletoe would change a gentleman's character. People have been hanging mistletoe over their doorways for centuries at Christmastime and so far there have been no rumors of mass molestation."

"Just because we do not hear of such tales doesn't mean it doesn't happen. If you must hang the stuff somewhere, why not the ballroom, where any impertinent behavior can be easily detected and therefore avoided?"

Madeline fixed her with a baleful glare. "Has it ever occurred to your addled brain that some people welcome such advances? I seem to remember you being much less prudish when your colonel pursued you in the rose garden."

Phoebe's face turned scarlet. "I beg your pardon?"

Deciding it was high time to intervene, Cecily said hurriedly, "I think we can begin rehearsals for the pantomime tomorrow. Doris arrived a short while ago, and I'm hoping she'll agree to help us with the production. Phoebe, have you contacted your dance troupe? How many can we depend on to help us with our presentation?"

After giving Madeline a final lethal glare, Phoebe turned a cold shoulder on her and smiled at Cecily. "At least six of the girls are eager to participate. They've missed the excitement of performing in front of an audience."

"I hope Doris knows what's in store for her," Madeline murmured. "She's accustomed to professional performers. It's going to be something of a shock when she has to deal with the Troupe Fiasco."

"I've asked you not to call them that," Phoebe said sharply. "It demoralizes them."

"That's nothing compared to what they can do to an audience." Madeline gave Cecily a sly look. "Are you sure Doris wants to be associated with Phoebe's band of clumsy clowns?"

"Doris will be happy to donate her talents, I'm sure," Cecily said, crossing her fingers in her lap. "In any case, a pantomime is not exactly an opera. It's supposed to be a display of amusement, with lots of jokes and good humor and audience participation. Who's going to notice if things are not quite perfect? And even if they do, really, who is going to care that much? It's all in the spirit of Christmas, is it not?"

"Exactly my sentiments," Phoebe declared, giving Madeline a triumphant smirk.

Madeline threw her hands up in defeat. "Very well. Don't say I didn't warn you."

"That's settled then." Cecily drew a sigh of relief. "When can you start the decorating, Madeline?"

"Right away, if you can tell me where to find the decorations." Madeline glanced at the clock on Cecily's sideboard. "Did you get another tree for the library?"

"I certainly did. I was just looking at it earlier. It's quite magnificent. I've decided to hold a private candle-lighting ceremony for my special guests in the library on Christmas Eve. You and Phoebe, and the colonel, of course, are all invited to attend. We'll have a wassail bowl and Christmas crackers, and roast chestnuts in the fire. We'll be hanging small gifts on the tree for the guests to be handed out on Christmas Day, so it will all look very festive with its candles burning."

"Oh, it does sound so heavenly!" Phoebe clapped her hands in delight. "I know dear Freddie will adore it." She glanced at Madeline. "I don't suppose you will be bringing the doctor, by any chance?"

Madeline's eyes were bleak when she answered. "For once you are quite correct, Phoebe. Dr. Prestwick will not be joining me this Christmas."

Cecily's heart ached when she saw the despondency on her friend's face. "But you will join us, will you not?"

"I wouldn't miss it." Madeline rose to her feet, her

peasant skirt fluttering in folds around her ankles. "I thought I'd ask Gertie's twins to help me with the decorating. It will give their mother a rest and keep them out of mischief."

"Oh, they'd love that, I know they would. If you ask Miss Bunkle where to find the decorations, I'm sure she'll be able to help you. Meanwhile, I'll talk to Doris and ask for her help with the pantomime."

Phoebe rose, too, smoothing her skirt down with her gloved hands. "And I must go in search of my husband. He is most likely getting lonely without me."

"If you've left him in the bar, he's most likely forgotten your existence by now," Madeline drawled.

Phoebe sniffed. "It won't take much to jog his memory. Pity you can't say as much for the good doctor."

Madeline smiled, though there was no humor in her eyes. "I can't imagine why you are so possessed with Kevin, Phoebe. Could it be that you are as enamored of him as half the female population of Badgers End?"

Phoebe tossed her head, at great risk of dislodging her hat. "If I were, Madeline dear, I would do everything in my power to make sure his attention was on me, and not on half the female population of Badgers End."

"Better women than you have tried and failed," Madeline murmured.

Phoebe was about to answer when a light tap on the door caught everyone's attention.

Cecily opened it, surprised to see Moira bobbing up and down in an awkward curtsey. "I'm so sorry to disturb you, m'm," she mumbled, "but Lady Lucille sent me. She asked to meet with you right away." Moira's gaze slid past

Cecily to the other two women. "She said it was important, m'm, that she speak with you in private."

"It's all right, Moira," Madeline said, gliding to the door. "We were just leaving." She transferred her smile to Cecily. "I will begin the decorating and I'll try not to get into anyone's way."

Caught up in wondering just what it was that Lady Lucille had to say to her, Cecily nodded absently. "Tell Miss Bunkle to give you enough candles to put on the tree in the library. I'd like a really good display of them."

Madeline nodded and passed through the door, then came to a standstill so abruptly Cecily thought she had bumped into Moira, who still hovered outside in the hallway awaiting further instructions.

But then she saw Moira standing to one side. Madeline, it seemed, had been seized by one of her trances. She turned slowly to face Cecily, and the stark expression on her face sent a chill coursing through Cecily's veins.

In that ghostly voice quite unlike her usual throaty tone, Madeline said softly, "Beware the candles. They are burning too brightly."

Cecily stared at her, trying to make sense of the words. "What is it, Madeline? What are you trying to tell me?"

Behind her Phoebe uttered a shocked gasp as Madeline's eyes seemed to glow with an unearthly light.

"I see you playing with fire, Cecily," Madeline whispered. "Take great care, or you will be horribly burned."

Moira let out a whimper of fear, while Phoebe said harshly, "Madeline! Enough of this nonsense."

Madeline seemed not to notice. She simply wafted off down the hallway and disappeared from view.

"Well," Phoebe said, sounding shaken. "What was that all about?"

Moira stared at Cecily with wide, frightened eyes. "M'm? Is the lady all right?"

Cecily pulled herself together. "Yes, I'm sure she's quite all right. Phoebe, you had better join your husband. It's getting late. Moira, please ask Lady Lucille to come here to my suite at her convenience."

Moira gave a frightened nod of her head and rushed off.

Phoebe left, too, shaking her head and muttering about Madeline not being right in the mind. Cecily closed the door and leaned against it.

There had been only a handful of times that Madeline had warned her in this way. And each time, she had found herself in deadly danger. She could only hope that this warning did not carry the same ugly threat.

CHAPTER
❦ 11 ❦

Less than ten minutes after Cecily had sent the message to Lady Lucille, a light tap summoned her to the door. Feeling somewhat apprehensive, she opened it and regarded the elegant woman, who stood looking down the corridor as if afraid someone might see her.

"Please, do come in," Cecily murmured, stepping back to allow her to enter. "Can I offer you some refreshment? I can have some tea sent up—"

"*Non, non, merci.*" Lucille trotted into the room in great haste. "I can only stay but a moment."

Cecily closed the door and indicated the nearest chair. "I hope there is nothing amiss with your room?"

"*Pardonnez-moi?*" Lucille turned anxious eyes on her. "Oh, not at all." She tugged at the fingers of her left glove, as if about to draw it off, then changed her mind and smoothed it down again. "Madame Baxter. I must ask of you a favor."

"Of course." Cecily waited until Lucille had seated herself, then took a chair across the room from her. "I'll be most happy to oblige if at all possible."

For a long moment it seemed as if the lady had trouble remembering what it was she had come to ask. Her hesitancy was such a marked change in her attitude that Cecily found it hard to realize it was the same woman.

Finally, Lucille lifted her chin and stared straight into Cecily's eyes. "My husband tells me that you returned the hat pin to him."

Having anticipated that Lucille's visit would have something to do with the hat pin, Cecily had prepared her reply. "Yes," she said smoothly. "I happened to be asking the other gentlemen if they recognized the pin when your husband declared that it belonged to you. It is rather distinctive, after all. An anniversary gift, I believe he said."

"*Oui.*" Lucille dropped her gaze. "You say you found it in the farmhouse?"

"Quite by accident, I assure you."

"You did not tell my husband where you found it?"

"No, of course not."

She looked up then, and to Cecily's surprise, her eyes filled with tears. "Madame Baxter, I know what you think of me. I am a weak woman, yes, but I have reason to seek attention elsewhere. My husband, he is a very busy man. He has many . . . interests that occupy much of his time. He does not have any time left for his wife. I might as well be a pretty picture on the wall for what little attention he pays to me."

"I'm sorry," Cecily murmured, at a loss as to how to respond to this outpouring of misery.

Lady Lucille shrugged. "He has a good position with the Inns of the Court. Why is he not satisfied with that? I do not understand why he needs all this extra work and demands. I tell him over and over again, I wish the others would leave him alone. If he wasn't so busy all the time, I would have no reason to . . ." She caught her breath on a sob, and hunted for a handkerchief in her sleeve.

Instantly intrigued, Cecily would dearly have loved to know what extra demands were taking so much of Sir John's time, and who "the others" might be. She was far too polite to ask, however. In spite of her disapproval of the woman's infidelity, Cecily felt a modicum of sympathy for her. It couldn't be easy to love a man and be ignored by him. Especially for a woman as seemingly passionate as Lucille. Sir John was making a grave mistake by neglecting his wife.

"Lady Lucille," she said softly. "It is not my place to pass judgment, nor is it any of my business. If you are asking me not to reveal to your husband where I found the pin, I assure you, your secret is quite safe with me."

Lucille pressed her handkerchief to her lips, her eyes still brimming. *"Merci, madame,"* she murmured. "You are most understanding."

Cecily studied her carefully. "Although, as I said, this is none of my business, I feel compelled to offer a note of warning. In view of the location where I found the pin, and since that is also the location where our former manager, Barry Wrotham, met his death, should there be an investigation forthcoming, I might have to mention it to the constables."

Lucille's eyes grew wide with apprehension. "An investigation? But I thought . . . I was told . . . Barry's death was an accident."

"It would seem that way, yes." Cecily deliberately paused, aware of the other woman's intense concentration. After a moment she continued, "There have been some questions raised, however, that need to be answered."

"Questions?"

"Yes. For instance, why Mr. Wrotham should be wandering around a deserted farm for apparently no good reason."

Lucille's expression was one of pure bewilderment. "But . . . I . . . I thought you knew. Mr. Wrotham, he came there to meet me."

Cecily felt her own eyes widen. "Barry Wrotham was your lover?"

"Mais, oui." Lucille lifted her hands and let them drop again. "I am sure you understand why I cannot tell the constables what he was doing there."

Cecily was still struggling with this latest revelation. She had been so certain that Lucille was involved with one of the Benchers. It had never occurred to her that this elegant, proud creature could have lowered herself to engage in an illicit alliance with Wrotham.

Apparently Lucille must have read her mind. "Madame Baxter, I have not always been a . . . how you say . . . member of society. When I met my husband, I was with the *Folies Bergère.* Sometimes, I miss the excitement of that time. Monsieur Wrotham reminded me of the woman I once had been." She raised a delicate hand to wipe her brow. "I do not expect you to understand."

"I understand better than you imagine," Cecily said

dryly. "Lady Lucille, I can't promise that your . . . association with Wrotham can remain a secret. Perhaps if you tell me what happened?"

Lucille shrugged. "I do not know what happened to him. I left when he was still in the house. We could not take the chance someone might see us together. I walked all the way to the town. I was to meet a car that would bring me back to the club. The same car that had taken me earlier. I told Raymond I was visiting the shops."

"So the last time you saw Barry Wrotham, he was alive and well in the farmhouse?"

"Oui." She sighed. "It grew dark as I left. Barry, he had been drinking the cognac, *n'est-ce pas?* I think he must have stumbled into the well and pouf!" She jerked a hand in the air. "He fell down it." She covered her face with her hands for a moment. "Imagine my great distress when I learned of Barry's death. I feel so terrible that this happened to him. If I had not responded to his attentions, he would remain alive to this day."

Cecily stared at her in silence, while outside in the hallway the jangling of a bell summoned the guests to dinner. "I see," she said at last. "Well, that would explain a great deal. I'm so glad we had this discussion, Lady Lucille."

"And you will tell no one what I have told you?" Lucille leaned forward, her hands outstretched in appeal. "You must understand . . . my husband . . . if he hears of this . . ."

"I see no need to inform the constables of our conversation," Cecily said slowly. "They have ruled Barry Wrotham's death an accident, and what you have told me seems to bear out that deduction."

"I am deeply grateful, *madame.*" Lucille rose, looking

more like her former self. "Now, if you will excuse me, I must join the others for dinner. I am sure they must be wondering where I am, *non?*"

Cecily got to her feet and walked with Lucille to the door. After seeing the lady out, she waited long enough for her to return to her suite, then headed down the stairs to the first floor. She couldn't wait to tell Baxter what she had learned. Nor did she have any qualms about discussing it with him. She had promised Lucille not to repeat anything that was said to the constables or to Sir John. She had not said anything about discussing the news with her own husband.

"You never did tell me how it was you got here a day early," Gertie said, bending down to unfasten the button on James's shoe. "I thought you said you still had a few customers to take care of."

"I did."

"So how did you get them all done so quick?" James kept kicking his feet so she couldn't get ahold of him. She made a grab at his pudgy leg and he let out a howl. "Oh, now, now," she muttered as she wrestled with the shoe. "Stop pretending that you're hurt. I didn't grab you that hard."

"Don't wanna go to bed," James yelled.

"Well, you're bloody going, so there."

Ross's voice, harsh with impatience, cut across the room. "For pity's sake, woman, can't you keep the bairn quiet for one minute?"

Gertie jerked her head up and stared at her husband. Ross was normally an even-tempered man, far less likely to get in a tizz than she was. This wasn't like him at all. "Sorry, luv. I'll get him in bed in a minute."

"Don't wanna!" Jamie yelled.

"You'll do as I *say!*" Gertie carried the squirming child to the bed, where Lillian was already half asleep. She dumped James in beside her and pulled the covers over his flailing arms. "Father Christmas is not going to fill your pillowcase with toys if you don't go to sleep right now."

James stopped yelling and blinked sleepy eyes at her. "Father Christmas is coming tonight?"

"Not tonight, no. But soon," she added hastily as James opened his mouth to scream again.

James gave her a suspicious look. "He won't know where to find us. He'll go to our house an . . . an . . . we won't be there. He'll think we don't want any toys . . ." His voice rose on yet another wail.

Gertie frowned. "Of course he'll find you. He's watching you right now from the North Pole. He knows if you're being naughty and it all goes down in his little book. Look at Lillian. She's being good. Father Christmas will bring lots of toys for her."

James pouted. "I want lots of toys, too."

"Then you'd better go to sleep right this blinking minute."

James turned immediately onto his side and closed his eyes.

Breathing a sigh of relief, Gertie crept over to where Ross waited for her by the door. "There, they'll be asleep any minute. Mrs. Chubb should be back soon. She went down to dinner an hour ago with Daisy and Samuel. Once she gets here, we can go down to dinner. I'm bloody starving, I am."

"Gertie." Ross sounded beaten, as if he'd been tramping Putney Downs all day instead of spending most of it resting in their room.

Gertie stared at him in concern. Now that she really looked at him, he looked really poorly. "Aren't you feeling well, luv?" She placed her hand on his arm. "What is it, then?"

"I've got something to tell you. I should've told you this morning, but I didna want to tell you in front of everybody."

His Scottish accent sounded even more pronounced than usual—a sure sign he was upset about something. Now she was really worried. "Tell me what, luv? What's wrong?"

He raised his chin to look up at the ceiling, then looked down at her with such sorrow in his face she wanted to cry out. Fear gripped her with a cold hand, and her lips felt numb with cold.

"I've sold the business, lass," he said at last. "I just couldna cope with it anymore."

Relief made her weak. "Is that all? Blimey, Ross, don't frighten me like that again. Don't worry, luv. Something will turn up. You'll have to get a job, that's all. Plenty of work around for a strapping lad like you."

"I don't know about that. I'm no' such a lad anymore. More like an old codger."

"Don't talk rubbish." She shook his arm. "Why, you're twice as big and three times as strong as any young lad I know. And four times as blinking handsome, and all."

His eyes softened, and he pulled her into his arms. "Ah, Gertie, my sweet, adorable love. What would I do without ye. Any other woman would be weepin' and wailin' at the news."

"Yeah, well, I'm not any bloody woman, am I. Things always have a way of working out, that's what I say, so what's the bleeding use of worrying about it."

Mrs. Chubb knocked on the door at that moment and Gertie welcomed the interruption. She'd made light of the situation, but her insides were churning like a keg of butter. It wasn't so much that Ross had sold the business. She was happy about that. She'd worried about him working such long hours in the harsh Scottish winters. And she was quite sure he'd soon find work again.

It was more the fact that he'd given up. Ross didn't give up easily on anything, and next to his family, the business was his life. Something had to be really wrong for him to get rid of something that had meant so much to him.

Making up her mind to have a word with Dr. Prestwick just as soon as she could, Gertie said good night to her babies and Mrs. Chubb, then took her husband's arm. They could never afford to stay in a posh hotel like this one. This was the one and only chance of a lifetime to live like the toffs for a little while, and she was determined to enjoy every single second of it.

Putting her worries out of her mind for the time being, she walked with her husband toward the stairs. In spite of the battles she'd had with Michel, she knew quite well that he was one of the best chefs in the country. She was really looking forward to her meal.

They were halfway down the corridor when she caught sight of someone moving in the shadows at the far end. The couple drew apart as they approached and the lady disappeared into a suite, while the gentleman turned his back and pretended to study a portrait hanging on the wall.

At the head of the stairwell, which was centered in the middle of the long corridor, Gertie glanced back at the lone figure farther down the hall. She'd recognized the

woman as the French wife of one of the toffs. Lady
Something-or-other. Now she recognized the gentleman.
It was the handsome bugger whose wife had all that flam-
ing red hair. Peebles, that was his name. Roger Peebles.

Intrigued, Gertie descended the stairs, wondering just
what the Frenchie was up to lurking in the corridor with
one of her husband's colleagues.

Jeannette grunted as she dumped the heavy tray of soiled
plates onto the kitchen table. "Look at this lot," she
mumbled to no one in particular. "It will take me all
night to get these washed and drained."

"It will if you stand there talking about it," Miss Bunkle said sharply. "Moira will be back any minute with
another load, so you'd better get started."

Muttering to herself, Jeannette rolled up her sleeves
past her elbows and stomped over to the stove, where a
cauldron of hot water sat bubbling and steaming. "All
this soap and hot water is drying out me skin. Me hands
look like they came off a crocodile."

Miss Bunkle grunted. "How would you know what a
crocodile looks like?"

"I seen one of them toffs wearing shoes made from
crocodile skin. Look just like me hands, they do."

Miss Bunkle gave her a sharp look. "I hope you haven't
been poking around amongst the guests' personal belongings again. You almost lost your job the last time when
Mr. Wrotham caught you snooping in the wardrobes. If
you get caught again doing that, you can say goodbye to
the Pennyfoot, that's for sure."

Jeannette sniffed, and wiped her nose with the back of
her finger. "This ain't the only place around here. I could

get a job anywhere doing what I do and getting better paid for it, too."

"That I doubt very much." Miss Bunkle shook a finger at her. "But you'll soon have the opportunity to find out if you don't get those plates in the sink this minute. And for heaven's sake, blow your nose. All that sniffing is driving me crazy."

"I'm getting a bloody cold, that's what." Jeannette grabbed the handles of the steaming cauldron and hauled it off the stove. She carried it to an empty sink next to the other two kitchen maids, who were feverishly plunging glasses, plates, and an assortment of cutlery in and out of the soapy water. "If I'm ill," she muttered, "you'll soon find out how much you'd miss me. What with all the guests here for Christmas and all."

"We'll cross that bridge when we come to it." Miss Bunkle picked up a fork from the other sink and examined it. "This fork isn't clean," she told the timid maid. "Make sure you scrub the prongs." She turned back to Jeanette. "Take some cod liver oil when you go to bed. That'll soon put you back on your feet. I'm going into the dining room. Make sure those plates are clean by the time I get back."

Jeanette waited until the kitchen door had swung to behind her before muttering, "Silly old cow." She mimicked Miss Bunkle's grating voice. "Take some cod liver oil."

The girl next to her giggled.

"I'd like to shove cod liver oil down her throat and see how she likes it." Jeanette swished a plate in the water and held it up to let the soap bubbles slide off it before placing it in the draining board.

The door swung open again and Moira staggered in,

bearing the weight of yet another tray of dirty dishes.

"Blimey," Jeanette said as her friend dumped the tray on the table. "How many bleeding more are there out there?"

"That's the lot, I think." Moira swiped at her forehead with the back of her arm. "There's just the coffee cups and saucers now."

"Thank Gawd for that." Jeanette beckoned to Moira. "Here, I want to ask you a favor."

Moira came forward with a good deal of reluctance. "What is it? The last time I did you a favor, it got me in trouble."

Jeanette made a face. "It weren't my fault. How was I to know they was Miss Bunkle's knickers hanging on the line? I just wanted to have a bit of fun, that's all."

"Miss Bunkle didn't think it was funny when she saw her knickers hanging on the cherub's head in the middle of the fountain. She knew I knew who dunnit. I should've told her it was you. She knew I was keeping her busy so she wouldn't see who did it."

"Well, you didn't tell her it were me and that's why you're me best friend." Jeanette nudged her with her elbow. "You are me best friend, aren't you?"

Moira shrugged. "I s'pose."

Jeanette glanced at the other two girls, both of whom were busy chattering about what they'd like for Christmas. Drawing Moira to one side, she whispered, "I have to go out tonight."

Moira stared at her. "Tonight? But it's not your night off. You can't go out tonight. Besides, you went out last night."

"No, I didn't. I had a big row with Wally and he went off in a huff."

"I know. I heard you. I thought you'd made it up with him."

"Well, I didn't. I went to bed early 'cos of me cold."

"Well, that was your night off. You can't just go tonight instead. Not without permission from Miss Bunkle."

"I'm not going to be that long. I just have to meet someone, that's all."

"Who, Wally? You going to make up with him?"

Jeanette shook her head. "Not Wally. We broke up."

Moira gasped in dismay. "Then who?"

"Never mind who. I just need you to tell Miss Bunkle that I'm not feeling well so I've gone to bed. I'll get these plates finished and then I'll leave."

Moira tightened her lips. "I'm not doing it unless you tell me who you're going to meet."

Jeanette glared at her in frustration. "I can't tell you, can I? At least, not now. I'll tell you later. I swear I will."

"Well, I don't know." Moira frowned. "I hope you're not getting yourself in no more trouble. You're in enough trouble as it is."

"Course not. I know what I'm doing. This is going to get me *out* of trouble, you'll see." Jeanette glanced at the clock on the wall. "And I'd better get on with these dishes or I'll be late. If you help me and tell Miss Bunkle I've gone to bed, I'll make it up to you. I'll do anything you want."

Moira sighed. "Well, all right. But you'd better be careful. If Miss Bunkle catches you, there'll be bloody hell to pay."

Jeanette grinned. "Don't you worry about that. The old biddy won't catch me. Thanks, Moira. I promise, I'll tell you everything just as soon as I know that everything's going to be all right again."

"Just be careful, that's all I ask." Moira turned back to the table. "Now we'd better get these plates washed, before we're both in trouble again."

Jeanette moved back to the sink and reached for another plate. She wished she *could* tell Moira who she was going to meet. It was so exciting, just thinking about it. But she'd promised, and until she was sure everything was going to turn out right, she had to keep that promise. She only hoped she wouldn't make a mess of things this time. Everything depended on what happened tonight. Everything.

CHAPTER

❧ 12 ❧

When Cecily arrived at Baxter's office, she was delighted to discover that he had completed his tasks for the day. "It would seem that you are finally catching up on all the work that Barry Wrotham's absence left behind," she said, giving her husband a warm hug. "I'm so pleased. I hated the thought that you might have to struggle with it all through the Christmas week."

"I would have put it all aside until after Christmas in any case," he told her.

"Piffle!" She smiled up at him. "You know very well you find it impossible to put aside work that has to be done."

"I seem to remember putting a great deal of my own work aside in order to come down here and manage this place for a month," Baxter said dryly.

"Ah, well, that was different." She glanced up at the clock. "In any case, since you are finished for the evening, what do you say to taking dinner in the dining room tonight? I'm tired of eating in our suite and snacking in your office. I would like to dine in style for a change."

"Anything you desire, my love. But I think it's a little late for Michel to cook us dinner now."

"Oh, they'll find something for us in the kitchen, I'm sure." She took hold of his arm. "Come, I have some delicious tidbits of news I'm just dying to share with you."

"Not gossip, I hope. You know how I abhor listening to gossip."

"Well, not strictly, no. This came straight from the horse's mouth. Besides, you'll be very pleased to hear that the mystery of Barry Wrotham's death has been explained. At least, I think it has. Though I can't help feeling that I haven't heard the whole story."

Baxter folded the ledger with a snap, then opened the door before turning out the gas lamps on the wall. "Well, my dear madam, you have succeeded in intriguing me. Let us proceed to the dining room this minute, so that we might satisfy both my curiosity and my appetite."

She accompanied him eagerly to the dining room, where to her delight, she found Gertie and Ross, still seated with Samuel and Doris, enjoying a lingering cup of coffee.

The men rose as she approached the table ahead of Baxter, who had paused to give their order to one of the serving maids. After greeting them all, she concentrated her attention on Doris, whom she barely recognized.

A picture of elegance in a high-throated gown of pale pink batiste, generously trimmed in Point de Paris lace, the young lady seemed nothing like that frightened little scullery maid who'd dropped everything she'd picked up and had spoken only in whispers.

Now a seasoned performer on the London stage, Doris had grown into a poised, glamorous young woman. Still not a star, perhaps, but definitely on her way there. Only her shy smile reminded Cecily of the child she once was.

"Doris!" Cecily grasped both of the young girl's slender hands. "How utterly marvelous to see you again. You look exquisite. Quite the London celebrity. How are you enjoying the stage?"

Doris's eyes glowed with warmth. "It's wonderful, m'm. I've never been so happy in all my life." Her smile faded a little. "Well, except for when I worked here at the Pennyfoot, that is."

Cecily laughed. "Come now, Doris, we can hardly compare to the excitement and glamour of the stage. But I hope you miss us just a little bit."

"Oh, I do, m'm." Doris waved a hand at Gertie. "I miss Gertie and Mrs. Chubb. And especially you and Mr. Baxter. You were like parents to me. I'll never forget that. Never."

Cecily felt a warm glow herself. "We've always considered the staff of the Pennyfoot our family. We miss you all very much."

Doris folded her serviette and placed it on the table. "Gertie was telling me you want to put on a pantomime."

"Yeah," Gertie said, laughing. "She asked me if I wanted to be in it. I told her I could be an Ugly Sister if we did *Cinderella*."

"I offered to be the prince," Samuel said, winking at Doris.

"Well, actually, I thought we might do *Aladdin*," Cecily said, looking hopefully at Doris. "Phoebe's dance troupe still have their *Arabian Nights* costumes. They were such a hit in the tableaux—"

"Except for the time Phoebe let a python loose on the stage," Baxter said dryly, having come up behind Cecily without her noticing. "I don't think the audience appreciated that little dramatic effect, judging by the amount of swooning ladies."

"Yeah," Samuel said with a grin. "The ballroom looked like a battlefield. After the python won."

They all laughed, greeting Baxter as if he were a long-lost friend. Cecily beamed on them all. It was so good to see her favorite people having such a wonderful time. It had been a good idea to invite everyone for Christmas, and now that the mystery of Barry Wrotham's death was solved, she could relax and enjoy the festivities.

Even so, as she preceded Baxter to a secluded table in the corner of the room, she couldn't quite dismiss the little niggling notion that Lucille had not been exactly truthful. Or perhaps she didn't want to pursue the possibility, just in case there was something sinister going on. Something that just might ruin Christmas for them all.

Right now everyone was happy and relaxed, looking forward with expectation to the big day. This was how it should be, and she could only hope that nothing would come along to spoil it all.

As for Madeline's dire warnings, she had been known to be mistaken before. Cecily decided just to put the whole thing out of her mind. Nothing was going to interfere with this Christmas Season. Not if she could help it.

*   *   *

The very next morning Doris called a rehearsal for the pantomime. Having appeared in a production of *Aladdin* the year before, she was well acquainted with the music and the general story line. Since most of the speaking parts were ad-libbed anyway, it was just a matter of prompting and prodding the actors.

Motor cars had been sent out to the vicarage so that Phoebe could round up her dance troupe, and various members of the staff had been invited to join in the fun. Raymond, who had been following Doris around all morning, was given the part of the genie, and Cecily agreed to juggle his duties among the footmen in order to allow him to take part. Doris herself was to play Aladdin.

Phoebe was beside herself with excitement, especially when told that her dance troupe could perform their tableaux as part of the backdrop, and even the colonel was recruited to act as a palace guard.

Despite Doris's pleas, both Cecily and Baxter declined to take part, citing their duties as being too numerous for them to spare the time. Gertie and Mrs. Chubb volunteered, however, and would be adding comic relief to the presentation. Though, as Baxter remarked in an aside to Cecily, just the appearance of Phoebe's dance troupe would provide plenty of amusement.

In all, the pantomime promised to be a spectacular addition to the Christmas events, and Cecily was well pleased with her decision. After leaving the excited cast to rehearse, she made her way to the kitchen. It had been some time since she had spoken to Michel, and she needed to go over the Christmas menu with him.

She was crossing the foyer when she spotted Percy Chatsworth entering through the front doors. He doffed his homburg at the sight of her, greeting her with a cheery "Good morning, Mrs. Baxter!"

She answered his greeting, and was about to pass him by, when she remembered something Lucille had said. *I do not understand why he needs all this extra work and demands . . . I wish the others would leave him alone.*

At the time, Cecily had wondered who "the others" might be, and what kind of business they were engaged in that Lucille found so distressing. It occurred to her now that Lucille might have been talking about the other Benchers.

True, it was none of her business, but curiosity had always been her downfall, and she really wanted to know what Lucille had meant by those words. Perhaps then she could finally banish that annoying little feeling that she had forgotten something that still taunted her mind.

Percy Chatsworth was a good deal older than his counterparts, and probably nearing retirement. It seemed a good place to start. "I trust you are enjoying your respite, Mr. Chatsworth?" She beamed at him. "Your work must bring such pressure to bear. It can't be easy to argue whether or not a man is guilty of a crime. It's a great responsibility."

"Indeed it is, Mrs. Baxter. Indeed it is." Chatsworth nodded his head emphatically in agreement.

"I imagine you are looking forward to your retirement. Your work must not give you time to enjoy much leisure. How fortunate that you are spared the time to visit with us here in Badgers End."

"Quite, quite." Chatsworth looked meaningfully at the grandfather clock. He was obviously in a hurry to be somewhere else.

"Though I suppose some of you manage to have business

interests outside of the courts, wouldn't you say?" It was a shot in the dark, but she was hoping he might shed some light on Sir John's activities.

To her surprise, Chatsworth's eyes had narrowed to thin slits, and the muscles in his jaw were so tight she could see them twitch. "That would be quite impossible, Mrs. Baxter. Masters of the Bench are prohibited from owning or being engaged in outside businesses. One would be instantly disbarred for life. Now, if you will excuse me, I am late for an important appointment."

She watched him stride off, his cape flapping around his ankles like an angry dog. It must have been something she said, though she couldn't imagine what it was. In any case, it would seem that Sir John's added demands were not connected to business affairs. Which made his lack of attention even more unreasonable. It was no wonder his wife was so upset with him. Feeling decidedly sorry for the woman, Cecily continued on her way.

Long before she reached the kitchen door, she could hear the uproar ensuing from behind it. The crashing and banging of pans sounded ominously familiar as an irate voice strove to make itself heard above the racket. "*Sacre bleu!* 'Ow am I supposed to provide ze meal with ze excellence my patrons expect from me when I 'ave such incompetence from ze 'elpers? You are all 'elpless, *oui?* You do not know 'ow to serve ze rack of lamb, *non?* 'Ow many times I tell you . . . put ze little white frills on top ze feet, not around ze bottom!"

Michel was on the warpath again. Cecily pushed open the door to the kitchen, just as a saucepan lid crashed to the floor.

Miss Bunkle emerged from the pantry carrying a huge tray loaded with hams. Moira leaped to help her and instead bumped into her. The flustered maid jumped backward, stepped back onto the saucepan lid, skidded on it, and sent it clattering across the red tile floor.

Miss Bunkle, unlike Mrs. Chubb, who would have raised her voice to scold the maid, simply sat the tray on the huge butcher table in the middle of the kitchen and said coldly, "Do try to be more careful, girl. We don't want any more broken dishes."

"Broken dishes?" Michel swung around from the stove, waving a wooden spoon in the air. "There'll be broken 'eads if I 'ave my way. I cannot work with such imbeciles—" Apparently catching sight of Cecily, he broke off, his eyes widening. "*Madame!* You are 'ere!" He swept her a flamboyant bow, sweeping yet another saucepan lid to the ground.

Cecily winced at the deafening rattle of its lopsided spin. Moira snatched it up before it could spin to a clattering stop. "Morning, m'm," she said, dipping a nervous curtsey.

"I'm sorry, madam," Miss Bunkle said, coming forward. "Things are a little disorganized this morning. One of our maids is ill and another has the half-day off and we are so busy we haven't had time to breathe."

"Oh, dear, we shall have to try to do something about that. Perhaps we should take on some extra maids over Christmas." Cecily smiled at Moira, who looked as if she were about to burst into tears. "It's all right, Moira. Get on with your work."

"Yes, m'm." The girl scurried over to the table and joined the other girls in polishing the silverware.

Cecily turned to the housekeeper. "Who is ill, Miss Bunkle?"

The housekeeper shook her head. "It's Jeanette, madam. She has a bad cold and went to bed early last night. The girl was sniffing all day yesterday. Now two of the others have started sniffing. If they go down with colds, we'll be in a right pickle."

"Has anyone attended to Jeanette this morning? Does she need a doctor?"

"I haven't had time to look in on her as yet, madam. I'll send someone to her room as soon as the midday meal is over."

"That won't be for another two hours or more." Cecily glanced at the clock. "I'll stop by there on my way out and see if she needs anything."

"Oh, no, madam, that won't be necessary. I—"

"Oh, *no, you can't!*"

Both Miss Bunkle and Moira had spoken at once. Or rather, Moira's protest had been more a cry of dismay. Everyone in the kitchen suddenly fell silent, as if sensing something important was amiss.

Cecily and the housekeeper stared at Moira, who appeared to be in great distress. She twisted her apron around her fingers as she stared wide-eyed at Cecily.

"What is it, girl?" Miss Bunkle demanded. "Speak up! Do you need to go to the lavatory?"

Moira's face flamed and she shot an embarrassed glance at Michel. "No, Miss Bunkle, it's just that, Jeanette, well . . ."

Cecily moved toward her, holding out her hand. "It's all right, Moira," she said soothingly. "What's the matter with Jeanette?"

"I don't know . . . that is . . . she's . . ." She sent a wild glance around the kitchen. Three of the maids stared back as if hanging on her every word, while Michel stirred a cauldron of soup with one hand and glared at the hapless girl.

"Perhaps we'd better step outside," Cecily said quietly.

At that Moira seemed even more agitated. "No, no, it's nothing, m'm, honest it isn't. Jeanette is quite all right, I know she is. She doesn't need nothing right now." She aimed a scared look at Miss Bunkle. "I can go and see her in a little while. She'll be all right until then. Honest. She'd rather be left alone."

Miss Bunkle walked right up to the maid and scowled at her. Although her voice was deadly calm, the knitting needle in her hair quivered as though attached to a rumbling volcano. "All right, my girl. *Where is Jeanette?*"

Tears welled up in Moira's frightened eyes. "I don't know, Miss Bunkle. Honest I don't."

"I assume she's not lying down in her room."

"I don't think so, Miss Bunkle."

"You share the room with her, don't you?"

The girl nodded, dabbing at her nose with the back of her hand.

"Then you know where she is."

"No, I don't, Miss Bunkle. She never told me where she was going." Once more she sent a worried glance at the other curious girls.

"Stop your gawking and get on with your work," Miss Bunkle ordered, jerking a hand in their direction. "We're behind enough as it is. Moira, you come with me." She grabbed the girl's hand and marched her out of the kitchen, with Cecily following close behind.

Once outside in the hallway, Miss Bunkle pushed her face into Moira's, nose to nose. "Now you're going to tell me where Jeanette is and what she is doing, or I'll have you scrubbing floors every night for a week."

Moira promptly burst into a storm of weeping, making it impossible to get anything out of her.

"Perhaps I should talk to her," Cecily suggested. "I'm sure you need to be back in the kitchen taking care of your chores."

Miss Bunkle hesitated, then gave Cecily a sharp nod. "Very well, madam. But I have to tell you, I am not happy with the way the staff behaves here. The maids are impertinent, and as for Michel, he's a drunken lout with a filthy temper. The staff have been allowed too many liberties if you ask me. Discipline, that's what these people need. They need to be treated like servants, not like members of the family. It's no wonder the whole place is so disorganized."

Cecily suppressed her resentment as best she could, saying evenly, "I'm sorry you feel that way, Miss Bunkle. Please return to your work. I'll take care of this matter with Jeanette."

Miss Bunkle muttered her begrudging thanks and disappeared into the kitchen. Moira still sobbed into her apron and Cecily patted her on the shoulder. "Come along with me, Moira. We'll talk in my suite."

Moira gulped and sniffed, and blew her nose into her apron, making Cecily wince. She made a mental note to supply all the maids with handkerchiefs. No wonder they were passing colds around to each other.

"I'd better not, m'm," Moira said, her voice quivering. "Miss Bunkle is really cross with me. I don't want to make her any more cross."

"Very well." Cecily smiled encouragingly at her. "You can go back now if you feel better."

"Yes, m'm. I do. Thank you, m'm." She turned to go, but Cecily laid a hand on her thin shoulder.

"But first, I think it might be a good idea if you tell me when you last saw Jeanette."

Moira gulped again, then whispered, "I gave my solemn promise I wouldn't tell."

"When was that?"

Moira's lips trembled. "Last night, m'm."

Cecily felt a pang of apprehension. "Last night? That was the last time you saw her?"

Moira gave her a reluctant nod of her head.

"And she didn't say where she was going?"

"No, m'm. She didn't. She said as how it were a secret."

"She stayed out all night?"

"Yes, m'm."

Now Cecily was really worried. "Did she say anything else that might help us know where she is? Did she give you any idea she planned on leaving for good?"

"Oh, no, m'm. She told me she was meeting someone and she couldn't tell me who it was, but that she'd tell me all about it later. I think she meant to come back, m'm. That's why I'm so worried." Her bottom lip trembled again and she caught it under her teeth.

"Does she have a young man?"

"Yes, m'm. Wally Diggett. But she weren't going to see him. She told me they broke up."

"Perhaps she was going to mend their quarrel."

Moira gave a definite shake of her head. "No, m'm. She was going to meet someone else. She told me that much, but she wouldn't tell me who it was." She started to cry again. "She's going to hate me for telling you, I know she is."

"Please don't worry, Moira," Cecily said gently. "I won't let her know you told me anything. Which room are you in?"

"Number three, m'm. And thank you." The girl managed a weak smile. "I'm much obliged."

The door closed behind her, and frowning, Cecily made her way down the hallway to the maids' quarters. Reaching the door with a brass number three on it, she tapped, gently at first. When there was no answer from inside, she rapped loudly. "Jeanette? Are you in there?" After a moment's hesitation, she turned the handle and went inside.

She had forgotten how cramped the maids' quarters were. The room was barely big enough to hold the two cots, which sat close together with a gap just big enough for knees to pass in between. A small wardrobe took up the space in one corner, and a narrow dresser bearing a washbasin and jug stood in the other.

The only mirror in the room was a small oval one in a carved metal frame that hung on the wall over the dresser. The tiny window looked out on the kitchen yard, barely ten feet of paving before it reached the high wooden fence on the other side.

No wonder the young girls were leaving the service in droves to find jobs in the city. The pay for a servant was small, the hours long, and the work arduous. The compensation of having room and board thrown in was hardly an incentive anymore, when compared with the freedom of returning to one's own home at night in the city. Even if that home was no more than a cramped room in a boardinghouse.

Freedom, that was the key word. Freedom to come and

go where and when one pleased, once the day's work was done. It made all the difference. Cecily sighed, and went to the wardrobe to open it. Two afternoon dresses hung there, and beneath them, two pairs of black patent-leather shoes. On the top shelf sat two large traveling bags.

After closing the door, she wandered over to the dresser. A hairbrush sat on one side of the washbasin, together with a face flannel, a comb, and a toothbrush. It certainly would appear that Jeanette had planned to return to the Pennyfoot. So now the question was, why hadn't she?

Cecily left the room and closed the door behind her. She had a very bad feeling in the pit of her stomach. It would seem that the ill luck that had haunted the Pennyfoot ever since James's death was still with them. She could only hope that the girl was safe and sound.

CHAPTER

❧ 13 ❧

Baxter seemed less concerned with Jeanette's disappearance than Cecily would have liked. "She's probably gone off with her young man for a day or two," he said, looking disdainful. "You know what these young girls are like nowadays. Disgraceful, that's what I call it. I don't know what's happening to women lately. This blasted Women's Movement is causing more trouble than I ever imagined. What with women digging up golf courses, breaking windows, and starving themselves in prisons, the whole world is going to rot. And for what? What do they really hope to achieve?"

"The vote, for one thing," Cecily said mildly. "To be on an equal footing with men, for another. To be allowed to enter any room in any establishment, such as the card

169

rooms and the bar of this country club. In other words, to be treated and respected as a human being."

"Are you saying I don't treat you with respect?"

"Of course not, dear. But then you are the exception." She smiled fondly at him. She had long ago learned that it was a waste of time to argue with his favorite grievance, much as she disagreed with his opinions. Ignoring his snort of exasperation, she poured out his tea from the silver teapot.

He had abandoned his office for a short while in order to take afternoon tea in the suite with her, a treat she truly enjoyed. Ever since they had arrived at the Pennyfoot, he had been closeted in his office for the most part.

Although he spent a great deal of time at home with his business, he'd at least had time to share meals with her, whereas here in the Pennyfoot, with the exception of a late supper at night, they were fortunate to snatch a few moments here and there over a cup of tea or a glass of sherry.

This afternoon, however, was a delightful departure from his normal routine, and she was determined to enjoy every moment. Even so, she'd deemed it necessary to inform him of Jeanette's unexplained absence.

"I'm particularly worried about Jeanette," she told him, "because Miss Bunkle said that she was coming down with a bad cold yesterday. I do hope she hasn't fallen ill somewhere and is lying in a hospital bed. She'd be so miserable and lonely with no one to pay her a visit."

"I think we would have heard if that had happened. Someone would have notified us by now."

"Well, Jeanette might seem a little frivolous at times, but she doesn't seem the sort to simply take her leave without a word to anyone."

"Who knows what these young girls will do just to please a beau."

"Moira told me that Jeanette was planning to meet someone other than her young man. Miss Bunkle is convinced that Jeanette stole her pearls and has gone off to London to sell them."

"Well. There you are then."

"I don't believe that for one minute. Jeanette was quite indignant that we should even suspect her of stealing the pearls."

"That could have been a well-executed piece of acting. You'd be surprised what these girls are capable of doing."

"I suppose." She sighed. "I hate to think of a young girl like that involved in crime at such a tender age."

"Well, I suggest we let the constables take care of it. Has anyone reported her as missing?"

"Not yet. We're all rather hoping she'll soon return with a feasible explanation."

"I wouldn't wait too long on that expectation." He lifted a miniature mince pie from the tray of pastries. "This is what I enjoy most about Christmas," he added after taking a bite with a look of supreme pleasure on his face. "I really don't understand why we can't have Christmas food all year long. It seems such a waste to wait until the end of the year to enjoy plum pudding and Christmas cakes."

"Ah, but you wouldn't enjoy them half as much if you could have them anytime you wanted." Abandoning her concerns about Jeanette for the moment, Cecily helped herself to a mince pie. "Besides, it's a tradition, such as Easter eggs and hot cross buns."

"Another waste, if you ask me." He leaned back with his cup and saucer balanced on his knee. "To blazes with tradition, that's what I say."

She burst out laughing. "Why, Bax, I never thought the day would come when you would give up on tradition. You're always fighting progress and change. Except for the motor car, that is."

"Ah, well, that's the only sensible thing to come out of all this rush to modernize the world. I'm thinking of asking young Samuel to teach me to drive an automobile. I think it would be a great asset for getting around in my business."

Cecily regarded him over the rim of her cup. "You always meet your clients at the club, which is a twenty-minute walk from our house. By the time you managed to crank up the engine of a motor car, climbed in, drove it to the club, deposited it, and got out of it, you could have walked the distance in half of that time."

Baxter frowned. "It's not the time involved, Cecily, it's the impression one gives when arriving in an automobile. Prestige!" He wagged a finger at her. "That is the key to a successful business."

"Well, my love, no one can deny that you have a very successful business, so your prestige must be in excellent condition already, in which case, you do not need a motor car to enhance it."

He frowned at her for a moment, then his face softened. "Has anyone ever told you, Mrs. Baxter, that you have an infernal way of turning an argument in your favor?"

She grinned. "I learned from a master. James could argue his way out of the dungeons in the Tower of London."

"Indeed he could." He studied her with a pensive expression. "You still miss him?"

"Not anymore." She got up from her chair, leaned over her husband, and kissed him. "How could I, when I have someone who fulfills me as you do?"

He sighed. "There are times when I feel I don't give you enough of myself. What with the business and now this . . ." He waved a vague hand in the air. "It seems we have so little time together these days. It was my biggest complaint when we worked here in the past."

She returned to her chair and reached for her tea. "Well, I must admit I was becoming a trifle bored at home, being left alone to my own devices. But now that I am back here at the Pennyfoot, I can find plenty enough to fill in my time. Though I will always welcome the chance to share a few minutes alone with you, my dear husband."

"It won't always be this way."

"I know." She sipped her tea, then replaced the cup in its saucer. "I am a patient woman, Bax. I know that one day we will have all the leisure time in the world together, and that is well worth the wait."

"I promise I will make it worth your while."

She smiled at him, content for now in knowing how much he cared for her. She was, indeed, a fortunate woman.

"It's very nice of you to invite us to help you decorate the tree, Miss Pengrath," Daisy said as she sat the twins down at a small table in the library. "The little ones have been looking forward to it all day, haven't you, ducks?"

Lillian nodded, while James looked bored. Daisy hoped he wouldn't give her any trouble. The twins had really grown up a lot since she'd last seen them. They were becoming quite a handful.

"I'm delighted to have the help," Madeline said in her low, musical voice. "It will give their mother and Mrs. Chubb some time to themselves."

Daisy wished fervently that she had a voice like Madeline's. She'd tried to speak like that now and then, but all she managed to do was sound as if she had a bad cold. "I know Gertie and Mrs. Chubb will like that." She beamed at the twins. "And it will be fun to help, won't it, luvs."

James pouted. "Don't want to," he muttered.

"Yes, you do," Madeline said firmly. She rummaged inside the large tapestry bag she'd brought in with her, and came up holding two peppermint sticks. "We'll have lots of fun, and this will be your pay for helping me."

Lillian's face lit up, and James held out a chubby hand. "I want it *now*," he demanded.

"Only when you've finished helping." Madeline dropped them back in the bag and pulled out a thick wad of paper strips. She laid them out on the table in piles of pink, blue, green, yellow, white, and red. Next she put out a large pot of paste with a brush fixed to the cap. "Now, this is how you make a paper chain."

Daisy watched her dab the paste brush on one end of a pink strip and fasten it into a circle. Then she threaded a blue strip through the circle and fastened the ends of it with the paste. "Now, do you two clever little people think you can do that?"

Lillian nodded eagerly and reached for a strip of paper. Even James seemed intrigued, in spite of his best efforts not to look interested. Daisy helped them put the paste on the strips and fasten the ends, then let them choose the next strip.

Out of the corner of her eye, she watched Madeline hang the glass ornaments, hand-sewn lace-trimmed hearts, and red velvet bows on the tree.

Seeing her at work, so graceful and serene, Daisy found it hard to believe the stories they told about Madeline in the village. In that white cotton dress with its little red bows, she looked just like an angel. A very beautiful angel. If she was dressed in a proper gown, she'd put all them toffs to shame. It didn't seem right that she wasn't married. But then, not many men would want to take the chance of marrying a witch.

"James took my paper," Lillian wailed. "I wanted that pink one."

"It's mine," James declared, holding the strip to his chest, where it promptly stuck to the bib of his apron.

Daisy peeled it off, tearing it in the process. Both twins wailed and it took a minute or two to restore harmony.

"Here," Madeline said as she lifted the uneven chain of paper from the table. "You can help me hang it on the tree now, and then we'll put all the Christmas crackers in between the branches."

"What are crackers?" James asked as he draped one end of the chain over a low branch of the tree.

"They have snaps inside them," Daisy explained. "You hold one end and I hold the other, then we pull and the cracker pops with a bang and a present falls out of it."

"And a hat," Madeline added. "Here, I'll show you." She hunted in her bag again, and then handed Daisy a box filled with long colored paper tubes, gaily decorated and frilled at each end. "Take one out and we'll let them pull it."

Daisy took a cracker out of the box and helped each

twin grasp the end of it. "Now pull," she told them.

They both tugged hard and the cracker popped open with a loud snap that made Lillian jump. Something fell to the floor and both twins dove for it. James came up holding a tiny silver horse, and Lillian pouted.

"He always gets everything," she wailed.

Madeline unwrapped the remains of the cracker and pulled out a paper hat, which she placed on Lillian's head. "Ah," she said softly, "but you are the one who is crowned the queen."

Lillian's tearful frown vanished, and she floated around the room chanting, "I'm the queen, I'm the queen!"

"Now it's time to put the candles on," Madeline said, handing some of the tiny wax sticks to Daisy. "You two can tell us where we should put them."

"Why are we putting candles on the tree?" James demanded.

"We're going to have a candle-lighting ceremony," Daisy told him. "We'll all stand around the tree on Christmas Eve and sing carols, and then someone lights all the candles and we turn all the lamps out and everyone gets a present off the Christmas tree."

"Will Father Christmas be here?" Lillian wanted to know.

Madeline laughed. "Father Christmas won't come until everyone is asleep. So you must be sure to go to sleep really quickly that night."

"Will the candles be burning when he comes?"

"No, we have to blow them all out," Daisy explained. "It would be much too dangerous to leave them burning on the tree. It could catch fire."

"Then how will he see to come down the chimney?" James demanded.

"We'll leave a lamp lit for him," Madeline promised. She reached up to fasten a candle holder onto a branch. "Don't worry, Father Christmas is accustomed to moving around . . . in the dark. He—"

Her voice stopped abruptly, and she seemed to freeze, her hands so still that Daisy thought she could have been a statue. Even the twins were silent, staring at Madeline's still figure as if they had seen a ghost.

The eerie silence that settled over the room made Daisy's blood run cold, then Madeline spoke, and her soft words sent chills all the way down Daisy's spine.

"There is evil in this room," she said, her voice close to a whisper. "Danger lurking everywhere. You must beware. *You must beware.*"

The warning seemed to float in the air, cold and menacing. Frightened now, Daisy drew the children close to her. She stared at Madeline, wondering frantically for whom the words were meant. Was it her? Was she in danger? The twins?

Madeline dropped her hands and turned to face her. "You can start putting the candles on the other side of the tree," she said, her voice perfectly normal again.

Daisy blinked. It was over so quickly she wondered if she'd imagined it, but the twins still stared at the other woman as if afraid of her.

Daisy pulled them around the other side of the tree with her and started talking very fast about all the things the children had to look forward to during Christmas. Before long they were chattering and laughing with her, and even Madeline joined in their silliness.

Daisy gradually relaxed, though she knew that it would be a very long time before she forgot the strange moment when Madeline saw something that no one else could see. Something evil and frightening, and perhaps still lurking in the shadows of the quiet library.

By the end of the day Cecily had to accept the fact that Jeanette was probably not going to return to the Pennyfoot. Miss Bunkle expressed her displeasure by announcing that she couldn't possibly cope with the Christmas Season unless she had another pair of hands.

Cecily promised to see what she could do about hiring another maid, but when Miss Bunkle insisted that she report to the constables that Jeanette had stolen her pearls, Cecily put her foot down.

"You cannot accuse someone of a crime without good cause," she told the infuriated woman. "Just because Jeanette has apparently left our employ does not mean she's a thief."

"Why else would she run away?" Miss Bunkle demanded. "It looks awfully suspicious to me. If she didn't steal my pearls, then where are they? They didn't just simply walk off on their own."

"Well, perhaps I can find out what happened to them. Just give me a little time."

Miss Bunkle tightened her lips. "Very well, madam. But if they don't turn up in the next day or two, I'm going to tell the constables everything."

"If I can't find out what happened to them, I'll call the constables myself," Cecily promised rashly. The last thing she wanted right now was a full-scale investigation going on in the club. Edward would never forgive her if she allowed the Christmas Season to be spoiled by a petty thief.

On a hunch she stopped by Moira's room and tapped on the door. Luckily the girl hadn't yet gone to bed, though she seemed extremely disturbed by Cecily's visit.

"I don't know nothing more about where Jeanette is, honest," she said when Cecily invited herself into the room.

"Actually, I came to ask if you had any idea where Miss Bunkle's pearls might be," Cecily said, seating herself on the edge of Jeanette's bed.

Moira looked frightened. "I told you, m'm, I had nothing to do with the pearls."

"Miss Bunkle thinks Jeanette might have taken them and that's why she ran away. What do you think about that?"

Moira's cheeks grew red, and she stared down at her feet. "I don't know nothing about that, m'm. But I got to thinking about things and I think I might know who Jeannette was meeting last night."

Taken by surprise, Cecily said sharply, "Then I think you had better tell me."

Moira fidgeted with the strings of her apron, winding them around her fingers so tightly they turned white. "I don't want to get no one in trouble, m'm, but if something bad has happened to Jeanette . . ." Her voice trailed off miserably.

"I'm sure nothing bad has happened to your friend," Cecily assured her. "And I promise you that you won't be getting anyone into any more trouble than they are already in, so why don't you just tell me who you think Jeannette was meeting and we'll see what we can do."

Moira sank onto her bed. "Well, I do know that Jeanette was sweet on someone. She was always talking about him, and once I saw her talking to him in the corridor."

"Did she tell you she was fond of this person? She could have simply been having a friendly conversation."

"Well, the other night Jeannette had a terrible row with Wally over him. I heard them arguing about it in the kitchen yard. Wally told her that if he wasn't good enough for her, she could run right back to her pretty boy lover."

"I see," Cecily said slowly. "And what did she say to that?"

"She said that's just what she was planning to do, and that if Wally didn't like it, it was just too bad. Wally laughed at her, and said that no toff would ever be caught dead with her."

Cecily stared at her. "A toff? Are you saying Jeanette was romantically involved with one of the guests?"

"I think so, m'm."

"Do you know who he is?"

Moira pressed her lips together, then blurted out, "You won't tell anyone I said anything, will you? I don't want to get no one in trouble. I just thought he might know where Jeanette went."

"I won't tell anyone you told me," Cecily promised. "But I must know who it is, Moira. It could be extremely important."

"All right." Moira carefully unwound the string from her fingers. "It were one of them barristers from London. The good-looking one. His name is Roger. Roger Peebles."

Cecily gaped at her. "Roger Peebles? Are you sure?"

Moira nodded. "Yes, that's him. Roger Peebles. He's the one. I think Jeanette was going to see him last night."

Cecily made an effort to collect her thoughts. The whole idea was so ludicrous. Jeannette was a nice young girl, but she was not exactly what one would call a beauty. She was certainly no match for Peebles's wife, Gretchen. Then again, there was no accounting for taste. Peebles wouldn't be the only one to turn to a serving girl to add a little spice to his life.

Making a mental note to talk to Peebles at the first opportunity, Cecily rose to leave. "Well, thank you, Moira. I appreciate you being so candid with me. You did the right thing by telling me what you know."

"Please don't be too angry with Jeanette, m'm," Moira pleaded. "After all, she's not the only one. I reckon all them barristers are the same. I saw the fat one, Mr. Fitzhammer, going into his room with a lady what wasn't his wife. I know that 'cos I saw his wife downstairs in the library right after I went downstairs again so it couldn't have been her I saw in his room."

What was the matter with these men, Cecily fumed inwardly. They had everything they could possibly want . . . money, prestige, a beautiful wife, and one would assume, a gorgeous home, and still it wasn't enough. As long as she lived, she would never understand the mentality of the human male species.

"I hope you won't repeat any of this to anyone else," she told Moira. "What goes on inside these walls must never be divulged to anyone. Is that clear?"

"Oh, I know, m'm." Moira nodded solemnly. "Me lips are sealed. I only told you 'cos I thought it might help find out what happened to Jeanette."

Cecily nodded. "Well, we'll have to see. Now get some sleep, Moira. You'll have a long day tomorrow if Jeanette doesn't return."

Moira's voice wavered when she asked, "What do you think happened to her, m'm?"

"I think she probably went off looking for adventure somewhere, and is probably wishing right now that she hadn't been so silly."

She closed the door behind her and headed back to the stairs. The answer she'd given to Moira's question had been deliberately vague. The truth was, she was far more concerned about the missing maid than she was willing to admit. She could only hope that Jeanette wasn't in more trouble than she could handle. The sense of urgency that had bothered her earlier was even more intense now. It was imperative they find the girl as soon as possible. She could only hope it wasn't too late.

CHAPTER
❧ 14 ❧

"These two are driving me blinking bonkers," Gertie announced the next morning. She and Mrs. Chubb had taken the twins for a stroll along the sands after breakfast, hoping to wear down some of the boundless energy that kept the children ceaselessly on the move.

The cold wind from the sea had whipped their faces, turning their little cheeks bright red by the time they'd returned to the Pennyfoot. Gertie was now huddled in Mrs. Chubb's room, trying to thaw out her frozen bones, while Mrs. Chubb did her best to prevent the twins from ruining the bedsprings as they bounced up and down with a little too much exuberance.

"Why don't you take Ross into the town and enjoy some of Dolly's baking?" Mrs. Chubb suggested. "You two haven't spent more than an hour or two together since he arrived."

"We've spent all night together," Gertie said, reaching out to break James's grasp on his sister's hair. She gave his hand a light slap. "Leave your sister alone or I'll tell your papa what a bad boy you are."

"I meant doing something outside the hotel. Go for a walk with him, or stop by the George and Dragon. Go and watch the ice-skating on Deep Willow Pond."

Gertie sighed. "I just been for a walk and my toes are ready to bleeding drop off with the cold. Besides, Ross is lying down. He don't feel very well."

Mrs. Chubb's eyes were full of concern when she looked at her. "He's not ill, is he?"

"I hope not." Gertie did her best to dismiss her pang of fear. "I think he's just tired, that's all. And fed up. I wasn't going to tell you this 'til after Christmas, but he's sold the business."

"Oh, my." Mrs. Chubb clutched her chest. "What is he going to do now?"

Gertie shrugged. "Oh, he'll find something, I know he will. It's just . . . it's not like him to give up like that."

Mrs. Chubb nodded. "He's not a young man anymore, Gertie. You have to remember that he's a lot older than you. He's ready to slow down a bit. And the business was taking its toll on him. I could tell that."

"Yeah, well, he'll be able to have a bit of a rest now, until he finds a job. The money he made on the business will keep us going for a bit. And I can always go back to work if needs be."

Mrs. Chubb grabbed Lillian's hand, just as she was

about to pull the washbowl and basin off its stand. "It would be hard on you, Gertie, after all this time."

"I don't think so." Gertie winced as James fell off the bed. He started wailing and she scooped him up and sat him on her lap. "I've sort of missed working since I've been married to Ross. I know I have plenty to do in the house, and Gawd knows the twins take up enough time, but they're getting older and I miss the company of the other girls. Being back here has reminded me of all the laughs we used to have, and all the adventures."

"We tend to remember the best of times and forget the worst."

"I know. Still, I do miss it." Her gaze met Mrs. Chubb's, and the older woman's wistful expression made her smile.

"I miss it, too," Mrs. Chubb confessed. "I mean, I love helping you take care of the children, but soon now they'll be going to school. What will two grown women do all day long in the house together without the little ones to worry about?"

Gertie shrugged. "Housework, I s'pose. Like we do now."

"Not very exciting, is it."

"No, it's not." She grinned. "Are you thinking what I'm thinking?"

Mrs. Chubb sighed. "It would be very nice to go back to work again, Gertie, but you know very well Ross would never allow you to go back to work and I'm getting too old for it now. Maybe we could take in some sewing or something, just to give us a little extra and keep us busy."

"Yeah, maybe." James wriggled off Gertie's lap and

promptly ran up to his sister and tugged on her hair again. "All right, that's bleeding it." She sprang up and slapped James on his rump.

He opened his mouth and howled, still holding on to Lillian's hair. By the time Gertie had untangled the long curls from his fist, Lillian was howling as well.

"We've got to get them out of here," Mrs. Chubb exclaimed as she gathered Lillian in her arms and hugged her to her generous bosom. "The other guests will be complaining about the noise."

"Let's take them for a walk around the grounds. They can throw stones in the fish pond or something. With the trees sheltering us, it might not be as bloody cold as it was on the beach."

"Good idea." Mrs. Chubb reached for Lillian's tam-o'-shanter and pulled it down over her ears. Then she wound a scarf around the little girl's neck and buttoned her into a warm coat. The boots were next, and it took her several minutes to fasten all the buttons with a button hook. Meanwhile Gertie struggled with James, who was still sniffling.

Several minutes later they were ready, and holding each child by the hand, Gertie and Mrs. Chubb emerged into the hallway and headed for the stairs.

Snowflakes floated down like soft white feathers as they stepped outside. Gertie had elected to go through the French doors in the library and out through the rose garden. There were no roses in bloom this late in the year, so there was no risk of the children trying to pick the blossoms off the bushes.

The wind from the ocean barely penetrated the thick hedges in the garden, and the twins spent a pleasant few minutes exploring the new territory and throwing snow-balls at each other, while Mrs. Chubb and Gertie sat on the wooden bench, enjoying the tranquil scene.

"These bushes look like they could use a bloody good trim," Gertie remarked, pointing at the rows of rose-bushes on either side of the crazy paving path.

"They do look a bit ragged." Mrs. Chubb frowned. "What happened to the arbor? It used to be so pretty with its archway of climbing roses."

"I knew something was missing." Gertie shook her head. "These gardens haven't looked the same since poor John Thimble died."

"I thought Ross did a good job of taking care of them when he worked here."

"Yeah, he did. But he really didn't have the time to do much before we moved back to Scotland."

"I've really missed living here," Mrs. Chubb said softly. "Scotland is very nice, but it's not Badgers End."

"I know." Gertie stretched out her booted feet. "It's too wild, too lonely. I miss the sea, and the shops, and the cliffs."

"And the people."

"Yeah, 'specially the people."

"Mama!"

The bloodcurdling shriek brought Gertie to her feet. "It's time we moved on before these two kill each other. Let's go for a walk around the tennis courts. By that time it should be close to mealtime again."

Mrs. Chubb rose a little stiffly. "All I seem to do here is eat."

Gertie grinned. "So what's bleeding wrong with that?" She grabbed James's hand as he raced by her. "We have a rehearsal this afternoon. Daisy said she'd look after the twins. It will give us both a bit of a break."

"I'm surprised Daisy didn't want to be in the pantomime," Mrs. Chubb remarked as she dusted a smear of dirt on Lillian's coat.

"Nah, Daisy doesn't like to be on show in front of everybody. She says she leaves that sort of thing to Doris. You know, it's a funny thing. I always thought Doris was the shy one, and Daisy was always so sure of herself, always ready to stand up to anyone what gave her lip. Yet now it's Doris what loves the stage and performing in front of people, and Daisy would rather be on her own than in a crowd."

Mrs. Chubb nodded. "Just goes to show, you never really know people as well as you think you do."

They rounded the end of the rose garden and came out on the edge of the bowling green. The grass had been allowed to grow a little too long, and needed a roller across it. The brief snow shower had ended, and a watery sun peeked out from behind the ominous clouds. As they neared the tennis courts, James tugged on Gertie's hand, anxious to explore this new and unusual playground.

"What's it for?" Lillian asked when they reached the high fence that surrounded the courts.

Gertie explained as best she could the rudiments of tennis. "It's a game, and you have a racquet and you hit the ball to each other across the net."

"I wanna play tennis!" James announced.

"Me, too." Lillian broke free from Mrs. Chubb's hand and rattled the gate. "I want to go in there."

Gertie unlatched the gate and opened it. The twins

raced onto the court and started chasing each other all around. "That'll get rid of some of that energy," she said smugly.

"You hope."

Even as Mrs. Chubb spoke, James came running back to them. "We wanna play the tennis game!"

"Well, you can't." Gertie waved a hand at the empty court. "Tennis is a summer game. You can't play it in the snow. Besides, there's no net, and no racquets and no balls. So you can't play tennis now."

"I wanna play!"

James stamped his foot, and Lillian joined in, chanting over and over, "Wanna play tennis! Wanna play tennis!"

"All right!" Gertie glanced over to the shed that housed the equipment for the tennis courts and the lawn bowls. "I wonder if the shed is locked."

"I doubt it. Judging by the way the grounds have been neglected." Mrs. Chubb looked at the expectant faces of the twins. "It's worth a look, I suppose."

"All right, you keep an eye on them while I go and look. If it's open, I'll just bring a couple of racquets back and some balls. They don't need a net."

"Wanna net!" James insisted.

Gertie rolled her eyes skyward and headed for the gate. After closing it carefully behind her, she crunched her way across the crisp, overgrown grass to the shed.

As Mrs. Chubb had predicted, the door had been left unlocked. It swung inward with a groaning creak that made Gertie wince. She stepped inside, holding her nose at the stench that greeted her. Must have been a skunk in there, she told herself as she glanced around.

Mounds of black tarpaulin hid the contents from view,

and sighing, Gertie advanced farther into the evil-smelling shed, wary of spiderwebs and whatever else might be waiting to snag her hat. She lifted the hem of her skirt with one hand, conscious of the thick layer of dust covering the bare floorboards. They creaked and snapped as she moved forward, making her jump with every sound. Then, without warning, the door swung to, plunging her into darkness.

For a moment she stood, heart pounding, waiting for her eyes to adjust to the dim light struggling to penetrate the small grimy window. Finally the shadows separated themselves, and she was able to make out the shapes again.

She was tempted to go back and open the door wide so she could see better, but instincts told her to grab what she wanted and get out of there. The stink was overpowering.

She reached for a corner of the closest tarpaulin and dragged it aside. To her relief, she saw a stack of tennis racquets lying on top of a folded net. She dragged them out to the middle of the floor. Now all she needed was a couple of tennis balls.

The mound next to the one she'd disturbed was smaller. It seemed a likely place to be concealing a box of tennis balls. She tugged on the tarpaulin, but it seemed caught on something, so she lifted it instead.

At first she thought someone had left a pile of clothes under there, but then she saw a pair of shoes sticking up on end. Something about the way they remained in that odd position made her go cold. They could only be that way if there were feet in them.

With a growing sense of horror, she tugged really hard on the tarpaulin. The thing under there rolled out into the open.

Gertie opened her mouth to yell, but no sound came out. Frozen with shock, she stared at the bone white face with its glassy sightless eyes. She barely recognized the maid, but there was no mistaking the uniform. The black afternoon dress was crumpled, and the white lace collar around her throat was soaked in something that was dark and horribly messy.

At last Gertie's voice exploded in her throat and her scream rattled the walls. It was the last thing she remembered as she fell to the floor.

Mrs. Chubb heard the scream and knew at once something dreadful had happened. She closed the gate on the twins and, despite their howls of protest, stumbled across the grass to the shed.

The door was closed, and she couldn't open it all the way. Peering through the gap, she could see Gertie's boot sticking out from under a pile of skirts. The rest of her body prevented her from opening the door far enough to squeeze her tubby figure through the narrow space.

Afraid to push too hard in case she hurt Gertie, she tried to peer farther into the shed to see the reason for Gertie's scream. But the shadows were too thick, and all she could see were mounds of tarpaulin and some old clothes. Wrinkling her nose against the foul smell, Mrs. Chubb banged on the door with her fist.

"Gertie! Ger*tay!*"

A low moan answered her.

"What's the matter, duck? What happened?"

The boot moved, and the door gave a little under Mrs. Chubb's hand. "Get me out of here," Gertie moaned. "I'm going to be sick."

Thoroughly alarmed now, Mrs. Chubb leaned on the door. It flew open and she stumbled inside, coming up short when she saw the crumpled figure lying in the middle of the floor. "Oh, good God, who's that?"

"It's one of the maids."

"Is she . . . ?" Mrs. Chubb let her voice trail off.

"She's bleeding dead, ain't she," Gertie snapped. She got unsteadily to her feet. "Let's get out of here, quick. We've got to tell someone."

Mrs. Chubb spun around, gulping down huge breaths of air, which didn't help much, seeing as the smell was enough to kill an elephant.

Gertie tugged the door open, stumbled outside, and promptly got rid of her breakfast.

Moaning, Mrs. Chubb surged forward after her. Her foot struck something and sent it skidding across the floor. She caught sight of it as she barreled through the door, and her stomach heaved.

"There's a knife in there," she gasped as Gertie turned a chalk white face toward her. "A big carving knife. I think it's covered in blood."

Gertie moaned and turned away from her again. "Bloody hell," she muttered when she was finished. "I used to have a stronger stomach than this."

Mrs. Chubb kept on taking deep breaths until she was reasonably sure she wasn't going to follow Gertie's performance with one of her own. "Enough to make any-one sick," she gasped at last. "You'd better go back to the club and find Mrs. Baxter. I'll bring the twins back if I can get them calmed down." She sent an apprehensive glance over to where both children stood with their fingers entwined in the fence, wailing loud enough to wake the dead, which was an unfortunate choice of words, she realized.

She hurried back to the enraged twins. Poor little mite. Who in the world would want to harm a young girl like that? A lot of sick people in this world, that was for sure. Poor Mrs. Baxter. She'd be beside herself when she heard the news. Couldn't have happened at a worse time, being Christmas and all. Though there was no good time for a murder to happen. What a mess.

She tugged open the gate and the twins hurled themselves through it, grabbing at her skirts and howling in a mixture of outrage and fright.

"What the matter with Mama?" James demanded between sobs, pointing at Gertie, who was rapidly disappearing in the murky distance.

"I want my mama!" Lillian stamped her foot. *"I want my mama!"*

"Then let us go find your mama." Mrs. Chubb grabbed a hand in each of hers. She felt better now that she was in charge again. Worrying about the children made her forget the ugly thing she'd seen in the shed. Though she had a nasty feeling that once she got to bed that night, she'd be seeing it all over again in her dreams. The prospect was extremely unsettling.

* * *

"We shall have to notify the constables now, of course," Baxter said when Cecily gave him the bad news. "They are bound to call in Inspector Cranshaw."

Cecily sat glumly in his office, wondering if there was anything she could have done to prevent this awful thing that had happened to the young girl. "I suppose there is no way we can avoid involving the inspector."

"None at all," Baxter said firmly. "The sooner we get this into the hands of the police, the better. We don't need the Pennyfoot involved in an investigation. It's obvious the girl was involved with someone of ill repute. Someone willing to buy the pearls she stole from Miss Bunkle. Probably one of those louts who hang around the George and Dragon all night. The sooner the culprit is arrested, the sooner we can put this behind us. All they have to do is find someone trying to get rid of a string of pearls. That shouldn't be too difficult for Cranshaw to handle, you'd suppose."

"I don't think it was someone from the village," Cecily said unhappily. She told him what Moira had told her.

"I don't believe it for one minute," he declared when she was finished. "Peebles and a kitchen maid? Never. The scandal could finish his career, not to mention his marriage."

"Exactly," Cecily murmured. "Perhaps that's why he had to kill Jeanette. She could have threatened to tell his wife and he had to silence her."

The icy expression she knew so well frosted his eyes. "Cecily, I absolutely forbid you to pursue this line of thinking. To accuse one of our most important guests without justification could cause a ruckus that would ruin the reputation of the Pennyfoot once and for all. We simply cannot take that kind of risk."

"I agree. Which is why I shall not inform the inspector at this time of my suspicions."

His shrewd gaze bore right through her head. "It is my firm belief that the maid was trying to sell Miss Bunkle's pearls to a hoodlum who decided to rid himself of the need to hand over the money. That is what I shall tell the constables. I sincerely hope that you let the matter rest there and allow the constables to do their job."

She merely nodded, hoping he wouldn't insist on her word. She had no intention of allowing the matter to rest there. What Baxter didn't know, however, wouldn't concern him. At least for the time.

Apparently accepting her silence for acquiescence, he reached for the telephone. After a lengthy wait for the operator, he managed to get his call put through to the police station.

She listened with one ear while he explained the situation. The rest of her mind worked busily on this latest development. She'd accompanied Raymond to the shed, where he'd locked it securely in case someone else should stumble upon the body before the constables arrived for their investigation.

She would have liked to conduct a far more intensive investigation herself, rather than the quick glance around she'd taken. She knew better, however, than to intrude on the scene and arouse the inspector's wrath. He was quite capable of closing down the Pennyfoot at the slightest provocation, especially when he learned that she was back at the helm, albeit on a temporary basis.

She and the inspector had drawn swords too many times for her to take a chance on antagonizing him now. Edward would never forgive her if she caused the cancellation of the Christmas Season. As it was, things were going to be somewhat disrupted. Unfortunately there was no doubt about that.

CHAPTER

❊ 15 ❊

Cecily's worst fears were realized when the inspector arrived an hour or so later. In spite of Baxter's theories about Jeanette's involvement with someone from the village, Cranshaw insisted that no one be allowed to leave until he'd had a chance to question potential witnesses. P. C. Northcott was given access to the current register, and generally made himself a nuisance while he copied down the list of guests currently staying at the club.

Baxter adamantly refused to remain in his office while Northcott worked on the list. His feud with the police constable went back a good many years. He'd once told Cecily that Northcott had stolen the young lady he was courting many years ago, but Cecily had always felt there was more to it than either man would say.

In any case, she volunteered to stay with Northcott until he'd completed his task, a decision that made the constable very uncomfortable indeed.

"It's not proper," he explained in his huffy voice, "for a gentleman to be alone in a room with a lady."

"A married lady," Cecily reminded him. "And a mature one at that." Nevertheless, she left the door open just a crack. There were a few things she wanted to ask the constable, and it was best that she wasn't overheard by the inspector, who was roaming the halls of the club looking for clues.

Northcott sat in Baxter's chair, the register open in front of him while he laboriously copied the names down in his notebook. She'd given him permission to remove his helmet, and he'd sat it on the desk next to him. The glow from the gas lamp gleamed on his bald head and the shiny buttons on his coat. He'd had a lot more hair the last time Cecily had seen him, and his pudgy face had lost much of its ruddy glow.

He looked older, and seemed slower in his movements, which had never exactly been swift. Every now and again he licked the end of his pencil before scratching it across the paper, and he muttered each name under his breath as if that made it easier to write it down.

Cecily pretended to be busy at the filing drawers for a while, until she was fairly confident that Northcott had relaxed. Then she sat down in her favorite chair in front of the desk. "This is like old times, Sam," she said pleasantly.

He seemed startled by her words when he looked up. "Yes, m'm. I s'pose it is. I must say, it's a pleasure to see you back in Badgers End. Not a very good reason to meet again though, is it."

"No, indeed. The poor girl." Cecily uttered a loud sigh. "I wonder who would have had reason to do such a dreadful thing."

"Well, I really can't say, Mrs. Sinclair."

"It's Mrs. Baxter now," she reminded him.

"H'oh, of course. I forgot you married '*im*.'"

The note of disgust in his voice was evident. Cecily tightened her lips, but managed to keep her voice even when she answered. "Does the inspector have any idea who might have been responsible for this dreadful act?"

Northcott's eyes grew wary. "Now, you know very well, m'm, I can't let on what the inspector knows. He'd have my guts for garters if I told you anything."

"He does have some clues then?" Cecily leaned forward. "What about the knife? Mrs. Chubb told me she saw a carving knife. I assume it came from our kitchen?"

Northcott's desire to seem important apparently overrode his fear of the inspector's wrath. He cleared his throat then, as if addressing a full court and jury, announced, "We 'ave h'ascertained that the lady in question did indeed h'observe a utensil wot turned out to be a carving knife. You are correct in assuming that said utensil originated in the kitchen of this 'ere h'establishment. A witness, who shall remain nameless, identified it as such."

"Miss Bunkle recognized the knife?"

Looking put out at her assumption, Northcott nodded reluctantly. "Proper mess she were'n all. Carried on something alarming, she did. Anyone would think it was her wot got knocked off, the way she was caterwauling. That's a fact."

Something else she would have to deal with later, Cecily thought ruefully. "The knife was used to kill Jeanette, I assume?"

Northcott twisted his florid features into a gruesome grimace and drew his thumb across his throat. "One quick slice and it were all over," he said with a relish Cecily found quite unnecessary.

"I see. I suppose the inspector will be questioning the staff?"

Northcott nodded. "And maybe one or two of your guests. He'll be conducting the interviews in the ballroom this afternoon."

Well, that would take care of the rehearsal, Cecily thought gloomily. Knowing the inspector, he would make a big production of it all.

"Well, it looks as if I 'ave all the names down now," Northcott announced. He gave his pencil a final lick and jammed it in the top pocket of his coat. "Thank you for your time, Mrs. ah . . . Baxter, and if the h'inspector should ask, I didn't tell you nothing. Mum's the word. All right?"

"Agreed," Cecily promised cheerfully. She was anxious for him to leave now. Ever since she'd spoken to Moira the night before, she'd been anxious to speak to Roger Peebles alone. So far she hadn't had that opportunity. All morning he'd been accompanied by his wife and one or another of his Bencher colleagues.

But now there was even more of an urgent reason to speak to him. Although well aware of her duty to pass on to the inspector what she knew, she was reluctant to do so until she'd had a chance to question the man herself. Baxter was right. There was no point in arousing suspicion of an esteemed guest if Moira had been mistaken.

She could only hope that if the girl was questioned by the inspector, she would keep silent about Peebles's possible involvement with Jeanette. At least until she'd had a chance to speak to him and, with any luck, learn exactly what Peebles was doing philandering with a lowly kitchen maid.

When Cecily went in search of Roger Peebles later, she was told that all four Benchers had retired to the card room for a game of baccarat. Resigning herself to a lengthy wait, she made her way to the library. She had promised Madeline and the twins that she would inspect their handiwork and no doubt they were waiting for her approval.

Upon entering the library, however, she found the four wives of the Benchers huddled around the fire, apparently engaged in deep discussion. They looked up as she approached, their faces lined with apprehension.

"Mrs. Baxter, is this dreadful news true?" Barbara Fitzhammer asked fearfully.

Cecily had hoped to keep the murder quiet for a little longer, but it seemed word had already spread among the guests. Even so, she was deliberately vague in the hopes she was mistaken. "I'm not certain to what news you refer, Mrs. Fitzhammer," she said cautiously.

"The death of that poor girl." Gretchen Peebles shuddered. "I heard that her throat was slit with a carving knife and that her frock was soaked in blood."

Cries of horror greeted that comment.

"What kind of establishment is this," Lady Lucille muttered, "that such an atrocity is allowed to happen?"

"Indeed." Amelia Chatsworth languidly waved a pink satin fan in front of her face. "Such a dreadful deed. I certainly hope the murderer isn't loose in this very club. We could all be murdered in our beds."

Barbara Fitzhammer shrieked so loudly it made Cecily jump in alarm. "I think we should leave at once."

Lady Lucille looked about to faint. "I think that is a very good idea," she declared. "All this has made me feel quite unwell."

The chorus of agreement worried Cecily. Hiding her concern, she announced firmly, "I can assure you, ladies, that everything is being done to ensure the safety of our guests. I doubt very much if the person responsible for Jeanette's death has lingered long in the area for fear of being discovered. In fact, the inspector and constables have already left to return to the police station. They are satisfied that there is no danger to anyone here at the Pennyfoot."

That wasn't strictly true, since according to North-cott's furtively whispered comments to her upon leaving, the inspector had not discovered anything that would lead him to the murderer. What's more, he planned to return to an urgent case in Wellercombe, leaving the investigation in the hands of his constables for the time being.

It was Cecily's considered opinion that had the victim been a member of the aristocracy, or perhaps one of these ladies who were staring at her with such apprehension, Inspector Cranshaw might have been a great deal more interested in hunting down the murderer. Obviously a common kitchen maid didn't warrant as much attention as the "urgent case" in Wellercombe—a fact that infuriated Cecily.

"But what about the Christmas festivities?" Amelia Chatsworth demanded. "What effect will this tragic event have on everything?"

"Yes, indeed." Gretchen Peebles gazed up at Cecily

with anxious eyes. "We wouldn't want to spend Christmas in a place of mourning. It would be far too demoralizing. It would completely spoil our Christmas."

"Perhaps it would be a good idea to look for a hotel in Wellercombe," Lady Lucille murmured.

"Yes, yes, do let's," Barbara Fitzhammer chimed in. "I just wouldn't feel safe here now."

Thoroughly alarmed now, Cecily hurried to reassure them. "I beg all of you to calm yourselves and try to put this incident out of your mind. As I've said, you are in no danger. The Pennyfoot Christmas Season will go on as planned. We have some wonderful festivities for you to enjoy, including a delightful pantomime and Michel is planning a spectacular Christmas dinner in the ballroom, with champagne and gifts for everyone. It would be a great shame to miss all that, especially when it would be most difficult to find room at another hotel this late in the Season."

"True," Amelia Chatsworth murmured. "And there isn't another country club within traveling distance, unless we return to London. Think how our husbands would feel if they couldn't spend their time in a card room. Everyone knows that it is illegal in a hotel to engage in such pursuits. It's the main reason my husband chooses to stay at the Pennyfoot."

"You're right," Barbara Fitzhammer said mournfully. "Lionel would never agree to go to a hotel now."

"Neither would Roger," Gretchen Peebles murmured. "I'm afraid we have no choice, ladies. We might as well make the best of it."

Having avoided disaster for the time being, Cecily left them chattering together and headed for the kitchen. It had occurred to her that the staff would also need some reassurance. Not to mention her own special guests.

Mrs. Chubb, the twins, and Gertie were lying down in their rooms, after having been questioned thoroughly by the inspector. Daisy, Doris, and Samuel had gone into town earlier that day, but would most likely have returned by now for the rehearsal, which would not now take place. Out of respect for Jeannette, Cecily had canceled everything for that day.

As she hurried down the steps to the kitchen, she realized she still hadn't inspected the tree in the library. That would have to wait until later now. There was just too much to be done.

As she entered the kitchen, it was obvious that Jeanette's death had a marked effect on the kitchen staff. The maids were all huddled by the sink around Moira, who sobbed loudly into her apron. The potatoes hadn't been peeled, the carrots had not been sliced, and even Michel stood aimlessly stirring his soup in apparent ignorance that the lengthy preparations for the evening meal were not being executed.

There was no doubt that the discipline Miss Bunkle kept talking about was sadly lacking. Looking around, Cecily was surprised to find no sign of the gaunt housekeeper. She was not in the pantry or the scullery, or even in the kitchen yard outside.

Clapping her hands to gain the maids' attention, she called out, "I want everyone back at their post immediately. We have a meal to serve in less than three hours, and by the looks of it, you haven't even begun your tasks."

At the sound of her voice, Michel had snapped to attention. "Hurry up, hurry up, you nitwits," he yelled, forgetting his fabricated French accent in his agitation. "Get a bloody move on, all of you!" His tall hat slipped sideways, and he made a grab at it, seizing it just before it slipped into the soup.

"Where is Miss Bunkle?" Cecily asked him as the maids scurried back and forth. "Why isn't she in here taking care of all this?"

Michel shrugged. "She is in her room, *madame*. She refuses to come out." He jammed his hat back on his head and in a thick French accent added, "I do not know what is ze matter with her. She wail and cry and carry on . . . like a baby. I tell you, *madame*, this kitchen was a lot 'appier to work in when Mrs. Chubb was housekeeper. *Oui?*"

"Oh, dear." Cecily glanced at the clock. "Don't fret, Michel. I'll take care of it."

Michel went back to his soup. "Someone needs to take care of things. I cannot work with such imbeciles."

Cecily hurried over to Moira, who stood sniffing mournfully at the sink, every now and then wiping her cheeks with the back of her hand.

"I understand all this is a great shock to you," Cecily told her. "I'll need to talk to you later, but right now, do you think you can manage to do your work? Michel really needs you now that Jeanette is no longer with us."

It was the wrong thing to say, Cecily realized as fresh tears poured down Moira's face.

"I *told* her not go out," she sobbed. "She wouldn't listen to me."

Cecily patted the girl's shoulder. "I know, dear, I know. I'm sorry, Moira. Please try to manage as best you can this afternoon and we'll have a little talk this evening, all right?"

The girl sniffed, wiped her nose with the back of her hand, and nodded. "Yes, m'm. I'll be all right. Really."

Feeling only a tad reassured, Cecily left the kitchen and hurried down the hall to Miss Bunkle's room. There was no reply to her sharp rap on the door, and giving up, she returned to the foyer and climbed the stairs to Mrs. Chubb's room.

Gertie had apparently recovered from her ordeal and was visiting with Mrs. Chubb when Cecily arrived.

"I really can't dawdle," she told them after making sure that all was well with them. "Miss Bunkle has locked herself in her room and refuses to come out. With Jeannette gone, the maids are short-handed. I must go back there right away to attempt some order."

Mrs. Chubb and Gertie looked at each other. Apparently a silent message passed between them as they both nodded.

"I could go down there and take over until Miss Bunkle feels better," Mrs. Chubb said, getting to her feet.

"Oh, I couldn't possibly ask you to do that," Cecily protested. "This is your Christmas holiday. I didn't ask you down here to work."

"I know, madam, but I'm getting bored sitting around doing nothing, and it will take my mind off things."

"I could help, too." Gertie jumped to her feet. "It'll be fun. Really, m'm. Just like old times."

"But what about the babies?" Cecily nodded in the direction of the bed where the twins lay sleeping peacefully.

"Daisy could take care of them. She asked me if she could anyway. She said she misses them."

Mrs. Chubb nodded. "It will do us both good, madam, and it will only be for a short while anyway. We'd really like to help out."

"Yeah, m'm, really," Gertie said earnestly. "Please let us do it."

"Well, if you're sure . . ."

Gertie's whoop of delight woke up the twins and they sat up, sleepily demanding something to eat.

"I'll go down there right away," Mrs. Chubb said, "just as soon as I can find an apron. Gertie, you talk to Daisy, and if she says it's all right, come down as soon as you can."

"Yes, Mrs. Chubb." Gertie headed for the door.

"And Gertie?"

She paused, looking back at the other woman.

"You should be able to find a uniform to fit you in the laundry room. Make sure you look neat and tidy. We want to set a good example to the rest of the staff."

"Yes, Mrs. Chubb." There was just a hint of irony in her voice as she rushed out of the room.

Cecily hid a smile. It was amazing to see the transformation in the two women. Up until this moment they had behaved more like mother and daughter, but now Mrs. Chubb was in charge again, and Gertie was once more relegated to the role of chief housemaid. Gertie was right. It was just like old times.

Cecily was on her way down the stairs to inform Baxter of the new arrangements with his staff when she heard the commotion in the lobby. At first she thought Colonel Fortescue had returned, but then she saw Raymond talking excitedly to the tall, stern figure of Sir John Gilroy.

Lady Lucille was at his side, leaning heavily on his arm, her face covered by a delicately embroidered handkerchief into which she loudly sobbed. She seemed not to notice Cecily, who had hurried over to them with a feeling of deep foreboding.

"Is something wrong?" she asked as Raymond turned his impassioned gaze in her direction.

"There's been an accident," he said, speaking so fast his words tumbled over each other. "The motor car went right off the cliffs. Landed upside down on the rocks, it did."

"Oh, my." Cecily's hand strayed to her throat. "I hope it wasn't one of ours."

"What the devil is all this racket about?" a deep voice demanded.

Cecily turned to see Baxter striding toward them, having apparently been disturbed by all the noise.

Lady Lucille was still weeping profusely, moaning something over and over that Cecily couldn't understand.

Raymond started chattering again, while Sir John remained silent, his jaw set in a grim line.

"Slow down, Raymond," Baxter said irritably. "Tell us exactly what happened."

"I was on me way into the town," Raymond said, his voice still trembling with agitation. He gulped several times, then continued, "I was going to Abbitsons to get some more chickens for the dinner tonight. I saw this motor car in front of me and it were going really fast, at least twenty miles an hour I reckon. Then he went over the top of the hill and started down the other side. Never made the first bend. Sailed right off the cliff, he did."

Lady Lucille wailed louder, and Sir John put his arm around her. "My wife needs to lie down. This has been a great shock. I need to inform . . . though God knows how . . . excuse me."

Cecily's sense of dread intensified. "Of course. Please let me know if there's anything I can do to help."

He barely acknowledged her offer with a slight inclination of his head before helping his wife up the stairs.

Apparently Baxter had come to a similar conclusion as he demanded sharply, "Raymond, did you recognize anyone in the automobile?"

Raymond nodded. "Not right away, though I went for help when I saw him disappear over the cliff. The noise was something awful. It were right across from Jim Biscott's farm. Jim climbed down with me to see if the driver were all right." Raymond gulped again. "One look at him and we knew he was a stiffun."

"Oh, dear." Cecily clutched Baxter's sleeve. "Who was it, Raymond?"

"One of them Bencher blokes," Raymond said unsteadily. "I'm not sure, but I think his name were Peebles. Yeah, that's it. Roger Peebles."

CHAPTER
❊ 16 ❊

"Unbelievable," Baxter said, closing the door to his office sometime later. "We arrive back at the Pennyfoot after a two-year absence and in less than a week we have two deaths on our hands."

"Three, if you count Barry Wrotham." Cecily seated herself on her favorite chair and watched her husband take his usual place behind his desk.

"Well, Wrotham's death happened before we arrived. And at least two of them were accidents." He leaned back in his chair and passed a hand over his hair. "I suppose we should be thankful for small mercies."

"I'm not so sure of that."

He stared at her, his eyes wary. "What does that mean?"

"It means that I'm not convinced that the other two deaths were accidents."

He groaned. "I thought we'd pretty much established that Wrotham fell into the well."

"In view of what has transpired this day, I'm beginning to have second thoughts about that."

"What does Jeanette's unfortunate end or Peebles's accident have to do with Wrotham?"

"Suppose that Peebles's death wasn't an accident."

He stared at her for a long moment. "Are you saying that Peebles deliberately drove his car over the cliff? I know people sometimes become depressed at Christmastime, but Peebles didn't strike me as the sort to do himself in."

"No, I'm not saying that." Cecily sighed. "I went to offer my condolences to Mrs. Peebles. She was quite distraught, of course, poor woman. She did, however, tell me that Peebles had been extremely irritable and short with her lately. Apparently they had a quarrel earlier this afternoon, and he left here in a great hurry without telling her where he was going. According to Mrs. Peebles, his behavior recently has been quite out of character."

"Well, then, there you are. He went out in a fit of temper and drove too fast. The road over Putney Downs has some very sharp bends. It was never meant for motor cars. That's the trouble with them. If you don't treat them with respect, they can cause all kinds of problems. If you ask me—"

"I think Roger Peebles was murdered," Cecily said deliberately.

Baxter shut his mouth with a snap, then after a moment said in an unsettling quiet tone, "Just how do you come to that conclusion?"

Cecily leaned forward. "I think he knew who killed Jeanette. Whoever is the murderer had to get rid of Peebles because he could identify him."

Baxter's frown was formidable. "This morning you were accusing Peebles of killing the maid. Now you're saying someone else killed her? How many more of our guests are you planning to accuse of murder?"

"I'm not accusing anyone just yet."

"I'm glad to hear it. I—"

The jangling of the telephone interrupted him. He lifted the receiver from its stand and said cautiously into it, "The Pennyfoot Country Club. Hugh Baxter speaking." He listened for a moment then added, "Thank you, operator. Please put him through." Glancing at Cecily he whispered, "Northcott. I—" Once more he broke off, listened, then said irritably, "Go on, I'm listening." Another pause, then he added, "And what about the girl?"

Cecily watched his face closely, and saw relief creep into his eyes. Muttering his thanks, he replaced the receiver and looked at her. "I was right," he announced. "Northcott has completed his investigation and has ruled Peebles's death an accident. As for the death of our maid, he believes, as I do, that she was killed while attempting to sell the pearls she had stolen. Probably trying to extort too much money from the wrong person. They are currently questioning people in the village in the hopes of tracking down the culprit."

"But—"

He raised his hand. "I suggest we cease concerning ourselves about a nonexistent murderer among our guests and concentrate on the task we came down here to do, which is to conduct a successful Christmas Season at the Penny-foot."

His pompous attitude infuriated her, but she curbed her resentment. It was pointless to argue when she had no proof to offer. All she had at that moment were supposi-tions and she knew better than to rely on such nebulous reasoning.

Rising to her feet, she murmured, "Very well. I shall go to the kitchen and see how things are faring under the new management."

"I think that's a very good idea."

After closing the door rather sharply behind her, she uttered a low growl of frustration. Her instincts told her that the deaths were connected in some way. Somehow she had to find out what that connection was, and who had reason to kill three people. And she knew just where to start.

She made her way to the foyer, but instead of going down to the kitchen, she climbed the stairs to the third floor.

As luck would have it, she found Samuel resting in his room. He opened the door with a book in his hand which, he explained, was helping him with his studies of mechanics.

"That's exactly what I came to talk to you about." Cecily glanced down the hall. "May I come in for just a moment?"

"Of course, m'm." He looked mystified, but stepped back to allow her to enter. Leaving the door slightly ajar, he beckoned a little self-consciously at the lone armchair in his room. "If you'd care to sit, m'm?"

"I won't take up more than a moment of your time," Cecily said, declining his invitation. "I need you to do something for me, if you will. Something that will have to be done with great discretion."

Samuel immediately looked interested. He threw his book on the bed. "Anything for you, m'm. You know you can always rely on me."

"Thank you, Samuel." Cecily lowered her voice. "I assume you have heard about the accident this afternoon."

Samuel nodded. "Moira told me. She was all upset about what happened to her friend, and now this. It took me a while to calm her down."

Cecily looked at him in surprise. "I wasn't aware you were acquainted with Moira."

He grinned. "Well, I wasn't when I came down here, if you know what I mean, m'm. But what with Doris not being around much anymore, well, a bloke has to take his chances where he can, so to speak."

"Oh." Cecily cleared her throat. "Yes, I see. Well, it's nice that Moira has a friend who can cheer her up. I'm afraid Jeanette's death has been a terrible shock for her."

"That it has, m'm. But I think she's getting over it a little now."

"Well, I'm glad to hear it. Now, about this little task I have for you." She quickly explained, and as she expected, Samuel was eager to help.

"I must ask you to keep all this in complete confidence for now," she said as she was leaving. "I don't have to tell you what this would mean if word got out."

"You can trust me to keep me mouth shut, m'm," Samuel promised her. "It wouldn't be the first time I had to keep a secret."

She smiled. "No, indeed, Samuel."

"Quite like old times, it is, m'm."

She was still smiling as she left, wondering how many times she would hear that phrase before this Christmas was over.

As she made her way down the hallway, she caught sight of Amelia Chatsworth ushering a weeping Gretchen Peebles into her room. Cecily waited until the door had closed behind the two women, then cautiously approached the Peebleses' suite. This was as good a time as any to put the second part of her plan into action.

After pausing to make certain she was unobserved, Cecily tried the door handle, uttering a little hiss of satisfaction when the door opened. This would save her the trouble of returning to her room for the set of master keys Baxter kept there.

She slipped inside the room and closed the door. The suite was in great disarray, with clothes strewn haphazardly across the bed and shoes lying on the floor. In the middle of the room a trunk stood with its lid open. Apparently Gretchen Peebles planned to return to London. Cecily could only hope the rest of the group wouldn't return with her.

Moving about the room, she opened drawers, then carefully closed them again. She wasn't really sure what she was looking for, except for the vague hope that she might find something that would point to where Peebles was heading in such a hurry that afternoon.

She opened the wardrobe and peered inside. Two men's day suits and an evening suit hung next to several gowns. Quickly Cecily searched the pockets of the suits, trying to ignore her voice of conscience that told her she was behaving like a common thief.

The pockets were empty, and she was about to close the door again when she caught sight of a shoe box on the upper shelf. It rattled when she shook it, and, intrigued now, she took it down and opened the lid.

Inside were several gambling chips, larger and a different design than those belonging to the Pennyfoot. A scrap of paper had been tucked underneath them, and she drew it out. Placing the box on the floor of the wardrobe, she unfolded the slip of paper.

It was an IOU in the sum of two thousand pounds. Printed across the top of the paper was a peculiar name. *Cureagambler.* The scrawl at the bottom was difficult to make out, but it could have been Peebles's signature. If so, then Roger Peebles was a lot more than a social gambler. What's more, he owed someone a very large sum of money.

She studied the printed heading again. Such an odd name. *Cureagambler.* She frowned. Spread apart, the words could read, *Cure a gambler.* Well, by the looks of it, Peebles certainly needed to be cured. Perhaps that was it. An organization that helped gamblers give up their addiction. Now, maybe if—

The sound of voices in the hallway outside startled her. After a moment's hesitation, she stuffed the note into her sleeve, then hastily replaced the box on the shelf before quietly closing the wardrobe door.

She had a nasty moment when she thought that one of the voices might be Gretchen Peebles returning to her room, but then the chattering guests passed by. After waiting another tense moment or two, Cecily slowly opened the door and peered through the crack. Once more the hallway appeared to be deserted. Holding her breath, she slipped out into the corridor and closed the door.

Her next stop was the kitchen, where she found a very different atmosphere than the last time she'd been there. Mrs. Chubb was bustling around, barking orders while maids scurried back and forth. Gertie stood at the table loading up a tray with crystal salt and pepper shakers.

She looked quite different in her black afternoon frock and a frilly white apron. Even her cap sat firmly on top of her head. In the old days it was always slipping sideways over her ear, while she constantly tucked stray strands of hair back under the pins.

She looked up as Cecily entered and gave her a lopsided grin. "I haven't forgotten nothing, m'm," she announced cheerfully. "It's all there in me head, just like I was here yesterday."

"I can't thank you enough, Gertie." Cecily picked up a fork and examined it critically. "Things have been a little slack in the kitchen. Miss Bunkle was always complaining about the lack of discipline but I don't think she had the gumption to enforce it."

"Not like the old battle-ax, anyway." Gertie jerked a thumb over her shoulder. "She'll soon whip 'em into bleeding shape. In her bloody element, she is."

Cecily managed a smile. "Well, it's a relief to know that things are under control in here again. After everything that's happened today, I need something to go right."

Gertie lowered her head toward her and whispered, "Terrible what happened to that toff, m'm. Raymond said he were crushed under that flipping motor car. Just goes to show what happens when you get careless in them things. What with that poor girl this morning and now this. Bloody terrible it is. Right before Christmas and all. Put a proper gloom around this place, it has." She jerked her chin at the rest of the staff, most of whom seemed to be tumbling over each other in their haste to follow Mrs. Chubb's orders.

The housekeeper caught sight of Cecily at that moment and came hurrying over. "There's nothing else gone wrong, I hope, madam?"

Before Cecily could answer, Gertie uttered a harsh laugh. "Gawd, I bleeding hope not. Two blinking deaths in one day is enough for anyone, if you ask me."

"That's enough, Gertie. Remember your place." Mrs. Chubb sent Cecily a look of apology. "Some things never change, I'm afraid."

"It's all right, Mrs. Chubb. It's a pleasure to have you both back at the helm."

"Yes, madam. We were sorry to hear of the motor car accident this afternoon. Though I can't say I'm surprised. The way some people go speeding around the bends in those things, I'm surprised there aren't more people dying in them."

"Yeah," Gertie said gloomily. "You'd think he'd know better. His poor widow won't have much of a Christmas this year, that's for sure. Though, mind you, it's no great loss in my opinion."

Cecily looked at her in surprise. "I wasn't aware you'd met Roger Peebles."

Gertie shrugged. "Bumped into him in the hallway. I don't like to speak ill of the dead, m'm, but he wasn't exactly the faithful husband, if you know what I mean."

"Gertie," Mrs. Chubb said sharply. "It's none of our business. I'm quite sure madam has better things to do than listen to idle gossip. I know I do."

"Don't let me keep you, Mrs. Chubb," Cecily said smoothly. "I'm sure you have plenty to do."

"Indeed I do, madam. And so does Gertie." She sent a meaningful look in Gertie's direction, then rushed over to the sinks, where two of the maids were arguing with each other in strident voices.

"I'd better get these bloody shakers into the dining room, m'm," Gertie said, lifting the tray. "Or the old girl will be getting her bleeding knickers in a twist."

Cecily followed her out into the corridor, holding the door open for her as she passed through with the heavy tray.

"Tell me, Gertie," she said as she followed her up the steps. "What did you mean when you said that Roger Peebles wasn't the faithful husband?"

Gertie paused, looking over her shoulder. "Well, m'm, don't tell Mrs. Chubb I told you, but I saw Roger Peebles taking a lady into his room. Yesterday it were. And it weren't his bloody wife."

"Did you happen to notice who it was?"

"Yes, m'm. It were that French toff, Lady Lucille."

Cecily stopped short, taken by surprise. "Are you quite sure?"

"Yes, m'm. Saw her plain as day, I did. Can't mistake her anyhow. All done up like a dog's dinner, she was."

At the top of the steps Cecily parted company with Gertie and walked across the foyer in deep thought. In her mind's eye she could see Raymond, arms waving in agitation as he informed a stern-faced Sir John Gilroy of

Peebles's accident, while Lady Lucille wept profusely into her handkerchief.

Was she weeping for a lost lover, perhaps?

Still engrossed in her thoughts, Cecily paused by the Christmas tree, pretending to be interested in the delicate ornaments nestled among its branches. Did Lady Lucille tell her that story about Barry Wrotham being her lover in order to cover up the identity of her true lover, Roger Peebles?

What if her original theory were correct after all, and Wrotham had discovered the two meeting at the farmhouse, perhaps threatening to inform Sir John unless they paid him to keep quiet. If Peebles were already deep in debt, he would have no choice but to silence him.

Then again, where did Jeanette fit in all this? Did Peebles's philandering include her as well? That simply didn't make sense.

She heard her name spoken in a low voice and swung around to confront Samuel, who had crept up behind her.

"Sorry, m'm," he said softly. "I didn't mean to startle you."

"That's all right, Samuel." She drew him closer into the corner, where they had less chance of being observed. "Did you manage to examine Peebles's motor car?"

"Yes, m'm, I did. I told the bobbies that Mrs. Peebles sent me to see if it could be repaired." He sent a furtive glance around, then added in a loud whisper, "It were the brake shoes, m'm. Both of 'em, snapped right off."

"I see," Cecily said, not seeing at all. "Was the damage done in the accident, do you think?"

Samuel shrugged. "Hard to say for certain, m'm, but if I had to guess, I'd say someone helped them along a bit.

Not likely they'd both go at the same time without a bit of nudging, if you get my meaning."

Cecily let out her breath. "Yes, I do. Thank you, Samuel. I'd had a feeling something like that might have happened."

Samuel glanced over his shoulder. "Who'd want to hurt that toff, anyway?"

"That's something we'll have to find out. I must ask you not to say a word to anyone about this. No one at all, you understand? If we are going to catch this person, we mustn't let him know what we know."

"Do you think it's the same person what did Jeanette in?" Samuel asked fearfully. "What if he's still lurking about, looking for his next victim?"

Cecily sighed. "This is exactly why we have to keep quiet about this. We don't need our guests to fly into a panic. After all, we're not absolutely certain that someone did tamper with the motor car. Just keep your eyes open, and if you see anything at all that strikes you as unusual or out of place, come and tell me at once."

Samuel nodded. "Don't worry, m'm. You know you can count on me."

Cecily left him in the foyer and headed down the hallway to Baxter's office. She had promised to keep him informed, but she wasn't certain at this point how much she wanted to tell him. So much of it was still conjecture.

He looked up when she entered the room. "Ah, there you are. I was just about to send one of the maids to look for you. How are things in the kitchen?"

"Better." She sank onto her chair. "Mrs. Chubb and Gertie have pretty much taken over everything for the time being, and even Michel seems in a better mood. I don't know what we would have done without them."

"Well, we might have to rely on them for longer than we thought." Baxter closed his ledger with a loud snap. "Miss Bunkle has given in her notice."

Cecily gaped at him in dismay. "No! Why? Did she say?"

"Apparently three deaths in less than a month have totally unnerved her. She is packing her bags and expects to be on the train to London early tomorrow morning."

Cecily sank back in her chair. "She might at least have worked out her notice. What are we going to do now? I can't ask Mrs. Chubb and Gertie to work through the Christmas holidays and it will be impossible to find another housekeeper at this late date." She covered her face with her hands. "Edward will never forgive us."

Baxter cleared his throat. "Perhaps we can persuade Mrs. Chubb and Gertie to help us out awhile longer if we give them generous compensation for their efforts."

Cecily lowered her hands. "Can we afford to do that?"

"Yes, I think we can." He opened the ledger, studied it for a moment. "We can certainly add another guinea each to the salaries."

"Well, that is generous. In that case, I shall have a word with them right away. I'll tell them about your offer and see if they are interested." She started to rise.

"Did you have a reason for this visit?"

Having momentarily forgotten why she was there, she sat down again. "Samuel thinks that someone tampered with Peebles's car," she said without preamble.

As she'd expected, a frown appeared on his face. "How did he manage to arrive at that conclusion?"

"He examined the motor car."

"Why did he do that?"

"Because I asked him to examine it."

"I might have known." He pressed the fingers of one hand against his forehead. "I was under the impression you had given up chasing after murderers and were concentrating your concerns on our Christmas Season."

"As long as there is the possibility of a killer in our midst, you know very well that I cannot rest until he is apprehended."

Baxter sighed. "Very well. What did Samuel discover?"

"He said it had something to do with the brake shoes, whatever they are. Apparently they were damaged."

"The motor car went off a cliff, fell over a hundred feet, and landed upside down. I'm not surprised there was damage."

"Ah, but Samuel believes they were damaged before it went over the cliff."

Baxter's frown intensified. "What makes him think so?"

"Well, I really don't understand too much about motor cars, but I do know that if one cannot stop them, it's entirely likely they won't slow down to manipulate a bend in the road. Which is what appears to have happened to poor Mr. Peebles."

Baxter sighed and laid his pen down next to the inkwell. "That's not what I meant. Has he informed Northcott?"

"No, I told him to keep it to himself for the time being. You know how P.C. Northcott is, always bungling things. I think we should be more certain of our facts before we trust this investigation to him."

"Perhaps you're right. After all, Samuel could very well be mistaken." He gave her his piercing stare. "Just as long as you remember your promise. At the very first sign of danger, you will turn this over to the constables."

"Of course, darling." Cecily rose to her feet. This probably wasn't a good time to tell him she'd been snooping around in Peebles's suite. It could wait until later. "Now I had better run down to the kitchen and pray that Mrs. Chubb and Gertie will take us up on our offer. If not, we could be in a real pickle."

"If not," Baxter said dryly, "we had better prepare ourselves for a disastrous Christmas."

CHAPTER
❊ 17 ❊

To Cecily's intense relief, Gertie was delighted to accept Baxter's offer. "This couldn't come at a better time, m'm," Gertie told her when Cecily presented the idea to her. She had just returned to the busy kitchen from the dining room, where the guests were already seating themselves in anticipation of another delicious meal.

"I didn't say nothing before," Gertie added as she piled tureens of soup onto her enormous tray. "But Ross sold the business, so right now he's out of work. I'll carry on here for as long as you need me."

"Goodness!" Cecily exclaimed. "I had no idea. It must have come as quite a shock to you."

Gertie shrugged. "Can't say I'm really surprised. Besides,

he needs a rest. He's been looking poorly lately. I think he should see a doctor."

"I'll ask Dr. Prestwick to stop by," Cecily promised. "Now I must ask Mrs. Chubb if she'll be willing to help out until we can get another housekeeper."

"I don't think you'll have any bleeding arguments with her," Gertie said, jerking her head in the house-keeper's direction. "Look at her. Having the time of her life, she is."

Gertie was right. Mrs. Chubb eagerly accepted the offer. "Though I don't think we'll be able to do the pantomime as well, madam," she said, looking anxiously around her bustling kitchen. "We'll have our hands full getting this lot in shape."

"Don't concern yourself about the pantomime." Cecily sighed. "I'm not at all sure there will be one, after all. No one has had a chance to rehearse that much, and the performance is scheduled for tomorrow night."

"I thought we were going to have it on Boxing Day."

"Doris and I decided to bring it forward. In any case, after what's happened, perhaps it would be considered in bad taste to continue with it."

"Well, if you ask me, madam," Mrs. Chubb said, raising a cloud of flour as she vigorously dusted her apron, "I think it will take everything off the minds of everyone. Do them good to have a laugh, that it will."

"Perhaps you're right," Cecily murmured. "After all, I have more or less promised some of the guests that we will carry on the Christmas Season as planned. I'll have a word with Doris and see what she can do."

"Very good, madam. And don't worry about the kitchen. Everything's in order now. You won't miss that sourpuss with the knitting needle one bit."

"'Ark at her," Gertie muttered as she swung by carrying the loaded tray above her head as if it were holding feathers instead of filled tureens. "All she has to do is yell bleeding orders. It's us flipping slaves what does the blinking work."

The door swung to behind her, and Mrs. Chubb winked at Cecily. "Business as usual, madam. Just like old times."

The next morning Cecily rang Dr. Prestwick and invited him to lunch at the Pennyfoot, then went down to the ballroom, where Doris was holding the rehearsal for the pantomime. Madeline was flitting around helping everyone with their costumes and giving instructions to Samuel and Raymond, both of whom had volunteered to set up the backdrops.

Doris assured Cecily that her cast would be ready for the big night, and that they could manage quite well without Mrs. Chubb and Gertie. Though she did warn Cecily not to expect a professional performance.

Having watched Phoebe struggling to control her unruly band of dancers, Cecily had already resigned herself to the usual comedy of errors. With any luck, the audience would be in a jovial mood and willing to accept a few mishaps.

Leaving Doris to cope with what seemed a dubious task, Cecily went in search of the Benchers. She spotted Lionel Fitzhammer in the smoking room, in deep conversation with Percy Chatsworth. Since this was yet another room where she was not allowed, she waited for some time before the two men emerged and she could talk to them.

"I wanted to offer my condolences for the loss of your colleague," she said after the two men greeted her with a polite nod. "It must have been a terrible shock to you all."

"Dreadful," Percy Chatsworth muttered. "I still can't believe Roger's gone. He should never have been driving while besotted with brandy."

Cecily stared at him. "Are you saying that Mr. Peebles was intoxicated when he left here in that motor car?"

"Of course he wasn't," Fitzhammer said curtly. "We'd had a couple of shots of brandy after lunch, but Roger could hold his damn liquor, that's for sure. Careless, that's what he was. Never did know how to take care of his automobile. I'll take a wager he didn't have his brakes examined before he left London. Some people shouldn't be allowed in the driver's seat, that's what I say."

"I still say he'd had one too many," Chatsworth insisted. "A little too fond of his brandy, was our Roger, if you ask me. And that French cognac they serve in the bar creeps up on you. Before you know it, it's hit you." He shot an apologetic glance at Cecily. "Not that I'm complaining, of course. Jolly good brandy, that is."

Cecily accepted this compliment with a smile. "Did either of you happen to know where Mr. Peebles was going when he left here yesterday?"

"Haven't the foggiest," Chatsworth muttered. "Bit of a dark horse, actually. Never did have much to say. Except in court, of course. Jolly good barrister, he was."

"He was, indeed," Fitzhammer agreed gloomily.

Cecily turned to him. "What about you, Mr. Fitzhammer? You were drinking with him before he left. Did he happen to mention anything to you about where he planned to go?"

Fitzhammer's beady eyes narrowed. "Not to me, he didn't. May I ask why you are so interested in Roger's appointment?"

"Just curious." Cecily gave him her most discerning smile. "He appeared to be in an enormous hurry. I was wondering if perhaps there was some emergency that needed to be taken care of, that's all. Mrs. Peebles didn't seem to know, so I simply wondered if you could shed some light on the subject. I mean, if he had an appointment, then someone must be wondering why he didn't keep it."

"As far as I know," Fitzhammer said carefully, "Roger wasn't planning on going anywhere in particular when he left here. He was in rather a snit, and I got the impression he needed a breath of fresh air. That's all."

"I see." Cecily smiled at both men. "Well, thank you for your time, gentlemen. "I'd like to remind you that the pantomime will take place immediately after supper tonight, in the Grand Ballroom. I trust you and your wives will be there? It might help to alleviate some of the heartache for all of you."

"My wife and I will most certainly be there," Fitzhammer said heartily. "The show must go on, and all that rot."

"My wife and I plan to accompany Gretchen to the train station this afternoon," Chatsworth said, sending Fitzhammer a sour look. "She will be returning to London with her husband's body. But we should return here in time for supper, though whether or not Amelia will be in any mood for a pantomime, I can't say for sure. I had the devil of a time persuading her to stay for Christmas as it was."

"Make her go, old boy," Fitzhammer said, slapping Chatsworth on the back. "It will do you both good."

"I hope Sir John and Lady Lucille will attend," Cecily put in.

Chatsworth sighed. "I imagine they will. Lucille twisted her ankle the other day coming down the stairs, but she seems to be managing to get around on it."

A vision flashed into Cecily's mind of Lady Lucille leaning heavily on her husband's arm yesterday. "Oh, I'm sorry to hear that," she said quickly. "Please tell her to let me know if there is anything I can do. The village doctor will be having lunch here today. I'm sure he will be happy to take a look at Lady Lucille's ankle if needs be."

"I'll convey your message to her." Chatsworth took out his pocket watch and flipped open the lid. "Now I have some business to take care of, so if you'll excuse me?"

"Of course." Cecily watched both men leave, then headed for the foyer. Just as she reached it, the front door opened to admit Dr. Prestwick.

He spotted her at once, and gave her an expansive grin, which she returned. He then doffed his trilby hat and offered her a low sweep of his arm. "Mrs. Baxter. You look as exquisite as always."

He was dressed in a dark gray lounge suit under a black topcoat and looked both debonaire and handsome. Cecily responded to his greeting by fluttering her eyelashes at him in mock adoration. "And you, my dear Kevin, are every bit as utterly engaging."

Moira, who was crossing the foyer at that moment, shot a curious stare at each of them before scurrying for the steps to the kitchen.

Cecily pulled a face. "Oh, dear, I'm afraid we might have generated some unwelcome gossip below stairs."

Prestwick chuckled. "That will teach you to trifle with

my affections. How is that handsome husband of yours?"

"Hale and hearty the last time I saw him." She glanced at the grandfather clock, just as the Westminster chimes began to strike. "Your timing is perfect, Kevin. Lunch will be served shortly. Let us retire to the dining room, where I can offer you an aperitif while we wait to be served."

"My pleasure, madam." He offered her his arm and accompanied her down the hallway to the dining room. "Baxter won't be joining us?" he exclaimed in surprise when they were seated at Cecily's favorite table set for two.

"He's taking his meal in the office," Cecily said a little guiltily. She hadn't had a chance to tell Baxter she was dining with the good doctor. Then again, she hadn't exactly made the effort to do so. Sometimes it was easier to explain after the fact than before.

"So tell me," Prestwick said after the aperitifs had been served, "What is the reason for this delightful rendezvous?"

She pretended not to understand. "There has to be a reason?"

"Isn't there always?" He smiled at her blank expression. "Come now, Cecily, we both know that this isn't a purely social visit. You want something from me, and hazarding a wild guess, I'd say it has something to do with either the accident that killed one of your guests, or more likely the death of your maid, does it not?"

She kept her expression of pure innocence. "Why, Kevin, I'm surprised at you. Surely you know me better than that?"

"Indeed, I do." He took a sip of his gin and put down

the glass. "Which is why I presume you have an ulterior motive. I'm certainly not vain enough to assume you have invited me here to bask in my considerable charm."

She had to laugh at that. "Oh, very well. What can you tell me about the deaths?"

"Not much that you probably don't already know. Your guest died from injuries received when his motor car went off the cliff. As for the maid, she bled to death from the wound in her throat. Someone slashed her with a kitchen knife, apparently from your kitchen."

"Which would seem to rule out the theory that it's someone from the village, as most people seem to think."

Prestwick's expression sobered. "Well, there is one thing that isn't common knowledge, though I'm not sure I should mention it."

"Well, now that you already have," Cecily said firmly, "you are duty bound to tell me what it is, unless you want me to hound you constantly until you give in."

"Well, if you phrase it in that manner, I suppose I have no choice." His tone had been light, but now he leaned forward and lowered his voice. "I found a pearl lodged in the girl's underclothing. The string must have been broken in the struggle. The constables believe she stole the pearls from your housekeeper and met with someone, most likely from London, in order to sell them."

"Then why was she killed?"

"Perhaps she wanted too much money, or refused to give them up. Thieves fall out all the time, for a number of reasons."

Cecily frowned. "But the kitchen knife?"

"She could have taken it along to defend herself, perhaps anticipating some form of violence from her client.

Mind you, he didn't get away unscathed. There was blood under her fingernails. She fought hard."

Cecily shook her head, remembering Jeanette's vehement protests of innocence when the pearls were first discovered missing. "I still can't believe that young lady was capable of such a deliberate crime."

"Ah, Cecily, you would not do well at Scotland Yard. You are much too reluctant to see the ugly truth about some people."

"I haven't done so badly in the past," she reminded him. "I have solved more than one murder behind these walls."

"More by luck than judgment, I'd venture."

She made a face at him. "You never were able to credit a woman with any grain of intelligence. That could well be the reason that you and Madeline are at such odds lately. Madeline is an extremely intelligent woman, and in my opinion, you are a little afraid she will outsmart you, especially when it comes to medicine."

His smile faded. "If you want our friendship to continue, Cecily, I must ask you to refrain from interfering in matters that don't concern you."

"But they do concern me. Madeline is one of my dearest friends, and it disturbs me to see her in so much pain when I know very well that you both care a very great deal for each other. It is such a dreadful waste. You two could achieve so much together."

Prestwick tapped the white linen tablecloth with his fingertips. His voice sounded casual enough, but his blue eyes mirrored his interest. "Madeline is in pain?"

Cecily crossed her fingers under the table. "Very much so, though she does her best to hide it. She is pining for you, Kevin. Isn't it time you swallowed some of that infernal pride and accepted the fact that Madeline Pengrath is exactly what you need to give your life purpose as well as pleasure?"

He gave her a long, thoughtful stare, then said slowly, "I'll take it under notice."

"Very well." Pleased with herself, she leaned back in her chair.

"Is *that* why you asked me here today?"

"Actually, I asked you here so that you might look in on Ross McBride, Gertie's husband. She's concerned about his health."

Prestwick stared at her a moment longer, then burst out laughing. "Cecily, you are priceless. Your husband is a lucky fellow."

She grinned happily at him. "Be sure to tell him that when you see him next."

For the rest of the meal she chatted with him about mundane matters, though never far from her mind were the questions she couldn't answer. Was Jeanette a thief, and was she killed by an accomplice? If so, where did Peebles's death fit in if, indeed, it was murder and not an accident? To whom did he owe such a large sum of money? Who or what was Cureagambler? And what about Wrotham's death? Was that an accident or yet another murder? There didn't seem any end to the questions, and none of them had answers. It would seem she still had a lot more digging to do.

The pantomime began promptly at eight o'clock that evening. Phoebe had persuaded the ballroom orchestra to provide the music, and the curtains opened to reveal Phoebe's dance troupe, clad in filmy trousers and quite scandalous upper garments that revealed bare arms to the shoulders.

The fact that some of the young ladies had gained a few pounds since their last appearance and were revealing a little more than decorum dictated aroused some horrified responses from the audience as the dancers pranced around the stage.

They were soon forgotten, however, with the appearance of Aladdin. Doris's beautiful voice soaring to the rafters kept the audience entranced, so much so that they generously forgave Raymond, in the guise of the genie, when he tripped over the lamp and sprawled on the floor.

Phoebe's loud hissing from the wings could be heard quite clearly at times, especially when her girls stumbled over each other, threatening to bring down the entire temple that had been hastily and somewhat haphazardly erected by Samuel and his assistants earlier. It didn't help matters when the colonel, resplendent in his guard's uniform, bellowed at Phoebe to "stop that blasted interfering."

The final scene called for Doris and a young maid to mount the lower steps of the temple and sing the final song together with the genie hovering behind them.

Phoebe's dance troupe had built a tableau, balancing precariously on various body parts of their companions. Due to the aforementioned extra weight, the unfortunate girls on the lower end were not able to hold their positions, and the entire human pyramid collapsed, revealing even more human flesh than was proper.

Raymond leapt down from his perch, obviously eager not to miss this golden opportunity to assist half-clothed damsels. Phoebe ran screeching onto the stage, then backed hastily off again as Doris gamely launched into her song, despite the mayhem going on behind her.

The audience, having recovered from their earlier shock, politely struggled to hold their mirth until Doris had finished her song and the curtains drew to a close. Then, as one, they surged to their feet, the men whistling and cheering while their wives demurely applauded.

Relieved that everyone had survived the ordeal without serious injury, Cecily went backstage with Baxter to congratulate everybody. She was intrigued to note that Kevin Prestwick had also wandered backstage and was engaged in an earnest conversation with Madeline. It would seem that her little chat with him had done some good.

Now she could only hope that the two of them could mend their differences and take this opportunity to work together, perhaps with an eye to a permanent relationship in the future. She couldn't ask for more for her friend.

"I suppose we should thank our lucky stars that it wasn't a total disaster," Baxter commented as they made their way back to the still crowded ballroom.

Several of the staff were hurriedly moving the chairs closer to the walls, so that the orchestra could take the stage and the room would be clear for an hour or two of dancing.

Cecily caught sight of Fitzhammer and his wife taking to the floor for a lively waltz, just as Baxter exclaimed, "Isn't that the Gilroys over there? His wife appears to be hurt."

Cecily followed his gaze. It was, indeed, the Gilroys, and they were almost at the door, proceeding slowly as Lady Lucille leaned on a cane while her husband supported her with an arm beneath her elbow.

"I heard that she sprained her ankle," Cecily said, quickening her pace. "I really should have a word with her." She caught up with the couple, followed closely by Baxter, who seemed reluctant to converse with the pair.

Lady Lucille appeared ill at ease, her fingers plucking at her husband's sleeve as if urging him to cut short the conversation.

As usual she wore no hat, and her hair, draped in a rather unique style covering most of her forehead and down her cheeks, was adorned with tiny silk violets.

She looked utterly divine in an exquisite pale violet ball gown, artfully tucked at the bodice in figured net over silk. Even the gold-topped cane could not deter from her sophisticated elegance.

"Lady Lucille," Cecily said breathlessly, having sped a little faster than she was accustomed. "I heard that you had injured your ankle. I do hope it isn't giving you too much trouble. I happen to have a doctor visiting us tonight. Would you like him to examine it for you? I'm quite sure he won't mind a bit."

Lucille glanced at Sir John, whose attention seemed to be caught by someone in the crowd of dancers. "Thank you, *madame*," she murmured, "but there is no cause to disturb the good doctor. It is merely a sprain and will soon mend."

"Very well." Cecily sought for a way to continue the conversation. "I must compliment you on your hair," she said, a little desperately. "It is such a charming style."

"*Merci, madame.*" Lucille tugged on her husband's sleeve. "It is the very latest fashion from Paris."

"Ah, I thought it must be." Cecily paused for a second, then added, "We are all deeply saddened by the death of

Mr. Peebles. It must have been such a dreadful shock for all of you."

This time it was Sir John who answered. "Please excuse us, Mrs. Baxter. My wife is tired and needs to rest." Without giving Lucille a chance to say more, he hurried her through the door and down the hallway, apparently oblivious to the way she hobbled painfully to keep up.

"Well, that was a bit abrupt," Baxter said, staring after the couple. "I wonder what's biting him?"

"I don't know," Cecily said thoughtfully, "but I have the impression that he didn't want to talk about Peebles."

"Probably still in shock," Baxter observed as he held the door open for his wife to pass through. "After all, by all accounts they were pretty close friends."

"Unless," Cecily murmured, "something happened to destroy that friendship. Now wouldn't *that* be interesting."

CHAPTER

❧ 18 ❧

The following morning Cecily waited until the morning rush was over, then went in search of Moira. Mrs. Chubb greeted her as she entered the kitchen, which was surprisingly quiet, thanks in part to the absence of Michel, who was taking a short respite from his busy schedule.

"I hear the pantomime went very well, madam," Mrs. Chubb said, her hands wrist deep in a large slab of bread dough. "Everyone said that Doris did a wonderful job. I wish we could have been part of it, but then again, I'd just as soon be right back here in my kitchen again. I'd quite forgotten how good it feels."

Cecily smiled. "I can't tell you how good it feels to have you here." She looked around. "Is Moira here?"

"Oh, she's taking a tray up to Lady Lucille. The lady

didn't come down for breakfast. Coming down with a nasty cold by all accounts. Seems to be doing the rounds, it does. Hope we don't all get it or this will be a poor Christmas, that's for sure."

"How are things working out with Gertie and the twins?" Cecily sat down on the nearest chair. "Is Daisy managing them? I imagine taking care of them can be hard work."

"Daisy is used to hard work." The housekeeper pounded the dough with her fist. "She loves those little scamps, that she does. She's so good with children, she should get a real job as a nanny. Be right up her alley, it would."

The door swung open and Moira rushed in with an empty tray. "Lady Lucille said to thank you for your kindness and—" She stopped short when she saw Cecily and dropped an awkward curtsey. "Good morning, m'm."

Cecily rose to her feet. "Moira, just the person I wanted to see. I'd like a quick word with you if you can spare the time?"

Moira glanced at Mrs. Chubb who, without looking up, answered for her. "She's got time."

"I won't keep her long," Cecily promised. She looked at Moira, whose face was creased with apprehension. "Perhaps we should step out into the hallway for a moment."

"Yes, m'm." Moira followed her out into the corridor, her fingers twisting the folds of her apron.

Cecily led her a few feet away, out of earshot of the kitchen. "I know you want to protect your friend," she said quietly, "but in order to know what happened to Jeanette, I need to know the truth. Everyone thinks she stole Miss Bunkle's pearls, especially since one was found hidden in Jeanette's clothing."

Moira gasped, her eyes wide above the hand she pressed to her mouth.

"You wouldn't want her to go to her grave with everyone believing she's a thief, now would you?"

Moira shook her head.

"I need to know, Moira," Cecily said gently. "Did Jeanette steal those pearls or not? If she did, then we'll say no more about it. After all, the girl is dead and can't be in any more trouble now. On the other hand, if she didn't steal them, I'm quite sure Jeanette would want everyone to know that. I know I would."

Moira lowered her hand, gulped, and looked down at her shoes. "I think I'd better show you something, m'm. It's down here in me room."

Cecily followed her down the hall to the tiny room Moira had shared with the dead girl. She watched the young girl dig her hand under the mattress on Jeanette's bed and withdraw a package, which she handed to Cecily with downcast eyes.

Carefully Cecily unwrapped the package and poured the contents into her hand. The lamplight glinted on the perfectly matched pearls, and Cecily caught her breath. "So she did steal them."

"No, m'm." Moira's voice rose a notch. "She didn't really steal them, m'm. She was only going to borrow them. She was going into Wellercombe with her boyfriend, Wally, and she wanted to dress up for him. Only they had a big row over that Mr. Peebles, like I told you, and somehow the string got broke."

"I see," Cecily said slowly. "And she was afraid to tell Miss Bunkle what she'd done."

"Yes, m'm. She picked up all the pearls and hid 'em.

She didn't have enough money to get them mended right away, so she was keeping them until she could get enough money. She was hoping to put them back before Miss Bunkle noticed they was missing, but then Miss Bunkle said they was stolen and Jeanette had to find the money in a hurry."

"I see." Cecily smoothed out the paper to wrap the pearls up again. As she did so, she noticed the printed heading at the top of the paper. It was a strange, yet familiar word. *Cureagambler*. The page had obviously been torn from the same notepad as Roger Peebles's IOU.

Baxter stared at the crinkled paper lying in front of him on his desk, his brows drawn together in a frown. "What *is* this?" he demanded. "Cureagambler? I've never heard of it."

"Neither had I until yesterday." Quickly Cecily explained about the IOU while Baxter's frown grew darker by the second. After delivering his usual lecture on the risk of invading the privacy of their guests, and the ramifications if she had been discovered, he calmed down enough to ask, "So what does it mean, this Cureagambler?"

"I'm not sure." She reached for a sheet of embossed notepaper, dipped Baxter's pen into the inkwell, shook the excess drops from it, then scrawled the name out on the paper. "Look, does this make more sense?"

"Cure a gambler," Baxter read out loud. "No, not really."

"I have a theory, if you'd like to hear it."

He gave her a look of pure irony. "Do I have a choice?"

She grinned. "Not really."

With a sigh he leaned back in his chair. "Oh, very well. Let's have it."

She paused for a moment to get her thoughts in order, then said, "Suppose that Cureagambler is an organization that helps cure people of a gambling habit. Suppose that Roger Peebles had a serious gambling habit, which judging by the IOU seems feasible. Now, Peebles was an important and respected Master of the Bench. If word got out that he had gambling problems, that surely wouldn't bode well for his career."

"I suppose not," Baxter said slowly, "but I don't see—"

"Wait." Cecily held up her hand. "I'm not finished yet."

"Pardon. One always lives in hope."

Ignoring his sarcasm, she went on, "Now, Jeanette also had a sheet of paper with the heading of this organization. Let us suppose that she discovered Peebles had a gambling problem. She could have found the sheet of paper earlier while cleaning his suite and reached the same conclusion we did. Then, when the string of pearls is broken, she needs money to have them restrung . . ."

"So she blackmails Peebles for the money."

She beamed, delighted that he had followed her train of thought so well. "Peebles already owes two thousand pounds that he can't afford to pay, since he has to issue an IOU. He certainly can't afford to pay a blackmailer."

"So he has to get rid of her instead."

"Precisely." She watched anxiously as Baxter thought it over.

"Well," he said at last. "If Peebles killed Jeanette, then his death must have been an accident. Just like Wrotham's."

Cecily sighed. "None of this really makes sense, does it. I still feel certain that someone tampered with Peebles's car, and I can't convince myself that Barry Wrotham fell into that well all by himself. It's all too close to be a coincidence. Yet there's absolutely nothing to connect them. So where do we go from here?"

"Nowhere," Baxter said firmly. "All of this is pure conjecture. Except for the theft of the pearls. Whether or not Jeanette planned to return them, she did steal them. In the eyes of the law, anyway. We shall have to report this to Northcott and see that these are returned to Miss Bunkle."

Cecily frowned. "I suppose we must. I just can't accept the fact that we'll never know what really happened."

"You might as well. The best thing we can do now is put this all behind us." Baxter replaced the pearls in their package, opened the drawer of his desk, and tucked them inside. "After all, if your theory is right and Peebles did kill Jeanette, he got his just reward."

Cecily scrawled aimlessly on the notepad, doodling circles around the words she'd scribbled earlier. "I wish I knew what this name really means." She looked up at him. "You have some influential associates in the city. I don't suppose you could ask some of them if they've ever heard of a company named Cureagambler?"

He narrowed his gaze. "I don't suppose you'll let it rest until I do."

She shrugged. "Just out of curiosity, that's all."

He sighed. "All right. I'll see what I can do. In the meantime, I'll give Northcott a ring and tell him to send someone for the pearls."

"Very well." Cecily rose from her chair.

"By the way," Baxter said casually, "I heard that you entertained a guest for lunch yesterday."

"Oh, you mean Dr. Prestwick." She headed for the

door, saying lightly over her shoulder, "I asked him here to look at Ross McBride. Gertie seemed most concerned about his health and I thought the doctor should take a look at him."

"Is that the only reason you invited him without telling me?"

She looked back at him. "No, actually I invited him here in the hopes that he would make up his quarrel with Madeline."

Baxter sighed, though his frown relaxed. "Cecily, when will you cease interfering in people's lives?"

"When everyone is as happy as I am, dear Bax."

To her relief, a smile warmed his face. "Amen."

With that, she left him to his work. There was much to be done before Christmas Eve, and she had neglected her work enough. Even so, the questions surrounding the three deaths still haunted her, and she knew she would not be able to rest until she had all the answers.

It was much later in the afternoon when Baxter caught up with her again. She was in the laundry room with Mrs. Chubb, trying to decide whether or not to invest in some new tablecloths for the dining room.

"Gertie told me you were here," Baxter said when Mrs. Chubb discreetly withdrew to leave them alone. "I thought you'd like to know that I have some news about Cureagambler."

Cecily dropped the pile of tablecloths onto the counter. "You found out what it is?"

"I did indeed." Baxter looked pleased with himself. "And it's not an organization to cure gambling, as we thought. Quite the opposite, in fact. It's a company, or rather a partnership, that owns two rather notorious gambling houses on the southeast coast. One is in Brighton, the other is in Southampton. Apparently both houses are quite well known among the more affluent citizens of London."

"Oh, my, how very intriguing." Cecily studied his face with interest. "Did you find out anything about them?"

"Only that there have been several brawls and incidents of . . ." He cleared his throat.

Cecily waited for a moment, then asked impatiently, "Incidents of what?"

"Well, it's a rather delicate matter, but the rumors have it that certain young ladies in the establishments are offering their . . . ah . . . services for payment."

Cecily opened her eyes wide. "A brothel?"

"Hush!" Baxter looked wildly around, though they were quite alone in the room. "A lady shouldn't even know the word, much less utter it."

"Oh, come now, Bax. I read the newspaper. Those women have been trading their wares since the beginning of time."

"That doesn't mean that it's a matter for discussion."

She stared at him, her mind busily digesting this latest information. "Roger Peebles must have visited those places, since he had their IOU slips in his pocket."

"Well, if so, I can certainly understand why he wouldn't want that to be common knowledge. From what I hear, the police are constantly raiding the place in an effort to shut them down, but so far the owners have been clever enough to avoid that."

"How interesting." She frowned. "I wonder who else knows about Peebles's indiscretions."

"I can't imagine he publicizes the fact."

"I wonder if this has anything to do with his death."

Baxter sighed. "Peebles's death was an accident. I thought we agreed on that."

"Now why would you think we'd agreed on anything?" She smiled sweetly. "I think, my dear husband, that you should have a word with the rest of the Benchers. Perhaps suggest you have some influential friends who are looking for somewhere out of town to indulge their habit?"

Baxter's pursed his lips. "And why, pray, would I do such a thing?"

"I think it would be most interesting to know who else knows about this Cureagambler. I have a feeling that it might have something to do with why Peebles died."

"A feeling," Baxter repeated. "You mean one of those infernal notions that invariably land you in trouble."

"And more often than not have led to some very satisfying conclusions."

"Not without hovering on the brink of disaster."

"Perhaps, but when a young girl in our employ is brutally murdered, isn't it our duty to discover why she was killed and by whom? Up until now we have been guessing. I think it's high time we made a concerted effort to solve this puzzle. Once and for all."

For several seconds their gazes clashed, then Baxter muttered, "Oh, very well. It can't do any harm, I suppose. I'll pay a visit to the card room, since the gentlemen in question seem to spend a vast amount of time in there."

"Thank you, Baxter." She laid a hand on his arm. "I

don't have to remind you to be careful not to let slip that we know about Cureagambler. After all, three deaths have occurred within a very short time. I'm not anxious to see a fourth. Particularly if it's yours."

"You surely don't suspect one of the Benchers of being involved in murder," Baxter exclaimed.

"I'm considering all possibilities, that's all." She smiled at him. "I know I can trust you to be discreet."

"Something tells me I'm going to regret this." He moved to the door, then paused to look back at her. "If you're free for lunch, perhaps you'd care to join me in the dining room."

"I would adore to have lunch with you."

"I think the staff should see us together, just in case they should have any false impressions about your tryst with Prestwick yesterday."

She controlled the urge to laugh and instead murmured demurely, "I think that's a very good idea."

Seemingly satisfied, he left.

Cecily turned back to the task of counting tablecloths. Poor Baxter. He couldn't forget that once Kevin Prestwick had pursued her, even though she had never entertained any notions of romantic attachment to him. Then again, it really didn't hurt to remind him every now and then. Just to keep him on his toes, so to speak. Smiling, Cecily started counting tablecloths.

It was an hour or so later before she had completed enough of her schedule to indulge in some free time with her husband. Baxter was waiting for her in his office, and she knew at once by his heavy scowl that something had upset him.

Somewhat alarmed, she hurried to his side. "What

happened? Surely there hasn't been another death?"

"No, no." He shook his head. "It's just those blasted Benchers. They were all in the card room, so I approached them and, as delicately as possible, broached the subject of gambling in general."

Cecily sat down, afraid of what she might hear. "So what did they say?"

"Well, the conversation went on and on, mostly rubbish that I didn't understand, about odds and bets and bluffs and a number of terms of which I had no idea of their meaning. I had to pretend interest, of course. I thought I was never going to get away."

Feeling somewhat disappointed, Cecily asked, "But did they mention Cureagambler?"

"Not one word. I mentioned the fact that I knew several wealthy gentlemen in the city who love to gamble, but who found our meager card rooms too tame for their adventurous spirits."

"That was extremely clever of you," Cecily said, beaming at him in admiration. "So what reaction did you get to that?"

Baxter shrugged. "Well, Sir John Gilroy's features remained carved in stone. Chatsworth looked interested but didn't say anything."

"And Fitzhammer? If anyone would spill the beans, it would be him."

"Well, he did hint that he might know a place where my gentlemen friends might find enough excitement to satisfy them. He suggested I join them in a few rounds of baccarat this evening, when we might discuss it. Naturally, I had to decline the invitation."

"Baxter!" Cecily sat up straight. "How could you? This

is the perfect opportunity for you to find out more about Cureagambler. Especially if Lionel Fitzhammer knows about it, too."

"I didn't say that. I merely said that Fitzhammer knew of a place. He didn't mention it by name."

Ignoring him, Cecily went on blithely, "We'll send in a few complimentary bottles of brandy and they'll be talking in no time. Lady Lucille complained of her husband taking part in something that didn't include her. Perhaps all of these gentlemen are paid members of these houses. If so, they would all have a motive for murder. You have to go to the game. It's the only chance we might have of catching all three of them unawares. You must pay strict attention to everything that is said."

His expression of sheer alarm was almost comical. "Have you forgotten that I know nothing about cards? I seem to remember you volunteering my participation in a poker game, giving my opponents the impression I had played professionally. I was hopelessly inept, and suffered agonies at that table. That was one of the most embarrassing and nerve-racking evenings of my life."

"We found out what we wanted to know, however," Cecily pointed out.

Baxter glared at her. "I *cannot* play baccarat."

"You can learn."

"In one afternoon?"

"Enough to get by. Yes."

"That's what you assured me about the poker game. And this time you won't be able to coach me as we play, since you're not allowed in the card rooms."

"Idiotic rules and regulations," Cecily muttered. "They should be outlawed."

"The rules are what make this a club and not a hotel."

"Exactly. That's my point." She drew a deep breath. "Darling, from what I hear, baccarat is much simpler to play than poker. We have the rules for them right here in your office. I suggest we have a leisurely lunch, then we'll return here and learn the rules of the game. You don't have to play with the Benchers all evening. Just long enough to find out what they know about Cureagambler, and anything else they might say."

"And how will that tell us who killed Jeanette?"

"I don't know," Cecily confessed. "But I can't help feeling it's all connected somehow. What's more, I think the Benchers know more than they are saying."

"Why are you so sure they are involved?"

Before she could answer, he held up his hand. "No, don't tell me. It's just a feeling."

She looked up at him in appeal. "It's a very *strong* feeling."

His sigh told her he'd capitulated. "I know I'm going to regret this, but all right. I'll make an attempt to learn the game. But I have to tell you, if I don't feel I know enough about it by this evening to put on a good show, then I'm calling it off. Agreed?"

Reluctantly, she agreed, though secretly she vowed that, come hell or high water, she'd make sure he learned how to play baccarat before the day was over.

During lunch Cecily deliberately kept the conversation away from the subject of gambling, or indeed, anything to do with the Benchers or their wives. She was half afraid that Baxter would change his mind. She would have felt a great deal better about the whole venture had she been able to join him in the card room. She made up her mind that, at the first opportunity, she would talk to Edward about changing some of the rules that offended her.

As soon as they had finished their meal, Cecily led the way back to Baxter's office, assuring him that their duties could wait until they had mastered the game of baccarat.

The game called for at least three decks of cards, and she had to wait for him to collect them, as well as the rules, before they could begin.

"This looks heinously complicated," Baxter complained after scanning the closely written rules.

"Not for a man of your intelligence," Cecily replied blithely. "Really all you have to do is know how to count to nine. You simply add two cards together, and take the last digit. For instance, if you have an eight and a five, you add them together, which is thirteen, so your count is three. It's simple."

Baxter looked unconvinced. "What's all this about a shoe? And what the devil is *cheval,* or *banco*?"

"It all depends on how you bet. The punters sit on either side of the banker and you bet on them being able to beat the banker's hand." She studied the rules over his shoulder. "Look, *banco* means the punter is betting the total value of the banker's funds."

Baxter shook his head. "This is not going to work. Why don't I simply ask them if they've heard of this Cureagambler? It would save a lot of trouble."

"Because no self-respecting barrister as important as the Masters of the Bench is going to admit he knows of a gambling brothel in Brighton."

Baxter winced, but refrained from chiding her for using the forbidden word. "Then what makes you think that playing this dratted game with them is going to open up their mouths?"

"It won't be the game that loosens their tongue," Cecily said smugly. "It's the free brandy they'll be pouring down their throats. Trust me, Bax. This will work. I have—"

"A feeling," he said in unison with her. "Very well, I'll do my best. I can only hope it doesn't turn into the disaster I experienced in the poker game."

"Don't worry, darling," Cecily said with a great deal more confidence than she felt. "You'll manage beautifully and I'm sure you will even enjoy it. Take my word for it."

CHAPTER
❧ 19 ❧

"So what did Dr. Prestcott say about Ross?" Mrs. Chubb asked, stirring her cup of tea vigorously with a delicate silver teaspoon.

Seated opposite her at the kitchen table, Gertie uttered a gloomy sigh. "He says he's exhausted. Needs a good rest. I could have told 'im that."

Mrs. Chubb lifted the cup to her lips and sipped cautiously in case it was still too hot. The steaming liquid stung her tongue and she hastily put the cup down again. "Well, he's getting that here, isn't he?"

"I suppose so. He's not very happy with me working, though. Even though I explained I was doing it as a favor for Mrs. Baxter. He said as how everyone would think it terrible for him to let his wife work and he's lying around doing nothing."

"Well, it won't be for long, will it." Mrs. Chubb tasted the tea again and this time managed to get a mouthful down without burning her tongue again. "Whereabouts is Ross now, anyway?"

"He's taking a walk around the grounds to get some fresh air, ain't he."

Mrs. Chubb watched in awe as Gertie chugged down the hot tea without even blinking. That girl had to have a constitution made of iron, that's all she could say.

"He wanted to take the twins with him," Gertie added, dropping her cup on its saucer. "But Daisy's taken them into town to look at the toy shops."

"Well, that's a mistake. Now they'll want everything they see on the shelves."

"Don't I bloomin' know it," Gertie said mournfully. "Course, they won't blinking get it, will they. We'll have to watch the bloody pennies now, that's for sure."

The maid seated next to her sniggered, and Mrs. Chubb gave Gertie a look that she hoped she would interpret as a command to watch her language. Gertie was trying, but she never could get rid of that smutty mouth of hers.

"Better not let Ross hear you say that," she warned. "He won't want to be reminded that he's not bringing home the fatted calf like he was."

"He's not even bringing home a scrawny chicken." Gertie picked up her empty cup and saucer and got wearily to her feet. "Never mind, that's what I say. He'll find something else to do before long, that I do know. Until then, well, I'm getting paid so that'll help."

Mrs. Chubb watched her carry her cup and saucer to the sink. Poor Gertie. She put on a good face, but it was pretty plain to her that the girl was worried sick. She could only hope that something good would turn up for Ross, or she might be out of a job herself. And that's what frightened her most of all.

That evening Cecily paced around her suite, unable to settle down. She had found a decent copy of Louisa May Alcott's *An Old-fashioned Girl* in the library and had promised herself she would read it at the earliest opportunity.

Knowing that Baxter was at that moment cornered in a card room with the Benchers was a distraction that made reading impossible. Sending him down there to find out what they knew had seemed a good idea at the time. Now that she'd had an hour or two to think about it, however, she was having qualms about the whole thing.

Baxter was right when he'd reminded her that he was no gambler. Without her there to prod or guide him, he could be getting in over his head, not to mention arousing the suspicions of three very influential barristers, all of whom possessed extraordinary intelligence, or they would not be in that particular profession.

They would easily see through Baxter's clumsy attempts to extract information from them, and could very well be extremely offended. On the other hand, if they did have something to hide, and were somehow connected to Peebles's death, the situation could actually be dangerous.

Once more she had acted on impulse, with dubious results. Now all she could do was sit and stew while Baxter dug a hole for himself that just might be too deep for him to climb out.

She was in such a state by the time the door to their suite finally flew open, that she wasn't at all surprised to see the heavy scowl on Baxter's face.

What did unsettle her was the cold fury in his eyes as he stalked across the room, dragged off his evening coat, and flung it on the bed.

Watching him stomp to the window, she tried out several questions in her mind and discarded them all. *How did things go?* was not a good one, since it was quite obvious from his dark expression that things did not go well at all. *What happened?* seemed equally precarious, and at that moment it didn't seem prudent to ask him if he'd found out anything helpful.

In the end, she kept silent, while viewing his stiff back with some trepidation. It wasn't often that Baxter lost his temper, but she'd learned to hold her tongue on the rare occasion he had become this incensed.

It seemed like an eternity before he finally spoke, and when he did, his voice was clipped and chipped with ice. "Well, you have certainly outdone yourself this time, Cecily."

As guilty as she'd felt earlier, she wasn't prepared to take all the blame for whatever disaster had transpired in the card room. Lifting her chin, she said quietly, "Perhaps if you explain what it is I'm supposed to have done, I might be able to understand why you are so angry."

He turned then, and this time the bleak expression on his face frightened her. "I tried to tell you I was no gambler. You wouldn't listen. I knew as soon as I started playing that dratted game that I had no business there, but there didn't seem any way I could withdraw without appearing to be a dishonorable, underhanded cad. So I stayed."

"I'm sorry if you were embarrassed—" she began, but he interrupted her with a roar that startled her half out of her wits.

"*Embarrassed!* Dammit, Cecily, if that were only all of it. I'm afraid there's a great deal more than embarrassment involved here."

She sat down, afraid of what she might hear next. "What happened? Did you find out more about Cureagambler?"

"No, I did not." He came toward her, his fists clenched at his sides. "I didn't find out a blasted thing. It was all for nothing, Cecily. All of it."

He stopped short, closed his eyes, and slapped a hand to his forehead in a way that at any other time would have seemed melodramatic.

At the moment, however, she recognized his anguish, and rose quickly to her feet. "You are frightening me, Hugh. Please, tell me, what is it? What's wrong?"

He lowered his hand and gazed at her with such sorrow her heart began pounding with fear. "It's all gone, Cecily. Everything we have. It happened so fast I found it hard to believe. I kept betting more and more, hoping to recoup at least some of the loss, but it just kept mounting up and . . ."

His voice broke, and she stepped toward him, her arms outstretched to comfort him.

To her shock and alarm, he turned his back to her. Regaining control of his voice, he said harshly, "We shall have to sell the house in London in order to pay the debt."

She uttered a cry of dismay. "No, it can't be that bad. Surely there is a way—"

"There is no way. This is your doing, Cecily. I hope you

are satisfied." With an abrupt movement he strode to the door and dragged it open.

She started after him. "Where are you going?"

"I don't know. I need to be alone. Go to bed. There is nothing you can do that you haven't already done."

The door closed behind him, and she sank onto her chair, utterly at a loss. Stunned with disbelief, she tried to make sense of what he'd told her. Sell the house? No, surely not. And what of his business? How would that fare if the house had to be sold? His office, all his associates, all the work he'd ever done was tied up in that house. To sell it now would surely mean ruin.

Now she was truly frightened. She couldn't wait for him to return, so that he could calm her fears and tell her he was simply overreacting to a distressing situation. Even Baxter, in all his ineptitude for gambling, couldn't have possibly lost that much money. No matter how humiliating the circumstances.

No, he was trying to frighten her so that she would never put him in that position again. In that, he had succeeded. She had already vowed to herself that very thing, even before he'd returned in such a temper.

Now all she could do was wait for his return and beg his forgiveness. Promise him anything he wanted as long as he did not look at her with that terrible coldness in his eyes.

She waited all night, but he did not return. And in the grayness of the next morning, as the snow began to fall once more, she faced the fact that this time she had gone too far. She could only hope that it wasn't too late for forgiveness, and that she hadn't lost the love and respect of the man she so greatly adored.

*   *   *

It was much later that morning when Baxter finally
returned to the suite. He changed his clothes and went
down to his office without saying a word to Cecily about
where he had been. Her brief attempt to open a conversation was met with a stony stare and a chilly silence and
she withdrew, knowing it would take time before she
could approach him.

After picking at a solitary breakfast in her sitting
room, she approached her desk with the idea of working
on a shopping list for Christmas gifts. The prospect of
Christmas with Baxter ignoring her was too dismal to
contemplate, and she pushed the list aside. She reached
instead for a pencil and started doodling aimlessly on the
blotting paper. She wished now she'd simply asked the
Benchers about the IOU she'd found in Peebles's
wardrobe. Or at least questioned Mrs. Peebles.

Then again, it would be difficult to explain how she
had come about it, or what her interest in it might be, and
since the other notepaper with the name of Cureagambler
on it had been wrapped around stolen pearls, that, too,
would have been a little awkward to explain.

She should have done as Baxter had suggested and left
well alone. She was no closer to solving the puzzle, and
now she had possibly lost her home. Though now that
she'd had time to think about it, she failed to see why she
should take all the blame. After all, Baxter had been foolish to the extreme, risking everything they had to salvage
his pride. This was every bit as much his fault as hers.
And she would point that out to him. Just as soon as he
got over his snit. If he ever got over it.

More dispirited than ever, she stared at the word she'd

written down. *Cureagambler*. It did seem odd that a company that apparently made a fortune from gamblers would form a name suggesting a cure for gamblers. That didn't make sense at all. The name must mean something else.

Her heart still ached so badly it hurt, and she did her best to keep her mind off her problems by rearranging the letters of the word that had caused so much trouble. Forward and backward, in and out. Nothing made sense. She began to play one of her favorite games, seeing how many words she could think of using the letters of Cureagambler. *Game, crab, blur, bar, luck* . . . no, there was no *k*. She crossed off the last letter, then stared at what she'd written. She started scribbling again, becoming more excited as she wrote. Then, with a small cry of triumph, she wrote rapidly on a piece of notepaper, then headed for the door. Angry at her or not, Baxter had to see this.

A few minutes later he answered her light tap with a curt, "Come in, come in then!"

When she put her head around the door, her heart sank at his forbidding expression. "I'm busy at the moment," he said shortly. "Whatever it is will have to wait."

She tightened her lips, but ignored his attempt to be rid of her and advanced into the room. After sitting herself down firmly on her chair, she slid the notepaper across the desk toward him.

For a moment she thought he would simply pretend it wasn't there, but evidently his curiosity got the better of him and he picked it up. "What the devil is this?"

Delighted to have drawn even that curt communication from him, she said quickly, "I broke the word *Cureagambler* down into four parts."

He made a sound of disgust and threw the paper at her

across the desk. "You simply do not have the sense to know when you have gone too far," he snapped. "Enough of this. I refuse to listen to any more wild conjecture about this company. No matter what it is. What these people do is none of our business, and quite frankly, the very thought of gambling right now is like waving a red rag at a bull. Please give me the courtesy of eliminating the subject from your mind, unless you want to conduct the rest of our lives together in silence."

All notions of attempting to placate him vanished in the face of this onslaught. Her own voice trembled with outrage when she answered him. "You are being most unfair. It wasn't I who gambled away our home which, in case you are under some misapprehension, is every bit as important to me as it is to you. Had you been more vigilant and less concerned with your insufferable pride, you would not have allowed the situation to arrive at such a disastrous conclusion. I suggested you attend the game, yes. I certainly did not sit there prodding you in the back while you recklessly threw away our entire assets. That is entirely on your shoulders, not on mine."

His chilling gaze was formidable, but she held her own without flinching. After a moment he said quietly, "This is not the time to discuss this matter."

"Perhaps not, but the very least you can do is listen to what I have to say. What I have discovered is of the utmost importance, and could very well shed a light on the reason why Roger Peebles died. Perhaps Jeanette, too. And be good enough to spare me the black looks until you have heard the entire story."

His mouth tightened, but he held out his hand for the paper she thrust at him. Taking it from her, he scanned it, then said brusquely, "I still do not understand what you are trying to show me."

"Look at the four names written there. Lucille, Gretchen, Amelia, and Barbara. Take the first three letters of each name, rearrange them, and you end up with . . ."

"Cureagambler." He stared at the paper. "My God. The partnership that owns those two gambling houses . . ."

"Unless it is an extraordinary coincidence, it would seem the partnership consists of the Benchers of Lincoln's Inn. I can think of no other reason for such an odd name."

"If this got out, the scandal could cost them their careers."

"Not could, but certainly would. According to Percy Chatsworth, the Masters of the Bench are prohibited from owning or being engaged in outside businesses. They would be instantly disbarred for life."

After another long moment, Baxter handed her back the paper. "Well, I see what you mean. This would certainly be a good reason to silence someone."

"Particularly if he or she threatened to disclose this interesting fact to the authorities."

"So you're saying that Roger Peebles discovered his fellow Benchers owned not only a business, but a disreputable one at that, and threatened to expose them? But why would he do that? What would he have to gain?"

"Professional jealousy, perhaps. After all, one must suppose that they are in competition with each other for influential clients."

"From what I understand," Baxter said dryly, "there are more than enough clients to keep them all busy. But what would this have to do with the death of our maid?"

"I have no idea at this point. Moira seemed to think

that Jeanette and Peebles were personally involved, since she saw them together. On the other hand, perhaps Jeanette knew about the partnership somehow, and threatened Peebles. Perhaps he killed Jeanette to silence her."

"Then one of the partners killed Peebles? That doesn't make sense at all."

"Nothing makes sense until we see the reasons behind it. In any case, I'm not really sure what I'm saying at this point. I haven't had time to think about it." She rose from her chair. "I've taken up enough of your time. I wanted your opinion in the hopes that you would help confirm my suspicions. Now I need to ponder on it all and try to remember what it is I keep forgetting."

He looked as if he would say something, then shook his head. "I can't think about this now. I have some serious work to do if I'm to salvage anything from the fiasco of last night."

Aware of the barrier still between them, she took her leave, her heart heavy with anxiety. If this catastrophe caused a permanent rift between them, she would never forgive herself. Or him. She could only hope that his coldness was a temporary condition that would soon be remedied. If not, this Christmas Season would be a depressing affair indeed.

Although Baxter shared her bed that night, he did not turn to her as he normally would, but instead presented her with his back and in a very short while was snoring heavily. She eventually fell asleep, but awoke sometime in the night, feeling decidedly chilly without the warmth of Baxter's body to comfort her.

He lay on the very edge of the bed, and although she was tempted to move closer, she refrained for fear she would tip him off onto the floor. He surely would not appreciate such a rude awakening in his present mood.

Instead, she lay on her back, staring at the shadows on the ceiling, and thought about the new development in the puzzle of Peebles's death. It was a risky venture indeed for the Benchers. The partnership must be extremely lucrative for them to take such a chance, though one would suppose it would not be difficult for barristers to keep such an enterprise a secret. After all, it was merely by chance that she had come upon it.

She tried to imagine the Benchers engaged in such a dubious association. It was difficult to imagine Sir John Gilroy in that role, or even Percy Chatsworth, who was so quick to advise her that Benchers were not allowed to own outside interests.

As for Roger Peebles and Lionel Fitzhammer, if Peebles killed Jeanette and Fitzhammer found out about it. . . . She sat bolt upright in bed, dragging the eiderdown from Baxter's shoulders. His snoring ended in a snort. He grunted, and tugged the warm covering back under his chin.

Cecily opened her mouth, then snapped it shut again. He would not appreciate being woken up in the middle of the night to listen to yet another of her rash theories. This would have to wait until the morning.

Excited now, she lay back down and reviewed the whole sequence in her mind. The thing she had buried in her memory had suddenly resurfaced, so clearly she couldn't imagine how she could have forgotten it in the first place.

It was when she'd offered her condolences to Chatsworth and Fitzhammer after the news of Peebles's death. Fitzhammer declared that Peebles was careless and most likely hadn't bothered to get his brakes examined before he left London.

But she was quite sure that Samuel had told no one that the brakes had failed, and she had told no one but Baxter. She could safely assume that he had not passed on the information, in which case, the only way Fitzhammer could have known was if he had something to do with it.

The memory of Samuel's soft voice came back clearly to her. *I'd say someone helped them along a bit. Not likely they'd both go at the same time without a bit of nudging.*

It would seem she finally had her killer.

CHAPTER
❈ 20 ❈

Unable to sleep now, Cecily wrestled with her thoughts. If Fitzhammer had killed Peebles, it was entirely likely that he had killed Jeanette, too. Perhaps even Barry Wrotham as well. The big question was, of course, if he had indeed killed three people, why had he found it necessary to take such drastic steps? If she thought about it long enough, perhaps she could determine the reason.

She frowned in the darkness. If only she could talk the whole thing through with Baxter. Curses on the entire gambling scene. Once she had been tolerant of the practice, particularly when it had been an integral source of income for the Pennyfoot, albeit illegal. But now she had nothing but disgust for gambling and the men who perpetuated it. Too many lives had been ruined by the habit.

And many more would certainly follow suit. Even murder.

She was convinced that the three deaths had something to do with the gambling houses. What if Wrotham were a gambler also, and had frequented the gambling houses, somehow discovering the identity of the owners. If he had suffered a loss comparable with Baxter's devastating misfortune, he might have hoped to recoup his money by blackmailing the partners. Or one partner such as Lionel Fitzhammer.

Wrotham would then have to be silenced. Jeanette might have found out about the murder and confided in Peebles, with whom she was apparently enamored, in which case Peebles might have confronted Fitzhammer, who then had to silence them both.

It was a possible solution, and pleased with herself, Cecily uttered a small sigh of satisfaction. That certainly made more sense than all her other scenarios, and would justify her conviction that none of the deaths was an accident.

Now the problem was, how to verify her suspicions, much less prove them. Inspector Cranshaw was hardly going to pay any attention to her vague theories, unless she had something substantial to provoke his interest.

Something else occurred to her. Something that disturbed her a great deal. If her suspicions were correct, then Fitzhammer was a very dangerous man. He apparently had no reservations about killing a close associate, not to mention an innocent young girl. It was entirely possible he had killed Wrotham because of what he knew. If Lady Lucille had been close to Barry Wrotham, then her life could very well be in danger, too. If Fitzhammer should decide that Lucille might suspect him and was a threat to him, he would have no hesitation in killing her as well.

No matter how vague her suspicions might still be, it was her duty to warn Lady Lucille, and Sir John Gilroy as well, that they could very well be keeping company with a mass murderer. Of course, that would mean she'd have to reveal what she knew about the Cureagambler partnership, but it couldn't be helped. It was up to her to see that another murder did not take place.

Having come to that conclusion, she finally allowed herself to fall asleep.

The next morning Baxter was still acting cold toward her, though he did answer her comments with a grunt or a nod. Somewhat encouraged by this first sign of thawing, she approached him as he was about to shave his chin.

One of the maids had brought a jug of hot water to their suite, and he was using the last of it in the washbasin. At the moment he was peering into the mirror at his lathered face.

As he brandished the long blade of his razor, about to stroke it down his cheek, Cecily said tentatively, "I've remembered what it was I'd forgotten yesterday."

She took his grunt for consent to continue and quickly told him about her conversation with Fitzhammer and the brakes on Peebles's car. When she received no response to that, she launched into her speculation of what might have happened, and why Fitzhammer might have seen fit to kill three people.

Baxter appeared to be listening as he scraped his chin and throat with the razor, though he kept his gaze squarely on the mirror in front of him.

"I think I should warn Sir John and Lady Lucille," she

said as she came to the end of her story. "If I'm right, then Lionel Fitzhammer is a very dangerous man. I think they should be aware that he could be a threat to them, especially Lady Lucille."

"*If* you are right," Baxter said pointedly. "If you are mistaken, as you so often are, you could be exposing yourself to a great deal of embarrassment. You will also offend some very influential members of this club, whose loss your cousin Edward would surely resent. Not that I expect you to heed my advice, Cecily, but if I were you, I would think long and deeply before you embark on such a dubious mission."

"Then what do you suggest I do?"

His glance at her was heavy with scorn. "Since when did you take notice of what I might advise? I see no point in offering my opinion, since you no doubt have already made up your mind and, in spite of what I might think, will indubitably take matters into your own hands. All I can ask is that you consider the consequences of your actions. And now, if you will excuse me, I have work to do."

"You are not taking breakfast with me?"

"I'll have something sent to the office."

Miserably she watched him head for the door. "Is there any word on the state of our finances?"

He paused and without looking at her muttered, "Contrary to what you might think, miracles are not performed every day, even at Christmastime. Nothing has changed. The house will be sold to cover the debt. I am . . . sorry." The door closed behind him with a snap.

She twisted her lips in a wry grimace. At least he

expressed some regret. It was a start in the right direction. Patience, that's what it would take. A good deal of patience on her part. She could only hope he wouldn't keep her waiting too long. She couldn't bear the thought of spending Christmas at odds with him.

She was about to follow him out when a tap on the door announced the arrival of Gertie, whose engaging grin went a long way to lifting Cecily's spirits.

"Just wanted to let you know, m'm, there's a gentleman waiting to speak to you on the telephone. I think he's ringing all the way from a foreign country, 'cos I heard the operator speaking to someone with a funny accent."

"I wonder if it's Michael, or Andrew." She hadn't heard from her sons in so long. The thought of talking to one of them right now was like a candle lighting up the dark.

"I don't think so, m'm. The operator said it were that Mr. Sandringham what bought the Pennyfoot."

"Edward? Oh, dear." For a moment Cecily was tempted to have Gertie tell Edward that she had gone out for the day. Things were bound to be awkward. She didn't want to worry him with the news that three deaths had occurred in as many weeks, but on the other hand, he should be told. Perhaps Baxter . . .

Shaking her head, she said briskly, "I'll come down right away, Gertie, thank you."

She hurried out the door and closed it behind her. "How are you all managing in the kitchen?" she asked as she followed Gertie to the head of the stairs.

"Very well, m'm, thank you. Mrs. Chubb has got everyone running around like a bloody blue-ass fly, but she's getting things done on time, which is what counts."

Gertie hesitated at the top of the stairs. "I know this isn't the time, m'm, but when you have a moment, I'd like a word with you if I may?"

"Of course, Gertie. I'll come down to the kitchen just as soon as I'm free."

"Thank you, m'm." The maid sped down the stairs ahead of her and disappeared around the turning.

Cecily frowned after her, wondering what was coming next. No doubt Gertie had seen enough of kitchen work. She was more than likely about to ask to be released from her duties. Not that she could blame her, Cecily thought desolately, but her absence would leave a huge gap. What's more, without Gertie's strong arms and brazen confidence to help things along, Mrs. Chubb might well decide to desert her post as well.

Cecily's stomach was tied up in knots by the time she arrived in the foyer to answer the telephone. Edward was bound to ask how they were faring. She could hardly blurt out to him that three people had died and the house-keeper had walked out on them, leaving them to the mercy of good friends who were now reaching the limit of their goodwill.

Her hand actually shook as she took the receiver and placed it to her ear. After speaking to the operator, who appeared to be in conversation with another faraway operator, there followed a series of buzzes, whistles, and shrieks, then a faint echo of Edward's voice crackled on the line. "Cecily? Cecily? Drat this interference. Is that you, Cecily? This is Edward."

"Edward, hello! It's good to hear from you."

She pressed the receiver closer to her ear as Edward

spoke again through all the crackling and buzzing. "Can't hear you, too well, so I'll make this brief. I'm off to Bermuda . . . probably be there for a while. I need to . . ." His voice disappeared beneath a barrage of buzzing and whistling.

She waited for an anxious moment or two, then shouted, "Edward? Hello? Hello!"

The buzzing quieted for a moment and once more Edward's voice could be faintly heard. "Cecily? Need you to find a new manager. All right? I'll ring you again after Christmas. Hope you have . . ."

This time the crackling went on even longer, then finally cut off. The operator's voice sounded so loud in her ear Cecily almost dropped the telephone. "I'm sorry, madam," she said, "but we have lost the connection."

"That's all right," Cecily said quickly. "Thank you, operator." She replaced the receiver and smiled at the desk clerk, who had been doing his best to look as if he couldn't hear a word she'd said.

Weak with relief, she made her way back to the stairs. She'd been saved the embarrassment of having to explain to Edward, in front of anyone who happened to be passing by, the events that had been taking place since she had arrived. Not that the deaths, or Miss Bunkle's defection for that matter, were much of a secret. Still, they weren't things she wanted to shout about.

She could have talked to Edward in Baxter's office, of course. It would have been more private. But frankly, the thought of facing that formidable stony face again that morning was more than she could tolerate.

She supposed she should let him know about Edward's

request to find a new manager. Then again, this probably wasn't a good time to give him that news. Better to wait until he had recovered his good nature.

She forced herself to stop thinking about her angry husband and concentrated instead on the beautiful work Madeline had put into the decorations. The stair bannisters had been swathed in fir and holly, and smelled divine. Huge red ribbons clung to the holly boughs, matching the firm red berries nestled among the shiny green leaves. Tiny sprigs of mistletoe peeked out at intervals, which would no doubt arouse Phoebe's contempt when she saw them.

Which reminded her, she hadn't seen the tree in the library since Madeline had decorated it. She would do that just as soon as she'd spoken to Sir John and had that word with Gertie that she'd promised. If Madeline had taken as much trouble with the tree as she had everywhere else, it would be quite a sight to see.

She missed her friends, Cecily realized as she climbed the stairs to the first floor. As soon as she had spoken to Sir John, she would send messages inviting both Madeline and Phoebe to tea that afternoon in her suite. They could sit and relax, gossip a little, and perhaps for a short while she could forget her troubles.

Feeling more cheered than she had in quite a while, she reached the top of the landing and headed down toward Sir John Gilroy's suite.

Her light tap on the door was answered by Lady Lucille, who seemed a little put out upon greeting her. Her eyes were watery and her red nose looked painfully raw from an overuse of a handkerchief.

In spite of her malady she still managed to look elegant,

though her hair still draped her face in that peculiar style, which really wasn't suitable for day wear, Cecily thought uncharitably. "I trust your cold is improving?" she inquired.

"It is a little better, *merci, madame.*"

"I'm happy to hear that. If there's anything you need, please let us know." She glanced into the room. "I'd like a word with Sir John," she added. "Is he here?"

"No, *Madame* Baxter, he is not here. He is in the card room, as always, with Mr. Chatsworth and Mr. Fitzhammer. Even the death of his very good friend does not prevent him from spending his time with those card games. *C'est si tragique.*"

Cecily stared at her. Until that moment she had forgotten that part of her conversation with Lucille earlier. She had been too engrossed with the woman's confession that Wrotham had been her lover. But now she remembered something else Lucille had mentioned. *I do not understand why he needs all this extra work and demands. I tell him over and over again, I wish the others would leave him alone.* Of course. Now she understood. The thing that kept him so busy was his partnership in Cureagambler.

Fitzhammer had already killed one of the partners. Could he possibly be planning on killing the others, in order to gain sole ownership of Cureagambler? It was something she hadn't thought of before, but now it seemed a distinct possibility.

"Lady Lucille," she said, advancing uninvited into the room. "I must speak with Sir John as soon as possible. It is a matter of great urgency. His life might very well be in danger."

Lucille's eyes opened wide, and she clutched her throat. "Whatever do you mean?"

"The accident that took the life of Roger Peebles."
Cecily drew a deep breath. "I have reason to believe that it
was not an accident. I must warn you to be on your guard.
Your husband, too. It is imperative that I speak with him
about this. Do you have any idea how long he plans to be
in the card room?"

Lucille's face looked white and drawn. She shook her
head, and her lips trembled when she whispered, "About
an hour, *madame*. No longer, I should think. He plans to
dine with me in the dining room." She gestured at her
ankle. "I am not feeling well, and I still cannot walk far
on my own. In any case, my husband prefers to accompany me when I am in public."

"In that case, perhaps you would be good enough to
ask him to meet me. I have to pay a visit to the kitchen,
but I shall be in the library after a while. I shall wait there
until Sir John can join me."

"I will be happy to pass on your message." Lady Lucille
limped to the door and held it open. "Thank you for your
concern, Mrs. Baxter. I pray that you are mistaken in your
fears. I cannot imagine anyone wishing to hurt my husband, or Mr. Peebles for that matter."

"Or Jeanette and Barry Wrotham, either. Nevertheless,
someone did."

Lucille's lips were colorless. "Barry, too? No, I cannot
believe . . ."

She swayed on her feet and Cecily looked at her in
alarm. "Lady Lucille, if you are feeling faint, I can send for
some salts . . ."

"No, *madame,* thank you." Her voice was stronger now.
"It was momentary, that is all." She turned her head as a

sneeze interrupted her, then added a little thickly, "I am quite well. Please, do not concern yourself."

"Very well." Reluctantly, Cecily moved to the door. She couldn't help feeling that she was making a mistake leaving this vulnerable woman alone, yet she could not spare the time to sit with her until Sir John returned. "If you should need assistance," she told her, "please don't hesitate to summon one of the maids. They'll be only too happy to oblige."

"*Merci, madame,*" Lucille murmured. "You are too kind."

Still feeling uneasy, Cecily made for the stairs and descended them swiftly. Her urge to confide in Baxter was strong, but she decided to delay it until she had spoken to Sir John. She intended only to warn him, since she could not accuse Fitzhammer of murder without more proof. But she also nursed a hope that the conversation might reveal something more tangible on which to hang her suspicions.

At that moment she would welcome anything that would make her case stronger when she presented it to Baxter later. If only she could convince him that her actions were justified, and that she was doing her utmost to apprehend a genuine murderer, he might find it easier to forgive her for pushing him into the situation that had cost them both so much.

For the time being, however, she had to take advantage of the morning lull to speak with Gertie, which could very well add yet another burden to their mounting concerns. Holding on to the hope that Gertie and Mrs. Chubb would at least see them through Christmas, Cecily headed for the kitchen.

The maids were seated around the main table, chatting among themselves as they shared creamy coffee and huge slices of Dundee cake. Mrs. Chubb and Gertie sat apart from them, their chairs drawn up in front of the stove. The doors were open, and emitted a fierce heat as the flames roared and rattled up the wide chimney pipe.

Cecily was surprised to see Samuel seated with them. She gave him a delighted smile as he leapt to his feet. "I thought you would be in the George and Dragon, Samuel," she told him. "It's past opening time already."

Samuel shrugged. "Gertie told me you was having a word with her this morning, m'm. I wanted to be in on it."

Worried now, Cecily took the empty chair closest to the stove. "Well, this sounds serious. You had better tell me what this is all about."

Samuel and Gertie looked at Mrs. Chubb.

"Don't look at me," she said sharply. "You go first, Gertie. Seeing as how you're the one who started all this."

Gertie's cheeks were flushed, though Cecily couldn't tell if it was from nervousness or the heat from the stove, which was already beginning to toast her own knees through the thick folds of her skirt.

"Well, m'm," Gertie began, "it's like this." She wound an apron string around her finger, then unwound it again.

"Go *on*, Gertie!" Mrs. Chubb said irritably. "Get on with it. We haven't got all day."

Gertie sent her a quick glance, then blurted out, "It's Ross, m'm. He's been walking around the grounds, you see, and well, now that he's sold the business and everything—"

Cecily uttered a muffled exclamation. "Of course. He must be upset. I'm so sorry."

"Oh, it's all right, m'm, really. It were getting too flipping much for him anyway. Riding around them streets in the snow on his bicycle. Couldn't keep up with it anymore, that's the trouble. Anyway, since he don't have no bleeding—"

"Gertie, you promised!"

She sent Mrs. Chubb a lethal glare. "I'm doing me flipping best."

"Just tell me," Cecily said quickly. "What's wrong with Ross?"

"Oh, nothing's wrong, m'm." Gertie's smile was lovely to see. "Well, he's tired, of course. Exhausted, the doctor said. Nothing what a bloody rest won't do him good."

Mrs. Chubb opened her mouth to speak, then shut it again when Gertie said hurriedly, "All right, I'm bleeding getting there, ain't I." She took a deep breath. "My Ross needs a job, m'm. He was wondering if you'd take him on as gardener. He's been looking around, like I said, and he can see what needs to be done. Bloody lot of work, so he says. He's really good at his job, he is, m'm. Mrs. Chubb will tell you. He does marvelous things—"

Cecily interrupted her. "Gertie, I would simply love to hire Ross as a gardener. I'm sure Edward would be overjoyed to have such an expert in his employ, but what about your home in Scotland? You can't live there without your husband."

Gertie shrugged. "Never did like it there, did I. I only stayed there because of Ross. I'd rather be living in Badgers End than anywhere else on earth, and that's the truth. Besides, me babies are bloody English, aren't they. They don't belong in Scotland. Different bleeding lot they are up there, m'm. Don't even talk English, half of 'em."

Cecily shook her head, bewildered by this turn of events. "Well, I'll be happy to talk to Ross, of course, and if this is what he really wants, I'm quite sure we can work something out."

"Well, that's not all, m'm." Gertie chewed on her bottom lip, then mumbled in a rush, "Me and Mrs. Chubb want to work here again, too, m'm. We missed it, we really did. Ross says as how he'd be all right with it as long as he worked here, too. And Daisy said she'd stay here as well, and look after the twins for me. With both Ross and me working, I could afford to pay her a proper wage. So I s'pose it's the three of us what want a job."

"Four," Samuel said, surprising them all.

Gertie looked at him in amazement. "Go on! You, too? What about your job in London? What about Doris?"

Samuel shrugged. "Doris don't care about me. She never did, really. She just needed a friend." He sent a worried glance at Cecily. "I'm not supposed to say nothing yet, but Raymond's thinking about going back to London with her. Doris reckons he can get a job with the theater. That'll leave you without a stable manager, m'm, and since I know about motor cars, well, I thought . . ." His voice trailed off, leaving them all sitting in silence.

Cecily did her best to gather her thoughts. She tried to speak, but the tightness in her throat prevented her for several seconds. Finally, she cleared her throat. "I think I need to remind you that Baxter and I won't be here for much longer—" She stopped short as a stupendous idea occurred to her.

"Oh, that's all right, madam," Mrs. Chubb said quickly. "We know that. We'll all miss you dreadfully, of course, when you go back to London, but you can come and visit us sometimes, and although it won't be the same without you, we'll still be here at the Pennyfoot."

"Yeah," Samuel said with a grin. He held up his cup as if offering a toast. "Just like old times."

CHAPTER

❈21❈

Overwhelmed by Gertie's surprising announcement, Cecily had some trouble finding words to say. She would have to keep her marvelous idea to herself for the time being, at least until she'd had time to discuss it with Baxter. The thought of everyone coming back to the Pennyfoot, however, was too wonderful to believe.

"I . . . can't tell you how happy this makes me," she said at last. "I shall have to address the issue with Baxter, of course, and we must have the final word from Mr. Sandringham, but in view of the difficulty in finding good people, I really can't see how either one of them could possibly refuse. I'm sure they will both be delighted to welcome all of you back to the Pennyfoot Hotel. I mean Country Club."

Gertie jumped to her feet with a yelp of joy. "I just knew this was going to be a bleeding great Christmas. What'd I tell you!" She nudged Mrs. Chubb's arm in her excitement. Unfortunately, the housekeeper was holding a cup of coffee in that hand, and the hot liquid spilled all over her lap.

Cecily used the ruckus that followed to quietly make her escape. Excited herself now, she rushed up the steps, across the foyer, and down the hallway to Baxter's office.

Without bothering to knock, she flung open the door and marched inside. Eager to share her idea with him, she'd forgotten all about his foul mood.

He looked up, one hand holding his pen poised above an open ledger. "What the devil—?" Dropping the pen, he surged to his feet.

"I have so much to tell you." She ignored his scowl, and plopped down on her chair. "So much I don't know where to begin."

"Don't tell me," he said dryly. "The entire male population of this club have been brutally murdered, and you have deduced that Father Christmas is responsible." He sat down and reached for his pen again.

Her smile faded. "I should think you would have more sensitivity than to jest about such matters."

He sighed. "You are quite right. My apologies. So what is it this time?"

Quickly, she informed him that Gertie, Mrs. Chubb, and Samuel had applied for permanent employment at the club.

He seemed pleased about it, though all he said was, "We will have to notify Edward, of course. He will have the final say. I'll send him a telegram."

"Well, that's the other part of it." She leaned forward, her hands clasped together. "Edward rang me on the telephone this morning."

He looked astounded. "From South Africa?"

"Well, I'm not really certain where he was ringing from, though it sounded more like France. I swear the operator on his end was French."

"Well, what did Edward want?"

"Oh, yes!" She beamed hopefully at him. "Well, he said he was being sent to Bermuda and he would be there for quite a while and he wanted us to hire a new manager."

Baxter frowned. "That might take a while."

"Exactly what I was thinking." In her eagerness she rose to her feet, forcing him to do the same. "Baxter, this could be the solution to our problems. Why can't we be the managers? It worked well for us before, and you know how I adore being here and you love being in a position of authority. We would have a place to stay while we get our finances in order—it would be too, too perfect."

The expression in his eyes worried her. "Please sit down, Cecily."

She sat, waiting anxiously for him to seat himself. For a long moment he said nothing, but sat tapping his pen on the paper. At last he sat back in his chair and smoothed a hand over his hair, a sign that Cecily recognized well. She braced herself.

"I'm going to give you the benefit of the doubt," he began, "and dismiss the possibility that you engineered this entire situation."

She stared at him in disbelief. "How can you possibly say that? I was not responsible for Barry Wrotham's death, nor Jeanette's. Certainly not Roger Peebles's death, either. How can you accuse me of manipulating everything?"

He shrugged. "You have to admit, it has all fallen rather nicely into your lap. You have never been truly happy away from the Pennyfoot, and it seems you have found a way to remedy that. I would be uncommonly suspicious of everything that has happened, were it not for the fact that I have to believe even you would be incapable of trickery on such a grand scale."

Relieved, she tried her best to smile. "You give me far too much credit, my dear husband."

"Nevertheless, I can't help feeling you had a hand in this somewhere."

"It is pure providence, I assure you." She watched his face, hopeful that she had won him over. "So you agree?"

"To what?"

"That taking over the management of the Pennyfoot would be the perfect solution to our troubles."

"No, I do not agree." He laid down his pen. "The perfect solution would be that none of this had happened, and that I still had a house and a business of my own. I do not relish the thought of working for Edward, managing a country club, at the beck and call of every pesky guest who feels it his right to make trivial complaints and waste my time. No, Cecily, it is not my idea of a solution."

She took a deep breath. "Well, then, let *me* do the managing. I can hire an accountant to keep the books, and I can manage everything else."

"And what am I supposed to do in the meantime? Sit and twiddle my thumbs?"

"No, of course not. I would certainly not expect you to while away your life unoccupied."

"Then what do you suggest?"

"There is no reason why you cannot conduct your business from here. You can use the bedroom in our suite for an office. It's certainly large enough. We would have a telephone put in there and you can be in contact with your associates just as you were in London. You might have to travel to the city now and then, but think how much your clients would adore spending a night at the seashore to conduct their business. You could start a whole new trend in business travel."

She had caught his interest—she could see it in his eyes. For a moment hope leapt like the flames up a chimney, then he said brusquely, "It's out of the question, Cecily. How the devil do you concoct such harebrained schemes?"

Dismayed, she rose to her feet. "But Bax, darling—"

His roar startled her. "Don't 'Bax, darling' me! I will not allow my wife to work, even if you are the cause of our financial ruin. Now, leave me! I have to finish these infernal accounts. Just leave me in peace."

Angry herself now, she placed both palms on the desk and leaned into him, nose to nose. "You had better watch that sharp tongue of yours, Hugh Baxter, *and* that insufferable attitude, or I might just be tempted to leave you altogether." With that, she spun around and headed for the door.

Unfortunately, her heel caught in the hem of her skirt, tripping her. Her outstretched hand slammed into the door, causing her to gasp in pain. Incensed now, she tugged the offending door open, ignoring Baxter's quick query of concern. To blazes with him. If she had broken her hand, she would not give him the satisfaction of knowing it.

More upset at ruining her exit than of any damage to her fingers, she stomped down the hallway to the library. Perhaps a few minutes admiring the magnificence of a Christmas tree would calm her.

Carefully she pushed open the door to the library and peeked inside. To her relief, the room was empty. She really wasn't in any mood for polite conversation. All she wanted was to have a few moments to herself, where she could cool her temper and collect her thoughts.

She wasn't about to give up on the idea of taking the manager's position. She was well qualified, having owned the Pennyfoot at one time, and even though Baxter would be attending to his business, he would be there to advise and guide her, should she need it. In any case, there had been a long period, when he had left her employ and moved to London, when she had managed the hotel quite well without him. Thanks to an incompetent replacement manager.

As for his objection to her working, that was adding insult to injury. He knew very well how she felt about such matters. Her association with the Women's Movement had been a bone of contention with him, but he had never openly opposed her opinions and beliefs in that respect.

Women were entitled to do what they wished, and if working for a living appealed to them, no one had a right to prevent them from doing so. Not even their husbands. Especially not their husbands. She had given up all thoughts of working upon marrying him because it was her choice. Even though she had allowed him to think it was his decision.

But now the decision was up to her, and the more he opposed her, the more determined she would become.

Sooner or later he would see things her way. At least, she very much hoped he would.

Her heart aching, she wandered over to the tree. She needed the solace of gazing at its lush branches, now laden with delicate ornaments and pretty velvet bows.

As she came closer, however, she could smell something other than the fragrant pine she had enjoyed earlier. A smell of burning? Surely . . . ?

She advanced around the side of the tree to where the back was hidden against the wall. In disbelief she stared at the tiny flames licking along the branches. Someone, it seemed, had lit the candles on the back of the tree. Not only that, but several of them were tipped over, so that the wicks lay on the dry needles. Who on earth . . . ?

Startled, she watched the flames suddenly leap to the branch above. Thoroughly alarmed now, she attempted to blow out the candles, but it was too late. Even as she gathered a deep breath, a loud pop sounded above her head, and the entire top of the tree became engulfed in flames.

Black, oily smoke poured from the melting ornaments, and glass popped and shattered at her feet. She backed away, aware that there was nothing she could do except summon help as quickly as possible.

She looked around for the bellpull, but it had been removed for some reason. No doubt Edward had thought it less troublesome for the kitchen staff if they were not constantly summoned to the library. She would have to go back to Baxter for help.

The smoke was already stinging her throat as she hurried across the room to the door. Grasping the handle, she turned it and tugged. To her amazement, the door refused to budge. In disbelief, she rattled the handle and tugged harder. There was no doubt about it, someone had locked the door.

Cecily frowned. The library was never locked as far as she knew. It certainly hadn't been when the Pennyfoot was a hotel. The key to it was on the set of master keys behind the reception desk, and presumably a copy on the set that was kept in the manager's suite. Someone must have used one of the keys to lock the library door behind her.

Turning back, she stared at the burning tree, now completely enveloped in the greedy flames. Whoever had lit the candles had to be the same person who had locked the door.

For a moment she thought it might be Lionel Fitzhammer, but then, in a burst of enlightenment, she realized who it was who wanted her dead. Of course. How stupid of her. She'd had all the clues right in front of her and hadn't put them together. Until now. Now that it could very well be too late.

Fearful for her life, she lifted her skirts and ran for the French windows. As she'd expected, they were jammed shut. A walking stick had been thrust through the handles. The smoke was choking her, burning her lungs. Heat from the burning tree made her feel faint.

Coughing uncontrollably, her eyes streaming with tears, she reached for her shoe. Her only hope lay in breaking the window and removing the cane. Even as she raised her hand with the heel of her shoe poised to strike, the strength sapped out of her knees and she sank to the floor.

As the darkness whirled around her, she heard the tree crash to the floor. She thought she heard Baxter's beloved voice calling her name. "Forgive me, my darling," she whispered, and knew no more.

*   *   *

Baxter took the kitchen stairs two at a time and strode swiftly across the foyer. He'd been looking for Cecily for the last several minutes. No one seemed to have any knowledge of her whereabouts. He'd sat for a while after she'd left his office earlier, fighting his own dratted pride. His anger had faded the moment she'd smashed her hand into the door, his concern for her easily outweighing his temper.

She'd left without a backward glance, and he'd nursed his hurt feelings awhile longer before surging to his feet. Enough was enough. It was time to make amends with his wife and put an end to this ridiculous squabbling.

If he were honest, he'd have to admit that her solution to their current difficulties held some merit. He hated the thought of losing his business, after working so long and hard to build it up. He was just beginning to make a name for himself in the city, and this time away had already cost him some transactions. He was itching to get back to it, and with Cecily managing the club, with his limited help, he could easily pursue his profession from Badgers End.

On his way to the suite, he'd faced the fact that no matter how he felt about his wife being employed, he was unlikely to prevent Cecily from doing what she wanted to do. As long as her work didn't interfere with their marriage, he could tolerate it. At least they would still be together under one roof, which was all he really could ask.

Disappointed at finding the suite empty, he had proceeded to the dining room. Moira had told him she'd seen Cecily go into the kitchen, so he'd gone straight there, only to be told that she'd left a few minutes earlier.

There was only one place where she could be now, and that was the library. As he hurried down the hallway, he was aware of a strange sense of urgency, and he quickened his pace.

He saw the smoke wreathing from beneath the closed door when he was still a few strides away. Raymond was coming toward him from the opposite direction, and Baxter shouted out to him. "Get everybody down here with buckets of water. We have a fire in the library. Now!"

After one startled glance at him, Raymond raced for the foyer, yelling at the top of his voice.

Thankfully Baxter heard him tell the clerk to ring for the fire brigade, though he knew it would be some time before they would arrive. His heart pounded hard in his chest when he thought what this could mean. If the fire took hold, the Pennyfoot could burn to the ground.

He turned the door handle, and was stunned when he realized it was locked. Apparently alerted by Samuel, two of the footmen were rushing toward him, and he yelled at them. "Help me break this down. All together, with your shoulders. Now!"

Within seconds the door burst open, sending all three of them stumbling into the room. One horrified glance told him the story. The room was filled with smoke. The tree had overturned and was lying across the fireplace. Fortunately, a good deal of the smoke was drifting up the gaping chimney, and the marble hearth had prevented most of the flames from reaching the floorboards.

He saw one corner of the carpet smoldering, and rushed to stamp it out. It was then that he saw her. His wife, lying on her side, her eyes closed and her dear face heavily smudged with smoke.

With an agonized cry, he leapt to her side and gathered her into his arms. Weak with relief, he saw she was still breathing, and he scooped her up in his arms.

He barely had time to register that a walking stick had been thrust through the handles of the French windows, before he lifted his foot and smashed it against the doors. They flew open, breaking the stick in two. With a muttered curse, he stepped through them and carried her into the life-giving fresh air.

Behind him in the library he heard people shouting to each other, while across the rose garden several men ran toward him with buckets filled with water, presumably from the fish pond.

In the distance, he could hear the faint clanging of the fire bell. They must have harnessed the horses in record time. Then he forgot about everything except for the white, lifeless look on the face of his beloved wife.

She was cold. So cold. Which was odd, because the last thing she remembered was the heat of the flaming tree. The fire! She had to escape!

She opened her eyes, and blinked. Instead of the burning room she'd expected to see, she saw instead the wide expanse of a gray sky. A snowflake drifted down and landed on her nose. She barely felt it. She was too engrossed in looking at her husband's face.

She was lying on the ground and he was huddled over her, chafing her cold hands in his warm ones, with tears clearly visible in his wonderful gray eyes.

"Thank God," he kept whispering over and over again. She was aware of several people standing around, murmuring expressions of relief. . . . and then they had disappeared and only Baxter remained.

Her throat hurt like the devil, but she managed to speak. "The last time we did this," she said unsteadily, "I seem to remember you proposing."

His smile warmed her heart. "Did you accept?"

"I think so." Her voice sounded odd, and she cleared her throat, then winced when the effort stung. She caught her breath. "The fire?"

"The fire brigade is here. They have saved the hotel, but I'm afraid the library and the suite above it will have to be renovated. The hallway, too, will need some attention, but we were lucky. The fireplace saved quite a lot of damage."

He reached for her suddenly, gathering her into his arms. "Oh, Cecily, what I fool I've been. What a stubborn, selfish fool. My pride would not allow me to take the blame for losing our home, and so I blamed you. Then, when I thought . . . all I could think about was how would I possibly survive without you?"

Vastly appreciating the warmth of his body, Cecily murmured, "You would survive quite well without my reckless behavior to impede you."

He sighed, resting his chin on her head. "Ah, but it is reckless behavior such as yours that brightens my world, and fills it with the spirit of adventure. Were it not for you, my love, I should be a lonely, miserable recluse, poring over my accounts like Ebenezer Scrooge."

She managed a hoarse laugh. "I shall remind you of this moment the next time you howl at me for landing you in trouble." She sobered, lifting her head to look at him. "I am truly sorry, Bax, for all the trouble I've caused. I am devastated that we have to sell the house, and I quite understand if you do not wish to stay here at the Pennyfoot. After all, it will serve as a reminder of everything we have lost."

"Perhaps, but then again, the Pennyfoot owes us a debt. This would be a good way to collect it."

She stared at him. "Are you saying you will stay on here as manager?"

"No." He smiled at her. "I'm saying that you will manage the Pennyfoot, as you so ably have done in the past . . ."

"With your help."

"And without it if I recall."

"And you will continue with your business?"

"Precisely."

"That is wonderful news." Now she really felt better. "There's just one thing I have left to do now."

He looked concerned. "I don't think you should be attempting to do anything just yet. You have just been through a traumatic experience. You need to rest."

"I will," Cecily told him. "Just as soon as we have taken care of one small task."

He shook his head. "What is so important that it cannot wait until tomorrow?"

She sat up, then waited for her head to clear before allowing him to help her to her feet. She felt a little weak, and none too steady, but she was determined to see this through. "First of all," she said more firmly, "you must ring the police station and ask Inspector Cranshaw to get here just as soon as he possibly can."

Baxter frowned. "The inspector?"

"Yes." Cecily lifted the hem of her skirt and stepped gingerly across the porch to peek in the shattered French windows. The scorched walls and burned curtains made her feel like weeping. Then she noticed the shattered stick at her feet. She had been extremely fortunate. She could well have died in there.

"Come," Baxter said, taking her arm. "We'll go around through the front door. And you can tell me why it is so urgent to send for the inspector."

"Because," she said as they walked briskly through the rose garden, "we are on our way to confront a particularly devious murderer."

CHAPTER
❦ 22 ❦

Cecily refused to answer Baxter's questions as he followed her up the stairs. She didn't want to argue with him again, as she knew he surely would do if she told him of her suspicions.

The smell of smoke clung to everything, overwhelming the fragrance of the pine that had pleased her so much. "We must open every window in the entire place," she told him as they reached the first landing. "Just as soon as possible. I want to smell Christmas again."

"I'll see to it," he promised her. "But right now I need to know where—" He broke off as she paused in front of the Gilroys' suite. "Sir John? Surely you don't suspect him of murder? This is ridiculous . . ."

"Shh!" She put a finger over his lips. "Just listen and

observe. I promise you, everything will be very clear in just a few moments." Without giving him time to argue further, she tapped on the door.

At first there was no answer to her summons, and she rapped again, louder this time.

"He is most likely in the card room—" Baxter began, but then the door opened a mere crack.

Lady Lucille's voice sounded muffled when she said, "Who is it?"

Cecily unceremoniously pushed the door open. "It is I, Lady Lucille."

The other woman fell back, her hand covering her mouth. Her eyes were wide with shock and disbelief, giving Cecily a grim sense of satisfaction.

"*Mon Dieu!*" Lucille muttered. "You are alive. I thought . . . I was told . . ." She recovered quickly. "I am so happy to see you are unhurt, *madame*. I heard about the fire. My husband . . . he came to me and demanded that we leave, but by the time we reached the ground floor, the fire had been put out. Such a shame to spoil the Christmas, *non?*"

Without answering her, Cecily barged into the room.

Lucille took several steps backward. "My husband is not here, *madame*. As you can see. He went back to the card room to finish his game."

Baxter hovered anxiously in the doorway. "Well, as long as he's not here, Cecily?"

"I'm not here to see Sir John." Cecily advanced on the cowering woman. "I believe Lady Lucille knows quite well why I am here."

Lucille violently shook her head. "*Non, non, je ne sais pas!*"

"Then I shall enlighten you." Cecily gestured at Baxter. "Perhaps it would be better if you came inside and closed the door."

Obviously reluctant, he did what she asked. "Cecily, if you are mistaken—"

"I am not mistaken, I promise you." Cecily faced Lucille again. "You lit the candles on the Christmas tree, knowing I went there to meet your husband. You were afraid of what I might tell him. You took the key from the reception desk and locked the library door behind me, then you jammed the French windows with your cane."

"I certainly did not, *madame*. How dare you accuse me—"

"You killed Jeanette, did you not?"

Again the violent shake of the head. "*Non, non, madame*. You are mistaken. I know not what you mean."

"I think you do." With a swift movement, Cecily reached out and dragged back a portion of Lucille's hair to reveal a deep scratch gouged into the woman's forehead. "An unusual style, Lady Lucille, but most assuredly not from Paris. I remember seeing an article in a magazine just a few days ago. The French have been cutting their hair quite short all year. You combed your hair in that peculiar style to hide the scratch that Jeanette gave you when you fought with her."

"I did no such thing! I—"

"You took the knife from the kitchen and went to meet her in the equipment shed, where you cut her throat."

Lucille whimpered, and drew back. "I do not understand why you are saying these dreadful things to me," she whispered.

"Yes, you do." Cecily advanced on her, heedless of Baxter's muttered warning.

"*S'il vous plaît, madame,*" Lucille pleaded, her hand at her throat. "I did not—"

"That's how you caught Jeanette's cold," Cecily went on ruthlessly. "And it's my guess that you didn't turn your ankle on the stairs, but that your ankle was injured when you struggled with Jeanette. I also believe that you pushed Barry Wrotham down the well. He was going to tell your husband about your association with him."

"*Non!*"

"As for Roger Peebles, he must have found out about Barry Wrotham. Did he threaten to tell Sir John, too? Is that why you killed him?"

"I did not kill him!" Lucille whirled on her. "It was Lionel. He did something to the brakes, I don't know what . . ."

Cecily withdrew the hand she'd kept hidden behind her back until now. "This is part of your cane, Lady Lucille. I recognized it. I'm giving it to the inspector when he arrives, which should be any minute now. You will go to prison for the murder of Jeanette and Barry Wrotham."

"Ah, Barry. *Mon amour.*" Lucille sank onto a chair, weeping profusely.

After a moment's hesitation, Baxter stepped forward and offered her his handkerchief.

She took it, and blew her nose. Then, between sobs, she said brokenly, "I never meant to hurt Barry. I loved him. He made me feel like a beautiful woman again. I was devastated when he died."

Cecily sat down opposite her and said, more gently now, "Tell me what happened."

Lucille gulped. "I know it would only be a matter of time before someone found out. It matters not, for nothing has been the same since Barry died. I care not if I go to prison, or if they hang me. I am dead inside without my Barry."

Cecily could almost feel sorry for her. "Then why did you kill him?"

Lucille sniffed, blew her nose again, then said softly, "It was an accident. We spent some wonderful afternoons in the farmhouse. It was all so cozy, so romantic. We had champagne, and sometimes I felt a little foolish, *oui?* Perhaps a little sorry for myself. One afternoon I told Barry that John spends all his time with his gambling houses, and never has time for me. I told him how he cares more for his partners than he does for his wife." She shook her head. "It was stupid, I know. It was supposed to always remain a secret. But I never imagined for a moment that Barry would use what I said against John."

"So Barry threatened to disclose Sir John's business dealings with Cureagambler."

Her eyebrows arched in surprise. "How did you know that name? How did you find out?"

"Never mind," Cecily said brusquely. "Go on with the story."

"Ah well, a few days after I told him, he said he had the money to start a new life. He wanted to buy a farm in Cornwall. He wanted me to run away with him. I could not do that. I loved him, *oui,* but I could not possibly live in a farmhouse cleaning the pigsty and cooking the meals. I told him I wanted everything to stay the same, but then he became angry. He left me alone, saying he was going to ruin my husband, so that John would not have the money to keep me in fine things. I ran after him. I begged him not to do it. He would not listen. I became angry myself. In my temper, I pushed him. So!" She lifted her palms and pushed them out in front of her. "He fell back against the well, he stumbled . . . and fell in . . ."

She began weeping again, and Cecily waited for her to control herself before saying, "And Jeanette found out what happened?"

Lucille shook her head. "No, she did not find out. She thought it was Roger who killed Barry."

Cecily frowned. "Why did she think that?"

Lucille dabbed at her eyes and blew her nose again. "After I told Barry about the gambling houses, he looked for . . . how you say? Ah, yes . . . evidence . . . to prove that John and the others had the gambling houses. He searched Roger's room and found papers, but Roger surprised him and caught him. Roger said he would call the police, but Barry told him he will tell everyone about the gambling houses and all of them would lose their seats on the Bench. He asked for money to keep quiet. Lots of money. So he could buy the farmhouse."

"I see," Cecily said slowly. "Then Barry was blackmailing Roger Peebles."

"That is what you call it, *oui*. But Jeanette, she must have been in the next room, listening. Because when Barry died, Jeanette went to Roger and said she would tell the police all about Cureagambler, and that he was giving Barry money to keep it quiet. She said she knew he had killed Barry and he would be arrested for murder unless he gave her the money."

"She wanted the money to have the pearls restrung," Cecily murmured.

Lucille looked puzzled. *"Pardon?"*

Cecily shook her head. "Never mind. But that doesn't explain why you had to kill Jeanette."

Lucille sat silent for a long moment, then in a voice heavy with weariness, she said, "Roger came to our suite. He was looking for John. He said he wanted to borrow money to keep Jeanette quiet about the gambling houses. He told me everything that happened. I was afraid. If he talked to John, he would find out about my rendevous with Barry and I could not allow it." She held her hands up in appeal. "What was I to do? If John knew I betrayed him, he would desert me. I would have nothing."

"So you killed Jeanette."

Lucille worried at her lip with her small, even teeth. "Roger made the appointment to meet Jeanette in the shed. I told him not to worry. I would talk to John and he would take care of everything." Tears started spilling down her cheeks. "I took the knife when no one was looking . . . I just wanted to frighten the girl, that is all. But she fought with me. I was afraid she would kill me . . . I had . . . to stop her. I raised the knife and . . ."

Cecily waited for her sobs to subside, then said gently, "That's why Roger Peebles had to die."

Lucille gulped and nodded. "It is wintertime. I did not think anyone would go into the shed until the spring. By then no one would know what happened or who killed her. But when she was found, Roger came to me. He was very upset. He thought John killed the maid and he told me he was going to see the constables that afternoon and tell them everything. I warned him he would lose everything as well, but he would not listen. He kept saying he would not be a part of murder."

"So you persuaded Lionel Fitzhammer to sabotage the brakes of his car," Cecily said, understanding at last.

Lucille nodded. She sent a quick, embarrassed glance at Baxter, then said in a low voice, "Lionel . . . he wanted . . . favors from me for a very long time. I told him Roger, he killed Jeanette and he deserved to die. I made him see we could not tell the constables, because everyone would know about Cureagambler. I promised him . . . just one night . . . in return. He was so besotted he agreed." She shuddered. "Thank heavens I have not yet had to fulfill that promise."

Baxter cleared his throat, and Cecily got to her feet. "It appears very likely you never will," she said. "I must ask you to remain here until the inspector arrives. Mr. Baxter will stand guard outside, just in case you should decide to leave without permission."

Lucille's misery was plain on her face when she looked up. "I am going nowhere, Mrs. Baxter. My life, it was over when Barry fell down the well. I knew it from that moment. I just did not want to believe it."

"I'm so sorry." Cecily nodded at Baxter, who opened the door for her, then followed her into the hallway. "It is better that you stay here," she told him. "Just in case, though I don't think she's going anywhere."

"You sounded genuine when you said you were sorry."

She sighed. "I do feel sorry for her. Everything that happened was because she made the mistake of falling in love with the wrong man. And even *that* wouldn't have happened if Sir John had paid less attention to his business interests and more to his wife."

Baxter caught her hand. "You could have died in that

library. I swear to you, Cecily, I will never neglect you for my business. Never."

She smiled sweetly at him. "Of course you won't, my dear Hugh. Because, quite simply, I won't allow it." She sailed off, preventing him from delivering the retort that was obviously hovering on his lips.

She had barely descended the stairs before P.C. Northcott arrived. He marched into the foyer, helmet slightly askew, notebook under his arm, and his chest puffed out with assumed importance.

"Mrs. Baxter," he announced the moment he caught sight of her. "I h'understand you 'ave h'apprehended one of your guests on suspicion of murder, is that right?"

"Not on suspicion, Sam," Cecily murmured. "I have a full confession. I trust the inspector is on his way?"

"Inspector Cranshaw has informed me he will arrive here within the hour. He asked me to keep an eye on things until he arrives."

"Well, the lady in question is confined to her suite." Cecily glanced at the grandfather clock. "As of now, her husband is unaware that she is being apprehended. I think perhaps you should inform him. You will find him in the card room."

Northcott seemed put out. "Well, as long as you have things under control so to speak, Mrs. B., I wonder if you might inform the gentleman. Ladies always do a better job of such delicate matters, that's what I always say."

Cecily sighed. "Very well. I left Baxter outside Lady Lucille's room to keep an eye on her. I'd be obliged if you would take his place and release him to get back to work. In the meantime I must hire someone to make repairs to the damaged rooms."

"Yes, I heard about the fire." Northcott rubbed his nose with the back of his fingers. "Nasty business that. Glad to see you're all right, Mrs. Baxter. So, it were one of them toffs, eh? And a lady, too. Would never have guessed that one. Not in a hundred years. You did it again, Mrs. B. The inspector will be pleased the case is solved." He leaned forward and added in a loud whisper, "I'd be much obliged if you'd put in a good word for me when you talk to him. Maybe tell him I gave you the idea, like?"

"I'll put in a good word for you," Cecily said, "if you promise never to call me 'Mrs. B.' again."

"Right you are. Sorry, m'm." He touched the rim of his helmet with his fingers. "Better get on with it, then. I'm hoping I'll have time for a quick visit to the kitchen. Got me mouth all ready for one of them mince pies, I have. I haven't had me elevenses yet, and I'm feeling a bit peckish, if you know what I mean."

"Well, I suppose Baxter can wait another minute or two." She started to move away, then added, "But I warn you, my husband has a nasty temper that is sure to explode if he's kept waiting too long."

"Gotcha, Mrs. B. . . . er . . . Baxter. Won't be more than a minute or two, I swear."

She watched him sprint for the kitchen steps, wondering what he'd say when he discovered Mrs. Chubb and Gertie back at their posts. She felt a little lift of her spirits when she envisioned telling them her good news. Perhaps, once this was all over, it would be a good Christmas after all.

At Cecily's request, the entire staff assembled in the ballroom late that afternoon. Having forgotten her invitation to Phoebe and Madeline, Cecily spent a few minutes recounting to them everything that had happened, then invited both her friends to join her for her official announcement.

Although Phoebe pestered her with questions, Cecily refused to tell either her or Madeline what the announcement would be, and they had to be content with joining the anxious group in the crowded ballroom.

Cecily was pleased to see a Christmas tree had been placed in two of the corners, which Madeline promised would be decorated in time for Christmas Eve. She had suggested leaving off the candles this time, but Cecily insisted that the tradition be followed as usual. Except the ceremony would now be held in the ballroom instead of her beloved library.

As she and Baxter took the stage, the chattering spectators fell silent. Cecily stepped to the center, and looked down on the sea of faces in front of her. She spoke briefly about Jeanette, announcing that her murderer had been apprehended, and asking everyone to remember the young maid this Christmas and pray for her soul.

Then she called upon Mrs. Chubb, Gertie, and Samuel to join her on the stage. She introduced them, explaining to the rest of the staff, amid a great deal of cheering and clapping, that the three new members were permanent.

Gertie left the stage grinning from ear to ear, while Samuel gave the crowd a jaunty wave. As for Mrs. Chubb, she marched off with her head held high, as befitting her esteemed position as housekeeper of the Pennyfoot Country Club.

When everyone had quietened down, Cecily turned to her husband. "Do you want to tell them, or shall I?"

"No, my love," he said with a smile. "This was your

idea and you deserve the entire stage. Enjoy this moment."
He walked off and left her alone.

She faced the crowd, who once again waited in silent
expectation. "I have one more announcement to make,"
she said, smiling down at them. "In view of the fact that
Mr. Sandringham will not be returning for a while, I have
accepted the position of manager of this establishment,
until such time other arrangements are made. With the
help of my husband, and you, my wonderful staff, I hope
to make the Pennyfoot Country Club the most favored
resort on the southeast coast. I look forward to working
with you all, and I wish every one of you a very happy
Christmas."

Cheers rang out again, and Cecily smiled when she saw
Mrs. Chubb and Gertie hug each other in delight. Things
had all worked out rather nicely after all, she thought as
she walked off the stage to join her husband. It was going
to be a good Christmas.

Later, as she and Baxter stood in the warm kitchen
accepting the congratulations of an excited Gertie and
Mrs. Chubb, she really felt as if they had come home
again.

After answering their questions as best they could,
leaving out the fact that Baxter had gambled away their
house, they joined everyone in a glass of hot cider punch,
celebrating the return of the Pennyfoot staff.

"I never would have thought that Lady Lucille would
have killed poor Jeanette," Mrs. Chubb said, her cheeks
glowing from the effects of the cider. "She looked like
such a delicate creature. As if one sneeze would knock her
off her feet."

"Just goes to show," Gertie said, smacking her lips in

enjoyment, "you never can tell with them toffs." She glanced at Cecily. "What's going to happen to them all?"

Cecily dabbed her mouth with a serviette. "According to the inspector, Lionel Fitzhammer and Lady Lucille will be charged with murder. Sir John will have to stand witness, I'm afraid. It will be hard on him. I imagine both he and Percy Chatsworth will lose their seats on the Bench."

"It's the bloody wives I feel sorry for." Gertie wiped her mouth on her sleeve. "That Mrs. Peebles lost her husband, Mrs. Fitzhammer's old man will be in jail, and Mrs. Chatsworth's will be out of a job. Not a very good Christmas for any of the buggers, is it."

"Well, by this afternoon they will all have left." Cecily put down her glass and stood up. "I must talk to the men who are working on the library. They have promised to have most of the mess cleared up by Christmas Eve, though I'm afraid it will be a while before we can use the library again."

"We're just glad you got out of there alive," Mrs. Chubb said with feeling. "Thank Gawd Mr. Baxter went looking for you."

In a rare public show of affection, Baxter placed an arm about her shoulders and pulled her close. She looked up at him, warmed by the love glowing in his eyes. For a while she had thought she might lose that devotion, and the prospect had terrified her. One never knew how much one had until one was in danger of losing it.

"Here, here." Samuel lifted his glass. "Right now I'd like to make a toast. To the staff of the Pennyfoot, and our new manager."

"Yeah," Gertie said, raising her glass. "It'll be just like old times!"

Everyone raised their glasses at once and chorused, "Just like old times!"

Cecily blinked back tears. "It is, indeed, like old times. I'm so happy we are all together again. Happy Christmas, everyone. And God bless you all."

Handsome, wealthy, and well-born, he had everything a gentleman needed to enjoy life to the fullest. Everything, that is, except the passion he would find in her bed.

Resounding praise for

Stephanie LAURENS

the Cynsters,
and
Temptation and Surrender

"Sinfully sexy and deliciously irresistible."
Booklist

"Laurens's writing shines . . .
an exceptional series."
Publishers Weekly

"A love scene written by Stephanie Laurens
is like an elaborate wedding cake: rich, decadent,
and covered in layers of sumptuous treats . . .
Her stories are well-crafted,
honest, and fast-paced."
Columbus Dispatch

"I'll buy anything with
Stephanie Laurens's name on it."
Linda Howard

Stephanie LAURENS

Temptation And Surrender
A CYNSTER NOVEL

AVON
An Imprint of HarperCollins*Publishers*

This book was originally published in hardcover March 2009 by
William Morrow, an Imprint of HarperCollins Publishers.

AVON BOOKS
An Imprint of HarperCollins*Publishers*
10 East 53rd Street
New York, New York 10022-5299

Copyright © 2009 by Savdek Management Proprietory Ltd.
Excerpt from *The Untamed Bride* copyright © 2009 by Savdek
Management Proprietory Ltd.
ISBN 978-0-06-124341-7
www.avonromance.com

First Avon Books paperback printing: October 2009
First William Morrow hardcover printing: March 2009

Avon Trademark Reg. U.S. Pat. Off. and in Other Countries, Marca
Registrada, Hecho en U.S.A.
HarperCollins® is a registered trademark of HarperCollins Publishers.

Printed in the U.S.A.

10 9 8 7 6 5 4 3 2

Temptation And Surrender

The Cynster Family Tree

Lady Eleanor···**SEBASTIAN**─┬─**Helena** Rebecce   Almira──**ARTHUR**──Louise
McEnery   5th Duke   de Stansion   Butterworth   Vennacombe
(d)   of St. Ives   Comtesse d'Lisle   (d)
               (d)

CHARLES
(d)

SYLVESTER *1*
DEVIL──┬──**Honoria**   **Michael**──**Caro**
6th Duke   *11*
of St. Ives

SEBASTIAN   MICHAEL   Louisa
Marquess
of Earith

RICHARD *3*
SCANDAL────┬────**Catriona**
         *

Lucilla   MARCUS   Annabelle

BARTHOLOMEW
[Tolly] (d)
                            8
                    Martin────────**Amanda**

MALE Cynsters in capitals   ✳ denotes twins
CHILDREN BORN AFTER 1825 NOT SHOWN

THE CYNSTER NOVELS

1. Devil's Bride   *4. A Rogue's Proposal*   *7. All About Passion*
2. A Rake's Vow   *5. A Secret Love*   *8. On a Wild Night*
3. Scandal's Bride   *6. All About Love*   *9. On a Wicked Dawn*
                                                     10. The Perfect Lover

❖ *Special—The Promise in a Kiss*

11. *The Ideal Bride*
12. *The Truth About Love*
13. *What Price Love?*
14. *The Taste of Innocence*
15. *Where the Heart Leads*
16. *This Volume*

1

Colyton, Devon
October 1825

I feel like tearing my hair out—not that that would do any good."

The dark hair in question fell in elegantly unruly locks about Jonas Tallent's handsome head. His brown eyes filled with disgusted irritation, he slumped back in the armchair behind the desk in the library of the Grange, the paternal home he would eventually inherit, a fact that accounted in multiple ways for his current, sorely frustrated state.

At ease in the chair facing the desk, Lucifer Cynster, Jonas's brother-in-law, smiled in wry commiseration. "Without intending to add to the burden weighing so heavily upon you, I feel I should mention that expectations are only rising with the passage of time."

Jonas humphed. "Hardly surprising—Juggs's demise, while being no loss whatsoever, has raised the specter of something better at the Red Bells. When Edgar found the old sot dead in a puddle of ale, I swear the entire village heaved a sigh of relief—and then immediately fell to speculating on what might be if the Red Bells had a *competent* innkeeper."

Juggs had been the innkeeper of the Red Bells for nearly a decade; he'd been found dead by the barman, Edgar Hills, two months ago.

Jonas settled deeper into his chair. "I have to admit I was first among the speculators, but that was before Uncle Martin expired of overwork and the pater went off to sort out Aunt Eliza and her horde, leaving the matter of the new incumbent at the Red Bells in my lap."

If truth be told, he'd welcomed the opportunity to return from London and assume full management of the estate. He'd been trained to the task throughout his youth, and while his father was still hale, he was becoming less robust; his unexpected and likely to be lengthy absence had seemed the perfect opportunity to step in and take up the reins.

That, however, hadn't been the principal reason he'd so readily kicked London's dust from his heels.

Over the last months he'd grown increasingly disaffected with the life he'd more or less fallen into in town. The clubs, the theaters, the dinners and balls, the soirees and select gatherings—the bucks and bloods, and the haughty matrons so many of whom were only too happy to welcome a handsome, independently wealthy, well-bred gentleman into their beds.

When he'd first gone on the town, shortly after Phyllida, his twin sister, had married Lucifer, a life built around such diversions had been his goal. With his innate and inherited attributes—and, courtesy of his connection with Lucifer, the imprimatur of the Cynsters—achieving all he'd desired hadn't been all that hard. However, having attained his goal and moved in tonnish circles for the past several years, he'd discovered that life on that gilded stage left him hollow, strangely empty.

Unsatisfied. Unfulfilled.

In reality, unengaged.

He'd been very ready to come home to Devon and assume control of the Grange and the estate while his father hied to Norfolk to support Eliza in her time of need.

He'd wondered whether life in Devon, too, would now feel empty, devoid of challenge. In the back of his mind had hovered the question of whether the deadening void within was entirely an effect of tonnish life or, far more worrying, was the symptom of some deeper inner malaise.

Within days of returning to the Grange he'd been reassured on that point at least. His life was suddenly overflowing with purpose. He hadn't had a moment when one challenge or another hadn't been front and center before him, clamoring for attention. Demanding action. Since returning home and seeing his father off, he'd barely had time to think.

That unsettling sense of disconnection and emptiness had evaporated, leaving only a novel restlessness beneath.

He no longer felt useless—clearly the life of a country gentleman, the life he'd been born and bred to, was his true calling—yet still there was something missing from his life.

Currently, however, it was the missing link at the Red Bells Inn that most severely exercised him. Replacing the unlamented Juggs had proved to be very far from a simple matter.

He shook his head in disgusted disbelief. "Whoever would have imagined finding a decent innkeeper would prove so damned difficult?"

"How far afield have you searched?"

"I've had notices posted throughout the shire and beyond— as far as Plymouth, Bristol, and Southampton." He pulled a face. "I could send to one of the London agencies, but we did that last time and they landed us with Juggs. If I had my choice, I'd have a local in the job, or at least a Westcountryman." Determination hardening his face, he sat up. "And if I can't have that, then at the very least I want to interview the applicant before I offer them the job. If we'd seen Juggs before the agency hired him, we'd never have contemplated foisting him on the village."

His long legs stretched before him, still very much the startlingly handsome, dark-haired devil who years before had made the ton's matrons swoon, Lucifer frowned. "It seems odd you've had no takers."

Jonas sighed. "It's the village—the smallness of it—that makes all the good applicants shy away. The countering facts—that when you add the surrounding houses and estates we're a decent-sized community, and with no other inn or hostelry in the vicinty we're assured a good trade—aren't sufficient, it seems, to weigh against the drawbacks of no shops and a small population." With one long finger, he flicked a sheaf of papers. "Once they learn the truth of Colyton, all the decent applicants take flight."

He grimaced and met Lucifer's dark blue eyes. "If they're good candidates, they're ambitious, and Colyton, so they believe, has nothing to offer them by way of advancement."

Lucifer grimaced back. "It seems you're looking for a rare bird—someone capable of managing an inn who wants to live in a backwater like Colyton."

Jonas eyed him speculatively. "You live in this backwater— can I tempt you to try your hand at managing an inn?"

Lucifer's grin flashed. "Thank you, but no. I've an estate to manage, just like you."

"Quite aside from the fact neither you nor I know the first thing about the domestic side of running an inn."

Lucifer nodded. "Aside from that."

"Mind you, Phyllida could probably manage the inn with her eyes closed."

"Except she's already got her hands full."

"Thanks to you." Jonas bent a mock-censorious look on his brother-in-law. Lucifer and Phyllida already had two children—Aidan and Evan, two very active little boys—and Phyllida had recently deigned to confirm that she was carrying their third child. Despite numerous other hands always about to help, Phyllida's own hands were indeed full.

Lucifer grinned unrepentantly. "Given you thoroughly enjoy playing uncle, that condemnatory look lacks bite."

Lips twisting in a rueful smile, Jonas let his gaze fall to the small pile of letters that were all that had come of the notices with which he'd papered the shire. "It's a sad situation when the best applicant is an ex-inmate of Newgate."

Lucifer let out a bark of laughter. He rose, stretched, then smiled at Jonas. "Something—or someone—will turn up."

"I daresay," Jonas returned. "But *when*? As you pointed out, the expectations are only escalating. As the inn's owner and therefore the person everyone deems responsible for fulfilling said expectations, time is not on my side."

Lucifer's smile was understanding if unhelpful. "I'll have to leave you to it. I promised I'd be home in good time to play pirates with my sons."

Jonas noted that, as always, Lucifer took special delight in saying that last word, all but rolling it on his tongue, savoring all that it meant.

With a jaunty salute, his brother-in-law departed, leaving him staring at the pile of dire applications for the post of innkeeper at the Red Bells Inn.

He wished he could leave to play pirates, too.

The thought vividly brought to mind what he knew would be waiting for Lucifer at the end of his short trek along the woodland path linking the back of the Grange to the back of Colyton Manor, the house Lucifer had inherited and now shared with Phyllida—and Aidan and Evan and a small company of staff. The manor was perennially filled with warmth and life, an energy—something tangible—that grew from shared contentment and happiness and filled the soul.

Anchored it.

While Jonas was entirely comfortable at the Grange—it was home, and the staff were excellent and had known him all his life—he was conscious—perhaps more so after his recent introspections on the shortfalls of tonnish life—of a wish that a warmth, a glow of happiness similar to that at the manor, would take root at the Grange and embrace him.

Fill his soul and anchor him.

For long moments, he stared unseeing across the room, then he mentally shook himself and lowered his gaze once more to the pile of useless applications.

The people of Colyton deserved a good inn.

Heaving a sigh, he shifted the pile to the middle of the

blotter, and forced himself to comb through it one last time.

Emily Ann Beauregard Colyton stood just beyond the last curve in the winding drive leading to the Grange on the southern outskirts of Colyton village, and peered at the house that sat in comfortable solidity fifty yards away.

Of worn red brick, it looked peaceful, serene, its roots sunk deep in the rich soil on which it sat. Unpretentious yet carrying a certain charm, the many-gabled slate roof sat over attic windows above two stories of wider, white-painted frames. Steps led up to the front porch. From where she hovered, Em could just see the front door, sitting back in shadowed majesty.

Neatly tended gardens spread to either side of the wide front façade. Beyond the lawns to her left, she spotted a rose garden, bright splashes of color, lush and inviting, bobbing against darker foliage.

She felt compelled to look again at the paper in her hand—a copy of the notice she'd spotted on the board in the posting inn at Axminster advertising the position of innkeeper-manager of the Red Bells Inn at Colyton. When she'd first set eyes on the notice, it had seemed expressly designed to be the answer to her prayers.

She and her brother and sisters had been wasting time waiting for the merchant who'd agreed to take them on his delivery dray when he made his round to Colyton. Over the previous week and a half, ever since her twenty-fifth birthday when, by virtue of her advanced age and her late father's farsighted will, she'd assumed guardianship of her brother and three sisters, they'd traveled from her uncle's house in Leicestershire by way of London to eventually reach Axminster—and finally, via the merchant's dray, Colyton.

The journey had cost much more than she'd expected, eating all of her meager savings and nearly all of the funds—her portion of their father's estate—that their family's solicitor, Mr. Cunningham, had arranged for her to receive. He alone knew she and her siblings had upped stakes and relocated to the tiny village of Colyton, deep in rural Devon.

Their uncle, and all those he might compel or persuade to his cause—that of feathering his own nest by dint of their free labor—had not been informed of their destination.

Which meant they were once again very much on their own—or, to be more precise, that the welfare of Isobel, Henry, and the twins, Gertrude and Beatrice, now rested firmly on Em's slight shoulders.

She didn't mind the burden, not in the least; she'd taken it up willingly. Continuing a day longer than absolutely necessary in their uncle's house had been beyond impossible; only the promise of eventual, and then imminent, departure had allowed any of the five Colytons to endure for so long under Harold Potheridge's exploitative thumb, but until Em had turned twenty-five, he—their late mother's brother—had been their co-guardian along with Mr. Cunningham.

On the day of her twenty-fifth birthday, Em had legally replaced her uncle. On that day, she and her siblings had taken their few worldly possessions—they'd packed days before—and departed Runcorn, their uncle's manor house. She'd steeled herself to face her uncle and explain their decision, but as matters had transpired, Harold had gone to a race meeting that day and hadn't been there to witness their departure.

All well and good, but she knew he would come after them, as far as he was able. They were worth quite a lot to him—his unpaid household staff. So traveling quickly down to London had been vital, and that had necessitated a coach and four, and that, as she'd discovered, had been expensive.

Then they'd had to cross London in hackneys, and stay two nights in a decent hotel, one in which they'd felt sufficiently safe to sleep. Although she'd thereafter economized and they'd traveled by mail coach, what with five tickets and the necessary meals and nights at various inns, her funds had dwindled, then shrunk alarmingly.

By the time they'd reached Axminster, she'd known she, and perhaps even Issy, twenty-three years old, would need to find work, although what work they might find, daughters of the gentry that they were, she hadn't been able to imagine.

Until she'd seen the notice on the board.

She scanned her copy again, rehearsing, as she had for the past hours, the right phrases and assurances with which to convince the owner of the Grange—who was also the owner of the Red Bells Inn—that she, Emily Beauregard—no one needed to know they were Colytons, at least not yet—was precisely the right person to whom he should entrust the running of his inn.

When she'd shown her siblings the notice, and informed them of her intention to apply for the position, they had—as they always did, bless them—fallen in unquestioningly and enthusiastically with her scheme. She now had in her reticule three glowing references for Emily Beauregard, written by the invented proprietors of inns they'd passed on their journey. She'd written one, Issy another, and Henry, fifteen and so painfully wanting to be helpful, had penned the third, all while they'd waited for the merchant and his dray.

The merchant had dropped them off outside the Red Bells. To her immense relief, there'd been a notice on the wall beside the door stating "Innkeeper Wanted" in bold black letters; the position hadn't yet been filled. She'd settled the others in a corner of the large common room, and given them coins enough to have glasses of lemonade. All the while she'd surveyed the inn, evaluating all she could see, noting that the shutters were in need of a coat of paint, and that the interior was sadly dusty and grimy, but there was nothing she could see amiss within the doors that wouldn't yield to a cloth and a bit of determination.

She'd watched the somewhat dour man behind the bar. Although he was manning the tap, his demeanor had suggested he was thinking of other things in a rather desultory way. The notice had given an address for applications, not the inn but the Grange, Colyton, doubtless expecting said applications to come through the post. Girding her loins, hearing the crinkle of her "references" in her reticule, she'd taken the first step, walked up to the bar, and asked the man the way to the Grange.

Which was how she'd come to be there, dithering in the drive. She told herself she was only being sensible by trying to gauge the type of man the owner was by examining his house.

Older, she thought—and settled; there was something about the house that suggested as much. Comfortable. Married for many years, perhaps a widower, or at least with a wife as old and as comfortable as he. He would be gentry, certainly, very likely of the sort they called the backbone of the counties. Paternalistic—she could be absolutely sure he would be that—which would doubtless prove useful. She would have to remember to invoke that emotion if she needed help getting him to give her the position.

She wished she'd been able to ask the barman about the owner, but given she intended to apply for the position of his superior that might have proved awkward, and she hadn't wanted to call attention to herself in any way.

The truth was she needed this position. Needed it quite desperately. Quite aside from the issue of replenishing her funds, she and her siblings needed somewhere to stay. She'd assumed there would be various types of accommodation available in the village, only to discover that the only place in Colyton able to house all five of them was the inn. And she couldn't afford to stay at any inn longer than one night.

Bad enough, but in the absence of an innkeeper, the inn wasn't housing paying guests. Only the bar was operating; there hadn't even been food on offer. As an inn, the Red Bells was barely functioning—all for want of an innkeeper.

Her Grand Plan—the goal that had kept her going for the last eight years—had involved returning to Colyton, to the home of their forebears, and finding the Colyton treasure. Family lore held that the treasure, expressly hidden against the need of future generations, was hidden there, at a location handed down in a cryptic rhyme.

Her grandmother had believed unswervingly in the treasure, and had taught Em and Issy the rhyme.

Her grandfather and father had laughed. They hadn't believed.

She'd held to her belief through thick and thin; for her and Issy, and later Henry and the twins, the promise of the treasure had held them together, held their spirits up, for the past eight years.

The treasure was there. She wouldn't—couldn't—believe otherwise.

She'd never kept an inn in her life, but having run her uncle's house from attics to cellars for eight years, including the numerous weeks he'd had his bachelor friends to stay for the hunting, she was, she felt sure, more than qualified to run a quiet inn in a sleepy little village like Colyton.

How difficult could it be?

There would no doubt be minor challenges, but with Issy's and Henry's support she'd overcome them. Even the twins, ten years old and mischievous, could be a real help.

She'd hovered long enough. She had to do this—had to march up to the front door, knock, and convince the old gentleman to hire her as the new innkeeper of the Red Bells.

She and her generation of Colytons had made it to the village. It was up to her to gain them the time, and the facility, to search for and find the treasure.

To search for and secure their futures.

Drawing in a deep breath, she held it and, putting one foot determinedly in front of the other, marched steadily on down the drive.

She climbed the front steps and without giving herself

even a second to think again, she raised her hand and beat a sharp rat-a-tat-tat on the white-painted front door.

Lowering her hand, she noticed a bellpull. She debated whether to tug that, too, but then approaching footsteps fixed her attention on the door.

It was opened by a butler, one of the more imposing sort. Having moved within the upper circles of York society prior to her father's death, she recognized the species. His back was ramrod straight, his girth impressive. His gaze initially passed over her head, but then lowered.

He considered her with a steady, even gaze. "Yes, miss?"

She took heart from the man's kindly mien. "I wish to speak with the owner of the Red Bells Inn. I'm here to apply for the position of innkeeper."

Surprise flitted over the butler's face, followed by a slight frown. He hesitated, regarding her, then asked, "Is this a joke, miss?"

She felt her lips tighten, her eyes narrow. "No. I'm perfectly serious." Jaw firming, she took the bull by the horns. "Yes, I know what I look like." Soft light brown hair with a tendency to curl and a face everyone—simply everyone— saw as sweet, combined with a slight stature and a height on the short side of average didn't add up to the general notion of a forceful presence—the sort needed to run an inn. "Be that as it may, I have experience aplenty, and I understand the position is still vacant."

The butler looked taken aback by her fierceness. He studied her for a moment more, taking in her high-necked olive green walking dress—she'd tidied herself as best she could while at Axminster—then asked, "If you're sure . . . ?"

She frowned. "Well, of course I'm sure. I'm here, aren't I?"

He acknowledged that with a slight nod, yet still he hesitated.

She lifted her chin. "I have written references—three of them." She tapped her reticule. As she did so, memories of the inn, and the notices—and their curling edges—flashed through her mind. Fixing her gaze on the butler's face, she risked a deductive leap. "It's clear your master has had difficulty filling the position. I'm sure he wishes to have his inn operating again. Here I am, a perfectly worthy applicant. Are you sure you want to turn me away, rather than inform him I am here and wish to speak with him?"

The butler considered her with a more measuring eye; she wondered if the flash she'd seen in his eyes might have been respect.

Regardless, at long last he inclined his head. "I will inform Mr. Tallent that you are here, miss. What name shall I say?"

"Miss Emily Beauregard."

W ho?" Looking up from the depressing pile of applications, Jonas stared at Mortimer. "A young woman?"

"Well . . . a young female person, sir." Mortimer was clearly in two minds about the social standing of Miss Emily Beauregard, which in itself was remarkable. He'd been in his present position for decades, and was well versed in identifying the various levels of persons who presented themselves at the local magistrate's door. "She seemed . . . very set on applying for the position. I thought, all things considered, that perhaps you should see her."

Sitting back in his chair, Jonas studied Mortimer and wondered what had got into the man. Miss Emily Beauregard had clearly made an impression, enough to have Mortimer espouse her cause. But the idea of a female managing the Red Bells . . . then again, not even half an hour ago he himself had acknowledged that Phyllida could have run the inn with barely half her highly capable brain.

The position was for an innkeeper-*manager*, after all, and certain females were very good at managing.

He sat up. "Very well. Show her in." She had to be an improvement over the applicant from Newgate.

"Indeed, sir." Mortimer turned to the door. "She said she has written references—three of them."

Jonas raised his brows. Apparently Miss Beauregard had come well prepared.

He looked at the sheaf of applications before him, then tapped them together and set the pile aside. Not that he had any great hopes of Miss Beauregard proving the answer to his prayers; he was simply sick of looking at the dismal outcome of his recent efforts.

A footstep in the doorway had him glancing up.

A young lady stepped into the room; Mortimer hovered behind her.

Instinct took hold, bringing Jonas to his feet.

Em's first thought on setting eyes on the gentleman behind the desk in the well-stocked library was: He's too young.

Far too young to feel paternalistic toward her.

Of quite the wrong sort to feel paternalistic at all.

Unexpected—unprecedented—panic tugged at her; this man—about thirty years old and as attractive as sin—was not the sort of man she'd expected to have to deal with.

Yet there was no one else in the room, and the butler had returned from this room to fetch her; presumably he knew who she was supposed to see.

Given the gentleman, now on his feet, was staring at her, she dragged in a breath, forced her wits to steady, and grasped the opportunity to study him.

He was over six feet tall, long limbed and rangy; broad shoulders stretched his well-cut coat. Dark, sable-brown hair fell in elegantly rumpled locks about a well-shaped head; his features bore the aquiline cast common among the aristocracy, reinforcing her increasing certainty that the owner of the Grange sat rather higher on the social scale than a mere squire.

His face was riveting. Dark brown eyes, more alive than soulful, well set under dark slashes of brows, commanded her attention even though he hadn't yet met her gaze. He was looking *at* her, at all of her; she saw his gaze travel down her frame, and had to suppress an unexpected shiver.

She drew in another breath, held it. Absorbed the implication of a broad forehead, a strong nose, and an even stronger, squarish jaw, all suggesting strength of character, firmness, and resolution.

His lips . . . were utterly, comprehensively distracting. Narrowish, their lines hinted at a mobility that would soften the angular, almost austere planes of his face.

She dragged her gaze from them, lowering it to take in his subtle sartorial perfection. She'd seen London dandies before, and while he wasn't in any way overdressed, his clothes were of excellent quality, his cravat expertly tied in a deceptively simple knot.

Beneath the fine linen of his shirt, his chest was well muscled, but he was all lean sleekness. As he came to life and slowly, smoothly, moved around the desk, he reminded her of a predatory animal, one that stalked with a dangerous, overtly athletic grace.

She blinked. Couldn't help asking, "You're the owner of the Red Bells Inn?"

He halted by the front corner of the desk and finally met her gaze.

She felt as if something hot had pierced her, making her breath hitch.

"I'm Mr. Tallent—Mr. Jonas Tallent." His voice was deep but clear, his accent the clipped speech of their class. "My father's Sir Jasper Tallent, owner of the inn. He's currently away and I'm managing the estate in his absence. Please— take a seat."

Jonas waved her to the chair before his desk. He had to stifle the urge to go forward and hold it while she sat.

If she'd been a man, he would have left her standing, but she wasn't a man. She was definitely female. The thought of having her standing before him while he sat and read her references and interrogated her about her background was simply unacceptable.

She subsided, with a practiced hand tucking her olive green skirts beneath her. Over her head he met Mortimer's gaze. He now understood Mortimer's hesitation in labeling Miss Beauregard a "young woman." Whatever else Miss Emily Beauregard was, she was a lady.

Her antecedents were there in every line of her slight form, in every unconsciously graceful movement. She possessed a small-boned, almost delicate frame; her face was heart-stoppingly fine, with a pale, blush cream porcelain complexion and features that—if he'd had a poetic turn of mind—he would have described as being sculpted by a master.

Lush, pale rose lips were the least of them; perfectly molded, they were presently set in an uncompromising line, one he felt compelled to make soften and curve. Her nose was small and straight, her lashes long and lush, a brown fringe framing large eyes of the most vibrant hazel he'd ever seen. Those arresting eyes sat beneath delicately arched brown brows, while her forehead was framed by soft curls of gleaming light brown; she'd attempted to force her hair into a severe bun at the nape of her neck, but the shining curls had a mind of their own, escaping to curl lovingly about her face.

Her chin, gently rounded, was the only element that gave any hint of underlying strength.

As he returned to his chair, the thought uppermost in his mind was: What the devil was she doing applying to be an innkeeper?

Dismissing Mortimer with a nod, he resumed his seat. As the door gently closed, he settled his gaze on the lady before him. "Miss Beauregard—"

"I have three references you'll want to read." She was already hunting in her reticule. Freeing three folded sheets, she leaned forward and held them out.

He had to take them. "Miss Beauregard—"

"If you read them"—folding her hands over the reticule in her lap, with a nod she indicated the references—"I believe you will see that I have experience aplenty, more than enough to qualify for the position of innkeeper of the Red Bells." She didn't give him time to respond, but fixed her vivid eyes on his and calmly stated, "I believe the position has been vacant for some time."

Pinned by that direct, surprisingly acute hazel gaze, he found his assumptions about Miss Emily Beauregard subtly altering. "Indeed."

She held his gaze calmly. Appearances aside, she was clearly no meek miss.

A pregnant moment passed, then her gaze flicked down to the references in his hands, then returned to his face. "I could read those for you, if you prefer?"

He mentally shook himself. Lips firming, he looked down—and dutifully smoothed open the first folded sheet.

While he read through the three neatly folded— identically folded—sheets, she filled his ears with a litany of her virtues—her experiences managing households as well as inns. Her voice was pleasant, soothing. He glanced up now and then, struck by a slight change in her tone; after the third instance he realized the change occurred when she was speaking of some event and calling on her memory.

Those aspects of her tale, he decided, were true; she had had experience running houses and catering for parties of guests.

When it came to her experience running inns, however . . .

"While at the Three Feathers in Hampstead, I . . ."

He looked down, again scanned the reference for her time at the Three Feathers. Her account mirrored what was written; she told him nothing more.

Glancing at her again, watching her face—an almost angelic vision—he toyed with the idea of telling her he knew her references were fake. While they were written in three different hands, he'd take an oath two were female—unlikely if they were, as stated, from the male owners of inns—and the third, while male, was not entirely consistent—a young male whose handwriting was still changing.

The most telling fact, however, was that all three references—supposedly from three geographically distant inns over a span of five years—were on the exact same paper, written in the same ink, with the same pen, one that had a slight scratch across the nib.

And they appeared the same age. Fresh and new.

Looking across his desk at Miss Emily Beauregard, he wondered why he didn't simply ring for Mortimer and have her shown out. He should—he knew it—yet he didn't.

He couldn't let her go without knowing the answer to his initial question. Why the devil was a lady of her ilk applying for a position as an innkeeper?

She eventually ended her recitation and looked at him, brows rising in faintly haughty query.

He tossed the three references on his blotter and met her bright eyes directly. "To be blunt, Miss Beauregard, I hadn't thought to give the position to a female, let alone one of your relative youth."

For a moment, she simply looked at him, then she drew in a breath and lifted her head a touch higher. Chin firming, she held his gaze. "If I may be blunt in return, Mr. Tallent, I took a quick look at the inn on my way here. The external shutters need painting, and the interior appears not to have been adequately cleaned for at least five years. No woman would sit in your common room by choice, yet it's the only public area you have. There is presently no food served at all, nor accommodation offered. In short, the inn is currently operating as no more than a bar-tavern. If you are indeed in charge of your father's estate, then you will have to admit that as an investment the Red Bells Inn is presently returning only a fraction of its true worth."

Her voice remained pleasant, her tones perfectly modulated; just like her face, it disguised the underlying strength—the underlying sharp edge.

She tilted her head, her eyes still locked with his. "I understand the inn has been without a manager for some months?"

Lips tightening, he conceded the point. "Several months."
Far too many months.

"I daresay you're keen to see it operating adequately as
soon as may be, especially as I noted there is no other tavern or gathering place in the village. The locals, too, must
be anxious to have their inn properly functioning again."

Why did he feel as if he were being herded?

It was plainly time to reassert control of the interview and
find out what he wanted to know. "If you could enlighten
me, Miss Beauregard, as to what brought you to Colyton?"

"I saw a copy of your notice at the inn in Axminster."

"And what brought you to Axminster?"

She shrugged lightly. "I was . . ." She paused, considering him, then amended, "*We*—my brother and sisters and
I—were merely passing through." Her gaze flickered; she
glanced down at her hands, lightly clasped on her reticule.
"We've been traveling through the summer, but now it's
time to get back to work."

And that, Jonas would swear, was a lie. They hadn't been
traveling over summer . . . but, if he was reading her correctly, she did have a brother and sisters with her. She knew
he would find out about them if she got the job, so had told
the truth on that score.

A reason for her wanting the innkeeper's job flared in his
mind, growing stronger as he swiftly assessed her gown—
serviceable, good quality, but not of recent vintage. "*Younger*
brother and sisters?"

Her head came up; she regarded him closely. "Indeed."
She hesitated, then asked, "Would that be a problem? It's
never been before. They're hardly babes. The youngest is . . .
twelve."

That latter hesitation was so slight he only caught it because he was listening as closely as she was watching him.
Not twelve—perhaps a precocious ten. "Your parents?"

"Both dead. They have been for many years."

Truth again. He was getting a clearer picture of why
Emily Beauregard wanted the innkeeper's job. But . . .

He sighed and sat forward, leaning both forearms on the desk, loosely clasping his hands. "Miss Beauregard—"

"Mr. Tallent."

Struck by her crisp tone, he broke off and looked up into her bright hazel eyes.

Once he had, she continued, "I believe we've wasted enough time in roundaboutation. The truth is you need an innkeeper quite desperately, and here I am, willing and very able to take on the job. Are you really going to turn me away just because I'm female and have younger family members in my train? My eldest sister is twenty-three, and assists me with whatever work I undertake. Likewise my brother is fifteen, and apart from the time given to his studies, works alongside us. My youngest sisters are twins, and even they lend a hand. If you hire me, you get their labor as well."

"So you and your family are a bargain?"

"Indeed, not that we work for nothing. I would expect a salary equal to a twentieth of the takings, or a tenth of the profits per month, and in addition to that, room and board supplied through the inn." She rattled on with barely a pause for breath. "I assume you wish the innkeeper to live on site. I noticed that there are attic rooms above, which appear to be unoccupied and would do perfectly for me and my siblings. As we're here, I could take up the position immediately—"

"Miss Beauregard." This time he let steel infuse his voice, enough so that she stopped and didn't try to speak over him. He caught her gaze, held it. "I haven't yet agreed to give you the position."

Her gaze didn't flinch, didn't waver. The desk may have been between them, yet it felt as if they were toe-to-toe. When she spoke, her voice was even, if tight. "You're desperate to have someone take the inn in hand. I want the job. Are you really going to turn me away?"

The question hovered between them, all but blazoned in the air. Lips thinning, he held her gaze, equally unwaveringly. He *was* desperate for any capable innkeeper—she had that right—and she was there, offering . . .

And if he turned her away, what would she do? She and her family, whom she was supporting and protecting.

He didn't need to think to know she'd never turned to the petticoat line, which meant her younger sister hadn't, either. What if he turned her away and she—they—were forced, at some point, to . . .

No! Taking such a risk was out of the question; he couldn't live with such a possibility on his conscience. Even if he never knew, just the thought, the chance, would drive him demented.

He narrowed his eyes on hers. It didn't sit well to be jock-eyed into hiring her, which was what she'd effectively done. Regardless . . .

Breaking eye contact, he reached for a fresh sheet of paper. Setting it on the desk, he didn't glance at her as he picked up his pen, checked the nib, then flipped open the ink pot, dipped, and rapidly scrawled.

No matter that her references were fake, she was better than no one, and she wanted the job. Lord knew she was a managing enough female to get it done. He'd simply keep a very close eye on her, make sure she correctly accounted for the takings and didn't otherwise do anything untoward. He doubted she'd drink down the cellar as Juggs had.

Finishing his brief note, he blotted it, then folded it. Only then did he look up and meet her wide, now curious eyes. "This"—he held out the sheet—"is a note for Edgar Hills, the barman, introducing you as the new innkeeper. He and John Ostler are, at present, the only staff."

Her fingers closed about the other end of the note and her face softened. Not just her lips; her whole face softly glowed. He recalled he'd wanted to make that happen, wondered what her lips—now irresistibly appealing—would taste like . . .

She gently tugged the note, but he held on. "I'll hire you on trial for three months." He had to clear his throat before going on. "After that, if the outcome is satisfactory to all, we'll make it a permanent appointment."

He released the note. She took it, tucked it in her reticule, then looked up, met his eyes—and smiled.

Just like that, she scrambled his brains.

That's what it felt like as, still beaming, she rose—and he did, too, driven purely by instinct given none of his faculties were operating.

"Thank you." Her words were heartfelt. Her gaze—those bright hazel eyes—remained locked on his. "I swear you won't regret it. I'll transform the Red Bells into the inn Colyton village deserves."

With a polite nod, she turned and walked to the door.

Although he couldn't remember doing so, he must have tugged the bellpull because Mortimer materialized to see her out.

She left with her head high and a spring in her step, but didn't look back.

For long moments after she'd disappeared, Jonas stood staring at the empty doorway while his mind slowly re-assembled.

His first coherent thought was a fervent thanks to the deity that she hadn't smiled at him when she'd first arrived.

2

Em walked briskly back down the drive and turned onto the lane that led to Colyton village.

She could barely keep from skipping. She'd got the job—convinced Mr. Jonas Tallent to give her the job—despite the thoroughly peculiar, thoroughly unnerving effect he'd had on her usually reliable senses.

Just the thought of him, the mental mention of his name, evoked the memory of how breathless his steady regard had made her feel, of how giddy she'd felt when she'd looked into his fathomless brown eyes, not soulful, as she'd noted from the first, but alive with intense and hidden depths—tantalizing depths her inner self had, entirely unexpectedly, longed to explore.

It was just as well he hadn't offered to shake her hand. She wasn't at all sure how she would have coped if his touch affected her to a commensurate degree as his gaze. She might have done something truly dreadful, like shudder revealingly, or shiver and close her eyes.

Luckily, she hadn't had to endure that trial.

Instead, all was well—*excellently* well—in her world.

She couldn't stop grinning. She allowed herself a little skip, an expression of pure exuberance, then looked ahead as the first cottages came into view, lining the road that ran north to south through the center of Colyton.

It wasn't a big village, but it was the home of her forebears, and that endeared it to her. To her mind, it was precisely the right size.

And they were staying.

At least until they found the treasure.

It was Monday, late afternoon, and other than herself the road was deserted. She looked about her as she walked to the inn, noting the blacksmith's forge a little way up the lane to the left, and beyond that the graveyard rising to the church, perched atop a ridge that formed the western boundary of the village proper. In front of the church, the common rolled down to a large duck pond, and then further, to eventually border the road. Directly opposite sat the Red Bells in all its flaking splendor.

Halting at the intersection with the lane, she paused to study her new responsibility. Other than the peeling shutters, the front façade would pass muster, at least for now. There were trestle tables and benches set outside; all could do with a good scrub, but were otherwise serviceable. Three window boxes stood empty, devoid of life, but that could easily be rectified—and they would benefit from a coat of paint, too. The window glass needed a good wash, and the rest could do with a thorough brushing, but beyond that, the front would do.

She looked up at the attic windows above; at least the rooms up there would have plenty of light—or would once the windows were cleaned. She wondered what state the other rooms—especially the guest rooms on the first floor—were in.

Glancing further along the road, she let her gaze sweep the line of small cottages facing the common, all the way to the larger house at the end of the stretch—the first house if one came in from the north.

She suspected that house was Colyton Manor, her family's

ancestral home. Her great-grandfather had been the last
Colyton to reside there, many years ago. She doubted anyone still living would remember him.

After a moment, she shook free of her thoughts, looked
again at the inn, and felt her smile grow. Time to put her
siblings' worries to rest. Her smile widening into a beaming grin, she headed for the inn door.

They were in the corner where she'd left them, their boxes
and trunks piled about them. She didn't need to say anything for them to know. One look at her face and the twins,
blue-eyed, blond-haired angel-demons, let out unladylike
whoops and came pelting up to fling their arms around her.

"You did it! You *did it*!" Caroling in unison, they danced
around her.

"Yes, but hush now." She hugged them briefly, then released them and walked on, her gaze going first to meet
Issy's blue eyes in quiet triumph, then, smile deepening, she
looked at Henry, who of them all remained somber and serious.

"Was it all right?" he asked.

Henry was fifteen-going-on-forty, and felt the weight of
every one of those years. Although taller than Em, indeed
even taller than Issy now, he shared Em's coloring—light
brown hair and light brown eyes, not as complex as Em's
hazel—while his face was a much stronger casting of his
sisters' delicate features.

She didn't need him to say it to know he'd worried that
someone at the Grange might take advantage of her. "It was
entirely civilized." She smiled reassuringly as she set her
reticule on the table they'd gathered around. "Mind you, it
turned out that the Mr. Tallent who's presently in charge is
the son, not the father, but he—Mr. Jonas Tallent—was perfectly gentlemanly." Seeing that that news hadn't allayed
Henry's concerns—quite the opposite—she smoothly added,
"He's not young. I'd say he's somewhere in his thirties."

Barely thirty would be closer to the mark, but the mention of the figure thirty—to Henry at fifteen an unimaginable age—was sufficient to dampen his worries.

Hopefully by the time he met Jonas Tallent, Henry would have realized that their employer posed no threat to either her or Issy. That, indeed, Jonas Tallent was a far cry from some of their uncle's friends.

His effect on her aside—and that hadn't been his fault but a product of her own unprecedented sensibility—she was entirely confident that Jonas Tallent was the sort of gentleman who played by society's rules, when it came to ladies probably to the letter. There was something about him that, despite her unsettled nerves, had made her feel entirely safe—as if he would protect her from any threat, any harm.

Unnerving he might be, but he was, she judged, an honorable man.

Freeing Tallent's folded note from her reticule, she brandished it to attract her siblings' attention. "I have to give this to the man behind the bar—his name is Edgar Hills. The only other person currently employed at the inn is the ostler—John Ostler by name. Now"—she looked pointedly at the twins—"please behave yourselves while I sort things out."

The twins dutifully sat on the bench alongside Issy, who smiled in wry if cynical amusement. Henry sat quietly and watched as, again carrying her reticule, Em walked to the bar.

Edgar Hills looked up as she neared, faint curiosity in his face. He'd heard the twins' exclamations, but wouldn't have been able to make out anything more. He nodded politely as she halted before the bar. "Miss."

Em smiled. "I'm Miss Beauregard." She handed Tallent's message across the bar. "I'm here to take charge of the inn."

Not entirely to her surprise, Edgar received the news with subdued and relieved joy; in his quiet, rather lugubrious way, he welcomed her and her siblings to the inn, smiling at the twins' exuberance, then showing them over the entire inn, before putting himself at their disposal for moving their trunks and boxes upstairs.

The next hours went in cheery, good-humored bustle, a much brighter and happier end to their day than Em could ever have dreamed. The upper rooms of the inn were perfect for her siblings—Issy, Henry, and the twins divided up the attic rooms surprisingly amicably; there seemed an ideal spot for each of them.

Somewhat to her bemusement, she found herself installed in a private set of rooms. Edgar shyly led her to a narrow door at the top of the stairs that led from one end of the common room up to the first floor. To the left of the stairhead, a wide corridor ran the length of the inn with the guest rooms giving off to both sides, overlooking the front and back of the inn. The door Edgar opened stood to the right of the stairs, facing down the corridor. It gave onto the innkeeper's domain—a generous parlor, leading to a good-sized bedroom, with a dressing room-cum-bathing chamber further back. The latter was connected by a very narrow set of stairs to the back hall beside the scullery.

After showing her through the rooms, Edgar murmured that he'd fetch up her things, and left her.

Alone—she was so rarely alone she always noticed and despite her fierce love for her siblings, she savored those moments of solitude whenever they came her way—she walked to the front window of the parlor and looked out.

The view was to the front of the inn. Across the road, the common was already bathed in purple shadow. Up on the ridge, the church stood starkly silhouetted against the still sunlit western sky.

She opened the casement window, breathed in the cool, fresh air that drifted in, spiced with the smell of green grass and growing things. The distant clack of a duck, the deeper bell-like tone of a frog, reached her on the evening breeze.

Issy had already taken charge of the kitchens. She'd done most of the cooking at their uncle's house. She was a better cook than Em, and enjoyed the challenges. Contrary to Em's expectations, Issy had reported that the inn's store-rooms and pantries were about half-stocked, with a variety of staples available for creating meals. She was presently in the kitchen, creating dinner.

Hitching her hip onto the wide windowsill, Em leaned against the open window frame. She would still need to re-plenish the inn's supplies. Tomorrow she'd investigate the wheres and hows.

Edgar didn't live in, but came in every day from a cottage on his brother's farm just outside the village. She'd asked him about his duties; aside from tending the bar, he was happy to continue to act as the main body manning the inn's counter. He and she had very easily come to an agree-ment; she would take responsibility for all the supplies, all the organization, and everything to do with getting the food and accommodation side of the inn functioning again, while he would oversee the running of the bar and keep track of liquor supplies, although she would order and orga-nize to have the liquor delivered.

She'd had Edgar introduce her to John Ostler, who lived in a room above the stables. Stables that were neat and clean; they hadn't had any horses in them for some time. John lived for horses; a shy, reticent man in, she judged, his late twenties, in light of the dearth of equine guests, he'd kept his hand in by helping out with the horses at Colyton Manor.

From him, she'd learned that the manor was indeed the large house further along the lane, and that it was presently the home of a family named Cynster—and the lady of the house was Jonas Tallent's twin sister.

Looking out into the deepening shadows, Em took men-tal stock of her new domain. The inn had only a single public room—the common room—but it stretched the length of the ground floor. The front door gave onto its cen-ter; the long bar stretched more to the right than left, leav-ing a good space in front of the door to the kitchen, to the left of center, with the staircase beyond, toward the rear left corner of the room. Set in the center of each side wall were large, stone-manteled fireplaces.

The common room could, she estimated, seat forty or more. There were various tables, benches, and chairs, including more comfortable wing chairs in a semicircle around one hearth. Long custom, it appeared, had made the area to the right of the front door the tap, with round tables with wooden chairs and benches along the walls. The area to the left of the door held padded benches and cushioned chairs, and more wing chairs, arranged in groupings about lower tables. Further back, between the hearth and the kitchen door, stood rectangular tables with benches—clearly the dining area.

From the dust that lay on the more comfortable chairs and the lower tables, Em surmised that area—presumably for women or older folk—hadn't seen much use in recent years.

That, she hoped, would change. An inn like the Red Bells should be the center of village life, and that included the female half of the population and the elders as well.

Aside from all else, having females and older folk in the common room would help modulate the behavior of the men. She made a note to set standards and institute some method to enforce them.

Edgar had already told her, in one of his quiet murmurs, that the clientele of the inn had dropped away over the tenure of her predecessor, a man called Juggs. Even the travelers who used to regularly break their journeys at the inn had, over time, found other places to stay.

She had a great deal of work before her to restore the inn to its full potential. Somewhat to her surprise, the challenge filled her with real zeal—something she certainly hadn't expected.

"Ooh—this is nice." Gertrude, Gert to the family, came into the room. Beatrice, Bea, followed at her heels, likewise round-eyed, exploring and noting.

Henry trooped in behind the twins; Issy, in a check apron and wiping her hands on a cloth, followed.

"Dinner will be ready in half an hour," Issy announced with some pride. She glanced at Em. "It's quite a well-set-out kitchen, once I unearthed the pots and pans. Someone had put them in the root cellar." She tilted her head. "Have you any ideas about kitchen help?"

Straightening from the windowsill, Em nodded. "Edgar's told me who used to work here as cook and the helpers she had. They're all locals, and likely still available, if we want them, which I said we do." She fixed Issy with a firm gaze. "I'll be glad of your help with the menus and the ordering, once I learn where to order from, but I don't want you cooking, only in emergencies." Issy opened her mouth; Em held up a staying hand. "Yes, I know you don't mind, but I didn't get you out of Uncle Harold's kitchen just to install you in another."

She let her gaze sweep over the others' faces. "We all know why we're here."

"To find the treasure!" Bea promptly piped.

Leaning back, Em grasped the latch and pulled the window shut; the twins' high-pitched voices carried, and no one else presently needed to know their reason for being in Colyton. "Yes." She nodded decisively. "We're going to find the treasure, *but* we are also going to live normal lives."

She regarded the twins, not entirely mock-severely; she knew their propensities all too well. "We've spoken of this before, but Susan sadly neglected your education. You cannot be Papa's daughters and not have the basics of a gentlewoman's upbringing. Issy, Henry, and I had governesses to teach us. You can't at the moment have a governess, but Issy—and I'll help when I can—can at least start you off with your lessons."

The twins exchanged glances—never a good sign—but then they looked at Em and dutifully nodded. "All right," they chorused, "we'll try them and see."

There would be no "seeing," but Em left that battle for

later. Issy, with whom she'd spent many hours discussing the twins' lack, nodded in quietly determined agreement.

Although they were all Colytons, all children of their father, the twins were the product of Reginald Colyton's second marriage. While Susan, the twins' mother, had been a lovely person, one Em, Issy, and Henry had taken to their hearts, her background hadn't been the equivalent of theirs. That hadn't mattered while their father had been alive, but after he died, when the twins were just two years old, the family had been separated. Harold Potheridge had been named Em's, Issy's, and Henry's principal guardian, and had taken them to his home, Runcorn Manor in Leicestershire, while the twins, naturally, had remained with Susan in York.

Although Em and Issy had corresponded regularly with Susan, and her letters in reply had always been cheery, after she'd died and the twins, orphans at nine, had appeared unannounced on Harold's doorstep, Em and Issy had learned enough from the innocent pair to realize that all had not gone as they'd thought—been led to believe—with Susan.

Certainly the marriage she'd told them of hadn't occurred.

And the twins had received no education whatever.

Em was determined to rectify that last, and luckily the twins were Colytons—they were quick and bright and learned quite well, when they could be convinced to apply themselves.

Unfortunately, as they were also Colytons in the sense of preferring exploring to all else, getting them to concentrate on lessons wasn't an easy task.

Em looked at Henry. He was never such a trial. He loved learning; it was his way of exploring far beyond his physical bounds. "We'll ask around and find a tutor for you. We mustn't let your lessons slide."

In his serious way, Henry nodded. "I'll still help with the inn, though. That's only fair."

Em acquiesced with a nod, but exchanged another glance with Issy. They would ensure Henry's studies had first call on his time. Part of the agreement Em had long ago struck with Harold—an agreement Henry had never been privy to—was that in return for hers and Issy's services in running his house, Harold would arrange lessons for Henry with the local vicar, who had studied at Oxford and was a keen scholar.

That was one bargain Harold had kept, knowing it would keep Em and Issy where he'd wanted them—willingly managing his house and seeing to his comforts, otherwise for free. So Henry was now well on the way to being the scholar he'd always wanted to be; he needed to start preparing for his entry to university, even though that was still some years away.

"Tell us about the treasure again." Gert bounced up and down in one of the armchairs, sending up a cloud of dust.

Bea immediately did the same in the other, with the same result.

"*If* you sit still," Em quickly said. As the story of the family treasure was one all her siblings never tired of hearing, the twins dutifully froze, eyes trained on her. Em glanced at Issy.

Who waved her on. "We've plenty of time. I've put a pot in the oven—it's taking care of itself."

Issy and Henry perched on the sofa. Making a mental note to dust thoroughly before she retired that night, Em glanced around at her siblings, then commenced, "Long ago, in the days of Sir Walter Raleigh and the Spanish conquistadors, one of the Colytons—he was a buccaneer and the captain of his own ship—captured a Spanish galleon filled with treasure."

She continued, describing the captain, his command, the voyage and the battle, concluding with the thrilling victory their ancestor had wrought. "As his share of the spoils, he brought home a chest brimming with gold and jewels. His wife, keeping house here in Colyton, pointed out that the family was already wealthy enough—she knew that if her husband and his brothers, adventurers all, as all Colytons are, kept the treasure, it would be frittered away on more ships and wild ventures. Instead, she suggested that most of the treasure be hidden in a place only Colytons could find, against the need of future generations who found themselves in difficulties. The intention was to keep the Colyton name alive, and the family financially secure, and with *that* all the Colyton men heartily agreed."

Pausing, Em smiled at the four rapt faces before her. "So the treasure was hidden in the village, and the location passed down in a rhyme from mother to child, and especially to the first son's wife, and so on down the generations."

"To us!" Gert beamed.

Em nodded. "Yes, to us. We're the last Colytons, and we need the treasure, and that's why we're here, back in Colyton village."

" '*The treasure of the Colytons resides in Colyton*,' " Henry intoned, repeating the rhyme they all knew by heart.

" '*In the highest house, the house of the highest, at the lowest level*,' " Issy continued.

" '*It lies in a box made for the purpose—one only a Colyton would open*.' " Em completed the directions to the twins' delight.

"So now we're here," Bea stated, "and we're going to find the treasure."

"Indeed." Em stood. "But first we're going to have dinner, and then tomorrow we'll arrange for Henry's lessons, and you two will start your lessons with Issy while I start to get this inn in order." Catching a hand of each, she drew the twins up from the chairs and herded them toward the door. "Now we're here, now we have a place to stay—one we can be comfortable in for months—and we all have things to do, then it's better we keep our search private, and only search in our spare time. Now we're here, there's no need to rush."

"So we'll keep the treasure a secret," Gert said.

"And in between other things, we'll *quietly* look." Em stopped her half sisters at the door and looked into their bright eyes. "I want you to promise me you won't go searching for the treasure—not even *quietly*—without telling me first."

She waited, too wise to demand they leave all the searching to her.

Gert and Bea smiled identical smiles. "We promise," they chorused.

"Good." Em let them go. They clattered down the stairs as she turned to Issy. "Now all we need do is feed them and get them off to bed."

By eight o'clock that evening, Em was satisfied that the twins, Henry, and Issy were comfortable and settled in their rooms, and that she'd removed sufficient dust from her own rooms to later allow a restful slumber.

After making up her bed with fresh linens, she left her rooms; she'd warned Edgar that she'd be down to assess the inn's patrons, to learn what type of clientele they presently had, the better to decide what sort of snacks and meals would best suit.

Quietly descending the main stairs, she paused halfway down the last flight, using the vantage point to swiftly scan the common room, noting the smattering of men propped along the bar, and the two pairs of older men sitting at tables about the tap's empty hearth.

The weather had been mild, but a fire would, she thought, add to the ambience. Continuing down the stairs, she added firewood to her mental list.

Stepping off the last stair, she was aware of the surreptitious attention of the inn's patrons, although none met her eye as she glanced around. They would, doubtless, have heard of her new appointment; sensing interest and expectation in their gazes, she flicked her shawl more definitely about her shoulders, then turned and went into the kitchen.

Circling through the empty kitchen, she stepped into the short hallway that lay between the end of Edgar's bar and the tiny innkeeper's office. She'd already investigated the office; other than a collection of aging receipts, she'd uncovered no records of any sort, no ledgers or accounts—nothing to identify the suppliers of goods Juggs had presumably dealt with.

How the inn had been run in the past was shrouded in mystery, but lifting the veil was a task she'd consigned to the following day. For tonight, she'd be content with getting some notion of the inn's current patrons.

Pausing before the office door, screened by the heavy shadows in the hall, she again scanned the drinkers, mentally creating lists of foods such men would pay for, and mulling over how many were married, specifically to women who might be tempted to patronize a clean and well-tended inn.

She duly added a large jar of beeswax, preferably scented with lemon or lavender, to her list.

She was studying one of the seated pairs when she sensed a large presence behind her—simultaneously felt a peculiar tingle slither down her spine.

"Hector Crabbe. He lives in a little cottage just south of the village."

She recognized the deep voice instantly, even though it was seductively lowered to whisper past her ear. Sheer pride had her folding her arms tightly beneath her breasts, all but physically holding back the impulse to whirl around. She fought to keep her voice light. "Which one is Crabbe?"

An instant's silence followed—no doubt while he waited for her to acknowledge his presence more appropriately. When she moved not a muscle, he replied, "The one with the beard."

"Is he married?"

"I believe so." She could almost hear him debating before he asked, "Why do you want to know?"

"Because," she said, finally driven by some benighted compulsion to cast a glance over her shoulder, "I was wondering if I might tempt Mrs. Crabbe and others like her to come to the inn on occasion, to use the common room as their communal gathering place, so to speak."

She turned back to the common room, fighting to ignore the sudden thudding of her pulse. His eyes at close quarters, even in the dimness, were so rich, their depths so alluring. "Do you happen to know where the women presently gather to chat?"

This time when he answered, she sensed arrested interest in his voice. "I don't know that they do."

She smiled, once again glancing up over her shoulder. "All the better for us, then."

Jonas met her eyes, felt again the power of her devastating smile.

He wasn't sure if he was disappointed or relieved when, after briefly holding his gaze, she turned back to the room.

"Who's the man Crabbe's speaking with?"

He told her. She progressed through the inn's customers, asking him to supply names, directions, and marital status for each. He could, and did, somewhat taken aback—faintly perturbed—that she could so easily not dismiss but brush aside the attraction between them. He might have wondered if she'd even felt it if he hadn't detected that initial breathlessness. Hadn't noticed how tightly she was clutching her elbows, as if holding on to them would anchor her.

He could appreciate the impulse; standing so close to her, close enough, in the dim shadows, to breathe in the scent that rose from her skin, from her gleaming hair, he felt a trifle giddy himself.

Which was . . . unusual. He'd never met a woman, let alone a lady, who so effortlessly drew him, who so easily captured his interest and held it.

And effortlessly was the appropriate word. He was perfectly aware that she hadn't intended to, still didn't intend to, affect him at all.

To attract him.

Heaven knew she was currently doing her damnedest to do anything but encourage him.

A pity that he was . . . even more stubborn than he sensed she was.

Their survey of the inn's current patrons completed, she half turned, in the gloom cast a swift glance up at his face. "I looked in the office, but couldn't find the inn's accounts. No records of any kind, in fact. Do you have them?"

He didn't immediately reply. His brain didn't immediately take in the question, too busy considering the scintillating possibilities of their current position. The hall was short, narrow, and relatively dark. He'd been standing quite close behind her. Now she'd turned . . . the top of her head barely reached his collarbone. To look into his face, she had to tilt her head back and look up . . . all the while standing so close that if he took a deep breath his coat would brush her breasts.

He looked into her eyes, even in the dimness saw her battle the urge to take a large step back—but he'd been right in thinking her stubborn. She all but swayed with the impulse to put distance between them, but held her ground.

The moment stretched, stretched—was on the verge of growing awkward when he capitulated, took a step back, and smoothly waved her into the office.

She went past him a touch quickly, crossing the tiny room to slip behind the desk, leaving its scarred expanse between them. She didn't sit, but looked up at him as he filled the doorway.

When he said nothing, simply stood there, watching her, a faint frown formed in her eyes.

He remembered her question. Propping one shoulder against the door frame, he answered, "There are no accounts or records—at least not for the last decade. Juggs didn't believe in writing anything down."

Her frown materialized. "How did he keep track of the profits, then?"

"He didn't. The arrangement he had with my father was a fixed rent per month, and he paid that, and kept whatever excess profit he made." He hesitated, then admitted, "In retrospect that wasn't the wisest arrangement to have made. Juggs didn't really care if the inn was successful or not, just as long as he made enough to meet the rent." He smiled. "The deal you and I struck was distinctly more sensible."

She uttered a small humph and deigned to sit, subsiding into the rickety chair behind the desk. Her gaze grew abstracted.

He watched her pretend to ignore him, but she knew very well he was there.

"Supplies," she eventually said. She looked up at him. "Is there somewhere the inn has an account?"

"There's a merchant in Seaton the estate uses for all supplies. You should deal with him on the Grange account."

She nodded, then opened the desk drawer and pulled out a sheet of paper and a pencil. She set the paper on the desk, held the pencil poised. "I intend to concentrate on building up the inn's culinary offerings first. Once people have reason to think of eating here, we're more likely to see them become regular customers." She made several notes, then paused, making a show of reading over what she'd written. "I believe," she said without looking up, "that we can make the inn the communal center for the village, not just for those who want a pint at the end of the day, but all through the day—a place where the women can come to chat over a pot of tea, and couples can stop in for a meal. All of which will greatly improve the inn's income, and thus its profits. As for the accommodation, I'll see to improving the rooms and amenities once we have something better—something more than just beer and ale—to offer paying guests."

She'd been steadily scribbling, making a list as she spoke. Now she looked up at him, faint but definite challenge in her eyes. "Does that meet with your approval, Mr. Tallent?"

Jonas, he wanted to say. He looked into her bright eyes, knew her challenge had a broader scope than just the inn.

But he hadn't missed her use of the royal "we." Whether she'd intended it or not, the word had reminded him that he needed her there, as the innkeeper of the Red Bells—that if he wanted her to remain and take the inn in hand, something he was increasingly confident she could in fact do, then he couldn't afford to rattle her to the extent she decided to leave.

She was defensive rather than skittish, putting up barriers, refusing to acknowledge the attraction between them.

He could break through her barriers easily enough; all he had to do was take one step further into the room, shut the door, and . . . but now was not the time to risk such a move. Quite aside from running the inn, he didn't yet know what had brought her there, brought her to this—to being his innkeeper. Until he did . . .

Straightening from the doorjamb, he inclined his head. "Indeed, Miss Beauregard. Your plan sounds . . . eminently practical." Lips curving, he swept her a bow. "I'll leave you to it. Good night, Miss Beauregard."

She inclined her head regally. "Good night, Mr. Tallent."

Without glancing back, he turned and left the office.

It was well after midnight by the time Em climbed the stairs and turned into her rooms. In the kitchen she'd found a fresh candle—a long one to see her through the night. She wasn't precisely *afraid* of the dark, but if she had a choice, she kept it at bay.

Darkness reminded her of the night her mother died. Why, exactly, she didn't know, but if she stayed in the dark for any length of time, it felt like a weight, an increasing weight, was pressing down on her chest, making it harder and harder to breathe—until she panicked and got back into the light.

Entering her parlor, she saw bright moonlight streaming across the carpet. She'd left the curtains open; she almost didn't need an extra light. Leaving the candle on the dresser, she went to the window. She stood before it, letting her eyes adjust to the darkness outside.

Silvery light spilled over the landscape, gilding trees and

bushes, washing over the common; in contrast the still surface of the duck pond looked like a piece of polished obsidian, black and reflective. Shadows shifted in the faint breeze, ruffling the moonlight. Atop the ridge the church stood in solid majesty, a watchful sentinel, pale gray against the black velvet sky.

She drew in a deep breath. Remained silent and still before the window, letting the unaccustomed peace slide over and through her.

She refused to think about Jonas Tallent, or the challenge she'd taken on with the inn. Refused to dwell even on her hunt for her family's treasure.

Through the dark of the night, calmness, serenity, and something deeper—something stronger, more enduring—reached her.

Soothed her.

When eventually she turned, picked up her candle, and headed for her new bed, she felt—unexpectedly—as if she'd finally come home.

The next morning at ten o'clock, Em stepped out of the front door of the Red Bells. With Henry beside her and the common to their left, she walked briskly up the road along the row of cottages.

She'd donned her Sunday bonnet, appropriate as they were off to visit the rectory. When applied to that morning, Edgar had suggested that she speak with the curate, a Mr. Filing, about tutoring Henry.

The inn's kitchen had been surprisingly comfortable when they'd gathered there for breakfast. Issy had happily supplied pancakes, and the tea discovered in one of the pantries had proved perfectly palatable.

Edgar had arrived at eight o'clock to open the front doors and sweep out the taproom. When, rather disappointed, Em had commented on the lack of morning customers, he'd broken the news that he rarely saw anyone before noon.

That would change.

By nine, Em had spoken with and rehired Hilda, the local woman who had previously served as cook—that she'd immediately started exchanging recipes with Issy had been an excellent sign—and also two girls, Hilda's nieces, to work alongside her. She'd also hired Hilda's cousin's strapping daughters, Bertha and May, to start on the dusting and cleaning.

As she'd informed Jonas Tallent, culinary improvements were at the top of her many lists. Once she had Henry settled, she would turn her mind to the very real imperative of replenishing the inn's supplies.

The day was fine, a light breeze whipping the ends of her bonnet's ribbons and flirting with the ties of the spring green spencer she wore over her pale green walking gown.

They'd just passed the duck pond when she heard a heavy footstep behind her.

"Good morning, Miss Beauregard."

She halted, drew a quick breath to steel her senses—and turned. "Good morning, Mr. Tallent."

His eyes locked with hers. The breath didn't help; her senses still leapt, her lungs still seized. He was wearing a light hacking jacket over buckskin breeches that molded to his thighs before disappearing into well-polished riding boots.

After an instant's pause, his gaze switched to Henry.

Who was studying him, one step away from bristling in her defense.

"Allow me to introduce my brother, Henry." To Henry she said, "This is Mr. Tallent, owner of the inn."

She hoped the label would remind her brother of the necessity of being civil to her employer.

Jonas found himself looking at a young but distinctly male version of his innkeeper; there was the same brightness in the youth's eyes, although they weren't of quite the same color. The lad was tall, almost a head taller than his diminutive sister, and lanky at present, although doubtless that would change. Regardless, no one seeing the pair would miss the connection, which explained, at least to Jonas who had a sister of his own, the incipient glower in Henry Beauregard's eyes.

Jonas held out his hand, nodded politely. "Henry."

The boy blinked, but grasped his hand and shook it, nodding in reply. "Mr. Tallent."

Releasing him, Jonas glanced at his sister. "Taking the air—or do you have a destination in mind?"

The latter was obviously the case; she'd been striding along at a determined clip. She hesitated for a second, then said, "We're on our way to the rectory."

Turning, she resumed her march. He fell in beside her, ambling, easily keeping pace while Henry ranged on her other side.

"If you're on your way to see Filing, then keeping to the road is the long way around." He indicated a worn path leading up across the common to a gate in the rectory fence. "That way's faster."

She inclined her head by way of thanks and diverted toward the path. As she stepped onto it, he put out a hand to steady her, lightly gripping her elbow.

He felt the subtle jolt that went through her; his fingertips felt hot. Once she was steady, reminding himself of his resolution not to intentionally rattle her—at least not yet—he reluctantly released her.

Halting, she faced him, the rising path making their gazes more level. Lips tight, she nodded. "Thank you. We can find our way from here—we won't need to trouble you further."

He smiled, all teeth. "No trouble at all—I'm going to see Filing myself."

"You are?" Suspicion was writ large in her bright eyes.

Lips twitching, he informed her, "We have business together." He waved her on.

Frowning, she turned and resumed the upward climb.

He followed, aware that Henry was watching him, glancing

frequently his way, prepared to be aggressively protective, but not yet convinced that was warranted; there was as much curiosity as suspicion in the lad's gaze.

Em was also conscious of Henry's evaluation of Jonas Tallent, and on that score found herself unexpectedly of two minds. While she had no intention of encouraging Tallent to concern himself with her or her family, she was achingly aware that for the last eight years, Henry had lacked any male mentor. Their uncle certainly hadn't stepped into their father's shoes in that regard. Henry needed male guidance—more, a male he could look up to—and while Filing might do for Henry's lessons, she doubted a curate-tutor could fill that other, less tangible, but no less important, role.

But Jonas Tallent could.

Aside from the unnerving effect he had on her and her witless senses, she'd yet to see anything in him to which she'd take exception. Indeed, his standing, social and financial, was in large measure the equivalent of her brother's, or rather what her brother's eventually would be.

As a role model for Henry, Tallent would do.

Assuming she discovered no black marks to hold against him.

The path up the common was steep, with steps cut into the side and braced with rock in places. The going was slow, and she had no reason to hurry. "Is it customary," she eventually asked, "for curates to be involved in business?"

There was amusement in Tallent's tone when he replied, "Not customary, but in Colyton it's become an accepted part of village life."

The comment made no sense, at least not to her. Frowning, she glanced back at him. "How so?"

"Filing keeps the accounts for the Colyton Import Company." Jonas decided she didn't need to know that the origins of the company lay in the smuggling trade. "It was created by my twin, Phyllida, some years ago. After she married, I took on the role of overseer, but Filing has always helped by keeping the records of the company's importations, and its dealings with the revenue office in Exmouth."

"What goods does the company import?"

"These days it's mostly French brandy and wines." Just as it had been in years past. "The brandy and wines the inn serves are supplied by the company."

She walked on for a minute, then said, "It seems a strange business for such a small village."

In his twin's defense, Jonas felt forced to explain, "It was Phyllida's solution to the end of the wars, which simultaneously brought an end to the smuggling trade, at least hereabouts. Rather than have those families losing the income they'd derived from the illicit trade, Phyllida turned largely the same enterprise into a legitimate venture. Gradually, over the years, it's become more conventional—the men now use a wharf and warehouse the company built at Axmouth to receive and store the goods, and from there distribute the tuns and kegs to the taverns and inns round about."

Brows rising, she looked ahead; he wasn't surprised when she grasped the central point. "So creating the company was a stabilizing influence, but it's subsequently grown beyond that."

More statement than question; she seemed to be turning the concept over in her mind—and approving.

Well and good. The garden gate of the rectory appeared before them. Jonas opened it and stood back, waving Henry through in Emily's wake before stepping through himself and relatching it.

Em looked up at the rectory, still a little way above them. "What's Filing like? How old is he?"

"He's in his early thirties—a sound man with an excellent education. We think ourselves lucky to have him. He more or less inherited the living, and found he liked the village and so he's stayed." Tallent directed his answer more to Henry than her; Henry nodded, grateful for the information. Tallent eyed her brother curiously, no doubt speculating on what business she with Henry in tow might have with the curate, but he said nothing more—asked no leading questions.

Of course, as he was following them up the steps to the rectory porch, he was going to get answers soon enough.

At her nod, Henry tugged the bellpull.

The door opened with an alacrity that suggested the man holding it had seen them climbing to his porch.

Em found herself looking into kindly blue eyes set in a pleasant, pale, aesthetic face. Filing—she assumed it was he—stood a little over average height, not as tall as Tallent at her back, and was somewhat slighter. His hair was a very light brown; both hair and attire—a gray coat and plain waistcoat over tan breeches—appeared fastidiously neat, their style conservative as befitted a man of the cloth.

"A sound man," Tallent had said; Em could see no reason to question that assessment.

She nodded politely. "Good morning. Mr. Filing, I presume?"

When he inclined his head in a half bow, regarding them all with an expectant air, she continued, "I am Miss Beauregard." With one hand, she waved vaguely over her shoulder—encompassing both Tallent and the inn below. "I've taken the position of innkeeper at the Red Bells, and wondered if I might talk to you about tutoring for my brother, Henry." Another wave indicated Henry beside her.

Filing smiled. "Miss Beauregard." He looked at Henry and offered his hand. "Henry."

After shaking hands, Filing returned his gaze to her. "It's a pleasure to make your acquaintance, Miss Beauregard. Please come in, and we can discuss your brother's requirements."

He stood back to let her and Henry enter; as she moved forward into what appeared to be the rectory's sitting room, Filing looked at the gentleman behind her. "Jonas. Thank you for coming."

"Joshua." Clasping Filing's hand, Tallent stepped over the threshold.

When Em turned around, he was looking at her.

He smiled at her, but spoke to Filing. "I'm in no hurry, so by all means deal with Miss Beauregard first. I know she has a lot on her plate."

Something she could hardly deny, especially not to him. Em felt her eyes narrow fractionally as they rested on Tallent's too-handsome face, but arranging tutoring for Henry was hardly a highly confidential matter, and Tallent already knew why they were there.

Rather frostily, she inclined her head. "Thank you, Mr. Tallent." Giving her attention to Filing, fixing it there, she launched into a description of Henry's studies to date and what they hoped to achieve over the next several years.

Her opinion of Filing escalated significantly when, after taking in all she said, he turned to Henry and questioned him directly about his likes, dislikes, and aspirations.

Initially reserved, Henry quickly lost his diffidence; silently observing, listening to Filing solicit Henry's opinions on various subjects and trade his own opinions and experiences in return, Em inwardly nodded in approval. Filing would do.

He and Henry agreed that Henry would return that afternoon at two o'clock with his books, and he and Filing would work out a plan of campaign, the ultimate aim, as she reiterated, being to gain entry to Pembroke, their father's old college at Oxford.

"We have contacts there, of course," she said as she turned toward the door. "As long as Henry can attain the required grades, there's a place for him there."

"Excellent." Filing went with her; Henry nodded a farewell to Tallent, then followed behind.

Halting before the door, Em faced Filing. "We should discuss your fee."

Filing looked down at her, his expression a medley of

pleased eagerness and kindliness. "If I might, I suggest we leave that discussion for later, once Henry and I have more definitely decided on the level of tutoring he needs." Filing glanced at her brother. "Henry's quite advanced—it may be that all he needs is guidance, rather than active teaching, and that, to me, is almost a pleasure."

Em nodded. "Very well—we'll work out an arrangement later."

Still very aware—her nerves seemed unable *not* to be aware—of Tallent standing by the window, she turned and bestowed a haughty nod. "Good day, Mr. Tallent."

His lips curved as he very correctly bowed. "Miss Beauregard."

Head rising, she swept out of the rectory door.

Filing followed, farewelling her and Henry on the porch.

Returning inside, Filing shut the door, then joined Jonas before the window. In companionable silence, they watched Emily Beauregard and her brother descend the common.

When they reached the road, Filing murmured, "How very curious."

Jonas snorted. "An innkeeper whose father went to Pembroke, who's set on ensuring her brother does the same. Definitely not your average innkeeper."

"The family's gentry at least, don't you think?"

He nodded. "At least. And before you ask, I have no idea what they're doing here, but Miss Emily Beauregard is indeed the new innkeeper of the Red Bells."

"She can only be an improvement on Juggs."

"Precisely my thought."

Shaking his head, Filing turned from the window. "An intriguing family—the boy is quite acute."

"As is his sister."

"Are there just the two of them?" Filing headed into the dining alcove where a cabinet contained the recent records of the Colyton Import Company.

"No—there's more. There's a sister who's"—Jonas dredged

his memory—"twenty-three, as well as a set of twin girls, who might be twelve but I think are younger."

When Filing raised his brows in question, Jonas shook his head. "A long and inconsequential story." He nodded to the papers Filing was hauling forth. "Are those the licenses?"

"Yes. There are three."

They sat at the table and worked their way through the latest formalities required to keep the company in legal order.

When they'd finished, Filing stacked the papers and set them aside. "The next ship should put in at Axmouth next week."

Rising, Jonas nodded. "I'll speak to Oscar and make sure he knows."

Filing accompanied him to the door and followed him onto the porch. They both paused, shoulder to shoulder, looking down the common—at the inn.

Filing shifted, as if to go inside. "I'll have Henry with me all afternoon—I'll let you know if I learn anything more about the family."

Jonas nodded, stepping onto the porch steps. "While he's with you, I plan to interrogate the lovely Miss Beauregard herself—I'll let you know if I extract anything interesting."

About to turn to the door, Filing paused. "She's wary of you."

"I know." Jonas smiled as he reached the bottom of the steps. "But I believe I have precisely the right carrot to dangle before her dainty little nose."

3

"Good afternoon, Miss Beauregard."

Em looked up from her pile of lists to discover Jonas Tallent blocking the doorway to her tiny office. She managed not to smile, but it took effort—he was a sight to please in a long, many-caped greatcoat that lapped at the tops of his highly polished Hessians. He'd exchanged his hacking jacket for a more formal coat and waistcoat; he looked like he'd stepped from a page of the *Gentlemen's Gazette*.

Battening down her unruly senses, she nodded briefly. "Mr. Tallent."

When he said nothing more, just looked at her, she felt compelled to ask, "Is there something I can help you with?"

"Actually, it's I who am here to help you."

Uttered in his deep, ineffably smooth voice, the words rolled over her. Her instincts rose in instant suspicion.

His smile only deepened, as if he knew. "It occurred to me that it might be beneficial for you to meet Finch, our supplier in Seaton, and look over his wares firsthand. I'm headed there now in my curricle, and wondered if you would like to come along."

Meeting her principal supplier, at his warehouse, with her employer—he who controlled the account she would be using—by her side . . .

She would have taken an oath that nothing would have got her physically closer to Jonas Tallent by choice, but . . . she set down her pencil. "How long will we be gone?"

"Two hours at most, there and back with time to talk to Finch." He nodded to the pile of papers under her hand. "Bring your lists, and you can give him your first order."

It was far too good an opportunity to pass up—something she was very sure Tallent knew.

What he didn't know was that she was perfectly capable of keeping him in his place, no matter what he thought or tried. That was one thing her years at her uncle's house had taught her; she was now an expert in the not-so-subtle art of keeping gentlemen in line.

Pushing back her chair, she rose. "Very well. If you'll wait while I fetch my bonnet?"

"Of course." He stood back to let her pass him. As she turned toward the common room, he added, "You might want your pelisse as well—the wind is always stronger closer to the coast."

Heading for the stairs, she smiled to herself. Any gentleman who instinctively thought of a lady's comfort was unlikely to pose any great threat.

She started up the stairs.

He paused at their foot. "My horses are frisky. I'll meet you outside."

Raising a hand in acknowledgment, she continued to her room.

Five minutes later, she joined him outside, and felt forced to amend her definition of "threat." The chestnut steeds prancing between the shafts looked like the devil's own.

He saw her hesitation, grinned. "Don't worry. I can manage them."

She looked up and met his eyes. "I've heard gentlemen say those words before—usually just before they overturn their carriage."

He laughed. The sound did disturbing things to her insides.

Transferring the reins to one hand, he laid the other over his heart. "I swear on my honor I won't land you in a ditch."

She humphed. Gathering her skirts, she reached for the curricle's side.

He held out his gloved hand to help her up; without thinking, she laid her fingers in his. His hand closed firmly about hers—and her world tilted.

Rocked.

He drew her up. She landed on the seat beside him, struggling not to gasp.

Good God! When would her wretched senses stop reacting?

When would they get over him?

He hadn't tried to hold on to her hand for any longer than necessary. He was wearing leather gloves, and so was she. Yet still the sensation of his fingers holding hers lingered, stealing her breath, making her heart pound.

Luckily, his horses, shifting restlessly, had claimed his attention. With just one last glance to make sure she was settled, he released the brake and loosened the reins. The chestnuts immediately surged, and they rattled out of the inn's forecourt.

He turned the pair south. "Seaton's almost directly south, more or less on the coast, and the roads are fairly direct."

She nodded, not yet trusting her voice. She waited for him to start questioning her—she would have sworn that's what he intended. Instead, once they were bowling along, he glanced at her once, but thereafter gave his attention to his horses, apparently feeling no need to converse.

The curricle rolled quite smoothly along, quite quickly, too, pulled effortlessly by the powerful horses. Her attention, too, fixed on the sleek pair. She knew enough to recognize prime horseflesh when she saw it; if Henry could see her now he'd turn green.

For his part, Jonas Tallent seemed an excellent whip—not showy or flashy, knowing just when to draw his leader in, when it was safe to lower his hands, just when to step in and restrain the highly strung pair.

"Have you had them for long?" She hadn't meant to initiate any discussion, to show any interest, but the words were out before she'd thought.

"Since they were foals." He didn't take his eyes from the road, but after a moment added, "My brother-in-law, Lucifer Cynster, has a cousin—Demon Cynster—who's one of the premier breeders of racehorses in England. These two are from his stud. He keeps those he considers better for racing, and the rest go to the family—which luckily for me includes anyone connected with the Cynsters."

Lucifer? *Demon?* She almost asked, but at the last minute decided she really didn't need to know. Instead . . . "Your brother-in-law—is he the one who lives at Colyton Manor?"

"Yes. He inherited the manor from the previous owner— Horatio Welham. Horatio was a collector, and Lucifer knew him through that. Horatio considered Lucifer the son he never had, so when Horatio died, Lucifer found himself the owner of Colyton Manor."

"And then he married your twin."

He nodded, glanced briefly her way. "You'll meet Phyllida soon—that I can guarantee. She'll have heard about you taking up the innkeeper's position by now—she'll be around to meet you as soon as she can get time away from her multiplying horde."

"Horde?"

"She and Lucifer have two sons—two noisy, boisterous imps who take up a lot of Phyllida's time. And multiplying because she's expecting another."

She let that, and his tone when he spoke of his sister and her brood, sink in. Eventually she asked, "Is there just the two of you—you and Phyllida?"

He glanced at her, mischief in his eyes. "Our parents always maintained two were enough."

Pure curiosity prompted her to ask, "But what about you—did you think it was enough?"

He didn't answer immediately. She wondered if he would, but finally he said, "Not all of us can be lucky enough to be part of a large family."

She looked ahead, thought of her family—and saw no reason to dispute his statement.

Now that the ice had been broken she fully expected him to start probing. Instead, they rattled on through the fine autumn afternoon in a strangely comfortable silence. Birds flitted and sang; the salty tang in the air grew increasingly pronounced as they crested the last rise before the gentle downward slope to the cliff tops.

Despite all recent distractions, the quest that had brought her to Colyton was never far from her mind. As he set his horses trotting evenly down the slope, she glanced at him. "Tell me about the village in the wider sense. I know about the manor and the Grange. Are there other large houses around? Places with staff we might persuade to use the inn?"

He nodded. "Quite a few larger houses, as it happens. Ballyclose Manor's the largest. That lies further along the lane beside the church. It's owned by Sir Cedric Fortemain. Then there's Highgate, owned by Sir Basil Smollet—that's out along the lane on the other side of the rectory. You should probably add Dottswood Farm to the list. Although it's not a house in the same sense as the others, it is a large holding supporting numerous families."

He glanced at her. "That's in the immediate area around the village. If you range further out, there are more, but the three houses I mentioned are . . . associated with the village, so to speak. All on those estates would consider Colyton their village."

She nodded. "That's what I wanted to know. Those are the people we need to draw in first." And one of those houses would most likely be "the highest house, the house of the highest" in which the Colyton treasure was concealed.

Ballyclose Manor sounded like the place to start their search. She was tempted to ask more, to confirm that the

Fortemain family, or whoever had lived at Ballyclose, had been the social leaders of the village long ago, but roofs came into view, lining the road ahead.

"Seaton." As he checked his pair, Jonas gave himself a mental pat on the back for having managed to sit next to Miss Emily Beauregard's slender form for nearly half an hour without triggering any frosty setdown—indeed, even better, she'd started to let her barriers—those she'd erected against him—come down.

They were still there, just not as heavily fortified as they had been; on a physical level he still had a challenge before him.

But his strategy for "interrogating" her seemed to be working. He'd reasoned that if he simply gave her the chance—horses and Cynsters notwithstanding—she would ask him things she wanted to know.

While her interest in the larger houses of the village might conceivably be due to her focus on expanding the inn's clientele, he didn't think that was the case; her mention of that had been an afterthought, an excuse for her question.

So she was interested in those houses—or one of those houses—for some reason. If he could restrain himself for the rest of the afternoon, who knew what he might learn?

He guided the curricle to Finch's warehouse. Drawing his horses to a stamping halt in the yard before the heavy doors, he tossed the reins to a young lad who came running, and jumped down.

The horses had had the edge taken from their energy. He could let them stand for at least a little while.

Rounding the curricle, he saw his passenger was about to attempt to jump to the ground. "No. Wait."

Poised on the edge of the curricle's raised floor, gloved hands locked on either side of the frame, she looked up.

He grasped her waist and lifted her down—she tried to jump as he did, throwing him off balance.

She collided with him, breast to chest. Her weight was

nowhere near enough to topple him; he staggered back a step, then halted.

With Miss Emily Beauregard in his arms.

Plastered against him.

For one finite moment, time stood still.

His brain seized; his heart stuttered, then stopped.

She wasn't breathing, either.

She was gazing up at him, and he was lost in her eyes . . .

Sensation returned in a rush. Warmth—heat. His heart kicked to life, thudding altogether too hard.

His fingers flexed, gripping her waist.

Just as she dragged in a huge breath—and her breasts pressed into his chest.

Just as he realized what would inevitably happen—was inevitably happening—with her warm, soft curves pressed so temptingly against him.

Just as he remembered that he didn't want to rattle her into taking flight.

Jaw setting, he forced his arms to work and set her back on her feet, a good half yard of clear air between them.

She dragged in a shuddering breath. "I'm *so* sorry."

I'm not. He bit his tongue, then managed to growl, "Never mind." Manners raised their heads. "Are you all right?"

No! Her senses were scrambled and her wits had flown. Em managed a nod. Her cheeks were flaming; she didn't want to think what she must look like. She still felt hot all the way down her front—wherever her body had touched his—an acutely unnerving sensation.

She was certainly unnerved. Drawing in another tight breath, too shallow to steady her giddy head, she turned and surveyed the warehouse just as an older man came out.

"That's Finch."

She tensed, expecting to feel Tallent's fingers close about her elbow. But he glanced at her briefly, then waved her forward, falling in by her side as she walked toward the man.

Her relief was tempered by that one swift glance. He knew he affected her, which was in no way comforting.

He cleared his throat and introduced her to Finch.

By ruthlessly forcing her mind to concentrate on Finch and all she'd come there to achieve—putting in a sizable order being just one part of her agenda—she managed to survive the next hour in a reasonable state.

Eventually, however, after an extended tour of the warehouse followed by discussions about deliveries and further orders, it was time to head back to Colyton. Which meant getting back into Jonas Tallent's curricle.

Which she couldn't do, certainly not before gentlemen, without assistance.

Just the thought of putting her hand in his again, and feeling his fingers close around hers, had anticipatory heat prickling along her arm.

Finch escorted them to the warehouse door, thoroughly pleased with her order. She'd put effort into charming the older man and knew she'd succeeded. He smiled delightedly as he shook her hand . . .

She smiled sweetly back. "Mr. Finch, I wonder if I could trouble you to hand me into the curricle? We do need to get on." Looking into the yard, she saw the boy struggling to hold the revived and impatient horses, and smoothly added, "And Mr. Tallent's horses are so restive."

"Of course, of course, my dear Miss Beauregard." Finch kept hold of her hand. "Here—do watch your step. There's a hole there."

She dutifully picked her way carefully along by Finch's side. As he helped her up, she glanced, briefly, in Tallent's direction.

And encountered a dark look. His lips had tightened into a line and his eyes were narrowed.

But he said nothing as he rescued his reins from the boy, stepped up into the curricle, and sat beside her.

She smiled once more on Mr. Finch—her unwitting savior.

"Thank you, sir. I'll look forward to receiving those goods tomorrow."

"First thing!" Finch declared. "I'll send the boy off with the dray at first light."

Tallent saluted Finch with his whip. Finch bowed as the curricle lurched, then rattled forward. Tallent deftly turned it out of the yard; the horses quickly settled into their usual smooth gait.

Em sat back, watching the houses of Seaton slip by. Studiously ignoring the louring weight in the air, emanating from the gentleman beside her.

She waited for him to say something, what she had no idea.

He waited until Seaton fell behind and they were bowling along at a clipping pace before stating, "I haven't met your sisters yet."

Not a question, yet given the tension in the air, she gratefully seized the topic and ran. "I've three—Isobel, Issy as we call her, is the eldest. As I believe I mentioned, she's twenty-three. The younger pair are the twins—Gertrude and Beatrice—Gert and Bea." She paused for breath, sensed that unnerving tension still there, and went on, "All three, Issy, Gert, and Bea, have blond hair and blue eyes, not like Henry and me. The twins especially look angelic, which is so very far from the truth it can be dangerous—people take them at face value far too readily. And I'm afraid they've run wild for too long. Their mother—Issy's, Henry's, and my stepmother—didn't cope well after my father's death, and she failed to educate them properly, as Issy and I subsequently learned when, after her death, the twins came to live with us. Issy's presently trying to instill some modicum of ladylike attributes into their unfortunately not always receptive minds."

She paused, glanced at him.

He nodded, frowning still, but whether it was over checking his horses or what she'd said—or what she'd done—she didn't know.

After a moment, she looked ahead; looking at his profile, all hard edges and planes currently set in uncompromising lines, wasn't an occupation likely to soothe her overactive nerves. "We hail from York originally. As I mentioned we've traveled quite a bit—we stayed in Leicestershire for some time before I took on those positions for which you saw the references."

There was a certain challenge—a certain thrill—in successfully skating around the whole truth. "The tavern at Wylands was quite lovely." She continued to color in her supposed background, inventing freely—filling the time.

Jonas stopped listening. He knew her references were false, ergo the memories she was now relating were fictional, fabrications. But she'd revealed more than he'd expected.

Thinking back over their conversations, he noted she hadn't reacted to his mention of the Cynsters. She had no knowledge of the family, which suggested she'd never moved among the haut ton. Combined with her father having attended Pembroke College, that gave him a clearer idea of the social strata to which she belonged—and she'd just told him she hailed from York. That, he thought, had been true.

And if she hadn't known that the twins weren't being educated, then her father must have died when the twins were quite young—say between seven to ten years ago—and she'd been acting as head of her family ever since. That was plain in the way she spoke of her siblings, in her attitude to Henry and his to her.

He glanced briefly at her; she was still holding forth about the inn at Wylands. Looking forward, he inwardly debated her age—twenty-four or five, at the most twenty-six, given her other sister was twenty-three. It was her maturity that made her seem older, gained no doubt through having to look after her siblings from an early age. That and . . . she'd definitely had experience of holding gentlemen at bay.

Those barriers she'd erected against him were too practiced; she was too watchful, too aware of the possibilities at all times.

It bothered him that she felt she needed to be so wary, so careful around gentlemen, especially him. It smacked of a loss of innocence, not in the biblical sense but in a practical, day-to-day sense, which in his book was regrettable.

Just how, where, and why she'd been subjected to unwanted attentions he didn't know—but for some reason he didn't comprehend, he felt compelled to learn the answers.

Felt compelled to . . . what? Defend her?

To his considerable surprise, he didn't—couldn't—dismiss that idea, much less the feeling behind it.

Which made him feel distinctly wary as well.

He drove on, her voice pleasant, almost musical, in his ears, and wondered what he should do—would do—next.

Wondered what he truly wanted.

Wondered how to achieve that.

By the time the first cottages of Colyton appeared, he'd made up his mind.

He needed to learn a great deal more about Miss Emily Beauregard. He needed to get answers; he needed to learn her secrets.

She would, of course, resist revealing them.

But he knew he could unsettle her by playing on the physical attraction between them.

Against that, he didn't want to lose her as his innkeeper. Given the strength of her barriers, given what he'd thus far seen of her will, he felt fairly certain that if he pushed too hard, she wouldn't hesitate to pack her bags and leave.

Leave him as well as Colyton, and that definitely wouldn't do.

He turned into the forecourt before the Red Bells and drew his horses to a halt. He stepped down, pinning her with a glance—defying her to try to jump down again.

She waited, not happily; that she was steeling herself to weather his touch without reacting was, to him, obvious.

She rose as he neared. He reached for her, grasped her waist, and swung her down.

And didn't let her go.

Not immediately.

Couldn't resist, despite his best intentions, taking just a moment to look into her bright eyes, and see her response, sense her locked breath.

And know that she was no more immune to the moment, to the closeness, to the sudden flaring heat, than he.

Drawing in a slow breath, he forced himself to let her go, forced himself to take a step back.

His eyes still locked on hers, he bowed. "I hope you enjoyed the drive. Good day, Miss Beauregard."

She tried to speak, had to clear her throat. Nodded. "Yes, thank you—the drive was pleasant. Good day, Mr. Tallent."

With another nod, she turned and walked to the inn door.

He watched until her figure was swallowed up by the gloom inside, then turned, strode around his horses, and leapt back into the curricle's seat.

Turning the equipage, he set off at a spanking trot for the Grange.

If he couldn't risk overly pressuring Miss Emily Beauregard for answers to his numerous questions, then he'd just have to be subtle and not step over her line.

Which was an excellent resolution as resolutions went, except that he had to, of necessity, first discover where her line—that point beyond which she would recoil and take flight—lay.

In pursuit of that goal—and hoping for more incidental revelations—Jonas walked to the Red Bells early that evening.

He stepped through the front door and, somewhat taken aback by the crowd, halted just inside to take stock.

That there was a crowd wasn't such a great surprise, but its composition and extent exceeded his expectations. Noise rose up and rolled over him in waves; laughter echoed from the rafters. And that wasn't all that was different.

The place *looked* different, yet he couldn't see anything—furniture or decorations—that hadn't been there before. The difference, which was quite remarkable, appeared to have been achieved by a thorough cleaning—was that lavender he smelled?—combined with better placement of cushions and the reappearance of doilies and table runners he hadn't seen in decades.

He glanced around again, dredged his memories. Decided the transformation had already been under way when he'd fetched Emily early that afternoon; he'd been distracted and hadn't paid close attention. And the change wasn't, he suspected, as glaringly obvious in the light of day as it was in the warm glow of brilliantly clean and polished lamps.

Scanning the tap-side of the room, he wasn't surprised to see that the occasional regulars were all there—among others, Thompson, the blacksmith, and his brother, Oscar, and from Colyton Manor there was Covey and Dodswell, Lucifer's groom. But in addition there was a solid representation of estate workers, farmers, gardeners, and household staff—some from even further afield than the houses he'd named for his new innkeeper.

Quite a few owners of said houses were present, too; Jonas spotted Henry Grisby and Cedric Fortemain talking animatedly, while Basil Smollet sipped an ale and chatted with Pommeroy Fortemain, Cedric's younger brother.

The cottages in the village were represented by Silas Coombe, Mr. Weatherspoon, and a sprinkling of other older males. What was notable was that many had their respective spouses perched at their elbows, women who hadn't darkened the inn's door since early in the late unlamented Juggs's tenure.

Even more remarkable was the throng, mostly feminine, to the left of the door. Every one of the more comfortable chairs was taken. Miss Sweet, Phyllida's old governess, was there, along with Miss Hellebore, almost an invalid but not to be outdone in the curiosity stakes. Both had noticed him and were watching him avidly, but he was accustomed to being the target of their bird-bright eyes.

The ladies from Highgate and others from Dottswood Farm were scattered in groups, chattering like magpies.

Jonas looked, but Phyllida wasn't among the throng. It was Aidan's and Evan's dinnertime, so that wasn't to be wondered at. He felt certain his twin would have looked in during the afternoon, but as Miss Beauregard had been with him, Phyllida might well have missed her mark.

That everyone had dropped by to see—and for the females at least, to if possible converse with—their new innkeeper went without saying. At that very moment, Lady Fortemain, Cedric's mother, held the floor. She'd captured Emily Beauregard and—Jonas knew her ladyship well—wasn't yet inclined to let her go.

Emily glanced up and saw him, but Lady Fortemain reached out and shackled a clawlike hand about Emily's wrist, reclaiming her attention.

Judging that his new innkeeper might require assistance in breaking free, Jonas strolled in their direction.

Em knew without looking that Tallent was approaching, and was disgusted at the inward dithering that knowledge provoked. One segment of her wits—or was it her instincts?—were prompting her to break off her interaction with Lady Fortemain—of Ballyclose Manor, no less—and seek safety in her office, or better yet in the female-stocked environment of the kitchen.

Another part of her mind—luckily the better part—was adamantly opposed to any show of weakness. She should stand her ground, refuse to be flustered or react in any way to his presence, at least not outwardly. And more important than all else, she should *listen* to what Lady Fortemain was saying. From all she'd learned that evening, Ballyclose Manor was at the top of the list to be their "house of the highest."

But with elegant danger approaching with near lethal grace, focusing on her ladyship wasn't all that easy.

Lady Fortemain, her birdlike claw still locked about Em's wrist, fixed her eyes on Em's face. "My dear, I know it's short notice, but I would be thrilled if you and your sister— I believe someone mentioned she's twenty-three—would consent to attend the parish afternoon tea at Ballyclose tomorrow afternoon."

Releasing Em, Lady Fortemain smiled encouragingly. "It's always been Ballyclose's duty to host the afternoon teas, and while my daughter-in-law as the current lady of the manor *ought* to be in charge, as she's so caught up in her burgeoning family, I still help out as I can." There was a hint of determination in her ladyship's eyes as they locked once more with Em's. "I really would take it as a *personal* favor if you would both attend."

Em kept her polite, noncommittal expression in place while her mind raced. Attending afternoon teas—even parish afternoon teas—wasn't, she suspected, something innkeepers normally did. More, she'd intended their presence in the neighborhood to be, if not a secret, then an unremarkable occurrence—but apparently becoming the local innkeeper wasn't compatible with being unremarked.

And while she held no illusions about why she and Issy were being invited—*they* would be the central attraction, at least until all those attending had looked their curious fill— there was, weighing against all the drawbacks, the undeniable fact that from all she'd gleaned, both from Tallent and from various patrons, Ballyclose Manor was most likely the hiding place of the Colyton treasure.

She needed to determine if they had cellars—she felt sure the house would—and then she would need to find some way to search them.

The informal nature of an afternoon tea might well afford the perfect opportunity for taking the next step in their still very necessary treasure hunt.

Letting her expression lighten, brighten, she returned Lady Fortemain's smile. "Thank you, ma'am. I'm sure I speak for my sister Isobel in saying we'd be delighted to attend your event."

"Excellent!" Sitting back, Lady Fortemain beamed. "Three o'clock then—anyone in the village can show you where we are." Her ladyship's gaze shifted to Em's left. "Jonas, my boy!" She held out her hand. "I'm hosting the parish afternoon tea, dear. I know it's no use asking gentlemen to attend, but if you should feel so inclined, we'd be delighted to welcome you."

Smiling his practiced, entirely noncommittal smile, Jonas half-bowed over her ladyship's beringed fingers. "I'll bear that in mind, ma'am."

Especially if, as it seemed, his innkeeper would be there.

"If you'll excuse me?" With a polite nod for Lady Fortemain and an even briefer one for him, said innkeeper moved away.

After a few smiling words with her ladyship, Jonas followed.

Of course, she tried to discourage him, constantly flitting from group to group among the women; with her burnished brown hair and hazel eyes, and the brown gown she now had on, she reminded him of a sparrow—which, he supposed, cast him as a hawk.

Smiling to himself, he ambled in her wake. Given he owned the inn, she could hardly escape him, but if she thought to catch him flat-footed and awkward in this milieu, she would need to think again. This was his village, where he'd been born and had spent most of his life; every female around knew him, and his having recently returned from years in London only lent added interest—at least for the ladies. They were more than ready to chat with him as he did the rounds.

Between their own careful behavior and the size of the crowd, he doubted his pursuit of Emily was obvious, even to dedicated observers like Sweetie and Miss Hellebore.

There was too much chatter, too much distraction, too many other things going on, for any to bother watching them for more than a few minutes.

Nine o'clock rolled around, and while some customers had left, more had arrived. The common room, much to Em's cautious satisfaction, was close to full.

Her nemesis finally ambled across to the tap-side of the room; he moved through the crowd as if he owned the place—which, of course, he did. With a combination of relief and damning disappointment—her emotions had clearly disengaged from her wits—she seized the opportunity to whisk through the kitchen, checking with Issy and Henry that all was well and the twins were safely abed, before slipping into the little hallway outside the office to cast an assessing eye over the crowd before the bar.

When she'd returned from Seaton, Issy had informed her of their afternoon's success. She and Hilda had decided to trial scones as an offering for the afternoon trade. They'd made plain scones—to be offered with raspberry jam and clotted cream—and raisin scones, and put them on show at two o'clock.

By four o'clock they'd sold out. The woman who did for the rectory had looked in, and bought half a dozen raisin scones for Mr. Filing, and a dozen for her own family. Others passing in the lane had sniffed, and looked in to buy two here, three there. Miss Hellebore's maid had come running in to buy some for her mistress's tea; apparently the delicious smells wafting from the inn's kitchen along the backs of the cottages had made Miss Hellebore's mouth water.

"Pies," Em had declared when they'd told her. "For lunch." It was the obvious conclusion, one with which Issy and Hilda had concurred.

Em looked out over the males strung along the bar and sitting or standing propped all about the tap. The small army in the kitchen had made smaller pastries and sandwiches, both substantial and delicate, for the evening drinkers, but it was difficult to tell which had been more popular as all had vanished some time ago.

Despite the size of the village, the inn could easily support a proper dining menu.

She was considering the balance of dishes that might suit while idly surveying the crowd, when she realized there was one head she couldn't see. She scanned again, then, confident she was well hidden in the shadows, stretched up on her toes . . . but she couldn't see him anywhere.

He must have left.

A deadening sense of deflation washed over her. She hadn't wanted him to pay her any attention—not as herself—but he might at least have commented favorably on the changes to the inn, let alone the significant increase in patronage, which both Edgar and John Ostler had informed her was remarkable.

He, apparently, hadn't thought to remark.

"Privately wallowing in your triumph?"

The words whispered across one ear; warmth slid across her nape and made her inwardly shiver.

She whirled. He was standing in the doorway to her office, shoulder propped against the frame.

All of six inches away.

She glared at him.

He smiled lazily down at her through the dimness.

"You're to be congratulated, Miss Beauregard." He glanced past her toward the packed tap. "The inn hasn't seen a crowd like this for more than a decade."

His gaze returned to her face. The sincerity in his voice left her scrambling for words, for some intelligent reply.

Thank you. I'll be sure to tell my staff was what she should have said. But her eyes had locked with his, and she'd somehow got wrapped in the warm richness of his gaze, and his murmured words seemed too personal, too private, to be returned with formal phrases.

It took a moment before she realized she couldn't breathe.

Before she realized that they were standing together, mere inches apart in the dark—mere feet away from the crowd in the tap, yet for all intents and purposes they were private and alone, unobserved and unobservable.

That his attention had focused solely on her.

That her senses had drawn in to encompass only him.

That her lips felt warm, almost throbbing.

His lids grew heavy. His gaze lowered to her lips.

They throbbed even more.

She could feel her heartbeat in her fingertips, feel some-thing within her stretch . . .

Heard him give a soft, almost inaudible sigh, then he straightened, slowly, his gaze slowly rising to her eyes.

His lips twisted in a gently rueful smile. "Good night, Miss Beauregard."

His deep voice was faintly gravelly.

He stepped back, easing away from the doorway, back toward the kitchen.

The darkness closed about him. "Sweet dreams."

4

❦

W ell." Em stood looking up at the front façade of Ballyclose Manor. "This could be it—our 'house of the highest.'"

The manor was a relatively nondescript structure of indeterminate age, yet its air of well-kept prominence, as well as the stream of women and the occasional man, all in their Sunday best even though it was Wednesday afternoon, arriving on foot and in gigs, suggested Ballyclose had a recognized claim to be the premier house of the area.

Beside her, similarly engaged in a survey of the house, Issy nodded. "We'll need to search their cellars."

"First we need to confirm that they actually have cellars, then we need to learn where they are." Determination infusing her, Em started for the front door, gravel crunching beneath her shoes. "If we can achieve that much today, I'll be satisfied." She glanced at Issy as they went up the steps. "While I'm as eager as the twins to find the treasure, now we've landed so comfortably at the inn, we don't need to rush or take unnecessary risks."

Issy nodded in agreement.

Gaining the portico, they decorously joined the line of people entering the house. Em had donned an apple green gown with a single flounce at the neckline and hem. A forest green spencer with satin ribbons defeated the October chill. In contrast, Issy was a vision in blue, her simple gown the perfect showcase for her willowy figure. With her blond curls, blue eyes, and more gentle nature, Issy was usually the sister most noticed, something Em counted on to give her greater freedom.

An imposing, rather supercilious butler was waiting just inside the open front doors, directing guests to the drawing room that ran down one side of the house.

With Issy at her elbow, Em entered the room in old Miss Hellebore's wake. The old lady was unable to move far or fast, yet remained mentally spry with sharp eyes and ears. Em seized the moment while Miss Hellebore exchanged greetings with Mr. Filing and was welcomed by Lady Fortemain to examine the old lady's companions.

Miss Sweet, a gentle, fluttery soul with features and smile to match her name, stood alongside Miss Hellebore, supporting the older woman. They were escorted by a lady with dark brown hair, a confident, direct manner—and very familiar features. Em wasn't surprised to hear Lady Fortemain greet the lady as "dear Phyllida."

Jonas Tallent's twin sister touched fingers with Lady Fortemain, then gathered Miss Sweet and Miss Hellebore and firmly steered them to a chaise in the center of the long room. Farmers' wives and various gentry were gathered in knots dotted about the room, chatting as they sipped from fine china cups distributed by a small army of footmen.

Summoning a smile, Em stepped forward and extended her hand. "Mr. Filing."

His practiced smile softening with approval, Filing shook her hand. "Miss Beauregard, I'm delighted to see you here. I must compliment you on your brother's diligence. He's a remarkably keen scholar—it will be a pleasure to guide his studies."

"Thank you, sir. For my part I'm very glad Henry's found such a knowledgeable teacher with whom he's so at ease." With a gracious nod, Em turned to Lady Fortemain and curtsied. "Ma'am. Thank you for inviting us." Smoothly turning to Issy, she continued, "Allow me to present my sister, Isobel."

Issy, who'd introduced herself to Filing and given him her hand, blushed faintly as she retrieved it. Turning to their hostess, she smiled and curtsied. "Lady Fortemain. It's a pleasure to be here."

Lady Fortemain's eyes widened fractionally as they traveled from Filing's face to Issy's. Then her ladyship beamed. "My dear, we're quite *delighted* to welcome you both to the village." She waved them on. "Please do go in. I—or Mr. Filing—will be along shortly to introduce you to the others, although I daresay most already know who you are. We don't stand on ceremony at these gatherings, you'll find."

Thus adjured, with easy smiles Em and Issy ventured deeper into the room. Issy didn't glance back, but Em did—in time to see Lady Fortemain recall Filing, staring after Issy, to his duty in welcoming the next parishioner.

Facing forward, Em glanced at her sister's profile, noted the slight blush still fading. And wondered. Filing was in his thirties—too old for calf love, something Issy occasionally inspired. But Em knew well enough to make no comment to her sister; Issy had transparently noticed Filing's interest and would make up her own mind how to react. Despite her gentle looks she was all Colyton beneath, and therefore capable of being as stubborn—no, stubborner—than any mule.

Nevertheless, Em couldn't recall any other gentleman who had made her sister blush—not like that.

They'd met a number of the other guests at the inn the previous evening; it was easy to move through the room, chatting and being introduced to yet others, learning people's names and placing them within the community.

The gathering encompassed a spectrum of social classes from the lady of the manor to farmers' wives, making the inclusion of the innkeeper and her sister rather less of an oddity. While in her role as innkeeper Em hadn't expected

to attend such events, her hesitation in accepting hadn't
been due to any anxiety that she and Issy would feel out of
their depth, but rather that in such a milieu their true colors
would inevitably shine through. They were both confident
and at ease in moving through the drawing room, accepting
and sipping tea and making small talk; the facility ran in
their blood, and neither of them was particularly good at
acting.

Em had accepted that there was nothing she could do
other than be herself. She hoped the more observant—
among whom she was perfectly sure she could class Phyllida Cynster—would conclude that she and Issy hailed from
a gentry family down on their luck.

Which was more or less the truth, at least for the moment.

She and Issy had decided that projecting such a background was the best tack they could take. Most people were
too polite to ask further questions.

In such a small community, however, gently bred was
gently bred, no matter how straitened their circumstances.

That, certainly, seemed to be Pommeroy Fortemain's attitude when he appeared at Em's elbow. "My dear Miss
Beauregard, allow me to introduce myself. Pommeroy Fortemain, at your service." He capped his speech with a flour-
ishing bow.

Although not all that old—perhaps Tallent's age—
Pommeroy Fortemain was well on the way to being portly.
His liking for nattily striped waistcoats with flashy buttons
did nothing to conceal his impending corpulence. Beyond
such sartorial gaudiness, however, his appearance was un-
distinguished; he shared little of the solid gravitas that
characterized his older brother, Cedric. Em waited until
Pommeroy straightened, then inclined her head and gave
him her hand. "Sir."

She'd separated from Issy, and having just parted from a
group of farmers' wives she was momentarily on her own.
Wondering what she might learn from her hostess's son, she

retrieved her hand from his overly enthusiastic clasp. "Tell me, sir, am I right in thinking it's your brother who owns the manor?"

"Yes—that's right. Cedric."

She'd briefly met Cedric at the inn the previous night.

"Rather older than I am," Pommeroy rattled on. "He's not in attendance this afternoon—holed up in his study, no doubt, busy with estate affairs." Pommeroy's tone suggested he was only too happy to leave all the work to his brother. "I always help Mama entertain the locals." He glanced around. "Truth to tell, there's not much else to do around here."

Em didn't know whether to laugh or look affronted. In the end she did neither; it was clear he'd intended no insult. "Did you grow up here—in the district?"

"Yes—this has always been home. Fortemains have been at Ballyclose since . . ." He thought, then looked faintly surprised. "I don't know when."

"Indeed?" She didn't have to fabricate her interest. More and more it appeared that Ballyclose Manor was the house they were seeking. She made a show of looking around, taking in the long room. "Is the house very large?"

Pommeroy shrugged. "So-so. Not as large as some."

"But in the immediate area?"

He pulled a considering face, then nodded. "It's probably the largest." His gaze fixed on her face. "But, I say, enough about this old pile. What brought you and your family to Colyton?"

She smiled, a touch tightly. "We came to manage the inn—I saw a notice in Axminster."

"So you hail from there?"

"Only in recent times." She didn't want to say anything further, didn't see any reason to feed the avid curiosity in Pommeroy's eyes. She strongly suspected that he was one of those men who loved to gossip. His mother certainly did, and he seemed very much his mother's son.

To her surprise, he leaned closer, his gaze fixing intently

on her eyes. "Perhaps I could take you for a drive around the area? Take in the local sights, that sort of thing."

She attempted to look regretful. "I'm sorry, but I'm the innkeeper—I have to run the inn." She eased back, preparing to move on.

"But you're an innkeeper-*manager*, really. You don't do the work—you tell other people what to do and *they* do it."

He was more right than wrong, but she wasn't about to engage in a discussion of her duties, not with him. She was hunting for the right words to discourage his notion that she had time to waste with him when she sensed someone approach.

Not just someone. Her employer.

A telltale tingle ran down her spine.

Lungs tightening, she swung to face him.

"Miss Beauregard." Jonas smiled into widening hazel eyes, then half-bowed. His innkeeper was looking particularly fetching—not at all like an innkeeper. "Allow me to present my sister, Phyllida Cynster."

Releasing his arm, Phyllida stepped forward, drawing Emily's bright gaze. Phyllida offered her hand; tentatively Emily clasped fingers. "It's a pleasure to meet you, Miss Beauregard. I must tell you we have great hopes that under your guidance the inn will once again be a place the whole village can and will visit."

His innkeeper rose to the occasion, inclining her head gracefully. "Thank you, Mrs. Cynster. That's certainly my ambition. I'm hoping the local ladies will help me define what works, and what misses the mark."

Phyllida grinned. "From all I've heard, your notion of scones was an inspired beginning."

Emily smiled. "The right food, the right ambience . . ."

"Indeed." Phyllida nodded briskly. "Build it and they will come. I'm sorry I missed you yesterday afternoon. I called at the inn, but I understand"—her gaze slid Jonas's way—"that my brother was introducing you to Finch in Seaton."

Jonas shrugged. "It seemed the least I could do, given Miss Beauregard needs to order from Finch."

Sensing some level of unvoiced censure—over what she couldn't imagine—Em hurried to say, "I was most grateful Mr. Tallent could spare the time to take me to Seaton—meeting a merchant face-to-face often avoids a great deal of unnecessary difficulty."

Phyllida studied her through dark brown eyes every bit as unfathomable as her twin's, then conceded, "With Finch that's probably true. He's easy enough when he knows you, but can be distinctly taciturn when he does not." She glanced again at her brother. "I'm glad to see you taking your responsibilities so seriously, brother mine."

Jonas pulled a face at her, but before he could respond further they were joined by another couple.

Em smiled through yet another introduction, forcing her mind to function, her senses to focus and not get distracted by the gentleman by her side. On her other side, Pommeroy Fortemain was entirely forgettable, but to her witless senses Jonas Tallent was utterly riveting.

It was irritating, and a touch unnerving. Her continuing—if she were truthful, escalating—obsession with Jonas Tallent was starting to make her uneasy.

Of herself, not of him.

Which for her was an entirely novel situation.

After that almost-kiss, the kiss that hadn't happened last night in the shadowed hallway at the inn, she wasn't at all sure of what might happen next. Of what she might do if he provoked her senses again.

When another trio joined their circle, distracting everyone, she grasped the moment to murmur her excuses and step back from the group. No one heard her, none of the others noticed, but as she turned away Jonas's head came around. He seemed about to follow, but his sister chose that instant to ask him a question, and he had to turn back to her.

Em slipped away, tacking between groups until she'd put most of the long room between herself and her employer.

There'd been something—some flash of intent—in that last swift glance that had made her want to run. She recalled that Lady Fortemain hadn't expected Jonas to attend, so why had he? Simply to pursue her?

"Nonsense," she muttered. Stepping to the side of the room, with a Herculean effort she shoved Jonas Tallent out of her mind, and turned it instead to her purpose in being there—unearthing her family's long-buried treasure.

Her next step was learning if Ballyclose Manor possessed the requisite cellar.

She looked around. The crowd wasn't that dense; locating Issy wasn't difficult. What was difficult was that Mr. Filing was with her.

More, as Em watched, she realized her sister, blushes and all, was "with" Mr. Filing. She was talking *to* him, with him, not merely conversing politely. They were standing together in the middle of the floor and apparently had eyes only for each other.

Even as Em watched, a local matron detached herself from a nearby group, glanced around, saw Filing and Issy, and headed their way, clearly intending to join them.

But then the lady slowed, halted, observed rather shrewdly, then, with a faint quirk of her brows, a subtle lift to her lips, changed course to join another group.

Leaving Issy and Filing talking earnestly.

Interesting. Even heartening. But . . .

Em glanced around. Her plan had been that she and Issy would search for the cellar together, Issy keeping a weather eye out for interruptions. But with Filing so focused on Issy, Em didn't think fetching her sister and together slipping away to explore the house would be at all wise. Filing, she suspected, would continue to watch Issy even if he were talking with someone else.

But they were inside Ballyclose Manor, and she was disinclined to let the opportunity slip. Who knew when another would eventuate?

There was no reason she couldn't search for the cellar alone—not with the steady stream of footmen trooping through the drawing room, still circling with plates of cakes or balancing trays with teapots, to lead the way.

The cellar door was most likely close by the kitchen.

When a footman bearing an empty platter slipped out of a nearby door, she followed.

The door gave onto a minor corridor. Her footsteps muffled by a thick runner, she hurried to keep the swiftly moving footman in sight. He didn't head back to the front hall and through the green baize door at its rear, but, via a series of ever-narrowing corridors, strode deeper into the house.

She walked openly in his wake, aware another footman or maid might come up behind her, or appear ahead, going in the opposite direction. If seen, she would say she'd gotten lost, then had spied the footman and was following him, assuming he'd lead her back to the drawing room.

As it happened, her skill at dissembling wasn't put to the test. Juggling his empty platter, the footman took one last turn; she followed, and halted at the top of a flight of stone stairs leading sharply down to a landing, then turning to the left and disappearing out of sight.

A door on the landing, facing the stairs, lay open, revealing the butler's pantry. From the cacophany rising up the stairs, they led directly into the kitchen.

"'Ere—don't be a dolt! Wipe that platter prop'ly before you take it upstairs. Have my head, her ladyship will, if you take it up like that, smeared with cream."

A rumbling grumble came in reply. Em didn't wait to hear what followed. Slipping away from the stairhead, she headed further along the corridor; a narrow door stood at the end, with a courtyard beyond. She needed to place the kitchen within the overall layout of the house, and that would most easily be done by viewing this wing from outside.

Reaching the door, she looked out, but couldn't see far;

the courtyard was narrow, limiting her view. Grasping the doorknob, she turned it—and was rewarded with a click. Opening the door, she stepped outside. After a cursory glance confirming that the courtyard was deserted, she silently shut the door.

Flagged with gray stone, the rectangular courtyard was walled on three sides. Beds bordering the walls hosted a variety of climbers that reached long fingers up the stone walls. The open end of the courtyard lay to the left of the door. One swift glance at what lay beyond had her smiling and walking quickly in that direction.

At the edge of the paving, she paused in the shadow cast by the wall at the courtyard's corner. The kitchen garden lay below her, spread out on a lower level, neat rows of vegetables marching down the plot, herbs straggling out of pots and over paths.

Stone steps led down; stepping onto the first, she peered around the building's corner and saw what looked to be a washhouse built onto the back of the house. A larger door sheltered by a narrow porch—presumably the back door leading into the kitchen—was set into the wall close by. But what drew her gaze, transfixed it, was the pair of low doors built into the wall halfway between the courtyard and the back door.

They had to be doors to the cellar.

She studied them, then glanced along the rear façade, then turned to view the surrounding gardens, noting trees to help her fix her position.

Eventually she brought her gaze back to the cellar doors. They were sturdy and had a small pane of thick glass set in their center; given the angle from which she was viewing them, she couldn't see through.

She was weighing going forward and peeking in—just enough to confirm the doors did indeed give access to the cellar—against the risk of someone coming out from the kitchen and seeing her, when a most peculiar panoply of sensations washed down her spine.

Abruptly swinging around, she stepped up, back into the courtyard—and nearly plowed into a wall.

A muscled male wall comprised of Jonas Tallent.

Her heart didn't just leap, it turned cartwheels. She instinctively inhaled, only to have the breath get stuck in her chest, doing her no good at all.

Eyes wide, she took a hasty step sideways. "What are you doing here?" The words came out perilously close to a squeak.

She swallowed and tried to steady her pounding heart, tried not to notice the alluring warmth that seemed to reach for her.

How had he got so close? Without her knowing? She'd realized he was there, but far too late. Why hadn't her witless senses noticed him and warned her, when they so consistently noticed him everywhere else? Why . . . ?

She was mentally babbling. Dragging in a huge breath, she held it and with an effort summoned a frown.

Recalled too late how unwise it was to look into his eyes, into the fathomless, fascinating depths . . . she fell in, and they held her.

He quirked one lazy brow at her. "I'd intended to ask you the same question."

She blinked. Question? He was standing half a foot away, towering over her—she could barely remember her name.

His lips curved. "What are you doing here?"

A hint of steel lay beneath the smooth words—enough to prod her instincts to action. She fought free of his spell, narrowed her eyes on his. "Did you follow me?"

Her tone made the question an accusation. Jonas raised both his brows in reply. "Yes." He held her gaze, then reached out and, with one finger, flicked back a gleaming brown curl at her temple. Sensed rather than saw her battle her reaction, felt an answering response that went marrow-deep.

He kept his eyes on hers—jewel green lit with golden sparks. "Are you going to tell me what you're searching for?"

Those lovely eyes flared. "No!" Her lips compressed to a thin, tight line, then, eyes locked with his, she muttered, "I'm not searching for anything."

He inwardly sighed. He'd tried being subtle, but that hadn't got him far. He'd tried being restrained; stepping back from her last night had taken more resolve than he'd known he possessed. Afterward, perhaps unsurprisingly, she'd inhabited his dreams, disturbing his rest.

Yet here she was, still holding firm against him.

Even if she was all but quivering with awareness.

An awareness that in turn affected him. Perhaps . . .

Heaving a melodramatic, put-upon sigh, he reached for her. Closed his hands about her upper arms and jerked her nearer. She uttered a strangled squeak as he released her—to slide his hands around her and link them, effectively caging her within his arms without having his hands on her.

Without crushing her to him, as every instinct he possessed was urging.

Instead of fighting or struggling, resisting in any way, she froze. Stopped breathing.

Linked hands resting at the back of her waist, he smiled intently into her wide, shocked eyes. "I'm not going to let you go until you tell me all. Until you confess what it is that brought you to Colyton—which I strongly suspect is the thing you're searching for." He raised his brows. "Am I right?"

Her eyes searched his. Her hands had instinctively risen, but she didn't know what to do with them; they hovered in the air between them, level with his chest. As he watched, her gaze dropped to his lips.

He sucked in a slow, impossibly tight breath, conscious of the debilitating effect, not just her telltale fascination with his lips, but the combined impact of having her so close, all but against him, and the more subtle allure of the scent of her hair—of her—was having on his control.

Mentally gritting his teeth, he hung on. Waited.

Mentally pleaded that she answer, soon, and save them both.

Managed to say, low and deep, his voice a rough murmur, "Emily . . . tell me all and I'll let you go."

Em heard, but found it impossible to concentrate. To focus on his words rather than the fascinating movement of his lips as he said them.

She watched his lips tighten, then soften as he again said her name, his tone one step removed from a plea . . . and suddenly she knew.

Two could play at his game, the game he'd started, the game he'd been playing last night at the inn.

One part of her mind insisted that she should be struggling, that she should plant her hands firmly on his chest and shove.

Most of her mind was on a different track.

Lifting her hands, she placed them on his shoulders, used the contact to steady her as she stretched up—and pressed her lips to his.

Kissed him. Just a kiss, a light one—enough to shock him and stop him from pursuing the question of what she was doing.

Just a quick kiss—because she knew, now, that he was as affected by her as she was by him—and she'd never been so tempted in her life.

Never been interested, never wanted to know, to understand why a man wanted her. But Jonas Tallent was different; with him, she had to know.

Distracting him from her search was her excuse, but just like all Colytons, discovery and exploration—plunging into the unknown with reckless abandon—were her true motives.

Discovery and exploration were uppermost in her mind. His lips were cool, firm, less soft than her own. Sheer shock had frozen him, his lips immobile, unresisting as with her own, she tested them.

Briefly. She knew she had to draw back. Reluctantly she started to lower her heels.

At her back, his hands moved. And then he was holding her, strong fingers spreading over her back, palms gripping her sides as he kept her where she was.

And took over the kiss.

Bent his head and pressed his lips to hers. Tested her lips as she had his.

But the result was quite different. Sensations washed through her, warm and enticing. A thrill, quite novel, played along her nerves. Seeped into her brain and seeded a suggestion, a thought, a want.

A desire.

To know more—to discover more.

The pressure of his lips on hers increased, subtly tempting. They shifted on hers, openly luring . . .

He drew back a fraction, then with the tip of his tongue swept her lower lip, gently coaxing, beckoning . . .

And she followed. For the first time in her life she wanted to know, to feel, to experience a kiss, all a kiss could be.

She parted her lips, and let him in.

Jonas all but shuddered. Felt ridiculously giddy as he accepted her invitation, felt immeasurably honored to have gained it. Her mouth was all sweetness, lusciously tempting; he took, pressed further, carefully claimed.

Carefully learned. Her innocence was transparent, at least to him; fresh and alluring—not the innocence of ignorance, not passive or shy, but alive and eager and elementally untouched.

She'd been kissed before, but not willingly. He was the first man she'd ever welcomed; that knowledge was certain, undisputed in his mind, and brought with it a responsibility, of which, as he found her tongue with his and gently stroked, he was acutely aware.

He hadn't expected her to kiss him, hadn't imagined she would—hadn't thought of it, hadn't been prepared—had no plan in place—to deal with the eventuality. He'd wanted to kiss her—had since he'd first laid eyes on her—but he hadn't seen it happening that day. Now it was . . .

Now she'd kissed him, then gifted him with her mouth, now she was standing before him, his hands holding her as they communed . . . now the moment was upon him, he couldn't think beyond the sweetness.

The simple, heady sweetness of her.

He couldn't get enough of it.

Had to have more.

Enthralled, Em let him explore as he wished—somewhat stunned, shaken off balance to find herself the object of exploration, instead of the explorer. The concept expanded in her mind, and made her shiver.

He sensed it, felt it; he angled his head and deepened the kiss. His tongue filled her mouth—fascinated, she permitted it.

Reveled in the heat, in the subtle tensing of his body, in the sensation of being soft and vulnerable in his hands.

She tensed at the thought. Realized on a rush of near panic that she was indeed helpless—a willing wanton, or at least had been.

But she didn't have to fight to free herself—didn't even have to whip up her vanished strength to struggle. He knew, read her reaction, and slowly but definitely brought the kiss to an albeit reluctant end.

She didn't need to think to know he was reluctant; the fact screamed in every slow, deliberate movement, in the reined grip of his hands at her sides. Yet that very control, the fact he'd stopped immediately when she'd wanted to, left her immeasurably reassured.

Reconfirmed that, as she'd thought, he was, indeed, an honorable man.

That she was, indeed, safe with him. Or at least, from him.

Where he was concerned, the danger lay in her.

Their lips parted—slowly. He lifted his head, set her back on her feet, only then raised his thickly lashed lids and met her eyes.

The heat in his was impossible to mistake.

It stole her breath, made her inwardly quake.

His eyes searched hers; at such close quarters his gaze was hotly piercing.

She tried to ease back. Again he had to tell his hands to let her go, but he did.

He straightened, his gaze still locked with hers. His face seemed harder, all sharp angles and rugged planes. "If that was meant to make me lose interest in you and your doings . . . permit me to inform you you've sadly miscalculated."

The gravelly tenor of the words—pure masculine possessiveness—made narrowing her eyes easy. "Me and my doings," she tartly informed him, "are no concern of yours."

Unrelentingly he held her gaze. "Before, possibly. Now?" His lips curved with pure predatory intent. "Not a chance."

She narrowed her eyes as far as they would go, pinned him with a fulminating glare, then swung around and stalked back to the door.

Turning his head, Jonas watched her go, then quietly reiterated, "Not a chance, Emily Beauregard. No chance at all."

Turning, he followed her back into the house.

5

If Emily Beauregard thought she could kiss him like that—and then look at him with stars in her eyes even though it had been broad daylight—and *then* expect him to let her be, she was not just sadly mistaken, she was . . .

"Daft!" Striding along the path through the wood on his way to the manor, Jonas kicked a fallen branch from his path. "Utterly, incomprehensibly daft."

Regardless, knowing the odd notions females were wont to take into their brains, he fully expected her to continue to try to dismiss him.

Much good would it do her.

After that kiss, he hadn't been able to think of anything else—other than kissing her again.

Other than what might follow—if he had any say in things, that *would* follow—beyond that next kiss.

In the meantime, he intended to get to the bottom of what had brought her and her family to Colyton. He was determined to learn what it was she was searching for. Clearly she imagined it might be at Ballyclose, although exactly where eluded him; the kitchen garden seemed an odd place to look. If she told him what she sought, he could ask Cedric, and then they would know.

Why she needed to keep her search, and presumably its

object, a secret, he had no clue, but he'd already considered—and discarded—the notion that it might be in any way illegal.

The idea of Miss Emily Beauregard involved in something untoward, let alone nefarious, was simply untenable. Indeed, laughable. How he could be so sure of that he didn't know, but he was. She was the sort who, on finding a shilling in the road, would insist on asking through the entire village *and* all the outlying farms to find the owner.

No. The reason Emily was keeping her real business in Colyton a secret was a matter of trust.

Once she trusted him, she would tell him all.

Until then . . . he would keep an eagle eye on her to make sure she didn't get into any difficulties while engaged in her secret search.

Why he felt responsible for her safety—especially considering her "me and my doings are no concern of yours" declaration—was a matter he didn't, at that point, deem it necessary to define. Regardless of all and any logic, he felt compelled to watch over her—and that was that.

Regardless of all else, it felt right.

The manor appeared ahead of him, its slate roof a gray glimmer through the trees. He'd already passed the side path leading to the back of the inn—had slowed, wondered . . . but then he'd lengthened his stride and continued on. Emily—Em—would be safe enough for the moment; there was someone else he needed to see.

Needed to recruit, to get on his side.

The path led to the manor's stables, and thence to the back door. Cutting through the wood, the path was the shortest route between the Grange and the manor; everyone from both houses used it frequently, especially since Phyllida had left the Grange and taken up residence with Lucifer at the manor. Jonas's appearance in the manor's kitchen therefore caused no great surprise. He saluted Mrs. Hemmings, Phyllida's housekeeper and cook; hands in a bowl of dough, she called a cheery greeting as he moved on to the butler's pantry.

There he found that worthy polishing silverware.

"Good morning, Bristleford. Any idea where m'sister is?"

"Good morning, sir. I believe you'll find the mistress in the drawing room."

Jonas frowned. "The drawing room?" Phyllida rarely sat in the more formal room, preferring the family parlor.

"Indeed, sir—she has the lady from the inn with her. Miss Beauregard."

"Ah." Brows rising, he nodded his thanks, noting Bristleford's description of Emily. Like Mortimer, Bristleford rarely mistook anyone's status.

Heading into the house, Jonas pushed through the door that gave onto the back of the entrance hall, then strode to the front room on the right.

He paused in the doorway, meeting both pairs of eyes that, alerted by his footsteps, had turned his way.

One pair, the same dark brown as his own, was filled with mild interest. The other pair, bright hazel, widened, but surprise was quickly superseded by wariness.

He smiled. "Good morning, ladies." Strolling to where they sat side by side on the chaise, he bent and bussed the cheek Phyllida offered, then nodded to Emily. "Miss Beauregard." He looked at the three books she had in her lap. "I take it you're a keen reader?"

Phyllida sat back, her eyes scanning his face. "Miss Beauregard inquired about the village's history. Naturally, Edgar sent her here." She glanced at Emily. "Lucifer's gone into Axminster, so I'm helping Miss Beauregard as best I can . . ." Phyllida returned her gaze to his face. "But I'm not sure where all the books on village history are. Do you know?"

He'd been watching Emily's face throughout, could clearly see chagrin behind her polite expression. Smiling easily, he held out a hand. "Let me see what you've discovered."

She handed him the books. He checked their spines, ignoring the speculation in Phyllida's eyes.

Being his sister—more, his twin—she was acutely sensitive to his moods, could all too often read his thoughts—often too well for his comfort. Despite neither he nor Emily having done or said anything in any way indicative, Phyllida had already noted the undercurrents between them—and was now alert and watching avidly.

"There are more books on the village than these." He handed the volumes back to Emily, caught her eye. "Were you interested in any aspect in particular?"

Em shook her head. "No—just the history in general." She glanced at Phyllida. "As I mentioned to Mrs. Cynster, as I hope to reinstate the inn as the center of village life, I thought to learn what, if any, traditions might apply." She turned her smile upward, to Jonas Tallent's face. "Beyond that, I am, of course, interested in the village I now call home."

He knew she wasn't telling him the whole truth; she could see his cynicism in his eyes. Sensed him hesitating, searching for some way to press her, she steeled herself to avoid revealing more.

A clatter of footsteps coming down the stairs, then rapidly pattering around the front hall, drew their gazes to the open doorway.

Abruptly Miss Sweet appeared, hands waving wildly. "Oh! There you are, Phyllida dear." Miss Sweet looked faintly stricken. "I'm afraid they've escaped and are on the loose."

Phyllida's eyes widened. She rose—just as an earsplitting shriek sounded from overhead.

They all looked up, then Phyllida sighed and shook her head. A smile tugged at her lips. "If you'll excuse me, Miss Beauregard, I fear I must attend to the causes of that disturbance." Her gaze shifted to Jonas. "But my brother will no doubt be able to help you further."

Em rose, gripping the three books. "Yes, of course.

Thank you for your time." She held up the books. "If you're sure I might borrow these?"

"Of course." Phyllida was already heading briskly to the door. "Books exist to be read—history books especially." Pausing in the doorway, she looked back at Jonas.

Who smiled. "I'll find some of the other books for Miss Beauregard, then come up and rescue you."

Phyllida laughed, inclined her head to them both, and left. Miss Sweet had already fluttered ahead.

As their footsteps faded, Em glanced at Jonas—Mr. Tallent—only to discover he was looking at her. Steadily. This was the first time they'd been together and alone since that unwise kiss the previous afternoon; she'd expected to feel awkward, even embarassed—she had kissed him first after all, and then invited more—but his focus on learning her goal left her no time to indulge in missish sensibilities. She hefted the three books. "These will very likely be enough—at least to begin with." She started for the door.

He raised his brows, and followed. "There are more books here—the ones you have are relatively general."

When she merely inclined her head and kept walking, Jonas added, "I thought your true interest lay in specifics— like houses." She glanced at him. He caught her eye. "Ballyclose Manor, for instance."

She halted, plainly torn. "Anyone who comes to the village would be interested in the background of a house like Ballyclose." Eyes on his, she said, "As your innkeeper, knowing more about the houses round about, those with staff who consider the village their home territory, is essential."

"So your interest in the surrounding houses is driven purely by your innkeeper's duty?"

She hesitated before nodding—then tried to make the action decisive. Convincing. "Just so."

He sighed. And stepped toward her.

Eyes flaring, she stepped back.

He repeated the exercise, once, twice, and had her neatly

backed into a corner with bookshelves stretching to either side. She realized, halted, then stiffened, tilted her chin, and glared at him. "Mr. Tallent."

He shifted a half step nearer, raised a hand to brush an errant curl from her cheek. Met her eyes. "Jonas."

She tried to draw in a huge breath, but her lungs had constricted. Just a touch, the lightest caress, and he'd distracted her. The knowledge sent a surge of unexpected lust through him—effectively distracting him.

Her lids had lowered, but beneath the screen of her lashes her gaze fastened on his lips.

He stopped thinking. Acted instead.

Raising one hand—slowly—he framed her delicate jaw, tipped up her face, and brought his lips down to hers.

Covered them gently, slowly, giving her plenty of time to resist.

She didn't—just sighed softly when his lips cruised hers.

He shifted still closer, and gave her what she wished—took what he wanted. Another kiss.

Different from the first. It was as if their lips, their mouths, knew the other's, recognized the touch, the taste, the texture. And hungered for more.

She had the three books locked against her chest, a barrier keeping their bodies apart. Leaving both of them focused solely on the kiss, on the melding of mouths, the rising heat of lips and tongues, the tactile communion.

He felt greedy, hungry, urgently so.

She seemed to be the same, if not quite so certain. She followed rather than led, but as the kiss grew hotter, deeper, she was with him every inch of the way.

Then she moved into him, and he felt his control quake.

An unprecedented happening sufficiently unusual to shake some of his wits back into place.

Blindly reaching to either side, he locked his hands on the bookshelves, once more caging her. Far safer than sweeping her into his arms, which was what his more primitive self was demanding.

He broke the kiss just enough to say, "What are you searching for?"

One small hand rose to his cheek to guide his lips back to hers. "Nothing." Her lips found his as she breathed, "Nothing."

He kissed her again, and she kissed him, and for a moment more nothing else mattered.

But he knew it couldn't go on. Not the kiss, nor his not knowing.

He drew back, broke the contact. Arms braced on either side of her, he waited until she drew breath and lifted her gaze to his eyes. "Tell me what you're searching for."

She held his gaze. The moment stretched. "No. As I told you before, it's none of your concern."

"You're wrong. It is."

She tilted her chin, between them gripped the books more tightly. "Mr. Tallent."

"Jonas." He looked at her lips, willed her to say his name.

Instead, the tempting curves compressed into a grim line. Using the books like a shield, she pushed against his chest. "If you please . . . ?"

He brought his gaze back to her eyes. Then, slowly, he released his hold on the shelves, straightened, and stepped back. "I can probably locate more books on the village."

She brushed past him. "Thank you, but no." She bustled toward the door. "These will be enough to begin with."

He followed her through the doorway and across the front hall. She stopped before the front door. Reaching past her, he gripped the knob, turned, then stopped. Caught her eyes. "For the moment."

Her eyes glittered with both temper and understanding, the comprehension that he wasn't talking about the books.

He opened the door and she swept past him. "Good day, Mr. Tallent."

Propping one shoulder against the door frame, he watched her march down the path to the gate. Opening it, she went through. She didn't glance at him when she turned back to latch it, but she knew he was there, watching.

He didn't hear her sniff, but he suspected she did before turning and marching off down the road.

Every instinct he possessed urged him to follow—to continue the discussion they'd started in the corner of the drawing room.

That discussion was far from over, but . . . straightening, he stepped back and shut the door.

Emily Beauregard was going to the inn, which he owned. Letting her escape—letting her imagine she had—wasn't a bad move; all the better to surprise her later.

Meanwhile . . . turning, he headed for the stairs. His purpose in coming to the Grange remained unfulfilled. Reaching the first floor, he set out to hunt down Phyllida.

Securing his twin's support was worth letting Emily Beauregard escape . . . for half an hour or so.

Em marched into the Red Bells in an uncharacteristic fluster—which, of course, she couldn't allow to show. She forced herself to slow, to smile easily at the customers already gathering in anticipation of the pies from which mouthwatering smells were wafting through the inn and out along the road.

The pies, clearly, would be a success. One thing she didn't need to worry her head about.

Indeed, bit by bit, element by element, under her guidance the inn was progressively transforming. She was now confident she could turn the Red Bells into the establishment she'd envisioned, the institution she thought it should be.

Its owner was the only fly in her ointment.

Her attraction to him was bad enough, difficult enough, but his attraction to her was even worse. The former she could control; the latter appeared to be entirely beyond her influence.

Making her way to her office, she set the three books on

the desk—then stood staring down at them, not truly seeing the spines and covers.

There could no longer be any doubt that her employer . . . had a certain interest in her. That he returned her interest in him in equal measure. What worried her was what he imagined that combination would lead to. She was his innkeeper, gentry or not; a liaison was the most that could exist between them—more likely an affair of relatively limited duration from what little she knew of gentlemen of his class.

Her class.

Which was the sticking point. Ladies of her ilk, innkeepers or not, didn't indulge in liaisons, let alone affairs, at least not before they were married and established and had given their husbands heirs.

She could pretend to be an innkeeper, but she couldn't stop being herself.

As Jonas—Mr. Tallent—could have nothing more than a liaison in mind, her way forward with respect to him was unquestionably clear. Wherever possible, she should avoid him at all costs, and when she failed in that, she would steadfastly keep pretending that he didn't affect her.

Didn't make her yearn for anything at all.

"There!" Lips tight, she stacked the books determinedly. "Decision made." Rounding the desk, she dropped her reticule into the bottom drawer, shut it, straightened and smoothed down her skirts.

Drew breath, lifted her head, plastered on an easy smile, and swept out to the kitchen.

She spent the next half hour with Hilda, working out the necessary ingredients for a week of various sorts of pies. Then Issy came in with the twins in tow. Seeing Em, the terrible two immediately started complaining about having to practice every morning on the old piano in the common room.

"And *then*," Bea stated, "Issy dragged us out and up that huge great hill."

Issy rolled her eyes. "Just up the hill to the church."

"It was windy!" Gert settled at the table. "But Issy said we had to go up there for inspration."

"Inspiration," Issy patiently corrected. She met Em's eyes. "Drawing lessons this afternoon."

Em nodded. She looked at the twins. "I hope you've both got a view in mind. I'll come up and see your drawings when you're finished."

They would have grumbled, but Hilda chose that moment to place pies fresh from the oven before them, and assuaging their appetites took precedence over all else.

Em exchanged a fond glance with Issy.

Hilda offered Issy a pie, but Issy waved it aside. "I'll eat later with the rest of you. I want to see how the pies do."

As it was Issy who, together with Hilda, had designed the various fillings, Em acquiesced. As long as Issy's culinary contributions were limited to designing recipes, she was content.

She, too, circulated through the common room as the pies were ferried out and placed before eager customers. Em watched the faces, saw eyes close as mouths chewed, before, with every evidence of gustatory delight, her patrons gave their full and undivided attention to devouring the pastries.

Across the room, she met Issy's eyes and smiled—content indeed. They'd be sold out within the hour.

Circling back to the kitchen door, she paused beside Issy and Hilda, who'd come to look. "Double the quantity tomorrow, I'd say."

"Aye." Hilda nodded, a beaming grin splitting her lined face. "Double tomorrow, and after that we'll see."

Em swanned back through the common room, intending to head through the tap to her office. Old Mrs. Smollet, seated near the door, waved her over to compliment her on the mutton pie.

"Thank you—I'll be sure to pass on your kind words." Turning away, Em paused in the shaft of sunlight streaming through the inn's open door. Taking a step back the better to survey her domain, she couldn't have been more gratified; their lunchtime crowd already exceeded the evening crowd prior to her appointment.

She was just thinking that her employer should be pleased when the light about her faded.

Even without turning, she knew he'd arrived—as if conjured by her thoughts—and was literally darkening her door.

Her first impulse was to rush—not walk—to the sanctuary of her office, but there was no safe haven there, not from him. She was about to move when it struck her that she was safer—as safe as she could be—where she was, in full view of a goodly portion of the village.

She settled back on her heels, every nerve aware that he was standing less than a foot behind her.

"You're to be congratulated, Miss Beauregard. The inn is prospering under your care."

The words rumbled past her ear, his deep voice converting the polite phrases into something close to a caress.

Without turning around, she somewhat stiffly inclined her head. "Thank you. I'll convey your approval to the staff."

"Do."

She heard the amusement in his voice, knew he'd goad her into some response if she didn't get away from him soon.

Even as she looked for it, salvation appeared. She waved to the plates one of Hilda's nieces was ferrying to a table. "Have you had luncheon? The mutton pies are already gone, but I can recommend the game pie."

She waited—sensed a certain hiatus behind her—then his voice reached her, pitched lower than before.

"Would that my hunger could be so easily assuaged."

She couldn't stop herself from turning around, could feel the heat rising in her cheeks.

The sight of him lounging in the doorway, one shoulder propped negligently against the frame—all that delectable maleness a bare foot away—didn't help. She had to force her gaze up to his face.

He met her eyes, arched a brow.

She narrowed her eyes at him. "If we can't tempt you with a game pie, then sadly we have nothing else to offer."

His lips curved. "Not on offer, perhaps, not yet, but who can tell what you might put on your menu one day soon?"

She understood perfectly—more heat flooded her cheeks—but she determinedly feigned innocence. "As a matter of fact, we were discussing chicken and leek pies only an hour ago."

"Is that so?" His dark eyes held hers. "Regardless, I believe I'll wait for something a little more . . . satisfying."

The deep brown of his eyes glinted, sinfully wicked. His lips held a suggestive curve. Far too clearly she could remember them on hers . . .

She cleared her throat. "I can't imagine what you might consider more satisfying than a game pie."

His smile deepened. "It's a secret."

Her secret. "I doubt any secrets will appear on the menu."

"We'll see. And then, of course"—his gaze lowered to her lips—"there's a certain sweetness to which I've discovered I'm decidedly partial."

She sucked in a breath, tried her best to summon a glare—difficult with her head spinning. "Sweet things are *definitely* not on our menu."

"Not yet, perhaps, but . . . we'll see."

He shifted, straightened, reached out, took her elbow, and moved her to the side, so the Thompson brothers could brush past and leave.

Both brothers, large and hulking, exchanged familiar nods with Jonas—Mr. Tallent!—to which he responded with graceful ease.

His attention returned to her, but she'd finally found her wits. Drawing herself up, she inclined her head. "If you'll excuse me, I must get back to running your inn."

He considered her for a moment, then nodded. "As you wish. But I'll be back, Miss Beauregard, however many times it takes, until I'm satisfied."

She couldn't bear to let him have the last word—especially not a word like that, loaded, positively burdened, with innuendo. "I believe you'll discover, sir, that your endeavor will be in vain."

She'd intended to move away, but his fingers tightened warningly about her elbow.

Then he bent his head.

She froze, thoughts scattering in panic. Surely he wouldn't kiss her in the common room before a dozen interested customers?

The answer was no. To her immense relief, all he did was lean close so no one could possibly hear him but her.

He lowered his voice, too, until his tone reverberated, resonated, through her. His eyes trapped hers; at such close quarters, his were mesmerizing.

"There's something you ought to know, Emily Beauregard." He spoke quietly, evenly, but there was weight behind every word. "I intend to learn all your secrets, and I intend to have you, and I'm a very determined and patient man."

Involuntarily, her eyes searched his, confirmed he meant each and every word. Her head swam; she struggled to draw breath. What could she say to cap such a bald-faced declaration?

Finally succeeding in dragging in a breath, she decided discretion was the better part of valor. Twisting her elbow free of his light grip, she swung around and set off for her office.

Then she halted, head rising, and swung back to face him. Eyes blazing, she met his. "We'll see about that!"

No one but he could interpret the phrase.

With a terse nod, she swung around and reset her course for the safety of the kitchen.

Three days later, as she sat in the church and listened to Mr. Filing's reading, Em was still congratulating herself on having successfully sent Jonas Tallent to the rightabout.

Since that fraught exchange in the inn doorway, she'd seen him, but only at a distance—across the tap or in the street. He'd made no attempt to catch her eye, or to speak with her, but she'd felt his gaze, dark and steady, on her whenever she was in his sight.

Which had occurred quite often; she'd hoped that given her trenchantly discouraging behavior, he would grow bored and lose interest, but she'd yet to see any sign of that. Indeed, it seemed that every time she turned around, he was there, his eyes on her.

The intensity of his gaze was unnerving, but if staring at her was all he did, she'd count her blessings.

He was in the church, but the Tallents had a family pew at the front, so she hadn't had to endure the weight of his gaze throughout the service. He hadn't turned and looked back at her—not once—for which, of course, she gave due thanks.

Reading ended, they all rose for a hymn. With comforting inexorability, the service moved through its customary stages, eventually ending with the benediction. Mr. Filing led the way outside. From the pew they'd occupied halfway down the aisle, she and her family joined the exodus slowly shuffling up the nave, falling in behind the first-pew families, who by custom were allowed to exit first.

In organizing the twins and setting them to walk before herself and Issy, Em had lost sight of Tallent's dark head. As she didn't feel the weight of his gaze on her back, she assumed he was ahead of her. With luck he would leave with his sister and her husband, and not linger to chat in the churchyard.

Reaching Mr. Filing, she gave him her hand, commended him on an excellent sermon—by which she meant short and to the point—then moved on to allow him to speak with Issy.

She paused on the last step to look around and discovered

herself the object of a good many curious glances. Initially mystified—the locals had had the past week to get used to her—as she stepped down to the path and called the twins to order, she realized it was them, and Henry, too, following behind Issy, who were the true focus of attention.

When Mrs. Weatherspoon, claiming the prerogative of experience—she had more children than anyone could count—beckoned, Em whispered to the twins to stay close and behave, and accommodatingly approached to let the old lady examine them.

Luckily the twins adored adoration; as they looked like angels, most people could be counted on to croon and compliment, all of which they lapped up. Which in turn kept them on their best behavior. Unusually docile, they allowed Em to steer them around the surprisingly considerable congregation. People had traveled from outlying farms to attend the service. Many stopped her with a word of encouragement about the inn.

All in all, a pleasant half hour passed while they chatted in the sunshine. Eventually, noting that Mr. Filing and Issy were once again deep in conversation, Em drew back to stand beneath a tree at the edge of the graveyard with Henry and the twins, to wait for their sister.

"Can't we go and get her?" Gert asked. "There's a lovely capon for lunch and it might be getting cold."

"Or overcooked," Bea added, her eyes on Issy.

"Let's just give her a little more time." Em glanced at the pair chatting before the steps, and thought they looked quite charming, Issy with eyes downcast, Filing head bent as he spoke quietly to her. "She's worked very hard all week on your lessons, and given up all of her time, so if she wants to spend a little of Sunday morning talking with Mr. Filing, it's only fair that you wait."

Silence greeted that suggestion. Em noted that the twins' gazes remained on Filing and Issy.

She wasn't entirely surprised when Gert eventually asked, "Is Issy sweet on Mr. Filing?"

"More importantly," Bea said, demonstrating a fine grasp of the nuances of life, "is Mr. Filing sweet on Issy?"

Briefly Em wondered what she should say, then decided truth was the wisest course. "I think *both* are very likely, don't you?"

The twins' heads moved in an identical side-to-side waggle, indicating they weren't quite sure, but they consented to wait without further protest.

Em was content to stand beneath the tree and let her mind wander.

When Jonas Tallent materialized at her elbow, it took a moment for her to realize he truly was there, that the sensations he engendered weren't simply a product of her overactive memory.

She turned to him. "Mr. Tallent—a lovely morning, is it not?"

"Indeed, Miss Beauregard." He caught her gaze, his own quizzical. "You seem to be in a brown study. Inventing new menus, perhaps?"

She would have narrowed her eyes at him and glared— this was what came of forgetting her resolution to avoid him at all costs and letting down her guard—but his gaze had shifted and lowered to the twins.

One glance at their faces told her they were quite fascinated. Hardly surprising; he was unquestionably the most handsome gentleman there. It wasn't just the cut of his London clothes that set him apart, but the faintly rakish aura that hung about him—as if he was safe on the outside, but not necessarily all the way through.

She supposed it was a case of like recognizing like that had him studying them, then commenting, "These are your angel-demons, I take it?"

"Indeed." Briskly she made the introductions, not at all sure how the twins would respond.

But after curtsying correctly, Bea piped up, "We're being very good at the moment."

Gert nodded solemnly. "Like angels." She fixed her blue

gaze on his face. "You're the one who took Em for a drive to somewhere—the one with the lovely horses."

"Brown ones, prancing." Her gaze on his face, Bea moved forward and brazenly slipped her hand into his much larger one. "It was a nice carriage, too."

Knowing all too well where her angel-demons were leading, Em was about to step in and head them off, when realization struck. Very few gentlemen could cope with two bold ten-year-old girls.

Brazen herself, she raised her brows and turned to Henry. "What was that?"

He gave her a puzzled look, but said nothing as she shifted to his side—leaving Jonas Tallent to her half sisters' tender mercies.

Jonas knew very well what she was up to, but while the prospect of dealing with the fair-haired twins made him inwardly quail, he wasn't about to be driven off so easily.

He drew Bea around to stand beside Gert, then fixed them both with a direct look. "Yes, I own those very lovely horses—and the nice carriage—it's a curricle, by the way—and if you're both very good and behave yourselves while in my hearing, I'll take you for a drive one day soon. Something like three weeks from now."

From experience with his nephews, he knew children had a poor notion of the passage of time, and three weeks, while sounding not too far away, was in fact long enough for them to forget any agreement before it came to pass. While his nephews were younger, he assumed the twins, too, would soon forget any agreement with him.

Their blue eyes had grown wide. They exchanged quick glances.

A twin himself, he knew precisely what that meant. "Do we have an agreement, ladies?"

Bea, the talkative one, narrowed her eyes at him—just like her eldest sister. "How will we know if we're behaving well enough? We can't be good all the time."

He fought to keep his lips straight and inclined his head

in grave acceptance. "Very true. You'll know you're being good enough if I'm not frowning at you."

They turned this over, communicating silently, then both looked at him and nodded. "Done," Gert said. "In three weeks, then—after church."

"Good." Jonas glanced around and saw Issy approaching. "In that case, I'll walk all you ladies back to the inn."

Rejoining the group, Em heard that proposition and looked at the twins in shocked surprise.

Before she could say anything, Jonas took her arm. "Come, my innkeeper—let me walk you home."

Issy merely smiled and took Henry's arm; they set off, following the twins, already ranging ahead, roast capon on their minds.

Finding her arm wound with Jonas's, Em had no real option but to let him steer her in her family's wake. They were among the last to leave the churchyard; the common was almost empty as they set off down the slope.

Puzzled, she studied the twins. How had he . . . ? Given it was the twins, she had to know. "What did you say to them?"

He chuckled, the sound warm and inviting. "I bribed them, of course."

"With what, for heaven's sake?"

"A drive in my curricle."

She considered long and hard, but eventually informed him, "You do realize they'll expect to handle the reins?"

"Over my dead body."

"I suggest you don't tell them in quite those words."

6

Em had avoided Jonas Tallent for three whole days, only, in a moment of weakness, to leave the way open for him to befriend the twins and earn points with Issy and Henry for gentlemanly courteousness in walking them home after church.

So she even more steadfastly avoided him for the next four days, hoping that would make him stop watching her like a hawk. She felt distinctly like a pigeon whenever he was about.

And *still* he kept watching her. Every time she turned around, it seemed he was there. The dark weight of his gaze was starting to feel familiar.

Luckily he couldn't see her thoughts.

She spent the first four days of the following week plotting how to search the Ballyclose Manor cellar. Not, as she discovered, an easy task. During the day the house was a hive of activity; there'd be no chance to search at any time while the household was awake. Inventing some story and inveigling her way in might have worked—if she could concoct a story that would excuse her searching the cellar, and then successfully lie through her teeth, neither of which seemed at all likely. Which left searching while the household was asleep, which meant breaking into the cellar, presumably through the outer doors she'd spied, praying all the while that she wouldn't get caught.

She'd be a nervous wreck.

Worse, it seemed that in this—actually laying hands on the treasure—she would be acting alone. She'd always assumed she'd have Issy beside her, or more to the point, watching her back, but Issy was spending what little free time she had with Mr. Filing—and there was no way on earth Em was going to interfere.

If Issy had a chance at happiness with the curate—at a future Em herself had had to lay aside—then she would do all she could to foster the romance; she would place no hurdle in her sister's path.

With the difficulties attendant on searching the Bally-close cellar mounting, she decided that before she embarked on any wild and dangerous scheme—something her Coly-ton soul would all too happily do—she needed to be completely and absolutely certain that Ballyclose Manor was indeed the "house of the highest" referred to in their rhyme.

On Friday morning, as soon as she'd seen the inn's increasingly regular daily schedule set in motion, she gathered the three books she'd borrowed and headed for Colyton Manor. She'd combed through the three tomes, but other than a passing mention of Ballyclose, and a minor reference to the Grange, there was nothing in them regarding the houses of the village that had existed in the late sixteenth and early seventeenth centuries, when the rhyme had come into being.

The "house of the highest" would be the house of the highest member of village society at that time, not necessarily now. Hence it might not be Ballyclose Manor—and she had to be sure.

Walking up the road past the cottages, she reached the low stone wall that bordered the manor's front garden. The garden was unusually lush, bursting with plants of all kinds—roses, lavender, honeysuckle, and countless flowering shrubs and creepers flung together in a glorious palette of color and scent.

The garden gate, set centrally, directly before the front door, was overhung by an arched trellis on which a climbing rose rioted, large apricot blooms bobbing in the light breeze. Unlatching the gate, she went in; closing it, she paused, breathing in the perfumes of the garden, then determinedly continued to the front door.

The butler, Bristleford, answered her knock. She waited in the hall while he went to ascertain if his mistress was receiving.

Em glanced around, checking for any evidence of a male visitor, but she doubted her nemesis would be about so early; his clothes screamed London—she assumed he was accustomed to London ways.

"Miss Beauregard." Phyllida Cynster appeared at the back of the hall. She smiled. "Please come and join us in the parlor."

Smiling in return, Em went forward. "I've brought back these books." She handed the volumes to Phyllida.

"Did you find the information you were seeking?" Taking the books, Phyllida stood back, waving Em past her into the parlor.

"I learned a little more," Em temporized, "but I'm still curious about the village's past, and that of the various houses round about, and the major families." She halted just inside the parlor, surprised to see Phyllida's husband, Lucifer Cynster, sprawled on the sofa with two little boys clambering over him.

He didn't seem to mind in the least, but restrained his sons enough to smile and half-bow. "Good morning, Miss Beauregard. I hope you don't mind joining us en famille."

She returned his smile. "No, not at all." One of the boys wriggled free, rushed across the rug, and grasped her hand.

Perhaps five years old, he shook it wildly. "I'm Aidan."

"And I'm Evan," came in a wail from the other, younger imp, still in his father's clutches.

Smile widening, Em looked down into dark blue eyes sparkling with life and mischief. "I'm very pleased to meet you, Aidan." She looked across the room. "And Evan, too."

"Now the courtesies have been observed," Phyllida said, "perhaps we can allow Miss Beauregard to sit." She waved Em to the heavily cushioned window seat.

Em crossed the room and sat. Aidan escorted her, waited gravely until she settled her skirts, then hitched himself up to sit beside her. She wasn't surprised when Evan quit his father's side to join them; he clambered up to sit on her other side, then slid one chubby hand into one of hers.

Phyllida saw and would have spoken, but Em caught her eye and, smiling, shook her head. "It's quite all right. I'm accustomed to children."

She'd missed seeing the twins at this age, and had always regretted it.

Lucifer Cynster sat up from his sprawl, assuming a more conventional pose. He was, Em judged, in his mid-thirties, a tall, vigorous man with black hair and the dark blue eyes his sons had inherited. He was, in her opinion, the second most handsome man in the village, and, like Jonas Tallent, a palpable aura of not-entirely-civilized male clung to his deceptively elegant shoulders.

"Phyllida mentioned," he said, "that you were interested in the history of the village."

Em nodded. "I make it a point to learn the history of each village in which I manage an inn. I'm particularly interested in the architecture of bygone days. It's a hobby of sorts—it fills the time and I often discover useful things."

Phyllida had left the books Em had returned on the low table in front of the sofa. Lucifer reached out and angled them so he could read the spines. "There are more books here—more informative than these—on Colyton village. I'll look some out for you before you leave." He looked up and met her eyes, smiled charmingly. "But first, how are you finding Colyton in the present day?"

"Very comfortable." Em released Evan's hand as he drew it away and slid off the seat to the floor. "Everyone's been so friendly—it's been easy to settle in."

"Yes, well, after Juggs, you and your brood are a welcome relief." Phyllida made an all-encompassing gesture. "I can't begin to tell you how awful the inn had become. After his wife died—and that was more than eight years ago—Juggs lost all interest, but the inn was all he knew, so he stayed."

"And stayed." Lucifer took up the tale. "No amount of hinting of fresh fields and new enterprises could stir a spark in his breast—and believe me, we all tried. His death, untimely though it was, was a release for him, and a new lease of life for the inn and the village." His charming smile warmed Em. "Which is why we're all so pleased with the way you're revitalizing the place."

"Getting Hilda and her girls back was a stroke of luck," Em said. "Without them—and Edgar Hills and John Ostler—finding my feet, let alone getting things moving, would have taken much longer."

Phyllida smiled. "But it's plain you hail from the country yourself—or at least understand its ways."

Definitely a leading question.

Luckily Evan appeared at Em's knee, giving her an excuse to avoid answering. He'd brought her a wooden toy, one for pulling along on wooden wheels. From the corner of her eye, she saw Phyllida open her mouth, then hesitate; with one hand, she signaled all was well. Eyes wide, she carefully took the toy. "Is it your favorite?"

When Evan nodded—big nods—she examined it. "It's very nice." She held it out to him. "Why don't you show me how it works?"

Delighted, he did, marching back and forth across the polished floor.

Nothing loath, Aidan slipped from Em's other side,

fetched his own favorite toy—two wooden soldiers—showed them to her, then once she'd shown her appreciation, settled to play on the rug at her feet.

Em couldn't help but smile. Looking up, she met Phyllida's gaze. "I remember Henry at this age."

Phyllida smiled back in a moment of complete understanding.

All three adults sat smiling fondly at the boys for a further minute, then Em sighed. "I really must be going." She rose. "When one manages an inn, one never knows what might eventuate hour to hour."

Lucifer and Phyllida rose, too. "We used to have many more travelers using the inn." Phyllida walked with Em to the parlor door.

"So I heard," Em replied. "I'm hoping to lure them back with Hilda's cooking and clean, comfortable beds. I've started planning what needs to be done to get the rooms up to scratch. I'll be speaking with your brother shortly on that score." Once she had a sufficiently long list of topics to ensure any meeting remained strictly business.

They stepped into the hall, Lucifer behind them.

"I'll find some other books on the village for you." As they walked up the hall, he gestured to left and right, inviting her to look.

Curious, she did, and through the open doors saw shelves in every room, even in the dining room.

"As you can see," he continued, "the collection is extensive, and while the volumes are organized by subject, books on history, on architecture, and on gardening, for example, are all in different places, and yet all might deal with, or include, sections relevant to Colyton. So to glean all the information we have, you'll need to work your way through all the likely groupings. For instance, the books you've already seen are from the drawing room and therefore about social aspects, rather than history per se."

Her smile felt a trifle tight. "As my interest is purely a hobby, luckily there's no rush."

But she wanted to find the treasure sooner rather than later.

Lucifer nodded. "In that case, let's see what we can find among the history and architecture books—they're in here."

He led the way into what was plainly the library, the room to the left of the front door. After a moment of watching him work his way along the packed shelves, Phyllida excused herself, farewelled Em, and returned to her sons.

Five minutes later, Lucifer piled four books into Em's arms. "These all have something about Colyton in them."

"Thank you." She stacked the books, then tucked them under her arm.

With elegant grace, Lucifer escorted her to the front door. She reiterated her thanks, then, content if still impatient, walked briskly back up the front path, through the gate onto the road, and headed back to the inn.

Lucifer stood in the doorway and watched her go. When the cottages cut her off from sight, he shut the door, then ambled back to the parlor. His sons greeted him with demands to join their game. He nodded. "In a minute."

Phyllida had sat on the sofa and pulled up a basket of the boys' never-ending mending; halting beside her, he met her gaze as she glanced up and raised her brows.

"What does Jonas think of his innkeeper's interest in village history?"

Phyllida was unsurprised by the question. "He thinks she's searching for something. The last time I spoke with him, he thought it was something to do with—possibly something at—Ballyclose." She studied his face. "What do you think?"

Lucifer's expression had grown serious. "I think he's right in that she's searching for something in one or more of the major houses. I noted she said 'houses' before 'families,' when most would list those things in reverse, and then there was the mention of architecture."

Phyllida frowned, her gaze still locked on his face. "Do

you think she's . . . well, a thief or something of that nature? Should we warn Cedric?"

Lucifer's expression eased. Lips curving, he shook his head. "Unnecessary, I'm sure—whatever Miss Emily Beauregard is, she's no thief."

"Jonas doesn't think so, either."

"Shrewd of him," Lucifer dryly replied. "Not many thieves go on the hunt with a large and very visible family in tow—much less organize for their brother to get lessons from the local curate."

Phyllida watched as he strolled to where their sons played, then subsided onto the ground, rearranging his long limbs, to join them. After a moment, she said, "I'm glad of that—I quite like her."

Lucifer nodded, already distracted by his sons' demands. "There's some mystery there—Jonas is right about that— and she is looking for something. Doubtless we'll learn the truth in time."

Em hurried back to the inn, slipped inside, and went quickly upstairs to her rooms. To her relief, she met no nosy gentlemen along the way. Setting the books on the dresser, she sent up a prayer that somewhere in one of the four she would find a clear answer as to whether Ballyclose was indeed the house she sought.

Her fingers lingered on the topmost book; she was tempted to sit down then and there and start looking through it, but she was an innkeeper now, and even if her duties were largely managerial, she still felt it important that she be downstairs—in her office, if not the common room or kitchen—simply by her presence keeping all on track.

If her staff had questions, she should be there for them to ask.

Going into her bedroom, now made rather more cheery with a chintz bedspread she'd found in one of the linen closets, she set her reticule down on the dressing table. She shook out her skirts, smoothed them down, then peered at her reflection in the mirror.

"Drat!" She poked at the curls that had sprung loose from the knot she'd anchored at the back of her head. Soft and wavy, the curls made a delicate frame for her face—to her mind only adding to the unfortunate image of a soft, delicate, not to say fragile female. That wasn't her at all; it certainly wasn't the image she wanted to present.

She grimaced at her reflection. "No time." Besides, ten minutes after she redid the knot, the curls would only spring free again.

Turning, she went downstairs. After casting an approving eye over the ladies' side of the common room, now infinitely cleaner and neater with lace doilies on every polished low table and cushions on most of the chairs, she cast a cursory glance over the tap—she could count on Edgar to keep that area respectably clean—then wended her way through the dining area, considering anew the trestle tables and benches.

Refinishing, followed by a good wax, would work wonders. She'd have to convince her employer that the cost would be worth it, but there was transparently a need for somewhere the locals could come for a good meal.

Entering the kitchen, she sniffed, and sighed with pleasure. No need to ask if everything was in hand, not with Hilda in charge. She paused to compliment the older woman, then check through her list of required supplies. List in hand, she headed for her office. .

"In truth, sir, I've no notion where she's gone, but she did say she'd be back shortly."

Em halted just before the opening to the hallway leading to her office; that had been Edgar speaking from behind the bar. It might be any man asking for her, but no doubt Jonas Tallent was now up and about—and as usual dogging her heels.

Stepping into the shadowed hall, she looked to her right, along the bar, and confirmed that it was indeed her nemesis propped against the counter, quizzing Edgar, who was setting out clean glasses, ready for the lunchtime trade.

Tallent was frowning. "How long ago did she leave?"

"Couldn't say exactly."

She must have moved—or perhaps he sensed her exasperation; his gaze swung her way, then he straightened.

Em narrowed her eyes in a fiery glare, then turned and went into her office.

She rounded her desk, deeming it wise to put furniture between them. She sat and pretended to be studying her list while working to keep the lid on her temper—he was her employer and she needed this job. Searching for the treasure would be a lot more problematic if she had to pursue some other line of employment, and where would the others stay while she did? Being the Red Bells' innkeeper-manager suited her to a T—and just because Jonas Tallent was a blessed nuisance was no reason to put her position at risk.

There was, of course, the curious question of why his attention even from a distance so annoyed, irritated, and unnerved her, but that was another issue entirely.

He filled the doorway all but literally. She watched him from beneath her lashes, but pretended not to notice he was there.

Lounging against the frame, he considered her. "I've been looking for you. Where have you been?"

She looked up, raised her brows haughtily. "I wasn't aware of any appointment. As to where I've been, as I've told you too many times to count, my affairs are none of your concern."

He sighed. "You may as well tell me—it'll save me asking around the village."

The words "You wouldn't dare!" were on her lips, but as she stared into his eyes, they died. He would, indeed, ask around—the fiend.

Exasperated, irritated, and oddly unnerved, she stood. "If you must know, I returned those books I borrowed from your sister."

"I see."

"Indeed, and now, if you're satisfied . . ." She stopped, recalling their earlier discussion using that word.

He smiled—wolfishly. "Not yet."

She glared, then marched determinedly around the desk. "If you don't mind, I have work to do." She brandished her list at him.

Amused, but knowing better than to show it—she resembled nothing so much as an irate sparrow—Jonas stepped back so she could exit the office. He fell in behind her as she stormed toward the kitchen. "Did you learn anything from the books?"

"No." Her steps faltered. She paused, then, head rising, amended as she marched forward again, "That is, the books were about local history, so I learned more about that."

"But not about what you wanted to learn?"

She turned down a narrow service corridor, barely more than an alcove, halted before a stout wooden door on the right, reached for the latch, then turned her head and sent him a scorching glare. "Mr. Tallent—"

"Jonas."

Her eyes couldn't get any narrower; her breasts rose beneath her olive green walking dress as she dragged in a huge breath. "What I might—or might not—be searching for is none of your affair."

Lifting the latch, she hauled open the door and disappeared behind it.

Reaching out, Jonas caught the edge—not that she tried to slam it shut. Curious, he edged around the door—open, it almost blocked the corridor—and looked into the tiny storeroom beyond.

It was the spirits cellar. His sparrow was industriously checking the small tuns and bottles while pretending he wasn't there.

Did she really think he'd simply go away?

Then again, he had patiently allowed her a week to get used to the notion of him always being around—in the transparently vain hope that she would learn to trust him enough to tell him what *he* wanted to know.

Namely what *she* wanted to know.

Clearly it was time to try a different strategy.

He stepped into the storeroom, leaving the door wide; they needed light and it was unlikely anyone else would come this way, not with the crowd flooding into the common room demanding pies for lunch.

The room was barely ten feet deep. Standing just inside the door, he watched her checking her list against the stock on the shelves.

In silence she worked her way further into the room. When she was at the end of the narrow aisle, he stepped down it. "You're wrong, you know."

She continued her cataloging and didn't immediately react, but then she threw him a frowning sideways glance. "Wrong about what?"

He halted beside her, blocking the aisle. "Wrong in thinking I'll go away if you ignore me."

She made a frustrated sound and swung to face him. "Just because I'm your innkeeper doesn't mean you're . . ." She waved both hands. "In any way *responsible* for me."

He frowned. "I don't feel responsible for you." He felt faintly disgusted and let it show. "In case it's escaped your notice, I'm attracted to you—I thought I'd made that plain. Helping ladies they're attracted to is what gentlemen like me do."

Eyes locked on his, she hauled in a huge breath. Tensely said, "It's also equally and undeniably true that just because I'm your innkeeper doesn't mean I'll welcome your attentions."

He blinked, then caught her gaze. "You don't welcome my attentions?" When she didn't immediately reply, he clarified, "You didn't welcome my attentions the last time we kissed?"

Her lips primmed. She lifted her chin. "I didn't know what I was doing."

"I see." His eyes narrowing, he studied hers, then softly said, "You're a terrible liar."

She blushed. "I'm not lying!"

She was, through her teeth. Why, he had no idea, but he'd reached the end of what little patience he possessed. He sighed, reached out, hauled her into his arms—and kissed her again.

Her lips softened under his, instantly responsive. Realizing, she tried to retreat, tried to hold back, but all resistance lasted less than a heartbeat, then she was with him again, all warm, honeyed sweetness and unalloyed enticement.

If this wasn't welcome, he didn't know what was.

He did know he hungered for it, and her, craved the sweetness of her mouth, of her innocent freshness.

Of the promise, more subtle, as she pressed closer, as her lips firmed and she returned the kiss without restraint.

Knew, as he gathered her into his arms, that he was already addicted.

Em knew—absolutely and with unimpaired clarity—that she shouldn't be doing this. That just because his lips were hungry didn't mean she had to feed them. Returning his kiss, kissing him back with even just a smidgen of the eagerness bubbling inside her was not just unwise, but the definition of counterproductive.

He would only pursue her all the more doggedly. She knew it—knew she should pull back, wrench free of his encircling arms, and put space between them—but instead of moving back, away from him, she pressed forward into the kiss.

A kiss she simply couldn't do without.

A kiss that somehow meant something to her, on a different plane she'd yet to understand.

With his lips on hers and his arms around her, the world melted away and she was safe and cared for.

When he kissed her, she understood why he wanted to protect her—sensed through the kiss that he wanted her in a possessive way, so protecting something he wanted as his was logical, rational.

Little else about the kiss, and all it made her feel, was either of those things. His lips had firmed, and parted hers; his tongue found hers and stroked, caressed, languid and slow. Her head reeled, her attention locked on the subtle communion of lips and tongue as he explored and claimed.

The sensations he evoked beckoned, lured, tempted her to explore, too, to seek more, learn more . . .

He angled his head and deepened the kiss. She feathered her fingers into his dark hair, lightly clutched . . . realized she must have raised one hand and burrowed her fingers into the dark, surprisingly silky mass.

Realized he was drawing her further, not just into the kiss but beyond . . .

Instinct stirred, raised its head. Looked around, assessed, then prodded. Sharply.

She lingered for an instant more, savoring the heat of his mouth, the seductive stroke of his tongue against hers, then drew back. Drew her hand from his hair, rested it on his broad shoulder.

Gathered her resolution, broke from the kiss, and pushed back in his arms.

He let her move away, but the aisle was only so wide; they were still far too close when her eyes locked on his. If she didn't look at his eyes, she would focus on his mouth instead, and she knew where that would lead, yet at such close quarters she felt mesmerized by his dark gaze.

"Are you going to tell me the truth?"

His low, gravelly, shockingly private tone slipped into her mind, slid around her shields, and tempted . . .

She blinked, mentally fought free of his sorcerous hold. Lips setting, she shook her head. Decisively. "I'm not telling you what I'm searching for—you don't need to know. I assure you it's nothing illicit."

Finding her list still clutched in one hand, feeling the other still tingling with the sensations of stroking his hair, she dragged in a breath and forced herself to turn away.

To step away, out of his arms toward the door.

Then she remembered, but kept walking and spoke over her shoulder. "And I'm *not* seeking your attentions, either."

"No need," he growled, following close behind her. "They're yours regardless. Anytime, anywhere."

She humphed as she stepped out of the storeroom into the corridor. "You shouldn't kiss me, not when I've said I don't want you to. That's not gentlemanly behavior—and you are, first and last, a gentleman."

Grasping the door, she waited for him to join her so she could close the storeroom.

He stepped into the corridor, and stopped. The look in his eyes, fixed on her face, was the epitome of exacerbated male frustration. "If you want to discourage me, you can't go around flinging down gauntlets and not expect me to pick them up."

"Gauntlets?" She let cynical disbelief color her tone. "What gauntlets?" Greatly daring, she planted one palm on his chest and shoved him sideways.

Stepping out of the doorway, he answered, "*We'll see about that?* Not to mention"—he waved back into the storeroom—"kissing me like a houri and then telling me you aren't seeking my attentions. If that's not a gauntlet—a challenge—I don't know what is."

"A *challenge*?" Closing the door, she turned to stare at him, then shook her head and faced forward. "Nonsense." She started down the corridor, back to the safety of the more inhabited areas of the inn. As she emerged into the hall, she scoffed, "Gauntlets. Really! Men get such strange ideas."

Jonas halted, watched her bustle to the swinging door into the kitchen, push past it and through. As the door swung closed, hiding her from view, he shook his head in abject disbelief. If she thought he'd simply give up and go away—desist and disappear—when she kissed him like that, her ideas were a great deal more strange than any he'd ever had.

Still shaking his head, he turned back to the tap. A pint and one of Hilda's delicious pies, and then he'd give his mind to devising the best way to educate his innkeeper as to the reality—his reality—of the situation between them.

The following evening, Em supervised the serving of the first dinner menu offered by the inn for nearly ten years.

Hilda and Issy had worked on the recipes for more than a week. Em had approved the selection of dishes on Thursday, and Hilda and her girls had set to with a will. Word had duly spread. The gratifying number of patrons who had chosen to grace the Red Bells that Saturday evening and sample the first night's dishes was a testament to their renewed confidence in the inn's level of service.

The dinner, indeed the whole evening, was on track to be an unqualified success. Em should have been savoring the triumph, but while she smiled and chatted, received compliments and took a degree of pleasure in conveying them to Hilda and Issy, when she drew back into the shadows, disaffection crept in and her smile faded.

She was not in a good mood; she was feeling uncharacteristically defeated—something alien to her Colyton nature.

She'd spent most of the past night, and every minute she could snatch through her busy day, leafing through the books she'd borrowed from the manor. As Lucifer had promised, all four books contained sections specifically devoted to Colyton village, its houses and their architectural features. Unfortunately, not one contained specific dates, not even anecdotes or accounts of long-ago occurrences from which she might deduce the true age of Ballyclose Manor.

Sir Cedric Fortemain and his wife, Jocasta, along with Lady Fortemain, were among the diners sampling the inn's cuisine. They'd been gracious and complimentary when they'd arrived. Hugging the shadows at the foot of the inn stairs, Em wondered if she could simply go up to Sir Cedric and inquire as to the age of his property.

She suspected she'd get the correct answer—the problem was, that answer would immediately be followed by other questions, ones she wouldn't want to answer, and would have difficulty avoiding. The Fortemains were widely considered social leaders in the area, the sort of people her innkeeper side needed to keep well disposed toward her and her family; the last thing she wanted was to make them view her askance.

So she couldn't ask directly, and bludgeon her brains though she had, she'd yet to divine any indirect way to elicit the information.

The leaden weight of defeat increased and dragged her spirits yet lower.

Folding her arms, she glanced moodily across the room—directly into the dark eyes of Jonas Tallent. He was sitting in the far corner of the tap; he'd arrived a little while ago, having presumably dined at home.

Since the interlude in the spirits cellar yesterday, they hadn't met, at least not to exchange words, but she didn't imagine he'd given up his obsession. Not only was he still watching over her—something most others, she'd discovered, assumed was due to his custodianship of the inn—but she sensed, since yesterday's interlude, that he was . . . making plans. He watched her, studied her, in a slightly different way, as if assessing her and her potential reactions.

Oddly, the sight of him still steadily watching sent a spurt of renewed zeal through her, strengthening her flagging, temporarily defeated determination, revitalizing her customary optimism.

There had to be a way to learn the age of Ballyclose Manor without revealing her reasons for wishing to know; she simply hadn't discovered it yet.

And discovery was one of those things at which Colytons excelled.

Reinvigorated, she once again surveyed the guests, paying particular attention to those dining. Finding all was well, she turned and pushed through the door into the kitchen.

Hilda was serving the last of the roast beef. She looked up, and grinned. "All gone. And the pot of pumpkin soup was wrung dry."

Em paused beside her. "The lamb's gone, too, I see." She patted the older woman's arm encouragingly. "Everyone loves your cooking." She hesitated, then said, "We must sit down on Monday and talk about your wages."

They'd agreed on the same rates that had applied early in Juggs's tenure, before he'd offended Hilda by demanding she cook with unfresh ingredients. "The inn's doing so much better now," Em went on, "and that's largely due to you and your helpers. It's only fair your wages rise accordingly."

Hilda eyed her shrewdly. "You'll need to speak with Mr. Tallent—more wages for us will come out of his pocket as well as yours."

Em nodded. "I will indeed speak with him, but I'm sure he'll agree."

She was, which was another point in Jonas Tallent's favor—not that she wished to remind herself of his virtues. It would be much easier to ignore him if he had fewer good qualities, and more bad ones.

To date the only bad quality she'd detected was his pig-headedness in pursuing her in the teeth of her protestations of disinterest. Admittedly said protestations were false, no matter how much she'd prefer them to be true, but the least he could do was believe her lies.

Heaven knew, she was having a hard enough time uttering them.

Hilda's niece appeared and whisked out the last order. Hilda started to clear her bench.

Em left her to it and circled through the large kitchen. She glanced into the scullery and smiled to see the three younger serving girls busy cleaning the first round of plates.

They were chattering nineteen to the dozen while their hands washed, dried, and stacked; Em didn't speak—she saw no need to douse their lively talk.

She'd taken one step toward her office when, on a gust of giggles and laughter, one of the girls said, "Claims to be the village historian, he does. Hard to believe, the way he dresses."

Em paused, then took a step back. The girls didn't notice; they chatted on.

"He has got all those books, though." Hetta rubbed a plate with a towel. "Maura, my cousin, knows Mrs. Keighley who does for him, and she says he has heaps and heaps of books about everything, and they collect more dust than she can keep up with."

"Maybe," Lily, the first speaker, her hands in the scullery trough, allowed. "But just having the books doesn't make him the village historian. I heard tell that was rightly old Mr. Welham, him as lived at the manor before he was killed and Mr. Cynster came."

"Well, I heard the same," Mary, who hadn't previously spoken, weighed in. "But I also remember hearing that Mr. Coombe was sort of in competition for the position with Mr. Welham. I overheard someone telling Mr. Filing that after church one day, so it's probably right."

Lily humphed. Suds splashed. She stopped to wipe some from the end of her nose.

Em nonchalantly walked in. "Hello, girls. I'm curious to learn more about the village, and I just heard you mention a Mr. Coombe who might know something about the village's history."

All three girls colored, but when Em merely looked curious rather than censorious, Mary nodded. "Mr. Silas Coombe, he is, miss. He lives in the cottage opposite the lychgate, just up the lane toward the forge."

Em smiled. "Thank you. I must speak with him." She turned, then remembered and looked back. "How does he dress?"

The three girls looked at one another, clearly searching for words. Mary said, "It's hard to describe, miss."

"Bright," Hetta volunteered.

"I think," Lily said, frowning, "that the proper word is 'gaudy.'" She looked at the others. They nodded.

"I see." Em smiled. "It won't be hard to spot him, then."

"Oh, no, miss!" all three girls chorused.

"You won't have any trouble at all," Lily assured her.

With a grateful nod Em left them; for the first time that day she had a spring in her step. She vaguely recalled seeing a gaudily—not to say garishly—dressed man in church the previous week. And tomorrow was Sunday.

7

The following morning, Em dutifully accompanied her family to church. They sat in the same pew they'd occupied the week before; the other members of the congregation had left it free. After just two weeks it felt as if they'd already found a place within village society.

Throughout the service she suppressed her impatience and concealed her interest in Mr. Silas Coombe, seated two rows ahead of them. Doubtless the sermon was Mr. Filing's usual concise effort, yet to her, each minute dragged.

At last the benediction was said, and she and her family joined the exodus from the church. As usual, people milled about in the clear space before the graves, exchanging news and opinions with their neighbors and catching up with what was going on in the district. The twins and Henry didn't need any encouragement not to linger; they were happy to set off for the inn by themselves, and from her position on the ridge Em could watch them all the way to the inn's door.

She and Issy circulated, chatting to their patrons, Issy waiting for Mr. Filing to be free, while Em kept her eye on Silas Coombe, biding her time, waiting for the right moment to approach him.

Jonas Tallent was in the crowd; although she didn't look

for him, she could feel his gaze, knew he was watching her. When she spoke to Coombe, she had to make the encounter look casual, just a normal furthering of acquaintance.

As the three girls had predicted, Coombe wasn't hard to spot. Attired in a vivid green coat complete with swallow-tails, a daffodil yellow waistcoat with large silver buttons, and with his cravat—admittedly the standard ivory white—tied in a soft, floppy bow, he stood out, a peacock among pigeons. As his stature was short, his form mildly rotund, the figure he cut was decidedly outlandish.

At least there was no mistaking him.

Finally free, Filing gravitated to Issy's side; Em turned to speak with Mrs. Weatherspoon, giving the pair a modicum of privacy. On leaving that redoubtable lady, she glanced at Coombe, saw him bow to Lady Fortemain, then part from her ladyship.

It was easy to make her path and his cross, apparently without intention.

"Mr. Coombe." She inclined her head, paused, and smiled encouragingly when Coombe's eyes lit.

He swept off his hat and made her an elegant bow. "Miss Beauregard! A pleasure, my dear. I must compliment you on the many excellent improvements you've made at the inn. It's positively restored—indeed, far better than it was."

"Thank you, Mr. Coombe. I've heard that you would know, being the village historian."

"Yes, indeed." Coombe gripped his lapels and puffed out his chest. "The inn has been the center of village life for centuries, you know. Why, I could tell you—"

"Oh, would you?" Em put a hand on his arm, stemming the tide; this was proving even easier than she'd hoped. "I would dearly love to hear all you can tell me, sir—but I've just noticed the time, and fear I must hie back to the inn to oversee the serving of luncheon." She looked a little hesitant—as indeed she was. "I hardly like to ask, but per-haps it would be possible for me to call on you—for instance this afternoon—to hear more? It really would be helpful to know what has gone before."

Coombe's smile turned to an outright beam. "Nothing would please me more, Miss Beauregard." He looked a trifle coy. "I did hear a whisper that you were interested in the history of the village in a wider sense."

Someone from the manor must have talked, but it made no difference. "Indeed, sir. I believe you have many books dealing with the village's past." Hand still on his arm, she leaned a trifle nearer and lowered her voice, the better to ensure the couple behind her wouldn't hear. "Quite aside from any knowledge of the inn, I would dearly love to view your collection."

Coombe's smile couldn't get any brighter. "*Delighted,* my dear—say no more. I'll look for you this afternoon— only too happy to place myself entirely at your service."

"Until then." Letting her hand fall, she stepped back. With a graceful nod and a secretive smile, she parted from Coombe. He seemed inclined to view their meeting in a conspiratorial light, but knowing Jonas was watching, as she wended her way back to Issy's side she counted that a blessing; Coombe was unlikely to rattle on about their appointment even if asked.

Their exchange had been brief; she'd spent no longer talking to Coombe than she had to others. Confident she'd succeeded in disguising her planned meeting from her employer's ever-watchful eyes, she collected Issy and headed back to the inn.

A t just before three o'clock, garbed in a dark red walking dress she rarely wore, Em walked quickly up the lane opposite the Red Bells. Her nemesis was currently ensconced in the tap, a pint of ale in his hand; she'd slipped out of the inn's back door, then circled around to escape his watchful eye.

His watchful glower. For some reason, his usual bland expression had changed. While he watched her just as unrelentingly, he was definitely not best pleased.

Perhaps he was starting to believe her disavowal of interest in him.

Strangely the thought didn't buoy her, which in turn made her frown. But before she could delve deeper into her recalcitrant emotions, the gate of the last cottage in the row lining the lane, the one facing the church's lych-gate, appeared beside her.

Halting at the gate, she looked swiftly around; seeing no one, she drew in a determined breath, then opened the gate and walked quickly up the path to the front door.

Coombe answered her knock himself, with an alacrity that suggested he'd been waiting on her arrival, very possibly hovering in the hall. A faint frisson of unease tickled her spine as, smile in place, she responded to his welcoming bow and stepped over his threshold.

Coombe shut the door, and with a grand gesture ushered her into a small parlor. "Please make yourself comfortable, Miss Beauregard."

Easier said than done; only now did she recollect the inadvisability of a lone lady calling at a bachelor's establishment. In truth, she hadn't seen Coombe as a bachelor, not even as a man, but as a route to information, yet her instincts were now warning her to be on guard.

With a choice between an overstuffed armchair half-buried beneath cushions and a small sofa, she chose the sofa—then wished she hadn't when Coombe joined her on it. She kept to her corner, and prayed he'd keep to his. The instant he'd settled his coattails, she asked, "Do you have any books dealing with the inn and its history, sir?"

"Indeed, Miss Beauregard." Coombe's expression turned superior. "But I fancy I can save you considerable time— I've made something of a study of the subject."

"How fascinating." She resigned herself to listening to all he knew about the inn. "Pray enlighten me, sir."

Coombe complied; she endeavored to look suitably interested and make appropriate noises whenever they seemed called for. In fact, Coombe imparted little she didn't already know, or hadn't already surmised.

One point puzzled her. "Has the inn always been owned by the Tallents?"

"Yes, indeed—it was their idea from the start. A watering hole for their estate workers—the village was, of course, much smaller then."

She frowned. "So the Tallents have been part of the village for . . . well, as long as anyone knows?"

Coombe nodded. "From the Conquest, most likely."

"So at one time the Tallents might well have been the leaders of village society?"

Coombe's brows rose. "I daresay, although I believe the Fortemains have been in the area for a similar time, and there's the Smollets, too, although I would have to say their antecedents aren't quite of the same caliber."

Em filed the information away for later examination. "What about the houses—the large ones like Ballyclose Manor and the Grange? I'm quite interested in the architecture of bygone days—the types of houses and rooms and amenities people had." She fixed her gaze on Coombe's face. "I was wondering in particular about Ballyclose Manor—do you have any books describing its history?"

Coombe wanted to say yes, wanted to impress her with his knowledge; she could read his expression with ease. But then he deflated. "Sadly, no. Horatio Welham, the gentleman who used to own the manor, a great collector, had the pick of the Ballyclose library years ago, and on his death, Cedric Fortemain bought back all the books on the manor. He also persuaded me to part with those few I had, so all the books on Ballyclose are now in the library there."

"I see."

Her disappointment must have shown. Coombe leaned nearer and laid a hand on her arm. "But never mind about Ballyclose, my dear Miss Beauregard. We have all the rest of my *collection* to consider." Eyes locked on her face, he seemed to be trying to draw her in . . .

"Ah . . . perhaps." Easing her arm from beneath his hand, she shifted toward the sofa's end. "But I tend to study aspects one by one, and at present I'm studying Ballyclose Manor."

Coombe's lips curved in a suggestive leer as he leaned nearer still. "Come, my dear—no need to be coy. We both know you're really here to study something quite different. You perceive me only too happy to tutor you in the art of dalliance, something that can only be fully explored with a gentleman of my experience and artistic temperament."

Stunned, Em stared, then she gripped her reticule and sprang to her feet. "*Mr. Coombe!* I'm not here to study anything of the sort. If you believe that you're not just mistaken, but willfully obtuse. As you have no further information to share with me, I am leaving—*now!*"

"Oh, I s-say . . ." Coombe's expression crumpled. He scrambled to his feet. "Miss Beauregard—I, that is, dear lady—believe me, just a misunderstanding—"

Em ignored his disjointed bleating. She marched out of the parlor to the front door and hauled it wide. On the front step, she recalled that there might be others passing in the lane, others who might see; dragging in a huge breath, she swung to face Coombe. He was standing inside the door wringing his hands, a comical look of dismay plastered across his face. Lips tight, she sent him a glare scorching enough to shrivel, then nodded tersely. "Good day, Mr. Coombe."

Swinging on her heel, she stalked to his front gate, opened it, and went through. With dreadful calm, she relatched it, then, without glancing back, headed off down the lane at a brisk pace. Her mind ranged over the encounter; she felt her cheeks burn. How Coombe could have imagined . . . then again, she was a lady-innkeeper—he must have assumed she was . . . desperate.

Emotions bubbled inside her—agitation, appalled conjecture, anger, and annoyed irritation that she'd misread him. As for him misreading her—good God! Incensed didn't begin to describe how she felt. As if she would—

"Did you find what you're after?"

The words made her falter in her headlong march, but then she drew breath, lifted her head, and forged on. "No." She heard a rustle of leaves as he left the shade of a nearby bush, then the soft thud of his boots as with a few long strides he caught up to her.

He strolled beside her. "If you tell me what you're searching for, I might be able to help."

She hadn't got any further in over a week. Issy was distracted; she was searching on her own. She could do with help, especially intelligent, local help, but . . . she shook her head impatiently. "I'm not searching for anything—I simply want to know."

"Well, tell me what you want to know—I might know the answer, or at least how to get it."

He sounded so reasonable . . . she halted and swung to face him.

Jonas halted, too, and looked down at her, watched while she searched his face, let her search his eyes. For the first time, she truly considered trusting him, letting him close, accepting his help—accepting him; he could see the debate raging in her eyes. And suspected it was that very last point that had her lips firming, had her, albeit reluctantly, shaking her head.

Facing forward, she walked on.

Disappointed, but not all that surprised, he ranged beside her again. Eyeing her profile, he wondered what it would take to overcome that last hurdle, make her willing to accept him and acknowledge his right to help her in whatever plan she was pursuing . . . only then noticed the color in her cheeks.

He felt himself literally grow cold, not from loss of heat, but from a sudden infusion of incipient icy rage. He drew in a breath, kept his voice steady. Chose his words carefully. "Emily—Coombe has been known to . . . misinterpret ladies' comments, reading into a lady's words what he wants to hear. I know he's done that in the past with Phyllida." Keeping pace alongside her, he ducked his head to look at her face. "He didn't misinterpret your interest, did he?"

Her returning blush was all the answer he needed.

He halted abruptly. "What did he do?" Reaching out, he caught her arm and drew her to face him.

Em blinked, stunned anew—nay, shocked—by his tone. Something far more primitive than mere gentlemanly protectiveness lay beneath his growl and smoldered in his eyes. Then his features hardened. Swallowing her surprise, she shook her head. "Nothing!"

He didn't noticeably relax; if anything his features grew grimmer. She reiterated, her voice strengthening, "He did nothing."

He couldn't tear Coombe limb from limb if he was following her in the opposite direction; she spun about and started marching again. After a fractional hesitation, he followed. She tipped her head his way. "Yes, he mistinterpreted, but if you imagine I'm incapable of putting a gentleman in his place, you're sadly—"

"Correct?"

His growl hadn't improved. She felt heat return to her cheeks as she recalled she'd yet to succeed in putting *him* in his place. Goaded, she retorted, "You're just boneheaded. Most men take my meaning—and correctly gauge my resolution—quite quickly."

He snorted, but his long strides lengthened as he settled to pace beside her again. She was about to congratulate herself on having won that battle, when he stated, flatly, "I'll still pay Coombe a visit."

Her temper frazzled. Frustration escaping in a sibilant hiss, she rounded on him. "No, you won't!" Fists clenched, she glared into his eyes. "I'm not your ward. I'm not *yours* in any way. What happened between Coombe and me is no business whatever of yours. Just because you kissed me—and I permitted it—and was misguided enough to kiss you back, none of that means *anything*, as you very well know!"

His expression had gone strangely blank. He looked down at her for a moment, then said, "It doesn't mean anything?"

Exasperated, she flung her hands wide. "What do you *want* it to mean? Something?"

Looking into her brilliantly bright eyes, Jonas discovered he didn't know the answer to her question. He hadn't thought of it, hadn't asked it of himself.

She searched his eyes, seemed to sense his blankness. She humphed. "Precisely." She turned away and started walking again. She spoke without looking back. "I've told you before, Jonas Tallent—*numerous times*—that I'm no concern of yours."

And he'd told her she was wrong.

Hands rising to his hips, he stood and watched her walk down the lane, let her words of denial, of rejection, once again slide through him—and on.

They didn't stick, didn't fit—because they were wrong.

They didn't match what he felt—or what she truly felt, either.

She'd asked a question, and neither of them actually had the answer. So what did he really want? What did all this mean?

Lowering his arms, he followed her down the lane.

Ten minutes later, Jonas sank onto a bench in the dim corner of the tap and took a long draught of the pint of ale Edgar had drawn for him.

He'd trailed Em back to the Red Bells. Head high, she'd swept in, looked around, then sought refuge in her office.

Rather than follow, he'd sought refuge in the shadows.

Intentionally or not, she'd flung another gauntlet his way.

Posed another challenge—a hurdle he would have to clear if he wished to continue his pursuit of her.

Specifically she'd asked him to define said pursuit, to explain what exactly he wanted.

It was, he had to admit, a fair and reasonable request.

She'd implied—and presumably believed—that his lack of an immediate answer meant he wasn't serious, but he was—deadly serious. Totally serious. He simply hadn't followed his intentions to their logical end and defined his ultimate goal. That omission didn't mean he wasn't intent on securing said ultimate goal—he just hadn't yet put it into words.

That last wasn't easy, not least because, where he and she were concerned, what was evolving between them didn't seem to have all that much to do with logic. Or rationality. He could analyze all he wished, but their interaction, increasingly at every level, was driven by feelings and emotions, and even more by their reactions to those—and such unruly manifestations defied logic at every turn.

Slumping back against the wall, he stretched his legs out before him, sipped his ale—and as the afternoon wore on watched Emily Beauregard flit about his inn, doing innkeeperly things and occasionally shooting narrow-eyed glances his way.

What did he want of her? From her, with her?

He knew various elements of the answer. He wanted her in his bed, wanted her to confide in him—for some reason felt compelled to lift all worldly cares from her slim shoulders. Associated wants grew clearer in his mind—he wanted to protect her, to share her life, and have her share his.

Encompassing all of those, what did he ultimately want with her? What was the real position he wanted her to fill?

And was he sure, beyond doubt, that that was what he needed?

By the time he rose and returned the empty pint pot to

the bar, then headed for the door, he had the answers to his questions as well as hers.

He'd defined his ultimate goal.

Now all he had to do was steer her to it. And convince her to agree.

8

The next morning, fingers tapping the blotter, her gaze fixed unseeing across the room, Em sat in her office and tried to decide how best to further her quest for the treasure. Learning the age of Ballyclose Manor before mounting any sortie to raid its cellar remained the most sensible course, even if that road appeared strewn with obstacles.

Her irritation with Silas Coombe remained, but beneath that lay a restlessness, a feeling of dissatisfaction, that troubled her more.

Ignoring both, she spent long minutes searching for a way forward, but no novel avenue spontaneously presented itself.

The morning was winging; there were things to be done. With a sigh, she resolutely put her quest aside—even more resolutely banned Jonas Tallent from her thoughts—and turned her mind to meeting the expectations her revival of the Red Bells had engendered in its now loyal patrons.

Increasingly the villagers, of all ages, genders, and conditions, flocked to the inn. Breakfast, morning tea and snacks, luncheon and afternoon tea were all well patronized, while they would have to institute a booking system for the tables at which they served dinners.

After consulting Hilda over the weekly order for Finch

and Sons, and checking the stocks of ale and beer with Edgar, Em retreated once more to her office to reconcile her accounts.

She was thus engaged when a clearing throat and a light tap on the open door had her glancing up.

Pommeroy Fortemain stood in the doorway, his gaze scanning the tiny room. "I say." He brought his gaze back to her face. "This is a bit of a broom closet, ain't it? When Edgar said 'office' I imagined something along the lines of Cedric's lair at the manor." Pommeroy glanced about again. "I'd bring this to Tallent's attention if I were you, Miss Beauregard. Hardly fitting, what?" Pommeroy looked down at her and beamed. "No fitting frame for such a lovely flower, heh?"

Em found it easy not to fall into raptures. She acknowledged the sally with a slight, tight curve of her lips, a faint frown in her eyes; two columns she was adding didn't match. "Can I help you with something, Mr. Fortemain?"

With a wave, Pommeroy advanced into the room. "No sense in formalities, my dear Miss Beauregard. Pommeroy's m'name, and I make you free of it."

She merely inclined her head. After Silas Coombe, she had no intention of smiling on those she didn't wish to smile upon; no sense in courting further misunderstandings. "Is there something you wanted, sir?"

"As to that"—Pommeroy beamed—"I come bearing an invitation from m'mother." Reaching into his coat, he drew out a card and presented it with a flourish. "Party—with dancing—at Ballyclose next Saturday evening. We hope you and your sister will attend."

Em stared at the ivory card, then reached out and took it. Attending parties was definitely not what she'd expected to be doing while engaged in their treasure hunt. However, as she and Issy had all their worldly goods with them, they did have evening gowns, albeit outmoded ones.

Although their uncle Harold had used them as his unpaid staff, outside his house he'd been immensely careful to keep up appearances, which had of necessity meant escorting herself, and later Issy, too, to various local ladies' entertainments; it had been that, or suffer untold calls from said local ladies intent on finding out how his nieces were.

Their gowns were outdated, but would pass muster. However . . . she was the innkeeper. Invitations such as this left her feeling she was straddling some uncomfortable divide—or should be, would be, if the locals weren't so intent on treating her and Issy as the young ladies they truly were.

Pommeroy had been studying her face, clearly puzzled by her lack of enthusiasm. "All the local gentry will be there, of course. Everyone attends m'mother's events—the done thing, you know."

Em nodded absentmindedly, her gaze locked on the card. There was nothing she could do about the locals' determination to invest her family with a status close to what they in reality possessed. And once they found the treasure, they would revert to being the Colytons of Colyton, and resume the social position the name commanded.

There seemed little point in clinging to her charade of being "nothing more than an innkeeper" when everyone was intent on behaving otherwise.

And—she was trying very hard not to let her danger-loving, reckless Colyton side loose—there was the undeniable fact that if she wanted to search through the books on Ballyclose Manor, those she'd learned were now residing in the library there, then a party—with dancing, no less—would create the perfect opportunity.

One too good to miss.

She looked up, met Pommeroy's eyes, and smiled. "Thank you, sir—please convey my compliments to Lady Fortemain. My sister and I will be delighted to attend."

"Good-oh!" Eyes alight, Pommeroy saluted her. "First waltz is mine, what?"

Em stopped smiling. "Possibly—we'll see." Her expression cool, she inclined her head. "If you'll excuse me, I must get back to my accounts."

Still beaming, Pommeroy waved and departed.

She stared at where he'd been, sighed, then got back to her recalcitrant figures.

By Saturday evening, she was champing at the bit, ridden by impatience to push ahead with her search. She might lecture the twins on not rushing into things recklessly, but exercising the same caution herself—worse, having willingly condemned herself to six days of getting nowhere—had sorely tried her self-control.

As she let John Ostler hand them down from one of the carriages the inn kept in its stable, then, with Issy beside her, fell in with the other guests climbing the Ballyclose Manor front steps on their way to the ballroom, instead of dreaming of waltzes, Em could barely wait to see the library.

Given the strength of the compulsion to slip away, she tightened her grip on her reckless Colyton self. Still, looking into a library during a party was a lot less risky than breaking into and searching the cellar.

Draped in blue muslin with embroidered ribbons at neckline and hem, her blond hair in gentle curls framing her face, Issy leaned closer to whisper, "I take it you didn't find even a hint in those books?"

"No." She spoke softly so no others could hear. "There were sections on all the major houses, Ballyclose included, but nothing to say that any of them were in existence prior to the eighteenth century." She looked at the façade above the main door. "I need to know when this place was built."

Issy frowned. "You've been doing everything. I can't let you slip away alone. I'll come, too, and keep watch."

Closing a hand about Issy's wrist, Em gently shook it. "Nonsense. I told you, I'll wait until the middle of the evening when everyone's absorbed. Filing told you he'll be here—there's no reason you shouldn't spend as much time with him as is permissable. Neither of us is so young we can't converse with gentlemen without a chaperone. Take advantage of the moment."

They broke off to nod and smile at the Courtneys, a family they'd met at the Ballyclose afternoon tea.

"And besides," she continued, voice low, "Filing will keep his eye on you regardless, so it's too dangerous for you to come with me. If you do, he'll likely follow, and then where will we be?"

Issy responded with a grimace. After a moment of shuffling forward in the reception line, she murmured, "If you're sure."

Smiling at another acquaintance, Em nodded. "I'm sure. Don't worry. What possible danger could be lurking in a gentleman's library?"

They eventually reached the head of the line, curtsied to their hostess and Jocasta Fortemain, Cedric's wife, then moved on into the large ballroom, which was reassuringly full. "See?" Em strolled into the throng. "It'll be easy to disappear for a while in such a crowd. No one will miss me."

Issy murmured noncommittally. Em followed her gaze and saw Filing's fair head moving purposefully through the sea of others toward them. Suppressing a delighted smile, she obligingly halted.

"Miss Beauregard." Reaching them, Filing bowed very correctly to her.

She gave him her hand and an encouraging smile. "Sir. It's a pleasure to see you in more convivial surrounds."

Filing smiled. "Indeed." At last he let his gaze swing to its lodestone. His smile softened as he bowed. "Miss Isobel."

Issy colored, glowing in a way Em had never seen, and gave him her hand. "Sir."

Em could barely restrain her smile; neither Issy nor Filing were dab hands at concealing their feelings. Their eyes were literally all for the other; she doubted anything less than a sharp prod would remind either of the world about them.

She touched Issy's arm, nodded to Filing. "I'll leave you two to chat."

Moving into the crowd, she wondered how long it would be before Filing asked for Issy's hand. Although her joy for her sister might be tinged with regret that, at twenty-five years old and with the twins and Henry to care for, she'd been forced to set aside all thoughts of marrying herself, her delight in Issy's blooming happiness was genuine and deep enough to make her feel like dancing.

It therefore seemed God-sent when the musicians, tucked away in the gallery at the far end of the room, played the opening chords of a waltz. It had been so long since she'd waltzed.

Jonas saw Em glance around as the music started, as if looking for a partner. As she'd arrived only minutes before and had spoken to no gentleman other than Filing, the position should be vacant; his feet were taking him in her direction before he'd completed the thought.

She looked . . . delicious. Fresh and crisp in a green silk gown with her brown hair gleaming under the light thrown by the chandeliers. For once she'd worn her hair in a knot on the top of her head, allowing the short curls she usually fought to restrain free rein to cluster about her face, a bobbing, living frame.

The silk clung lovingly, revealing her neatly rounded figure, delicate feminine shoulders and graceful arms, full rounded breasts, a waist a man's hands would easily span balanced by lush hips, and, despite her relative lack of height, surprisingly long legs. A pocket Venus was the description that sprang to mind.

Certainly his mind.

It took only a moment to reach her, to reach out and capture her hand.

An "Oh!" on her lips, she spun to face him.

Raising her hand, he brushed his lips over the backs of her fingers—and watched color rise in her cheeks. He smiled. "Well met, Miss Beauregard."

She drew in a breath, and nodded, trying to make her expression severe. "Mr. Tallent."

"Jonas, remember?"

She looked away, across the room—toward the dance floor. Through his hold on her fingers, he could sense her impatience to join the couples heading onto the cleared expanse. To whirl. She was like a well-bred filly reined in, but quivering to be off.

"Might I beg the indulgence of this waltz, Miss Beauregard?"

Her gaze snapped back to his face.

At sight of the consideration filling her bright eyes, he smiled. "I promise not to bite."

She hesitated for an instant longer, then nodded. "Thank you. I would like to waltz."

An understatement he felt sure. Setting her hand on his sleeve, he led her through the crowd—only to have Pommeroy Fortemain step into their path.

"Miss Beauregard!" Pommeroy looked faintly shocked. "You must have forgot—you promised the first waltz to me."

"Good evening, Mr. Fortemain." Em recalled her words clearly. "With regard to this dance, if you recall I did not accept your suggestion that the first waltz should be yours. There seemed no reason to make such a decision at that time." She smiled politely. "If you'll excuse us?"

She'd hoped Tallent would take the hint and lead her on. Instead, he stood rooted, looking at her curiously.

Giving Pommeroy time to protest. "But I say . . . expectations and all that. I thought . . ."

Em looked at Jonas, willing him to rescue her. Amusement was dancing in his dark eyes. All he did was raise a questioning brow.

Leaving her to make an issue of choosing him over Pommeroy. She ought to change her mind, but . . . there really was no choice. Choosing Pommeroy to deny Jonas would be cutting off her nose to spite her face. She didn't know for a fact that Jonas could waltz well, but he'd spent time in London—of course he could waltz. Pommeroy on the other hand . . .

She met his gaze. "I regret, Pommeroy, but I made no promise."

He started to pout.

If she and Jonas didn't get to the floor soon, the whole question would be moot. She drew in a breath. "Perhaps the next dance." Which almost certainly wouldn't be a waltz.

Pommeroy looked glum. "Oh, very well, then. The next dance it'll be."

She fabricated a smile.

With a nod to Pommeroy, Tallent consented to escort her on—to the dance floor where other couples were already waltzing.

He turned and drew her into his arms.

Distracted by Pommeroy, she went without thinking, without steeling herself against the sudden onslaught of sensations. She stepped into Jonas's arms, and very nearly gasped, felt her eyes widen as they started to twirl. She stiffened—as if that could hold back the tide, could stop her senses, her wits, from crazily whirling.

He seemed not to notice, but masterfully swept her into the dance.

Into the lazy revolutions.

And she was floating on air; her toes barely touched the floor as he effortlessly whirled with her in his arms.

"You dance very well, Mr Tallent." The compliment was on her lips—plain fact that it was—before she'd thought.

He looked down at her, smiled. "Thank you. It helps to have a partner who isn't trying to lead."

She normally did; normally she danced so much better than her partners that she could rarely refrain. But with him . . . she hadn't consciously thought of it, but there was plainly no necessity. He knew what he was doing.

He demonstrated by expertly steering her through a tight turn, then once more, in perfect physical accord, they settled into the looser revolutions as they traveled up the long room.

"I do have a complaint, however." Again trapping her gaze, he arched a brow. "He gets to be Pommeroy, but I'm Mr. Tallent?"

There was weight—that weight she was, heaven help her, growing far too accustomed to—behind his dark gaze. She met it, tried to hold firm . . . pulled a fleeting face at him. "Oh, very well. Jonas, then."

He smiled brilliantly, and her breath lodged in her chest. The first thought to seep back into her temporarily blank brain was one of fervent gratitude that he hadn't smiled at her like that before.

Her eyes were still trapped in his; his gaze was too piercing—too perceptive—for her peace of mind. Shifting her gaze so it fell above his left shoulder, she tried to think— of something, anything, that wasn't Jonas Tallent.

That wasn't about what it felt like to be lightly caged in his arms, whirling so freely down the floor. About how it felt to be constrained, yet not, to be led, dictated to, yet to feel so responsive, so attuned.

To feel so much two halves of a whole, moving as one.

She'd waltzed often enough in the past, yet with no other man had it felt anything like this.

Anywhere so pleasurable.

She could still feel his gaze on her face, but didn't dare meet it. She felt so alive, so aware of him—of his chest mere inches from her breasts, of his long, strong thighs as they pressed between hers through the turns, of the strength in his arms, in all his lean frame as they checked and whirled around the room—she felt sure, if she looked at him, he'd be able to see her heightened sensitivity in her eyes.

He didn't need any encouragement. He was still pursuing her; although he'd made no move to further engage her through the last few days, that, she knew, would be part of his plan. He'd probably reasoned that after their last argument, where she'd pointed out his lack of an honorable goal, giving her space and not pressing her would make her more receptive to his next advance.

As it had. If she'd had any sense at all, she'd never have agreed to this waltz, let alone refused Pommeroy to claim it.

But she'd wanted to waltz, and, despite all, she'd wanted to waltz with him. With Jonas.

She inwardly frowned. She would have liked to tell herself she'd wanted him because she'd guessed he would be an excellent partner, but she couldn't delude herself; that hadn't weighed heavily in her scale.

Which meant something else—some idiot impulse she hadn't yet tamed—had sneaked past her well-honed defenses and guided her.

Her Colyton nature had reared its head.

She would need to guard against it—and if he was what the adventurous side of her had fixed its reckless sights upon, she would need to guard against him.

It was with real regret that she heard the closing bars of the dance. He swirled her to a halt; she stepped back, out of his arms, and curtsied.

Rising, she inclined her head. "Thank you. That was . . . pleasant." Distracting was more like it, and now she felt something akin to loss at being no longer so close to him, held within the cage of his arms.

He smiled as if he knew.

It occurred to her that, beyond that first sally, he hadn't spoken—or rather, he'd kept his tongue still and let his dancing, and her too-aware senses, speak for him. She started to narrow her eyes at him.

"Ah—Miss Beauregard. Ready for the next dance?"

She turned to see Pommeroy, bright-eyed and waiting, heard the calling chords for a cotillion.

Here was penance indeed. Plastering on a smile, she held out her hand. "Mr. Fortemain."

Taking her hand, he patted it as he led her back to the floor. "Pommeroy, my dear. Pommeroy."

Resigning herself to calling gentlemen by their first name, she surrendered to fate, and to the next measure.

Jonas watched her go, then set off to hunt down Phyllida, who he'd earlier spotted whirling in Lucifer's arms.

His sparrow was trapped for the moment, and all was well with her; no dangers were permitted in Lady Fortemain's ballroom. He had time to hunt up his twin and see whether she'd learned from her husband which books he'd lent Em, and whether from that they could deduce anything more about her goal.

And after that, he'd claim another waltz.

She'd felt like thistledown in his arms, unbelievably light on her feet. There wasn't that much of her—her head didn't clear his shoulder—but her vibrant eyes were matched by the vibrance, the sheer vitality she held within her. He knew she'd enjoyed waltzing with him, but the dance had definitely been a shared pleasure. He'd been thoroughly grateful that she wasn't one of those females who had to fill every silence with prattle; he'd been able to simply enjoy the dance, and the satisfying pleasure of having her in his arms.

Not that he was satisfied—not yet—but he would be. Now he knew his goal—had finally put into words and accepted as truth that he wanted her as his wife—he would be dogged and relentless. As he'd warned her, he was a determined and patient man.

E m had had no idea she would be in such demand. After the dance with Pommeroy ended, he gave every sign of intending to monopolize her. His increasing attentiveness set her nerves flickering; she was casting about for some way to escape him when to her relief his brother, Cedric, strolled up to convey a summons to Pommeroy from Lady Fortemain. Openly chagrined at being denied her company, Pommeroy nevertheless grudgingly left. Cedric remained chatting to her; she debated innocently inquiring as to the age of his house, but decided to explore his library first. Then he surprised her by claiming her hand for the next dance.

After that, she danced with Filing. Separated from Issy, who was dancing with Basil Smollet, Filing shamelessly picked her brains about her sister's likes and dislikes. Em laughed and answered readily; quite aside from approving of Filing as a suitor for Issy's hand, she honestly liked the man.

He seemed to like and approve of her, too. They spent some time discussing Henry and the twins, then Issy returned to Filing's side, and Em took herself off—only to fall victim to the second most handsome man in Colyton. He, too, solicited her hand for the next dance, which happened to be a country dance, but one that allowed them to converse.

"Why Lucifer?" She had to ask. "You couldn't have been christened that."

He laughed. "No, indeed. It's a nickname from my earlier days."

"As in being a devil?"

His grin widened. "No. As in being a dark, fallen archangel."

It took a moment for her to digest that. She fixed him with a mock-censorious look. "I take it it wasn't gentlemen who gave you that name."

"It was the ladies of the ton, if you must know."

She held up a hand. "I believe I know enough. No need for further details."

"Just as well—I seriously doubt Phyllida would approve of me revealing further details."

"I daresay. So—" She paused while they twirled around each other, then came together again. "How are your sons?"

"In their usual rude health. Tell me, were those books I found for you of any particular interest?"

She opened her eyes wide. "Yes, indeed—I've been poring over them." She'd spotted Jonas speaking with his sister and Lucifer; she could now make an educated guess as to the topic of conversation.

Given she was now so close to learning if Ballyclose Manor was indeed their "house of the highest," with luck there would no longer be any reason to pursue information via books from Colyton Manor.

She smiled. "One thing you can tell me."

Lucifer's dark brows arched; his deep blue eyes sharpened. "Yes?"

"Miss Sweet is such a dear—has she been with Phyllida for long?"

His lips tightened. She wasn't at all sure he believed her innocent expression, but then his features eased. "She's not a native of the village. She came as a governess for Phyllida and Jonas when they were three, and became part of the family."

From that beginning, it wasn't hard to ask about all the other older people in the village. Her inquiries had nothing to do with her search; she was simply interested.

She parted from Lucifer and found Basil Smollet waiting to escort her to his mother.

Old Mrs. Smollet had taken a keen interest in Em, her family, and the resurrection of the inn. She was one of the oldest inhabitants and demonstrated as proprietary an interest in village affairs as anyone.

"Keep it up, dear"—the old lady patted her hand—"and you'll have our undying gratitude. You're restoring village life to what it should be."

Em felt the compliment warm her heart. It wasn't the first she'd received that evening; others had paused beside her to tender their thanks for the inn's transformation. The most frequent comment was that now it was a place the ladies, women, and their daughters could use, too.

After conveying her own thanks and parting from Mrs.

Smollet, Em rejoined Issy. Filing was dealing with one of his parishioners off to one side of the room; Em seized the moment of privacy to repeat the comments made to her.

"I feel rather chuffed, truth be told," she confessed. "I had no idea we would make such an impression, or achieve something that clearly means so much to so many—not from what was initially merely a means to an end."

Issy smiled her soft smile. "Perhaps, but in the circumstances I'm not sure it's truly all that surprising that, intentionally or not, we'd seek to make things better for the village—we are the Colytons of Colyton, after all, even if the rest of the village don't know it."

Em raised her brows. "Very true. Perhaps helping Colyton and caring for the village truly is in our blood."

Filing returned, and after a few exchanges, Em strolled on.

Despite all distractions, she'd kept one eye on the clock and the other on the partying throng. Now she circulated, gauging the moment. One more dance and it would be time to slip into the shadows. From idle comments made at the afternoon tea, she'd deduced in which wing the library lay; if she had it right, it was off the same main hall as the ballroom, but on the opposite side.

Another series of dances was about to commence. The first would be a waltz. Hugging the walls, she circled the room, making for the door to the hall. Given she wanted to slip away, she didn't intend to participate.

"There you are."

A large hand closed about hers and made her jump. Not from shock, or even surprise. Pure sensation jolted up her arm, telling her more clearly than her eyes or ears who was so cavalierly appropriating her.

"Mr. Tallent!" She swung to face him.

He was smiling at her—that same brilliant smile with a touch of rogue about the edges. "Jonas, remember?" Winding her arm in his, he turned toward the dance floor. "It's time for another waltz."

She sucked in a huge breath. "Jonas—we've already waltzed once."

"Indeed. And as it was such an enjoyable experience for us both, there's no reason we shouldn't repeat the exercise."

"Yes, there is," she muttered, trying to keep her Colyton self restrained. "People will talk."

"People are already talking about you. If you don't want the world to speculate, you shouldn't present it with such a contradictory mystery."

She frowned up at him as he turned and drew her into his arms; she instinctively raised hers, letting him grip her right hand, putting her left on his shoulder, and then she was whirling—while still trying to puzzle out his last comment. "I'm not a mystery, let alone a contradictory one."

"Oh, yes, you are. A young lady who sets herself up as an innkeeper, but who remains very much a young lady, and insists her whole family keep to the same social line. 'Why?' is what everyone wants to know."

"But . . . I thought they'd all assume we were gentry fallen on hard times—which we are."

He bent a mock-disappointed look on her. "My dear Em, permit me to inform you that 'gentry fallen on hard times' do not possess silk evening gowns, nor do they wear pearl combs in their hair"—he looked pointedly at the comb anchoring her unruly curls—"nor do they hire tutors for their brothers with the stated aim of preparing said brothers to enter Pembroke College."

His dark brown eyes held hers. She looked into them, and wondered anew. Pommeroy Fortemain set her nerves flickering in clear warning. Jonas set them flickering even more, but in exactly the opposite way.

And, drat him, the attraction between them wasn't any longer purely physical. Beneath the undeniable glamor, there was something very *steady* about Jonas Tallent. Something that appealed to her in a way that almost scared her.

She could feel it like a physical tug, the growing impulse

to tell him, to confide their Grand Plan to him and let him help. If that impulse had arisen from needing his help, she might already have told him and asked for it, yet although he probably could help, she was confident they'd succeed in finding the treasure on their own; she didn't need to tell him to find the treasure—at least not at this point.

The reason she wanted to tell him, what fed the impulse to do so, had more to do with sharing, with telling him who she really was so they could hunt the treasure together. Uncovering her family's treasure would unquestionably be one of the major adventures of her life—and because of that reason she couldn't quite define, she wanted to share that adventure with him.

She'd been alone for more than a decade, in charge of her siblings for all that time. All alone. Just herself. To suddenly feel the compulsion to include someone else shook her, unnerved her.

More than anything else, it confused her.

She wasn't sure she was capable of thinking clearly when in Jonas Tallent's arms.

Certainly not while waltzing with him.

Especially not when his dark gaze grew warmer, more mesmerizing; especially not when he drew her closer, his large hand on her back burning through the silk of her gown.

She was floating again, barely touching the earth, and in that altered state could sense, feel . . . could almost believe . . .

The music ended, he swirled slowly to a halt, and she fell back to earth.

To the reality that he was her employer, and she was the keeper-manager of his inn.

He might scoff at her charade, yet she was still that; in taking the position she'd stepped off the pedestal of ladyhood, and that was something not even he could deny. She couldn't believe—would be foolish to believe—that he was thinking in terms of anything more than an affair.

She turned, scanned the room, in reality avoiding looking into his eyes—eyes that where she was concerned too often saw too much.

He didn't release her hand, but closed his more firmly around her fingers. "Em—"

"Here's Mrs. Crockforth, with her daughter." Em smiled encouragingly at the matron who had chosen that moment to approach. The next dance would start in a few minutes, and she and Jonas had already waltzed twice; she wouldn't be dancing with him again that night.

Innkeeper or not.

Jonas perforce had to bow and smile, and shake the young lady's, Tabitha's, hand.

Em had to tug surreptitiously to get him to release her hand, but with that achieved, she joined forces with Mrs. Crockforth to ensure her Tabitha shared the next dance with the patently reluctant, but incapable of being impolite, Mr. Tallent.

Delighted, Em watched the pair head for the dance floor, then parted from Mrs. Crockforth with mutual commendations. She remained watching until Jonas turned the other way, then stepped back into the crowd and slipped from the room.

The library was where she'd thought it would be, and helpfully deserted. Somewhat to her dismay, it was on the large side and lined with bookcases, all of which were crammed with books.

Lots and lots of books.

She didn't have time to waste grumbling; she started with the bookcase nearest the door. She quickly discovered there was a system to the shelving; she started to scan the shelves, checking the spine of the first book on each.

She'd progressed down one long side, and down one short side of the room, when finally in the corner behind the huge desk she came upon the books on local history—which included two books specifically on Ballyclose Manor!

Her fingers all but tingling with excitement, she pulled

both books out. Setting one atop the other, she opened the cover and started to read.

She rapidly learned a great deal about the house—except what she wanted to know. She'd flicked through half the book without finding any reference to the date the house was built, when her nerves flickered—in alarm.

She looked up.

A puzzled frown on his face, Pommeroy was advancing around the desk, his footsteps muffled by the thick rug. "What are you doing?"

"Ah . . ." She bludgeoned her wits into order. "I . . . think I might have mentioned I have an interest in local architecture. Especially of old houses. It's my hobby."

Pommeroy's puzzlement vanished at the word "hobby." He gave a silent "Oh," and nodded.

Then he looked at the books in her hand—tipped his head to check the spines—and frowned again. "Ballyclose?" Surprised, he met her eyes. "Wouldn't think it merited any serious consideration—well, it's nice and all that, but it's hardly old."

She blinked. "Old? You mean . . . it isn't old?"

Smiling, Pommeroy shook his head. "Not old at all—built by my grandfather about fifty years ago."

"Fifty?" She shut the book. Mentally scrambled. She'd been so sure Ballyclose was their target. "But . . . perhaps it was built on some older structure." She fixed Pommeroy with a hopeful look. "Many old houses are like that—new, but with older sections, or incorporating old walls, or foundations, even cellars."

Smiling smugly, Pommeroy shook his head. "Big family secret—or at least the family never let it be said. M'grandfather built this place on top of an old farm cottage after it crumbled to rubble."

It was Em's turn to frown. "But Fortemains have lived in the village for centuries—I know that much. So where did your family live before Ballyclose?"

Pommeroy rocked on his heels, patently enjoying being

the focus of her attention. "Wasn't the same family—or, leastways, not the same branch. M'grandfather hailed from near London. He moved here when one of his cousins died and left him the farm—the Ballyclose lands. That's when he built the house."

She drew closer, willing Pommeroy to give her the critical information. "Where did that cousin live—do you know?"

"Just in one of the cottages near the inn."

None of which were sufficiently grand to have ever been termed "the house of the highest."

She sighed and drew back.

Pommeroy raised his brows. "I could show you around the house, if you like. Better than returning to the party, what?"

She shook her head. "Thank you, but no. I'm only interested in older houses—ones that date from centuries ago." Remembering the books she still carried in her hands, she turned back to the shelves and returned the volumes to their place close by the corner.

Straightening, she swung around—into Pommeroy's arms.

"Pommeroy!" She tried to push him away, but he had his arms locked about her. And, as she discovered with her first attempt to break free, he was a lot stronger than he looked. She started struggling in earnest. "What are you *doing*?"

He leered at her. "I helped you with your hobby—only fair I get a reward." Tightening his arms, he leaned in and tried to kiss her.

"No!" Ducking, she managed to evade his thick lips.

She pushed against his chest with all her might. Her dress was getting horribly crushed, yet she couldn't seem to gain any leverage, certainly not enough to break from his hold. And the more she struggled, the more he seemed to think it was some game—that she wasn't in earnest, but teasing him! The sounds he was making were all of escalating excitement.

Panic bloomed. Her earlier comment regarding the dangers to be found in gentlemen's libraries returned to taunt her.

She lifted her head, peeked—and he came at her again. She shrieked and ducked again; his lips collided with her head just above her forehead. The thought of those lips on her skin—anywhere—was too awful to even contemplate. She redoubled her struggles. Tried to stamp on his foot. All but screamed, "Stop it, or I'll tell your mother!"

"Nonsense—no harm in a bit of—*oophmm!*"

He was suddenly gone. Just like that, he was plucked from her and sent sailing into the opposite corner. He fetched up against the shelves like a bag of potatoes, dully rattling, then slowly slid down, stunned, to sit on the floor.

He blinked at her, dazed, then transferred his gaze to her rescuer.

Jonas.

Em knew it was him although she hadn't yet glanced his way. She was, she discovered, short of breath, and panicky, and just a touch giddy. The first order for the immediate moment was to breathe—to gain enough breath to calm her wits and steady her nerves.

For a long moment, no one said a word. Then, her breathing gradually evening, her hand at her throat, she looked at Jonas.

His face was all hard angles and planes. He was looking at Pommeroy as if debating the ethics of dismembering his hostess's son.

He felt her gaze.

She knew he did because a different sort of tension infused his long frame.

He turned his head slowly and met her gaze.

And she stopped breathing again.

They were close enough for her to see his eyes, see the emotions roiling in their dark depths, violent and powerful.

He waited, but she couldn't find her tongue. Faced with what she could see in his eyes, she couldn't lay her wits to any words, let alone find the breath to utter them. Primitive instinct had her in its grip. She wasn't sure it was safe to make a sound.

Jonas turned back to Pommeroy. A compulsion unlike any he'd known had him in a merciless grip; it was all he could do not to haul Pommeroy up just so he could knock him down again. Rational thought had little purchase in his brain. He was all instinct and impulse; some dark side of him had broken loose from all civilized bonds and now roared.

Pommeroy seemed to sense that; eyes wide, he flailed, trying to sit up.

Jonas trapped his gaze. "You've just developed a hideous headache, Pommeroy, and you're going to retire to your room. Now."

Managing to sit upright, Pommeroy goggled at him. "I-I am?"

Grimly, he nodded. "And if you have any trouble feigning feeling ill, I'll be only too happy to make it easier for you." He spoke through clenched teeth. "Do you understand me, Pommeroy?"

Pale, Pommeroy looked from him to Em, who glanced up from straightening her gown to glare ferociously. Pommeroy looked down. Mumbled, "Not well. Think I'll go to m'room."

"Very good." Turning to Em, Jonas reached for her arm. "Meanwhile, we'll finish our stroll on the terrace."

She let him take her elbow and steer her toward the French doors. She glanced into his face, frowned. "What stroll?"

"The stroll all the guests in the ballroom are going to see us returning from." Hauling open the door to the terrace, he met her gaze. "That stroll."

"Oh." She hesitated, then stepped out onto the terrace.

He followed, closing the door, sparing not a glance for Pommeroy, struggling to his feet in the corner.

She'd halted, looking down the terrace; it ran the length of the house. At the far end, a pair of French doors stood ajar, spilling light and noise, the sounds of gaiety, into the night, but as the October evening was chilly, no other couples had ventured outside.

Somewhat stiffly, he offered her his arm.

She considered it, then consented to place her hand on his sleeve.

He resisted the urge to clamp his other hand over hers and not let go. He was hanging on to his temper by his fingernails, and was determined to make no further comment; speech of any kind was too dangerous in his current, highly charged state. Fury, outrage, a ferocious protectiveness, and something exceedingly more primitive, coursed his veins. The touch of her hand on his sleeve, the smallness, the fragility of her dainty fingers felt through the fabric, only heightened and exacerbated that primitive response . . .

They'd taken no more than five paces along the terrace when against his better judgment, all but against his will, he growled, "I can't believe you plotted to go apart alone with that nincompoop Pommeroy."

From the way she'd assisted Mrs. Crockforth in urging her daughter on him, he'd known she was planning something—that she was about to make some move.

He'd seen her slip from the ballroom. He'd had to wait until the end of the dance and he'd parted from Miss Crockforth before he'd been able to follow. Knowing she'd been searching through books, the library had been his first port of call. He hadn't been surprised to find her there, but he'd been stunned to discover her in Pommeroy's arms.

Then he'd seen she was struggling, had heard her shriek, and instinct had taken hold.

He tried to tell himself it would have been the same with any other young lady he'd discovered in Pommeroy's clutches.

He wished he could believe that, but while he would certainly have gone to the aid of any female in such a situation, he wouldn't—he knew he wouldn't—have felt the raw black rage that had swamped him, all because it was her.

She didn't immediately reply to his remark; she tipped up her nose and took three more steps before saying, "*Not* that it's any concern of yours, but I didn't plot, plan, scheme, or in any way *arrange* to meet privately with Pommeroy Fortemain. It's beyond my comprehension why you think I would." Her tone had grown increasingly heated. Pulling her hand from his sleeve, she halted and swung to face him. "Why the devil would I want to have anything to do with him?" Fists clenched, she glared up into his face as he halted, too. "Next you'll accuse me of having designs on him!"

He glowered back. "I would hope you'd have better taste. But how else—" He broke off. "He followed you?"

"Well, of course he followed me! That's how he found me alone and tried to take advantage."

"He couldn't have found you alone if you hadn't slipped off to search for whatever it is you're damned well searching for."

Em narrowed her eyes on his. "I was about to thank you for your timely intervention, but regardless of any gratitude I might feel, nothing—I repeat *nothing*—gives you the right to dictate to me about where I might go, and when, or even with whom!" Sheer aggravation brought her up on her toes; she jabbed a finger at his nose. "*You* are not my keeper! No one elected you to that role. It's beyond my comprehension why you believe you have any claim to interfere in my life. What do you imagine gives you that right?"

His expression hadn't softened, but it had gone strangely blank. He stared at her as the seconds ticked by.

She was about to humph and rock back on her heels, judging her message had finally struck home, when he reached for her.

Hauled her into his arms, up against his chest, bent his head, and crushed his lips to hers.

9

Wild, passionate, intense—from the first meeting of lips the kiss swept her away, far beyond rational thought.

Her wits whirled into a maelstrom of delight, of heat and sensation, the epitome of temptation.

Something new, wonderful, fascinating—a new world to explore, a scintillating new horizon that called to her Colyton soul, to that part of her that thrived on the novel and the wild, that craved adventure and the thrills of exploration.

Far from reeling back in shock, she seized the moment and plunged in.

Into the heat, into the fire, into the searing wonder of the kiss.

Her hands were trapped against his chest. Instead of pushing, they clung. Her fingers hooked into the fabric of his coat and closed, holding him to her every bit as much as the steel bands of his arms held her to him.

Crushed her to him. She could feel the heavy muscles of his chest, his ridged abdomen, all down her front.

His tongue thrust boldly, enticing, igniting. His arms tightened as he angled his head; his lips locked on hers, devouring, claiming.

She kissed him back, hungry and greedy, some slumbering part of her brought alive by passion undisguised, by desire unveiled.

Both might be new to her, but some part of her recognized and knew them for what they were, and rejoiced.

Greedily incited. Beckoned and invited.

As the kiss continued and the heat spun out, her breasts grew heavy, swollen, and achy, their tips ruching into tight buds.

She wanted to get closer, to press kisses on him, to ease the unfamiliar restless ache by pressing herself to him. She tried to move into him, but apparently sensing her need, he instead moved into her, backing her step by deliberate step until she felt the cool wall at her back—a shocking contrast to the heat of him, of which she couldn't get enough.

His hands clamped about her waist and he shifted closer, his heavy body pressing into hers, fitting against hers. One long, hard thigh wedged between hers, bringing her up on her toes. A sharp thrill cascaded down her spine; delicious heat and wanton sensation erupted in its wake, then flowed, flooded, raced through her to pool low in her belly.

She clung to the kiss, an equal participant, overwhelmed by sensation entirely by choice. Glorying and savoring and wanting more.

Eager, enthusiatic—demanding.

Jonas drank in her response, sensed it to his bones, felt sensual anticipation grip and sink its claws deep.

He couldn't catch his breath. Couldn't find the reins. He'd somehow relinquished control of the exchange—not to her, but to the conflagration that between them they'd ignited.

A fire that was familiar yet not, more intense, too intense, almost frightening in its power.

Unbidden, his arms had tightened and he'd gathered her in, hard against him. Enough lucidity had remained to make him back her into the shadows, trapping her soft form between him and the wall, holding her there, savoring how she, her curves and hollows, cradled his long frame.

At the mercy of some force stronger than his will, he couldn't stop from steeping himself in the glories of her mouth, in the evocatively feminine caress of her body, couldn't stop himself from kissing her with a passion so raw and undisguised he shocked even himself.

That anything could be so powerful as to strip away his civilized veneer rocked him to his toes. Shattered his heretofore absolute belief in his self-control.

What had erupted between them was both sweet and hot, a combination he found impossibly alluring. The kiss had turned ravenous, a flagrant mating of mouths, one she fed as much as he.

He had to fight not to press his hips to hers, to suggestively shift against her. Even in his current fraught state, he knew that would be one step too far, at least at this point.

Yet although she should have been fighting to make him stop, frightened by the intensity of the exchange, instead she was fighting to make him continue. Tempting him to.

Therein lay a good part of his problem.

He knew she'd never been kissed like this before—the evidence was there in her innocent eagerness, her unbounded unfettered delight. He doubted she knew, had any idea of, what she was doing.

What she was inciting. Inviting.

How dangerous playing with this particular fire could be.

Her hands, until then clutching his coat, eased their convulsive grip and slid upward. Pressed over his collarbones, cruised the sides of his throat to gently frame his jaw, to oh-so-gently hold him while she rose even higher on her toes and kissed him like a wanton angel.

Her touch sent awareness of a different sort through him, awoke, drew forth, another part of what he felt for her, one until then overwhelmed.

They were on the terrace, in full view should any other guests decide to take the air.

Her reputation would be severely damaged if they were

seen like this; for that matter, given she was now the village darling, so would his.

What they were doing was dangerous. They had to stop.

So much easier said than done.

Drawing back from the exchange took every ounce of resolution he possessed. In the end he had to force his hands from her, plant both palms flat on the wall, and slowly brace his arms to make himself pull away.

He finally succeeded; their lips parted, the kiss ended.

It took still more effort to lift his head, and not plunge back into it.

He was breathing rapidly; so was she.

He looked down at her face, watched her lids rise . . . on eyes starry with awakened desire.

The sight shook him, drew him.

Abruptly he pushed away from her, managed to take a single step back.

Through the dimness he held her wide eyes.

"That"—his voice was a gravelly threat—"is what makes me your keeper. What gives me the right—no, lays on me the duty—to watch over you and keep you safe."

She blinked; in her eyes he could see awareness returning, hand in hand with her stubborn resistance.

"You can deny it for however long you choose, but I won't." He held her gaze. "It's real. All of it. And I have no intention of ignoring it, or turning my back on it. This"—he gestured between them—"comes but once in a lifetime. I don't intend to let the chance pass."

Her expression had shuttered, her eyes slightly narrowed; her lips slowly set in a firm line.

Still holding her gaze, he drew in a deep breath. "You asked me before what I thought, and wanted, this—what's between us—to mean. To me, it means—can mean—only one thing. You're mine. *Mine*. Mine to hold, mine to defend, mine to protect. And no matter how long it takes, I fully intend you to see that, too—and to agree."

Her eyes had flared, denial bright and absolute filling them. Decisively she shook her head. "No." Her voice was low and husky. She swallowed, then went on, "You might think— might believe, might have decided—that I'm yours, but I'm not." Her chin firmed as she lifted it. "And I never will be."

He nodded grimly. "Yes, you are—and will be. What's more, you'll definitely agree."

Her eyes narrowed to bright slivers; she held his gaze belligerently, stubborn to stubborn. She longed to have the last word, he knew—he waited to hear what it would be.

Instead, tipping her nose higher in the air, she swung on her heel and stalked off.

He watched her walk down the terrace; recalling where they were, he settled his coat and followed. Catching up to her just short of the ballroom, he wound her arm in his. She cast him a sharp look, but allowed it, and permitted him to escort her inside.

She was going to concentrate—wholly, solely, to the exclusion of all else—on locating the Colyton treasure.

The next morning, Em sat in the church pew—fast becoming her family's pew—and pretended to listen to the Sunday sermon. Given Filing was delivering it, Issy was paying rapt attention—enough for them both. Em felt not the slightest guilt in giving her mind over to her hunt.

If their "house of the highest" wasn't Ballyclose Manor, then the next most likely house was the Grange.

Unfortunately the Grange would be even harder to search than Ballyclose. It was a smaller, neater house, with a smaller but highly active staff, all of whom knew her, at the very least by sight. And it was Jonas Tallent's home, his lair, an even bigger complication.

Without conscious direction, her eyes locked on his dark head. She could still hear his "mine" echoing in her ears. As usual he was in the front pew; at least he couldn't gaze, unrelenting and unsettling, at her.

Regrettably her gaze seemed irresistibly drawn to him, to his well-shaped dark head with its silky near-black hair, to his broad shoulders exquisitely encased in sober gray superfine.

His declaration replayed in her head. Even more than the words, it was his tone—diabolically, blatantly possessive—that had affected her. Still affected her, even as a memory, in a thoroughly unsettling way.

Just what it made her feel she wasn't sure; she'd never experienced such a reaction, had no prior knowledge on which to base a judgment. Regardless, she was perfectly certain gentlemen weren't supposed to go around declaring young ladies "theirs."

She kept telling herself she should shift her gaze, kept intending to, yet it remained locked on him.

Filing's sermon proved no competition for her attention.

She drew breath, felt tightness in her chest. She might not be able to deny the attraction that flared between them—after that interlude on the terrace denial in any form would be so much wasted breath—but she could still resist it, resist giving in to her wilder side and letting it and him lead her onto paths she hadn't yet trod. Paths she'd assumed she never would explore—never have the chance to, not with her family so reliant on her.

Paths she didn't have time to even ponder, not now.

The service drew to a close and they all rose. On exiting the church, she paused to exchange greetings with others of the congregation. She steadily moved further from the door, eventually reaching the first of the graves. Turning, she scanned the gathering for her siblings. The twins had gone down the steps just ahead of her; they were playing a game of tag in and around the gravestones. With their blond hair gleaming golden in the sunshine, they looked like angels flitting about; far from earning censure, the departing congregation smiled on their antics.

Issy had hung back by the door; she was now talking to Filing, both fair heads close.

As for Henry . . . for a moment, Em couldn't spot him—
he was in the last place she allowed herself to look, standing at the bottom of the church steps with Jonas Tallent.

Speaking with Jonas Tallent. Em felt her eyes narrow as
she took in her brother's eager, animated expression. She
wanted to go and retrieve him, yet hesitated; getting closer
to Tallent wasn't on her agenda. But what was he saying to
make Henry, so often too sober, so enthusiastic?

She learned the answer a minute later. Parting from Jonas, Henry looked about, searching the crowd—for her.
Jonas, who knew exactly where she was, met her gaze and
smiled—smug, knowing, yet she sensed a certain challenge
in the gesture.

Henry spotted her and trotted over. His eyes were alight.
"I say—Jonas—Mr. Tallent—said he'll take me for a drive
in his curricle this afternoon. He's going down the coast
road to check on something, and asked if I wanted to come
along." Eagerness shone in Henry's eyes. "He said he'd teach
me how to handle the reins. It's all right if I go, isn't it? I've
already said I would—I didn't think you'd mind."

Denying the temptation to narrow her eyes in Jonas Tallent's direction, Em kept her gaze on her brother's face. What
she could see there, glowing in his eyes, lighting his whole
face, made it impossible to do anything other than acqui-
esce. "Yes, all right. As long as you're back in good time for
dinner."

Henry crowed, beamed her a brilliant smile, then turned
and rushed back to confirm the arrangement with Jonas,
who'd wisely kept his distance.

"How come he asked Henry instead of us?"

Em glanced down at Gert, who'd come up in time to hear
Henry's news. Bea stood a step behind, an incipient pout on
her lips.

"Age before beauty," Em informed them. "Now come
along—we need to get home."

Home being the inn; strange how it had so easily become
their place. Herding the girls before her, Em glanced at

Issy, who had noticed the signs of their imminent departure; taking her leave of Filing, she hurried to join them.

Glancing at Henry, Em caught his eye and beckoned. He nodded. As she turned down the hill, from the corner of her eye, she saw Henry set out—with Jonas Tallent beside him.

But then Filing called to Jonas and he halted, then waved Henry to go on without him. Jonas turned back to speak with Filing. Em breathed easier; she wasn't yet ready to converse with her employer, not if she could avoid it.

With Issy smiling contendedly by her side, she followed the twins down the slope and around the duck pond. Henry caught up, then eagerly strode ahead.

She knew Jonas was trailing somewhere behind them; she could feel his gaze on her back. She in turn studied Henry. Wondered if she was being too cynical in thinking that Jonas had invited her brother to go driving to get into her good graces, reasoning—correctly—that being kind to her siblings would achieve that goal. A goal he was intelligent enough to know he needed to achieve.

But perhaps she was seeing ulterior motives where there were none.

Regardless, if Jonas Tallent was spending the afternoon out driving with Henry, he wouldn't be at home at the Grange.

It was only sensible to strike when opportunity presented itself. At a few minutes after two o'clock that afternoon, having seen Jonas drive off with Henry beside him, Em knocked on the back door of the Grange. Gladys, the housekeeper, answered the door.

"Miss Beauregard! Good gracious me—you should have come to the front, miss." She glanced back over her shoulder. "Or is Mortimer napping and not heard you knock?"

"No, no—it's quite all right. I came this way deliberately—it's you and"—Em nodded to the presence in the cozy kitchen beyond—"Cook that I came to see."

Gladys looked surprised, but entirely amenable. "If that's the case, dearie, you come right in and sit yourself down."

Em complied, exchanging smiles and greetings with Cook—never known as anything but Cook—who was standing at the kitchen table kneading dough. "Orange scones," Cook said in response to her inquiring look.

"Ah! Well, that's what I've come to speak with you about. I wanted to pick your brains about recipes, those that are special to this area. I've been thinking that the inn should concentrate on local dishes." Her excuse was genuine; the idea had indeed been fomenting for some days. "It will give the Red Bells a point of distinction—something we could say we did that no one else did, dishes and menus unique to Colyton. But that would depend on getting enough local special recipes."

Cook exchanged a look with Gladys. "Well, I should think we'd be able to help you with that."

Gladys nodded. "You'll want to ask Cilla at Dottswood, and Cook at Ballyclose, and Mrs. Hemmings at the manor, too."

"And Mrs. Farquarson," Cook said. "She has a great old book of recipes from her aunt who lived in Colyton all her life. The aunt's gone now, but the recipes are still here."

Em pulled paper and pencil from her reticule and began to take notes. Gladys made tea. Mortimer joined them. It took Em a little while to find the right moment, but eventually she said, "The cellars at the inn are surprisingly extensive." She glanced at the wooden door just visible along the corridor to the scullery. "Is that normal for houses around here, do you know? Was there a particular need for such large cellars?"

Mortimer smiled. "I don't know about need, but the cellars here, too, are quite large. Rooms leading into more rooms. Perhaps, being such an old house, in days gone by those who lived here had more of a need to store food and the like. They even had underground tunnels linking the various outbuildings, like the stables and buttery, to the house cellars."

It required no effort for Em to look interested. "How old is this house?"

"As to that, I couldn't say, miss." Mortimer set down his teacup. "But Mr. Jonas would know."

The one person she didn't want to ask. She smiled and let the subject slide, returning instead to her pursuit of local recipes.

Two minutes later, a tap on the back door was followed by it opening to reveal Miss Sweet, with Phyllida Cynster behind her.

"Good morning, Gladys, dear." Miss Sweet breezed in. "Oh, Miss Beauregard. How lovely to see you here . . ." Miss Sweet's expression showed she was at a loss as to why Em was sitting in the kitchen.

With a smile, Em greeted her and explained her errand. Miss Sweet promptly waxed enthusiastic.

Phyllida, too, was encouraging. "Mrs. Hemmings has a number of particular recipes I'm sure she'd be happy to share in such a cause."

It transpired that Phyllida had walked Miss Sweet to the Grange merely to keep an eye on the older woman along the woodland path. "I must get back—my imps can't be trusted to stay out of trouble for long."

"If you don't mind," Em said, gathering her notes, "I'll walk with you. I've finished here, and while I know there's a path that leads to the back of the inn, I'm not sure of the way."

Phyllida smiled. "I can show you. Indeed, I'll be glad of your company."

Em thanked Gladys, Cook, and Mortimer, and farewelled Miss Sweet, then she and Phyllida set off along the path.

Phyllida waved ahead of them at the narrow beaten path just wide enough for them to walk along side by side. "It leads from the rear of the Grange almost directly north through the wood. Further along, there's a path leading off to the left which will take you to the inn's back door. Beyond that, the path skirts the rear of the cottages along the lane, eventually ending near the stables at the manor."

"So it's a shortcut between the manor, the Grange, and the inn."

Phyllida nodded. "Jonas and I use it most, and have for decades. He'll occasionally send the Grange gardener along to clear the way, but it's been there for as long as I can remember."

They strolled along in companionable amity. "I mentioned the cellars at the inn," Em said, "and was told that you, or your brother, might know more about their history."

"Ah, yes." Smiling, Phyllida nodded. "The connection between the Grange, long the home of the local magistrate, who happened to own the inn and therefore placed the local holding cells in the inn's cellars rather than his own."

"Is that what those rooms are? I did wonder."

"They're rarely used," Phyllida assured her. "Indeed, the last person to have been incarcerated there was Lucifer." When Em looked shocked, she laughed. "It was a mistake, but he was unconscious at the time. I had to rescue him, and we looked after him at the Grange until he came to his senses."

Em was tempted to inquire further, but decided it was more important to ask, "I'm still trying to get a feeling for the village's history, and the role of the major houses in that. Can you tell me anything about the Grange?" She glanced at Phyllida. "I understand it's been in your family for generations."

"Oh, indeed—almost since the Conquest. Of course the current building isn't that old—the oldest parts of it date from the early fifteenth century, although it's been extensively added to over the years."

"And your family's been the local magistrates, or equivalent, for most of that time?"

"More or less." Phyllida glanced at Em, smiled. "And

now if I might ask, where does your family hail from, Miss Beauregard?"

Em smiled back. "Please call me Emily, or Em, as most do."

"If you will drop formality and call me Phyllida."

Em inclined her head. "As to your question, my grandfather moved around the country somewhat, but then settled in York. My father was born there—within sound of the cathedral bells, as he often said—and lived there all his life. My mother was from a local family, and so was my stepmother—the twins' mother."

"Ah—so they're your half sisters."

"Yes, but all of us have always been close. When their mother died, they came to live with us."

"Oh—so you were separated for a while?"

She hadn't meant to divulge that. "After my father's death, we—Henry, Issy, and I—lived with our maternal uncle for a time. But then it became necessary for us to make our way, and I started managing inns." She was straying onto shaky ground, and sought to come about. "I understand the manor's as old as the Grange."

Looking ahead, she noted the opening of a side path to the left.

"As far as I know. I went to the manor on my marriage—I'm not as au fait with its history as I am with the Grange's. You should ask Lucifer."

Em was pleased to have skated successfully over the thin ice of her recent past. "I'll try to remember the next time I meet him." She halted at the intersection of the paths. "This must be my turning."

"It is." Smiling, Phyllida held out her hand. "I'll no doubt see you in the inn. Your revitalization is proceeding apace—it's wonderful to have such a comfortable place even ladies can use."

"It's certainly proving popular." Em shook hands, then turned toward the inn. "I just hope we can live up to expectations."

"I'm sure you will." Phyllida waved, then headed on along the path.

Thinking, wondering. There was absolutely no doubt in her mind that Emily Beauregard was well born, more, of the same social class as herself. When they were together without others about, there was a . . . camaraderie, for want of a better description, that Phyllida recognized. It was the same sense of shared experiences, shared types of lives, that she felt with the other Cynster ladies—the wives of Lucifer's brother and cousins.

They were not all the same, not by any means, yet they shared the same goals, the same problems, the same ambitions. She recognized all those aspects in Emily Beauregard; she was a kindred spirit.

The manor appeared ahead. Phyllida strolled through her kitchen garden, taking note of what was up and what needed cutting back. She went in through the kitchen, stopped to consult with Mrs. Hemmings as to dinner, then continued on into the house—to the back parlor, where she'd left her handsome husband in charge of their sons.

All was strangely silent behind the parlor's closed door. She quietly eased it open; the sight that met her eyes brought a smile, a softly glowing one, to her face.

Lucifer was sprawled on the rug before the sofa, on his back, arms at his sides, each cradling one son as said sons slumbered. Whatever he'd been doing with them had clearly tired them out.

She crept in, not sure if he, too, was asleep. Sliding onto the sofa, she sat and looked down lovingly at the three faces, the younger two softer, more rounded versions of their sire's. Even in respose, his held the hard lines and angular planes that so unambiguously marked him as a member of the aristocracy.

Slowly his ridiculously long black lashes lifted and his eyes—those dark blue eyes that always seemed to see straight to her soul—looked into hers. He smiled. "What have you been up to?"

He'd spoken in a whisper. She whispered back, "I walked back with Miss Beauregard—Emily." She paused, then asked, "Do we know anyone in York?"

She explained what she'd learned about their new innkeeper. "She didn't mention Ballyclose at all, but she did ask after the history of the Grange."

"What about the manor? They're of much the same vintage."

Phyllida shook her head. "She mentioned it in passing, but I got the impression she was now concentrating on the Grange."

Lucifer's brows rose. "Interesting. What it means, however, I can't begin to guess."

A footstep on the hall tiles had Phyllida glancing at the door. It cracked open, and Jonas looked in. Seeing the family tableau, he grinned, and as Phyllida had, crept in.

Coming to stand by the end of the sofa where Lucifer could see him, he nodded in greeting, then glanced at Phyllida. "I just returned Henry Beauregard to the inn— we went out driving. Em wasn't there—have you seen her?"

Phyllida's brows rose. "As it happens, I have." She explained, and recounted what she'd learned.

None of them knew anyone in York from whom they might inquire of the Beauregards.

Phyllida studied Jonas. "Did you learn anything from Henry?"

Jonas shook his head. "The instant I make any inquiry as to his family's past, he becomes very careful and circumspect. He's too intelligent to trick in any way. If he doesn't want to discuss an issue, he simply won't, so I got no further there."

He hesitated, then looked from Phyllida to Lucifer. "I've come to the conclusion that whatever Em's quest—her goal—is, whatever it is she's searching for, the most sensible way forward is to help her to it. To tell her whatever she wants to know."

Lucifer grimaced. "It would help if she asked direct questions, or better yet, told us what she's after."

"She might soon, now she's getting to know us," Jonas suggested.

"Her interest seems to have switched from Ballyclose to the Grange." Phyllida raised her brows. "I wonder why?"

Jonas frowned. "If you see Pommeroy about, you might ask him whether Em spoke to him about Ballyclose. At the moment, he's avoiding me." He wasn't about to explain why, although Lucifer's suddenly sharpened gaze suggested he, at least, could guess.

Phyllida was nodding. "I get the impression that whatever she's searching for, it's something old—something connected to history and days long gone. And it definitely is a 'something'—some actual object."

Jonas nodded in agreement. "If only we knew what."

If only they knew what Em was searching for, they'd very likely be able to help her to it, and then . . .

And then he might be able to get her to concentrate on him and what was evolving between them, rather than on her search.

The following morning, Jonas cantered through his father's fields, following the line of the River Coly upstream from where it joined the Axe. He'd been to check the weir downriver; finding all was well, he was heading back to the Grange, casting his eyes over his father's domains and thinking of Emily Beauregard.

His wish to have her undivided attention wasn't the only reason he wanted her search brought to a quick and satisfactory conclusion. It had finally occurred to him just why her secret project made him so uneasy—because her very secrecy implied there was potentially danger involved, from some direction, one he couldn't begin to identify given he didn't know what she was searching for.

The thought of her being in danger wasn't one he could

bear with any degree of equanimity; having finally accepted what she meant to him, he even understood why.

Frowning into the morning sun, he guided Jupiter, his black gelding, on.

He wouldn't have spotted the errant pair making their way through the corn if they hadn't giggled—loudly enough for Jupiter to take exception, to shake his head and lay back his ears.

Reining in by the side of a copse, Jonas watched the two bright heads striking across the field—directly for the riverbank.

The Coly was a small enough river, and given it was October, wasn't running high, but beneath the gently rippling surface, the current was, in places, strong, and there were deep pools scattered along its length.

Too deep for young girls to risk slipping in.

Jonas hadn't intended to reclaim their attention, not until they'd forgotten about his promise to take them driving. Besides, as Em had foreseen, the pair made him, if not nervous, then wary. He'd grown up side by side with Phyllida, but dealing with a sister wasn't the same as dealing with the twins, prospective sisters-in-law though they might be.

Still . . . they continued on, skipping and leaping through the corn.

Jonas sighed and urged Jupiter into a walk—toward the pair. He angled closer, then before they saw him, he tapped his heels to Jupiter's sides, setting him to a trot, bringing him onto a line between the girls and the river.

He drew rein directly in their path.

Startled, they halted. They looked up at him—recognized him—and smiled. Brilliantly.

Before delight could completely overtake them, he arched a brow at them. "Do your sisters know where you are?"

The question brought them up short—cut off their exclamations of joy. Instead, they exchanged a long glance, deciding what to tell him, then looked up at him.

"No," said Gert.

"We're supposed to be upstairs *drawing*." Bea made the activity sound like the biggest waste of time ever invented. "But it was far too nice to stay indoors."

Their expressions stated that they fully expected him to understand and sympathize; the truth was, he did. He pulled a face, letting that show. "Understandable, *but* . . . while these fields and the river might look safe enough, there's dangers aplenty. For instance—" He let his imagination free and listed a number of potential hazards. While the girls didn't look all that deterred, when he pointed out how upset their sisters would be if anything happened to them, and no one knew to save them because they'd slipped out without permission, their expressions turned serious, enough to encourage him to conclude with, "And just at the moment, what with the inn and her search, Em has enough to worry about without you two adding to it, don't you think?"

At that they exchanged glances, and looked truly contrite.

"We just wanted to explore, just a *little*." Bea offered him a wavering grimace.

Convinced, now, that they wouldn't run from him, he swung down from the saddle. "Come on—I'll walk you home."

They turned away from the river and cut across the field, then followed the next hedgerow back toward the wood. The girls ranged on either side of him as he tramped along, Jupiter's reins in his hands. The big gelding snorted, not pleased by having to walk instead of run.

"We wanted to see what was out there," Gert stated, eyes on the ground as she marched along. "To explore a bit, seeing we're going to be here for a little while."

If he had any say in the matter, they'd be here for a good long while.

"It's what Colytons do," Bea stated, as if that explained all.

Jonas knew the stories of the village's founders, all of whom, so the tales went, had been irrepressible adventurers; it seemed the twins had heard the tales and decided that simply living in Colyton demanded such enterprise—at least gumption enough to learn what lay over the nearest horizon.

"Be that as it may," he said, "I doubt your sisters would approve."

Bea pulled a horrendous face. "Pr'bly not."

"They like us to be safe." Gert was eyeing Jupiter. "Is he a *good* horse?"

Jonas glanced back at his steed, who appeared to have resigned himself to having his gallop cut short. "Good enough." He glanced at Gert, then Bea. "You must be getting tired—would you like to sit on his back for the rest of the way?"

They did, of course. He lifted them up, but didn't shorten the stirrups. Jupiter's back was wide enough that they were in no danger of sliding off. "Don't giggle," he warned as he started off, leading the big black. "He doesn't like giggling—most horses don't. He might decide he doesn't want you on his back if you giggle."

They were suitably silent for the next ten yards. Then they started asking questions about what they could see from their elevated perch. As he knew the area—could see it in his mind's eye—he could answer with ease. They were still posing questions when they walked into the stableyard at the back of the inn.

John Ostler stuck his head out of the kitchen door, then drew back. A moment later, Em emerged. Looking thoroughly surprised, she hurried up.

Jonas answered the question he could see in her eyes before she got close enough to utter it. "They're well, unharmed, perfectly fine."

Halting, locking her hands on her hips, Em looked up at her half sisters. "Where were they?" She narrowed her eyes at the pair, who appeared not one whit abashed.

"I found them heading for the river. I've explained to them why that isn't a good place to explore. Nor yet the further woods." Jonas reached up and lifted Gert down, then turned back for Bea. "I've suggested they confine themselves to the wood this side of the path for now—and to always make sure they get your permission before they venture forth."

He stepped back and looked at the pair. They returned his gaze and nodded solemnly—first to him, then to Em.

She looked at them and wondered.

She held to her awful silence for a moment more, then said, "You'd better get inside and apologize to Issy, then take yourselves upstairs and resume your lesson."

With identical angelic smiles, the two skipped off.

She watched them go, then sighed. "I'll have to remind Issy that they need breaks—she'll have to take them out and about in between their indoor lessons."

"That would be wise." Jonas remained beside her, showing no inclination to leave.

She glanced at him, met his eyes. "What did you promise them?"

He held her gaze for a moment, his expression uncommunicative, then he grinned. "I told them about various places round about—places they can't possibly reach on their own—then suggested that if they behave and don't go wandering alone and without telling you for the next month, that I might—just might—find time to take them to explore one or two of those distant places."

A carrot perfectly fashioned to keep the twins in line. "Thank you." She heard the relief in her voice, knew she felt it. "That's . . . very kind of you."

His horse snorted, shifted, coming between them and the house. He glanced at the big black beast, who obediently settled.

Then he looked down at her.

Considered her for a moment before saying, "I didn't do it for them—I did it for you."

Looking into his dark eyes, she knew he spoke the truth, tried unsuccessfully to steel herself against it. She inclined her head. "Once again, thank you. I . . . Issy and I would have been frantic when we discovered them gone."

He nodded. He made no move to depart. Instead, his eyes still on hers, his lips curved in a distinctly unsettling way, as if he knew something she didn't.

She frowned at him. "What?"

"I was just thinking that I deserve a reward."

Every instinct leapt—in various different directions. "What reward?"

"This reward."

His arm slid around her waist and cinched her to him, scattering her wits even before he bent his head and pressed his lips to hers. First his tongue teased her lips apart, then plunged into her mouth and tasted.

Taunted, tempted.

She kissed him back, her best intentions flown, dimly aware that his huge horse stood between them and the house, an effective screen should any look out. Their legs might be visible, their nearness suggestive, but no one could see as he angled his head, deepened the kiss—and she slid her arms up, wound them about his neck, and stretched up against him.

The better to kiss him. The better to revel in the sweet exchange. To give, and receive, and share the moment in all its simple yet exciting, illicit yet thrilling, pleasure.

It was just a kiss, she told herself. A kiss and nothing more. Yet within seconds the exchange became a game, a battle of give-and-take, although who was taking and who was giving kept changing and blurring. Which was better, which each preferred, which was the route to greatest delight were all considerations whirling in her brain when, to her dismay, he brought the kiss to an end.

Lifting his head, Jonas looked down into her face, watched her eyes blink open, read in them her utter and complete distraction.

He could barely contain his triumph.

Ignoring the proddings of his baser self, he forced himself

to ease his hold on her. Once assured she was steady on her feet, he released her and stepped back.

Saluted her; he couldn't keep a smile from his lips as he murmured, "Until next time."

The next time he did a good deed for her, or the next time she rewarded him—or possibly the next time he found her alone.

From the look in her eyes, she couldn't tell which he meant.

As he didn't know either, he tugged on Jupiter's reins, led the gelding a little way on, then swung up to the saddle and rode home.

Leaving her watching him, wondering.

10

Late that afternoon, Jonas returned Henry to the inn after another drive down the nearby lanes. Reins in his hands, Henry drove the curricle sedately into the rear stableyard, surprising Em, crossing the yard from the kitchen garden.

Startled, she halted in the middle of the graveled expanse.

"Drive around her," Jonas suggested.

Henry carefully guided the grays around his sister, who looked at first amazed, then, pirouetting to keep them in sight, laughed and applauded.

Drawing up before the stable, Henry turned a beaming face to Jonas. "Thank you! I'll never be able to thank you enough."

"Nonsense." Jonas smiled. "I'll think of something."

Henry laughed, then, still beaming, handed over the reins and leapt down to face his sister. "It was wonderful! I drove for most of the time. Jonas says I've got good hands."

"Indeed." Tying off the reins, Jonas stepped down from the curricle. John Ostler stuck his head out of the kitchen door to see if he was needed; rounding the curricle, Jonas waved him away, then smiled at Em. "He'll be a creditable driver with very little effort. It's easy to teach someone who understands the difference between steering and pulling."

Henry glowed.

His expression easy, Jonas nodded his way. "I'll call by in a few days—see how you're getting on with your lessons and arrange a time for another drive."

"Again, thank you!" Henry saluted him jauntily, then turned and hurried off to the inn.

Jonas and Em watched him go.

Em frowned. "I suppose he's hungry." Her tone suggested that reason accounted for much strange behavior in males of Henry's age.

Jonas suspected Henry's abrupt departure was occasioned more by the conversation they'd had while tooling about the countryside—a conversation initiated by Henry, regarding Jonas's intentions toward Em. Once he'd assured Henry those were honorable—that he wished to marry Em and the only true hurdle was finessing the moment and getting her to agree—Henry had brightened considerably; his rapid exit was blatant encouragement.

"These aren't your horses."

He glanced down to find Em frowning at the grays. "No—they're my father's. They needed the outing and they're much more staid than my chestnuts. Much as I approve of your brother's hands, I wouldn't trust him to them."

She cast him a look. "Him to them, or them to him?"

He smiled tightly. "As I said. They'd sense his inexperience and make off with him. He'd probably never try to drive again."

She studied him for a moment, then shook her head. "So I find I must thank you again." A suspicious glint lit her fine eyes. "You aren't, by any chance, being kind to my siblings in order to curry my favor, are you?"

Leaning one shoulder more definitely against the curricle's side, he smiled down into her eyes. "The thought did occur, I'll admit, but against all expectations I'm quite enjoying my times with your brother and sisters. They're entertaining, not boring as most children of their age are." He held her gaze for a moment, then added, "You've guided them well."

A faint blush rose in her cheeks. "They're inherently good—just sometimes high-spirited."

He nodded. "Sadly not everyone appreciates the difference. You're to be commended for not suppressing their verve. It can't have been easy with no parents."

She didn't know what to say to that. She considered him for a moment more, verifying he was sincere. Before she could thank him again—then try to go in—he reached for her, smoothly drew her to him.

"What . . . ?" Her hands grasped his arms, but she didn't try to hold him off. The glance she cast was a furtive one directed toward the inn.

"No one can see us," he murmured, then covered her lips with his.

Kissed her—drank in her sweetness for the second time that day. Wished he could taste her more often. Safe in the shadow of the carriage, he straightened and drew her fully to him—determined to savor that, too—the inexpressibly heady sensation of her slender, slight frame hard up against his.

She tried to hold firm, perhaps meant to resist; she quivered on the cusp, but then relaxed into the kiss, into his embrace. She was all softness and feminine curves, feminine mystery and allure. Her body called to him on some primal level; she wasn't at all what he'd previously thought his ideal—she was more, better, infinitely more appealing.

His palms itched to sculpt her curves. He longed to lift her in his arms, off her feet, and take her to where he could; only an instinctive tracking of what she would allow—what would and wouldn't alarm her—prevented him from doing just that. From lifting her and waltzing her into the empty stable behind them.

But he had to woo her step by step, kiss by kiss. Had to gradually awaken her—awaken her desire—until she wanted him. Until she needed him as he needed her.

Already needed her—not a thought to soothe his more primitive side.

He pushed the taunting, incendiary truth away, concentrated instead on keeping his hands still while he savored her luscious lips, the honeyed delight of her mouth. While he took, steeped his senses, and drank his fill—at least for now.

He had to end the kiss, had to lift his head, had to set her down, had to let her go. He forced himself to do so, then to look into her flatteringly dazed eyes, and smile—with just the right amount of teasing taunting. He couldn't let her see more—see how much he wanted her, what he wanted of her—not yet. Later, yes, but not now.

Now he didn't want her to take fright, to draw back.

Today, he wanted her curious, tempted, lured.

Seduced.

Into wanting more.

Her bright gaze refocused, searched his face. A frown started to form in her eyes.

She opened her lips—

Before she could say a word, he tapped the end of her nose. "Good afternoon to you, Sparrow. I'll see you later."

With an inclination of his head—as jaunty as Henry's had earlier been—he stepped around the curricle, climbed up, loosened the reins, then with a last salute, gave the grays the office and steered them out of the yard.

Left once again standing in his wake, her lips throbbing, her wits only just settling, Em narrowed her eyes on his departing back. "Sparrow?"

Admittedly she was wearing brown.

She narrowed her eyes even more, inwardly berating her Colyton self for growing far too fond of his kisses. She should resist, refuse, yet *not* resisting was so much more interesting. So much more intriguing. More thrilling, more exciting. And despite all, with him, even trapped in his arms, she felt safe.

A conundrum.

How to manage their mutual attraction was something she'd yet to define. With all other men, her instincts would have leapt into action and held them off; with him, they simply didn't. They lay quiescent, unaroused. Accepting. Yet another conundrum.

She stared after his curricle until he turned into the road and disappeared from sight, then with a shake of her head, she headed inside.

He should never have told the terrible twins about the local sights. Too late Jonas realized his error.

Too late he learned just how expert in the art of badgering the pair were.

They cornered him that evening in the tap. The instant he sat down and placed his customary pint pot on the table before him, they appeared and promptly set about cajoling him into taking them to see one of said sights the following day.

He smiled and tried to distract them—then tried to confuse them, overwhelm them, delay them, dismiss them. Nothing worked.

In the end, he agreed to take them for a ramble to a nearby lookout the following afternoon, simply to gain some peace.

Simply to be able to sit back, sip, and watch their elder sister flit about the inn as she did every evening, smiling and nodding to the patrons, stopping to chat with many of the women. Many looked for her, even the men, although most just nodded and went back to their ale.

As did he, with a sense of peace he hadn't previously known, but was quickly growing accustomed to.

He duly reported at the back door of the inn the following afternoon. His nephews might routinely forget arranged outings in the bustle of their innocent young lives, but the twins, he now accepted, would be waiting.

They were. Em stood in the corridor behind them; from her expression she wasn't sure whether to depress her sisters' pretensions and rescue him from the coming ordeal, or smile at the sight of him in thrall to the two terrors.

In the end, she stood in the doorway and waved them off. In somewhat horrified trepidation, he tramped off for the Seaton lookout flanked by two angel-demons chattering like magpies.

They returned a little before dusk and found Em waiting to gather them in. "How was it?" she asked.

"Lov-er-ly," Gert averred. "Lots of views all about the countryside."

"All the way to the sea." Bea yawned. "We might draw some tomorrow."

Em's brows rose. She looked at Jonas, arched a brow as the twins headed for the kitchen.

"It was . . ." He thought, then admitted, "Better than I expected. They kept up quite well, but they'll be tired."

"Come in and have some tea. Hilda's experimenting with buns—come and give us your opinion."

He needed no encouragement beyond the delicious smells wafting from the kitchen. Following Em into the warmth and cheery bustle, he couldn't help but recall how cold, dull, and empty the inn's kitchen used to be.

Now it was literally a hive of activity. As well as Hilda and her two helpers, Issy was there, and John Ostler. The twins helped themselves to buns, then escaped upstairs.

The big ovens pumped out warmth and delicious aromas. At Em's wave, Jonas pulled out a chair at the big deal table and sat—more to get out of everyone's way than anything else.

Henry was already seated, a half-eaten bun in one hand, a pencil gripped in the other, a book open on the table before him, and a frown on his face.

A bun on a plate and a mug of tea appeared before Jonas. He looked up, smiled his thanks at Em, then picked up the bun and bit into it.

The tang of preserved fruit and cinnamon burst on his

tongue, tantalized his taste buds. It was so good he might have moaned.

Em shot a glance his way. "Good?"

He simply nodded, and took another bite.

In contrast, Henry ate his bun absentmindedly, without reaction. Curious over what could deaden anyone's senses to such a degree, Jonas peered at the book. "What is it?"

"Latin homework." Henry glanced up. "I'm not as advanced with my Latin as I need to be. I have to catch up."

Jonas took another bite of bun, then nodded to the book. "So what are you wrestling with—declensions?"

"Among other things."

Jonas inwardly shrugged and volunteered, "I still read a fair bit in Latin—in the interest of saving you from premature wrinkles, I might be able to help. Which verb?"

Passing behind the pair, Em heard Henry answer. Heard Jonas reply. While she moved about the kitchen checking this and that, slipping out to the tap, then returning, she kept an eye on the pair at the table. They'd quickly become oblivious to all around them, sliding deeper into discussion of both verbs and the philosophy text Henry was translating.

He didn't accept help easily; of them all, he was the most reserved, the quietest and most private. She often worried that if something were wrong, he wouldn't say, not wanting to add to the burden already on her shoulders.

The only male in their small household, he felt both responsible, and largely helpless. Em understood enough to sympathize; he felt he should take care of them, but his age and inexperience meant she and Issy had always taken care of him.

Although she'd never told him of the bargain she and Issy had struck with their uncle—their unpaid labor in return for his schooling—she'd long suspected he'd guessed, if not all, then enough to feel obligated to her and Issy evermore.

Neither she nor Issy expected nor wanted such thanks; that wasn't why they'd made their bargain. But she understood that Henry felt that way—she would herself in such circumstances—and that his inability to repay what he viewed as a huge debt chafed.

She wanted to find the Colyton treasure for all of them, but for Henry most of all. Not just so he could have his share of it, but so he would know they—all his sisters— were provided for.

The treasure and her hunt for it loomed large in her mind—all day, every day, through every hour. Now that she'd focused on the Grange, as she'd done with Ballyclose she was checking all the available sources, hoping to verify its claim to being "the house of the highest" in the late six- teenth century before she undertook the far more difficult task of searching its cellars.

Unlike with Ballyclose, she'd found mentions aplenty to confirm that the Grange had at least been in existence as a major house in the village all those years ago.

She hadn't yet reached the point of mounting a sortie on the Grange, and this week she had numerous matters to settle at the inn, but soon . . .

Movement at the table drew her eye. Jonas—when had she started thinking of him by his first name?—pushed back his chair and got to his feet.

Henry glanced up at him and smiled. "Thank you. I didn't think I'd finish this tonight, but now I will."

Jonas grinned. "Ask Filing to give you Virgil—he's rather more interesting."

He glanced around the room and located her. Em waited by the back door as he wended his way around the table and the benches to her.

Having found her, his eyes didn't leave her; by the time he reached her and took her arm, she had, to her irritation, stopped breathing.

She drew in a breath, let him turn her to the door. "Again I owe you more thanks."

He was looking ahead as he opened the door; he glanced back as he drew her through and down the single step, let- ting the door shut behind them. "I don't want your thanks."

Dusk had closed in; the rear yard was full of shadows. She was about to arch her brows haughtily when he smoothly grasped her hand, twirled her about—

And she suddenly found herself with her back to the wall, with him before her, head bent as he leaned closer.

"What I need"—his voice was a gravelly purr—"is my reward."

Her lips throbbed, softened, even before his closed over them. This time she didn't wait, didn't try to fight the inevitable, but pushed one arm up, over his shoulder, and with one hand clasped his nape and kissed him back.

Eagerly. Fervently.

He moved closer, his long, hard frame pressing into her, the planes of his chest hard and welcome against her peaking breasts. He angled his head and deepened the kiss, and she clung and held him to her.

The yard was wreathed in thickening shadows; there was no one about to see as they—he and she both—sank ever deeper into the embrace as she surrendered to the kiss, to sensation, to the thrill and excitement of new experience. As she reveled in discovering more.

She knew that he was luring and tempting her—seducing her in truth—yet she couldn't hold back, couldn't hold against him. At least, not knowing she was a Colyton, he couldn't know why he was succeeding, couldn't know on what plane he was appealing to her—he couldn't know that like all Colytons, she possessed an explorer's soul.

His tongue stroked hers, and she inwardly shuddered, felt a hot lick of desire slide down her spine, felt the heat pooling within swell and grow—hotter, more urgent.

He was all strength and latent power, all muscle and heavy bones, before and around her, surrounding her. The wall at her back was a mere prop; his hands—one spread at the side of her waist, gripping, the other cradling her head—held her securely. Trapped her, anchored her, as he filled her mouth, and fed.

She met his hunger, sensed it, tasted it—did her best to

appease it, yet knew he wanted more. The kiss had changed, his desire no longer so restrained, no longer veiled or screened, but still reined, so she could see it, sense it—wonder at it—but not feel threatened.

Whether he'd intended that or not she didn't know—was too inexperienced in the ways of seduction to guess. Regardless, the sense of being able to go forward without risk was tempting.

To her Colyton soul it was the ultimate lure.

Why not? If there was no good answer forthcoming, then she would. That had proved the guiding principle in her life—her natural, innate lodestone. So she gave in to the need to touch—pressed her other hand, trapped between them, to the hard planes of his chest, felt the heat and strength of him burn her palm.

Jonas felt the deliberate touch to his marrow. Had to drag in a ragged breath and kiss her again—even more deeply—to quell, to suppress, his response. That exploratory touch was a message—a sign; he knew it, but equally knew he had to give her time to pursue the new avenue at her own pace. He couldn't force her to go faster. Couldn't force her to want him. She was a curious blend of innocence and abandon, of determination and caution. Before she moved, she thought, considered, weighed, but once she'd made up her mind there was nothing tentative about her actions—just as there'd been nothing tentative about that touch.

She possessed boldness and naïveté—an explosive mix. One that could shatter his control. He clung to it as her small hand explored, learned, assessed.

Fought not to yield to the impulses she evoked—battled not to permit his will to be suborned. His primitive side was wide awake and ready to take charge, to bring to life, into being, the images that rolled through his mind. That more primitive side whispered—about how easy it would be to slide his hand down between them and touch her, caress the soft flesh between her thighs, even through the cotton of her gown.

And once he had, and she'd melted, he could lift her skirts, lift her, and . . .

He kissed her more fiercely, even more ravenously, fighting to banish those images from his mind.

The way she kissed him back—all hot and eager sweetness—defeated him. Without conscious thought his hand eased from her waist, skimmed up her side, and closed about her breast.

She gasped through the kiss, swayed—but then kissed him back, and the flames between them flared hotter, higher.

He dived into them, into her mouth in greedy desperation; she met him, matched him, clung as his fingers stroked and learned, sculpting her firm flesh, then he located the tight bud of her nipple, circled it slowly—when she shifted and pressed closer, he gently squeezed.

Her response, uninhibited, unrestrained, flagrantly inviting, left him giddy.

A giddiness no amount of ragged breathing while still kissing her could cure. A giddiness that weakened his hold on his baser impulses.

And still she pressed on. Still wanted, still avidly sought . . .

They had to stop. Now. Before his impulses overcame him and he pressed her for more—and she acceded.

Taking her against the inn wall was definitely not part of his plan.

He told himself to draw back, to ease back, step away.

He tried to tense his muscles and force them to work, but her clinging nearness sapped his strength. He was fighting a battle he didn't want to win, and his baser self knew it.

It wasn't possible for her grip to be strong enough to hold him, yet he couldn't break free. Desperate, he lowered both hands to her waist, gripped, then swung around—swung her around, too, so his back was to the wall and she stood before him.

Lifting his head, he dragged in a breath, rested his head

back against the hard wall, locked his eyes on hers, shadowed and unreadable as with considerable effort he straightened his arms and set her back—away from him.

She was breathing quickly, ragged and urgent. For one long moment, their gazes held, locked, merged.

He swallowed. "Go inside." The words were a dark, deep rumble. "Now."

Instead of turning and fleeing from the threat any featherbrain would know he posed, she stood blatantly studying him as the moments ticked by.

Finally, *finally*, she inclined her head. "Very well."

She turned to go, but with her hand on the door, looked back; he couldn't be sure, but he thought her lips had curved. "Good night. And . . . thank you."

Her eyes on his, she smiled—definitely smiled—then turned and went inside.

He let his head thump back against the wall, stayed slumped against it as the minutes ticked by, staring blankly into the gathering darkness, waiting to catch his breath, to let the cool of the evening douse his heat, while he wondered. Pondered.

He wasn't at all sure he approved of that smile.

"Further to the left." Em stood in the middle of the inn's rear yard and directed her small army of helpers. Now that they'd started preparing rooms for paying guests, a refitting of the washhouse had been necessary, and that in turn had called for a washing line.

If there'd ever been one before, no one could remember it.

She'd mentioned the project in the common room the evening before; both Jonas and Filing had heard and volunteered to help. Thompson, the blacksmith, said he knew where suitable posts could be found. Phyllida had donated spare ropes she never used. Before she'd turned around, Em had had all the pieces required to construct the inn's washing line, and enough willing hands to do it.

Everyone had gathered that afternoon; only Edgar, tending the bar, wasn't there. The kitchen staff and John Ostler had the afternoon off, but the three girls from nearby farms who Em had hired to work as laundresses were waiting in the shadow of the open washhouse door, eyes wide, their first batch of laundry in baskets at their feet.

Issy stood to one side, carrying various tools in a trug. The twins jigged impatiently by the kitchen door, their arms full of the ropes, pulleys, and anchors to be mounted on the crossbeams.

"Just a little more." Em waved to Jonas and Filing. Coats off, pints of ale supplied as sustenance already consumed and set aside, they'd earlier worked to assemble the uprights for the ends of the line—two tall posts each anchored by a stone lashed to the center point of two heavy crossed timbers that served as a stabilizing foot. They'd already placed the first upright to her satisfaction and were now positioning the second.

Henry stood nearby, holding the crossbeam that would need to be lifted into its slot across the top of the post, then bolted on.

"How's that?" Jonas straightened to sight the other post.

"It's very close." Em strode forward to stand between the posts, checking the line between them, mentally measuring the clear distance in terms of sheet widths. She nodded. "Yes, that will do."

Filing straightened from his half crouch with an audible groan. Issy went to his side; he looked into her eyes and smiled, shaking his head to dispel her concern.

Jonas waved Henry forward. They each took one end of the crossbeam, then hefted it into the notch on the upright, sliding it onto long bolts set through the notch. Filing took a heavy wrench from Issy. With one hand, Jonas reached into his pocket and pulled out two nuts; he handed them to Filing, who quickly secured one bolt, then the other.

They all stepped back, considered the result, then Jonas turned and beckoned to the twins. "Ropes next."

The girls rushed up, ropes with attached pulleys and anchors bobbing.

Jonas and Filing sorted out the ropes, then with Henry holding one end, and all four sisters strung out along the lines holding the ropes up, they worked together to hammer the anchors into position, first on one crossbeam, then on the other.

Then they tensioned the ropes with the pulleys, and all was done.

All of them stood back in the shadow of the inn and viewed their creation.

Em nodded. "Excellent."

She waved the laundresses forward. "You can hang the sheets. I know it's late"—she glanced at the sky to the southwest—"but I doubt it will rain tonight. They can stay hanging until tomorrow."

Picking up their baskets, the girls ran out, eager to try the new lines. Jonas showed them how to raise and lower the ropes. The twins, too, drew close to see. Em watched them eagerly question, and wondered what devilment their fertile brains were hatching. She was on the brink of walking over and warning them off, when, leaving the laundresses to their task, Jonas turned and directed his gaze and various words to the twins.

They looked up at him, wide-eyed. When he finished speaking, they smiled and shook their heads, their expressions all angelic reassurance.

Em inwardly snorted in cynical disbelief, but then the twins exchanged glances, plainly weighing their options, then of their own accord, headed back to the inn.

Still suspicious, she watched them go.

Gravel crunched as Jonas joined her, shrugging on his coat, settling his sleeves.

Her gaze returned to her sisters. "What did you say to them?"

"I reminded them of the agreement we struck a few weeks ago—that if they were good—good enough so I didn't have to frown at them—I'd take them for a drive in my curricle."

She turned her head and looked at him. "That was brave of you."

He caught her gaze. Shrugged lightly.

Turning, he joined her in a last survey of their most recent field of endeavor. The laundry girls were giggling, swiftly pegging out the sheets; the pale cotton billowed in the light breeze.

She was very—hideously—aware of his nearness, of the heat that emanated from his large body. Of the temptation that posed to her wayward senses, the debilitating effect it had on her will, her resolution. She cleared her throat. "You've been so helpful, I can't keep just saying 'thank you.'"

And she certainly couldn't keep rewarding him. He'd glanced at her; before he could suggest just that she hurried on, "Issy and I wondered if you and Mr. Filing might join us—just the family—for lunch on Sunday, after the service." She faced him, met his eyes. "If you're free."

He looked into her eyes; his were so dark she couldn't read his thoughts as he studied her face. Then he smiled. "Thank you." He captured her hand, lifted it to his lips, brushed a light kiss to the backs of her fingers.

She felt her inner shiver all the way to her toes.

"I'd be delighted to join you." His words were low, very male—too knowing.

Ignoring the impulse to glance away, she continued to meet his eyes. She couldn't keep kissing him, but she knew herself well enough to know she *would* keep kissing him if he kept kissing her. So she had to stop him kissing her, had to avoid giving him opportunity and reason to do so. She forced herself to nod briskly. "Good. After church, then."

She would have turned and swept away, but his gaze held her. Between them, he still held her hand.

His thumb shifted, stroking lightly, gently, slowly back and forth.

Lost in his eyes, she felt her world, her senses, stretch, warm, sigh.

With a small, satisfied smile, he released her. He nodded as he stepped back. "I'll look forward to it."

She stood and watched him stride to the wood, watched until he'd disappeared down the path that would eventually lead him back to the Grange.

Issy came up and wound her arm in hers. "Joshua accepted."

"Jonas did, too."

"Well, then!" Issy turned back into the inn; unresisting, Em turned with her. "We'd better give some thought as to what to serve."

S he couldn't find the twins.

The following afternoon, knowing Issy had gone to help Miss Sweet with the church flowers and that Henry would be with Filing at the rectory, in midafternoon Em had left her accounts to go upstairs to check on her sisters, supposedly reading in her parlor upstairs, only to discover the parlor empty and the twins gone.

She hadn't panicked. Assuming they'd gone to the kitchen in search of sustenance—Hilda's latest buns, the fragrant aromas of which were filling the inn, for example—she followed, but the twins hadn't been seated at the deal table. Neither Hilda nor her helpers had sighted the pair since lunchtime.

That was when she'd started to worry. If the aroma of currant buns hadn't drawn the twins to the kitchen, they weren't in smelling range.

They weren't in the inn.

Grabbing her shawl from her office, she headed out to the stables. John Ostler hadn't seen them, but that meant nothing. She combed the tack rooms, looking under benches, peered into every stall, then climbed to the loft and fought her way over mountains of bales—but they weren't hiding in any snug corners, either.

Descending to the ground, shaking straw from her shawl and skirts, she left the stables. There was no one in the yard. The sheets had been taken down and folded; the laundry maids had headed home for the day. Crossing to the entrance to the path through the wood, she paused at its mouth; arms folded, she considered the shadowed depths.

Would the twins have plunged into the wood? Usually the answer would have been an instant affirmative, but Jonas had warned them of the dangers and had—most tellingly—promised them a drive in his curricle if they remained "good." Given the incentive, she honestly didn't think they would have done anything that might cost them that treat.

Frowning, she swung around and stared at the inn, visualizing the regions beyond. Where might her angel-demons have gone? She could just see the church's roof and tower, high up on the ridge; she was debating marching up there and enlisting Issy's help when the light breeze carried a high-pitched shriek to her ears.

Faint though it was, she instantly knew the shrieker was Bea—and wherever her sister was, she was enjoying herself hugely.

Em humphed, tightened her shawl about her shoulders, and marched around the inn. Once past the building's muffling bulk, she could more clearly hear the sounds of children playing—laughs, shrieks, calls—drifting down from the common.

Crossing the road, she walked onto the green expanse, climbing to skirt the upper edge of the duck pond. Gaining the higher ground above the pond, she paused and looked down on a scene of bucolic charm.

On the other side of the duck pond, where a level stretch of green lay between the road and the rise of the hill, twelve children, the twins included, were playing a spirited game of bat and ball.

There were no adults in sight, bar one.

Jonas sat on a bench a little way away, well above the players, watching over them.

Em watched him for several minutes, wondered if the bat and ball were his. Decided she wouldn't be surprised to learn they were.

She looked again at the children playing on the grass. Looked at her sisters, at the laughing light in their faces, watched them interact with the other children openly, without reserve.

The twins didn't make friends easily. Being twins, they always had each other; they tended to turn inward, to each other, and with the bond between them so strong, no outsider could normally impinge. Although she'd only seen them at this age over the past year, she'd noticed their lack of socializing and the concomitant social skills. But it was hard to make them expand their horizons; all they needed was each other, and her, Issy, and Henry, their family. They saw no need to make other connections.

Yet there they were, joining in, a trifle cautious—she could see that even from a distance—but they were making the effort to be part of a larger whole.

After watching for a minute more, she went forward. Halting beside the bench where Jonas sat, she kept her gaze on the game below.

He looked her way; she felt his gaze on her face. When she didn't react, she felt it slide slowly down her body, yet still she didn't turn to meet it.

She couldn't decide if he'd done what he had by chance, or if he'd knowingly set out to pave the way for the twins— to open a door for them into the wider group by instigating the game . . . then she recalled he was a twin himself.

"Thank you." She looked down into his eyes. "It's always been so difficult to get them to . . ."—she gestured at the children below—"bother."

He smiled, then looked back at the children. "I know

what it's like. But there's no substitute for childhood games, and the games two can play are limited." After a moment, he glanced at her again. "I saw them hanging out of the upstairs parlor window. They said they weren't doing anything and were free to come out."

She shrugged. "True enough. They don't have to tell me if they're not going far."

He nodded. "They need to learn to be responsible for themselves." His gaze returned to the children.

Leaving Em free to study him. To wonder. Eventually she murmured, "You don't need to do this, you know. You've already impressed me."

He chuckled, glanced briefly up at her, dark eyes alight. "I know." Looking down the slope again, he paused, then drew a deep breath. "But . . ."

A long moment passed. She thought he wasn't going to finish the sentence, but then he continued, "It's possible that it's I who should thank you—and your family, especially the angel-demons." Again he paused, then after a moment went on, his tone softer, more musing, "I'm starting to think this is what I've been missing. That this—watching over the village, the next generation especially—is a large part of my true calling. A major part of what I'm meant to do." His voice grew fainter. "What I'm on this earth to do."

Em watched his face, knew he was serious, that the words were introspective, directed more at him than her. She made no comment, but stored the revelation away for later cogitation, for when she lay in her bed at night and thought of him.

His gaze had remained fixed on the game. Without looking up, he reached for her hand, unerringly captured it, and gently but relentlessly drew her down—until she surrendered, stepped around the end of the bench, and sat beside him.

Neither said anything, they simply sat and watched the game. Smiled at the antics, at the exuberance and enthusiasm.

Yet throughout he held her hand, captured, engulfed in his, his thumb lightly, gently, stroking her fingers.

Lunch that Sunday was the most entertaining meal Jonas had ever sat down to—and he suspected Joshua Filing would say the same. The Beauregards, en famille, were a boisterous lot. They'd elected to dine and entertain their guests in the long room—a general parlor of sorts—on the upper floor of the inn.

Joshua was an only child, and although Jonas had Phyllida, as twins with no other siblings they were but one step removed from being only children. Both he and Joshua were initially taken aback by the cacophany—not so much by its volume as its constancy; there seemed always to be someone talking and as Henry was relatively quiet, that someone was usually female.

Luckily all the Beauregard females had pleasant, rather musical voices.

Both Jonas and Joshua gradually learned to tune their ears to the babel.

There was a dumbwaiter at the end of the wing above the kitchens, designed to ferry dishes back and forth; at one point early in the proceedings, he and Joshua were called on to extract Bea from it. Once she was safe, Em scolded, but her heart wasn't in it; she seemed to be having trouble keeping her lips straight. Issy, meanwhile, descended to the kitchen to explain and calm the kitchen staff, some of whom had thought the inn had sprouted a ghost; from below she commandeered the freed dumbwaiter for its intended purpose.

He and Joshua, the family's guests, were quickly shooed back to their chairs. Henry, Gert, and Bea set themselves to be entertaining while their sisters delivered the dishes to the table.

Celery soup and crisp, crunchy bread formed the first course, followed by a fine trout with almonds. Then came roast goose and a plump duck, surrounded by vegetables of numerous kinds. Bread-and-butter pudding with raisins followed, with a final course of fruits and cheese.

Edgar had shyly produced a bottle of wine and begged them to try it, confiding that he'd hidden a few of the better vintages from the maraudings of the unlamented Juggs. The wine inside the old and dusty bottle proved to be very fine indeed, which significantly contributed to the mellowness around the table.

They lingered as long as they could, content and comfortable; for his part, Jonas couldn't recall the last time he'd felt so companionably at ease. But at last, with real regret, Joshua rose to leave.

"I must prepare for the evening service." His tone made it clear he would much rather have stayed. He squeezed Em's hand and thanked her, then turned to Issy.

She smiled warmly and wound her arm in his. "Come—I'll see you out."

Jonas watched the pair walk to the door, Issy's head angled close to Joshua's shoulder, the better to hear his softly spoken words. They looked like a couple—very much two people who belonged to each other.

He glanced at Em and found her watching the pair as well, a gentle, hopeful smile on her lips.

Reaching out, he tapped the end of her nose. "Come on, Sparrow—you can see me out, although I'm going in the opposite direction."

She fell in beside him and they walked to the door. She frowned. "Since when did I become 'Sparrow'?" She looked down at her green gown, then up at him, brows raised.

He smiled and stood back so she could precede him through the door and down the narrow corridor. He followed at her heels. "Actually the appellation occurred to me virtually the first time I saw you."

She grimaced. "I must have been wearing brown."

He chuckled. "It wasn't the color of your gown that made me think it."

Starting down the stairs, she cast him a narrow-eyed look. "I'm not sure I want to know, but what, then?"

He let his smile deepen. "Your eyes." He looked into them as, surprised, she glanced at him again. "They're bright and . . . curious. Just like a sparrow's."

"Hmm." She continued down the stairs without further comment.

They paused in the kitchen to chat with Hilda, then went out through the back door.

Hilda's nieces were in the kitchen garden, digging up carrots. One of the laundry maids was working, moving in and out of the washhouse. Em told herself she was glad of the company; he couldn't possibly kiss her today.

She halted in the middle of the yard, and held out her hand. "I hope you enjoyed the meal."

He took her hand; quite how he managed to make the simple contact both casual and yet almost intimate she couldn't understand. He looked into her eyes; his thumb moved over her fingers, a caress that sent an achy longing sliding through her.

No kissing, she told herself, inwardly strident.

He smiled as if he could hear. "This time it's I who must thank you. The meal, and the company, was . . ." His smile faded. "Beyond perfect." He hesitated, as if he would say more, but then he smiled softly, privately, again; raising her hand, he brushed his lips across the sensitive backs of her fingers.

Even though she'd steeled herself against the sensation, a shiver skated down her spine. He sensed it; his gaze sharpened.

His gaze lowered to her lips. Beyond her control, her gaze fell to his.

Around them, the world faded. Some tangible force drew them closer, a magnet drawing her into his arms. Her resistance weakened, melted away; she teetered . . .

He drew a quick, tight breath and stepped away.

She raised her eyes to his, felt her lips throb.

He met her gaze, hesitated again, but then, rather stiffly, inclined his head. Releasing her hand, he stepped back. "Until later."

The words were deep, laden with reluctance, but with a last salute he turned away.

Em watched him stride onto the path, watched until the shadows of the wood swallowed his broad-shouldered figure.

Waited while her senses calmed and her nerves settled.

It wasn't sensible to fall in love with a gentleman who declared he wanted her as his. "His" as in being his mistress.

She knew very well that such a position wasn't for her, and never would be. *But . . .*

In her experience of life thus far, there usually was a "but"—the other side to every coin. In this case, the "but" was more than plain; it was the reason one part of her—her reckless Colyton side, the real heart and soul of her—was pulling, hard, in the opposite direction to her prosaic, wiser, sensible self.

She knew what temptation Jonas Tallent was dangling like a carrot before her, understood the basis of his seduction, yet . . . would this—this opportunity with him—be her only chance, the only one that came to her in her life, to explore the wonders of lovemaking, a region in life's landscape into which she'd not ventured? She hadn't previously had any real interest in it beyond an academic wish to know. Now . . . her need, her wanting to know, was anything but academic. It was fueled by some power she didn't truly comprehend, only felt—a compulsion that drove her to . . . want to kiss Jonas Tallent, and want him to kiss her, and more.

While her prosaic, wise, and sensible self knew well enough not to yield to the temptation, she wasn't at all sure what her reckless Colyton side had in mind.

"Miss?"

Em turned to see Hilda framed in the doorway.

"Could you come and try this custard for me?" Hilda called. "I think it might be a touch too sweet."

Em nodded, and headed back to the inn.

11

Monday morning dawned brilliantly fine. Em bustled about, filling her time with her innkeeper's chores. Jonas would be calling midmorning to look over the books; all was in readiness—she really didn't need to dwell on the event beforehand.

Customers rolled in for their morning teas and to partake of Hilda's latest batch of scones. All was progressing smoothly—the common room, more than half-full with the morning trade, truly looking the part of a successful inn—when, flitting between her office and the hall, Em heard light carriage wheels crunch over the gravel forecourt.

Assuming Jonas had driven there in his curricle, she quit her sanctuary and headed for the open inn door. Before her wiser self could ask what she thought she was doing, she put her head out—

And immediately pulled it back.

The gentleman stepping down from a gig wasn't Jonas.

And he'd seen her.

Regardless, sweeping around, she hurried—rushed—back to her office, but she wasn't in time. She'd just reached the bar counter when a stentorian voice bellowed, "Here! *Em!* Where the devil are you off to, gel?"

Every single person on both sides of the common room

stopped talking and turned their heads to stare. Delicious scones lay forgotten as they took in the large, somewhat rotund gentleman who stood in the doorway, an expression of severe pique firmly fixed on his choleric visage.

Caught, trapped, Em could only stare along with everyone else at her uncle, Harold Potheridge, he of the manor in Leicestershire with no paid servants.

He frowned and flourished his cane at her. "Been searching for you everywhere." He moved heavily forward; he was nattily, just a trifle too colorfully, dressed, and while he affected the cane, he didn't need it—he was still quite vigorous, if rather past his prime.

From the corner of her eye, Em saw Edgar slide out from behind the bar; she half-expected him to come up beside her, but he didn't reappear. Instead Harold came steadily on, bowling belligerently down the center of the room with a sublime disregard for everyone else there.

"What did you mean by it, eh?" Halting in the clear space where the central aisle met the bar, clearly relishing having an audience, he leaned on his cane and glowered at her. "Leaving my house like that after I'd taken you and your sister and brother in—and even suffered you to keep those brats of half sisters with you instead of casting the harpies out, as I'd every right to do."

A soft gasp rose from the female side of the room—at Harold's back; without seeing the expressions of incipient outrage that went with it, he smiled craftily, imagining it was her behavior in leaving his house that had caused the reaction.

Em forced herself to stand and face him; it was too late to undo the damage he'd already done. Issy was with the twins upstairs—they shouldn't hear the commotion—and Henry was safe at the rectory with Joshua. She could deal with Harold on her own.

She inclined her head distantly. "Good morning, Uncle Harold. I did leave you a note—you'd gone off to the races, if you recall."

"I recall very well, gel!" Harold was back to glowering. "What I fail to comprehend is why you left my house—how you dared to simply get up and go!" He thumped the floor with his cane for emphasis. "*I'm* in charge of you. And I say your place—and that of your sister and brother—is with me." He waved his cane at her, half-turned to the door. "Go get your things—you're coming back with me to Runcorn immediately."

Em raised her chin. "I think not, Uncle."

His face started to turn purple. She hurried on, "If you consult with Mr. Cunningham—our solicitor, remember?— he'll confirm that as of my twenty-fifth birthday—more than a month ago—I became my own person and assumed guardianship of the others, replacing you as our guardian. Consequently, where we choose to live is no longer any concern of yours."

She sensed a familiar presence at her back. Jonas had arrived. He was close, but not so close as to make matters worse.

"Indeed." She kept her attention fixed on the real threat in the room. "What we do with our lives—any of us—is no longer up to you."

Harold's beady blue eyes shifted swiftly to right, then left, then fixed on her face. "I don't care what that ferrety solicitor says—I'm your uncle, flesh-and-blood family, and I know what's best for you." He thumped the floor with his cane again.

She sensed Jonas shift restlessly. "I'm afraid, Uncle, that you'll have to think again." She lifted her chin. "We're very comfortable here."

Harold's expression turned apoplectic. "Dammit! You'll do as I say! Get your things *now*—and fetch that cipher of a sister of yours and your damned brother as well!"

"No." Em stood her ground. All she could do was let the truth out; as defenses went, it was solid. "We're not going back to Runcorn to continue to be your unpaid staff. You've used us—your flesh-and-blood family—for the past eight years, but now that's at an end. I suggest you return to Runcorn and start looking for staff—I imagine it must be quite uncomfortable alone in that big house and you'll want to get staff settled before winter."

Harold's expression stated he couldn't believe his ears. "This," he stated at full volume, "isn't *right*—no matter what that weasely solicitor says!"

For the first time he looked around at his audience, seeking support; his gaze passed over the fascinated, riveted expressions, skated over the women, then more slowly over the men in the tap—and finally came to rest on the male two paces behind Em's left shoulder. Jonas. "Who's the magistrate in this place, heh?"

The intonation suggested "this place" was beneath his notice, but Jonas smiled. From the corner of her eye, Em saw and decided if he smiled at her like that she would run.

"As it happens, my father's the magistrate," Jonas replied. "But he's away from home and not expected back for some time." He omitted to add that in view of his father's lengthy absence, he'd been deputized in his place.

Harold brought his glare to bear on Em—who didn't quail in the least. "I'll *wait*," the old beggar growled.

Beady blue eyes fixed on Em, he smashed the floor with his cane one last time, and half-turned to the door before vindictively stating, "The law will see I've the right. The magistrate will hand you back to me, and then, missy, your half sisters will be out in the streets, and you and your sister will be back scrubbing floors at Runcorn—mark my words!"

Jonas stepped up to Em's side, but the old braggart had finished. He swung on his heel and strode out of the inn—before Jonas or Joshua, who'd slipped into the inn a few minutes before, or any number of men who'd risen from their seats, showed him out.

Knowing Em's liking for having the last word, Jonas was faintly surprised when none followed her uncle—was he truly her uncle?—from the inn.

He looked at her. Head high, spine straight, she stood

watching the old man leave, watched him pass through the door . . . then she started to shake.

Em found herself pushed into one of the wing chairs. Jonas was giving orders, Joshua overseeing. Lady Fortemain and old Mrs. Smollet sat on either side of her, each patting one of her hands, both assuring her in their very different ways that everything would be *all right*.

Then Hilda arrived, nudging everyone aside to place a mug of tea, made just as she liked it, in her hands.

"There now. You get that into you and you'll feel much better." Hilda glanced at Jonas, who was standing, hands on hips, looking rather grimly down at Em. "And then we'll all work out what to do."

Turning, Hilda poked Jonas in the chest, although he wasn't really in her way. "Give her some space, do. Needs to catch her breath, she does." With that, she headed back to her kitchen.

Em sipped and tried to steady her wits, tried to focus, tried to think. She'd seen Harold off, but he'd be back. Nothing was more certain.

A slight commotion heralded the arrival of Phyllida with Lucifer behind her. Phyllida looked at her twin; Jonas didn't even meet her gaze, but she seemed to read all she needed in his face. Smoothly leaning down, she grasped Em's arm and lightly squeezed. "Sweetie told us what happened. Whatever you need, we're all here."

Em looked into her dark eyes, and blinked rapidly. A quick glance around showed every head bobbing in agreement, including Jonas's.

Lady Fortemain leaned closer. "Was it true—what you said? That he—your uncle—had you and the others working as unpaid servants in his house?"

"Yes." Em paused, then drew in a breath and let the truth free. "We lived in York. Our mother died when we were young, and then later our father died—".

She gave them the whole story, all of it, with only two omissions. She didn't reveal their real surname—that, after all, changed nothing—and she omitted to mention what had brought them specifically to Colyton, namely their family's mysterious treasure.

Glancing around as she spoke, she thought that the village outside the inn must have emptied; everyone had crammed in to hear what had gone on, and the explanation. Only her siblings remained oblivious, but they were safe and out of Harold's reach; Joshua had earlier told her that Henry was still at the rectory, his nose buried in a book, and Issy and the twins were still upstairs.

At the conclusion of her tale, Miss Hellebore, ensconced in one of the heavily padded armchairs, leaned forward on her cane, her expression one of abject regret. "My dear, I'm *so* sorry. I fear I've let my room to the blackguard—I had no idea he was here to cause you trouble." Her many chins wobbled in distress. She earned a little pin money by letting her downstairs room.

Em sat up and leaned across to squeeze the old lady's hand. "It's not your fault—you're not in any way to blame."

Miss Hellebore sniffed. "Well, it's kind of you to say so, dear, but I don't want trouble coming to you from under my roof." She glanced up at Lucifer and Joshua. "If someone will help me, I'll go home right now and evict him."

The men were transparently eager to assist, but . . . Em held up her hand. "No—please. Quite aside from the fact I like the idea of Harold having to pay you—as you can guess he's the most dreadful miser—but if he doesn't stay with you, he'll try to stay here—" A dark murmur confirmed he wouldn't succeed. "But," she went on, "he's stubborn and dogged, so he'll find somewhere, and . . . well, I'd much rather know where he's staying while he's here." She looked around, her gaze coming to rest on Jonas. "Eventually he'll realize we're not going to budge, and he'll go away."

Others grumbled; most of the men were in favor of evicting Harold from the village altogether. Em hoped wiser heads would prevail; she knew Harold—he was stubborn, but she and her siblings could be even more so. They'd escaped and were very definitely not going back.

Lady Fortemain gripped her wrist quite fiercely, a martial light in her eyes. "You're not to worry, dear. We won't let that horrid man have you. He simply can't." She made a gesture that eloquently dismissed Harold and his claim on them. "You *chose* to come here, and now you're one of us. You belong here." She gestured around them. "You've made the inn a lovely place again, and we're not going to let him bully you into leaving."

Heads nodded all around, some belligerent, others earnest—all adamant.

Em found it amazing how strongly everyone patently felt; never had she had others—a community of others—stand up for her before. "Thank you." Her voice was a trifle husky. She glanced around. "All of you. And now—" She slowly rose from the chair. "I must get back to my duties." She turned to the room and smiled. "I hope you'll stay and enjoy Hilda's scones."

With that, her smile still in place, she made her way through the crowd, heading for her office. Everyone she passed had a kind word for her, or a pat on the shoulder. She was clinging to her composure by the time she won free, slipped through the small hall and into her office. Her empty office.

Not that that lasted for long.

Nevertheless, Jonas gave her time to slump into the chair behind the desk, then, in an effort to put Harold and his threats, however misdirected, in perspective, she rearranged the account ledgers before her and fiddled with a pencil, waiting . . .

She looked up and Jonas was standing in the doorway, steadily regarding her. He met her gaze, his own unreadable, his expression the same.

After a moment, he stepped into the room, and for the first time since she'd been using the office, he reached out, caught the door; the babble of voices from the tap faded as, his gaze locked on her, he closed it—then leaned back against the long panel.

She held his gaze. "I'm sorry I lied to you."

Head resting against the door, he considered that. "I understand why you did, I can understand why you told me—and everyone else—the tale you did. That doesn't trouble me— escaping from your uncle Harold couldn't have been easy. But·. . ."

As always, there was a "but"; she waited to hear what his was.

He grimaced. "Are there any other well-fleshed skeletons in your closet? Even less well fleshed?"

Against all the odds, the question made her smile. Effectively defused the tension between them. She shook her head. "No. Just Harold. But believe me, he's quite enough."

He pushed away from the door, came forward to pull out the chair before the desk and sit. "That I can readily believe."

She hesitated, then asked, "When are you expecting your father to return?"

He grinned evilly. "Not for some time . . . and I'm the magistrate in his absence, anyway."

"You are?"

He nodded. "And as the local representative of the law, I can assure you no one is going to be aiding Harold in any way. Incidentally, what is his full name, just in case I need to know?"

"Potheridge. Harold Gordon Potheridge."

Jonas nodded. "Right." He let his gaze fall to the ledgers on the desk. "Now . . . what's the state of my inn?"

She blinked, but readily opened the ledger and proceeded to demonstrate just what an excellent innkeeper she was.

Jonas paid attention, asked questions whenever possible— and from behind his businesslike demeanor, watched her like a hawk. Focusing on the inn—on all the wonders she'd performed with the place—helped put her bothersome uncle from her mind, and allowed her to concentrate on something she enjoyed.

That she enjoyed running his inn was beyond doubt.

He sat back while she told him her further plans, satisfied on all counts.

I would like to speak with my niece, sirrah. Fetch her, if you please."

Seated behind the desk in her office, Em heard Harold's arrogant demand. She wasn't the least surprised to hear it. He'd let twenty-four hours go by, and was now back to have another tilt at intimidating her. Because she'd given in all those years ago—when he'd been their legal guardian and she hadn't had any choice—he thought it merely required the application of more pressure to have her capitulating now.

Edgar, uncharacteristically sharp, said he'd "inquire"; she heard his footsteps slowly nearing.

She debated whether to have Harold shown into the office—but the office was very small.

Inwardly sighing, she got to her feet. Waved Edgar back when he appeared in the doorway. "Yes, I heard. I'll speak with him out there."

In the common room, where she had supporters aplenty.

Harold saw her coming around the bar. He stiffened, but then seemed, with difficulty, to recall his manners. He took off his hat.

She halted two paces away, nodded politely. "Good morning, Uncle Harold. What can I do for you?"

An unfortunate turn of phrase; Harold chose to take it literally. "You can forget this nonsense and come back to Runcorn." His tone was peeved, aggrieved; he heard it and moderated his approach. He tried a patronizing smile. "Really, Emily, you must see how inappropriate it is for you to be managing an inn. Your dear mother would turn in her grave to see you waiting on such people, at the beck and call of the hoi polloi. If you have any proper family feeling, you'll see that the right thing to do is to return to Runcorn—"

"And devote myself to seeing to your comfort for the rest of your days?" Raising her brows, she folded her arms. "I think not. I'm quite comfortable here, and so are the others. The village has been welcoming—and here, at least, our labors are appreciated."

Harold snorted. "Poppycock! Not as if Runcorn was a cave—and as for appreciation—"

"Uncle Harold." She held up a hand to stem his tide. "The situation is simple. *I* don't wish to return to Runcorn. *The others* don't wish to return to Runcorn."

"Have you asked them—even told them I'm here?"

She nodded. "I have. They don't wish to see you, they don't wish to speak with you—and legally you have no right to demand to see them."

Issy and Henry had specifically *not* wished to see him; neither had a kind word to say of him, and what they would say if they faced him wasn't likely to help anyone. Both had agreed to let Em handle Harold as she saw fit.

Refolding her arms, she continued, "That's how matters stand—and that's the end of it."

Color flooded Harold's face. Features contorting, he wagged a finger in her face. "Listen, missy, I—"

"Seems to me," a slow, lugubrious voice cut in, "that it's time you left, sir. Begging y'r pardon, but you seem to have outstayed your welcome."

Oscar, Thompson's, the blacksmith, younger brother, had come up to loom at Harold's side. The foreman of the Colyton Import Company, Oscar was smaller than his elder brother. He was still a very large man; he didn't have to exert himself to intimidate.

Harold's color turned ugly. "Now see here, my good man—"

Mild as cheese, Oscar ignored the bluster and looked at Em. "You finished your discussion, miss?"

Lips set, Em nodded. If Oscar was offering, she was willing to accept. Anything to get her point through Harold's thick skull. "Thank you, Oscar." She looked pointedly at Harold. "I believe my uncle is just leaving."

Harold huffed, puffed, but when no one gave any indication of backing down, he jammed his hat on his head, spun on his heel, and stalked out.

Em watched him go, but doubted she'd yet seen the last of him. Once he'd disappeared, she smiled at Oscar. "Thank you."

"My pleasure, miss."

"Let me get Edgar to draw another pint for you. Ale, was it?"

Once she'd seen Oscar settled with a frothing mug, she walked slowly back into her office.

Harold finding them hadn't really changed their situation all that much. It had, however, made them all feel less safe, less secure. Less sure of themselves.

Especially less sure financially. Both Issy and Henry were starting to worry, although neither wanted to say anything that would increase the burden already on her shoulders.

It was a burden she'd willingly taken up, and would again were the circumstances the same.

Sitting back in her chair, she murmured, "We have to find the treasure sooner rather than later." Once she'd located it, Harold—and even more importantly the insecurity his arrival had fostered—would go away.

Once she found the treasure, they would all be free to get on with their lives.

The thought of having a life to live freely, one she could shape as she wished, more than tempted, but exactly what life she would choose, the details of it, remained nebulous, hazy. Then she thought of the way everyone in the village had defended her and hers. If nothing else, here in Colyton, home of her forebears, she'd found a place among others, others she liked, and who liked her. In terms of reshaping her life, that wasn't a bad start.

She hadn't given much thought to where they would go, what they might do, once they'd found the treasure, but . . .

"First I have to find it." Determined, she reached down and opened the bottom drawer of her desk, pulled out a heavy tome, and set it on her blotter.

Opening the book to a marked page, she settled to read about the Grange.

Jonas sat at his desk in the library of the Grange, and tried to keep his mind focused on the crop tallies he was checking. Contrary to the amount of time he'd recently been spending there, the Red Bells Inn formed only a very small part of his father's estate—the overseeing of which currently fell to him.

He needed to be free to help Em if and when she needed him, and to do that with a clear conscience, he had to see all his other responsibilities brought up to date.

Once he had . . . the next issue on his plate was to find some way to move matters between her and him forward at a faster rate. He could feel a certain pressure building within him, something he'd never felt before—a need, an imperative, to make her his, a compulsion he'd never felt over any other woman; no other had evoked it.

If he didn't make her his soon . . .

He sat back, stared at the figures he'd lost track of minutes ago, and sighed.

A tap on the door had him looking up almost eagerly.

Mortimer looked in. "Mr. Filing, sir. Shall I show him in?"

"Yes. Do." Jonas tidied away his notations on the crop yields, then stood as Filing entered. He held out his hand. "Joshua."

"Jonas." Filing shook his hand. He looked decidedly grim. "I wondered if you'd heard the latest about the uncle."

Jonas felt every muscle tense. "No. What happened?"

"Nothing untoward, as it transpired, but . . ."

Relieved, Jonas relaxed enough to wave his friend to a chair. "Tell me." He resumed his seat as Joshua sat.

"He—Potheridge—called again at the inn this morning, trying once again to browbeat Em into leaving and returning to his home." Joshua's expression was as severely disapproving as it ever got. "Em resisted, of course. She sent him to the rightabout—with a little help from Oscar."

Jonas tensed. "She needed help?"

Joshua nodded. "I called on Issy last evening. She told me more about their past with Potheridge. Believe it or not, he would indeed thrust those innocent children—the twins, I mean—out into the streets. And his only reason for wanting Em, Issy, and Henry is to have them work for him gratis, as they'd previously had to do. As far as I can gather, the tale Em told was severely understated. Potheridge should be . . . well, perhaps not hanged, but certainly booted a good long way."

Jonas would have smiled at the sight of his usually intensely peaceable friend so roused, if he hadn't been feeling the same emotions himself.

Before he could say anything, Joshua looked up. "I'm going to marry Issy—my mind was made up even before Potheridge arrived. And now I'm even more determined to marry her and remove her completely from his orbit—and being her husband will place me in a better position to make sure he doesn't further pressure Em or Henry. It seems he has no interest in the twins—presumably they're too young to be of use to him, and, of course, they're not directly related."

Joshua met Jonas's eyes. "I'd marry Issy tomorrow if I could, but she won't hear of it, not at present, because that will leave Em alone to cope with the others."

Jonas frowned. "But you'd be there, and so would Issy—you're not proposing to take her away."

"Precisely! But despite her gentle looks, she has a steel rod for a backbone. She's as stubborn as . . . well, hell—and I can't shift her." Joshua looked at Jonas.

And waited.

Jonas pulled a face at him. "Yes, all right—you've guessed correctly. I intend to marry Em, but . . ." He frowned. "Why are there so many 'buts' in life?"

"A philosophical question to which no one has yet found an answer." Joshua waved it aside. "You were saying?"

Sliding his hands into his pockets, Jonas sat back. "I was about to say I'd marry Em tomorrow—we could stand up beside you and Issy—except that I'm having infinite difficulty getting her to focus on the issue. She's forever distracted— forever being distracted. What with the inn, the twins, and Henry, there's always something demanding her attention."

He paused, eyeing Joshua. "And as you're going to marry Issy, I should tell you that Em—and I presume Issy and the others, too—are here in Colyton because they're searching for something."

Succinctly he outlined what he knew, what he'd learned.

Joshua frowned. "Henry hasn't shown any interest in the local houses."

"Nor have the twins, but I suspect—call it intuition if you like—that all of them are in on the hunt. They all know what Em's searching for, but she's the only one actively turning stones."

Joshua frowned, clearly thinking.

Jonas sighed. "So, you see, there's a great deal more mystery about the Beauregards than just their disreputable Uncle Harold."

Joshua shrugged. "Whatever the mystery is, whatever they're searching for, it makes no difference to me." His jaw set, he reiterated, "I'm going to marry Isobel Beauregard come what may."

Jonas laughed. "Naturally. I didn't tell you that to warn you off—I just thought you ought to know."

Joshua acknowledged that with a nod. "Knowing said information has clearly not warned you off Em."

Jonas grimaced. "No—it only adds to the pressure. If

she's keeping whatever she's searching for a close secret, then there has to be some danger involved."

"Secrecy does suggest that."

"Indeed." He tapped a finger on the desk. "But the main problem for me is that the search is important to Em and the rest of them, and she's so singleminded she clearly intends to resolve that issue first before turning her mind to other things. Me and the rest of her life, for instance."

Joshua waggled his head; he was struggling to keep a straight face. "Definitely a difficulty."

Jonas smiled tightly. "It's as much a difficulty for you as for me."

It took a moment for Joshua to work it out. "Damn! Issy won't marry me until Em at least consents to marry you."

"Precisely. So here we are, stuck and waiting on Em and her search."

Joshua raised his brows. "We could help."

"Indeed we could—indeed, we *would*—if only the benighted woman would tell us what she's searching for. *But*, if you recall, that's a secret."

Joshua frowned. After a moment he said, "You're right—there are too many 'buts' in this world."

Silence fell.

Eventually Jonas broke it. "I don't know about you, but I'm highly disinclined to sit and wait. Which means it's imperative we learn what Em's searching for."

Grimly Joshua nodded. "So we can help her to it, and thus gain relief."

"Precisely. It's that or go blind."

12

Jonas brooded for the rest of the day and into the evening.

If Joshua hadn't told him about Potheridge's second visit to the Red Bells, he wouldn't have known anything about it—wouldn't have known Em had been subjected to her uncle's bullying again—and that irked.

He knew why it so irritated, but that didn't ease the nagging itch. When the clock in the library struck ten o'clock, and he couldn't remember where the last two hours had gone, he surrendered and set off along the path to the inn.

As he'd hoped, Em and Edgar were closing up. She was straightening mats and doilies on the other side of the common room while the last patrons downed the dregs of their ale before drifting home through the night.

Thompson and Oscar spotted him as he stood in the hall beside the bar; both called a greeting as they lumbered toward the door.

He returned it, drawing Em's attention. After one arrested glance, she continued with her tidying.

Propping a shoulder against the wall, he watched her.

Em wasn't sure why he was there. She didn't think there was any business matter pending between them, but she'd had a tiring day, one of nonstop dramas; her brain felt scatty, her thoughts fractured—she might have forgotten something.

Despite all the support, despite knowing Harold logically posed no threat, he nevertheless loomed large in her mind. Until he left the neighborhood, she'd be tense and on guard; she'd long ago learned not to trust him. Even once he accepted that she wouldn't be returning to keep house for him—and he was still a long way from that—he was the sort who would make trouble purely out of spite.

His presence had already affected the twins. They knew he didn't like them, so were wary of him, but knowing he was her, Issy's, and Henry's relative, they tried to please over anything to do with him; no matter that she'd told them otherwise, they thought it was somehow their fault that he didn't like them. She'd had to work to convince them that it wouldn't help for them to take him a plate of Hilda's scones as a peace offering.

She felt beset, hemmed in by worries, not least of which was that she'd had no time to further pursue the treasure; she knew Jonas was waiting, but the mechanical chore of tidying soothed and helped her thoughts settle.

Edgar came out from behind the bar. He paused in the center of the room. "All done, miss." He hefted his keys. "I'll lock up behind me."

She summoned a smile. "Thank you, Edgar. Good night."

"'Night, miss." With a respectful nod, Edgar left.

Leaving her alone with the inn's owner.

The front door closed; the lock clicked. Tidying done, she circled, checking the shutters were secure, then, with no further excuse for procrastination, approached her nemesis.

Halting before him, she arched a brow.

He straightened from the wall. "I heard you had another visit from your uncle."

She nodded and stepped past him, toward her office. "And I'm sure there'll be more. He won't give up that easily."

"I'll speak to him."

"No!" She whirled, frowning. "He'll go away eventually, but regardless, as I've told you umpteen times before, I'm not yours. You're not responsible for me. You don't have to fight any battles for me."

He glowered, actually glowered at her. She sensed him hesitate; in an effort to aid him rein in his overdeveloped protectiveness—or was that possessiveness?—she changed direction, doused the last lantern left burning on the counter, then, in the dim glow from the fires banked in the hearths, headed across the common room, her destination the stairs and ultimately the safety of her rooms.

Instead of letting her go, he followed close behind her; lowering his head, he growled in her ear, "I *want* to be responsible for you—I *want* to fight battles for you, slay any dragons that menace you."

The low words sounded rough, as if they were dragged from deep inside him. She walked faster, but he easily kept pace.

"Damn it, I *want* the right to stand up for you—to protect you and yours from the likes of your uncle Harold." He caught her arm and spun her to face him. "Obviously I mean to claim that right."

"Obviously?" She twitched her arm from his hold, looked him in the eye. "Whatever bee you have in your bonnet it's not obvious to *me*."

He frowned even more blackly. "Damn it—how I feel can hardly be a surprise. I've all but spelled it out. What the devil did you think this"—arms wide, he waved his hands between them—"is all about?"

She lifted her chin, categorically stated, "I'm your *inn-keeper*."

Turning, she started up the stairs. He was simply incapable of letting that argument—the one about protecting her—go, and she was too tired, too woolly headed, to argue. The only thing she felt sure about was that he was set on placing her under his protection.

On becoming her protector.

She would be wise for them both and retreat.

She continued to march up the stairs. "Good night, Mr. Tallent. You'll think more clearly in the morning—you can thank me then."

"Jonas. And you're like no bloody innkeeper ever born." Jonas followed her up, sorting through her words, intent and determined to prosecute his case. "And what the devil do you mean about me thinking differently come morning? I've been *wooing* you for weeks. Don't you dare tell me you haven't noticed."

Reaching the top of the stairs, she swung to face him, blocking the way, forcing him to halt two steps down, leaving her face level with his.

So she could glare directly into his eyes. "You haven't been *wooing* me—you've been *seducing* me. Trying to. One absolute reality is that gentlemen like you don't marry innkeepers."

His temper rose; he narrowed his eyes on hers. "Another reality you might like to ponder, one equally absolute, is that gentlemen like me don't *seduce* innkeepers. It's considered poor form."

Her eyes slitted, bright shards in the shadows. Her lips compressed into a stubborn line, then she nodded curtly. "As I said, good night, Mr. Tallent."

Em swung on her heel, stalked to her parlor door, flung it open, and sailed through.

She would have stopped and shut the door, but he growled—literally growled low in his throat—as he followed close behind.

"This is *ridiculous*!"

"I couldn't agree more." She swung to face him, intending to order him out—only to discover he was a lot closer than she'd thought. Hands on his hips, head lowered as he glared at her, there was a light in his eyes, a set to his expression, that had her heart thumping. One lock of dark hair had fallen across his forehead; he looked positively dangerous. She took a step back.

And another as he kept advancing, looming over her.

She pointed at the door—and kept backing. "You should go home. Now."

"No." Eyes locked on hers, he reached back, caught the edge of the door, and sent it swinging shut. "I'm not going to go, and you're not going to flee—and there's no one else about to distract either of us. We're going to get to the bottom of this—sort it all out so you understand."

"I do understand! You're delirious. You've lost your wits—you don't know what you're saying." And she didn't have clear space in her head to work it out, either. She was too tired; her wits were whirling. "Things will seem much clearer after a good night's sleep."

She turned and rushed into her bedroom, sure that—gentleman that he was—he wouldn't follow her in there.

He did.

Turning to shut the door, she found him right behind her.

She squeaked—went to take a step back, tripped on her hem, and started falling—he caught her upper arms, set her back on her feet.

Didn't let go.

"Stop pretending this—what's between us—doesn't exist." His dark eyes held hers, warm—hot—emotions roiling in their depths.

They took her breath away. "T-this?"

His gaze hardened. "*This.*"

He bent his head and kissed her. Not forcefully—that she might have resisted—but coaxingly, temptingly—almost pleadingly.

As if he truly wanted her to look and see, to understand what this—the welling, swelling heat that inexorably rose through the kiss—really was. As if he wanted her to feel what it was, appreciate it for the symptom it was—and acknowledge what that meant.

All that reached her through his lips, through the heavy stroke of his tongue against hers. He gathered her into his arms, and her heart, her senses, leapt. There was still more for her to gauge in the way he held her, securely, possessively, yet for all that so tenderly. More for her to appreciate, to learn—to see because he let her, because he laid it out before her—the symptoms of how he felt.

Of its own volition, one of her hands rose to lightly, wonderingly, touch his lean cheek. He desired her, wanted her. Perhaps even needed her.

What she felt in return, in response, what leapt in her veins and spread along every nerve, was far less restrained. A hunger, blatant and powerful, open and greedy.

And this time she was ready to be swept away. It wasn't that she lacked for distraction—she hadn't had a moment to think all day—but what with Harold's appearances and the twins' consequent worries, let alone Henry's and Issy's increasing concerns, she needed—desperately needed—distraction of a different sort.

She needed something to whisk her away, to take her from this world for a little while—and he was there, he was offering, and other than with him she might never know . . .

And he wanted her.

She slid her arms about his neck and kissed him back—flagrantly, without reserve.

Felt his sudden hesitation, his surprise.

She ignored it and moved boldly into him. Felt her nerves frazzle, felt his immediate response, the hardness that infused every muscle, that tightened the steely arms banding her back. Encouraged, heartened, she incited, then plunged into a duel of tongues, a heated exchange, one she sensed he was helpless to deny, to hold back from.

Her Colyton side, wild and reckless, scented opportunity, saw a wide and new horizon—and rose up, seized the initiative with both hands, and ran.

Amazed, Jonas found himself following, mentally stumbling in his haste to catch up with her. To rein her, and his more primitive side, in. It was like managing two runaway steeds, one set of reins in each hand; together, they—she and that elemental male she appealed to in him—were too strong.

That was a shock—and a wonder. One she brazenly fed with kisses that grew increasingly passionate, increasingly urgent. Her lips were soft, pliant, but ravenous beneath his, inciting and inviting a similar response; she seemed to glory when he lost all restraint, cupped her face between his hands, and devoured.

Without thought, he backed her until her hips hit the raised mattress of her bed. The faint jolt, the sensation of her bending slightly back, her stomach cradling his erection, shook awareness, albeit distant, into his brain.

Enough to realize he—and she—had skipped several steps in the customary progression. Enough to think that perhaps he should back off, or at least slow down—and see where she wanted to go, what she actually wanted to do.

That distant part of his brain that still functioned couldn't quite believe she truly intended this interlude to lead where it was presently headed.

Gathering his strength, and his resolution, he tried to ease back, tried to moderate the kiss from ravenous to merely hungry. But she wasn't of a mind to allow any abatement; the instant he eased the pressure of his lips, she compensated with a fiery, passionate demand that shredded his will and had him complying—instantly, beyond thought or control.

She wasn't going to let him back away, wasn't going to let him think or reason—not wise, given the power of his desire for her, the restless, greedy passion she evoked.

Dragging in a mental as well as physical breath, he locked his lips on hers, filled her mouth—and gave her what she clearly craved, what she was so insistently demanding. Releasing her face, he slid his palms from her shoulders slowly down her back, savoring the graceful feminine planes, the supple strength. Tasting her deeply, drinking unrestrained from her yielded mouth, he let his hands pause at her waist, fingers lightly flexing, holding her before him, trapped between his body and the bed, letting that knowledge—that she was there, willing and patently ready to satisfy him—sink in and soothe his clamorous needs.

She was all promise and bounty, warmth and rich treasure, pleasure distilled within a slight human frame. And she was his. Whether intimacy followed tonight or tomorrow was immaterial; that she was his was incontestable, something that simply was, and forever would be.

That seemed her thought as well as his; she moved into him, pressing against him in flagrant invitation.

He took her at her unvoiced word; releasing her waist, he slid his hands down, over her hips, pressing into the mattress to trace the luscious curves of her bottom.

She shivered, trembled, but then pressed closer still. He cupped the full globes and molded her to him, held her there as, beyond restraint, he shifted suggestively against her.

A statement of claiming, of things to come—she only grew wilder, more urgent and demanding. He'd never doubted that she would want him when the time came. Now it apparently had, the realization she did was heady beyond belief.

Hands anchored in his hair, Em clung to the kiss, to him as her wits whirled, as her senses danced and the world as she knew it gave way to one that was richer, more exciting, more tantalizing and enthralling. A world she wanted to explore—one full of novel sensations on which her Colyton soul could gorge.

She'd stepped beyond all hope of restraint, had let her adventurous soul free; she didn't imagine she might rein it in—had no intention of even trying.

Moments like this were beyond price—moments in which she could feed her inner self and be whole, be all she was meant to be. Without worry, beyond care; even if only for a few reckless minutes, she wouldn't count the cost.

The feel of him, all hard muscle and heavy bones, against her, his very male body trapping her against the bed—that moment of startling vulnerability when he'd backed her against it—were all nectar for her parched soul.

His fingers flexed, gripped. His palms on her bottom burned like brands through the skirts of her plain gown, but she needed more. Wanted more.

Much more.

She found his tongue with hers, stroked, and sensed his arrestation. Using her whole body, she leaned into him, seeking to ease the ache building in her breasts, tight, swollen, heavy, the peaks furled and so sensitive.

He understood, thank heaven! Releasing her bottom, he shifted so his hips and legs held her against the bed. His large hands skated up her sides, then closed, flagrantly possessive, over her aching breasts.

The relief was so sharp she gasped, sensed his approval as he drank the exhalation from her lips. Her mouth was all his, surrendered from the first; the way he feasted, languid yet claiming every soft inch, sent sensual shudders down her spine.

His strong hands shifted on her breasts, learning, assessing. He cupped the mounds, firm and taut, squeezed gently, then kneaded. His questing fingers found her nipples, circled tantalizingly, tauntingly . . . until she sank her fingers into his skull, clutched, and shifted boldly, invitingly, against him.

His fingers closed about her nipples and she felt her spine arch, heard a distant moan. Realized it came from her. He rolled her nipples until she thought she would scream, then palmed her breasts once more . . . but it wasn't enough. She needed more—and she was increasingly certain how to make her wishes known.

Twisting a fraction, she angled one hip, sending it riding against his erection. She might be an innocent, but she was far from ignorant; she knew what the hard ridge thrusting against her stomach was—knew what it signified, knew what he might do with it, if she could tempt him that far . . .

Her Colyton soul trembled with anticipation at the prospect.

His sharp intake of breath was her first reward; her second was even more satisfying. He kissed her—ravished her mouth—while his hands left her breasts, locked about her waist, and lifted her . . .

Jonas sat her on the edge of the bed, with one hand tugged her skirts up enough to press her knees wide and step between. He eased back from the kiss, let her have the reins and respond as she wished, while he reached up with both hands, caught her wrists, drew her hands from his hair, drew her arms down and back until he could set them on the bedspread behind her.

Then he resumed control of the kiss—tried to—found she wasn't inclined to relinquish the reins, and he had to sensually wrestle her for them. For supremacy, something that was customarily his for the taking.

The moment rang a warning bell—a distant one, one he ignored.

Now was not the time to heed any call for caution, not when through their increasingly frenzied mating of mouths he could sense her need, taste her desire. He leaned into her, forcing her to ease back, to take her weight on her arms—leaving his hands free so he could set them to work on the buttons closing her bodice.

It was the work of a mere minute to slip the tiny buttons free, to tug her laces loose so he could cup both hands about her throat, kiss her deeply, then skate his palms outward over her shoulders and collarbones, pushing the neckline and sleeves of her gown wide, eventually easing them over her shoulders and partway down her arms—effectively trapping them, and her, in the pose he wanted.

Only then did he draw back from the kiss, but he didn't straighten. Didn't step back.

Instead, drawing his lips from her still hungry ones, he skated them along her jaw, then tipped it back and spent a moment placing lingering kisses in the hollow beneath her ear, before stringing nipping caresses down the taut line of her throat. She tipped her head further back, gave a shivery sigh.

He paused at the base of her throat to savor her thudding pulse while his fingers found and unraveled the ribbon bow that secured her fine chemise.

Cotton, not silk, but of so fine a weave it was translucent. He spent a moment in contemplation of her puckered nipples and the softly flushed swells of her breasts imperfectly veiled by the delicate fabric.

She stirred, restless, then he felt her gaze on his face.

Slowly he lifted his gaze to meet it. Saw desire and curiosity rampant in her eyes. He let his lips curve, then looked down. Brought his hand once more to her breast, cupped it, through the thin fabric teased her nipple—until it tightened so much she arched and gasped.

Hooking a finger in the gathered edge of the chemise, he drew it down, exposing one breast fully, then bent his head and set his lips to the delicate skin. As fine as apple blossom, it heated beneath the caress; he sampled the curves, then bared her other breast and sampled that, too, avoiding the strawberry buds begging for his attention, instead listening to her breathing grow more ragged, more desperate.

More urgent.

Until, restless and needy, she moaned and shifted; tightening one hand on her waist, anchoring her, he acceded to her incoherent demand and closed his lips about one nipple, kissed, then licked, laved, finally drew it into his mouth and gently suckled.

Em gasped again, arched helplessly, shocked by the acute delight; head back, eyes closed, she gave herself up to the sensations, let them flood and cascade through her, lancing sharp, then hot and molten, drew them to her, held them to her, drank in all he would give her . . . then wordlessly, shamelessly, begged for more.

She should have been shocked—if she could think she undoubtedly would be—but feelings and emotions left no room for thought in her overwhelmed mind. It felt sinfully delicious letting him unwrap her like a present, encouraging him to; the moment held such an illicit thrill she hadn't been able to resist. Hadn't wanted to resist, lured by the promise of heat in his eyes, by the certainty of delight, and the impulse—more, compulsion—to feel his hands on her skin.

His lips on her skin, the hot, wet caress of his mouth on her breasts, the subtle tug on her nipples that seemed to spread, reach, and pull low in her belly, were all novel—for her unimagined—sensations, delicious, illicit—addictive.

Building. The heat his hands, his lips, sent cruising through her only seemed to grow. To swell until it felt like a river, a current of hot desire sweeping her along. Driving her to indulge, to treat her senses, to revel and know and be sensually consumed.

To be sensually overwhelmed. Such a novel, thrilling, exciting lure, one tailormade for her reckless soul, yet even as she let herself flow with the tide of pleasure he conjured, she couldn't help but wonder at herself, at how easily, how completely, she'd given herself to him.

Couldn't help wonder, in some lazy, languid part of her mind, why she had.

Knew only that with him, in his arms, she felt confident, assured—and safe.

Protected, even from him. Leaving her free to explore . . . this.

This thing that had grown and was flowering between them.

More than just him, more than simply her, it was riveting and commanding. It demanded, and she had to give. It soothed, through him delighted, and she accepted—that was the way it worked, it seemed.

She could only ride on through the moment, accept and let him steer her, guide her. She knew the basics, the theory, but not enough of the physical reality to take the lead.

So she waited—and when he paused, checking, between

ragged breaths searching her eyes, she encouraged him to
go on. There was something infinitely precious, infinitely
dear to her, infinitely alluring in the way he wordlessly consulted her and waited for her to make her wishes known.

So she did; her breasts flushed and damp, hot and swollen
and tightly peaked, heated almost beyond bearing by his
expert attentions, she gasped, managed a breathless, achy
"*Please* . . . ," and waited for what came next.

Waited, breath bated, to see what he would do. What next
delight he would introduce her to.

His lips returned to hers, waltzing her into a soul-deep
kiss, submerging her mind in a whirlpool of sensation.

Distracting her, she realized, when he eased back from
the kiss enough for her to feel his hand on her bare knee. To
feel him skate it slowly upward, his palm to the sensitive
skin of her thigh—inexorably tracing, blatantly claiming,
all the way up to where thigh and torso met. With one blunt
fingertip he traced the crease inward, lightly ruffled the
curls covering her mons, then lifted his hand, pushing her
skirts higher so he could trace the crease on the other side,
once again inward until his finger reached her curls.

He broke the kiss; lifting her heavy lids, through her
lashes she saw him glance down, saw him watch as he
touched her curls lightly, stroked.

She closed her eyes, heard her softly urgent breaths as
poised on the cusp of the unknown, she waited. She was sitting on her bed, leaning back on her arms, her knees spread
wide, her skirts rucked to her hips, her breasts bared—and
all she could think of was the hot throbbing of the soft flesh
between her thighs.

And what might assuage it.

His fingers slid lower and he touched her there, and her
world quaked. He stroked, traced, then blatantly explored
the slick, swollen folds. Caressed her knowingly, expertly,
until she bit her lower lip to stifle a moan, until, helpless,
she shifted her hips restlessly, parted her thighs further,
wanting yet more, inviting more.

His lips returned to hers, and he gave her what she wanted. Capturing her hungry lips, he teased, taunted, then filled her mouth once more, while between her thighs one long, blunt finger circled her entrance, then pressed in. She tensed against the novel intrusion, but the penetration continued, slowly, relentlessly, until his finger was deeply buried in her sheath.

Giddy, she broke from the kiss, hauled in a shuddering breath—lost it as his hand shifted and his thumb found the sensitive nubbin shielded beneath her curls, brushed, then pressed.

She gasped, tensed, but his hand moved and he continued the intimate caress; his thumb circled, stroking; his finger retreated then returned, filling her slick sheath. He nudged her head up, kissed her again, and his tongue mimicked the continuing play of his finger, easing her, filling her.

Driving her up some incredible peak of escalating tension, escalating heat.

Every thrust of his finger into her sheath, every pressing caress of his thumb, fed fire and pulsing excitement down her veins, sent both swirling through her, igniting, burning, feeding the empty furnace that had grown inside her, until the flames roared, then coalesced.

Until they tightened unbearably, white hot and intense.

He drew back from the kiss, murmured against her lips, "Let it happen—let go."

From under his lashes, Jonas watched as she teetered on the very peak, on the brink of orgasm, as, her skin gloriously flushed, her lips swollen and parted, her breathing beyond ragged, she clung with sensual fingernails, tried to hold against the waves of pleasure he sent coursing through her, threatening—about to—sweep her away.

He could imagine her first time would be shocking. Amazing, astonishing—something new, beyond her previous ken. He concentrated on ensuring delight—and the desire to feel the sensations again—was the assured outcome. Shifting his hand, he pressed deeper into her tight sheath, stroked, then with his thumb nudged her over the edge . . .

She fell with a soft cry.

He watched pleasure wash across her features as her sheath clamped tight about his finger, as her womb clenched, then throbbed. The ripples of her release slowly ebbed, all her tension gradually fading as she relaxed on a pleasured sigh.

Savoring the moment, he waited, then withdrew his hand from between her thighs. It took a major exercise of will, but he edged back from the bed, let her skirts fall to her knees. Locking his hands about her waist, he leaned over her and kissed her—drank long and deep, but fought to disguise his hunger, the need that ate at him, the unsated urge that clawed for release.

He knew what he wanted, what his body ached for, but given this had been her first taste of paradise, *that* might be taking things too far, too fast. He wouldn't, couldn't, rush her; he wanted her to want him in the same way, with the same unquestioning certainty, the same undeniable intensity—most importantly for the same reason—as he wanted her.

The right time for the next step would come. He assured himself of that as he, with impossible to conceal reluctance, drew his lips from hers.

Before he could straighten, she shifted, freed a hand, and seized his lapel; she clutched, holding him there, a mere breath away. Opening her eyes, still hazed with pleasure, she studied his, then searched his face.

Her eyes narrowed fractionally, as if sensing his intent—and not approving. Then she tilted her head, locked her eyes on his. "I want you to teach me more. All. Now."

Her voice was a sultry siren's song, but beneath the seductive tones determination and decision rang clearly.

Clearly enough for him, after the briefest instant of searching her eyes to confirm he wasn't dreaming, to tighten his hold on her waist and lean forward.

But . . .

His lips all but brushing hers, he hesitated. Forced himself to ask, albeit in a low, gravelly—almost incomprehensible—growl, "Are you sure? Absolutely sure?"

At close quarters, their eyes met, held. With mere inches between them, nothing could be hidden. He searched her eyes while she searched his; he sensed rather than saw her smile—sensed an emotion behind it that made his head spin.

"Yes," she whispered. "I'm sure." It was she who closed the tiny gap; her lips were curved as they touched his, and on a breath she sighed, "I'm absolutely sure."

They kissed, neither in the ascendancy, for one long moment indulged in a true sharing.

Then she shifted, grabbed his other lapel with her other hand—and no longer braced, fell back on the bed, pulling him down with her, toppling him down on top of her.

He made a heroic effort and managed to twist to the side, landing beside her.

She wriggled, turning to him; her lips recaptured his and she kissed him with such ferocity that for one finite minute she held him in thrall. In complete and absolute abandonment to the moment.

But then she wriggled some more, trying to get closer, getting her skirts even more rucked up between them and sending her thighs sliding against him in a way guaranteed to wake his demons and urge them to ravening heights.

One nicely rounded hip caressed his groin.

He sucked in a breath, shifted his concentration from her lips and mouth, from the naked breasts his hands had—entirely of their own volition—reclaimed. Through the fog of desire hazing his brain, he realized from her fuddled fumblings that she had some basic notion of the physical act, but the basics weren't going to get him and her to where he wanted them to be.

This would be her first time, and first times had to be absolutely right. Especially hers, with him, given his intention was to make the exercise a mutual habit. So he took charge.

Was only mildly surprised to discover he had to exert himself to do so.

He had to lean over her and bear her back on the bed, had to use his weight to subdue her. Even then, when she lay pinned beneath him, her hands continued to tug . . . forced to ease back from the rapacious exchange their kiss had become, he registered that she was wrestling with his coat rather than him; she was trying to push it off his shoulders, in her present position something she simply couldn't do.

He dove back into the kiss, let his hunger show and flare; although she met him, matched him, and wantonly invited more, she didn't stop tugging.

On a muttered curse, he abruptly drew back, broke the kiss, and sat up. Hands going to his coat, shrugging it off, he pinned her with a commanding stare. "Stay there. Don't move."

Standing, in short order he dispensed with coat, waistcoat, and cravat, then set his fingers to the buttons closing his shirt.

Em watched him, fingers instinctively flexing, waiting—beyond impatient—to get her hands on his naked skin. His hands had felt so good on hers, she wanted to return the favor—and see where that led. See if it made him as helpless, as wantonly yearning, as his caresses made her. She wanted to learn more—everything—now.

When the pleasure he'd wrought had flooded her, burgeoned, then imploded in ecstasy, in the immediate aftermath she'd experienced a moment of blinding, startling clarity.

He was right—she needed to know, to understand, *this*. *All* about this.

How else could she be sure—how else would she know? With whom else would she ever learn?

It was him, here and now—or never. Or so her Colyton soul believed.

Are you sure? he'd asked. *Yes*, she'd replied, and had never been more certain of anything in her life.

So she waited, her breathing shallow, constrained, her eyes hungrily, greedily surveying the wide acres of lightly tanned skin, the sculpted planes of his chest, the ridges of his abdomen, noting and drinking in every aspect as it was revealed. The broad curve of his shoulders made her palms itch. She wanted to touch, to skim her hands over every inch of skin, to explore the tactile contrast provided by the dark hair that grew in a band from one side of his chest to the other; it dipped in the middle to trail down, eventually disappearing beneath his waistband.

She looked up and met his eyes—saw he'd noticed her following that tempting downward trail. His eyes were dark pools she could lose herself in; they held heat enough to liquefy steel.

He tossed aside his shirt, not even glancing to see where it landed, and returned to settle beside her; leaning over her, his hips to one side of her thighs, with one elbow and forearm on either side, he caged her.

His hands, large, strong, infinitely gentle, framed her face. He looked into her eyes, then lowered his head.

Before he could kiss her—steal her wits, cloud her mind, and make her yearn again—she placed both hands palms flat to his chest and held him back.

He could have ignored the restraint, but didn't. He paused, looking down at her; she could see curiosity in his face, over what she wanted, what she intended.

Letting her lips curve, she showed him. Let her hands drift tantalizingly over his chest, and was rewarded with a soft hiss of appreciation. Reaching the points of his shoulders, she pressed her palms more definitely to his skin, marveling at the resilience of his flesh, the contrast of smooth, hot, pliable skin stretched tautly over hard, heavy, immovable muscle.

His chest was a tactile feast; she let her hands explore, let her senses absorb, then sent her hands skating lower, tracing the fascinating ridges of his abdomen, the muscle bands tense, tight, almost quivering.

She reached lower, tried to, but he shifted, caught her hands, first one, then the other, raised them to his shoulders, but retained his hold as he leaned in and kissed her, parted her lips and filled her mouth, as he lowered his chest to her breasts.

Her senses leapt, skittered, fractured; her nerves seared, then burned.

All of her burned. Not just her nerves, and her skin where he touched it, not just her breasts, but all of her.

And this time the flame was hotter, deeper, broader—more intense. More demanding—just as he was more demanding, more commanding as he filled her mouth, ravaged her senses, then settled to dictate their play.

To control, yes, but in this instance she needed him to guide her. Needed him to show her the way.

Needed him to gently strip away her gown, her chemise, to set his hands and clever fingers to her skin.

So that she burned even more.

Burned hotter, brighter, hungrier still, with an emptiness inside that ached to be filled.

Ached for him to fill it, to fill her, claim her, take her—show her all.

He was slow, but thorough; she tried to wordlessly urge him on, but he was adamant, refusing to shift from his steady pace, unrelenting and determined.

She could hardly complain. He gave her what she'd asked for—all and even more than she'd demanded. Yet she wasn't about to refuse whatever pleasure he sought to bestow—because it was all pleasure, all delight and bright sensation, as she discovered passion and desire in his arms.

Jonas fought not to rush, not to let his baser self accept any of the wanton, not to say abandoned, invitations she issued; that way lay failure—too easy gratification at the expense of her satisfaction, and, ultimately, his. He wasn't about to make such an error. He held his goal, his aim, before him, clung to it in the face of her blatant acceptance of anything he chose to do—each caress, each kiss, each evocative pressure she welcomed like a houri and sought— even fought—to respond in kind—but he knew very well that she couldn't know what she was doing, inviting, that no matter her assurance, her will and determination, she was lying in a man's arms for the first time.

So he stripped her slowly—and some wiser, more mature and sophisticated part of him reveled in the act. In its slowness and certainty, in the time he took to examine and savor, to tempt, then lavish ever more evocative caresses upon her.

He held them both back; with a ruthless hand on his reins, and hers, he held them to an excruciatingly slow beat. To a pace where every touch, every lingering caress, was answered, where every gasp, every moan he wrung from her, was appreciated to the full—both by him and her.

More than any other woman he'd known, he wanted her—completely, absolutely, beyond all reason. And part of that want, that all-consuming desire, was to have her want him in the same way.

So the long moments spent in such extended foreplay were, to him, not just a wise but a necessary investment. The effort he had to expend to hold his demons back, to stop himself from simply surrendering and ravishing her, was the price he had to pay for perfection.

To achieve the perfect introduction to intimacy.

For her. With her.

For all that he wanted the moment to mean.

She was hot, heated, restless almost to the point of desperation, her naked body and long, bare limbs lightly flushed and damp with desire, when he drew back and finally removed his shoes and trousers, then lifted her higher on the bed, laying her on the bedspread, then joining her.

Hazel eyes, bright and burning with open passion, glinted at him from beneath her heavy lids; lips swollen and sheening from his kisses, her skin flushed and rosy, breasts full and swollen, their peaks tight buds, she reached for him. He let her grasp, let her tug—and slowly eased his body down on hers.

He parted her thighs with his, settled between; she readily shifted to accommodate him. His erection was a heavy, rigid rod, its bulbous head nudging at her entrance.

The touch of it there made her tense, close her eyes, suck in a tight breath, then she shivered, released the breath slowly, gradually relaxed.

Gradually let the heat and the need and the passion reclaim her, gradually, knowingly, sank into that heated sea.

Are you sure? The words burned on his tongue, but looking into her face, reading, sensing, beneath the flushed blankness of passion, her determination—her courage and unquenchable desire in forging so far with neither resistance nor hesitation—the question seemed redundant.

Even insulting.

She'd made up her mind and she was there, spread naked beneath him, willing and very ready to take him in.

So he bent his head and found her lips, covered them, filled her mouth, and waltzed her back into the full heat of their shared passion, then flexed his spine and slowly entered her.

Em caught her breath, held it as he pressed in, struggled not to tense as he forged deeper into her body, as the pressure built and he stretched her, filled her, inch by slow inch claimed her.

An inkling of why such words applied—possessing, taking, claiming—seeped into her mind, already reeling with sensations both novel and . . . tense-making. Her hands locked on his upper arms, nails sinking in, she clung, hung on, her spine instinctively arching. The feel of his erection pushing into her was nothing like the earlier intrusion of his finger. This was so much more, so . . . enthralling.

Then she felt a slight, but building, resistance; he hesitated, then he kissed her so voraciously she had to drag her mind from its preoccupation and focus on their melded mouths, on kissing him back and appeasing the fiery demand in his kiss.

He withdrew just a little, then thrust in—powerful and relentless. Distracted, she didn't immediately realize, then felt a searing pain, enough to make her jolt, make her tense, but the sensation faded to mere discomfort so rapidly she started to relax in the same breath . . . then a tide of raw awareness crashed over her, overtaking, subsuming, submerging all else. Her skin prickled, came alive, every nerve stretched taut as she realized, felt, finally experienced the reality of having him buried deep within her.

Having his body merged so intimately and completely with hers.

He held still—whether to impress the moment on her or savor it himself, she couldn't tell—but that instant of mutual hiatus seemed infinitely precious, like a perfectly formed dewdrop in the instant before it fell. Something precious that lasted for only an instant in time.

The moment passed. He murmured her name against her lips, a question in the guttural sound. In response, she kissed him, then, unknowing but waiting to learn, shifted encouragingly beneath him.

He caught his breath, withdrew and slowly, carefully, thrust in again. This time there was no pain; she eased her hips beneath him, through the kiss sought to reassure . . .

Attuned to her every move, every breath, every heartbeat, Jonas received her message with abject relief. He eased his desperate, metaphorically white-knuckled hold on his reins, and let himself slide into the familiar dance.

She responded immediately, quickly learning the rhythm of thrust and retreat; soon—too soon—she started to experiment, to angle her hips and take him deeper, to tighten the muscles in her scalding sheath and clasp him even more tightly.

That last made him catch his breath, made his head spin. Made it just that bit harder to keep control of their ride—especially as she didn't seem to want him to. Having committed to the interlude, she clearly saw no reason to cling to inhibitions; he wasn't entirely surprised—or shocked—by her headlong dive into intimacy—her eager, enthusiastic, even greedy wish to experience more, learn more, know more.

Especially about him. Her hands had come alive, skating over his chest, his shoulders, sliding lower to stroke his buttocks and thighs. Fingers spread, she seemed to be imprinting all of him on her senses; he couldn't—didn't want to—discourage that, quite the opposite, but the effect of her blatantly exploring touch had him reeling.

Had him feeling like surrendering and simply doing whatever she wished, however she wished, regardless of any agenda of his own.

Regardless of all wisdom.

That she could reduce him to such mindless acquiescence with the luscious clasp of her body, with the sensuous feel of her firm curves, supple limbs, and soft feminine skin undulating beneath him, with her hands laying fire over his skin, shook a few wits into place, enough to have him refocus on the reality that an extended engagement wasn't in her best interests, and therefore his, not this first time.

He kissed her more firmly, slid deep into her mouth and claimed her softness—and her attention. Used the moment of her distraction to lower his body to hers. Steeling himself against the subtle lure of her breasts pressing against and cushioning his chest, he settled more fully upon her, caught one of her questing hands, engulfed it in one of his, held it, and led her on.

On, steadily on, down the path to fulfilment and release.

The tempo of their dance increased, until she was writhing beneath him, her body wantonly begging, eloquently urging him on. She brought her free hand to his cheek, laid it against his jaw—then kissed him, lips and tongue combining to convey a ferociously blatant demand, one so explicit and strong that against all the odds she snapped his reins.

And they were suddenly whirling in heat and flames, writhing together, wrestling in sensuous abandon, striving, pressing, wanting, clinging, gasping as together they ascended the peak.

They flung themselves over the edge. He sent her winging with one last thrust; she clung, her climax dragging him with her.

Into that moment of unutterable ecstasy, of imploding sensation, of feeling so sharp it cut, so brilliant it blinded.

Of emotion that, for him unprecedently, sent warm tendrils twining about his heart.

For one defined instant they hung, caught, captured, suspended in that moment of crystal clarity.

Then they fell. The bright sensations drained as they spiraled back to earth, secure in each other's arms, pillowed, cushioned, buoyed on the waves of golden aftermath that rolled in and swept them away.

13

Em stirred—and wondered why the sheets were so scratchy.

Eyes still closed, she frowned—unable to remember why she'd gone to bed naked, without her nightgown—indeed, without a stitch on.

Then she registered the heat—and the body from which it was emanating—wrapped all around her.

It wasn't the sheets that were lightly abrading her suddenly sensitive skin.

Awareness, then memories, flooded her. On a stifled gasp she opened her eyes—and confirmed the conclusion of her senses.

Those memories weren't dreams.

She was lying on her back with Jonas slumped facedown beside her. She stared at the heavily muscled, hairy arm lying across her breasts, then shifted her gaze to stare at the long, large frame—decently screened beneath her coverlet—stretched alongside her, one heavy, naked thigh anchoring one of hers.

Had she really . . . ?

Yes, she had. She'd invited Jonas Tallent into her bed, into her body. He'd followed her up to her room under his own steam—arguing about something as she recalled. She couldn't remember what—could remember very little of what had transpired before she'd thrown her cap over the proverbial windmill. She could remember all that had followed— all her explorations, all she'd learned, all the incredible sensations—in remarkable detail . . .

Distracting detail.

Blinking, she realized long minutes had ticked by while she wallowed in what had been—on what their *this* had encompassed.

Understandable enough, but . . . what now?

Having invited him in, how did she get him to leave?

She wasn't sure of the etiquette, but assumed she should, somehow, see him out. Certainly he couldn't still be in her room come morning.

What was the time? A small clock stood on a chest of drawers against the wall alongside the bed; she squinted at it, couldn't quite make out the hands . . .

"It's just after midnight."

The low words rumbled past her ear, making her start. Making her nerves, her skin, sizzle with awareness. Making her turn her head toward him.

He'd turned his head on the pillow to watch her. He lay close; enough moonlight washed across the bed for her to see his features, but his eyes remained dark pools—she couldn't read their expression.

She could see his lips, saw them curve in what appeared to be a richly self-satisfied smile. One that bordered on the smug.

She would have frowned—intended to—but he moved his arm, and his hand, his long fingers, brushed the side of her breast. A start of a different sort lanced through her, memory rendering anticipation that much sharper. Her gaze on his face, her attention—every last bit of it— locked on his hand, on his questing fingers as they found, stroked, weighed, caressed . . . she nearly squirmed with remembered delight, with damning, building, expectation.

She licked her lips. Saw his gaze fall to them. Forced herself to say, "Shouldn't you . . . leave?"

His gaze rose to her eyes, held hers for an instant, then his lips curved more definitely. He shook his head; his gaze lowered to where, beneath the covers, his hand continued to caress—to reclaim—her breast. "I'm precisely where I want to be."

And he had no intention of leaving, not until consideration for her reputation drove him out at dawn. Jonas couldn't remember ever feeling so content, so satisfied.

Emily Beauregard was his. Incontrovertibly, beyond question or doubt.

He lay naked in her bed, and she lay with him, also naked—and despite her fluster, despite her weak attempt to suggest he leave, her body was responding encouragingly to his caresses, if anything with even greater fervor than before.

Heaven help him. Her fervor, her eagerness, were apparently ingrained. Once she'd made up her mind, made her decision, she'd flung herself wholeheartedly into the engagement.

Which augured well for what would occur once she made her final decision to be his wife; the events of the night were clearly her first step along that road. The realization buoyed him; he was perfectly willing to give her whatever time— whatever reinforcement—she needed to make up her mind.

"But shouldn't you . . ." She waved vaguely. "Leave? Now we've . . . oh!"

That last was occasioned by him sending his hand skating, openly possessive, down her body. Her eyes widened as with one finger he found, then stroked the slick flesh between her thighs.

Smiling, he leaned closer to nudge the coverlet down with his chin and nuzzle one pert breast. "Later."

She hesitated, then he felt her nod. "All right," she whispered. "Later . . ."

He looked up and saw her eyes close, her spine arching lightly as he slid his finger deeper into her heat. He probed, and she shifted restlessly, breath hitching, her hands groping, then fastening on his upper arms, clutching.

He needed no further invitation. Withdrawing his hand, he lifted over her; spreading her thighs wide, he settled between. Glancing at her face, he saw her bite her lower lip to stifle a moan. He entered her with one long, powerful thrust, and she lost the battle.

The sound of her urgent breathing, of her breathy little moans, drove him on.

And this time the act was more blatantly a claiming. She was with him, wanton and eager, yet this time she seemed content to not just let him take the lead, but to consistently follow—watching, gauging, learning.

Not more about lovemaking per se, but about him making love to her.

If he'd been in any state to disguise things, to draw a concealing veil over the emotions that gripped him, that were revealed in all their stark power in the moonlight as she welcomed him in and he rode her to mutual pleasured oblivion, he would have done so, but the moment stripped him of all ability to hide anything—not from her, and even less from himself.

Never with any other woman had he felt as he did for her—with her, over her. Never had being inside a woman meant so much, or felt so right. So incontestably his destiny.

He pushed her further, drove more deeply, more powerfully into her, and she responded wholeheartedly, embracing him, holding him—clinging as she shattered, cradling him as he followed her into pleasured bliss.

Em woke in the morning—alone. She lifted her head, looked around the room, but there was no sign of Jonas. Then her gaze fell on the bed—the rumpled bed with sheets all askew, the coverlet wildly tangled . . . and she smiled.

With a sigh, she fell back on the pillows and beamed at the ceiling. What an exciting, enthralling, thoroughly entrancing night—the night she'd spent in his arms. He'd answered all her questions regarding lovemaking—had throughly demonstrated what *this*—the attraction that had risen between them—was, what it meant, where it led . . .

She frowned. She was now a fallen woman. Shouldn't she feel more . . . cast down? Dismayed, guilty—at least regretful?

She consulted her inner self—and could find not a trace, not a single one, of any of those feelings. Instead . . . she felt on top of the world, as if waking to a sunny day with not a cloud on her horizon.

Yet the more she thought, the more her mind wrestled with the likely ramifications of their activities last night, the more she realized how very far from the truth, how divorced from reality, how misleading that feeling was.

She was in Colyton to find her family's treasure. She was masquerading, albeit not terribly successfully, as an innkeeper in order to facilitate hunting for said treasure. It formed no part of her plans to become her employer's—or anyone else's—mistress.

Worse, jumbled in amid her memories of the past night was a hazy recollection that, in the moment he'd collapsed upon her a second time, spent and wondrously, gratifyingly helpless, she'd heard—or thought she'd heard—the words "You're mine. All mine."

The problem was . . .

She grimaced, then flung back her covers and—steadfastly ignoring her naked state—got up. Locating her robe, she shrugged into it, belted it, then determinedly set about getting ready for the day; she could hear Hilda and her girls already moving about in the kitchen below.

While she washed and dressed, she wrestled with her

memory, trying to bring that revelatory moment back, clearer in her mind. And failed.

Putting the last touches to her hair, she pulled a face at the mirror, then rose and headed for the door.

Her problem was she couldn't remember if she'd heard *him* growl those words—or if *she'd* been the one to think them so strongly she'd heard them ringing in her head.

The instant she stepped out of her rooms, the inn and her family claimed her. She had no time to ponder the whys and wherefores, let alone dwell on the likely outcomes, of her illicit night. She plunged into a veritable whirlpool of activities, of managing this, giving orders for that, making decisions, and— wonder of wonders—welcoming the inn's first residential guests in, so she'd been informed, more than five years.

"Heard in Exeter that the Red Bells was back up and running properly again," one of the travelers, a Mr. Dobson, said. "I used to stop here often, years ago. I pass by every few months. Thought it was worth a try again—especially when I heard about the food."

Em smiled welcomingly. "We're very glad you did. Now if you'll just follow Mary here, she'll show you to your room. Your bags will be brought up shortly. Do let Edgar know if you require anything else."

The man tipped his hat and followed Mary—one of the two girls from nearby farms Em had hired to help with cleaning the rooms and maid duties—up the stairs. Under her guidance, both girls and the three laundry maids had slaved to get the chambers upstairs habitable again. She'd been rather surprised and pleased with the result. Now it remained to see how their new—and returning—patrons reacted to the freshly whitewashed walls, the crisply clean sheets, and the freshly restuffed pillows and mattresses. Curtains and upholstery had also needed to be cleaned; all in all it had taken over a week for her to be satisfied with the state of four of the rooms at the front—all they'd thus far reopened for use.

She spent the morning chatting with the locals, overseeing orders—and welcoming more guests. At eleven o'clock, after Mary had seen an older couple, traveling the country taking in the sights, up to the third of their prepared rooms, she suggested to the girl that she bring her sister with her the next day, so they could work faster on getting the rest of the inn's bedchambers refurbished and ready; heaven forbid she had to turn a potential customer away! Given anyone who stayed overnight at the inn necessarily ate and drank there, too, the increased profits more than compensated for hiring extra staff.

She made a mental note to mention the increase in staff to Jonas—her employer; determined not to let thoughts of him and the previous night claim her, she thereafter resolutely banished him from her mind. Pausing in the little hall outside her office, she looked around the common room. It was gratifyingly busy with those lured inside by the smell of Hilda's cinnamon buns.

She was about to retreat to her office when a newcomer walked into the inn. Bag in hand, he paused just inside the door and slowly looked around; his casual survey seemed to take in everything.

The inn's patrons weren't backward in taking in everything about him. He was an arresting sight, an attractive one to a good portion of the inn's customers, namely those sitting on the other side of the common room.

Given the locals' scrutiny, Em felt confident in labeling him a stranger. He was tallish, well set up, with black hair long enough to be wind-tousled, and a well-shaped but craggy, tanned face. Em glanced at the hand wrapped around the handle of the bag he was carrying; it was also deeply tanned. A sailor at one time was her guess.

He was no ancient salty tar, but somewhere in his late thirties. His clothes marked him as a man not engaged in menial trades. His dark blue coat was of decent cut, with a plain waistcoat beneath and an unremarkable cravat. His trousers were of the same dark blue as the coat, but of thicker weave. Em recognized the work of a provincial tailor; the man—there was something about him that made her shy from labeling him a gentleman—no doubt hailed from one of the shires.

His survey complete, the stranger bent and hefted another, odd-shaped, flattish, angular parcel he'd left resting against the door frame. With that under his arm, his bag in the other, he walked to the bar. He nodded to Edgar. "Good morning. I heard you have rooms. I'd like to hire one, if possible."

Engaged in pulling a pint, Edgar nodded back. "Aye—we should be able to put you up." He glanced at Em, a questioning quirk to his brows.

Lifting her head, she walked out from the shadows and along behind the bar. Seeing her, the stranger straightened. She smiled. Passing Edgar, she picked up the register from under the counter, halted before the newcomer, and set the book on the counter between them. "Good morning, sir. You're in luck—we have only one room left."

She looked up and discovered the stranger had slate gray eyes. They were fixed on her, then he returned her smile.

He was really quite handsome; she wondered why her senses only yawned. Presumably Jonas had worn them out.

Keeping her pleasant, welcoming smile in place, she opened the register, then turned it to the newcomer. "Your name, sir?" She indicated the column in which he should write the information.

"Hadley. William Hadley." He picked up the pencil tied to the register and duly filled out his name, then signed alongside.

Em took back the book and filled in the day's date. "Are you planning on staying long, Mr. Hadley?"

She glanced up, expecting him to say a day or two.

"I'd like to take the room for a week, to begin with." His eyes met hers as she blinked. "Will that be a problem?"

"No, no." She hurried to reassure him. "We're happy to accommodate long-term guests." Just as long as they paid.

She calculated rapidly. "In the circumstances, we'll need four night's lodgings, if you please." She named the sum.

Without hesitation, Hadley pulled out a leather purse and counted out the amount.

Taking it—reassured Hadley was no trickster—her smile grew more natural. "I take it you have business in the district?"

Hadley, too, seemed to relax. "After a fashion." He gestured to the strange-shaped parcel. "I'm an artist. I travel around the country sketching old monuments. I heard that the church here is well worth a visit—I'm told it has some of the finest monuments in the country."

"Indeed?" Em recalled that the statues inside the church were well wrought, many quite intricate. She smiled more brightly. "In that case, I hope your stay is a pleasant and productive one. Mary"—she indicated the little maid who'd come hurrying up to bob a curtsy—"will show you to your room. If you require anything further, please let one of our staff know."

"Thank you. I will." Hadley nodded politely, hefted his bag and parcel—Em now recognized the outline of a folded easel—and turned to follow Mary, her cheeks pink as she led the way to the stairs.

Striding in her wake, Hadley noticed the various women gathered on that side of the common room, all openly studying him. His lips curved; he inclined his head politely. "Ladies."

The deep rumble elicited a few careful nods; others ducked their heads, while yet others simply continued to stare.

Hadley turned and climbed the stairs, following Mary. His audience continued to watch in silence; only once he'd disappeared from sight along the upstairs corridor did a fascinated titter flit about the room.

Em noted it, but distantly, her mind weighing the more pertinent tidbit Hadley had let fall. If their church really was such a drawcard for artists—especially for sketching, a pastime many ladies indulged in—perhaps she—and her employer—should consider ways to attract the attention of the artists' societies. Indoor monuments could be sketched in any season; considering the benefits of a steady stream of patrons whose attraction to the neighborhood wasn't dependent on the weather, she drifted back to her office.

The rest of her day passed less pleasantly.

Harold came in just after they'd finished serving lunch. Ordering a pint, he sat at a table at the rear of the tap—and broodingly glowered at her whenever she hove in sight.

Oscar kindly offered to throw her uncle out on his ear; she debated, but in the end declined. She'd rather have Harold under her eye than sneaking around behind her back.

He was still there when the twins came down after their afternoon lesson with Issy. Descending the stairs in the girls' wake, Issy noticed, and deftly distracted her half sisters with promises of scones, and thus diverted them into the kichen. Leaving them under Hilda's matronly eye, Issy sought out Em in her office.

Looking up from her order book, Em nodded. "Yes, I know he's there."

Issy looked worried, and a touch torn. "Are you sure it's all right for me to go to see Joshua? I don't need to go if you need me here."

Shutting the book, Em shook her head. "No—go. I'll stay with our two terrors and make sure they don't do anything they shouldn't."

Issy usually walked to the rectory once her day with the twins came to an end; she would meet Henry and Joshua there, spend a little time with Joshua on his front porch while Henry finished his work inside, then she and Henry would walk home.

All perfectly innocent and aboveboard, and Issy deserved the moment of peace and pleasure after taking care of the twins all day.

Standing, Em shooed her off. "Go on—we'll manage perfectly well."

Issy pulled a face at her. "If you're sure?"

"I'm sure. Go!" Em pointed in her sternest fashion. Issy laughed, and went.

Smiling, Em followed her out of the door. She stood watching while Issy, utterly ignoring Harold—or was that, in light of her preoccupation as attested to by the soft smile on her face, not seeing him at all?—walked through the inn's common room and out of the door.

Standing in the concealing shadows of the little hall— such a useful spot it had proved—Em continued to watch their uncle until she was sure he wasn't going to follow her sister.

Relieved on that score, she headed for her next responsibility—keeping the twins occupied.

Contrary to Issy's belief, the twins had seen Harold. Em spent the next hours being highly creative in keeping her half sisters out of the common room, where they normally gravitated in the late afternoon—usually to sit by the hearth, ears flapping as they listened to the older women gossip, and otherwise providing attractive color with their angelic little-girl looks.

They nearly drove her demented, but in the end she prevailed. Not, however, without a few acid thoughts about inn owners who might have helped had they thought to call.

Somewhat to her surprise, said inn owner didn't come by that evening, either. She'd grown used to seeing him in the rear corner of the tap, nursing a single pint through the evening, chatting with the locals and otherwise fixing his dark gaze on her whenever she passed by. She missed feeling its weight, that was all; she told herself that was the cause of the niggling disquiet—a sense of something not being right—that insensibly grew through the evening.

Harold eventually departed after regaling himself with dinner and a bottle of red wine; whenever she'd glanced his way, he'd glowered at her. She wasn't pleased to see him return later, when there were many fewer in the common room. He called for a glass of whiskey. Edgar glanced her way, and at her nod, obliged; she knew Harold's drinking habits—one glass would have no effect whatever.

It didn't, but . . . her sense of unease grew as she noticed he was no longer directing black looks her way, but rather at everyone else.

He was waiting for them to leave . . . so he'd have her to himself. And for once, her white knight wasn't there.

As the minutes to closing time ticked by, Em revised her opinion of protective gentlemen. She felt herself growing tenser and tenser, waiting for the moment when the last customer left and Harold made his move. What would it be this time? In the end, however, Harold's ploy was defeated by an alliance of locals, who, suspecting his motives and deducing that he intended to wait them out, moved in on him instead. Led by the sometimes garrulous, sometimes belligerent Oscar, they surrounded Harold, offered to buy him a pint so he could share in their bonhomie, then, despite his declining, proceeded to regale him with the highlights of their lives.

As it became perfectly plain they were prepared to continue into the future, and if necessary into the afterlife, Harold capitulated and with very bad grace—and a filthy look her way—left.

Everyone heaved a sigh of relief. She thanked her unexpected saviors and promised them a drink on the house the following evening; the instant they left, Edgar locked up, then departed.

Alone at last, she heaved a massive sigh, then turned down the last lamp and headed for the stairs.

And her room—her empty room—and her equally empty bed.

Climbing the stairs, she lectured herself that that was how it should be. How it ought to be. Always.

Some part of her—the Colyton part of her—grizzled and grumped, sulked and slumped. She went into her parlor, closed the door, then, picking up the lighted candle Issy had left burning on the dresser for her, crossed to her bedroom. She didn't want to even let the thought form, but she couldn't duck the knowledge that her wearying evening would have been a lot less tiring, a lot less trying and wearing on her nerves, if Jonas had been there.

She would have felt much safer, much more confident— not nearly as watchful and wary.

"Humph!" Grimacing, she sat before her dressing table, lighted the two candles in the holders flanking the mirror, then started pulling pins from her hair. She'd had to hunt high and low for them that morning; they'd been scattered over the bed and on the floor.

She'd just shaken her hair loose, was running her fingers through the tresses, when she heard the stair tread one from the top creak.

Her heart leapt to her throat, but then she heard a firm footstep—recalled they now had guests staying at the inn. One must have gone downstairs . . . why?

Before she could start imagining unwelcome scenarios, a light rap sounded on her parlor door.

Frowning, she rose and headed for the door between bed-chamber and parlor—froze in the doorway as the parlor door swung open . . .

Jonas walked in.

He saw her, smiled, shut the door—and locked it. Then he walked toward her.

She blinked, shook free of her senses' distraction. Frowned up at him as he neared. "What are you doing here?"

His brows rose. Halting before her, he set his hands to her waist—and steered her back into her bedroom. She realized and tried to dig in her heels, but by then she was in the room, and so was he.

With one booted foot, he nudged the door closed behind him. Expression impossibly mild, he held her gaze. "Where else would I be?"

She glanced pointedly at the clock. "In some room at the Grange?"

He shook his head. Lips curving, he turned away, shrugged out of his coat, and carefully set it over the back of a chair. "It's time for bed."

"Precisely!" She stepped to the chair, picked up his coat, and held it out for him to put back on. "So you should go home to your room and your bed."

He looked at the coat, then raised his eyes to her face—all the while unbuttoning his cuffs. "I prefer this room—and your bed. At present it has a highly pertinent advantage over mine." Cuffs undone, he set his fingers to the buttons on the placket of his shirt.

She frowned, watched his fingers move down the row of buttons . . . realized, bludgeoned her wits into order, forced herself to think. Felt compelled to ask, "What advantage?"

He grinned—wickedly. "Your bed has you in it."

She narrowed her eyes, dropped his coat back on the chair. Just as, buttons all free, he stripped off his neckerchief and shirt. Her eyes went wide. "Jonas!"

Dropping both garments on the chair, he raised his brows. "What?" His expression remained studiously mild, yet amusement lurked in his dark eyes.

Dragging in a breath—difficult given her reaction to the blatant display of male charms—she pointed a finger at his chest, waved to encompass the expanse. "You can't—we can't . . . you shouldn't be here, doing this."

"Why not?"

"Because, despite last night, *this* cannot be. I will not be your mistress." She hadn't had time to think things through, but of that she was certain.

"Of course not." He sat on the chair and proceeded to remove his boots and stockings. "I couldn't agree more."

She stared at him. "But . . . if I'm not to be your mistress, what are you doing here?"

He cocked a brow at her. "After last night, I would think you'd be able to answer that yourself."

She felt totally at sea, but she wasn't going to simply surrender—to him or to her inner self's urging. Folding her arms, she fixed him with her sternest look. "While I realize last night might have given you an incorrect impression, I will not consent to being your sometime lover."

He frowned, opened his mouth to respond—she silenced him with an upraised hand. "No—just listen. Regardless of any inclinations, this—you and me and *this*—simply cannot be. We cannot indulge our passions at will."

Slowly his brows rose in question.

She frowned him down, tightened her arms beneath her breasts. "You know very well *why*. My reputation would be ruined, and as this is such a small village, in the circumstances you wouldn't escape unscathed, either. And on top of that, we're both working to restore the inn to its former glory, and any scandal will immediately drive away all the females we've managed to attract. Regardless of how we feel, our reputations and the inn are too important, not just to us but to many others as well, for us to so cavalierly risk all."

His eyes had narrowed on her face. He nodded, rather curtly. "Very true."

She inwardly frowned at his suddenly terse tone. "So you agree?"

"You haven't said anything I haven't already thought of."

She let her puzzled frown materialize. "Then why are you here?"

His lips thinned; he looked down, then rose. "I never imagined you as my mistress, and even less as a 'sometime lover.' And while all you said is indisputably true, there's a simple solution, one that will allow us to eat our cake and have all that, too."

She tried to think of it, failed. "What solution?"

He looked at her then, met her eyes. His were very dark. "All you have to do is marry me, and all will be well."

His tone was all reasonableness on the surface, but strong emotions roiled beneath.

"Marry you." She'd stared at him before; now she felt as if her eyes would pop. "*Marry* you? But . . . but . . ." He held her gaze; in his eyes she saw his strength, the rock-solid steadfastness she'd sensed from the first. Her head whirled, her wits in absolute disarray. She uttered the first words that came into her head. "Are you serious?"

His eyes narrowed to glinting shards. "I always was."

Jonas looked into her face, saw the depth of her astonishment, knew it was real, and felt his temper race. "I'm *deadly* serious. What the devil did you imagine my pursuit of you was about?"

She blinked, searched his eyes. "Passion. Desire. Uncontrollable urges. How was I supposed to know you meant marriage?" She flung her hands wide. "I'm your *innkeeper,* for heaven's sake!"

"You were supposed to know because I *told* you I was wooing you." His jaw tightened. "I also pointed out that gentlemen like me don't seduce innkeepers." He jabbed a finger in the direction of her nose, making her weave back. "And *don't* bother telling me you're my innkeeper! Everyone in the village knows you're a lady who—presumably to escape your uncle Harold, an entirely understandable endeavor—have *temporarily* taken a position as an innkeeper. No one believes you're *actually* an innkeeper, because you aren't."

He locked his gaze with hers. Eyes bright, awash with uncertainty, she stared back. Her expression, her frown, underscored her confusion. She honestly hadn't realized . . . and didn't know how to react.

That last gave him pause. Her refusing to be his wife didn't feature in his plan.

The mere idea doused his temper, allowing the wisdom of not scaring her, or in any way pushing her so that out of stubbornness or uncertainty she uttered the word "no," to take root in his mind. Once she refused, she would feel obliged to stick to her guns, and his road would be much harder. Getting her to make up her mind in his favor was one thing; getting her to *change* it was a task he didn't wish to face.

Straightening, he lowered his hand, manufactured a long-suffering but patient sigh. "Em—" He broke off, then cocked a brow at her. "Is that your real name?"

She considered him, then nodded.

"Beauregard?"

She lifted her chin. "That's my real name, too."

It just wasn't her surname. Em felt as if she'd stepped from one reality into a completely different one. Marriage? She'd been mentally revisiting their encounters, all he'd said, why she'd thought . . . and had to concede that yes, he might have meant marriage all along, *but . . .*

More sure of herself, she folded her arms—the stance made her feel safer—and frowned more definitely at him. "You never actually said. If you'd uttered the word, or any of the associated ones, I would have known."

He looked a little peeved at her tone. "Yes, well . . ." He held her gaze, then grimaced. "I knew it was marriage I wanted from the first, *but . . .* I didn't accept that conclusion, not straightaway. That was what was in my mind from the first, but I didn't want to admit it, not in words to you, or even to me. It wasn't until a week ago that I realized there was no point fighting it, or pretending my intentions were anything else."

He moved to stand directly before her, his dark gaze trained on her face. "But I intend to marry you and that was always my aim." His jaw tightened again. "And—"

"And it was wrong of me, knowing you're an honorable gentleman, to imagine you intended anything else." She nodded, accepting the rebuke and his justifiable anger. "*But . . .*" She returned briefly to her recollections of their earlier encounters, then refocused on him. "While I admit I encouraged you, you *did* seduce me."

"Only because I intend to marry you." He reached out and caught first one wrist, then the other, and drew her folded arms apart and down. "I thought perhaps you needed a little help in making up your mind, and as we are going to marry, there's no harm in indulging ahead of the wedding bells, as it were."

She narrowed her eyes as he released her wrists, reached for her waist, and drew her to him. "So this—*this*"—she felt her pulse leap at his touch, his nearness, the promise of it, could sense his hunger through his hands—"is by way of persuasion?"

He lowered his lips to hers. "Among other things."

She wasn't sure—not of anything to do with him, much less them—but the kiss drew her in; he parted her lips and his tongue found hers, tempted . . . and she was following again, eager again to tread the path to pleasure hand in hand with him.

In that moment, it truly seemed that simple; there was him, there was her, and between them blazed a flame that never seemed to completely wane. It flared at just a touch, just one long, evocative caress, his open hand sweeping from the hollow of her throat, down over her breast, pausing there to capture, to weigh, to claim, then tracing lower, to her belly, lightly testing its tautness before pressing lower, to the juncture of her thighs and lightly, blatantly, possessively cupping her there.

And she was lost, cast adrift on a swirling, heated sea of desire—hers and his. Passion rose and whipped her on; yearning and need burgeoned in its wake, and compelled.

Clothes drifted to the floor, hers and his; who unbuttoned this, who tugged off that was immaterial; it was suddenly important to be skin to skin, an urgency that afflicted him as much as her. Then they were naked, and hands grasped, fingers gripped, clung; she pressed closer still, as if in doing so she could merge their bodies—succeeded in firing his passion to new heights.

They were standing naked in the middle of her room, the moonlight streaming in laying cool, silvery light over their heated bodies. He broke the kiss, on a muttered oath stepped back, grasped her hips, and lifted her.

"Wrap your legs about my waist."

The words came in a deep growl. She only just made out their meaning—instantly, without question, complied.

And he brought her down over his straining erection, drew her down so she was impaled.

In the silvery light she closed her eyes, let her head fall back on a moan. Felt him pull her relentlessly down, press inexorably deeper—of her own accord, she greedily sank lower, still lower, encasing him in her body, taking him in, hungry for the sensation of fullness, for that moment of feeling complete.

Wanting him. Needing him.

Loving the feel of him at her core.

She clasped him tightly, and for one second heard "mine, all mine" echo in her head—this time knew from the purring tone that it was her reckless Colyton self who spoke so smugly.

But then the fire was upon them; it rose up, flared high, and roared. Raced through them, through their veins, flashed down their nerves, spread under their skins, and she didn't have time to wonder or think.

Could only lock her lips on his, lock her arms about his shoulders, and cling as she welcomed the steady, evocative plundering of his tongue that echoed and emphasized his repetitive possession of her body, the indescribably erotic thrust and retreat of his erection into her slick sheath.

Steady and relentless, he filled her, and all she could do was glory. His hands were wrapped about her hips; she couldn't move other than at his direction. Could only gasp, cling, and moan as he moved her upon him, over him, so he could penetrate her more deeply, then more shallowly, causing an ebb and flow in the tide of their passions, slowing the inevitable journey to that moment when her nerves and senses would be overwhelmed . . .

Jonas strove, battled, fought to hold her back, to rein in the inner beast that wanted simply to devour. He'd already taken her sensual measure, hence, given his fell intention to persuade her, he hadn't availed himself of her bed.

She liked . . . adventure. New things, novel positions, more intense and erotic stimuli, fresh fields to explore—and he was perfectly prepared to cater to her tastes. From their first kiss, he'd sensed—known and recognized at some level—that streak of wildness, of reckless, open-hearted courage, the ability—even tendency—to abandon herself wholeheartedly, without reservation, to new experience.

In her case, effective persuasion lay in inventiveness, in having something new and novel with which to entice her. Showing her a new landscape she could explore with him and only him, and coloring it vividly, was the most certain path to realizing his aim.

He didn't have to think to comprehend all that; the knowledge was at his mental fingertips, instinctive and complete.

So he knew as he finally, *finally* let them scale the last steps to the inevitable peak, that the road he'd chosen was right. That possessing her physically, completely and absolutely, was also the way to making her his.

His wife, his lover—his to hold, to possess, to protect.

As she climaxed in his arms, and with a roar he stifled in the curve of her throat he allowed himself to let go—to thrust deep into her welcoming heat and fill her with his seed—having a woman, possessing a woman, had never felt so right.

So deeply and completely satisfying.

So deeply and completely making him whole.

14

Persuasion, Em realized, could come in many forms. Jonas apparently considered ecstasy to be a potent persuader; she wasn't sure she wanted to disagree.

Certainly the three times he'd brought her to gasping, senses-reeling delight over the previous night suggested he was willing to invest considerable energy in convincing her to accept his suit.

To be his wife.

As she settled into what had become her morning routine—catching up with the twins, Issy, and Henry over breakfast, then doing a round of the inn, chatting with every member of staff before retreating to her office to deal with the orders and accounts—she was still trying to bend her mind around his declaration. To accept it, and decide how she felt.

Finally finding herself in her office chair, the order ledger open on the desk before her—with no orders entered—she humphed, gave up the pretense of focusing on work, closed the book, and gave herself over to considering the matter that currently filled her mind.

The prospect of marrying Jonas Tallent.

Most ladies in her position would, she suspected, be dancing with joy, happiness, and even gratitude at such a chance. She, however, felt . . . unsure.

Uncertain over how she felt. Even less certain of how she *should* feel.

It wasn't that she doubted him, either his direction or his determination; last night had amply demonstrated both—three times. He was resolutely definite about marrying her.

She didn't know if she wanted to—or should—marry him.

Her difficulty—her uncharacteristic uncertainty—stemmed from one simple fact: She'd never expected to marry.

Never thought of it, except to shrug the notion aside as impractical. She'd neither dreamed nor imagined that she might, someday, walk up any aisle, not after her father's death had left her in charge of her siblings.

So there'd never been a moment when she'd consciously laid aside marriage—acknowledged she'd wanted it and made a deliberate sacrifice. Marriage had never seemed a viable option, so had never featured in her plans—not through all the years she'd spent as her uncle's glorified housekeeper, and following their escape from his house, she'd assumed marriage for her had grown even less likely—what gentleman would marry an innkeeper?

More, she was twenty-five. Definitely on the shelf, although perhaps not for long enough to have gathered dust.

Yet now, against the odds and so very much against her expectations, Jonas wanted to marry her.

She frowned at the closed order book. "What does a sane and sensible woman look for in marriage? What does she look for in a husband?"

The muttered questions illustrated her utter lack of knowledge on the subject. And despite managing to formulate those questions, answers weren't spontaneously arising in her brain.

"Miss?"

She looked up to see Hilda standing in the doorway, wiping her hands on her apron. "Yes?"

"If you've a moment, miss, could you come and taste

these pasties? I think the crust's light enough, but I'd value your opinion."

"Of course." She pushed back her chair and rose. She was perfectly sure Hilda's pasties would be scrumptious, but knew the older woman appreciated her verdict.

True enough, the pasties were mouthwateringly delicious. She made a face signifying extreme pleasure. "They're superb, Hilda. Yet another excellent addition to our menu."

"These are every bit as good as your pies," Issy concurred. She and the twins had taken a break from lessons, lured irresistibly by the baking smells. They'd quartered a pasty between the four sisters. Em saw Issy licking her fingers delicately; the twins were already looking around for more.

She looked at Hilda. "How many of these can you have ready by lunchtime?"

"I've twenty ready to go. We could manage maybe another twenty before the regulars arrive."

Regulars. The word was music to any innkeeper's ears. The taste of the pasty still tantalizing her taste buds, Em nodded. "Yes—let's make that our main offering for lunch in the tap today. Those who miss out will make sure they come next time we serve them."

"Miss?" Edgar put his head around the kitchen door. "The Martins, the couple that's staying, would like a word with you."

"Yes, of course." Turning, she bustled into the dining area, wondering whether the Martins had found anything amiss. Seeing them by the end of the bar counter, she plastered on a smile and swept up. "Mr. and Mrs. Martin, I do hope you've enjoyed your stay with us."

"Oh, yes, dear!" Mrs. Martin enthused. "It's been wonderfully comfortable—and the food!" She shared a quick glance with her husband, then confided, "We wondered if we might stay for a few days more. Is that possible?"

Delighted, Em whisked behind the counter and picked up the register. "I believe that can be arranged."

As she wrote the Martins in for two more days, Mr. Martin confessed the Red Bells was the first village inn at which they'd spent more than one night. "We usually only stay multiple nights in the major towns, but there's just something soothing about this village. We were thinking of spending a day in Seaton—I understand the inn has a gig we can hire?"

Em assured them the inn could meet their requirements, and thanked heaven for John Ostler, who had kept the inn's carriages in good condition and would know from whom to hire a horse. "I'll speak with our stableman right away," she told the Martins. "When would you like the gig?"

After ferrying the request to John Ostler, she returned indoors, debating the options of hiring the occasional hack or carriage horse versus buying animals that ate and required care regardless of whether they were used or not.

Glancing out at the tap—more reflex than intention as she headed for her office—she saw Lucifer chatting with Thompson, who as well as being the blacksmith was also the local farrier. She paused, hesitated, then went out to ask their opinion on the best way to secure the use of horses for the inn.

After that, her morning went in a whirl of checking, arranging, consulting, and ordering, supervising the cleaning of the rooms—true to his calling, Mr. Dobson had moved on, as had the other overnight guest, yet they still had two rooms occupied—and with luck Mr. Dobson would spread the word; Edgar mentioned he'd been highly complimentary before he'd left.

Mr. Hadley seemed to be settling in; she noticed him propped at the bar, relaxed and easy, talking to Edgar, then later, when the regulars started arriving for their midmorning snacks, she saw him elbow to elbow with Oscar, no doubt swapping tales of life on the waves.

Despite her distraction, marriage—the institution— hovered at the edge of her mind. Pausing in the kitchen and finding Hilda taking a well-earned breather now that her pasties were in the ovens, Em poured herself a cup of tea and sat alongside the older woman at the deal table.

After sipping companionably for a minute, Em murmured, "You've been married a long time, haven't you, Hilda?"

Hilda snorted, but her lips lifted lightly. "Aye—decades. And some mornings it feels like it, let me tell you. Then again"—she shrugged philosophically—"at others it seems like just yesterday we was walking out."

"If you had to say what was most important about marriage—not your husband, but the state itself—what would you say?"

Hilda slanted her a curious look, but when she said nothing more, duly ruminated, sipped, then offered, "Being settled. Having a home, knowing where you fit in the scheme of things." Lowering her cup, she paused, then lips firming, nodded. "Aye—that's it. When you're married, you know who you are."

Em raised her brows. "I hadn't thought of it like that." Sipping, she considered the point, then drained her cup. "Thank you." With a nod to Hilda, she rose, set her cup in the scullery, then headed once more for her office.

Who you are, Hilda had said, but as she settled in her chair and prepared to concentrate on the day's orders, Em rather suspected Hilda had meant *what* you are. Marriage, whether within the gentry or among farmers, gave a woman a certain status, a position within and recognized by society.

But was that—achieving that—sufficient reason to marry? Specifically for her to marry? As innkeeper—albeit like no other innkeeper ever known—she was perfectly satisfied with her role, her position within the village. She didn't feel any lack in that regard, the respect the locals gave her.

She couldn't see that she needed marriage to define either who or what she was.

No help there; Jonas hadn't suggested she needed to marry him for any such reason. Indeed, he hadn't made any case for marriage at all, simply stated he meant to marry her; his declaration hadn't even been a proposal. He hadn't asked, solicited, in any way offered for her hand. He'd stated his intention—as if her eventual acceptance was assumed, if not quite taken for granted.

The order ledger still closed before her, narrow-eyed she stared unseeing across the room—and wondered whether she shouldn't just leave the subject hanging until he mentioned it again, and then make him propose properly, and as part of that, state his reasons for marriage.

She would certainly push him to argue his case, but . . . she'd already had ample evidence of his reticence on that subject—how long had it been before he'd actually uttered the word "marriage"? Indeed, he'd told her himself he'd been reluctant to acknowledge the idea, not at first.

While he might *know* he wanted to marry her, did he know why? Why he felt that way, why marrying her from his perspective was a good idea.

Or had the idea simply taken root?

She had a suspicion the latter would be the case. Regardless, she couldn't rely on his view of marriage to guide her. He, after all, was the other party to that contract.

Until he made a proper offer, she didn't have to give him an answer; his not having proposed gave her time to define her stance. She suspected she'd be wise to have some inkling of her wishes before he asked formally and she found herself having to respond.

Her gaze focused on the order ledger. With a frown, she shook her head and opened the book. Defining her stance regarding marriage was not a task that could be adequately addressed squeezed in between a plethora of other activities; she would have to find some better time. "Meanwhile," she muttered, "I have an inn to run."

She knuckled down to the task in all its many and varied forms. Part of her duties, or at least those she'd assumed, was to wander through the common room often during the day, especially during mealtimes. Every one of Hilda's pasties was spoken for even before they'd started serving luncheon; Phyllida and Miss Sweet came in early, and paused to compliment her as they left.

"You've worked wonders," Phyllida assured her, smiling broadly. "Juggs will be turning in his grave."

Em returned her smile; if Phyllida hadn't been Jonas's twin she would have been tempted to ask for her opinion on marriage, on its most important elements. Then again . . . she stood in the inn's doorway watching Phyllida and Miss Sweet turn into the road, only to meet Lucifer coming down from the forge. The emotion that softened Lucifer's harsh features as he approached his wife, the answering glow in Phyllida's face, strongly suggested that Phyllida was avidly devoted to the married state.

Em could hazard a very good guess what Phyllida's response to her question would be. Love. The sort of love that existed between a man and a woman, that in popular conception was the best foundation for marriage.

The sight of the departing couple, arm in arm, dark heads bent close as they walked home with Miss Sweet fluttering along beside them, left her wondering.

Was she in love with Jonas? Did he love her?

Or was *this*—that unnamed and indefinable mix of emotions that flared between them—merely lust?

Lust, desire, and passion.

Limited though her experience was, in her opinion all three had been present—were still present—between her and Jonas. But what of love?

As she understood it, that was the most pertinent question, the question of all questions when it came to marriage.

Was love there between them, or growing between them? Was it a seed planted but yet to germinate, or had it already sprouted?

Were there degrees of love, or qualifications?

Raising a hand, she rubbed a finger in the center of her forehead, vainly trying to erase her frown. Would that she could erase her ignorance as well. As she couldn't, she'd have to seek education and wisdom on love and marriage from those who knew.

"Excuse me, miss."

She jumped, realized she was blocking the inn door. "Yes, of course." She stepped aside, saw it was Mr. Scroggs from along the lane waiting to exit. She smiled. "Did you enjoy your pasty?"

"Delicious, it was." Hat in his hands, Scroggs bobbed his head. "Compliments to Hilda. The missus and me'll be back this evening—the missus says she'd rather eat Hilda's cooking than her own."

Em laughed. "We'll save places for you, and look forward to serving you both."

Scroggs bobbed his head again and left, crossing the inn's narrow front yard to head up the lane to his cottage.

Turning to go inside, Em noticed a familiar back, shoulders hunched, at the last of the tables and benches set along the front of the inn.

Harold, still lurking. He was deep in discussion with someone; she shifted, peered around him, and saw Hadley seated across the table. The artist was listening, occasionally nodding; Harold was doing most of the talking.

She retreated into the inn before Hadley noticed her and alerted Harold. Edgar had mentioned that Hadley had gone up to scout out his best prospects in the church. He must have returned and inadvertently lunched with Harold, who, she had to admit, could be pleasant enough when he wished.

She circled through what was fast becoming known as the "Ladies' Tap," the front half of the common room opposite the tap itself. The luncheon rush, which had started early because of the allure of Hilda's pasties, was dying down. She spied Lady Fortemain at the table in the window that was already designated as "her ladyship's." She'd just finished delicately demolishing a pasty; laying down her cutlery, she pushed the plate away, picked up her teacup, and sipped.

Smiling, Em made her way to the table; there were no others close enough to overhear a quiet conversation.

Lady Fortemain saw her and smiled. "Emily, dear. Dare I hope you have time to pass a few minutes with an old lady?"

"You're not that old," Em dutifully responded, slipping into the chair opposite her ladyship.

They exchanged views on the pasties, and on the various improvements to the inn, before Em drew in a breath and said, "Issy and I were discussing our futures, and as you know, our mother died long ago. I wondered if you had any advice to offer regarding what a gentlewoman should look for in her marriage."

Lady Fortemain beamed. She laid a hand on Em's wrist. "My dear, I'm honored to have you ask. And indeed"— her ladyship re-formed her features into a most serious expression—"that's a subject all young ladies would do well to explore at length before making any choice."

She sat back, clearly formulating her advice. Em waited patiently.

"If I had to define what is most important to look for in marriage, I would say it's a combination of two elements, which are themselves linked in a way." Lady Fortemain met Em's eyes earnestly and lowered her voice. "It's the man, my dear—marriage is all about the man. You want him to be devoted to you, utterly devoted beyond question, and he must have an adequate standing—no one respects a lady who marries beneath her—and suitable wealth, although wealth is relative, of course."

Em nodded.

Her ladyship rolled on, one finger raised for emphasis. "*And* you need a gentleman who knows what is due to his position—one who pays attention to the little things that underpin that position, and therefore that of his wife. For instance, although it pains me to say it, Cedric has grown a great deal too lax and easy in his ways, too ready to rub shoulders with his workers, which in my view does his position no good at all. Pommeroy, on the other hand . . ." Lady Fortemain smiled brightly into Em's eyes. "Suffice to say, my dear, that Pommeroy will make some young lady an *excellent* husband."

Em registered the sudden intentness in Lady Fortemain's eyes; she managed not to let her own flare in alarm. "Yes." She nodded decisively. "I daresay he will. It's a pity there are so few young ladies hereabouts. But I daresay he intends to seek a wife in London—one with the polish and connections he deserves."

Her last comment gave her ladyship pause. She pursed her lips. "I hadn't thought of matters quite like that, but . . ." Abruptly she shook her head; looking up, she smiled— fondly—again at Em. "You might well be right, my dear, *but*—"

"Pray excuse me, ma'am—I believe I'm needed urgently." Gently detaching her ladyship's clawlike grip on her wrist, smiling charmingly, Em rose, bobbed a curtsy, and managed to leave Lady Fortemain still smiling.

She'd been right in thinking someone was waiting in the hall outside her office. Dulcie, one of the laundry maids, was bobbing up and down in the shadows; when she saw Em coming, she jigged even faster. "Miss, come quick! One of the twins—Bea, I think it is—has gone and got her hair tangled in the mangle. We turned away for just a minute, and next thing we knew—"

"She was trying to straighten her hair." Em nodded briskly, more relieved than concerned; Bea had tried that trick before. "I'll come and get her out."

The next quiet moment Em got to consider marriage and the insights she'd thus far gained was when she sat down alone to a late luncheon. Issy and the twins—Bea now freed, no worse for wear—had retired upstairs to continue their lessons; although they still grumbled and groaned, Issy reported they were progressing with their arithmetic and their reading and writing. Ladylike skills such as drawing and playing the pianoforte were more difficult; the twins were at the tomboy stage; such occupations didn't appeal.

As both Em and Issy could sympathize, neither was strident in forcing those issues. Colytons as a whole were a more adventurous breed, ergo not well suited to sitting at home embroidering.

Henry was with Filing; Hilda and her girls had cleared the kitchen and retired for a well-earned rest until it was time to prepare dinner. Edgar was cleaning his bar and nattering to a few locals in the tap. For once, Em actually had time and space to herself.

She quietly munched her way through the pasty Hilda had saved for her while weighing Hilda's and Lady Fortemain's opinions, contrasting them with what she imagined Phyllida's response would be, metaphorically trying the notions on, seeing how they fit.

While she could understand Hilda's view, and acknowledged Lady Fortemain's position as wise, it was Phyllida's imagined attitude—that love was all—that resonated best with Em's Colyton soul.

She had no doubt whatever that her forebears were the sort who would count the world well lost for love. And she knew herself too well to imagine she could go against her inherited grain; while she might pretend otherwise for a short time, ultimately her innate tendencies would out. Like all the Colytons, she was a Colyton through and through, and if love was the mast to which her family habitually nailed its flag, then she, too, would have to embrace that nebulous but powerful emotion.

She would have to learn of it, enough to recognize it, have to learn to understand it, nurture it, protect it—and all the rest, whatever that rest was.

Being a Colyton, her correct response to Jonas's intentions would be governed by love—by whether she loved him and he loved her.

But—as always there was a "but"—he didn't, as yet, even know who she truly was. She couldn't in all fairness expect him to love—to admit to loving—a lady whose family name he didn't know.

More, she herself didn't know, at this point, what her status truly was—was she nearly penniless, the small portion inherited from her father frittered away in pursuit of the Colyton treasure?

Once they found the treasure, she would know precisely where she stood . . .

The more that thought revolved in her mind—the more the fact that she was dealing with Jonas in part under false pretenses abraded and irked—the greater and more urgent grew the need to make a serious effort to locate the treasure.

Once that was done—once the treasure was found, and she and her siblings were financially secure and could reclaim their true name and station—then all else, all the pretenses between herself and Jonas—and those equally pertinent between Issy and Filing—would be resolved.

And *then* she would be able to properly assess whether Jonas loved her and she loved him, and whether she should accept his proposal and marry him.

"I have to find that damned treasure." There was no one around to hear her muttered words as she stood and cleared away her plate.

Standing at the scullery sink, she looked out of the window—at the hot, drowsy afternoon outside. It was an unseasonably warm day, a sleepy summer afternoon in October.

The Grange remained the most likely resting place of her family's treasure. She'd often wondered why it had been buried somewhere other than at Colyton Manor, but the rhyme seemed fairly clear on that point. Of the houses in the immediate area, the Grange fitted the description of "the house of the highest" best; indeed, there seemed no other house it could be.

She brought up a vision of the Grange in her mind. Mentally walked around it, turning over in her mind ways and means, and possible stories, to gain access to its cellar in sufficient privacy and for long enough to mount a meaningful search.

It lies in a box made for the purpose—one only a Colyton would open.

Thus went the last line of the rhyme. Presumably when she saw whatever receptacle or hiding place the treasure was concealed in, she would know. She couldn't imagine what the box referred to might be; she'd long ago given up trying. She would know it when she saw it; she had to believe that.

But first she had to get into the Grange cellar. The door to the cellar opened from the main kitchen; if she went in that way, she'd need a convincing excuse that would lead Mortimer to leave her down there alone for an hour or so.

No adequate story occurred to her, but thinking of Mortimer brought to mind something else he'd mentioned . . .

She refocused on the yard beyond the window, and the section of wood visible beyond. It was so warm, the Grange's staff would as far as possible remain indoors; it was unlikely anyone would be about to notice someone searching the outbuildings—like the buttery, which according to Mortimer was linked by an underground tunnel to the cellar.

All was quiet at the inn.

She escaped with only a quick word to Edgar that she was taking a walk and would return in a few hours. She did walk, briskly, along the path through the wood—toward the rear of the Grange.

The wood ended at the edge of the wide clearing in which the Grange and its associated buildings stood. She halted just within the treeline; from the shadows, she scanned the rear yard of the old house. All was, as she'd predicted, quiet and still, the heat hanging oppressively heavy over all.

The path led on, through the kitchen garden to the back door. To her right, beyond the kitchen garden, lay the stables. She looked, strained her ears, but it was difficult to tell if there were stableboys or grooms somewhere in the largish structure.

To her left, abutting the house, lay a long, low building that looked like the washhouse. Further out from the house, closer to where she stood, another smaller square building sat, sharing one stone wall with the washhouse, but with its own wooden door and wooden shutters secured over two windows, one set into the stone on either side of the door.

The small square building had to be the buttery.

To reach its door, she could hug the treeline for a little way, but the last stretch was over open ground; she would be clearly visible from the house.

She weighed the risk for all of a second before her Colyton self dismissed it as inconsequential; she'd come prepared to take risks in pursuit of the treasure.

Grateful that, by pure chance, she'd that morning donned a forest green gown, she drew breath, then boldly stepped out—as if she knew exactly where she was going and had every reason to be there; walking briskly, she skirted the edge of the clearing, then cut across the last open stretch. Reaching the buttery, she grasped the wooden latch, lifted it—and literally sent up a prayer of thanks when it smoothly rose. Pushing open the door, she whisked inside. One glance was enough to assure her there was no maid or footman tapping any butts; she quickly and silently shut the door, then waited for her eyes to adjust to the dimness.

The shutters allowed a little light to seep in, enough to see, but the thick stone walls kept the area within cool; after the warmth outside, she shivered and rubbed her arms.

Gradually her senses adjusted. She took stock of the room, of the butts of ale and various foodstuffs deemed better stored there than in the chillier, damp cold and absolute dark of the cellars. The area was well organized, with orderly rows of different types of staples stacked on the floor perpendicular to the door. Shelves circled the walls, with goods in sacks sitting beneath on the flagstone floor.

There was no wall likely to house any tunnel, and no door other than the one through which she'd entered. Given the buttery floor was aboveground, and the house cellar was definitely below, then the tunnel between presumably ran below the floor, suggesting a trapdoor.

She paused to plan her search, then set out, carefully walking the aisles between the rows of stacked goods, studying the old flagstones, paying particular attention to the mortar between. Mortimer hadn't suggested the tunnels to the cellar were still in use; she doubted they would be, but even if they were, they would most likely be used in winter, when a heavy snowfall made reaching the buttery from the kitchen difficult.

It was well into autumn, so it was possible the trapdoor hadn't been opened for nine or so months. Regardless, there should be some wear on the flagstones around it, some irregularity or mark made through long-term use.

If there was, she couldn't see it. Reaching her original position by the door, she blew out a breath, then, refusing to be disheartened just because it hadn't been easy, she went to the beginning of the first row and started to shift the goods so she could examine the floor beneath them.

She was bent over a sack of meal, with one finger tracing a gouge in a flagstone, when the buttery door opened.

Startled, she straightened and spun around—so fast she swayed and had to flail to keep from falling backward over several sacks.

Regaining her balance, her heart pounding, she found herself looking into Jonas's dark eyes. Amusement glinted in their depths; his lips weren't straight as he stepped over the threshold and closed the door.

Eyeing her, no more than a yard away in the small, cramped space, he leaned back against the door and arched a brow. "What are you searching for?"

"Ah . . ." She blinked, tried to think—of some tale he might believe. "I . . . ah . . ." She dragged in a breath and lifted her chin. "As you know I'm interested in old houses, and Mortimer mentioned there were tunnels connecting your stables and buttery to the cellar. I was passing"—she glanced around at the sacks she'd disarranged—"and couldn't resist taking a peek to see what sort of tunnels they were, what sort of doors." She shrugged and met his gaze. "That sort of thing."

She'd always heard that when lying, it was best to stick as close as possible to the truth. Fixing him with an innocently inquiring gaze, she asked, "So . . . can you show me the tunnel?" She didn't need to fabricate eagerness; if he showed her, she could use the tunnel to search the cellar at night.

He held her gaze for a long moment before pushing away from the door. "The tunnels collapsed long ago. They've been filled in for as long as I, or even my father, remember." Halting before her, he looked down into her eyes. "Why do you want to find the tunnels?"

"Distraction." That was what she needed now—to distract him. Raising her hand to his lean cheek, she smiled. "It's a quiet afternoon at the inn, a sleepy time with few people about." Letting her gaze lower to his mouth, she stretched up and brushed her lips over his. "I was bored, so I thought to come here to seek excitement."

All true enough.

Her senses shivered, quivered, as she felt his hands slide around her waist, spanning, then gripping, holding her before him. She raised her gaze to his eyes; his dark gaze searched, then, slowly, he bent his head.

She stretched up the last inch and kissed him, then gave him her mouth as he kissed her.

The result, the conflagration, was instantaneous, as if they'd stepped off some platform directly into a furnace of growing, ravenous heat. A heat that sparked, flared, then roared, that sent fire racing down their veins to burn beneath their skins, to make them hungry, make them yearn, make them want.

To reduce them to some primitive state where they suddenly simply had to find surcease, to come together and quench the heat, to plunge into the flames and be consumed.

His hands were on her aching breasts, kneading, possessing; through the fine cotton of the simple round gown his fingers found her nipples and wickedly tweaked. She gasped; her head spun, even as she wrestled with the buttons of his jacket.

He broke from the kiss, shrugged out of the jacket, then swept her into his arms, hard against him; his lips recaptured hers in a searing kiss—and the flames raced hungrily, greedily on.

Down every vein, scorching every nerve.

Reducing inhibitions to ash.

Lifting his head, as breathless as she, his dark eyes wild and burning, he glanced swiftly around, then scooped her up in his arms, swung around—and tumbled her onto a pile of stacked sacks so she sprawled on her back, her skirts rucked up above her knees.

Before she could react and push her hems down, instinctively close her thighs, he stepped between, tossed her skirts higher, up to her waist, set his hands on her knees and spread them even more widely.

His gaze locked on hers, his own filled with dark fires, with emotions both powerful and raw, he paused . . . a mere heartbeat of time that seemed to stretch, when she knew he was waiting, if not precisely for permission, then for some hint she actively wanted this, him—more.

Eyes locked on his, she licked her lips and shifted restlessly, an evocative—patently inciting—movement of her hips.

The hiatus holding him shattered, splintered; all restraint fell away.

The planes of his face grew harder, sharper edged, hewn granite as he looked down at the delicate flesh between her thighs, fully revealed to him courtesy of her sprawl. Then he bent and set his lips to her softness.

She shrieked at the first contact—just as she had last night. Knuckles pressed to her lips, she fought valiantly to stifle the impossible-to-suppress sounds he wrung from her, then his lips moved on her, his tongue thrust in and she moaned.

He licked, supped, suckled, and savored; even more artfully than he had the previous night, he steadily drove her up the long rise to a shattering, breath-stealing, senses-imploding climax; she had to clamp her hand over her mouth to mute her scream.

As she gasped, panted, her heart still racing, the furnace inside her still molten, still empty and waiting, he straightened, looked down on her, then he smiled.

Wickedly. Dangerously.

To her surprise, he tugged down her skirts, then gripped her hips and, lifting her, flipped her over onto her stomach, drawing her hips back so her legs dangled down the front of the sacks; the pile was so high her toes didn't reach the ground.

Curious, she struggled up onto her elbows.

Just as he lifted the back of her skirts, tossing them high, over her waist.

Exposing her bottom.

The cool air of the buttery washed over her already heated skin.

She caught her breath, started to turn her head.

Just as his palm touched her fevered curves.

She froze, then sucked in a breath, held it. Bit her lip against a moan as his hand boldly cruised, fingertips tracing every line, possessing every inch of skin, sending damp heat flushing hotly beneath. Then his hand slid down, around; beneath the curve of her bottom, between her thighs, his fingers pressed into her slick heat and probed.

The moan escaped, a shivery sound; she pressed back

against his hand, wanting more, wantonly demanding. Begging for deeper, more satisfying penetration.

She was scalding hot, so ready and willing, Jonas could barely think as with his other hand he undid the buttons at his waist. His erection sprang free, fully engorged; he wasted no time positioning the empurpled head at her entrance, then with one solid thrust, he filled her.

Felt her clamp tight about him, walls closing in eager welcome to hotly embrace him.

Felt more than heard her gasp, sensed in the sound her delighted shock.

He hadn't entered her from behind before, hadn't taken her like this, with the ripe globes of her bottom bare before him, delectable and beyond arousing.

She shifted her hips experimentally in a slow, rolling motion, caressing the length of his rigid shaft, making his eyes all but cross with lust. Closing them, he withdrew and thrust in again, deeper this time, letting her feel his strength, and her vulnerability, her relative helplessness.

Not that she seemed at all bothered; the little gasp she uttered was all feminine excitement, fascination, and enthrallment. Again she shifted her hips, more blatantly urging him on. Accepting her invitation, he withdrew and thrust yet more forcefully into the scalding haven of her sheath, then settled to a measured, relentless rhythm—one that quickly escalated beyond his control.

Braced on her forearms and elbows she pushed back, forcing him deeper, rolling her hips with each long thrust, rocking as he filled her, working her sheath over him until he felt the tension in her coil, tighten . . . her head came up, he thrust strongly in and she shattered.

The contractions of her sheath pulled him in, on, milked him greedily until he couldn't hold back. With a smothered roar, he pumped his seed deep inside her, then collapsed forward, arms braced to keep from crushing her.

Head bowed, lungs sawing, he tried to take in, to absorb

every sensation. To drink in the wonder of her body slumped so illicitly pleasured beneath his. To let the feel of her bare bottom pressed to his groin while he was buried so deeply inside her imprint on his memory—one memory he intended to reexperience frequently.

His arms wouldn't hold him; slowly he let himself down to his elbows. She humphed, turned. He quickly disengaged. The movement threw him off balance; trying to right himself he leaned too heavily on the sacks and they started to slide . . .

She giggled. Continued to snicker, then to laugh as, cursing, he tumbled with the sacks.

He pulled her down with him. She landed atop him, now helplessly giggling. He couldn't help but smile, then laugh, too.

Lying back on the sacks, he gathered her to him, settled her on his chest.

Just lay there and savored the moment, with the dim warmth of the buttery all about them, the musky scent of their joining another aroma among many, although none were as sweet as her, lavender and roses and some other fragrance he couldn't define.

She lay in his arms, quiescent, sated. Undemanding. Accepting.

After a moment, staring up at the ceiling, he asked, "What are you searching for? Is it in the cellar?"

She stilled, but somewhat to his surprise, she didn't tense. So he waited.

Em knew why they'd elected to keep their quest for the treasure a secret; they'd assumed the village would be populated by strangers—by people who might pose potential threats, who might want the treasure for themselves.

That had been their vision before they'd reached Colyton. Now . . . now they knew the people, had been accepted by them. The villagers of Colyton, high and low, were a close-knit group—as close as an extended family. And her family had been embraced and taken in, accorded a place in the larger whole. Was there any longer a need for absolute secrecy?

It was a matter of trust, and she'd come to trust in the good of the villagers of Colyton. As for Jonas . . . here she was, lying in his arms, having taken him into her body, having trusted him physically, and to some extent emotionally as well.

She already trusted him. She already knew he was an honorable man.

Regardless of whether she married him or not, he would help her, and he posed no threat to her or her family—of that she was absolutely sure.

She drew in a long, deep breath. Where to start?

"I told you my name is Emily Beauregard. My full name is Emily Ann Beauregard Colyton." His body started beneath hers; before he could interrupt, she went on, "My great-grandfather was the last Colyton to live in the village. My grandfather and father—"

Briefly, succinctly, she outlined her family's history; the story of the treasure held him in the same fascinated silence as it habitually held the twins. She kept nothing back; there seemed little point. Her native caution was perfectly sure she had nothing to fear from him.

She concluded with, "So that's what I've been trying to locate—the treasure box only a Colyton would open, on the lowest level of the house of the highest."

He shook his head in amazement. She'd wriggled around so she could watch his face as she made her revelations; all she'd seen in his eyes and expression was sincere, honest, intrigued astonishment.

Meeting her eyes, he grinned. "So you're really a Colyton—one of the Colytons of Colyton."

"Yes." She wasn't sure why that point so delighted him; to her it was a pertinent but less important detail. "So—will you, can you, help me find the treasure?"

He blinked. "Of course." He looked away, across the buttery in the direction of the house, then he urged her up. "No time like the present. I agree that the Grange is most likely your 'house of the highest'—my family's been the magistrates for the area for centuries, so that fits. Let's go and search the cellar."

They got to their feet, rearranged their clothes, then he opened the buttery door and they headed for the house.

Mortimer met them in the hall beside the kitchen.

"Just the person," Jonas said. "Miss Beauregard is searching for a long-lost box her family might have left here—possibly for safekeeping—centuries ago. Her information is that if it's here, the box will be in the cellar. Do you know of any such mystery box?"

Mortimer shook his head. "No, sir. But we can certainly look."

Em pushed past Jonas. "I'll help."

"We'll help." Jonas caught her hand and held her beside him as he waved Mortimer ahead of them. "Lead on."

He led them into the kitchen. Em greeted Gladys and Cook, then turned to the heavy door Mortimer had opened.

Lighting a lantern, Mortimer raised it and led the way down the stairs. Jonas waved Em ahead of him, then followed.

The cellar of the Grange was in daily use; Jonas couldn't see how any unknown box of any sort would have escaped Mortimer's, Cook's, or Gladys's notice, much less that of their numerous predecessors. But they had to look nonetheless.

Mortimer and Em went ahead, Mortimer lifting the lantern high as he explained what each room—each successive cavern separated by stone arches from the ones flanking it—now contained. They reached the far end of the cellar, which ran under most of the house.

"Right, then." Em looked around, eyes gleaming in the lantern light. "Let's start searching here, and work our way back to the stairs."

They did; it wasn't hard to be thorough because everything in the cellar was frequently rearranged, re-sorted, and tidied—as Mortimer mentioned—at least twice a year.

He glanced at Em, puzzled. "Are you sure your box was left here, miss? If it was supposed to be hidden away, then this cellar isn't a good hiding place. It's been in constant use for centuries—the kitchen doesn't have enough space, and the staff have always relied on the cellar for storage."

From the disappointment evident on Em's face, she'd come to the same conclusion. "I'm not sure, no." She blew out a frustrated breath. "As far as we know, the box was put wherever it is around 1600, maybe a bit earlier, and hasn't been moved—at least not by the family—since."

"1600? Hmm." Mortimer pursed his lips, then suggested, "The most likely place for something that old—if it's here at all—is the small rooms off the wine cellar."

They decided to be thorough and finish the search they'd started, ending back at the stairs to the kitchen with nothing to show for their efforts. Then Mortimer unlocked another sturdy door and led the way into the wine cellar. They searched it, and all the smaller caves off it, to no avail.

"It's not here." Em knew that was true. The Grange cellars were simply too tidy to imagine they'd missed anything. The only possibility . . . she glanced at Jonas. "Is there any other separate place—like another coal cellar reached from some other point—or perhaps a priest hole under some room?"

He shook his head. "There is a priest hole, but it's on the second floor, and the secret stair leads—used to lead—to one of the tunnels."

"What about the entry to the tunnels?" She looked around. "Where they join the cellar, perhaps?"

"No. Apparently when the tunnels started crumbling, they were completely cleared, then solidly filled." He walked over to one wall, tapped an unremarkable piece of stone.

"The tunnel from the stable came out here." He pointed to the edge of the stone, and then followed the line around. "If you look carefully, you can see the outline of the archway which was later filled in."

She looked, saw, then sighed. "It seems this isn't the right house after all."

Jonas studied her face, then reached out and took her hand. "Buck up. We've other houses that might fit. If I can suggest . . . ?"

She met his eyes, then raised her brows.

"I think we should go and tell Phyllida and Lucifer what we know. They'll help—and the manor library is the place to look for clues."

She hesitated, considering, then nodded. "Yes—all right. Let's go to the manor."

I simply can't believe—" Phyllida broke off, then, eyes shining, continued, "Well, of course I believe, but I'm just so *thrilled* to learn that you're Colytons. Colytons of Colyton. It's wonderful to have some of the original family return to the village."

Em mentally shook her head. Just like Jonas, Phyllida had focused on the family, not the treasure.

She and Jonas had climbed out of the Grange cellars, paused to check with Gladys and Cook, neither of whom knew of any mysterious box anywhere in their domains, then they'd set off for the manor via the path through the wood. They'd found Lucifer and Phyllida both at home. Leaving Aidan and Evan with Miss Sweet, at Jonas's suggestion they'd repaired to the drawing room; with the door shut, Em had retold her story.

To her relief, Lucifer seemed more inclined to concentrate on the real issue. "So the treasure's not at the Grange—and I have to admit I've never heard the phrase 'house of the highest' applied to either the Grange or the manor—but are you sure it isn't here? Even though we don't have, and as far as I know have never had, cellars, but a sprawl of out-buildings instead?"

Em grimaced. "This was the family home—the rhyme seems expressly designed to point to some other place."

Jonas nodded. "If the treasure were here, the rhyme would probably not exist—there'd be no need for it, certainly no need to specify a house."

Lucifer nodded. "True enough. So it's not the Grange, not the manor, and you've already established it's not Ballyclose because of its age. So what does that leave?"

A question no one could answer.

Lucifer leaned forward, his harshly handsome face serious, his expression focused. "Correct me if I'm wrong, but we need a house that was here in the 1500s, exactly when you're not sure, and by 1600 it was known as 'the house of the highest'—presumably meaning the house of the person with the highest standing in the area or district at the time."

"There've never been any princely retreats or royal residences of any sort in this region." Phyllida glanced at Lucifer. "I remember checking long ago, when I was a young girl."

"Kings and princes being the sort of thing girls dream about." Jonas pulled a face at his sister, who merely smiled back superiorly.

Lucifer shook his head. "I keep thinking of the way that phrase 'house of the highest' is couched in the rhyme. In 1600, this would have been a very small, relatively isolated community. The house of the highest—the rhyme uses that phrase as if it should be obvious which house is being referred to, suggesting it *was* obvious to the locals in 1600."

They were silent as they considered that point, then Phyllida looked at Em. "You've already looked through a handful of our books and found no reference to this mystery house. Let's go through the others." She glanced at Lucifer and Jonas. "It won't take long with four of us, not if we concentrate on the time around 1600."

The other three exchanged glances, then all nodded. Rising, Lucifer led the way into the library.

Over the next hour, they scoured the collection, finding a number of travel diaries that described Colyton at that time, and two other village descriptions from the early sixteen hundreds, but none mentioned any large houses other than the Grange and the manor, nor made any reference to any "house of the highest."

"Nothing." Em sighed. She'd hoped . . . Swallowing her disappointment, she glanced at Jonas. "What now?" She looked at Phyllida and Lucifer. "Any suggestions?"

Lucifer seemed as stumped as she and Jonas, but after a moment Phyllida, head tilted as she thought, raised her brows, then she met Em's eyes. "If I were you, I'd let your family's real name become known. It'll gain you more support from the locals—and on the back of that, I'd ask around the village, especially among the older folk, to see if anyone has ever heard the phrase 'the house of the highest.' Chances are it'll mean something to someone. Others will have stories handed down through their families—we might find someone who knows of the place in some other context."

Jonas nodded; he looked at Em. "I'll second that suggestion. Let people know who you really are."

Em frowned. "What excuse would I give for initially concealing our identity?"

"That's easy," Phyllida said. "You wanted the job of innkeeper and to be accepted by the village for the people you are, not just embraced and put on a pedestal because of the name you bear."

Em raised her brows, considering.

Lucifer nodded. "That's eccentric perhaps, but not inconceivable."

She glanced at Jonas, who nodded, too. She drew in a breath. "All right. We'll let it be known that we're Colytons." She frowned again. "How long do you think it will take for word to spread?"

Phyllida smiled. "We can help with that." Crossing to Em, she drew her to her feet, wound her arm in hers, and turned them both to the door. "Let's leave these gentlemen racking their brains, while you and I have a little chat with Sweetie."

15

My dear, I couldn't be more *delighted*!" Lady Fortemain sat back, eyes wide. "To think you, and your dear sisters and brother, too, are Colytons. Well!"

"Yes, well . . ." Em glanced at Jonas, who was smiling an I-told-you-so smile. They'd let Sweetie loose in the common room all the previous evening; that morning Jonas had called with his curricle, offering to take Em around the neighborhood to speak with the older folk. Lady Fortemain at Ballyclose Manor had been first on Em's list, and, of course, she'd heard their news.

"As I mentioned," Em persevered, hoping to avoid any lengthy recounting of the family's recent history, "we're trying to identify which house in the neighborhood used to be referred to as 'the house of the highest' many years ago. Centuries ago, in fact, so we know it isn't Ballyclose Manor. Have you ever heard the phrase?"

"'The house of the highest?'" Tapping one finger to her lips, Lady Fortemain frowned in concentration. A movement in the hallway caught her eye. "Oh, Jocasta! You must come in and hear this news!"

Jocasta, also Lady Fortemain, wife of her ladyship's older son, Cedric, appeared in the doorway. A dark-haired, dark-eyed woman with a quiet, pleasant nature, she smiled at Em and Jonas and came in. "Good morning. I heard the news last night. It seems so appropriate to have you and your family back in the village, and specifically resurrecting the Red Bells."

"Thank you." Em returned her smile.

Jonas caught Jocasta's eye. "As another local from a long-time village family, Jocasta, have you ever heard the phrase 'the house of the highest'?"

Jocasta pursed her lips, but eventually shook her head. "I can't say I have—although it does sound like the sort of phrase one of the Fortemains might have used about Bally-close. Why do you want to know?"

Jonas smoothly replied, "Some house that was in the village a long time ago—long before Ballyclose was built—was referred to by one of Miss Colyton's forebears in a cryptic family rhyme, and we're trying to locate the place."

Jocasta gave a silent "Oh," then added, "I'm certain I've never heard the phrase, but you might try Mother. She has all sorts of odd tidbits like that about the village tucked away in her brain."

Em rose. "Mrs. Smollet is next on our list to see."

Jonas abandoned his stance before the drawing room hearth and joined her. "We also thought we'd try Muriel Grisby and old Mrs. Thompson."

Jocasta nodded. "Those are the people I would ask. Miss Hellebore is old—I think she's the oldest person in the village—but she only arrived a few years before Horatio Welham." Jocasta smiled at Em. "That makes her a relatively recent addition, and I know her family wasn't from around here."

"Thank you," Em said. "Miss Sweet thought that was the case, but we weren't sure." She turned to Lady Fortemain. "Thank you for seeing us, ma'am."

Her ladyship waved her hands. "Oh, but you will stay for morning tea, won't you?"

"Thank you, but I'm still wary about leaving the inn—and the twins—to their own devices for long." Em curtsied.

Lady Fortemain grimaced. "Your devotion can only be commended, my dear. Perhaps next time?"

Em and Jonas made their farewells to both ladies.

Jocasta walked with them to the door. "I'll ask Cedric if he's ever heard that phrase. I daresay we'll see you at the inn tonight."

"Thank you." Em let Jonas help her up into his curricle, then waved as he drove them away.

E m had spoken the truth; she was reluctant to leave the inn's staff totally unsupervised. "Not that I expect anything to go wrong," she told Jonas as, later that afternoon, they took advantage of the quiet time between luncheon and afternoon tea to drive out to Highgate, the home of Basil Smollet, Jocasta's brother. "It's just that if anything does go wrong, they have to shoulder the responsibility for making whatever decision needs to be made—but that's my job, and it's unfair for them to have to do it. It's one thing if I make a mistake, but it's worse if they do, and then feel responsible for things going badly."

Jonas glanced at her; his lips curved appreciatively as he took in the determined cast of her features, then, smile deepening, he gave his attention to his horses. He took the chestnuts up the long hill beyond the rectory at a smart clip, then slowed as Highgate came into view.

Mrs. Smollet was in and receiving, at least in the physical sense. Unfortunately, as they rapidly discovered, that meant little in terms of her mental presence.

"A Colyton. *More* than one Colyton, and you've come back—fancy that! I didn't know any of your family well—I was too young." Mrs. Smollet nodded her gray head. "Those were the days. I remember . . ."

She trailed off, plainly caught in her memories.

Basil, her son, had come in to join them and hear Em's tale firsthand. Shifting forward in his chair, he laid a hand on his mother's, slack in her lap. "Mama? Can you remember what house people used to call 'the house of the highest'?"

Mrs. Smollet abruptly focused surprisingly shrewd eyes on his face. '"The house of the highest'?" She frowned, looked away. "That sounds vaguely familiar."

Em held her breath; so did Jonas.

They waited, Basil patiently still and silent.

Mrs. Smollet shook her head. "No. I can't remember. But it wasn't this place, and not Ballyclose, either, no matter what that frippery woman might say."

There was little love lost between Lady Fortemain and Mrs. Smollet.

Mrs. Smollet's expression relaxed. "But I do remember the Mitchell boys—they lived in that old house by the cliffs. Dead now, all of them, long gone, but they were rascals. I remember—"

Her voice rising and falling, she rambled softly on about a long ago summer.

Basil sighed and drew back. He threw a sympathetic look at Em and Jonas, then rose.

They did, too.

Mrs. Smollet, her gaze fixed in some distant past, didn't notice. Basil beckoned and headed for the door.

They followed.

In the front hall, Basil turned to them. "She's physically quite hale, but her mind isn't strong. Some days she's acute, almost bright, on others . . ." He shrugged. "I'll ask the maids who sit with her to let me know if she says anything about any 'house of the highest.' I'll send word if she does."

"Thank you." Em smiled gratefully.

Jonas nodded. "We've spoken with Lady Fortemain, and plan to see Muriel Grisby and old Mrs. Thompson. Is there anyone else you can think of who might know more?"

Basil considered, then shook his head. "I can't think of anyone living who would have longer memories than those four, not of the village. I can't even think of anyone who's moved away."

"Phyllida and I couldn't, either." Jonas held out his hand; Basil gripped and shook it.

"Thank you for your time, Mr. Smollet." Em gave him her hand. "And for your help with your mother."

Basil smiled, surprisingly charmingly. "Anything for the returning Colytons—especially the one who's rejuvenated our inn."

Em laughed as he bowed over her hand.

She had to wait until the next morning to visit Dottswood Farm in pursuit of Muriel Grisby. Muriel, who by then had heard the latest village news, was only too happy to grant Em and Jonas an interview.

"So delightful to have Colytons in the village again! Such a blessing that you've made the inn usable again, too." Surprisingly nimble and spry, Muriel waved them to chairs. "I remember your great-grandfather—quite a figure he cut, so impressive with all that wild white hair. I was only a girl then, of course, but I remember as if it were yesterday."

Em tried not to let her hopes rise. Using Jonas's version of events—that they were trying to solve a cryptic family rhyme, which was only the truth—she asked if Muriel had any light to shed on their mysterious phrase.

"No." Muriel shook her head decisively. "Never heard of it."

And that was that.

After three disappointments, Em didn't hold out much hope of old Mrs. Thompson, Thompson's and Oscar's mother, knowing anything pertinent, but Jonas called for her that afternoon, and chivvied her into at least trying.

In the lull between luncheon and afternoon tea, they walked up the lane to the forge.

The forge fronted the lane; Thompson's cottage was set well back beyond it. He was working, in full leather apron standing before the furnace pounding horseshoes into shape; he waved as they went past.

"I mentioned last night that we might call on his mother." Holding open the gate that led into the narrow yard before the cottage, Jonas studied Em's face, sensed her flagging spirits. "You never know. Mrs. Thompson comes from a completely different social strata than the other three—she might have heard something, learned something none of the others did."

Em's answering smile was weak, but when Mrs. Thompson opened the door to his knock, she brightened. "Good afternoon, Mrs. Thompson. I hope we're not disturbing you?"

"No, no, dearie—come in, do." Mrs. Thompson waved them into her small front room. "Such a thrill to have Colytons among us again. Just as it ought to be, and you've made the inn such a lovely place—who would have imagined it after what Juggs had done to it."

Jonas hung back in the doorway, letting the women take the two small armchairs in the room. It had always been a mystery to him how a female so tiny and birdlike as Mrs. Thompson could possibly have borne two strapping sons of the likes of Thompson and Oscar. There was another brother, too, and two sisters, yet Mrs. Thompson looked so frail and delicate, as if a good wind would blow her away.

Her mind, however, was like a steel trap.

"I remember your great-grandfather well—an imposing gentleman, he was, but always with a cheery smile. He'd been a sailor—captained his own ship, if memory serves—but I knew him long after that. He lived at the manor—Colyton Manor, that is—until he died. His son—that'd be your grandfather, I expect—was already settled elsewhere, as were the rest of the old man's children, so the house was sold."

"Indeed." Em nodded. "My great-grandfather was the last Colyton to live and die here. We—my sisters, brother, and I—have returned to, among other things, trace the meaning of an old family rhyme. The rhyme describes a house as 'the house of the highest.' Have you any idea which house that might be?"

Mrs. Thompson screwed up her face in concentration. After several moments, she shook her head. "No. I don't . . . but I have to say the words sound familiar."

She refocused on Em, then patted her hand. "You let me think on it, dearie. If it's meant to be, it'll come."

Jonas could almost hear Em's dispirited sigh as she rose and, with a smile that looked a trifle worn, took her leave of Mrs. Thompson.

He did the same, then escorted Em from the small cottage, past the forge and into the lane.

Pacing beside her, he glanced at her face. Had to duck his head to do so; she was, uncharacteristically, trudging along rather glumly, head down. "Don't feel dejected. You've only just started asking around. Those ladies will turn the phrase over in their minds, and mention it to their female friends. And just as Mrs. Thompson said, the answer will come."

When Em didn't respond, he jogged her elbow with his. "Give it time."

She nodded once, then drew in a breath and lifted her head. Looked down the lane at the inn dead ahead. He could almost see levers in her mind shift as she switched focus.

He forestalled any comment. "The inn's doing well." A gross understatement; the revitalized Red Bells was doing a roaring trade above and beyond what even the most starry-eyed optimist could have dreamed.

"Hmm. I just hope all's in train for dinner tonight. We're fully booked for the first time—did I mention?"

"No, but I'm not surprised." It was Saturday, and not just the villagers, but all those from the surrounding estates and farms seemed to have taken the new Red Bells to their hearts; the inn was busier than it had ever been.

Hands in his breeches' pockets, he continued to walk beside her, undemanding and silent, knowing from her expression that she was thinking of inn things—which was better than dwelling on their thus far less than satisfactory results in hunting for her family treasure.

He had no real interest in the treasure himself beyond a distant curiosity; he'd agreed to help search for it because it was important to her. More, while she hadn't expressly stated it, he'd got the impression that she wanted to find the treasure first, before she turned her mind to making her decision to marry him. Ergo, it was in his best interests to help her retrieve said treasure with all speed.

Yet even more than that, he wanted her happy and content, and, for her, finding the treasure seemed critical.

He'd spent the past two nights in her bed; he had no intention of relinquishing a position he'd already won. In the quieter moments when she'd lain in his arms, she'd told him, explained to him, more about the treasure—revealing how she saw it, why it had grown to be important to her.

It wasn't the treasure per se that she sought, but what it represented, and that not just for herself, but even more importantly for her brother and sisters.

The treasure would secure Henry's future, and reestablish the family at the social level to which they'd been born. It would provide dowries for her sisters, and replenish her own that—if he'd read correctly between her lines—she'd severely depleted in funding their escape from Harold.

All of which was well and good, but from his viewpoint immaterial. If she married him, her brother and sisters would come under his protection, and thus would be adequately provided for regardless.

As for her dowry, he didn't care if she had not a penny. Thanks to his association with the Cynsters and through them the bright world of investing, he was more than merely well-to-do.

Of course, she didn't know that—and he had to admit it was refreshingly pleasant to have no hint of monetary considerations weighing in either his or her decision to wed. However, regardless of his wealth and the consequent fact that there were no circumstances in which she and her siblings might find themselves destitute—or even condemned to being innkeepers all their lives—he understood, appreciated, and definitely approved of the emotions that drove her.

Family support, family pride. Not a prideful pride, but a respectful one, a sense of what was due to the name one bore, a responsibility to see it protected, to have it respected by others as it should be.

That wasn't a simple emotion, not in any way, nor was it one everyone felt. But it seemed ingrained in her—and it was something he, too, subscribed to, even more so after his return from the capital and his newfound appreciation of his own roots.

A belief in family, in place and tradition, was something they shared.

Because of that he would help her find her treasure—somehow, some way, regardless of what effort it took. Because that belief was worth the price.

Their feet crunched on the gravel in the inn's narrow forecourt. The open doorway stood before them, a pleasant buzz of muted conversations wafting out welcomingly.

He followed Em into the common room.

She paused just inside to scan the room—taking in the few customers whiling away the afternoon—then headed for her office. "I must check whether Hilda needs any extra help for tonight."

Ambling in her wake, Jonas nodded to old Mr. Wright and the Weatherspoons, noted the artist—Hadley—sitting in a dim corner, a sketchbook open on the table before him. Bringing his gaze back to Em, he spoke to the back of her head. "I'll drop in on Lucifer, check if he's turned up anything in his reexamination of those books, and then I think I'll visit Silas Coombe."

Reaching the end of the bar, Em halted and looked at him, brows rising.

He smiled, all teeth. "His collection isn't as extensive as

the manor's, but Silas's tastes are eclectic. He might be able to find some reference to the description we have, and if I ask, I suspect he'll find it in him to oblige."

She looked into his eyes; hers narrowed, but then she nodded and turned to her office. "Very well. But just remember that he's been behaving himself perfectly ever since our misunderstanding."

He humphed and followed her into the office.

Heard the little sigh she gave as she set her reticule down on the desk.

Smoothly he closed the distance between them, slid his arms around her, and drew her against him, her back to his chest, enclosing her in a protective embrace. Leaning his chin on her sleek head, he simply held her. Rocked her just a fraction, murmured, "Don't get too disappointed. You may have been searching for a while, but *we've* only just begun. And we means not just me, but Lucifer, Phyllida, Filing, Miss Sweet, and everyone we've asked. Someone will know, the answer will come, and we'll find your treasure." Shifting his head, he pressed a kiss to her temple. "Trust me—you'll see."

Em closed her eyes and relaxed back against him. For one finite instant, drank in something she'd couldn't remember being offered by anyone at any time in her life. Comfort, support—unconditional and steadfast. A simple thing, but so poignantly helpful.

So right.

A footstep, light and quick, sounded in the corridor outside. Jonas's arms fell reluctantly from her; equally reluctantly she stepped away from his warmth and turned to face whatever crisis was approaching.

In her experience, footsteps tapping in that way generally heralded a crisis.

Issy appeared in the doorway, a slight frown on her face. Other than that, she evinced no sign of panic or distress.

Em was beginning to wonder if her instincts had lied and

there was no crisis—merely her dejected mind assuming the worst—when Issy asked, "Have you seen the twins?"

Silence held for a moment, then Em answered, "No." She kept her tone even. "Where are they? Or rather, where were they?"

Issy stepped into the office. "I said they could play for half an hour after lunch, and then come to the upstairs parlor to help me with the darning. I've been trying to teach them the basics." She glanced at Jonas, then looked back at Em. "I wasn't exactly surprised when they didn't arrive. I just kept darning, expecting them to turn up with all sorts of excuses, but they didn't."

Em glanced at the little clock on a cabinet. "It's after three."

Issy nodded. "I realized and started looking a few minutes ago. I've searched upstairs—they're not up there— then asked Hilda and the girls, but no one's seen them, not since they went out into the yard after lunch."

More than two hours ago. "They can't have gone far." Em told herself they'd gone blackberrying, or seen something that had distracted them—that they'd turn up shortly full of apologies and excuses. She waved Issy back toward the kitchen. "I'll come and help look."

"*We'll* come and help look." Jonas followed her from her office. "I'll see if they're anywhere on the common—if they're not, I'll check the rectory."

Em nodded and hurried after Issy.

Jonas stepped into the tap and strode for the door.

Em was waiting for him in the common room when he returned half an hour later, Joshua and Henry at his heels.

He didn't need to ask if she'd located the twins; her anxious expression said it all.

One glance at his face, at Joshua's and Henry's, told her

they hadn't sighted the girls, either. Hands clasped too tightly before her, she met his eyes. "Where can they be?"

He hesitated, then asked, "Have you tried—" Systematically he ran through all the possible places, all the potential attractions for a pair of girls as adventurous as the twins within easy reach. He knew from experience that being together, having each other for support, they would go further than a single child would.

John Ostler came in, reporting that he'd found no signs of the pair at the places he'd gone to check.

Between them, they'd searched the inn and its immediate surrounds.

Jonas looked down at Em, then asked because it had to be asked, "This isn't usual for them, is it? Just up and disappearing like this?"

Her expression openly worried, she shook her head. "Normally they only wander when left to their own devices. If they're supposed to be somewhere to do something at a certain time and know someone will be waiting, they usually arrive, although they might be late. This isn't just late."

"No. It isn't." This felt serious.

Pale, Issy came to stand beside Em. "They've been so good lately—as if they've finally accepted that they do need to learn the things I've been teaching them. They haven't even tried to talk their way out of lessons—not for weeks."

Joshua stepped forward and took Issy's hand, nodded to Em. "Don't worry. We'll find them."

Looking into Em's eyes, Jonas didn't bother stating the obvious. "Wherever they are, they can't be far—it's been less than three hours since they were here."

Lifting his head, he scanned the customers in the common room, both in the tap and on the ladies' side. A good number of villagers had gathered to partake of the inn's afternoon tea. Naturally everyone was listening avidly to the unfolding drama. In a voice that carried clearly throughout the room, he announced, "We need to organize a search."

* * *

Everyone volunteered, even Miss Sweet and Miss Helle-bore, who had come in to sample Hilda's currant scones.

Em was touched. While Jonas conferred with the men and those women more able to hike about the countryside, assigning different areas to each, she sent Issy to fetch paper and pen, and organized for Miss Sweet and Miss Helle-bore to take everyone's name and the area they would search before the searchers left the inn. "If people report in after they've searched, then we'll at least know where the girls aren't."

Jonas left with John Ostler and Dodswell, Lucifer's groom, to beat through the wood behind the inn. "We'll go as far as the river. If we see any sign they've gone that way, or crossed it, I'll send Dodswell back to let you know while John and I keep after them."

Em nodded, pressed his hand, and let him go. She hoped—prayed—that finding her half sisters would simply be a matter of looking in the right place.

Joshua, with Hadley, would search the church, as well as the crypt and bell tower. "The crypt and tower are locked, but the key's in the vestry, hanging on a nail for all to see, and I wouldn't put it past them to have noticed." He grimaced. "Both the crypt and the tower have very steep steps. It's possible they've panicked and got stuck."

Em was about to assure him that was unlikely—the twins delighted in climbing trees and wriggling through small spaces—but before the words left her lips, another thought occurred. She looked at Issy—and saw the same apprehension in her eyes.

If one of the twins had had an accident—fallen and broken her leg, for instance—the other wouldn't leave to go for help. They'd stay together and wait to be rescued.

"Wherever they are, they can't be far." She repeated Jonas's words for her own benefit as well as Issy's.

Her sister drew breath, then nodded. "Henry and I will call at the cottages along the lane. Even if they're not there, someone might have seen them."

Em waved them toward Miss Sweet and Miss Hellebore, then looked around. Other than the two old ladies, only she and Edgar, behind the bar, and Hilda and her girls preparing dinner in the kichen remained. Everyone else was out searching.

Drawing in a steadying breath, she went to the bar. "For anyone who's been out searching, their next drink is on my account."

Edgar leaned across and patted her hand. "Don't you worry, miss. They'll find those two angels safe and sound, and have them back in no time."

She tried to smile.

She waited, but although the searchers returned in good time, none brought any angels with them. On her orders Edgar opened the tap early, serving frothing ale to the thirsty crew.

Gradually fewer and fewer searchers remained out and looking. Miss Sweet and Miss Hellebore looked increasingly concerned as the list of areas in which the twins weren't grew. When Jonas, John Ostler, and Dodswell, the last of the searchers, walked back into the inn—and Jonas looked at Em and shook his head—a hum of concern rose from the assembled throng.

Em felt the blood drain from her head. She swayed back against the counter.

Jonas closed the last yards, grasped her arm. Looked into her eyes—steadied her with his touch, his attention, his simple presence. "I'm going to send to Axminster for the constable."

Em tried to take it in, managed a nod. If he thought that was necessary—

A stir around the door drew her attention. The crowd parted; Harold swaggered in.

He was smiling, nodding genially as he passed those he

recognized. Puzzled by his jovial attitude, as he headed for her, everyone in the room muted their discussions and watched. Listened.

She was equally taken aback. Surely Harold couldn't have missed hearing the news? People had come in from the outlying farms because they'd heard and wanted to be there, ready to witness or help.

Harold wouldn't be there to help, but why was he smiling?

Fighting to keep a frown from her face, she waited as he approached down the center of the room. Jonas turned back from the men he'd been consulting over driving to Axminster; he remained by her side, facing Harold.

In the periphery of her vision, Em saw Issy, with Joshua beside her, at the front of the now subtly encircling crowd.

Coming to a halt before her, Harold beamed down at her with undisguised smugness, a gloating pleasure. "Well, miss—are you ready to see sense and pack your bags, heh?"

Em felt ice slide through her veins. Spine stiff, she locked her eyes on her uncle's puffy orbs. "Uncle Harold." Her voice—its awful, restrained tone—made him blink. She drew in a huge breath, tightly asked, "Have you seen the twins?"

He opened his eyes wide. "Well, of course I have. That's what I'm here to tell you, ain't it?"

Relief flooded her. "Oh, thank God."

"Aye—so I think." He fixed her with a stern eye. "I've packed them into a carriage and sent them off to Runcorn— where they, and you, and that sister and brother of yours, belong. So if the three of you"—he glanced at Issy and Henry—"will just pack your bags, we can be off."

A stunned silence ensued. The entire population of the common room stared, unable to take it in.

Em felt a surge of pure fury rise through her; hauling in a breath, she grabbed hold of it, hung on. She couldn't afford to lose it—loose it—not until she had the twins back. "Just so that we're clear, Uncle Harold."

He'd noticed the silence and was glancing around, more curious than alarmed, so insensitive he didn't detect the rising tide of animosity directed his way. He brought his gaze back to her.

She caught his eye. "You found the twins, lured them away, and took them where?"

He snorted. "Musbury. Silly twits wanted to learn to drive a curricle, so I offered to teach them to drive my gig. Drove them to Musbury where I had a coach waiting, popped them into it with some female I hired, and dispatched them with a coachman and groom to Runcorn."

"And they went willingly?" She couldn't believe it.

"Oh, there was plenty of wailing and carrying on, of course—you know what girls are." Harold waved dismissively. "Tied them up with scarves, shut the door on them, and told the coachman to drive off quick." He clapped his large pudgy hands together, rubbed them in gloating expectation. "Well, then. Are you ready to follow, heh?"

Jonas turned to Em. "They can't have got far. I'll drive after the carriage and fetch them back."

He had to do something—something that got him out of the common room before his raging temper snapped its leash, and he dealt with her uncle as he deserved.

He squeezed Em's arm in comfort and support. Releasing her, he looked at Potheridge with open contempt, then walked past him and strode for the door.

"I'll come, too."

It was Filing who'd spoken; Jonas heard the same suppressed fury he felt in his friend's voice. Glancing back, he saw Joshua cast a condemnatory look at Potheridge, then step past him.

Potheridge turned, his expression apoplexically affronted. "Here, now! None of your business what I do with my nieces."

As Joshua halted beside Jonas and, fists clenched, turned back to look at Potheridge, Jonas leveled a disgusted look at the older man. "On the contrary. As I understand it, the twins are not your nieces. You are not their guardian—you have no right to do anything with them at all. And I believe you'll discover kidnapping is still a crime."

"Kidnapping!" Potheridge goggled. "Nonsense!" He finally glanced around, finally seemed to realize that no one present was on his side. He puffed out his chest. "Well, upon my word! This is a nice thing. All I want—"

"What you want," Jonas cut in, "is neither here nor there. It's what those girls want, and what Em as their guardian wants, that's important." He looked at Em, nodded. "We're off. Don't worry—we'll get them back."

His gaze returned to her uncle; he couldn't stop his lip from curling. "If you weren't old enough to be my father, I'd teach you a lesson you wouldn't soon forget."

"And if I wasn't a man of the cloth," Joshua grated, "I'd help."

Eyes widening, Potheridge took a step back.

Jonas turned and strode out of the inn, Joshua behind him.

Em watched them go, wished she could go with them, but knew she had to stay at the inn—and deal with Harold.

She steeled herself as her uncle, choleric color rising in his mottled cheeks, gobbling like an insulted turkey-cock, swung to face her.

The crowd around them rippled, surged; Thompson emerged. He stepped between her and Harold. Facing Harold, he fixed him with a measuring look. "The way I see it," Thompson said, speaking in his slow, soft, country drawl, "you and I are much the same age, give or take a year or two. And heaven knows I'm no man of God. So . . ."

In one neat, economical movement, Thompson plowed his huge fist into Harold's jaw.

Ducking to see beneath the blacksmith's raised arm, Em gasped—watched as Harold's eyes rolled up and he slowly toppled to land in a sprawl on his back.

For one instant, she stared—as did everyone else—at Harold's still form, then she lifted her gaze and through the open doorway and saw that Jonas and Joshua had paused in the yard and looked back.

Grimly satisfied, Jonas saluted Thompson.

Thompson waved him on. "We'll take care of things here—you two go and fetch those angels back."

Raising a hand in acknowledgment, Jonas swung on his heel and left.

16

Em didn't have to do anything. The entire village rallied around—she wasn't allowed to lift even a finger.

Summoned by Miss Sweet, Lucifer and Phyllida, who'd been at the inn earlier but had gone home to tend their sons, arrived just after the confrontation—just in time to see Thompson and Oscar, one at Harold's feet, the other gripping his arms, lug her unconscious uncle out of the inn. Lucifer took one look at Harold—and jaw firming, directed Thompson to leave him propped on one of the benches along the inn's front wall.

"I want him out of my house." Miss Hellebore, looking uncharacteristically belligerent, rapped the floor with her cane.

Em stiffened; she wasn't sure her uncle, even now, would go away. And if he demanded to stay at the inn . . . she looked up and found Phyllida's dark gaze on her.

With an almost imperceptible nod, Phyllida crouched beside Miss Hellebore's chair. "Actually," she said, "if you can manage not to throttle him, it might be best if we let him take himself off. If you evict him, he'll likely try to insist that Miss Colyton put him up at the inn." A murmur of disapproval rumbled around the room. Phyllida nodded in acknowledgment. "And that simply won't do."

When the matter was put like that, Miss Hellebore was only too ready to agree to allow Harold to stay under her roof. He wouldn't, of course, be welcome, not there or anywhere in the village; that was understood by all.

Waiting, patiently or otherwise, had never been Em's forte; her Colyton nature didn't tolerate the activity at all well. And as the hours rolled by, with the whole village crammed into the common room, all insisting on doing absolutely everything for her—offers she found impossible to refuse—and thus being denied the distraction of her duties, she grew increasingly tense.

Increasingly anxious.

She trusted Jonas and Filing to rescue the twins—absolutely, without question—yet until she saw the pair, until she held them in her arms again and felt their smaller, thinner arms clutching her, she could know no peace, could not relax.

As matters transpired, with all the noise in the common room no one heard the crunch of wheels on the gravel outside.

The first Em or anyone knew of the twins' return was the patter of their shoes and their high-pitched voices calling, "Em? Em?"

The crowd opened, and they spotted her before the bar; picking up their skirts, they pelted to her and flung themselves into her opened arms.

She grabbed them, caught them to her, blinked like fury to keep the welling tears back; she had to be able to see to check them over. Once satisfied, she couldn't help patting them, stroking their shining heads. She smiled mistily as Issy joined her.

Led by the Thompson brothers, the entire inn cheered—making Gert and Bea, never averse to being the center of attention, glance around curiously.

Quickly tiring of being petted, the twins pulled back—just to arm's length. Enough for Gert to exclaim, "It was that horrible man!"

Bea fixed huge eyes on Em's face; her lower lip wobbled. "He *lied* to us!"

The twins knew they weren't supposed to lie; the notion that an adult would lie to *them* was entirely beyond their comprehension.

"We know he's your uncle." Gert's eyes flicked from Em, to Issy, to Henry, who'd come up.

"But he's not a nice man at all," Bea declared. "We don't think we should go to stay with him."

Em nodded. "We're not. Not now, not ever again."

Bea slid her hand into Em's. "Good." She turned to survey the crowd. "Is there a party?"

Many laughed. Lady Fortemain smiled and beckoned. The girls left their older sisters and went to socialize, to tell their story, no doubt with various histrionic embellishments.

Issy shook her head, but she was smiling. "Their heads will be turned. They'll be dreadful come morning."

"But tomorrow is another day," Em said, "and I'm too thankful to have them back to cavil. We can haul on their reins tomorrow."

Another rousing cheer drew all attention to the door—to the heroes of the hour, Jonas and Joshua. Both men played up to the reception, making the crowd laugh, but their focus was clearly on attaining Em's and Issy's sides.

Em saw their difficulty. She turned to Edgar. "Call drinks all around—on the house."

Grinning, Edgar did, creating an instant diversion; Jonas and Filing seized the chance to push through the melee.

Em held out her hands to them both. "Thank you."

Filing smiled and squeezed her fingers, then released her and turned to Issy, also very ready to tender her thanks.

As the pair moved away, Jonas caught her gaze, briefly raised her hand to his lips.

She looked into his dark eyes. "I can't thank you enough."

His lips kicked up at the ends. "You can try—later."

She laughed.

He set her hand on his arm and turned to survey the crowd. "Anyway, I told you that you and yours are mine—several times, I believe."

She slanted a glance up at his face. "Is this what you meant?"

He nodded. "Mine to protect. Among other things."

"Even terrors like the twins?"

"Even such terrors. They were spitting like cats when we found them, incidentally, ready to take on Harold and shred him. Lucky for him it was Filing and me hauling them out of that coach. Harold's minions weren't at all hard to convince to give them up. They were all hired from Musbury, and had no idea they were participating in any kidnapping—Harold had told them he was the twins' guardian."

"He knows he's not—he just does what suits him."

"Speaking of terrors, where is he?"

"Thompson and Oscar left him on one of the benches outside. When he came to his senses he must have taken himself off. A little while ago Miss Sweet went to check for Miss Hellebore to see if he'd gone back to his room in her cottage, but he wasn't there."

"Presumably he's wandering the lanes, dwelling on his misdemeanors."

She couldn't stifle a snort. "A lovely fantasy, but unlikely."

Sobering, Jonas looked down at her. "If he comes back—"

"Oh, he will, but he won't try anything like this again. I expect he'll return, pretending to be contrite, and try once more to plead his case, but that's all." She glanced at him. "Nothing I can't handle."

His lips thinned. After a moment, he said, "If there *is* anything more, promise me you'll tell me."

She hesitated; it felt odd—strange and not quite right—to *promise* to ask for help.

His gaze searched her face. "Think of it as my boon for retrieving your minxes."

She met his eyes, could read in their rich dark brown that he was intent on gaining that promise at least. From the moment she'd first met him, his protective tendencies had been on show. They seemed ingrained, an intrinsic part of him; she couldn't truly imagine him without them.

Accepting his proposition still felt strange, but she inclined her head. "Very well. If there's any further problem, I'll let you know."

Her answer was clearly satisfactory; he nodded, relaxed, then Phyllida waved, beckoning him to her. Em went to move the other way, but he caught her hand and towed her with him to speak with his sister.

Much later, when everyone had finished celebrating and gone home, Jonas followed Em up the back stairs to the rooms above the inn's guest rooms that her siblings had made their own.

The twins, lagging after their ordeal, had gone up at nine o'clock. Issy and Henry, likewise worn out by the day's events, had retired an hour ago. Em went past two rooms with their doors shut to the last room at the end of the narrow corridor.

The door stood ajar; within the room a candle flame flickered as she gently eased the door further open and peeked in.

Across the room, two single beds stood with their heads against the wall. Each held a sleeping angel. Golden tresses spilled across the pillows on which delicately flushed, cherubic cheeks lay cushioned.

Surveying the scene from over Em's head, he heard her soft sigh. Relief, love, and contentment infused the gentle sound.

Each twin had been restless enough to disarrange her

covers, leaving soft rounded limbs, hands, and feet exposed to the cooling night air. Em tiptoed in and straightened the covers, tucking each girl in, dropping a kiss on each forehead.

Shoulder propped against the door frame, his hands in his pockets, Jonas watched her. Saw the undisguised love that lit her face, and the caring that grew out of that, infusing every touch, every silent look.

The want, the need, to have her look at his son or daughter with that same all-embracing love in her eyes gripped him. Powerfully. Raw, poignant, the novel desire held him effortlessly.

Satisfied, she left her sleeping sisters and returned to him. Raising a finger to her lips to enjoin his silence, she waved him back, then stepped into the corridor and drew the door almost closed.

Looking up, she smiled at him, then moved past; silently they retraced their steps along the corridor and down the back stairs. On the first-floor landing, she opened a shadowed door; he followed her into the small bathing chamber behind her bedroom.

She led him straight through.

Thinking she meant to lead him to her parlor, as they crossed her bedroom, he reached for her hand—just as she halted and swung to face him. She looked into his face, locked her eyes on his, smiled—and moved into his arms, into him, slid her arms around his neck, stretched up on her toes, and kissed him.

Deeply. Freely. Openly giving.

His hands instinctively fastened about her waist. He took a moment to savor her gift; he was about to take charge, and take more, when she drew back.

Lowering her heels, her eyes bright even in the dim light, she smiled. "Thank you."

He looked into her face, studied her eyes, arched a brow. "I don't want your thanks." He moved into her, gathering her more securely against him. "I don't even want your gratitude."

Quiescent in his arms, her hands resting on his shoulders, she looked her question.

"I just want you."

The simple words held absolute conviction. Em tilted her head and through the soft moonlight that seeped into the room studied his face. "Why?"

The most important question she wanted him—needed him—to answer. Honestly, straightforwardly, without obfuscation or guile.

He seemed to understand; he didn't turn the query aside with a glib reply. He thought, then softly, more hesitantly, said, "Because . . ." He drew in a breath, then went on, "Because without you my life won't be complete."

Oh? She would have asked for further clarification, but he'd apparently run out of words. He drew her closer, bent his head, and kissed her.

From the first touch of his lips on hers, she sensed . . . had to wonder if this was part of his answer, if he was showing her, demonstrating what he couldn't, or wouldn't, say in words.

He'd always been inclined to draw back and gauge her response before forging on to the next sensual stage, the next visceral delight. This time, however, there seemed more to it, more behind his easing back from the kiss to, in the moonlight, touch her lips, trace the lines of her face with his fingertips.

His touch was lingering, almost worshipful. Then he bent his head and sealed their lips again, and whirled her into the fire.

Into the familiar rising heat, the swelling, welling flames of their passion. Their joint, shared, mutual passions, fueled by desires that had only grown stronger, more confident, more demanding.

Perhaps it was experience, her growing more accustomed

to the searing pleasures, that allowed her to take in, to absorb, his focus, his attention. His intentness as he slowly stripped away her clothes, letting them fall to the floor disregarded as his eyes, his senses, locked on the next treasure revealed, the next part of her bared to him. Given, surrendered to him.

So that he could savor. Claim, appreciate, and possess.

Yet it wasn't any simple, greedy possession. Even though her wits were whirling, her senses waltzing with delight, this time she saw—perhaps because she was alerted to look for it—his devotion. The reverence born of deeper feelings, of emotion that came from his core, that was tangled with passion and desire, yet was infinitely more powerful.

Powerful enough to make him pause as, naked, they tumbled onto the bed, to draw back from the conflagration of their kiss, to, with his hands and eyes, palms, and fingers, sculpt her body, tracing every line, every curve, laying a web of red-hot possession over her skin, before repeating the exercise, from ear to toe, with his lips, his mouth, with his warm, rasping tongue.

Reaching her feet, he spread her legs and worked his way up the inner faces. She was gasping, arching; her hands buried in his silky hair, she was blatantly urging him on long before he consented to bury his face between her thighs and send her rocketing into paradise.

He lapped, savored, then rose up, moved up the bed, covered her body with his, and filled her with one long thrust.

She gasped, arched beneath him to meet the more definite invasion; eagerly she opened to him, welcomed him, embraced him.

Took him deep within her body and felt emotion well and pour through her. Felt the molten tide swell and grow—a sea ever deeper, broader, more powerful.

More addictive, more enthralling.

More binding.

Caught in its waves, in the throes of rising heat, she reached up and laid a hand against his cheek. Guided his lips down to hers, for a kiss that on her part invited, offered, surrendered all.

Braced on his arms over her, Jonas groaned, his spine flexing powerfully as he relentlessly drove into her. She was all supple feminine curves beneath him, her scalding sheath slick and tight, her willing body the epitome of delight.

Grasping one knee, he hooked it over his hip, then did the same with the other, opening her more fully to him, so he could thrust yet deeper into her delicious heat, could fill her and take her and make her his.

Brand her as his.

She seemed to understand, to comprehend his desperate need; wrapping her legs about his hips, she tilted hers, giving him an extra inch he immediately, greedily seized.

It still wasn't enough, not for whatever power now drove him. Coming down on one elbow, taking his weight on that side, with his other hand he reached down, around, slid his palm over her hip, grasped one firm globe of her bottom and tipped her up to him, held her there, trapped and vulnerable and his, and filled her, thrust deep into her body and claimed her, again and again and again.

She shattered; on a muffled scream she came apart in his arms.

The intensely powerful contractions of her sheath caught him, pulled him on, dragged him over the edge of sharp delight.

And he was plummeting through the void with her, shuddering as his release claimed him—as she claimed him and held him and anchored him in the world.

He collapsed upon her, swamped with sensation, with the indescribable bliss of satiation soothingly seeping into him, through him. Like a cooling hand laid on his fevered brow, assurance, calmness, and a serenity he'd never previously known sank to his soul.

Beneath him, she lay boneless, warm, and quiescent, her expression blissful, totally sated, eyes closed, a gentle smile curving her lips.

After uncounted moments, he summoned enough strength—and will—to move. To disengage and lift from her so he was no longer squashing her into the bed. Flopping onto his back, he drew her to him; she came, settled her head on his shoulder, exhaled a soft, immeasurably contented sigh.

One small hand lay spread over his chest. Over his heart.

He looked at it for a moment, then raised his hand and covered hers with his. Held her hand there, on his heart.

His voice, when he spoke, was a dark yet definite rumble in the night. "You came here, to Colyton, and made the village complete." Another moment ticked by. "You do the same for me."

Em heard every word, understood that she'd been right—that this, all of it, including those words, that elemental admission—was his answer to her question.

When it came to her questions, he had the answers. The right answers, the ones that spoke to her soul.

She lay absorbing that truth, letting it sink into her heart and mind, then she shifted the hand he held trapped against his chest just enough to hook her thumb over his much larger one, and link them.

Closing her eyes, she let sleep wash in and claim her. Slid into slumber in his arms, her hand on his heart.

The next day being Sunday, Em attended church with Issy, Henry, and the twins. Jonas didn't appear; she suspected that might have something to do with the relatively late hour, sometime after dawn, when he'd finally left her bed. Regardless, he'd said he would see her later, and with that she was content.

Indeed, she was content through and through, a state that had never before been hers, at least not that she could remember. Jonas wanted to marry her, and she felt increasingly sure that she wanted to marry him, increasingly certain that the reasons behind his proposal were the right ones, the sort of unwavering reasons it would be safe to put her faith in, to trust in and build a future upon.

There was the treasure yet to find, but it was Sunday and after the trials of yesterday, she was willing to set aside her quest and savor the beauties of the day, the inexpressible comfort of being able to follow the twins—dancing and skipping and laughing—back down the common to the inn, with Issy beside her, a delicate smile that spoke of happiness curving her lips, and Henry, hands in his pockets, striding along on her other side, absorbed with practicing his declensions.

Lifting her head, she felt the light breeze flirt with the ribbons of her bonnet, and the faint warmth of the sun on her cheeks. And smiled.

Today was a good day.

She was looking forward to many more, but she still had an inn to run.

More guests had arrived. Edgar, not a churchgoer, had dealt with them. She approved his dispositions, then looked in on Hilda and her girls. Everything was in readiness for serving lunch; Hilda shooed her away and with a laugh, she left.

Issy would oversee the serving of the family's lunch— they'd invited Jonas and Joshua in light of their sterling efforts of the day before—but there was still half an hour before Em would be summoned upstairs. Glancing into the common room, she saw the usual small crowd of familiar faces. Smiling, she went out to chat.

She circulated freely among the men in the tap and the ladies on the other side of the room. Mr. Hadley was seated in what was fast becoming his corner of the tap. It was a shadowed nook, but the position allowed him to glance out of the window across the inn's front yard to the common and the church.

Halting beside his table, she smiled. "How is your sketching progressing?"

Lips curving, Hadley met her eyes. "Very well, thank you." He swung around the large sketch pad his hand had been resting on, flicked it open. "See for yourself."

She looked down at an excellent likeness of the carving that stood to one side of the altar. The detail was quite extraordinary. She raised her gaze to Hadley's face. "You're very talented."

He inclined his head, obviously pleased. "Thank you." He waved her to join him. "Please—look at the rest. I'd value your opinion."

She sank onto the stool opposite him and turned to the next page. An accurate rendering of one of the other carved monuments filled it. Advancing through the well-used pad, she found countless studies as well as complete sketches. The precision with which Hadley had captured the monuments was striking, so much so she could almost imagine she was looking at the real thing, except for the lighting. There wasn't a great deal of light or shade, or even texture in the majority of sketches; it was only in those where the monuments stood in shadow that Hadley had thought to capture something of the atmosphere—and some of those were quite eerie.

She smiled and said as much, closing the pad.

He shrugged. "I just draw what I see."

"You see with a very fine eye, then. But you were a sailor, were you not? I've heard that sailors' eyes are very keen."

He laughed. "Aye—there's many who would say that. They also say that sailors have roving eyes, yet in my case, I'd say I've roved the world and seen many sights—not quite the same thing."

She propped her chin on the palm of her hand, elbow on the table. "Tell me of some of the sights you've seen."

He obliged.

It wasn't hard to appear fascinated as he outlined some of his travels, yet it occurred to her that Hadley was exerting himself to charm her. The notion didn't bother her; men occasionally charmed simply because they could.

While she listened, smiled, and nodded, it came to her

that while Hadley appeared to be an open book—a creature who lived fully in the light—his affinity in his drawings seemed conversely for the dark. The point struck her as curious, made her a touch more curious about him.

High-pitched voices drew her—and Hadley's—gaze to the window, to the scene beyond it; Filing, approaching the inn, had been waylaid by the twins. Chattering nineteen to the dozen, each grabbed a hand and towed the curate into the inn.

Good-naturedly laughing, Filing acquiesced, allowing himself to be paraded through the common room like a conquering hero. Everyone smiled. Too intent on their procession, the twins didn't see Em sitting in the corner. Filing did; he smiled and nodded her way, but then the twins reclaimed his attention. They towed him through the dining tables and on into the kitchen.

Chuckling, Em turned back to Hadley. He'd leaned back, deeper into the corner of the bench seat; his affinity for shadows struck her anew.

Hadley smiled his easy smile. "Your sisters seem fond of the curate."

"Indeed. He's an estimable man."

"It must have been a huge relief to have the girls back."

"It was." She felt a familiar weighty gaze and glanced around to see Jonas emerge from the hall by her office. "I'm very grateful to everyone who helped search." Jonas waited. She turned back to Hadley with a polite smile. "If you'll excuse me?"

His smile was a trifle perfunctory as he reached for his sketch pad. She left him with a nod, her thoughts and senses instantly focusing on Jonas.

She joined him with a smile, one infused with a warmth that came from deep inside her. She laid a hand on his arm; he covered it with his. "They'll be waiting upstairs. We should go up."

His dark eyes roamed her face; the hard lines of his features softened. "Yes—let's."

He stepped back into the hall, drawing her with him. As the shadows swallowed her, she cast a last glance over the common room's customers—and noticed Hadley's gaze locked on her and Jonas.

Despite the distance, his expression seemed harsh.

Could the artist be jealous?

She smiled to herself, dismissing the notion as fanciful; Hadley was doubtless just broody, as artists were. She turned to follow Jonas—just as he halted, drew her to him, and kissed her. Thoroughly.

How could a kiss with no heat be all-consuming?

This one was—a kiss between lovers who knew where they stood, it still left her wits reeling, her senses purring, her mind . . .

He'd ended the kiss, lifted his head. She opened her eyes, glanced at his face, took in his smug, satisfied expression, and cleared her throat. "Lunch," she declared.

He chuckled and closed his hand around hers. "Lunch, then—if that's what you want."

She told herself it was. Of course it was.

A trifle flustered, she led him through the kitchen to the stairs beyond.

The next morning, as they had on previous Mondays, Jonas and Em met as innkeeper and inn owner, and with all due attention worked through the inn's accounts.

"You were right." Jonas turned pages in the ledger, comparing earlier weeks' takings with the most recent. "The profit—which you'd already improved greatly based purely on local patronage—leaps dramatically when we have paying guests."

"So you agree I can hire Riggs to paint the front shutters, and take on more girls to help with opening, and then servicing, more guest rooms?" Across her desk, Em cocked a brow at him.

He sat back. "I would think you must have already hired all the available girls round about."

"Almost. But Mrs. Hillard at the farm by the crossroads has two daughters she was going to have to send into service, but she'd much rather send both girls to work here, at least while they're so young. She or Hillard could fetch them home every night, so everyone would be happy."

He considered her for a long moment, then said, "I agree with you about the Hillard girls, but we have to be careful not to overreach ourselves."

She knew precisely what he was really saying; she smiled and looked down, scribbling a note. "You're perfectly right—we can only hire people we need. I talked with Phyllida about the Colyton Import Company and how it started. I agree with her philosophy that it's important for their own self-worth for people to know they're valued for what they contribute, and that they're not just being kept busy for charity's sake." She completed her note with a flourish. "We're a sound business operation, not a charity."

She looked up—just as a flurry of pattery footsteps sounded out in the common room.

"Miss Colyton! Oh, Miss Colyton!"

"That's Sweetie." Pushing back his chair, Jonas got to his feet as, rising, Em came around the desk. He followed her through the hall and into the common room, where Sweetie was indeed jigging and fluttering with impatience.

Eyes bird-bright, she pounced on Em, grasping her wrist. "There you are, dear." She beamed at Jonas. "And so fortunate that you're here, too, dear boy." Conspiratorially Sweetie glanced around, then edged closer and lowered her voice. "The thing is, Harriet—Miss Hellebore—thinks she may have solved your riddle. The one about the highest house. Mind you, she's not sure." Suppressed excitement all but rolled off Sweetie's diminutive figure, but she made an effort and managed to compose her features into a semblance of seriousness. "She asked me to come and fetch you so you can decide if what she's thought of makes any sense."

Em glanced at Jonas, hope lighting her eyes.

He nodded, glanced around as he put his hand to her back. "We can go now. The accounts will keep."

He ushered them through the common room to the open inn door. Four new visitors, two ancient farmers and a handful of regulars, and—back in the shadows of the tap's far corner—Hadley, head down, busily sketching, were the only ones about to witness Sweetie's excited fluttering and the glow of rising hope in Em's face.

Jonas held few illusions about his fellow man; while he had no idea if the Colyton treasure would prove to exist, let alone be of significant value, he saw no point in taking chances and broadcasting the possibility of hidden treasure to all and sundry.

Being circumspect about the object of their hunt had from the first struck him as wise, and while Sweetie's excitement would raise little more than a smile, Em, normally far more prosaic, would raise eyebrows and awaken curiosity if she appeared too openly thrilled.

Miss Hellebore's cottage lay just along the road, standing alongside the manor's fabulous front garden.

Jonas held the little gate in the low stone wall open for Sweetie and Em to pass through, then followed them up the short path to the door.

It opened just before they reached it, and Harold Potheridge stepped out. He looked as taken aback to see them as they were to see him.

Her face expressionless, Em edged aside. Sweetie did the same.

Potheridge hesitated, then stepped past them with a distant nod.

Letting him pass, Jonas watched until, with only one glance back as he shut the gate, Potheridge departed down the road.

Sweetie shivered histrionically. "Such an *uninspiring* man."

Jonas glanced at Em and saw her lips twitch.

"It's a good thing he left," she said. "We don't want him eavesdropping."

"No, indeed." Sweetie led the way into the house, waited for them to join her in the hall, then shut and locked the door behind them. "Now we can't be interrupted or over-heard." She waved them to the front room. "Harriet's wait-ing in the parlor."

They found Miss Hellebore in her favorite chair between the hearth and the window; she was as excited and bright-eyed as Sweetie.

"This place you've been searching for. It suddenly came to me." Miss Hellebore waited, while they subsided onto the small sofa, and Sweetie slipped into the other armchair, before continuing, "I was sitting here, just glancing out at the common, as I so often do . . . and there it was."

With a wave, she directed their gazes to the window and the wide view beyond. They saw the far edge of the road, the common with its duck pond, and beyond that the slope of the ridge rising to where the church sat on the crest.

She waited while they looked, took the sight in, then qui-etly intoned, " 'The highest house—the house of the high-est.' I think you need to take those phrases as two *separate* parts of one description. As two clues, not the repetition of one. You also need to know that this village has always been devoted to its church—that's why the monuments in it are so old and so grand. And lastly you need to remember that in olden times, the Lord's house was often referred to as—"

" 'The house of the highest,' " Em breathed. Eyes locked on the church, silhouetted against the blue of the morning sky, she slowly shook her head. "It was there, in front of us, all along."

"If you think of it as the Lord's *house,* then the church is the highest house—physically the highest in the district. And the lowest level . . ." Rising, Jonas dragged his gaze from the church and glanced at Em. "That must mean the crypt."

She met his eyes. " 'A box only a Colyton would open.' A Colyton tomb?"

"Very likely. We'll have to go and look."

She bounced to her feet, eagerness lighting her face as she turned to Miss Hellebore. "Thank you so much, ma'am."

"No need to thank me, dear." Miss Hellebore waved them to the door. "Just come and tell us what you find, and, come to think of it, what this is all about, when you've found it."

Em grinned. "We will." She hurried to join Jonas at the door.

They let themselves out, then strode across the road and up the common. Lifting her skirts, she hurried as fast as she could; he paced alongside her.

"I can barely believe it," she puffed, "yet I'm sure she's right. It was there all along—we just didn't see it."

"The rhyme was well written—it would have been obvious to anyone living in the village back then, but obscure, in fact ambiguous, to anyone who didn't know the place." He looked up at the church. "Or, as has been the case, anyone who lived so far in the future that 'house of the highest' was no longer a common phrase for a church."

Reaching the church, they walked around to the side door facing the graveyard; it was always left open, day and night.

Jonas pushed the door wide; Em went in and he followed. "We'll need the crypt key." Opening the vestry door, he unhooked the key—large as a man's palm, attached to a ring big enough to fit a fist through—from the nail just inside, then waved Em to the steps to one side of the nave that led down to the crypt.

"I've been meaning to come down here and look for the graves of my ancestors ever since we arrived." Em stood back and let Jonas go down the stone steps ahead of her, then holding her skirts carefully, followed. "Other things always . . . happened."

"Never mind." Halting before the door at the bottom of the steps, he fitted the key in the lock and turned it. "We're here now, and with a purpose."

He pushed the door open; it swung easily and noiselessly on well-oiled hinges. "The crypt is still occasionally used as a store for the Colyton Import Company, so it's in reasonable state—not too much dust."

Em was glad to hear it, also to note, as she hung back in the doorway waiting for him to light the lantern left ready on the nearest tomb, that there was no evidence of clinging cobwebs festooning the crypt's arches.

Tinder sparked, light flared, then settled to a steady glow. Jonas blew out the taper, closed the lantern, then picked it up and held it high. She stepped into the crypt barely able to contain the excitement bubbling and welling inside her. "I hadn't expected to find the treasure today."

Jonas glanced back at her, then went forward to hang the lantern on a hook embedded in the ceiling, from where it spread a soft glow throughout the cavernous crypt.

She spun around, peering through the thinning shadows. "Yet here I am." She threw Jonas a smile. "Here we are, just one step away from unearthing it. Seeing it, touching it. Something left me by my ancestors all those centuries ago." She all but shivered in anticipation.

Smiling, too, he looked around. "We need to find the Colyton tombs. I can't recall seeing them, but I've never paid much attention to the names down here."

"We'd better be organized then." She considered the long, roughly rectangular room. Quite aside from the tombs and memorials lining the walls, large tombs filled much of the floor space, leaving little walkways between, some barely wide enough for her to squeeze along. Some of the floor tombs were doubles, and some had canopies that merged into the crypt's ceiling. If she hadn't been so buoyed by excitement and hope, she might have balked. "Where should we start?"

They quartered the room and methodically set about their search. They clambered over tombs, poked along the wall niches, brushed dust from the lettering on long-forgotten memorials.

Em lost count of the tombs she checked. Her excitement gradually waned, replaced by a sense that there was something wrong—something not quite right with their deductions. Still, she forged on, slipping between tightly spaced tombs to peer at their inscriptions.

They were thorough and systematic—and entirely unsuccessful.

Returning to the center of the room, she frowned. "This is nonsensical. The Colyton tombs *have* to be here." She looked around, then looked at Jonas. "Where else could they be?"

His expression said he was as mystified as she. "Let's go and talk to Joshua. He must know—or at least have records—of where the Colytons of Colyton are buried."

He returned the lantern to its resting place, then waved her ahead of him out of the door.

Skirts held high, she reluctantly trudged up the steps. "They were the premier family in the village—the founding family. They must be here somewhere."

Frustrated disappointment rang in her tone.

Jonas locked the crypt door and followed her up the steps. "They aren't buried in the graveyard, are they?"

"No." Reaching the top of the steps, she released her skirts, shook them, then smoothed them down. "I checked. There are no Colyton graves out there. I assumed most would be in the crypt, but thought there might be a few buried outside—but there aren't."

Waiting while he replaced the crypt key on its hook in the vestry, she shook her head again, utterly at a loss. "They have to be buried *somewhere*."

"Filing must know." Returning, Jonas took her hand. His gaze went past her, and he paused.

Turning her head, she followed his gaze to the far corner of the church. Within a grid of shafts of morning light and lingering shadow, Hadley was sketching a statue of an angel set on an ornate plinth. Half turned away, he was so absorbed he hadn't noticed them.

So fixated had she been on searching the crypt, she hadn't noticed if he'd been there when they arrived.

Being inside a church, she and Jonas had been speaking in hushed tones. While their voices must have carried to Hadley, they clearly hadn't been loud enough to break his concentration.

Jonas tugged at her hand; when she looked up, he tilted his head toward the door. She nodded, and they quietly walked out and headed for the rectory.

17

I t's been an abiding mystery—one I've yet to solve." Filing shook his head. "Once I heard there'd been a family of
that name, and they were indeed the founders of the village,
I couldn't understand why there are no Colyton tombs in
the crypt."

Em sank onto the sofa, disappointment writ large in her
face, but then her chin firmed. "They have to be somewhere."

Henry had been studying at the table when they'd come
in, but once Em and Jonas had related Miss Hellebore's
deductions and described their subsequent search of the
crypt, he'd deserted his books and perched on the end of
the sofa beside Em. He looked down at her. "There were
Colytons living here for centuries, weren't there?"

She nodded. "Generations and generations of them."

Standing beside Filing, Jonas said, "To restate the obvious, the Colyton remains must be *somewhere*. Somewhere
in the village, which means somewhere in the church. And
the fact we've found *no* Colytons of any age or gender suggests that, wherever they are, they're all together."

Filing nodded. "Indeed. Unfortunately I came to this parish after the death of the previous incumbent, so I had no
chance to ask questions—or learn any secrets." He turned

to the alcove he used as a study. "I'll show you what I've found. Let's see if you can make anything more of it."

Going to a bookcase, he scanned the volumes, then drew out a very old, leather-bound tome. Pushing Henry's notes aside, Filing laid the book carefully on the table; Em, Jonas, and Henry gathered around as he opened it, revealing thick pages yellowed with age.

"This is the burial record for the church. The first burial recorded is in 1453, and as far as I can tell, the record has been diligently kept through the years—as it's supposed to be." He turned back from the pages written in his own neat hand, to ones with more spidery writing. "When you look back through the centuries . . ." He stopped flipping pages and pointed to one entry.

The others crowded around.

" 'Colyton, James,' " Em read. " '1724. Dead of consumption. Age fifty-four. Buried in the Colyton crypt.' "

"As you would expect, there's more, many more, Colytons listed." Filing gently riffled the pages' edges. "And that's what all the entries say. 'Buried in the Colyton crypt.' But they're not there."

Em looked at Jonas. He shook his head and traded a glance with Filing. None of them could think of an explanation.

Henry slid back onto his chair at the table, sliding the old book around so it sat before him. Em watched as he carefully turned the pages back so he was reading the very first page. He turned over the next. Paused.

"This entry," he said, frowning, "says the Colyton *vault.*"

"Crypts were often referred to as vaults." Filing shrugged. "The words were interchangeable."

Henry looked up at him, then at Em. "But what if they weren't?"

When she frowned, Henry hurried on, eagerness growing in his voice. "What if we're getting confused because the family name is the same as the village name. What if

'Colyton crypt,' or in this case 'Colyton vault,' doesn't mean the crypt of Colyton church, but—".

"A different place." Jonas nodded, his dark eyes shining. "You're right—you must be. We've too many tombs to account for—they have to be somewhere, ergo they're in some *other* crypt."

"Let me see that." Filing took the book from Henry, quickly turned more pages. "Here's another—Colyton vault. And another." He kept flicking pages. "Here's the point where the first incumbent gave way to the second—see the different writing?" He continued flicking through entries in several different hands, then stopped. "Yes, this is where a new incumbent stopped calling it the Colyton vault, and instead wrote 'Colyton crypt.'" Filing straightened. "That both entries occur in this book suggests they're one and the same place, and wherever it is, it's part of the church."

"Either vault or crypt, it has to be underground." Jonas looked at Filing and pulled a face. "The access could be off the church crypt—with a door that's now hidden—or via a door somewhere else in the church—"

"And that could be just about anywhere." Filing grimaced back. "It might be off the vestry, or even the tower."

"A door could be concealed in a wall or the floor. Behind paneling or in stone." Jonas looked at Em. "We can search for the door—it has to be there somewhere—but it would be easier if we could find some way to narrow the search."

She stared at him for a moment, her mind scurrying to take in all they'd learned . . . she looked at the burial record, still open before Filing. "My great-grandfather was the last Colyton to live here—I'm sure he was buried here."

Filing nodded. "I've checked. His entry says 'Colyton crypt.'"

"But what was the date?"

Filing met her gaze, then looked down and quickly hunted through the pages. "Here it is."

Henry peered around Filing's shoulder. "1759."

Em looked from Filing to Jonas. "His funeral—the last Colyton of Colyton—would have been a village event. Are any of the women in the village old enough to remember it?"

Jonas exchanged a glance with Filing. "Mrs. Smollet is old enough, but whether she'd remember . . ."

Filing nodded. "The other who might know is Mrs. Thompson. But there's only those two—they're the oldest in the village by far. There's no one even in the surrounding area who's as old as they."

"And, I suspect," Jonas said, "that they're only just old enough for our purposes."

Em nodded decisively and turned to the door. "We'll try Mrs. Thompson first."

Jonas set off after her.

Filing and Henry exchanged glances, clearly not relishing being left behind. It was Filing who called after them, "Come back and tell us what you learn."

Em looked back from the doorway. "Of course. But it might take a little while."

She was praying that it wouldn't, that old Mrs. Thompson, spry and bright, would recall her great-grandfather's funeral perfectly and be able to say where the burial had been, *but* . . .

As she'd expected, it didn't prove to be that easy.

They found Mrs. Thompson in the cottage behind the forge, waiting for Oscar to bring her back one of Hilda's pasties for lunch. She was only too happy to sit around her table and chat.

"Oh, I remember the funeral—big to-do it was." Her bright gaze distant, staring into the past, Mrs. Thompson nodded her gray head. "Everyone put on their best black and went—the whole village, of course, but there were lots of nobs and others from all about. I was only seven or so, mind, but I remember it like it was yesterday."

Em leaned forward, hands tightly clasped. "Can you remember where they took the coffin for burial?"

Mrs. Thompson glanced at her, then shook her head. "No, dearie. I was too young to go to the funeral—there was no room, anyways. But . . ." She frowned, gaze distant again as she looked back over the years. "I was outside, playing in the graveyard, so I know they never brought the coffin outside." She refocused on Em. "I thought he was buried in the crypt. Isn't he?"

Em smiled weakly. "He might be, but we're trying to find exactly where. It might be in a different part of the crypt than the part used these days."

"Ah." Mrs. Thompson nodded her head sagely. "That was a long time ago."

Jonas rose. "Thank you for your time, ma'am."

"And your memories." Em stood, too.

Mrs. Thompson got to her feet to see them out. "Well, I don't see as I've helped you much, but if you want to find out where your great-granddad is buried, I'd try asking old Mrs. Smollet. She would have been ten years old or more then. Precocious child she was, Eloisa Smollet. Always had to know everything about everything going on."

Pausing at the door, Mrs. Thompson met Em's eyes and nodded. "You go and ask her. She wouldn't have been at the burial itself, no more than I was, but her older brothers would have been—they'd have been among those from the village who would have witnessed it. And I'll eat my Sunday bonnet if later Eloisa didn't demand and insist on being told every detail."

Mrs. Thompson shifted her bright gaze to Jonas. "Mark my words, if anyone still living knows where the last Colyton of Colyton is buried, it'll be Eloisa Smollet."

They stopped for a quick bite at the inn, by mutual agreement avoiding giving any hint of the latest developments to anyone, especially the twins. That necessitated keeping Issy in the dark, too, but Em whispered to Jonas that it was better that way. "Issy's useless at dissembling, and the twins are simply too sharp—once they sense she knows something, they'll wheedle it out of her, and then we'll have them under our feet."

Protectiveness still lurking beneath his calm—he was confident he could keep Em safe during their search as he planned to stick by her side, but add the twins to the mix and he'd be trying to look in three directions at once— Jonas was perfectly willing to keep their current interest secret.

As soon as they could slip away without evoking undue curiosity, they walked through the wood to the Grange for his curricle and chestnuts, and he drove them out to Highgate.

Basil was out, but old Mrs. Smollet agreed to see them. They found her in her parlor, a piece of embroidery lying half-forgotten in her lap.

She was pleased to see Em. "I've been a mite poorly for the last few days, so I haven't been able to get down to the village. So!" She fixed Em with an expectant look. "You can tell me what's been happening."

Em smiled and obliged; Jonas learned that one of Hilda's nieces was walking out with Thompson's son, and that one of the farmer's wives at Dottswood was expecting another child.

Not the sort of things he needed to know, but from her pleased nods, such tidbits were exactly what Mrs. Smollet had wanted.

Eventually Em steered the conversation to their quest. "We've been trying to locate my great-grandfather's grave. You would have been just a girl at the time of his funeral, but we thought you might remember . . . ?"

That was precisely the right way to word their request. Old Mrs. Smollet beamed. "Oh, yes—I remember that well. One of the biggest funerals I've ever seen. I even remember him—he was a very distinguished old gentleman, your great-grandfather. Everyone round about knew him—and he knew them. The whole county came to pay their respects."

Em sat forward. "Do you know anything about the burial? I realize you wouldn't have witnessed it, but . . . ?"

Mrs. Smollet all but preened. "I was at the service, but in those days females weren't allowed to witness interments." She sniffed disparagingly. "My brothers—I had two much older—were among the pallbearers. They had to have more than the usual number because of all the steps."

"The steps down to the crypt?" Jonas asked.

Mrs. Smollet nodded. "Quite an effort it was to get such a large and heavy coffin down such steep and narrow steps. Everyone waited in the church while it was taken down— my brothers said the hardest bit was remembering not to swear. He—old Mr. Colyton—was buried in the family mausoleum, or so my brothers said." She frowned.

So did Em, but before she could interrupt, Mrs. Smollet continued, "I always wondered about that. I meant to get them to show me where it—the mausoleum—was, because when Mitzy Walls and I slipped down to take a look the following week, we couldn't find it." She glanced at Jonas. "And I could never understand what my brothers meant about it being so hard to get the coffin down *both* flights of steps."

Jonas felt his pulse leap. From Em's puzzled expression as she looked at him, she didn't understand the significance. He caught her gaze, reminded her, "There's only one flight of steps down to the crypt."

They left Mrs. Smollet with effusive thanks, which she assured them quite made her day, and raced back to the rectory.

Filing and Henry leapt at the chance to leave their respective books. Together with Em and Jonas, they hurried along the path and into the church. Filing grabbed the key to the crypt and led the way down, Henry at his heels. Jonas stood back and let Em precede him; he glanced around the church, peering into the shadows, then followed her down.

Hadley must have gone back to the inn for lunch. His easel was stacked in the corner; it didn't look like he planned to hurry back. To Jonas's mind that was just as well. The fewer who knew there was any treasure involved—even knew of their search for the Colyton tombs—the better.

Filing lit the lantern, set it on its hook. "A mausoleum, vault or crypt, opening from this one, with another flight of steps leading down."

"The church stands on top of a limestone ridge," Jonas pointed out. "Another room could lie in any direction."

Scanning the walls, they gathered in the center of the room. The crypt was carved out of the ridge; the ceiling was still rough-hewn, bearing the marks of picks and adzes, but the walls had largely been hollowed out, then bricked in to form niches, alcoves, or frames for tombs. Most of the original rock had disappeared behind the more decorative stone and brick work, much of which was ornate.

Locating a door concealed within the myriad structures wasn't going to be a simple, let alone quick, task.

Jonas doubted any of them felt daunted; on the contrary, this latest hurdle only added to the challenge. The crypt was roughly rectangular. "Let's each take a wall."

The others nodded. Em walked forward to the north wall. Jonas turned and claimed the south. Filing went east, Henry west.

Silence descended as they searched.

Initially Em tapped the wall, hoping to hear some difference in tone, but she soon found that different types of stone gave different sounds when tapped, regardless of whether they had a secret passage behind them. Thereafter she resorted to pulling and pushing every brick, every rosette, every ornate corbel, and poking at every line of mortar with a shard she'd found on the floor.

She'd started in the northwest corner. After what seemed

an age during which she'd advanced barely ten feet, she glanced around and was relieved to see the others were no faster, no further forward than she.

Returning her attention to the next niche to be investigated, she continued her careful examination. Somewhat to her surprise, she didn't find it hard to concentrate, to suspend her impatience; hand in hand with adventurousness, her Colyton self possessed a certain doggedness, a determination never to be beaten and defeated by mere circumstance.

Straightening and stretching to ease her back, she glanced at the others. She wasn't surprised to see Henry as focused as she, but Jonas and Filing were equally intent, equally blind and deaf to all else as they steadily worked through their sections.

Then again, Jonas wanted to marry her, and had devoted himself to her problems, taking them on as his own. His devotion shouldn't surprise her—and by the same token, she supposed she understood Filing's motivation; once the treasure was found, Issy would feel free to marry him.

Turning back to the north wall, she stepped to the right, to the next section of stonework to be examined—an arched alcove framing a statue of an angel atop a small tomb. She considered it, then stepped back—as far as she could go—and, head tilted, studied alcove and angel some more.

She frowned.

The alcove was larger than any of the other alcoves or niches; she looked around the crypt, confirming that was true. Its top—the zenith of a perfect arch—was over six feet clear of the floor. The highest part of the angel—the tops of its wings—was significantly shorter, not even five feet. The alcove was also deeper than any of the others, nearly three feet deep, enough so shadows screened the rear wall behind the angel. The composition—angel in alcove— looked wrong, as if the alcove was too big for the angel . . .

She looked at the angel, bent to read the inscription on the tomb—a child's tomb from its size—that formed the statue's base. "Fortemain."

Turning, she looked across the narrow aisle at the large and imposing tomb she'd backed into, the one opposite the alcove. The inscription was still sharp-edged and clear: Sir Cedric Fortemain.

She checked the dates, confirming it was most likely the current Sir Cedric's grandfather. She looked at the surrounding tombs spread over the crypt floor. They were all Fortemains. In contrast, those along the wall to either side of the alcove were Binghams to one side, Elgars to the other. Looking again at the angel, she murmured, "What are you doing over there?"

On impulse, she turned, and standing before the angel, surveyed the Fortemain tombs. And saw the place the angel should have been—a neat space between the foot of Sir Cedric's tomb and the next. A quick check of the inscription on the latter tomb suggested it was Sir Cedric the elder's mother, and from the dates, the child beneath the angel was one of her offspring.

Em looked at the angel. "You should be over there."

Filing heard. From the corner of her eye, Em saw him lift his head, but when she said nothing more, he went back to his search.

She frowned at the angel. She needed to check the alcove behind it, but although not that tall, getting around the wings would be a tight squeeze.

She wasn't a Colyton for nothing. She drew in a breath, then, shard gripped tightly in one hand, she breathed out, ducked under one wing, wriggled and squeezed—and eventually popped through to the other side. Breathing again, not wanting to know if there'd been any cobwebs on the angel's lower wings that might now be decorating her hair, she eased her way upright behind the angel.

Facing the back of the alcove.

And the dusty stone plaque at eye level, directly before her face.

COLYTON

She couldn't breathe, couldn't move—could only stare.

Then she dragged in a breath to shriek—and discovered her vocal cords had seized.

She remembered the stone shard in her hand. Looking to left and right, she saw a line of stonework one brick wide bordering the back face of the arch; the rest of the face was also stone but laid in a different, horizontal pattern, incorporating the plaque in the center of what had to be a door. Holding her breath, with the sharp sliver of stone, she probed the line of what looked like mortar between the curving border stones and the ones she thought were the face of the door . . . the shard slid in easily. All the way. When she pulled it out, dust came with it, leaving an empty line between the border and the door . . .

"I've found it," she breathed. Following the border around, she noticed a large, dense spiderweb. Gritting her teeth, she lifted a fold of her skirt and quickly brushed it away—a keyhole lay behind it.

She cleared her throat, almost desperately raised her voice. "I've found it!"

A second's silence followed, then, "Where are you?" Henry called.

"Behind the angel." She shuffled and wriggled around, putting her back to the door. Reaching beneath the angel's wing, she waved one hand. "Here!"

"Good Lord." Jonas looked over the angel's wings.

Filing came up behind him and looked as well.

Em pointed excitedly behind her. "The back of this alcove is really a door and there's a plaque with Colyton carved into it."

"I thought it was just the angel's place." Filing looked bemused.

Jonas crouched at the foot of the angel statue. "This can move—it has been moved, although not recently."

Em jigged. Pointed. "It's a Fortemain. It should be over there—between Sir Cedric and his mother—it's her child. *That* Sir Cedric died two years after my great-grandfather.

They must have moved the statue so they could set his coffin in that great tomb—"

"And then they forgot to move the angel back." Filing had gone to check the Fortemain dates. "You're right."

She was sure of it. "And as there were no more Colyton burials here—my great-grandmother had already passed on and their children all died far away—then nothing occurred to remind them that the angel was in the wrong place—"

"Blocking the entry into the Colyton vault." Jonas put his hands on the statue's base. "Let's return the angel to its proper place. Em—stay where you are."

She did and helped by pushing as they edged the heavy statue out of the alcove, then maneuvered it across the aisle back into its rightful place.

Then they all turned to the now revealed door. Henry stepped close, reading the plaque, then looked at the door, pushed. "It's locked." He glanced at Filing. "Do you have the key?"

"The only key I have"—Filing took it from his belt where he'd hooked it—"is the crypt key." He handed it to Henry. "Try it."

Em stood beside Jonas and watched, all sorts of emotions coursing through her as the last male Colyton of their line slid the key into the hole.

Henry tried to turn it. Frowned. "It fits, but it's stiff."

Jonas started to move, but then stilled. Waited.

Henry wriggled the key, pressed hard—with a horrible grating screech, the key turned.

"That's it!" He looked up at the door, pushed, then set his shoulder to it; the door inched forward, then stuck.

Jonas stepped past Em. He braced both hands on the edge of the door above the lock. "On the count of three," he told Henry. "One, two—three!"

Jonas shoved, Henry pushed, and the door creaked, groaned, and gave. Jonas stepped back as Henry kept pushing.

Em expected a musty smell—the vault had been sealed for decades, after all—but instead a stream of cool air wafted out.

Jonas exchanged a glance with Filing. "The vault must connect with one of the cave systems."

Filing nodded. "I was surprised the crypt itself didn't, but perhaps it did, but the connecting chamber was made into the Colyton vault and subsequently sealed."

The door almost fully open, Henry halted just over the threshold. Em joined him as Jonas fetched the lantern from its hook, then returned to hold it above their heads—shining down into the chamber beyond the door.

It was instantly apparent that Mrs. Smollet's brothers had had cause for their complaints—the stone steps that led down into the rock were precipitous, and the walls and roof of the stairwell were so close they left barely enough space to imagine grown men getting a large coffin down the slightly winding steps.

The cavern below ate the lantern's light. There was only enough illumination to make out the ghostly shapes of tombs close by the steps, with the barest hint of yet more tombs beyond.

Filing looked at Henry. "You're fastest. There's another lantern in the vestry."

Henry nodded, turned, and, his face alight, raced off through the crypt, then pattered up the steps.

He was back a bare minute later, the other lantern in his hand.

Filing took it. As he lit it, he remarked, "This might explain that last line in the rhyme—'in a box only a Colyton would open.'" He nodded at the stone door. "Traditionally, this vault door would only be opened by a Colyton—or more precisely *for* a Colyton. Either to bury one, or for family members to visit the dead."

"Not a bad place, then, to hide a family treasure," Jonas said.

Em nodded. Her insides felt knotted with a species of dread excitement. She'd dreamed of the treasure for so long, dreamed of finding it—had embarked on a quest to hunt for it—and now there she was, standing on the threshold of solving the last part of the riddle of its location—and she could barely breathe for the anticipation welling inside her.

Filing handed the first lantern back to Jonas. "We may as well take both—no need to leave one here."

Jonas nodded. "From the looks of the size of the Colyton vault, we'll need both to search it."

He and Filing looked at Em, waited. She glanced into the crypt of her ancestors; no matter she wanted to rush in, it was still dark. She waved Jonas ahead of her. "Light the way."

He moved past her and started down the steps. Lifting her skirts, she followed.

The Colyton crypt, vault, or mausoleum, call it what one would, was enormous, if anything larger, certainly more spacious, than the church crypt. Where tombs were squeezed together in the latter, here they were well spaced and generously proportioned. Many had ornate canopies; all were large, full-sized tombs, even those for children.

Henry and Filing had followed Em down the steps. The four of them spread out, moving silently through the short avenues of tombs.

"What are we looking for?" Henry whispered.

"A box." Em answered in similar hushed tones; it seemed only fitting. "A receptacle that could hold treasure."

Jonas glanced her way. "Do you have any idea what size of box the treasure required?"

She shook her head. Halting, she surveyed the room, mentally counted . . . there had to be more than one hundred edifices dotting the space.

Jonas put her thoughts into words. "It'll take weeks to open and search all these tombs. Do you have any idea which one, or ones, the treasure will be with?"

Resting a hand on the tomb of a long-dead Colyton, she

thought back to all she'd ever heard about the treasure, about the rhyme. "The rhyme supposedly came into being in the early sixteen hundreds, so the Colyton involved was from that time or before. *But . . .*" She grimaced; as always there was a "but." "There's nothing to suggest that the treasure—presumably in some sort of box—will be associated with any particular tomb."

Filing had been surveying the extent of the crypt. "I suggest we search first for any boxlike structure—whether associated with a tomb or not. If nothing turns up via that avenue, then we can think about which tombs to open first."

Em, Jonas, and Henry murmured agreement. They set to work in pairs, each pair with one lantern; Jonas and Em walked to one end of the crypt, while Filing and Henry took the other half, working from the center toward the far wall.

Reaching the last of the tombs, Em and Jonas saw that the crypt extended some way beyond. Jonas held the lantern high and peered. "There's a tunnel leading away—probably to some other cave." He glanced at Em. "That explains the relatively fresh air. This area is riddled with cave systems."

"There's another tunnel there." Henry's voice reached them through the gloom.

He pointed to another darker area on the wall opposite the steps.

"By my reckoning," Filing called softly, "all the tombs I would expect for the Colytons are in here. There's plenty of room still left in here, so I doubt we need search for any others elsewhere."

Jonas signaled that they'd heard. He and Em turned their attention to the tombs around them. Searching for possible boxes wasn't a simple matter; the tombs came in a large number of configurations, with lots of segments built into their construction; in essence each tomb was a conglomeration of rectangular shapes buried beneath ornate stonework. Only by careful examination of each tomb, verifying that each boxlike segment was an essential part of that particular tomb, could they discount it as a potential treasure chest.

It was slow work, especially with only the light of two lanterns. They could only effectively search where the light fell; immediately beyond that, the shadows cast by the larger canopied tombs, or the more ornate edifices, broke up the light.

Em eventually halted. While there was nothing in the family's stories to suggest the treasure chest was associated with the tomb of the Colyton who'd won it, there was nothing to say it wasn't, either. She looked around. "I'm going to see if I can find the older tombs."

Absorbed with one of the larger structures, Jonas nodded.

He'd set their lantern on the top of the tomb; Em glanced around, checking how far the circle of light extended. Far enough, as it happened, to allow her to check the dates of about fifteen surrounding tombs. Picking one with a soaring angel as a marker, she commenced her survey.

By the time she returned to the soaring angel, on a tomb from the seventeen hundreds, her eyes had grown accustomed to the dimmer light. While all the tombs she'd thus far checked had dated from the late sixteen or seventeen hundreds, the next section of tombs beyond the angel looked different. Most incorporated effigies, for one thing, and the decoration on them seemed simpler, more stylized—of a different style certainly to those she'd been examining.

Moving silently forward, she searched for the dates. Some were on obvious plaques on the stonework, but others were buried within the carving; those were much harder to decipher. All had to be brushed free of dust and grit before she could make out their meaning.

She was so far from the lantern she was using her fingertips to trace letters and numbers, when she realized with a sharp jolt of excitement that the tomb she was examining— that of one Henry William Colyton—stated he was a sea captain who had died in 1595.

"Jonas." Her voice quavered; she strengthened it. "Bring the lantern—I think this is the tomb of the Colyton who amassed the treasure."

She'd spoken in little more than a whisper. Jonas looked her way, then glanced down the chamber, but Henry and Filing hadn't heard.

Straightening, he lifted the lantern and wove through the tombs to where she stood.

She patted the top of the tomb. "This is him—I'm sure of it." Excitement thrummed through her; anticipation bubbled through her veins.

In the stronger light, Jonas read the inscription she'd brushed clear. He set the lantern down. Glanced at her. "This is a simpler sort of tomb. Not so many sections to check." But he bent and set about examining the plinth, then the body, then the long rectangular top for any openings or detachable sections.

Em checked the effigy itself—trying the stone bible resting on the man's chest, then tugging at the block beneath his head—all to no avail.

Jonas stood and looked at the top of the tomb. Walking to its end, he set his hands to one corner, braced, and pushed—hard—but the heavy stone didn't shift. He straightened. "We'll need a few others, and a crowbar."

Em pursed her lips. The rhyme repeated in her head—while it might mean the treasure was inside a tomb, she had an instinctive aversion to opening a tomb, especially of one of her own ancestors; surely the Colyton wife who had hidden the treasure would have felt the same way.

Frowning, she lifted her gaze—and focused on the next tomb. The effigy was that of a woman.

"Wait." Em moved to the woman's tomb. Brushing aside the dust, she read the inscription, much easier now with the lantern so near. "Yes," she breathed. "This is his—the captain's—wife." She looked at Jonas. "It was she who caused the treasure to be put aside, rather than spent on more ships, more adventuring."

Jonas moved to her side. "In that case." He crouched and started to examine the base of the tomb.

Em looked at the effigy, wondered if the face on it was anything like her long-ago, many-times-great-grandmother. Moving to the head, she pushed and pressed the sides of the box-shaped headrest, but nothing seemed remotely giving.

The woman was much shorter than her husband; Em inwardly snorted—lack of inches was apparently one Colyton trait she'd inherited. The woman's soles rested against another stone box, necessary to balance the placment of the effigy on the tomb's top. Going to the foot of the tomb, Em placed her hands on the corners of the box, and, as she had so many times before, pulled.

The box shifted. Not by much—just a fraction of an inch. Barely able to believe it—not breathing at all—she released it and went to peer at the box from the effigy side—and saw a newly formed gap between the effigy's soles and the back of the box.

A real box—one that was meant to be lifted away.

"I think this is it." Her voice wobbled. She felt . . . dizzy, nauseous, and so excited she could barely stand.

Jonas appeared beside her. She pointed to the box. Prodded it with a fingertip. "I think it pulls out." Her whisper was a mere thread, but he heard.

He frowned at the box. "There are words engraved on it."

They both stepped nearer; standing side by side at the foot of the tomb, they stared as with his cuff—now beyond redemption anyway—he wiped the letters free of dust.

The words cleared. Em traced them—just to make sure. " 'Here lies the future of the Colytons.' "

"Very neat," Jonas murmured. "Anyone who didn't know about the rhyme and the treasure would imagine that refers to an infant's burial, perhaps a miscarriage, given there are no dates and this is a private crypt."

"It might have referred to her." Em nodded at her ancestor. "It might be thought to mean that she was the future of the Colytons, and she'd died before her time."

"True." Jonas nudged her aside. "But we—we think—know better. So let's see."

Gripping the sides of the box, he braced, steadily pulled, and the box inched forward.

Em peered into the widening gap at the effigy's feet. "It's on carved runners."

Jonas grunted. He wriggled the box side to side, then pulled again, and it slid slowly forward, then came more easily. He stopped before it came totally free, glanced around. "Stand back." He braced, pulled the box off the tomb, took its weight—nearly staggered, but managed to swing around and set it down heavily on the flat top of a later tomb. "Gads—it's heavy!"

Filing and Henry heard the thump and looked up.

Em waved. "We think we've found it."

Pent-up excitement had sent her voice up several octaves. She felt like jigging, yet her stomach was churning. What if there was nothing but rocks in the box? Or worse, bones?

She pushed the disturbing thought from her mind, dragged in a huge breath as Henry and Filing rushed up.

While they exclaimed over the box, and where it had lain, she felt Jonas's steady gaze on her. She met it. When he quirked a brow, she managed a weak smile, mouthed, "I'm all right."

Folding her arms, she rubbed them. She wasn't cold, but . . . she turned her attention back to the box. "Can we open it, do you think?"

All three males poked and prodded, shifting the lantern so it cast better light first on this face, then that.

"There's a sort of catch here." Henry picked at one of the longer sides. "It's made of stone—set into the stone. Like one of those Chinese puzzles."

None of the others could see, but then a click sounded, and Henry straightened. "That's it." He glanced at Em.

She nodded. "Go on—open it."

Easier said than done; although unlocked, the heavy lid's

hinges seemed stuck. Jonas and Filing tried to help, but no amount of pulling with fingers worked.

Filing stepped back. "The encrustation of the ages."

"It'll open," Jonas said. "But we'll need a crowbar to lever it up."

He looked at Em, to see her frowning at the edge of the lid. "It did lift, just a little." She raised her gaze to his face; hers seemed a trifle pale. "Do we have anything we can jam in the gap?"

Henry, Filing, and Jonas checked their pockets; the only thing they had that might work was the ring on which the crypt key dangled; it had a thinned edge.

Filing handed it to Em. "We'll lift—you slide it in."

Together with Filing and Henry, Jonas grabbed hold of the lid; at his nod, they pulled in unison. Peering at the edge, Em wedged the thin iron in the gap, wiggled it. "I've got it."

She turned to grab the lantern. Releasing the lid, the men came around to look.

Henry was beside her as she crouched before the box. Eyes level with the thin slit of an opening they'd managed to create, she directed the lantern light in . . .

"Gold!" Henry said.

After a moment of shifting the light this way and that, all Em could manage was a weak "Oh, my." She looked up and found Jonas watching her. "Jewels." She paused to clear her throat. "They have to be jewels—blues and reds and greens. And pearls. Gold coins, and other gold things, too."

Excitement was building, strengthening her voice, carrying her away on a euphoric tide.

A slow smile spread across Jonas's face. "It looks like you Colytons have found your family treasure."

They had. They'd actually done it—and there really was a treasure. A *real* treasure. Em could barely take it in.

Getting the box up and into the light brought her back to earth. It was so heavy, and so hard to keep a good grip on, that Jonas and Filing together could only manage to shift it a few feet at a time.

Maneuvering it up the steps to the crypt was a major undertaking even with all four of them lending a hand, in fact two. Managing the last flight up to the church was equally difficult.

Sitting it on a nearby pew, they stopped to catch their breath.

At the front of the church, Hadley looked up from his sketching. Filing saw and waved him over. "Just what we need—more hands."

Setting aside his pencils, Hadley rose and walked over. "What is it?" he asked, looking at the box.

"Our family's treasure!" Henry could barely stand still. "We always knew it was somewhere here, and today we found it. It was in the family crypt."

"Is that so?" Smiling easily, Hadley nodded to Em, then looked at Jonas and Filing. "What are you planning on doing with it now?"

"We need to take the box back to the inn. We'll need tools to open it—the lid's jammed." Jonas looked at Henry. "Thompson's working at the Grange today, but Oscar should be around the forge. Why don't you run and see if you can roust him out and bring him here?"

Henry nodded and took off, racing out of the door and all but leaping down the path to the lych-gate. His hands had proved too small, his arms too weak, for him to support the box even with Jonas or Filing on the other end.

"So what's in it?" Hadley nodded at the box.

"We're not sure yet," Em answered. "Most likely gold and jewels, but we need to open it to see."

"How did it come to be there?" Hadley asked.

While they waited for Henry to return, Em briefly related the tale of the treasure and the rhyme.

Hadley grinned. "Quite an adventure, then, leaving your

uncle's house and coming all this way, searching for it, and then finding it."

"Indeed." Em smiled as Henry bounced back into the church, Oscar stumping along behind him. Oscar, too, had to hear the story, but he was perfectly willing to listen as he and Hadley spelled Jonas and Joshua as they carried the box, one at each end, down the path to the lych-gate, then followed the lane to the road and the Red Bells.

By the time they reached the inn's front yard, they'd gathered an audience, an increasingly excited one as the story of the treasure spread.

Hadley halted. "I need to go back and pack up my sketches."

John Ostler promptly took his place.

"Thank you," Em called.

Hadley saluted, then turned and jogged back up the lane.

They wrestled the box—which only seemed to grow heavier—into the inn and let it thump down onto one of the tables near the bar.

Edgar pulled Jonas and Filing a pint while John Ostler went to fetch a crowbar from his tack room.

Henry fetched Issy and the twins. Like Em, Issy had difficulty absorbing that their hunt was finally over. That the treasure sat before them, albeit sealed in a stone box.

The twins had no such difficulty. They danced and jigged and exclaimed.

Thompson came in with John Ostler, the crowbar already in his hamlike hand. He looked at Em for permission.

"Please." She waved him to the box.

Henry released the stone catch again, held it open while Jonas directed and Thompson carefully inserted, then wriggled and pushed the end of his bar into the box . . . with a long, low groan, the lid eased up, then swung up to reveal . . .

Enough gold coins, jewels—sapphires, rubies, and the white fire of diamonds winking amid the jumbled mass— ropes of pearls and jewel-encrusted gold goblets to satisfy anyone's version of what a buccaneer's treasure should be like.

"Oh. My. God." Hands to her face, Em stared.

Beside her, Issy was speechless.

Even the twins were reduced to round-eyed "Ooohs" as they peered into the box.

Silence held the inn for a finite instant, then someone cheered—and everyone took it up. The name "Colyton" shook the rafters.

Em suddenly felt weak, giddy, dizzy.

"Here—sit down." Jonas's hand closed on her shoulder. She felt the edge of a chair behind her knees; she all but fell into it.

Filing had Issy in hand, sitting her beside Em at the table on which the fabulous treasure lay.

Em glanced up, found Jonas by her shoulder, raised her hand to cover his, looked up into his face. "Thank you."

His smile was confident and proud. He squeezed her hand, then looked up, across the table. "Ah—just the man we need."

Lucifer stood looking down at the treasure, then he looked at Em and smiled. "Congratulations."

"Thank you." Em waved at the hoard. "Now we have it, I confess I'm overwhelmed. I don't know what to do with all this." A thought struck. She sat up and peered at the sparkling pile. "Is it even real?"

"Oh, I think so." Smiling, Lucifer raised a brow at her. "May I?"

She waved her assent. Under cover of continued exclamations and untold conversations and speculations about the newfound treasure, Lucifer trawled through the mass, long fingers turning over coins, picking out bright jewels and holding them up to the light. Setting one particularly bright gem back in the box, he grunted, then ran a long rope of pearls through his fingers.

Phyllida came up beside him. "Stop performing. They're real, aren't they?"

Lucifer looked at Em. His lips curved; dark blue eyes bright, he nodded. "Very real. These are some of the finest rubies I've seen in a long time, and the sapphires are flawless. The emeralds have excellent color, and I can't recall ever seeing ropes of pearls with such perfect sizing. They must be old."

"My grandmother told me they were taken from a Spanish galleon in the late fourteen hundreds," Em said.

Lucifer nodded. "That would explain the gold doubloons, which, I might add, are also in excellent condition and on their own"—he lowered his voice—"are worth a not inconsiderable fortune. Add them to all the rest and . . ." He gestured to the treasure. "Your family treasure is literally worth a king's ransom." He caught Em's gaze. "It's a very good thing you pursued it and found it. Or at some point in time, someone else would have."

"Good God!"

The exclamation came from behind Em. She swiveled in her chair to see Harold a few feet away, goggling, slack-jawed, at the treasure.

His mouth worked, then he managed to utter, "*That's* the Colyton treasure? Well, my word—I always thought it was just a silly story, a fairytale made up to entertain children."

"Clearly not." Jonas's clipped accents were a warning, one Harold didn't seem to hear.

"No, indeed." His eyes gleamed avariciously. He licked his lips; eyes fixed on the treasure, he rubbed his hands together.

It was blatantly obvious to everyone watching that he was considering ways to get his hands on the treasure. Gradually the excited chatter faded, then died. A rather oppressive silence descended.

Harold remained oblivious.

Jonas sighed. "Potheridge—I believe you should leave."

"Heh?" Jerked from his contemplation of the treasure, it nevertheless took Harold a moment to transfer his uncomprehending gaze to Jonas's face.

What he saw there brought him to himself. He noticed the silence, quickly glanced around—finally registered the suppressed animosity directed his way.

He humphed. Looked at Em, opened his mouth, then abruptly closed it, swung on his heel, and stalked out.

"Good riddance, I say." Thompson bent to lean his crowbar against the front of the bar. "Less we all see of that one, the better."

A dark murmur of agreement circled the room.

Jonas exchanged a glance with Lucifer, then caught Edgar's eye. "Call drinks on the house." As Edgar did, Jonas looked down at Em and smiled. "My treat, while we decide what to do with this."

She nodded and looked at the treasure, a great deal more sober after what Lucifer had said.

Jonas pulled up a chair beside her; Phyllida and Lucifer pulled a bench to the other side of the table and joined them.

Em glanced from Jonas to Lucifer. "I've never had anything like this to deal with before. Can you advise me?"

Lucifer nodded. "I can appraise it for you—that will give you a much better idea of its worth. After that . . . to be blunt, I would urge you to sell it, at least a good portion of it."

Em wrinkled her nose. "It's what the inscription says it is—the future of the Colytons. It was placed there to help us when we were in need. If it's really as valuable as you say, then we'd only want to take what we need—enough to set Henry up properly, as is due the Colyton name, and portions for us, his sisters—and leave the rest for the next generation of needy Colytons."

Lucifer nodded. "A laudable aim, but you can't put the treasure back, not where it was. And regardless, I'd strongly urge you to sell it all and convert what you want to leave for future generations into investments. Jonas and I can help you with that—so that the next generation of needy Colytons don't have to embark on any wild treasure hunt fueled only by belief in a family tale."

Em smiled. "Thank you—although I have to point out that Colytons actually enjoy treasure hunts."

"Perhaps so," Filing said, "but with this much at stake, it simply wouldn't be safe."

"No, indeed." Em stared at the treasure. What lay before her, gleaming and winking, far exceeded her wildest dreams. She was still having difficulty believing it, absorbing it. Truly grasping that her quest was over, and all her prayers for her family had been answered—comprehensively.

She looked at Issy, still stunned, still staring, then at Henry. He was smiling, but kept shaking his head every now and then, as if he, too, was having trouble taking it in.

Only the twins, bright-eyed and focused intently on the treasure, seemed to have accepted the entirety of it without the slightest quibble. They, she suspected, had believed without doubt, unconditionally trusting in the tale, and by their easy acceptance must have always imagined the treasure would be as magnificent as it was.

Now . . . she glanced at Jonas, then looked at Lucifer. "Now it's here, and we can see what it is, where can we safely store it?"

"I know just the place." Jonas caught her gaze as she turned to him; to her surprise he raised his voice so the inn's patrons all around could hear. "We'll put the treasure in the cells below the inn. No prisoner has ever escaped them— and no one has ever broken into them, either."

18

T hat was well done." Lucifer nodded to Jonas as they stood outside one of the cells in the inn cellar, looking through the doorway at the stone box they'd deposited on the bench inside.

Closed once more, its brilliant contents concealed, the box looked incongruous—a strange inanimate prisoner.

Jonas swung the heavily barred door closed and turned the large key. "I wanted to make sure everyone knew there was no point trying to steal the newly unearthed Colyton treasure." Although he spoke in response to Lucifer's comment, it was Em his eyes rested upon.

She nodded, understanding completely. Not just that the treasure was now indisputably safe, but also his reasons for making his announcement; she was learning to appreciate his protective streak.

"Here." He held out the key to her. "You need to keep this safe."

Accepting the heavy key, she slipped it into her pocket; its weight dragged. "I'll think of a safe place to leave it."

The entire day still seemed like a dream; she was half-convinced she would wake up shortly and discover none of it was real.

They climbed the cellar stairs and returned to the common room, still comfortably crowded. Many had come to learn what was going on, and had stayed to dine. When she looked into the kitchen, she found Hilda like a general in the midst of organized chaos.

"They're waiting dinner for you in the family parlor," Hilda directed. "You and Mr. Tallent and Mr. Cynster should go up. Mrs. Cynster's already there with Mr. Filing, Master Henry, and your sisters."

Thus dispatched, Em climbed the stairs with Jonas and Lucifer. The others were already at the table, waiting; as soon as they'd taken their seats, Joshua said grace. Never before had she murmured a more sincerely fervent thanks for God's bounties. As soon as the dishes were set before them, she dismissed the two maids to their own dinner in the kitchen, leaving the family, and Jonas, Filing, and the Cynsters, free to converse as they pleased.

While she, Issy, and Henry were still grappling with the enormity of their windfall, the twins were much less awed; in their imaginations the Colyton treasure had always been fabulous. The reality had simply lived up to their expectations. Consequently they'd already concocted some quite startling plans as to what to do with it.

The girls' ebullient, exuberant spirits were infectious. Two hours passed swiftly; Em barely had a chance to think between dealing with suggestions such as "I think we should buy a house in London," and "We need to buy a ship and sail to the Indies," and maintaining some degree of polite discourse.

Phyllida understood. She caught Lucifer's eye, indicated the door, then turned to Em and patted her hand. "Your head must be whirling. My one piece of advice, and I'm sure Lucifer will agree, is not to rush things. Take your time and let things sink in—give other options a chance to present themselves before you make any decisions." She smiled, and Em could see the likeness to Jonas. "You've found the treasure and it's safe, and so are you and your brood here in Colyton."

Glancing at Jonas and Filing, both discussing some point with Lucifer, slowly getting to his feet, Phyllida added, "As I'm sure you realize, you, Issy, Henry, and the twins all have a place here among us." She stood.

Meeting her dark gaze, Em inclined her head. "Thank you. That's excellent advice."

Collecting her husband, Phyllida left. Leaving Issy and Joshua watching over the twins, at last flagging, Em insisted on going down to show her face—the innkeeper's face—in the common room.

Jonas sighed, but didn't try to dissuade her. He accompanied her down the stairs, then sat in the tap with the other men, chatting and sipping ale, and watching Em flit back and forth, checking on this, having a quick word with some lady, then buzzing back to the kitchen to convey something to Hilda before reappearing at Edgar's shoulder behind the bar.

He suspected it was her way of bringing herself back to earth. Finding and laying hands on the treasure had been exciting, but discovering the extent of her ancestors' legacy had been a shock. An entirely understandable shock, one that would knock any lady for a loop, but most especially one who had spent the last months walking a knife-edge of incipient penury, all in pursuit of a dream.

A dream that had converted into a staggering reality.

He, of course, felt distinctly mellow, if not a trifle smug. Now she had her treasure, her newfound wealth would obviate a good number of the difficulties she would have wrestled with in accepting his suit. He wouldn't have cared if she was penniless, but she would have. Now she would have a decent portion, enough to allow her to accept his hand without quibble.

And with Henry and her sisters' futures now assured, she would soon have time to turn her mind to him, and his proposal.

Would soon have more time to devote to him, and the role he wished her to fill.

He was feeling distinctly in charity with the world when, the last stragglers waved on their way and the inn secured for the night, he followed Em up the stairs to her rooms.

Ignoring the candle left burning on the dresser, she led the way through the parlor into her bedroom. He followed, noting with a certain triumph her lack of hesitation, of consciousness in having him there.

She slowed, then halted in the middle of the room and turned to face him. Moonlight flooded in through the uncurtained windows, laying a pearlescent silver sheen wherever it touched. Her gaze scanned his face, then she looked down. "I think, if you don't mind, that I'd rather you kept this."

Following her gaze, he saw that she was holding the heavy key to the cell in her hand.

Something in him stilled.

An instant ticked by, then he forced himself to ask, "Are you sure?" Sure she wanted to entrust him with her family's future.

Her moon-silvered lips curved. "Yes, I'm sure. Take it, please. You can hide it at the Grange. There are too many people coming and going at the inn these days, especially now we have paying guests." She drew in a breath, lifted her head, looked him in the eye. "I'd feel much more comfortable if I knew it was with you."

His hand closed about hers, removing the key from her open palm. His eyes locked on hers, he saw full comprehension of the moment in her face, in her expression; sliding the key into his coat pocket, he reached for her.

She came readily into his arms; reaching up, framing his face with her small hands, she looked into his eyes, then kissed him. Longingly, lingeringly, enticingly—a clear invitation.

They both had so much to celebrate.

He gathered her in, fitting her against him, where she belonged. He kissed her back, as gloriously hungry, as joyfully elated as she.

As intent on seizing the moment, on sharing the triumph, on celebrating their success—and all that it meant.

She was with him every step of the way as he steered them unerringly into the heart of the flames. This was indeed a moment to savor, a night to recognize, accept, embrace, and give thanks for the bounties that had come their way.

The Colyton treasure, yes, but along the way they'd discovered something with far greater potential, something more enduring than gold and jewels, and infinitely more precious.

She yielded her mouth, and he took, claimed, unrestrainedly plundered, then surrendered the reins and let her have her way while he set his fingers to her laces and the buttons closing her gown.

Clothes drifted to the floor.

Hers, his, until a drift of fabrics lay about their feet in the moonlight.

Naked, she was eager and urgent; he let her help him remove his boots and stockings, then yielded to her insistent demand and let her kneel before him and peel his breeches down.

Quickly he shrugged free of the shirt she'd already opened, eyes locked on her, reading the wild passions, the considerations and speculations gleaming in her bright eyes. Before she could act on any of them, he stepped free of his breeches, seized her by the shoulders, and lifted her onto her feet, then pulled her into his arms.

Skin met skin.

Em gasped, senses reeling in delight at the contact. With heated deliberation, she wound her arms about his neck, sinuously stretched up against him, seized an instant to glory in the feel of his rougher skin and harder body riding against her softer curves, then, with eager abandon, she locked her lips on his.

Yielded her mouth, his to possess, as she moved into him, pressing her breasts, already aching and heavy, against the solid planes of his chest as she fitted her hips against his thighs and wantonly undulated, stroking the rigid rod of his erection with her taut, silky-smooth belly.

Hands grasped.

His closed about her bottom, evocatively kneading, sending molten desire sliding through her, pooling at her core. His fingers drifted, traced, probed. Her skin grew fevered, damp.

He gripped, hoisted her up; instinctively she spread her legs, wrapped them about his hips, with eyes closed caught her breath on a shuddering gasp as he held her steady and pressed into her, released that breath in a shuddering moan as sensation, primitive and undeniable, washed over and through her.

Her hands clutched his shoulders, fingers gripping tight. His hands locked viselike about her hips, holding her immobile as he steadily, relentlessly, claimed her. Filled her, completed her. She gasped, arched, and took him in; her body welcomed him, embraced and clung, surrendered and seized.

Once he was fully seated, he held her securely and walked the short distance to the bed. He set her down on her back on the coverlet, her hips only just supported on the mattress; his hands curving possessively over the heated curves of her bottom, he held her, held her senses captive as he straightened, then, his gaze locked with hers, he withdrew, almost to her entrance, then with a sharp thrust of his hips, he solidly filled her again.

It felt different, the sensations of possession heightened given they were only touching there—she had no other tactile sensation to distract her; her mind, all her senses, locked avidly, greedily, on where they joined.

The slick friction from the steady rhythm he set, each long stroke filling her to the hilt, built and intensified until each solid penetration sent waves of pleasure pulsing down her veins, tightening her nerves.

Gradually overwhelming her mind; she closed her fingers,

fisted her hands in the coverlet, flung her head from side to side as the bright fire within grew, heard her own moan as she felt the flames coalesce and ecstasy beckon.

But she wanted him with her. Tightening her legs about his hips, she pulled him closer, deeper, arched her spine as much as he would allow . . .

Jonas gasped as he felt the reins slide from his grasp, as his body answered her wild call. Chest heaving, he released her hips, leaned over her, arms braced on either side to hold him above her; head bowed, his gaze locked on her face as she writhed beneath him, he thrust again and again, taking every inch she offered, demanding her surrender.

Giving her his.

In response she demanded still more, craved more, her body luscious and heated beneath his, open and embracing; beyond his control, his body responded, thrusting deeper, harder, more powerfully.

A celebration in truth, but of something more primal, more primitive and elemental; it swelled, rose through them, flowing in a rush from where they so uninhibitedly merged.

A firestorm of passion, desire, and need, and something even more potent.

The flames roared through him, through her, and took them. For one blind instant, in an explosion of senses, sundered them from this world.

Transported them to one where ecstasy was the very air; they drew it in and it filled them. Overflowed . . .

The tumult faded into memory, leaving them gasping, clinging, awash on a golden sea.

From beneath drooping lids, their gazes met, held.

Their hearts slowed, beat as one, as knowledge seeped into their souls.

She smiled. Slowly, the gesture spreading across her sweet face, lighting her golden eyes with jewel green.

His lips curved in reply; he felt a chuckle rumble through his chest.

Disengaging, he lifted her, laid her higher on the bed, then joined her.

Felt vindicated, honored, and blessed—and felt certain she felt the same as she curled into him, settling her head on his shoulder.

Contentment held him, born of the certainty that she had to know, as he did, that *this* was true glory, that what had burgeoned and grown between them, and now slid, the finest elixir, through their veins, the power that caught them and held them, addicted and helpless, that shattered them only to fill them with bliss—that this—being that power's pawn—was true heaven on earth.

As he sank into her bed, drew her into his arms, and flicked the covers over their cooling limbs, he was never more certain that *this* was meant to be, that this, and she, was his true destiny.

"A-hem!"

Em looked up from the open ledger on her desk to see Silas Coombe standing in the doorway of her office. "Mr. Coombe." She pushed back her chair and started to rise. "Can I help you?"

"No, no, dear lady!" Smiling unctuously, Coombe advanced, waving her back to her seat. "It is *I* who have come to offer my poor services to *you.*"

Perfectly willing to keep the desk between them, she sank back into her chair and politely raised her brows. "How so, sir?"

"If I may?" Coombe indicated the chair before the desk; when she nodded he slipped into it and leaned forward to speak in a confidential tone. "It's about the . . . ah, Colyton treasure, my dear. I'm not sure if you're aware, but I'm an expert of sorts, an authority on antiquities of various kinds."

His expression one of scholarly seriousness, he continued, "Cynster is an expert on jewels and jewelry—you'd be wise to seek his advice on such items as fall within his scope. But one of my specialities is coins, old coins. I'd be very happy to assist you in evaluating and disposing of the doubloons and any other such items in the cache."

Em had no doubt whatever that Coombe would be very happy—ecstatically happy—were she to hand the coins over to him for assessment and sale. She smiled, but the gesture didn't reach her eyes. "Thank you for your offer, Mr. Coombe. I will certainly bear it in mind, but at this point my siblings and I have yet to decide what we will do with the treasure—what we will sell, what we will keep, whether we sell anything much at all."

She rose, her smile still polite, but clearly one of dismissal. "I will, of course, inform you if we wish to avail ourselves of your kind offer. Thank you for dropping by."

Good manners brought Coombe to his feet. He stared, mouth opening and closing several times before he realized she'd left him little choice but to accept her dismissal with good grace.

He drew himself up. "Indeed. Don't hesitate to let me know if I may be of service. Your servant, Miss Colyton."

He bowed rather stiffly and made his exit.

Em watched him go, then slowly sank back into her chair.

She'd spoken truly in saying that she and her siblings hadn't yet made any decision regarding the treasure. For herself, she was still coming to grips with its scope. She'd been expecting a pouch of gold coins, perhaps a small cache—just a handful—of good gems. The staggering quantity they'd uncovered cast the family treasure in a significantly different light; dealing with it now loomed as a responsibility—both to her siblings and future generations. The decision of what to do with it had acquired a gravity it hadn't previously had.

The cautious streak that ran alongside her Colyton recklessness urged her to heed Phyllida's excellent advice. She would take her time, and make the right decisions.

Regardless, she wouldn't trust Coombe, not even with a handful of coins. Lucifer, however, was a different matter. She'd never trusted easily—life had taught her to be careful from an early age—but she trusted her instincts, too, and they hadn't taken long to accept Lucifer . . . in much the same way they'd accepted Jonas. As an honorable man.

More, along with Phyllida, Lucifer had somehow—entirely without pushing—achieved a status, not just with her but also with her siblings, as being almost family. She would, she decided, accept his offer to appraise the treasure, and then she would discuss with her siblings, and with Jonas, Joshua, Phyllida, and Lucifer, what would be the wisest thing to do.

It seemed odd to have others—other adults as well as Issy and Henry—with whom to share her deliberations. Strange to have people on whom she could call whose opinions and advice she valued.

She found her lips had spontaneously curved. Admitted to herself, as she picked up her pencil and refocused on the accounts, that having such people around felt good.

Her day was as busy, if not busier, than ever. Those from the outlying farms came in to hear the story of the treasure. Even though it was locked away and not on show, there were many in the common room, male and female alike, who had seen it the previous day and were happy to describe its fabulousness to their less fortunate neighbors.

"It's inevitable," Jonas said when, later that night, with the inn quiet about them, he followed her up the stairs. "This is the country—the news will spread far and wide. However, said news will also include where the treasure presently is, and the fact that the cells below the inn are impregnable."

"There is that, I suppose." Reaching the top of the stairs, Em turned to the door to her parlor; she sent it swinging wide—and recoiled on a gasp.

"What?" Jonas was instantly behind her, his hands closing protectively about her shoulders as he looked over her head.

At the devastation inside.

Shock held them immobile for a full minute, their gazes taking in the upended furniture, the cushions flung this way and that, the dresser with drawers hanging open, their contents strewn over the floor—bare boards with the rug flung aside.

"What the hell?" Grim-faced, Jonas set Em gently aside and moved into the room. Nothing seemed broken; this was not wanton destruction.

He scanned the room, then stalked to the bedroom door. It swung wide at his touch; inside the scene was a repetition of that in the parlor—the bedcovers dragged off the bed, the mattress upended, the armoire doors open, every drawer pulled out and emptied on the floor. Even the thick curtains had been pushed aside.

"They were searching for the key." Em spoke from just behind him.

He glanced down into her pale face. Nodded. "It looks like it."

Leaving the doorway, he picked his way across the room. The bathing chamber had fewer places to search, but it, too, had been thoroughly ransacked.

The door beyond, leading to the back stairs, stood ajar.

Lips thinning, he walked to the door, examined the latch. "No lock." There wasn't even a bolt Em could slide to secure the door. He turned to find her staring at her disarranged towels. "If you're agreeable, I'll have Thompson around here tomorrow to put bolts on this door."

His voice seemed to draw her from her shock. She looked at him; it took a moment for her to work through his words, then she nodded. Wrapping her arms about herself, she shivered. "Yes, please do. Otherwise I'll never be able to sleep here alone again."

She'd never be sleeping alone again, here or anywhere

else, but he bit back the words; now was not the time to push.

She suddenly looked up, horror in her eyes. "The twins. Issy."

She hurried toward him; he opened the door and stood aside, then followed her up the back stairs to the upper floor.

Em rushed straight to the twins' room, but they lay asleep in the moonlight, innocent and undisturbed. Hugely relieved, she waved Jonas back. She stuck her head around Issy's door, and Henry's, but all her siblings were safe and sleeping in rooms showing no signs of pillage.

Heaving a huge sigh, she met Jonas's eyes, flashed him a relieved smile. Silently they made their way back to her rooms.

She halted in the bathing chamber, picked up a towel and started folding it. "Thank goodness whoever it was didn't think to search up there."

Or knew better than to bother. Jonas didn't voice his suspicions, but tucked them away for later examination. He pointed through the bedroom to the parlor. "I'll get started in there."

Em nodded. "I'll get these things tidied away, then come and help."

He left her to sort through her more personal belongings; returning to the parlor, he righted the furniture and set it back in place. When she joined him, he left her putting back the smaller things dumped out of the drawers, and went into the bedroom. After reassembling the bed, he returned drawers and furniture to their proper place, then set about untangling the covers.

Em came in, saw him, and smiled.

Flicking out the sheet as he'd seen Gladys do countless times, he grunted. "I can manage here. You do the other stuff."

Her smile widened briefly—he wasn't at all averse to having her laugh at him, just as long as she laughed—then she turned to the mess the intruder had made of her clothes.

By the time she'd finished tidying and closed the last drawer with a sigh, he'd made a passable job of the bed. There was no point in it being picture perfect; they'd be disarranging it almost immediately.

She came to him, put her arms around him, and laid her head on his chest. "Someone's after the treasure."

Although neither spoke the name, both knew who had to be classed as the principal suspect. He dropped a kiss on her brow. "We can think about that tomorrow." With one hand, he tipped up her chin, looked into her eyes. "For tonight . . ." He searched her eyes, then bent his head and kissed her.

Covered her lips with his and sensed for the first time that while she was willing, she was distracted. Thinking too much about, worrying too much about, the intruder who had searched her rooms.

"He's gone," he murmured against her lips. "He won't be back." He supped lightly, tantalizingly. "Not tonight. Not tomorrow. Not again."

He nipped her lower lip—caught her attention. And with ruthless devotion seized her senses and hauled her, not resisting but for once passive, into a landscape of sensation powerful enough to suspend her thoughts, to circumvent them, to hold her mind in thrall, to take her from the disturbing present and later, he hoped, allow sleep to soothe her.

That was his aim as he kissed her voraciously and with unwavering determination waltzed her into the welcoming heat of their mutual, consuming passion.

That one look into her eyes had been enough to confirm that she was already fretting, concerned, worried—all those weighty cares that came to her by habit. That habitually she'd shouldered alone, by herself. Until now.

Now he was there, to take the weight from her, metaphorically and practically; he'd already claimed that role. And there was nothing to be done until morning.

Until then, she needed to stop thinking, stop worrying.

Yet she hovered on the threshold of the moment; even as his lips parted hers and he plundered her mouth, she was still not fully engaged.

There was only one thing he could imagine strong enough to drag her thoughts from her cares.

So he gave it to her.

Lavished it on her.

Unleashed all he felt for her and purely through their kiss pressed his desire, passion, and need upon her—until she couldn't resist, couldn't hold back, until she, the adventurous woman who ruled her heart and soul, had to seize with both hands and plunge into the whirlpool of their passions.

Hands rising to clasp his face, Em gasped, struggling to ride the fiery tide he'd so recklessly let loose, trying to find mental feet she'd already lost in the tumult now raging between them.

This—*this*—was something else. Stronger, more powerful, than she'd yet experienced, the sheer intensity of feeling—of driving relentless need—rocked her, would have shocked her had her Colyton soul not stepped forward and, in awe, metaphorical eyes sparkling, murmured *Yes*.

His arms held her trapped, then his hands were on her, not in gentle persuasion, but in blatant demand. His lips, his kiss, held her wits captive, disengaged, flown, leaving her a prisoner of her senses—senses he suborned. That he made his, his tools, his weapons as, palms hard, his touch almost rough, he closed his hands about her breasts.

Weighed, squeezed, then through the thin fabric of her gown he captured her nipples and rolled, tweaked them to hard, tight buds. His strong fingers played, sending lancing sensation spearing through her, down nerves and veins to pool hotly between her thighs.

He gave her no time to think, no opportunity for her head to clear, for her wits to break free. Releasing her breasts, he skated his hands down her body, over her waist, openly, possessively over her hips, to grasp her bottom, to fill his hands and flagrantly, evocatively grip and knead.

Pressing his hips to her, holding her against his rigid erection, he steered her back until she met the side of the bed.

For one long instant, he held her there, trapped between the bed and him—making her feel what she did to him, impressing every last facet of his arousal on her. Throughout he ravenously kissed her, feasted on her mouth until she felt giddy, weak.

Then he lifted his head, stepped back, spun her around, then stepped in again, so she was trapped facing the bed, with him behind her.

She felt his fingers on the laces of her gown. Felt his gaze—on her breasts.

"Look into the mirror."

His gravelly command—it was that and no request—had her lifting her gaze. Directly across the bed, against the far wall, sat her dressing table with its wide mirror. The window beside it allowed moonlight to flood in; it was a clear, crisp night—there was more than enough illumination for her to see her own reflection—and see him, a large, dark shadow looming behind her.

She couldn't make out his eyes, his expression, but his face seemed hard, graven, passion etched.

The sight sent a frisson of lustful expectation sliding down her spine.

An expectation more reckless than any she'd entertained before.

An expectation that only heightened as, with ruthless efficiency, he stripped her gown, petticoats, and chemise from her.

Dropping her clothes to the floor, he brought his hands back to her body, closed them about her breasts once again—and made her gasp as, his hands darker against her pale skin, she watched him possess her sensitive flesh anew.

Releasing one breast, he skated that hand slowly down the front of her body, pausing to splay his fingers over her taut belly and press in as he moved in even closer, and she felt the wool of his trousers lightly abrade the backs of her bare thighs, the already damp curves of her bottom.

Felt his erection, hard and rigid, in the small of her back.

His wandering hand continued assessingly down; his fingers brushed her curls—in the mirror a dark triangle at the apex of her thighs—then his hand moved on, over and around, to fondle her bottom.

Then, from behind, he pressed two long fingers between her thighs, stroked the slick, already swollen flesh, then parted her folds and thrust slowly in.

In . . .

With a gasp she rose on her toes. Eyes wide, she felt his hand flex; his fingers retreated, only to return an instant later, more forcefully, more definitely.

Her senses tightened, teetered; her skin came alive as he stroked again and again, pushing her on, but before she climbed too high, he withdrew his hand. Released her breast.

"Don't move."

His voice was so low, so rough, she only just made out the words, but, her skin tingling in the cool moonlight, ultra-sensitive and aroused, she waited, expecting him to dispense with his clothes—instead he went down on one knee and divested her of her stockings and shoes.

She stepped out of the latter, then went to swing around; she was now totally naked, but he was still fully clothed. But before she could turn and set her hands to his coat, he grasped her hips, held her as she was, still facing the bed, as he rose once more behind her.

She looked at him in the mirror. This was not her gentle, persuasive lover, but someone else. This man wanted her, and had stripped his need bare, let it loose, revealing the reality behind his façade.

Looking over her shoulder at the beauty he'd revealed—his for the taking—Jonas barely recognized himself. He hadn't intended this, much less what, some part of him knew, would follow; his script was already, ineradicably, set in stone. He'd had no idea that dropping his emotional guard and simply letting what he felt for her—his love, if he were honest—free would result in this—this unwavering, unrelenting need to possess.

To possess her, far more deeply than he yet had.

To make her his—incontrovertibly, beyond question, thought, or reason. To impress on her the reality not just of his need for her, but of the rightness of it, the rightness and inevitability of her place beside him.

Beneath him.

Some more primitive side of himself had taken charge, taken absolute control, and now drove him.

Drove him to, while locking his gaze on hers in the mirror, close his hands about her waist and lift her; setting her on her knees on the edge of the bed, he stepped between her spread calves.

Sent one hand to claim her breast once more, possessively enough to make her catch her breath; the other palm he set skating over the ripe globes of her bottom, down and around, then with his fingers he delved into the scalding slickness between her thighs. Thrusting one finger into her heated sheath, with another he found the tight nubbin that testified to her arousal, and caressed. Stroked as his other finger repetitively penetrated.

He heard her breath hitch, tangling in her throat. Saw her lids lower as she desperately tried to draw in a tight breath. Lips parted, skin flushed, she held still, letting him do as he wished, a sensual, sensory captive as he had his way with her—as he prepared her body and her senses for the possession to come.

In the mirror his gaze roamed her body, then he raised his eyes to her face.

"Open your eyes. Watch what I'm doing to you."

Em heard the guttural order—very clearly an order—and, even though it was an effort to lift her weighted lids, complied without hesitation. She looked at herself, naked in the moonlight, realized she, her hips, were undulating, riding his fingers, searching for relief.

Her whole body felt taut, alive and burning, passion's heat very real beneath her skin. Never had she felt so . . . stretched, her senses so racked, so drawn . . . so expectant. So poised on the cusp of some far greater stimulation.

A sensory explosion that would overwhelm her, that would sweep her away, rip her from this world . . .

A sensation she couldn't wait to experience, but . . . she knew she had to wait. Wait until he judged the moment right, when he would give her . . . what she truly wanted.

Him. All of him. Not just the gentle lover he'd already shared with her, but this side of him, too. This more forceful, primitive male who wanted her.

Needed her.

That last was engraved on his face, in the harsh lines of his expression, in the rugged set of his jaw.

She had something he would give his all for.

She was in his power . . . and he was in hers.

He was conqueror and supplicant combined; increasingly ravenous expectation a sharp brilliance, bright and true, gilding every nerve, sliding through every vein, she waited—for him to take her.

His gaze had dropped again to her body; she could feel the burning heat in his dark eyes. Then he raised his head and saw her watching him.

Releasing her breast, he caught one of her hands, until then lying forgotten, loosely resting on her thighs. And guided it to the apex of her spread legs. His hand wrapped over hers, he guided her fingers into the slickness he'd drawn forth.

"Feel how wet you've become for me." Head bent, his voice was a dark growl in her ear.

She shuddered as, under his, her fingertips slid along her swollen folds, caressed.

Her lungs impossibly tight, her senses focused between her thighs, she let her lids close.

His hand tightened on hers, stilled. "Open your eyes."

She did, dragged in a desperate breath and obediently locked her gaze on her reflection, on the subtly shifting curves gilded to pearlescent ivory by the moonlight.

On where his dark sleeve reached around and across her, his hand tucked between her legs, cupped over hers.

Satisfied, he continued, his voice a deep murmur in her ear as he pressed her fingers deeper between her thighs. "Watch yourself feeling me readying you."

She had no choice but to do so; the sight stole her breath, overwhelmed her mind. The combined sensations—of his hard hand holding her fingers, pressing them into the hot wetness, locking them where she could feel two fingers of his other hand slowly, repeatedly, thrusting into her body, of that fist flexing beneath her bottom, of her sheath stretching and giving against the invasion—completely ensnared her, drove every last thought from her head.

Then the hand surrounding hers shifted. He curled his thumb into her palm, and she felt him caressing the tight nubbin of pleasure beneath her curls—felt both the sensations his touch evoked, as well as his finger stroking against her palm.

It was all too much. The explosion she'd been waiting for flared brightly, hotly, then imploded, cindering her senses, leaving her physically and mentally gasping, reeling . . . yet still unfulfilled.

Beyond her control, her lids had fallen; before she could summon the strength to lift them, his hands left her completely, left her bereft. She sensed him shifting behind her, then felt him guide the thick rod of his erection between her thighs, felt the broad head stroke, then settle at her entrance.

She forced her lids up—as he locked one arm around her hips, anchoring her, holding her steady—then he thrust hard and deep, into her willing body. Her surrendered body.

Head rising, she uttered a breathless scream—not of pain

but of pleasure. Pleasure so intense it ripped away any lingering anchors with the world and sent her spinning on a sea of pure sensation.

Jonas felt the ripples of a small climax caress his shaft, but he wanted—lusted after and was determined to wring from her—far more than that.

The primitive self who now ruled him, who had completely overtaken his civilized self, saw absolutely no reason not to make her scream again—much more loudly.

He set himself, his heated body still fully clothed, to the task. He'd only opened the placket of his trousers to take her, knowing she would realize—would feel the abrasion of cloth against her bottom and the backs of her thighs, that she would see and feel the fabric of his sleeve crossing her soft belly as he held her steady so he could plunder without restraint.

So he could thrust as forcefully as he wished—as powerfully as she wanted.

That she wanted was beyond question; the soft mewling sounds that fell from her lips was music to his primitive ears. Hands locked on his arm, half-tipped forward, she rode every thrust. Peeling the fingers of his other hand from her hip, he raised it to her breast, heard her keen as he played, possessed, pressed.

She shattered again, more deeply this time, her breathless scream a primal sensual benediction.

But he wasn't yet finished with her.

In extremis, she slumped forward, catching herself on one arm.

He withdrew from her, lifted her; placing one knee on the bed, he moved her higher, then laid her down on her stomach on the coverlet.

Dispensing with his clothes took no more than a heated minute; his body felt too large for their constraint, his skin overheated, his muscles taut and tight. Her eyes had remained closed, her cheek resting on the softness of the bed; she didn't stir as, naked, he stretched out alongside her.

Ignoring the throbbing urgency of his erection, he laid a
hand on her shoulder, ran his palm down over the indenta-
tion of her waist, lovingly tracing the evocative curve of her
hip and derriere, skin bare, still flushed and dewed, and
flagrantly exposed to his gaze.

He took the time to savor the sight of her slumped, wrung
out with passion, his to take and fill at his leisure . . . the
prod of his own passion, his own rabid need, grew too
great. Grasping her knee, he pushed it higher on the bed,
opening her to him; lifting over her, he settled, half-braced
on one arm, his hips below her bottom in the space between
her thighs.

She was more than ready; he nudged into her, slowly
eased deeper, then slid fully home. Closed his eyes as sensation swamped him, as her sheath closed tightly about him
once more, bathing him in her passion.

The sensation of her bare bottom riding against his groin
had been arousing before, when he'd been mostly clothed.
Now as he rode her, naked skin to naked skin, the sensation
bloomed on an even more evocative, more intensely primitive plane.

One more deeply arousing as she stirred, then joined him
in the dance, as she worked her hips against him, beneath
him, sliding her sheath over the impaling length of him
until he thought his eyes would cross, until the flames
roared and the all-consuming fire swept in and took him,
razed him, burned through him.

And her.

As he shuddered over her, head bowed as his release
claimed him, the sensation of her sheath rippling about
him, milking every last drop of his seed, cut through the
fire's heat to blazon across his mind, his reeling senses.

Drained, more sated than he'd ever been, he slumped
over her. And felt his more primitive self at last ease its
grip, draw back, and let him free.

He felt her back rise beneath his chest as she drew in a
long, slow breath. His heart still thundering, his muscles

quivering, he pressed a gentle kiss to her shoulder, then eased sideways, slumped deeper into the mattress beside her, and surrendered.

To her, and to sleep.

Half beneath him, his body a large, warm, muscled blanket pressing her into the mattress, the weight both soothing and comforting, Em mentally sighed and drifted in the golden glow of aftermath. Never before had he been so . . . flagrantly possessive. Never before had she felt anything to compare with the sated bliss that coursed her veins, that slid through her body, deep into her heart and soul, and reassured.

This was what it felt like to be wanted beyond reason, to be needed as a vital part of a man's life.

Relaxed and comfortable in the hazy world between paradise and the mundane, her mind finally had a chance to look—and see clearly. Clarity and its consequent certainty infused her. She'd spoken to others to learn what love was, but it was both the same, and different, for everyone, for every couple.

For her and him . . . love, she now knew, was always being there. It was the selfless devotion that had had him lowering all his shields and letting her see how much she really meant to him. That he'd intended to comfort and distract her she didn't doubt, yet when faced with the strength of her absorption he hadn't shrunk from doing what was needed to capture her attention—utterly and completely.

This interlude had been about many things—about possession, about caring, about . . . love.

About a gentle kiss on her shoulder.

And the way he even now held her in sleep.

The message borne on those heated moments had been crystal clear—he wanted her, needed her, and would give anything she or fate demanded to have her, hold her, protect and care for her.

From the moment she'd met him, his dedication to the latter two aspects had been unswerving; only tonight had he allowed her to see how much the former two meant to him. But he had, and she knew the revelation was not something to be taken lightly; it was something to cling to, cleave to, hold on to, a mast of certainty that would see her and him through all the storms of life.

As the moonlight washed over them in gentle benediction, she realized she had a smile on her face.

And a belief that was unwavering, and unquestionably clear.

No decision was required.

Love, for them, was trusting, sharing, protecting, caring.

Her heart and her soul knew the essential truth, and as she was a Colyton, they'd made up her mind.

19

They'd all agreed the treasure was in the safest place it could be.

The next morning, after consulting with Lucifer and Phyllida at the manor, Jonas set off for the Grange via the path through the wood.

After leaving Em at dawn, he'd headed back home to change and think. The previous night had evolved into something far removed from what he'd planned; in setting out to distract her from the attempted burglary, he'd forgotten that he, too, might have a reaction to that occurrence—namely, over the potential danger had she happened to stumble on the burglar in action. His response to that scenario had led to his more primitive self gaining the upper hand; he'd been somewhat apprehensive over her reaction, but if the smug smile that had curved her lips when he'd left her at dawn had been any indication, he hadn't harmed his standing with her, not in the least.

Just as well. In his present state, he wouldn't handle any attempt to distance herself from him with any degree of equanimity.

After considering the situation, he'd gone to the manor for breakfast, to alert Lucifer, Phyllida, and their household to the latest development.

The most troubling aspect was the timing. Whoever had ransacked Em's room had known, not just about the treasure, but about its hiding place. Specifically that the only way through the cell door was with the key. He'd checked the cell before he'd left the inn that morning; there had been no marks about the lock, no attempt to break in.

Everyone in the village knew about the cell and its impregnability. Everyone who'd been at the inn when they'd brought in the treasure had seen it and known where it had been secured.

Yesterday the tale would have started to spread beyond the village borders, but *during* yesterday, when Em's room had been searched, only those who lived locally, those who'd learned the tale on the first night, would have had time to mount such a well-engineered search.

While Em's rooms were empty through most of the day, the area around the foot of the back stairs was not; only at certain times would it be safe for someone who wasn't part of the inn's staff to venture into that region just beyond the kitchen.

The only other way to Em's rooms was via the main stairs, but with Edgar a fixture behind the bar, and with so many others coming and going in the open common room, it simply wasn't feasible to imagine that someone who had no right to be on the guest floor of the inn had managed to go up and later come down without anyone noticing and mentioning the matter.

It couldn't have been a case of some outsider hearing the news and somehow knowing just how to access Em's rooms, and when it would be safe to do so. Ergo . . . whoever was searching for the key was someone they knew, someone who'd been there on that first night, cheering and drinking to the Colytons' health.

The prime suspect was clearly Harold Potheridge. He'd been around the village, specifically hanging about the inn, long enough to know where, how, and when to search.

Hands in his pockets, eyes on the ground, Jonas trudged on.

Lucifer had agreed with his assessment; he'd volunteered Dodswell, his groom, to keep an eye on Potheridge. On hearing the news, Dodswell had been happy to take on the assignment; he was one of those people who possessed an uncanny ability to be seen but not noticed.

Meanwhile, Jonas intended to spend the next hour or two dealing with business, then after lunch he would return to the inn, taking advantage of the postprandial lull to question Hilda and her girls, especially the scullery maids and the laundresses, to see if anyone had spotted someone unexpected in the region of the back stairs.

The treasure was safe while the key was safe. He'd left it in his room at the Grange. No one would think to look for it there, and the Grange, with its full complement of staff and no guests to confuse matters, wasn't anywhere near as easy to waltz into as the inn.

A branch cracked, all but on his heels.

He started to whirl—

Pain exploded in his skull.

He saw nothing, heard nothing, knew nothing else as the ground rushed up to meet him.

A list of items to be ordered in her hand, Em had just walked into the inn kitchen, looking for Hilda to discuss the menu for the next week, when movement beyond the window caught her eye.

She looked—saw Jonas, staggering, weaving, one hand to his head as he tried to cross the inn's backyard . . . she was out of the door and racing to him before she'd thought. Hilda and her girls and John Ostler were close behind.

"Jonas!"

She clutched his coat, steadied him as he halted, swaying, eyes closed in obvious pain.

"Someone hit me on the head. On the path through the wood."

"Here." John ducked a shoulder under Jonas's arm.

Em quickly caught his other arm and looped it over her shoulders. "Let's get you inside."

Hilda called for a bowl of water and some cloths; she hurried ahead of Em, Jonas, and John, shooing her girls before her.

By the time Em and John eased Jonas into a chair at the kitchen table, Hilda had everything in hand. She wrung out a cloth and applied it gently to Jonas's head. She parted the thick hair, peered, then dabbed solicitously. "A very nasty bump."

Em itched to take over, but Hilda was clearly an expert.

Jonas winced as she worked, then squinted up at Em. "Send John to fetch Lucifer and Filing."

She nodded, looked up to find that John, hovering by the door, had heard. He saluted and went.

When she turned back to Jonas, he caught her eye again. "You might want to ask Edgar which men have been in the tap—" He broke off. "Damn! I don't know how long I was unconscious for." He frowned even more blackly, then his face cleared. "Ask Edgar which men have been in the common room and haven't left at all since ten o'clock."

Em nodded and left.

She returned as Hilda was winding a wide bandage about Jonas's head. Hilda tied it off. "That'll do you for now. No doubt Gladys will have it off to take a look at the damage when you get back to the Grange."

Jonas grimaced. "No doubt."

Footsteps sounded outside the kitchen door, then Phyllida appeared, Lucifer behind her. Her gaze went immediately to Jonas, then she glanced at Em. "Don't worry—he has a hard head."

Jonas glanced Phyllida's way and grunted.

"We came through the wood," Lucifer said. "Your attacker was waiting for you. I found the spot where he stood just off the path—the ground was soft enough to hold vague footprints. You walked by him, then he stepped out behind you."

"I was thinking." Jonas supported his head with his hands. "I wasn't paying attention to what was round about. He went through my pockets—they were inside out when I came to my senses."

"The pertinent point," Lucifer said, "is that whoever it was knew you were at the manor, and that you'd take the path through the wood when you left."

Frowning, Phyllida slipped into a chair. "A local?"

Lucifer grimaced. "It would have to be someone who knows Jonas's habits well enough to know he generally uses that path."

Em slowly subsided onto the chair beside Jonas. Was the Colyton treasure going to prove to be a curse?

Filing came in from the tap. He nodded to everyone. "I just heard." Glancing at Em, he added, "John called me outside to tell me—I left Henry in ignorance, busy with his books. I didn't think you'd want him involved at this stage."

"No—he'd just worry." She smiled a trifle weakly. "Thank you."

Jonas reached along the table and closed his hand about hers. "You don't need to worry, either. Whoever's doing this—searching for the key to get to the treasure—we'll find him. This is too small a village for him to hide for long." He met her gaze. "So what did Edgar say?"

She grimaced. "At ten there were only the older men—Mr. Weatherspoon and his cronies—by the fire. No one else, although a few others have stopped by since for a snack, but most don't linger at this time."

Jonas grunted. "No help there. I didn't imagine it was Mr. Weatherspoon who coshed me."

Lucifer leaned against the table. "Theoretically, I grant you, it could be any able-bodied male, anyone with sufficient knowledge, but do we really suspect any of the locals?"

"Even if they laid hands on the treasure," Phyllida said, "what would they do with it? They'd have to dispose of it somehow—and even if they could find a way, chances are they'd be caught." She shook her head, looked at Em. "Aside from all else, I have to say I find it difficult to imagine any of the locals stealing from one of our own, but most especially from the Colytons. To the village—all of the village—your family is special. Everything I've heard since you've let your identity be known suggests everyone is pleased, even thrilled, to see you and yours back in Colyton, and the treasure is part of that wonderful tale. Any local trying to steal it would be risking—well, village infamy and social eviction, so to speak. I just can't see it."

Filing nodded solemnly. "I would have to concur."

Em nodded, too, but more slowly. "In general, I agree, but . . ." She met Jonas's eye. "Mr. Coombe called yesterday. He wanted me to entrust him with the coins in the treasure—to appraise and sell them. He would have been quite insistent, I think, but I cut him off."

Jonas snorted. He frowned at their linked hands, then said, "Be that as it may, unless he's grown more desperate than we know, Silas is unlikely to resort to physical violence—it's not his style. And I think whoever struck me was taller than he is. Bigger."

"The truth is," Lucifer said, "it's unlikely to be a local—and much more likely to be Harold Potheridge."

Em pulled a face. "He hasn't been into the tap this morning—I asked Edgar."

"Other than Potheridge," Jonas said, "we've only Hadley as an outsider still about." He glanced at Em. "Have any of the other inn guests stayed on?"

She shook her head. "All who stayed last night left this morning—except for Hadley, but he always intended to remain, even before we found the treasure."

"I think," Lucifer said, pushing away from the table, "that I might take a wander around the village. See who I can see."

"I'll come with you," Filing said.

Jonas nodded, and winced.

Em exchanged a look with Phyllida, then rose. "And you," she addressed Jonas, "should come upstairs to my parlor and rest."

Jonas tried to say he was all right where he was, but Hilda weighed in and told him he was in her way. Evicted from the kitchen, he tried to deny he needed coddling, but between Phyllida and Em, they steered his footsteps up the back stairs and through Em's quarters to her small front parlor.

She determinedly guided him to the sofa; she'd grabbed a pillow from her bed along the way. "You should stretch out here—it's quiet and no one will bother you."

Face paler than before, lips tight, Jonas slowly eased down, then, without further complaint, stretched out and laid his head gently on the pillow.

Em exchanged another, more worried glance with Phyllida.

Gathering her shawl about her, Phyllida sat in one of the armchairs. "I'll stay for a little while."

Em nodded. "I'll go and fetch a jug of water and a glass, and bring up my account books—I can do them here as well as I can in my office."

"Take your time," Phyllida said. "I'll stay until you get back."

Both glanced at Jonas. One arm raised, shading his eyes, he simply lay there and didn't respond. Didn't tell them they were fussing unnecessarily.

Em turned and left the room. Closing the door softly behind her, she hurried down the main stairs.

Lucifer looked in more than an hour later. Jonas was resting, but not asleep. He lifted his arm from his face, but didn't move his head as his brother-in-law came into the parlor and quietly shut the door.

Noticing Jonas's open eyes, Lucifer glanced at Em, sitting in an armchair, her account ledgers open in her lap.

"Phyllida had to get back to your boys," Em said.

With a nod, Lucifer dropped into the other armchair so Jonas could focus more easily on his face. "I found Hadley sketching in the church. Filing said he'd been there earlier, in the same spot, when Filing went to tend the altar at nine o'clock. I strolled up and asked if I could look at his sketch. Hadley permitted it without a qualm. He was using charcoal, and the work—the strokes—looked fresh and consistent, and he'd done quite a bit. I don't know how fast he can work, but it was a reasonable body of work for a good artist for an entire morning. In short, when I asked and he said he'd been there since before nine, I had and still have no reason to disbelieve him. So Hadley doesn't look to be a suspect."

"What about Potheridge?" Jonas asked.

"He's another story entirely." Lucifer looked grim. "He left Miss Hellebore's at around nine, stepped into the lane, and hasn't been sighted by anyone since. He could have gone for a long walk, of course, but . . ."

Em snorted softly. "He's not one for bracing rambles through the countryside—he'd be more likely to ride."

Lucifer shook his head. "I checked with John Ostler—Potheridge hasn't hired a horse."

"So as we all thought"—Jonas let his head sink into the pillow—"the most likely suspect is Harold Potheridge."

"The most likely, yes." Lucifer met his eyes. "However, I couldn't find Silas, couldn't locate anyone who's seen him this morning, not after nine o'clock—so he, too, must remain on our suspect list. At least for now."

Em found it difficult if not impossible to concentrate on anything else while Jonas lay prostrate on her sofa.

Hale and whole he was distracting beyond belief; ill . . . all her senses, all her being, seemed to focus on him.

She'd never considered herself an obsessive worrier, but even though she knew—and he'd assured her—that he wasn't seriously injured, until he was well again, himself again, she couldn't seem to, knew she wouldn't be able to, damp down her flaring concern.

By a consensus of opinion, including his, Jonas remained on Em's sofa until his senses cleared and the throbbing in his head dimmed to a dull ache. Although he would much rather have been laid out on his own bed, or at least somewhere long enough to properly accommodate his frame, while he was incapacitated he wanted to keep Em near; he needed to know she was safe. And the easiest way to achieve that in his less-than-robust state was to permit her to fuss over him as she wished.

Through the remainder of the morning, and over luncheon and into the afternoon, she was constantly in and out of her parlor, looking in on him, bringing him some broth to eat and, when he requested it, a roast beef sandwich especially prepared by Hilda herself.

By three o'clock in the afternoon, he was feeling considerably improved, although he still found it difficult to concentrate enough to think.

When Em next popped her head around the door, he was sitting in an armchair, waiting to smile reassuringly her way.

She frowned and came in. "Shouldn't you still be resting?"

He let his smile brighten several degrees. "I'm much better. I'm going to go home." Using the chair's arms for leverage he slowly got to his feet, pleased to find he was perfectly steady and the room didn't threaten to spin.

Her frown darkened, her lips thinned.

Before she could protest, he tapped her nose. "You can't argue. I can't remain here, in your private apartments, not in such circumstances."

She considered, then humphed. "At least let me fetch my shawl, and I'll come with you." She headed for her bedroom.

He wasn't at all reluctant to have her company, but . . . when she emerged, swinging a knitted shawl about her shoulders, he said, "I think we should take John Ostler with us, just in case I stumble along the way."

Her curt nod suggested she'd thought of the same thing. "We can pick him up on our way—I think he's in the kitchen."

He let her guide him down the back stairs. His insistence on John's company was more for her benefit than his; he didn't want her returning to the inn alone, not with his attacker potentially still lurking.

John was in the kitchen. Dodswell had just dropped in; he offered to keep an eye on the inn's stables while John accompanied them to the Grange.

"I still haven't laid eyes on Potheridge." Dodswell said the name as if Em's uncle were already a convicted felon. "Miss Sweet says he's not been back to Miss Hellebore's. Thompson glimpsed him making his way up the lane toward Ballyclose about eleven o'clock, but Sir Cedric was in just before, and he hasn't set eyes on him."

Jonas went to nod, remembered just in time how painful that might be. "Let me know when Potheridge gets back— I'll be at the Grange."

"Right you are." Dodswell saluted, then followed them out and headed for the stables while the three of them— Em, Jonas, and John—set off along the minor path that joined the main path through the wood.

By the time they reached the Grange, Jonas was clenching his jaw against the pain. Em saw the telltale tension, but bit her tongue against any protest—what help would that be? If she'd been coshed, she'd want to lie down on her own bed, too.

But in order to gain his bed, Jonas had first to run the gauntlet of Gladys's concern and subsequent ministrations, egged on by Cook, who ran a close second to the housekeeper in the fussing stakes.

Em viewed their insistence—and Jonas's abject if reluctant surrender—with relief. If he had to be out of her sight, then him being under Gladys's stern and watchful eye was the next best thing.

Standing a little way from the bed, she watched while Gladys carefully removed Hilda's bandage, clucked over the injury, then gently applied some salve.

Hands clasped tightly—to stop herself from grabbing and gripping one of his—Em tried to remain detached while noting every little flinch, every tightening of his lips, the line that seemed etched between his brows.

She still felt . . . exercised. Alert, poised to react, with her senses still fixed on him. If she'd learned anything that day, it was how much he now meant to her—how incredibly precious to her he now was.

All of which had come as something of a shock. It was a novel experience, an emotional upheaval she'd not previously had to weather, never before having had another adult—someone not connected to her by blood—to whom she was so attached.

While being concerned was hardly surprising, the part that shocked was the depth of her feelings, the breadth, the life-shaking intensity of her response; even in her relative inexperience she knew well enough that that intensity was a direct reflection of her attachment, of how much she now cared for him.

How much she loved him.

While her Colyton soul reveled in new experiences, this was one she could have done without. Seeing him in pain, knowing there was little she could do to ease it, tied her in tense, tight knots.

Finally Gladys was satisfied. She stood back and surveyed her patient. "You just rest there quietly now, and sip that lemon and barley water if you're thirsty. I'll come up and check on you before we prepare dinner."

Stretched out on his bed, Jonas smiled weakly. "Thank you, dearest Gladys. I promise to do exactly as ordered."

With a skeptical humph, Gladys nodded deferentially to Em, then left; the door snicked closed behind her.

Jonas looked at the door, let his brows quirk; clearly Gladys knew more than she was—thankfully—letting on.

Transferring his gaze to Em's rather pale face, he let his features relax into a smile. He held out his hand, fingers beckoning. "Come and sit with me."

She came, sliding her fingers into his hand, hitching a hip up onto the bed. He looked up at her, smiled, and slowly, deliberately, drew her down until their lips met in an easy, gentle, soulful kiss.

It ended on a sigh, one she gave, one he felt.

Rather than let her sit up again, he closed his arms around her and settled her across him, let her wriggle, then lay her head on his chest.

Simply held her.

Drew comfort and warmth from her nearness, from the closeness that was more than merely physical. Felt soothing calm seep into his limbs, wend its way inexorably through his body, simply from having her warm and alive in his arms, from feeling her soft feminine form against him.

Holding him, wanting him in ways that had nothing to do with the physical, needing him, accepting him as he was.

In that long-drawn, silent moment of peace, he sensed and learned more about the power of love, of the strengths that went hand in hand with its weaknesses. Of the comfort and support that were the other side of the coin to love's inherent vulnerability.

And felt blessed.

Em lay in his arms and listened to his heart beat steadily, strongly, beneath her ear. An infinitely calming, pounding thud, it anchored her, reassured and wiped away the tension of the past hours, of her discombobulating day.

She didn't close her eyes, but her mind wandered along paths she hadn't before trod. Seeing, sensing, knowing, reaching through the quiet closeness that held them, cradled them, to a place, a state, where the world seemed golden.

Quiet calm, the beat of a heart not her own, yet one to

which all her senses were attuned. And a presence, physical flesh and blood and more, a pervasive sense of shared strength, of mutual, communal peace.

How long she lay in his arms, cocooned against the world, how long that aura of peace transfused her she didn't know, but eventually she stirred; lifting her head, she looked into his face, and felt restored, renewed.

His features were so relaxed, so pain-free, she thought he'd fallen asleep. She studied his face, then leaned in, and dropped a feather-light kiss on his chin, hesitated, then repeated the caress on his lips.

They curved.

His lashes rose just a fraction, enough for her to see the dark glint of his eyes. "Are you going?" His voice was a deep, sleepy rumble.

She smiled. "I should." She let her gaze rise to the bandage about his head. "You have to rest and get better."

"I will, but I'll be fine later." Raising a hand, he tucked an errant curl behind her ear. "I'll come and see you as usual tonight, although I might be late."

She frowned, opened her lips on a protest—one he silenced with a finger across her lips. "No—don't argue. You're here with me now. By the same token, I'll be with you tonight."

She searched his eyes, understood what he was saying— that he understood how she felt, and felt the same in reverse. He was right; she couldn't argue, not if she wanted to claim the same rights to care for and protect him as he'd been so insistent on claiming with her.

"Very well—but you have to promise you'll take care. Especially coming through the wood at night."

He smiled. "He won't catch me twice. Last time I wasn't watching, and anyway now he knows I don't carry the key with me, he has no reason to search me again."

She grimaced. "I suppose not."

"Indeed not. But incidentally . . ." Opening his arms,

letting her free, he turned his head to look at the bedside table; she slipped off the bed, brows rising. "Open the drawer," he said. "The key's in there."

Sliding the drawer out, she saw the key sitting right at the front.

He slumped back on his pillows. "If ever you need it and I'm not around, that's where it is."

She looked at him, then closed the drawer. "It's safe where it is."

He'd closed his eyes again. She leaned over and kissed him one last time. "I'll see you tonight."

"Hmm." His lips gently curved.

Infinitely more reassured than when she'd arrived, she slipped out of his room and quietly closed the door.

It was nearly nine o'clock when Dodswell found her in the common room and handed her a note.

"From his highness," he said with a grin. "Said I had to put it into your hand and no other, and that I couldn't find my bed until I did."

Em smiled. "Thank you." She bit back an inquiry as to "his highness's" health; doubtless that was what the note was about.

She stuffed it into her pocket, where it burned a hole while she forced herself to finish chatting with the latest travelers who'd decided to make the Red Bells their temporary home.

News of the inn and its food and refurbishment was spreading faster than she'd dared hope. She'd opened two more rooms, and had filled them every night; the girls she'd hired to help were slaving to have two more ready in the next few days.

She saw the travelers upstairs, then whisked into her office and pulled Jonas's note from her pocket. Unfolding it, she smoothed the sheet and tipped it toward the lamplight.

Dearest Em,

It is with immeasurable regret that I have to inform
you that, when upright, my head still threatens to
spin rather too much to risk making the journey to
the inn.

I've asked Lucifer to look in later to make sure all's
well.

I'll see you tomorrow—until then, take all due care.

Yours, etc,
Jonas

Em read the note twice, then humphed. "All very well for
him to tell *me* to take care! I'm not the one with a goose egg
on my head."

She stared at the note for a full minute—considered,
debated—then whirled and sat in the chair behind her desk.
Pulling out a fresh sheet of paper, she flicked open her ink
pot, dipped her nib, and quickly scrawled a note of her
own.

After blotting, folding, and addressing it, she slipped out
and found John Ostler, and dispatched him, note in hand, to
the Grange.

"I'm not expecting any reply," she called after him.

He saluted and went, striding into the wood.

Em looked at the dark, dense trees, and inwardly shivered. Turning, she hurried back into the warmth and light.

Just after ten o'clock was the inn's usual closing time.
Lucifer duly appeared in the tap at that time, and assisted
with good-naturedly evicting the customary stragglers, a
task Jonas had fallen into the habit of performing in recent
times. The tap cleared, Lucifer waved to her, then headed
home.

It was close to eleven o'clock before she farewelled Edgar
and retired with the last lamp. Climbing the stairs, she

refused to let herself question her plan, the one she was about to put into action. There was no quibble in her mind over whether or not she should—it was more a case of whether or not she could.

She went through her rooms to the back stairs and thence to the attics, checking on the twins, Issy, and Henry, and finding them all fast asleep. Safe and well.

Returning to her rooms, she gathered a small bundle of necessities, tied them in an old scarf, then threw her warmest shawl around her shoulders. Picking up the lamp, she checked the level of oil and, finding that satisfactory, adjusted the wick so it threw a glow just bright enough to light her way, then, with nothing else to check or do, she went down the stairs, past the bar and her office, and out of the inn's back door.

She locked it carefully behind her, then—without letting herself think—walked steadily across the yard and onto the minor path that led to the main path through the wood.

Doggedly she thought of other things—of the church in sunlight, of the warmth and light in Hilda's kitchen, of the bustle in the laundry, the babel of the tap—anything to keep the black darkness beneath the trees from swallowing her senses.

She didn't want to think about the dark. She wasn't exactly afraid of it; it was simply that her senses tended to freeze, that being shrouded in inky blackness seemed to paralyze her. Keeping her eyes locked on the pale shaft of light thrown by the lamp, concentrating on keeping her feet steadily moving, one foot in front of the other, she came to the intersection with the main path and turned south toward the Grange.

The huge old house lay ahead of her, somewhere through the trees. She drew in a breath, tighter than she liked, fought not to let the shadows distract her, to let them pull her attention sideways, into the solid gloom beneath the branches.

She could feel her heart climbing slowly upward, into her throat. The compulsion to pick up her skirts and run—flee down the path—steadily grew, but she was determined not to race into Jonas's room in hysterics.

Jonas.

His image formed in her mind; she seized upon it like a drowning soul, clung to it, felt her senses lock and hold, tightly enough to withstand even the insidious pull of the dark.

She trudged on beneath the trees, under the overhanging branches, her breathing still tight, but calmer now, her eyes locked on the beam of lamplight, her feet moving more confidently, with a surer purpose, her senses fixed on the beacon that glowed in her mind's eye.

And then she was stepping into the open, into the faint moonlight, free of the trees. Out of the dark. She could almost feel the tendrils of her latent fear fall away, stretch thin and break as she walked along the path through the Grange's kitchen garden.

She went straight to the back door. Lifting the latch, she pushed it open and went inside. There was a candle left burning on the dresser, waiting for her. She smiled and blessed Mortimer as she blew it out, preferring to take her lamp upstairs.

In brazen contravention of all acceptable procedure, she'd written directly to Mortimer and baldly asked him to leave the kitchen door open for her, saying she wanted to check on Jonas before she retired for the night.

All perfectly true.

Locking the back door, she resettled her shawl, picked up her lamp and, silent as a mouse, made her way through the quiet house to the main stairs and climbed them.

Jonas's door was shut. Carefully screening the lamp, she opened the door, glanced in, and saw him sprawled under the covers. Moonlight streamed in through curtains left wide, providing more than enough illumination; she doused the lamp, then slipped inside, and quietly shut the door.

She set the lamp down by the wall, then approached the bed. He was asleep, but restless; as she watched he stirred, head turning on the pillow, long limbs shifting beneath the sheets. He wasn't wearing a nightshirt. With the bandage no longer swathing his head, he didn't look injured at all, but unsettled.

The observation confirmed her assumptions, firmed her resolve. Laying her small bundle—her brush and a change of clothes—on his dresser, she set her fingers to the laces of her gown.

It took a few minutes to peel the gown down and step out of the skirts and her petticoats, then strip off her garters and hose. Feeling the touch of the cool night air, she hesitated, but then quickly pulled her chemise off over her head.

Naked, she lifted the covers along one side of the bed— the side she normally ended upon—and slid under.

Heat enveloped her; he wasn't fevered, but his large body radiated a familiar and comforting warmth. She instinctively snuggled closer, trying not to disturb him, intending to comfort simply by her presence.

He sensed her; he turned and wrapped his arms about her, gathered her against him, settling her within the circle of his arms, her head on his shoulder, as he always did.

She thought at first that he'd woken, but the vagueness in his touch and the slow, steady rhythm of his breathing said otherwise. Lips curving, she laid her hand over his heart, relaxed into his embrace, and closed her eyes.

He might be asleep, but he remained restless, stirring again and again. At first she thought it was dreams that were disturbing his rest, but watching his face, she realized he was still suffering from occasional pain. From pangs strong enough to disturb, but not wake.

She watched, waited, but he didn't truly settle, not properly; his sleep remained light, constantly fractured.

The need to do something to alleviate his pain, to bring him peace, built until it flooded her. She couldn't ignore it; the compulsion was too strong, too inherent a part of her.

But what could she do?

Her mind considered and rejected a host of options; her

thoughts circled, then returned to just one. She'd heard that pleasure—physical, especially sensual, pleasure—could mute pain, override it, at least for a little while.

Possibly long enough for him to fall more deeply asleep.

Pleasure, after all, distracted her utterly; she was fairly certain it distracted him, too.

The thought tempted, tantalized, yet she hesitated, then he stirred again, this time more fretfully, and she set aside her reservations; hands splayed on his chest, she stretched up against him and kissed him.

Gently, lingeringly, lips supping without urgency or haste, tasting, coaxing.

He responded, and yet . . . she didn't think he was awake. His hands spread and slid over her skin, touching, tracing, possessively caressing before gripping and supporting her where she was, leaning over him.

So she could kiss him more deeply, could take advantage of his parted lips and with her tongue claim his mouth as he had so often hers. He let her, not quiescent, but accepting each increasingly lavish caress as his due—as if he were some pasha and she his pleasure slave.

The notion slid into her mind and her Colyton soul leapt in reckless anticipation. In wanton abandon, urged and compelled her to seize the moment.

To slowly slide her body over his until she was lying atop him, then to part her legs until her knees found the bed on either side of his waist. Slowly, flagrantly lingering, she drew back from the kiss, but only to slide lower and set her lips to his chest.

To trace with lips and tongue the broad, muscled expanse, to with her teeth test and tease the flat nubbins of his nipples concealed beneath the mat of springy dark hair.

One large hand rose to cup her nape as she eased herself lower, feeling his erection, solid and rigid, pressing against her midriff. Wantonly wicked, she wove her body back and forth, using her soft, smooth skin to caress the turgid shaft, the sensitive bulbous head.

His grip on her head tightened, strengthened; his chest swelled as he drew in a long, shallow breath and held it.

Inwardly smiling, certain now that she was on the right path, that the pain that had so constantly niggled could no longer reach him, she trailed her lips lovingly down the narrow band of hair that arrowed to his belly. Muscles tensed, tightened, as she wriggled lower still, as she lifted her head and eased her hips down to rest between his widespread thighs, and brought one hand up to cradle his erection.

To fondle, stroke, caress, to with her fingertips trace, then she bent her head and followed the same trail with the tip of her tongue.

He stopped breathing. Excitement skittered along her spine; a sense of wonder bloomed—that she could so thoroughly please him, pleasure him, that he forgot to breathe.

Emboldened, she licked—and muscles bunched and shifted. She settled to lave and felt him slowly tense beneath her. Felt the muscles surrounding her, cushioning her, turn to steel.

She parted her lips and took him into her mouth, curled her tongue and tasted. Went back for more, the salty tang very much to her liking.

Delighting him, pleasuring him, was a pleasure in itself. She gave herself over to it, taking as much as giving, thrilled and enthralled that she could give him this, give of herself to him in this way.

Her hair had come loose; it fell in rivulets over her shoulders to lightly brush his naked skin. Jonas felt the silken touch, featherlight, elusive, working in tandem—in sensual contrast—to the hot, wet suction of her mouth, the earthy rasp of her tongue cindering any thoughts he might have had, leaving him wanting—craving—more.

More of this dream.

More of her.

He let himself slide into the moment, into the drugging

delight, let the sensations wash over him, capture him, ensnare him.

Let them sink to his soul and imprison him.

Trap him and hold him in pleasured delight.

The throbbing in his head had eased, the throbbing of his erection taking precedence. She drew his engorged flesh deep, suckled, and he gasped, felt his spine helplessly arch as he locked his hands about her head, sank his fingers into her soft curls, and held her there.

While she took him deep and slayed him with her passion, seductively flayed him with her tongue, with the steady deliberation of her devotion.

He knew she was real, that this was no dream, that she was there, tangling with him in his bed, but that only deepened the fantasy, heightened his delight.

The knowledge that she had come to him of her own accord, sought to please him, ease him, that she would willingly engage with his primitive soul in such a blatantly erotic way, was the elixir of paradise to him.

To the him who wanted her, needed her, coveted her—who wanted her to want him with the same fervor, the same unequivocal devotion. The same abject surrender.

She was an innocent adept when it came to pleasing him; her hands toyed, weighed, gently squeezed, and while he valued her actions, treasured her attentions, he couldn't take any more of her giving, not like that.

He wanted her, wanted more of her. He'd already surrendered in every possible way, yet there was more he would give her, gift her, yield to her, lavish upon her—to him that was his role; to him giving to her had become a major part of his reason for being.

Tightening his grip on her skull, he urged her up; she released him reluctantly, but yielded to his direction—let him draw her up so he could fill her mouth with his tongue, so he could capture her senses while he drew her knees up on either side of his waist. Releasing them, he set his hands to her shoulders, eased them down the long planes of her back, testing the supple muscles, then he gripped her hips and held her steady, and nudged the heavy head of his erection into the scalding heat between her thighs.

She gasped through the kiss, but he held her to it, with his tongue possessed her mouth while slowly he pushed past her entrance, slowly drew her down and filled her.

With a short, powerful thrust of his hips he seated himself within her, impaling her on his full length, making her catch her breath, letting her break from the kiss, suck in air as she straightened and felt him high inside her.

Her face was a mask of sensual surprise; she looked down at him, bright eyes glinting from beneath her long lashes. "My God," she breathed.

His face felt graven, stone etched by passion. Eyes locked on hers, he gripped her hips and lifted her, then slowly brought her down again.

"Oh . . ." She breathed the sound out on a long, slow exhalation, eyes closing as she sank lower, as he filled her completely again.

He repeated the movement once, but then she took over— eagerly, joyously, smiling in pleasure as she quickly learned, experimented, and tested, then settled to ride him with her customary abandon.

Bringing his hands up, he closed them about her breasts, kneaded evocatively, then half-rose beneath her to take one pert nipple into his mouth and feed.

Feed the conflagration that had flared, swelled, and raced through them, that burned so hotly their skins grew flushed and damp, fevered. That consumed in a rush of heat and passion, and left them both gasping as she reached the pinnacle.

And shattered.

Gasping, fingers clenched on his chest, head back, she struggled to breathe, struggled to stand against the tide of sensation that poured through her and swept her away.

Releasing her breasts, he gripped her hips and anchored

her, watched her and gloried, drank in her abandon, took
pleasure in her passion, then he surged up and rolled, taking
her with him, pressing her beneath him. Settling her there,
in his bed—gloriously naked, her skin hot, already burning,
her supple legs spread wide, his hips already between.

His erection sunk deep in her body.

He withdrew and surged in again, in one long, slow thrust
filling her sheath, stretching her, pinning her, only to draw
back and repeat the exercise.

Slowly.

It was he who gasped, who, eyes closed, lowered his head,
who found her lips with his. Took her mouth, urged her to
take his, to anchor him as he started to move within her.

She gave him her mouth, her tongue, her body, rose once
again to the primitive call.

Lips melded, tongues dueling, tangling, mouths urgently
greedy as their bodies merged, they gave themselves over
to, submerged their senses wholly in, the familiar slick
dance of retreat and penetration. She reached up and tugged;
he surrendered and let himself down upon her, so she could
wrap her arms about him and cling. She kicked back the
covers and wrapped her legs about his hips, flagrantly, erot-
ically begged.

For more, for all of him.

He gave her what she wanted, took what he needed, lost
himself in her welcoming body. His heart and soul were
already hers, yet he gave her those anew, pledged them to
her as she crested the peak—and effortlessly caught him
and hauled him with her, into a deep sea of pleasured bliss.

Em could barely breathe; she certainly couldn't think, yet
as he collapsed on top of her, her lips curved irrepressibly.
Having his dead weight slumped upon her, crushing her
into the bed, felt like a sensual badge of honor—eclipsed
only by the joy that slid through her veins when his harsh
breathing slowed, and with her hands gently stroking his
back, he fell deeply asleep.

20

Jonas woke the next morning energized, but alone. Nevertheless, he couldn't stop smiling. Crossing his arms beneath his head—no longer even aching—he beamed up at the ceiling.

It had almost been worth getting knocked on the head.

He no longer had the slightest doubt that Em would marry him; the previous night wouldn't have happened if she hadn't already made up her mind.

It was a heady realization; lying still, he savored it for several long minutes before impatience to see what the day would bring impelled him to sit up.

He waited, checking to see if the giddiness that had assailed him the day before would return, but no hint of dizziness remained. Swinging his legs out of the bed, he stood, waited, then smiled.

Reaching up, he felt the bump on the back of his head— winced as he probed, but that, too, felt a great deal better.

Just as well. He had plans for the day, and they didn't include being coddled and kept abed.

He and Lucifer would work through the Colyton treasure, appraising it formally, this morning. They would have done it yesterday if he hadn't been attacked.

After that, after having lunch at the inn and spending an

hour or two with Em, he intended trawling quietly through the village. He had questions to ask of two of the present inhabitants—Coombe and Potheridge. He intended being persuasive; one way or another he intended to get answers.

He rang for his washing water, then sorted through his clothes. The day was fine and he had things to do.

Em felt oddly nervous as she hovered in the doorway of the cell beneath the inn, watching as Lucifer, assisted by Jonas, inventoried her family's treasure. Lucifer would examine each item, then describe it and name a price, all of which Jonas noted down on carefully ruled sheets.

She'd invested such a lot in finding the treasure, not just financially but even more emotionally; now they'd found it . . . strangely the relief was difficult to assimilate. She still couldn't quite believe it was real, couldn't quite believe she no longer had to worry—about anything.

Just listening to the amounts Lucifer murmured to Jonas, it was abundantly clear the family no longer had the slightest financial concern; selling only a small portion of the treasure would set them all up for life.

She'd looked in on the pair from time to time over the past two hours. They were nearly finished—there were only a few more coins yet to be examined—so she lingered, waiting for the verdict and to discuss what should be done with the hoard.

Lucifer examined the last coins, gave his opinion, then stacked them with the others. He looked up and smiled at Em, then took the sheets Jonas offered, briefly perused them, then checked Jonas's addition. The final sum had him raising his brows. "Well, my dear." He looked up at Em. "By my best guess, there's a sizable fortune here." He named a sum that was well beyond her wildest expectations. "And that's a conservative estimate—if realized, it will almost certainly amount to more. Have you decided what you want to do?"

Em met Jonas's dark eyes; chin firming, she nodded. "As coins and jewels, the treasure is too easy to steal—it will always be a temptation to some scoundrel, and as I understand it, coins and jewels like these are impossible to trace. We want to sell the whole, and convert it into funds and investments, things that can't easily be stolen."

So neither Jonas, nor her family, would be in any sort of danger. She looked at Lucifer. "We need monies set aside for the girls—portions for Issy, and the twins—and—"

"Another portion for you." Issy appeared at Em's shoulder. "Henry and I have discussed this, and while we agree with everything else you have in mind, we feel it's only right you have the same benefits from the treasure as me and the twins, *plus* you should be repaid for the funds you expended to get us here so we could find it. That's only fair. You used almost all the money you had from Papa, and you should get that back." Issy's gentle features set in a stubborn expression Em knew meant she wouldn't be gainsaid. "You can't expect us to agree to anything less."

"Indeed." Lucifer nodded to Issy. "Your point is more than valid."

Em looked at Jonas. He nodded in agreement. She grimaced. "Very well. But—"

"No buts." Issy looked at Lucifer. "Em's portion from Papa was five hundred pounds, so that should be added to her amount."

"Four hundred and eighty," Em corrected. "I still have twenty pounds left, but—"

"*No* buts." This time they all chorused it.

She shut her lips.

Lucifer was making notes. "So we have portions for four girls, plus an extra four hundred and eighty pounds to refund Em's expenditures. Then there's funds for Henry."

"We want him to go to Pembroke," Em stated, "and then after he completes his studies, have enough to live comfortably. He'll need to buy a suitable house, and be able to support a wife and run a decent household."

She watched Lucifer make notes on another sheet of paper, adding and calculating swiftly. Jonas leaned over and pointed to a sum, and murmured something about "income streams from investments."

Lucifer nodded and murmured something back. After a few more jottings, he looked over what he had, then looked up at Em and Issy. "The most effective way of using the funds to achieve what you wish is—"

He suggested setting up a series of accounts, one for each sister and a larger one for Henry, and explained how, if the money were invested, they could comfortably live off the income. Em understood enough to see the value in his proposal.

"And the rest—the remainder of the funds realized from selling the treasure—can be set aside in an investment trust for future generations." Lucifer looked at Em and raised his brows. "Is that the sort of arrangement that would suit?"

"Yes." She nodded decisively. "That's exactly what we want. Can you help us arrange it?"

"With pleasure." Lucifer gathered his notes. "I'll have this copied, so you can keep the original. I'll send letters out this afternoon to some of the London dealers I'd trust with such a hoard—they'll come down and do their own appraisal and we can proceed from there. Meanwhile, I'll also contact Montague." He glanced at Jonas, who nodded.

"Montague," Jonas explained, "is an excellent man-of-business. You'll need someone like him—someone you can trust implicitly to do the best for your family—to set up the accounts and manage them."

"And this Montague person is trustworthy?" Em asked.

"Beyond question." Jonas smiled. "We—Lucifer, all the Cynsters, and I, and various other connected family members—use him and his firm for all our investments. He's the best there is."

"In that case." Em looked at Lucifer. "Please do contact him on our behalf."

Lucifer nodded and rose. "I'll write to him this afternoon. Who knows? We might even tempt him to visit Colyton."

After lunching with Em and her small tribe, Jonas headed back to the Grange, strolling, senses alert, along the path through the wood. Filing had come down from the rectory with Henry to check on how matters were progressing; he, too, had stayed and joined the family about the long table in the attic parlor the younger members had made their own.

It had been a comfortable family meal. Thinking of how at home he'd felt, Jonas couldn't imagine how he—and Filing, too—had filled their days, indeed, their lives, before the return of the Colytons to Colyton.

Apropos of which, he'd heard Filing arrange with Em to take Issy for a drive to Seaton that afternoon. He wouldn't be at all surprised if they returned with news of the matrimonial kind. Now the treasure had been found, and confirmed to be significant, and as Filing and Issy, and indeed everyone, knew Jonas intended to marry Em, the good curate was no doubt planning on persuading Issy to say yes and name a date.

Which, Jonas hoped, would in turn focus Em's mind on setting her own date. He felt certain Issy would insist that in the circumstances Em and he were married first, a point with which he was in complete agreement. It would be difficult for Em to procrastinate under the combined persuasions of her family and him.

And she could no longer claim the inn and the village needed her attentions on a daily basis. She'd organized matters so successfully that the inn and its staff were increasingly operating smoothly on their own. When he'd walked in that morning, he'd been struck by how much, under her guidance, the inn had altered from its previous state. Under Juggs, at ten in the morning the common room would have been deserted. Instead, it had been more than half-full, with locals gathering for a late breakfast or morning tea, and guests finishing their breakfasts before leaving.

He couldn't recall, under Juggs's reign, how long it had been since he'd seen one guest at the inn, let alone the five who'd stayed on the previous night.

Everything was in place for Em to name the date; he was, he discovered, impatient, champing at the bit to take the next step. To declare she was his to the world, to establish that fact beyond question.

And to start a family. He and Em would take the twins and Henry under their wing, but he was surprised at how often in recent times his mind had drifted, imagining Em with a child—his child—in her arms. The vision had remained in his brain, and returned every now and then to tempt him. Prod him.

Not that he needed further prodding in that regard.

Everything was settling perfectly into place. There remained only one fly in his ointment, and he intended to remove that forthwith.

Reaching the back of the Grange, he strode through the kitchen garden and went in through the back door. He would return the cell key to its hiding place, then head out in pursuit of his goal.

He'd let Em think he would be at the Grange through the afternoon; he hadn't wanted her to worry about what might transpire when he interrogated the two suspects most likely to be behind his attack.

Harold Potheridge was at the top of his list; according to Dodswell, Potheridge hadn't returned to Miss Hellebore's cottage until late last night. But he rather thought he'd try Silas Coombe first.

With the key safely stored, he left his room, descended the stairs, and set off for Silas's cottage.

* * *

At three o'clock, Em climbed the stairs to the attics, looking for the twins. In Issy's absence, she'd told them they could play for half an hour after lunch before reporting to her office to practice their arithmetic under her watchful eye.

When they hadn't appeared at precisely two-thirty, she hadn't been either surprised or worried, but when they still hadn't come in by a quarter to three, she'd closed her ledger and embarked on a search.

After their experience with Harold, she felt sure they would be somewhere near. She'd expected to discover them with the laundry maids, or harassing John Ostler, but neither the stables nor the laundry had yielded any clues; no one had seen them since lunch.

Puzzled, she headed for their room; as it was fine outside, it would be unusual for them to stay indoors, but perhaps one of them wasn't feeling well.

Reaching the room at the end of the corridor, she opened the door—and saw two empty beds, and a note prominently displayed on the nightstand between. Frowning, wondering what their latest start would be, she crossed the room, picked up the note—and felt a jolt of apprehension on seeing it was addressed to her in bold block capitals, not either twin's childish scrawl.

A chill touched her spine. For an instant, she simply stared at the note, then she unfolded it. Read:

IF YOU WISH TO SEE YOUR SISTERS AGAIN, GET THE TREASURE, PUT IT IN THE CANVAS BAG BELOW, AND TAKE IT BACK TO WHERE YOU FOUND IT. FURTHER INSTRUCTIONS WILL AWAIT YOU THERE. ACT NOW—YOU HAVE ONLY AN HOUR FROM THE TIME YOU READ THIS TO RETURN TO THE TOMB. TELL NO ONE ELSE OF THIS. I'LL BE WATCHING. IF I SEE YOU COMING WITH ANYONE ELSE,

YOU'LL NEVER SEE YOUR SISTERS ALIVE
AGAIN.

Reaching the end of the note, Em looked down—and saw
a canvas bag at the bottom of the nightstand, by her feet.

By the time her wits returned enough for her to think,
she was on the path through the wood, hurrying to the
Grange.

Harold. It had to be he, surely?

Halting, she pulled the note from her pocket and looked
again at the script, but the block capitals defeated her; she
couldn't tell if he'd written it or not. Stuffing the note back
in her pocket, she picked up her skirts and ran on.

The rear of the Grange came into view. She halted just
inside the trees, scanned the kitchen garden, and gave
thanks there was no one there. She peered at the laundry
alongside, strained her ears; from the swishing, there were
maids working at the troughs. If so, their backs would be to
the door. Hauling in a tight breath, she quietly walked up
the path to the door.

No one hailed her. Exhaling, she opened the door; Gladys
had mentioned it was always left unlocked during the day.
She crept into the little hall beyond, closed the door silently,
listened for a moment, but all seemed quiet in the kitchen.
With any luck, at that hour both Gladys and Cook would be
napping in their rooms; neither was young, and they would
have been up since dawn.

Drawing in another breath, she closed her eyes, uttered a
short prayer, then walked silently past the doorway to the
kitchen, and on around to the main stairs. Without even
glancing toward the library door, she quietly climbed the
stairs and made her way to Jonas's room—praying nonstop
that he wouldn't be there, but in the library.

She opened the door, scanned the room, heaved a sigh of

relief that it was empty; whisking inside, she shut the door, then crossed to the bedside table.

The key was where it had been before. She lifted it out, slipped it into her pocket, and shut the drawer.

Telling Jonas of the note had occurred to her, only to be instantly dismissed. The instructions were specific; she had to act now, and act alone. If the villain saw her with anyone else, he would kill the twins.

That was something she couldn't risk—not by word, deed, not by anything at all—and she knew Jonas well enough to be absolutely sure he would never agree to her going into the mausoleum to face the villain alone.

Yet she had to.

And she had no time to argue. She'd wondered how anyone could know at what time she'd read the note, but then she'd realized the twins' nightstand stood directly before a dormer window. Anyone on the common opposite the inn could have seen her as she stood there reading the note.

Whoever the villain was, he'd planned well.

So her time was finite; an hour was truly all she had to gather the treasure and get it back to the Colyton mausoleum.

Turning from the bedside table, her gaze fell on the bed. The closeness, the precious joy of the hours she'd spent in Jonas's arms, flared brightly in her mind.

That was what she was risking by going alone to rescue her sisters. She wasn't fool enough to think the kidnapper would readily let them go; the twins must know who he was, and presumably she would, too, once she saw him. All she hoped to gain in return for the treasure was to see her sisters—and have at least one chance to rescue them, and herself, if she could.

One chance, and she would grab it, and see what she could make of it. For once she embraced her reckless and courageous Colyton side with open arms. Somehow she would win through—or die trying.

It was the thought of the latter, and of how Jonas would

feel, that had her glancing at the clock on his dresser. Estimating she had ten minutes she could spare, she quickly crossed, not to the door, but to his writing desk.

Dropping into the chair before it, she drew a crisp, clean sheet onto the blotter, picked up his pen, and rapidly wrote.

Everything. What had happened, what she was doing, where she was going—that took only a few lines—then, scribbling madly, she wrote down all she felt.

She didn't have time to censor her words—not even to make them totally coherent. She just let them pour out of her, out of her heart, through the pen and onto the page.

Unfortunately, writing the words—condensing all she'd dreamed of into stark black on white—only made all she was risking more real, only made the coldness that was settling about her heart weigh more heavily.

She wanted, more than anything, to cling to the promise of life, of a future and a family, that Jonas represented. She didn't want to go into danger—didn't want to risk all she would have, all she now knew and believed with all her heart and soul she would have with him, as his wife, as the mother of his children.

But she had no choice. Her half sisters had only her to rely on—she couldn't fail them now.

She ended her message with a simple statement: I love you—I always will.

Barely able to draw breath past the lump in her throat, she signed the missive, set the pen down, left the note where it was, rose, and rushed to the door.

She didn't breathe freely again until she was in the wood, racing back to the inn.

Whoever the villain was, he'd planned well.

That thought echoed in her head as she pushed the heavy key into the lock on the cell door, turned it, then swung the door wide.

The villain's timing was nothing short of remarkable. At

this time of day, all the regular inn staff were taking advantage of the customary lull between the lunchtime and later afternoon trade. Other than Edgar behind the bar—easy to avoid—there'd been no one else she'd had to dodge.

Whoever the villain was, he knew the inn well.

Canvas bag in hand, she studied the stone box of her ancestors and thanked whatever saint was watching over her; the heavy lid was back on the box, but not perfectly aligned. There was just space enough for her to insert the end of the small crowbar they'd left beside the bench past the lid's edge, and lever the lid sufficiently open for her to slip her hand into the box. Setting the crowbar back down, she reached inside, quickly pulling out handful after handful of coins and jewels.

Then she slowed. How could the villain know how much was in the box?

She glanced around the cell; there was no window, and if she left the lid as it was, from outside the cell no one could see if she left some of the treasure—even a lot of the treasure—behind.

Looking into the bag, then peering into the box, she decided to take not quite a quarter of the total. She would take what was roughly her share and that of the twins, and leave the rest for Henry and Issy and future Colytons. What she was taking would be enough to convince anyone who hadn't seen the entire treasure spread out, free of the box—and the only people who had seen it like that were Lucifer, Jonas, herself, and Issy.

"He must have seen it when we opened the box in the common room," she muttered.

Aside from all else, as she hefted the canvas bag she realized she could never have carried the whole treasure anyway.

Her decision confirmed, the canvas bag solidly full, she tied the attached cords about its mouth, then stood, swung the door to the cell shut again, and locked it.

What to do with the key?

She stared at it for a moment, then hurried up the cellar stairs and into her office. It was the work of a minute to drop the key into the inn strongbox, where inevitably, at some point in time, Jonas would find it.

Glancing at the clock, she saw she had seven minutes left to reach the Colyton mausoleum. Grabbing her cloak off the hook by the door, she wrapped the canvas bag in it, then rushed out into the tap.

"Edgar—I'm going out for a quick walk."

From his usual position behind the bar, Edgar nodded. "Aye, miss. I'll tell any who come asking after you that you'll be back in a while."

"Thank you," she called as she hurried out of the door.

She reached the church and the head of the crypt stairs without seeing anyone, without having to concoct any story about where she was rushing to at that hour. She'd steeled herself to make some excuse if she met Joshua in the church, then remembered he'd gone driving with Issy.

She wondered if he'd offered for Issy's hand. Prayed he had, and that her sweet sister had accepted him. Issy had stood at her back for years; she deserved nothing but good out of life.

Pausing in the vestry to, with shaking hands, light one of the lanterns kept ready there, she noted the key to the crypt wasn't on its hook. Presumably the way was open, and the villain was already down there—waiting for her. Picking up the lantern, hefting the canvas bag in her other hand, she hurried to the stairs and started down.

She made plenty of noise so he—whoever he was—would know she was coming. With luck the twins would hear, too, and know she would be with them soon.

That was another point that suggested the villain wasn't anyone as fundamentally unthreatening as her uncle; she couldn't imagine the twins going anywhere with him again. They were young, but they weren't witless, far from it. No matter what he'd said or promised, she doubted they would have believed him.

As for Silas Coombe, the twins, with the usual bluntness of youth, thought him supremely silly. He'd have no luck at all in luring them away.

Which meant the villain was . . . someone she didn't know at all. Someone she couldn't predict, couldn't make plans for dealing with.

As she descended into the darkness of the crypt, lantern held before her, the only thing she did feel sure of was that whatever was to come, she would need to keep her wits about her if she and her sisters were to survive.

She slowed as she reached the last steps, looking around, swiftly scanning. The tombs and monuments blocked her view in many directions, but she couldn't hear anyone, no breathing, no scuff of a shoe.

Holding the lantern higher, she looked toward the mausoleum's entrance. The door stood open.

Stepping down to the crypt's stone floor, she went toward the gaping maw of her family's communal tomb.

Treasure or curse?

How ironic if, after all her searching, she found her family's treasure only to die prematurely because of it—in the family vault.

She shook aside the morbid thought; she wasn't going to die, not if she could help it.

Her gaze went to the mausoleum's door; the key—the crypt key—wasn't in that lock, either. Which presumably meant the villain had it and could therefore lock her—and her sisters—in the vault.

If that happened . . . luckily, if they survived the encounter only to be locked in the vault, Jonas, once he found her note that night, would know where they were. That eventuality, at least, she'd guarded against.

There wasn't anything more she could do to prepare. She had to go down and face the villain.

Drawing in a deep breath, she lifted her chin, lifted the

lantern, raised the canvas bag, and stepped forward onto the narrow steps that led down to her family's tombs.

She didn't rush, but took each downward step deliberately. He had to know she was coming; there was no reason to rush blindly forward.

The lantern light played over the various monuments and effigies, setting monstrous shadows leaping over the walls. There was no other source of light in the vault—no sign of the lantern normally left in the crypt. The villain had to have it if he'd come down here ahead of her; the crypt, and even more the mausoleum, would be . . . as dark as the grave without the saving light of a lantern.

Perhaps he was behind her?

The thought made her whirl on the last step and look back. Her heart thudded, but even straining her senses, she could detect no hint of movement, no sound to suggest there was anyone in the crypt or even on the stairs leading down to it.

Turning back to the mausoleum, she swallowed her rising panic—partly expectation over who she would shortly meet and what might happen, and partly born of her irrational fear—and doggedly stepped down to the roughly hewn floor.

When she'd been there before, she'd been with others—others she trusted. She hadn't, then, been all that aware of the eeriness of the place, of the oppressive pressure of the hovering dark. Now her nerves were screaming, instincts on high alert, a primitive sense of impending doom urging her to flee—back to the light, out of the dark.

She swallowed again, forced herself to hold the lantern high and look around. She was sure she'd see someone—someone evil—but increasingly the sense of being alone intensified; she was alone with the dead.

She reminded herself they were *her* dead—Colytons all, her ancestors. If anyone had anything to fear there, it was he who wanted to steal the family legacy.

Remembering the villain's instructions, she slowly made

her way to the tomb of her many-times-great-grandmother, she who had been farsighted enough to hoard the treasure and hide it so cleverly.

Reaching the tomb, she raised the canvas bag and set it down where the treasure box had previously been, letting the coins and jewels clink loudly.

The noise echoed in the dark. She waited, wondering, senses stretching in an attempt to locate the direction from whence danger might spring. She slowly pirouetted, and still she saw no one.

"Emily."

Her name reached her as a ghostly whisper; at first she wasn't sure the sound wasn't a figment of her imagination.

But then it came again, more insistent, faintly taunting. "Em—ily."

The voice was coming from the nearer of the two dark holes in the wall, the tunnels leading deeper into the heart of the limestone ridge.

"Em—ily."

More insistent still. A man's voice, definitely not her half sisters', yet not a voice she recognized.

She hesitated, then picked up the canvas bag and went to the opening. She held the lantern high—prayed she would see the twins—but all that met her eyes were the walls of a narrow passage leading away.

Leading into pitch blackness.

"Emily."

There was a chiding, almost disapproving note in the voice now. Clearly she was supposed to go forward, into the tunnel.

Panic was a wild, fluttering bird in her chest. Just the thought of what she was about to do sent the blood draining from her face.

But she couldn't swoon, couldn't faint—couldn't back away. The twins were relying on her; she was their only hope.

Dragging in a short, too shallow breath, struggling to calm her galloping heart, she tightened her hold on the canvas bag, clenched her fingers even tighter around the handle of the lantern, and, holding it aloft, stepped into the abiding dark.

21

It was late afternoon before Jonas headed back to the Grange. He'd searched high and low for both Silas and Potheridge, and found neither. However, according to Miss Hellebore and Mrs. Keighley, who did for Silas, both men were in the village, or at least were returning to their beds there every night.

Both, it seemed, were playing least in sight.

Which left the possibility open that one, or even both, knew something about the attack on him.

He was increasingly certain the man who'd struck him hadn't been Silas, and the stealth of the attack made him doubt it had been Potheridge; the man was corpulent and heavy on his feet. Jonas doubted he could move silently on a clean stone floor, let alone on a woodland path.

But Potheridge was a bully, one Em had thwarted; from what she'd let fall her uncle was one of those for whom spite alone was sufficient motive for violence. And Silas might be in sufficiently desperate straits to make the treasure simply too good an opportunity to pass up. Neither might have been the man who'd struck him, but he wouldn't wager that one or both hadn't hired a thug and told him where to wait.

Indeed, hiring someone to do their dirty work was a trait

he had no difficulty at all crediting to both Silas and Potheridge.

He returned to his home via the front drive. Rather than bother Mortimer, he circled the front porch and went in through the side door. Reaching the front hall he headed for the library, just as Gladys came through the green baize door.

"There you are! Just the person." Bustling forward, she waved a folded note. "Jenny, the upstairs maid, found this on the desk in your room. It wasn't folded then, but she can't read, so she wasn't sure if she should clear it away or not, so she brought it down to me. I didn't read it either—not my place—but I did see it's from Miss Emily, so I thought you'd want it."

Jonas took the note, unfolded it. Started to read.

Gladys headed back to the kitchen. "Mind you, I've no idea how it got on your desk—no one came in this morning that I know of."

Her voice faded as she passed through the baize-covered door, and it swung shut behind her.

But Jonas was no longer listening. His eyes locked on Em's panicked scrawl, his mind was captured, riveted by what she'd written . . . the latter part of the letter would have filled him with joy to see her love for him so clearly stated, *but* his eyes, his mind, immediately returned to the first few lines.

He could barely believe what they conveyed.

She'd gone into danger alone—by herself was trying to deal with a kidnapper—Potheridge?—and rescue the twins. She was going to hand over the treasure, the family future she'd worked so hard to secure, hoping to survive—it was patently clear from her tone that that last was only a hope.

"Damn it!" Jaw setting, he shoved the note into his pocket. She'd promised—*promised*—to tell him of any problem, to share it and allow him to help. True, she'd written, but she clearly hadn't expected him to find the letter until later . . .

He glanced at the clock. He'd left her at two; it was now just past four. Allow her time to hunt for the twins, find the kidnapper's note, come there and get the key, then gather the treasure and take it to the church . . . he couldn't be far behind her.

Before he'd completed the thought he was striding for the back door. Pushing through it, he started to run; when he hit the tree line and the path through the wood, he lengthened his stride and raced.

The fastest way to the church was via the inn.

Chill fingers touched his nape; icy dread bloomed and wrapped about his heart. He knew she would pay the ransom, that she'd hand over the treasure to save her sisters—as would he. But kidnappers were inherently desperate, and especially desperate to conceal their identity, and how would the villain do that once she—and the twins—had seen him?

The answer was obvious; he ran faster, his boots pounding along the track in time with his heart.

To have his love returned only to have her snatched away—*no*. That wasn't going to happen. He would give anything, including his life, to keep her safe.

Em felt as if the mountain had swallowed her. The narrow passage led on and on, barely wide enough for a man to pass through, sloping gently downward. The dark beyond the circle of lantern light was so intense it seemed to swallow reality; the only piece of the world that existed was contained within the glowing sphere of light.

Abruptly the front edge of the lantern's glow diffused and softened. She slowed, then realized she'd reached the end of the passage. She halted on the threshold of . . . a cavern? Holding the lantern high, she peered through the gloom, but the light didn't illuminate any walls or ceiling. It didn't illuminate anything at all except the floor before her.

That floor was uneven, pocked and fissured; playing the

light further afield, she saw bright white columns, rough and irregular, formed by water dripping from the roof she couldn't see.

"Emily."

She was starting to hate that voice; it definitely held a note of taunting smugness. Assuming the beckoning call to mean she should go forward, she did. Moving slowly across the cavern floor, picking her way through clumps of fragmented rock, through dips and over small rises, slipping past numerous slimy whitish columns, she moved steadily, cautiously on, keeping the lantern directly in front of her and following its guiding beam.

The cavern, if cavern it was, seemed enormous. She was about to halt, to force the disembodied voice to speak again, when she heard . . . something.

She swung the lantern beam this way and that, then stopped, held her breath, listened for all she was worth—and made out soft muffled thumps and thuds, and what sounded like muffled cries . . .

Fixing the direction, she grabbed up her skirts, held the lantern high, and hurried toward the sound. "Gert? Bea? Are you there?"

The muffled thuds increased in vigor—more like drumming. The girls were drumming their heels on the rock floor.

She hurried on. A stand—more like a coppice—of white columns rose before her. She dodged them and saw a low wall—a place where the rock of the cave hadn't worn down as much as the surrounding areas; the sound of drumming heels was coming from beyond. Rounding the wall, she beamed the lantern behind it—and saw her terrified half sisters bound and gagged, lashed together with their hands behind their backs.

"Thank God!" She rushed forward. Setting the lantern down, she fell to her knees and hugged both girls to her. "I'm here—you're safe."

Releasing them, she pulled down the scarf around Gert's mouth, then turned to do the same for Bea.

"But we're not safe," Gert hissed, her voice the merest whisper. "He's here—he called you in."

Bea nodded vigorously, eyes round, as Em tugged off her gag. "He has to still be here."

The sheer terror in Bea's voice refocused Em. They were right. But . . . "Who is he?" She'd already untied the rope lashing them together; she urged Bea around and started untying the ropes securing her wrists.

"Mr. Jervis!" Gert hissed.

When Em looked her confusion, Bea blurted, "Mr. Jerry Jervis—Mama's gentleman friend from York."

"York?" Em couldn't place any such gentleman. "But—"

"He was Mama's *especial* gentleman friend, but he was a sailor and had to leave on some ship—we haven't seen him in ages." Gert wriggled around so Em could get to the ropes about her wrists.

"He told us Mama had asked him to look in on us and he'd finally found us at the Red Bells." Bea pressed close, keeping her voice low. "He asked us to go for a walk with him on the common—"

"We told him about the treasure." Gert pulled her wrists free. "He asked us to show him where it had been hidden . . ." She met Em's eyes in the dimness. "We didn't think there'd be any harm in that, but—"

"He caught us"—Bea grabbed Em's arm—"and he tied us up and left us here."

"Why?" Gert's face was all puzzled hurt. "Why would he do such a thing?"

Em remembered the treasure, glanced at the sack lying beside her. She'd found the girls, but she still had the sack.

The lantern started to flicker, then fade.

Her fear of the dark, until then held at bay, rushed in, rolled in like a wave threatening to swamp her, to drown her and sweep her away . . .

She sucked in a breath, focused on the girls—saw their eyes grow round with fright.

Then they screamed and pointed behind her.

"Hello, Emily."

She swung around just as the lantern died, plunging them into darkness.

For an instant, she couldn't breathe, felt smothered, suffocated—then she remembered the treasure and reached for the sack.

It whisked past her fingertips, already seized.

The air about her swirled as someone large, standing very close, swung about. He didn't try to mask his footsteps, but walked confidently away through the dark.

For a moment, panic and surprise held her silent. She rose uncertainly to her feet; the girls scrambled up, clinging on either side. She couldn't understand how the man could walk so easily through the dark over such terrain—then her eyes adjusted, and as he drew further away she saw a narrow shaft of dim lantern light playing before the faint silhouette of a largish man.

Chill desperation gripped her. "Wait! You can't leave us here!" Gathering the girls, she stepped out from behind the low stone wall.

He paused, turned his head. "Yes, I can." A moment passed. "You'll either find your way out, or die here. Regardless, I'll be long gone, and for my pains I'll be rich beyond my wildest dreams."

There was something about his voice . . . She frowned. "Hadley?"

The man laughed. "Good-bye, Emily Colyton. It was . . . rewarding to have known you." He chuckled, was about to walk on, then paused once more. "It's a pity, really, that you wanted Tallent. If you'd been amenable to wanting me, I might have taken you with me, but then again, like Susan, you'd never have left those brats behind."

Em could just discern the mocking flourish he made her.

"So farewell, my dear—I doubt we'll meet again." He resumed his steady march out of the cavern.

Leaving pitch blackness behind.

"Hadley!" Even she heard the terrified desperation in her

voice, but the rest of her appeal died on her lips as, in a brief strengthening of lantern light, she saw Hadley outlined as he entered the distant passage.

The light faded, and he was gone.

The darkness thickened.

Em looped an arm around each girl, holding them to her, and fought to steady her racing heart. She swallowed. Dragged in a breath, then another—forced herself to exhale. "We have to get out of here."

"But we can't see," Bea whispered.

"No." Em pushed herself to speak in a normal, reassuring tone. "But I know which way the passage is from here." She did know that much; she was facing the passage entrance. "Come along. We just have to put one foot in front of the other, and we'll reach the passage."

She took one step, and her shoe brushed the empty lantern. "Wait." She stooped and picked the lantern up; it was a sturdy one with a solid iron base. It was no longer of any use in casting light, yet just having it in her hand made her feel marginally better. "Right, now—you stay on that side, Gert, and Bea stays on the other. Hold on to my skirts tightly—you'll be able to follow where I go. Just walk with me—think of it as one of your games."

"All right," Bea said. "But I don't like the dark."

Em *hated* the dark, abhorred it, was all but terrified of it—but she didn't have time to indulge that old fear. Their lives—all their lives—depended on her keeping her head. So she would.

They now had full lives to live, and people they loved who loved them; all she cared about was ensuring both continued, and that meant finding their way out of the cavern and back to the light of day.

"Come along—let's go." Not even her old fear was going to keep her from seeing Jonas again, from lying in his arms, from kissing him, from being held by him—from being protected and cherished and loved by him. She put one foot directly in front of the other, then repeated the exercise. One hand held out before her to keep from running into the columns that lay between them and the passage—how she would navigate around even one and then get back to their correct course she'd yet to work out—she determinedly went forward.

One foot in front of the other.

They reached the coppice of columns about twenty footsteps along. She was trying to remember how many there'd been, and how they stood in relation to the passage entrance, when a breath of cool air played over her face.

Just the veriest waft, the merest caress, but the air was otherwise so still and even-temperatured, the cool touch was distinctive.

She halted, wondering if her imagination was inventing answers to her prayers, but then the cool waft came again, increasingly clear to her dark-sharpened senses. Despite everything, she smiled. "Girls—can you feel the breeze?"

An instant passed, then she felt them both nod.

"It's coming from the passage." She *thought* it was coming from the passage; there were other possibilities, but she saw no benefit in dwelling on those—as far as she could tell, the gentle flow was coming down the passage from the mausoleum. The chill, clammy clasp of her fear eased a notch. "All we have to do to find the passage is keep walking into the breeze. Come along."

With a great deal more confidence, one hand waving wildly before her, she led them around the coppice of slimy columns, then got them back on track, walking into the faint breeze.

Their progress was still painfully slow; although the breeze gave them their direction, they still had to feel for every step—both girls as well as she. The floor of the cavern seemed much more rocky and broken, the dips and rises much steeper, in the absolute dark.

Regardless of her resolution, the dark still weighed heavily on her, like a smothering blanket that threatened to steal away her next breath. She still had to battle for every breath, to push back the fear that made her lungs seize.

Hope kept her moving forward—that, and Jonas—the fixed, immutable conviction that she had to be, needed to be, *would be* with him again, that her destined place, her ordained future, was at his side in the daylight, not there in the suffocating dark.

So she pressed on, one step after another, carefully placing one foot before the other, keeping the faint breeze on her cheeks.

J onas raced into the church and swung down onto the crypt steps. He'd paused at the inn to ask Edgar where Em was—faint hope—but Edgar had confirmed she was "taking a walk."

He'd sworn and sent Edgar to fetch Thompson and Oscar from the forge and meet him at the church. There'd been no time for explanations; he'd left Edgar to it and pelted up the rise to the church. With Filing and Issy gone for the day, and Henry out walking, there was no help to be had from the rectory, and no time to summon Lucifer and his men.

With luck one of the locals who'd been in the tap would carry the news to the manor.

He slowed on the precipitous steps. The door to the crypt stood open, but within all was dark. He went down the last steps quietly; he was virtually at the bottom before he could confirm that the mausoleum door stood open. The faintest of faint glows came from within. Remembering that Em had to return the treasure to where it had been found, he slowed still more and cautiously, silently, approached the mausoleum.

Pausing at the top of the mausoleum steps, he listened intently. At first, nothing but aching silence reached his ears, then, faint and distant, but distinct, he heard muffled footsteps.

Not Em's footsteps—a man's.

Jonas silently flowed down the mausoleum steps, pausing on the last to scan the darkness—instantly seeing that the reason the lantern glow was so dim was that the source was approaching along one of the underground tunnels that gave off the mausoleum, leading back into the limestone ridge.

God—and presumably the villain—knew what lay beyond the tunnel.

The lantern bearer was nearing the mausoleum proper. Jonas stepped down to the rough floor and slipped into the dense shadows; choosing a large tomb, he crouched behind, looking around its corner at the tunnel entrance.

A man came striding out of the tunnel. He stepped clear of its mouth and looked up. Hadley! Jonas frowned. Was he the villain, or had he simply been curious and gone down to see . . . ?

Then Hadley lifted the hand not holding the lantern, and Jonas saw a canvas sack—heard a telltale jingle.

He was looking at the villain who'd been pursuing the treasure, who'd attacked him, and stolen the twins away— then lured Em away.

Where was she? And the twins?

Hadley walked to the nearest large tomb and set the sack down on the flat lid. Placing the lantern alongside it, he opened the drawstring closing the sack, then tipped it up, spreading some of the contents on the tomb lid.

Gold and jewels winked in the lamplight.

Hadley's smile was pure avarice. It remained in place as he scooped the items—the Colyton treasure—back into the sack and retied the drawstring. Then he picked up the lantern and, still smiling, headed for the steps.

Jonas slipped around the tomb behind which he was crouching, chose another close by the foot of the steps. He waited, listening to Hadley's footsteps near, watching the lantern glow brighten.

At just the right moment he stood and swung into the

narrow aisle—directly in Hadley's path, blocking his way to the steps.

Startled, Hadley halted.

Jonas seized the sack and wrenched it from the artist's grasp. "I'll take that."

Hadley came to life with a snarl. He lunged for the sack.

Jonas fended him off and flung the sack far behind him. It clattered against the end wall.

Reversing the direction of his arm, he plowed his fist toward Hadley's gut. Hadley leapt back and used the lantern to push the blow aside.

Hadley lost his grip on the lantern; it fell, rolling away, the light flickering wildly. Regaining his balance, Jonas saw Hadley groping in his pocket, furiously tugging to free . . . a pistol?

He didn't wait to find out, but launched himself at Hadley.

Hadley left off freeing his weapon to grapple with him. Gripping each other's arms, they swung this way, then that, wrestling in the restricted area between the tombs.

Although Jonas was an inch or so taller, Hadley was heavier; neither had any real advantage as they lurched back and forth in the confined space. The tombs of long-dead Colytons battered them as they bounced between the unforgiving stone, neither able to gain the ascendancy.

Then he managed to free his right arm; he plowed his fist into Hadley's jaw, the blow fueled by fury and escalating uncertainty over Em's and the twins' whereabouts, their safety, their well-being.

Hadley reeled back, weakening his hold on him. With a gasp, Hadley grabbed the chance, broke from his clutches, and rolled back and over a free-standing tomb. Before he could move, Hadley popped up on the other side, a pistol in his hand.

Jonas dived to the side, but felt the ball rip a fiery path across his upper left shoulder.

Hadley didn't wait to check the damage; he flung the now

useless pistol after Jonas, making him duck again, then raced around the tomb, heading for the spot where Jonas had flung the treasure.

Voices reached them from the crypt above. Hadley skidded to a halt.

"He must be down there." Thompson's bass rumble boomed down the mausoleum's steps.

"So let's go down and look, then." Oscar's reply was followed by heavy bootsteps on the stone stairs.

Jonas used one of the tombs to get back on his feet. "Quickly! Down here!" Edging backward, he put himself between Hadley and the tunnel from which he'd come.

Eyes wide, Hadley looked from him to the stone steps—the only way up, now blocked by the descending bulks of Oscar and Thompson.

Hadley glanced toward the treasure, out of sight at the far end of the mausoleum, then glanced over his shoulder—at the mouth of the second tunnel at the opposite end.

If he went after the treasure, he'd be trapped at that end of the mausoleum with Jonas, Oscar, and Thompson between him and all exits.

With a snarl of frustrated fury, Hadley seized the dropped lantern, still alight, whirled and fled—across the mausoleum and down the second tunnel.

Frowning, Jonas watched the light fade.

Coming down the steps with another lantern, Oscar had seen Hadley flee, too. Sweeping the lantern beam around the mausoleum, he located Jonas in the deepening gloom. "What's up?"

Jonas wasn't sure, but finding Em and the twins was his priority. He waved. "Give me that lantern. Do you have another?"

"Aye." It was Thompson who answered, following his brother down the steps holding another lighted lantern high. "These are the last two, as it happens. There should be four—don't know where the other two have got to."

"Hadley—he's our villain—just ran off with one lantern down that tunnel." Jonas indicated the far tunnel with his head. "I think Em must have the other." He hoped she did; he had a suspicion—more an impression—that she didn't like being in absolute dark.

He turned to the tunnel behind him, playing the lantern light into its mouth. "Hadley came out of this tunnel, carrying the sack Em must have put the treasure—or at least some of it—in." In a few succinct phrases, he outlined Hadley's scheme, and what he believed Em had done in response. "I flung the sack against the wall back there—you could retrieve it and hold on to it."

"Aye." Thompson nodded his big head. "But you're bleeding. Was that a shot we heard?"

Jonas flexed his shoulder, suppressed a wince. "Just a flesh wound. The pistol's lying around the tombs somewhere—Hadley hasn't got it, and I doubt he's carrying a second."

"So where do you think Miss Emily and those girls are?" Oscar asked.

Jonas walked to the tunnel he'd been studying. "I think Hadley's left them somewhere down this tunnel."

"Gawd! Hope they haven't wandered off." Oscar shuddered.

Jonas hoped so—prayed so—too. People got lost—forever—in the caves. "I'm going down to look, but you two stay here." He looked to the other tunnel, the one down which Hadley had fled. "I don't know where that tunnel leads, either, but I suspect Hadley is waiting for all of us to go after Em and the girls, letting him slip out behind us."

"Well, he won't do that." Thompson settled his lantern on a tomb, his expression the epitome of belligerent. "But you take care down there, and give us a 'hoy' if you need help getting those ladies back out."

"I will." Jonas paused on the threshold of the tunnel. "If I need to go too deep"—if Em and the girls had wandered away—"I'll come back and tell you first."

The brothers mumbled agreement. Raising the lantern, Jonas strode into the tunnel.

It was longer than he'd hoped. He hurried as much as he dared, as fast as the unfamiliar terrain allowed. The pain in his shoulder made jogging unwise; he'd be no use to Em and the twins if he swooned.

Oscar's and Thompson's voices faded as he pressed deeper into the ridge. His mind ranged ahead, assessing the probabilities of what he might find. It had been years—decades—since he'd gone caving, and as the mausoleum had been shut for all those years, he'd never explored these tunnels, or the caves they most likely connected with.

One heartening discovery was the dearth of connecting passages; he didn't have to wonder which way he needed to go.

Hurrying as fast as he was able, he prayed he wasn't—wouldn't be—too late.

They'd heard a muffled bang in the distance, soft but distinct, and a long way away. Em didn't want to think what it might have been. Hadley slamming the mausoleum door, sealing them inside?

She told herself not to think of such things, to concentrate on getting all three of them safely to the passage, and then back to the mausoleum. Jonas would find her note sometime that evening, and then he would come and free them.

All they had to do was reach the mausoleum and wait there.

All in absolute, utter, and complete darkness.

Don't think about it.

She focused instead on the continuing, fractionally strengthening, brush of cool air past her face. More definite now, she had no difficulty using it to steer them, but their progress was still excruciatingly slow. The rocky and uneven floor was bad enough, but the slimy columns that they had to find by touch were worse. She often had to detour a considerable way to find space enough for all three of them to pass; entirely understandably, neither twin would let go, or even change their position at her sides.

Arms outstretched, the lantern swinging from one hand, she shuffled and stumbled along, the girls doing the same on either side. Regardless of her self-lecturing, the dark was so dense it felt like a physical weight pressing on her eyelids. She'd closed her eyes long ago; it was too disorientating looking into blackness dense enough to have one questioning whether one's eyes still worked.

Despite telling herself that the faint breeze meant they really weren't shut in there, that the dark was just dark, and there truly wasn't anything else alive in the cavern, her fears were starting to build, swelling like a balloon in her chest, squeezing against her lungs, making it difficult to breathe.

But the twins were relying on her to lead them out of there; she had no time to swoon.

"Are there mice down here?" Bea whispered.

"I doubt it." Em answered in as matter-of-fact a tone as she could muster. "No food, so no mice."

"Oh." Bea fell silent.

Gert piped up. "What about spiders?"

"Too damp." Em certainly hoped so. She had enough fear to handle without such crawly creatures.

Suddenly the flow of air increased. She frowned; that should mean they were getting close to the passage entrance, but she thought they were still some distance away.

Could there be two passages?

She hadn't seen another, yet . . . the gush of air coming toward her seemed . . . broader.

Halting, she forced herself to take stock. Eyes closed, concentrating on the flow of air across her cheeks, slowly she turned her head in an arc from left to right.

She—her senses—weren't wrong. The air was now flowing to them from two different angles.

Two different passages.

Which was the one leading to the mausoleum and safety?

All that Jonas, and later Henry, had let fall about the massive, interconnected cave systems in the region, and how people got lost in them, never to be seen again, replayed in her mind.

Keeping her voice as unconcerned as she could, she asked, "Did either of you notice another passage or tunnel near the one from the mausoluem?"

"There was another opening," Gert said. "Another passage like the one Mr. Jervis brought us down. It was to our left when we came into this place."

Thanking heaven for observant children, Em nodded. "Good. So from this direction, the passage to the mausoleum is the one to our left."

Making decisions about directions with one's eyes closed was unnerving. Opening hers, she turned her face so the breeze from the wrong tunnel, the one to the right, was blowing directly in her face. That, she told herself, squinting into the dark, was the wrong direction.

She frowned, and squinted some more. Was it a trick of her eyes, or her mind, or were the walls inside the wrong passage starting to lighten? To become visible.

Out of the silence, echoing footsteps reached them.

Men's bootsteps. Hadley? Or rescue?

Or both?

Her hyperacute senses detected two sets of footsteps coming toward them—the first and nearer pounding along, almost running, the other further away, quick strides hurrying, but not at the same clip as the first man.

The nearer man was approaching via the tunnel to the right, while the other, slightly slower man was coming from the mausoleum.

The only fact she could discern from the sound of the steps was that both men were wearing heeled boots, not the flat-soled workboots laborers wore.

Hadley-Jervis-whoever-he-was had been wearing boots. Jonas always wore boots.

Ahead of them, still yards away but not as far as she'd thought, the end wall of the cavern to which they'd been heading grew more distinct, defined by the strengthening glows increasingly illuminating each tunnel.

Both men had lanterns.

One man was rescue and safety, the other was danger.

Which was which?

The twins stayed blessedly silent; she felt their grips tighten on her skirts.

In a burst of clarity, she realized that while she and the twins would be able to see the men clearly, the men wouldn't immediately be able to see them. She and the girls were still far enough back from the tunnel mouths to be outside the immediate sweep of a lantern. The cavern about them seemed limitless, swallowing all light, yet with their eyes accustomed to the dark, they could now see clearly.

She scanned their immediate surroundings; several paces back, on their right, stood a series of the ubiquitous limestone columns. They were what had screened them from the airflow from the passage to the right until they'd stepped beyond them.

She glanced down at the twins, then shifted to gather one in the curve of each arm. She bent low. "Stay quiet," she ordered in the barest whisper.

She steered them a few steps back and across behind the screening columns. "Let's get down," she breathed. She crouched, and they obediently sank down beside her, pressing close. Setting the lantern on the rocky floor before her, she draped her arms protectively over both girls. Head bent to theirs, she murmured, "I want you to let go of me, just in case I have to move." She felt their fingers slowly, reluctantly, uncurl, releasing her skirts. "I need you to keep your faces down—don't look up. Stay here, huddled down, unless I or Jonas call you out."

The man in the right passage thundered toward them.

"No sound," was the last thing she dared say.

Hadley burst into the cavern, breathing hard. He pulled up just inside, weaving, then held his lantern high and swept the light in a wide arc, peering deep into the cavern.

The light passed over their heads; Hadley's attention was fixed far beyond them.

He muttered a curse, then raised his voice. "Emily!" His call was a forceful whisper, quite different from his earlier taunting.

When nothing but silence replied, he went on, "I've changed my mind. Come out and I'll lead you to safety."

Em smothered a derisive snort.

The second man was coming steadily closer; the nearer he came, the clearer his footsteps, the more certain she was that it was Jonas.

Safety. Protection. Security.

How he'd known to come looking for her down there, and so soon, she didn't know; she could only be thankful that he had.

Under cover of the echoing footsteps, she breathed to the twins, "Stay down. Don't move."

Hadley could hear Jonas coming; still breathing in gulps, eyes wild, after one last searching look around the cavern, he turned to face the other passage.

A second passed, then he looked down at his lantern. He moved, keeping to the right of the mausoleum passage, then carefully set the lantern down, angling its beam at the entrance of the other passage.

To shine in Jonas's eyes as he stepped into the cavern.

As Hadley straightened, Em saw his right hand slide from his pocket, saw light glint along a blade as, softfooted, he stepped back from the lantern and swiftly circled around the glow of light.

He passed within two feet of them.

She held her breath, but, his attention fixed on the passage from which Jonas would come, Hadley was no longer looking for them. He didn't so much as glance their way as they cowered in the lee of the columns.

As he passed between her and the oncoming light, she more clearly saw the wicked-looking knife in his hand.

Jonas's footsteps echoed, growing louder and louder.

Hadley swiftly continued until he stood to the left of the mausoleum passage, so when Jonas stepped into the cavern, he—Hadley—would be on the other side to the lighted lantern.

Jonas would look toward the lantern, and then . . .

Silently Em rose; picking up her spent lantern, she started to move, to glide around, circling without a sound until she stood two yards behind Hadley.

The light from Jonas's lantern filled the mouth of the passage; he stood holding it aloft, directing light around the cavern, squinting against the glare from the other lantern.

He'd halted just inside the passage; poised to leap murderously forward, Hadley couldn't yet pounce.

Then Jonas stepped into the cavern. "Em?"

Hadley moved.

"Hadley has a knife, Jonas! He's this way."

Hadley whirled, blinking furiously as he tried to see her, but he'd been looking into the light, and she was far enough away from the stationary lantern's beam to be all but invisible.

Her muscles twitched, but she held her ground. As long as she didn't move, he wouldn't be able to see her.

Jonas had swung her way. Then Hadley moved sideways—Em heard Jonas curse as the light from his lantern washed over her.

Hadley's eyes locked on her. With a snarl, he lunged for her—hand extended, fingers hooked to grab her.

Jonas flung his lantern at Hadley. It struck him on the back of the neck, the blow enough to make him stagger, then swing back to face Jonas—turning away from Em.

Jonas dove after the lantern. The blackguard wanted to

use Em as a hostage—that's why he'd raced back to the cavern.

He collided with Hadley and they went down; in the heat of the moment, he'd forgotten his shoulder wound, but a searing jolt of pain as he landed reminded him.

Hadley hadn't forgotten the wound, nor Jonas's head wound, either. His face contorted in a vicious snarl, he fought to put pressure on Jonas's damaged shoulder, Jonas's weight as well as all he could bring to bear.

Jonas gritted his teeth and clung to consciousness. The only way to ease the building pressure was to flip onto his back, putting his still-tender skull on the rock floor, simultaneously allowing Hadley the advantage of being on top.

An advantage Hadley immediately pressed, trying to strike downward with the knife clutched in his fist.

Jonas caught Hadley's hand and fist, wrapped both his hands about them, and braced his arms as Hadley bore down.

His arms began to tremble.

Circling the shifting men, Em saw the quiver in Jonas's arms.

Saw the blood on his shoulder, seeping into his coat around a nasty-looking tear.

Anger, red hot, erupted through her. Setting her lips, she hefted her until then useless lantern, weighed it, gauged her swing, then stepped forward and swung the heavy base at Hadley.

With a solid *thunk*, it connected with his skull.

He froze, then, easing back, dazedly shook his head.

Jonas dragged back one fist and plowed it into Hadley's jaw.

The sharp crack echoed through the cavern; Hadley's head snapped around, then his body slowly followed, eyes closing as he slid sideways to topple onto the rocky floor.

Off Jonas.

Em looked down at the result of their joint efforts—Hadley was well and truly unconscious—then she dropped the lantern and flung herself on her knees beside Jonas. "You're bleeding!" She gently touched his shoulder. Her face paled. "Good God—did he actually shoot you?"

Turning her head, she sent a glare Hadley's way. "Hadley, Jervis, whoever he is."

"It's just a flesh wound." Sitting up, lips compressed, Jonas set her aside, then managed to get to his feet, along the way confiscating the knife that had fallen from Hadley's hand. He pocketed the blade, then turned to face Em as she rose.

Felt anger, and more, erupt as the last minutes—especially the moment in which Hadley had lunged at her—replayed in his head. He met her bright eyes, felt fury blaze in his. "What the *devil* did you mean by coming here without me?"

She blinked, taken aback. "You must have read my note—I had to pay his ransom and rescue the twins."

He nodded. "That much I comprehend. What I don't understand is why you didn't see fit to tell me even though you'd promised you would—when you *promised* you'd share any troubles. Remember that?" Planting his hands on his hips, he thrust his face close to hers, ignoring the throbbing ache in his shoulder. "And while we're about it, what about minutes ago, when you deliberately called his attention to you?" He jabbed a finger at her nose. "And don't try to tell me you didn't know he had a knife!"

She'd backed one step, but his last comment, somewhat to his surprise, had her narrowing her eyes, spine stiffening as she abruptly stood her ground. "Don't be a dolt. He was going to leap on you—with his knife! What did you expect me to do? Stand there and watch him stick you with it?"

He wasn't going to let her use such an excuse. "What I *expected*—"

"Can we come out now?"

The plaintive voice floated out from the dark, effectively

cutting through their mutual absorption. Both drew back, then exchanged a fraught look.

"Later," Em said, voice low, eyes still narrow, lips still thin.

He nodded tersely. "Later." That discussion wasn't over, not by any means.

Em turned to where she'd left the twins. "Yes, it's all right to come out now. You're safe."

She wasn't sure she was, and was even less sure Jonas was, but with Hadley stretched out at her feet, her sisters indubitably were safe once more.

22

Leaving Hadley in the dark, they ushered the twins back up the passage all of them had come down.

"The other passage must lead to the mausoleum, too." Jonas followed Em along the tunnel. They'd relit his lantern, which had gone out, from Hadley's, so he and Em each had one to hold the dark at bay; they'd left the lantern she'd used to knock Hadley over the head—it was out of fuel. "Hadley raced away from the mausoleum to escape Thompson, Oscar, and me—we thought he'd just run blindly into the caves."

"Instead, he ran back to find me," Em said.

Tight-lipped, Jonas nodded; his head was all right, but his shoulder was throbbing. "He wanted you, or one of the twins, to use as a hostage, so he could demand the treasure back again, along with a chance to escape." He frowned at the twins' shining heads. "Gert, Bea—how did he persuade you to go with him? I would have thought you would have learned your lesson after Harold."

With great dignity, the twins explained, informing him that Hadley was their mama's "especial gentleman friend from York."

"But he was Mr. Jervis, then."

"*And* he had a big beard."

Facing forward, the girls marched on; they seemed not a whit the worse for their adventure. Indeed, from the whispers they were exchanging, it seemed they were honing and polishing their tale for the villagers' consumption.

Jonas exchanged a look with Em. "I suspect he's Mr. Jervis still."

She nodded. "Susan—the twin's mama—knew about the treasure. I'm not sure if she knew the rhyme, but the twins have heard it from their earliest years, from me, and Issy and Henry."

Bouncing along ahead of them, Bea swung around to say, "Mr. Jervis was the one who, after Mama went to live with the angels, told the constable we should be sent to live with Em at her uncle Harold's house."

"Did he?" From her expression, that was news to Em. "Well, that was one kind thing he did."

Gert snorted. "He didn't do it to be kind. I overheard him saying he hoped it would put more pressure on you." She glanced back at Em. "But we're not 'pressure,' are we?"

"Mr. Jervis is clearly a bad man," Em said. "You should never believe anything bad men say."

When, reassured, Gert and Bea faced forward again, she exchanged an even more meaningful look with Jonas.

He slowed his stride; she did, too. As, whispering, the twins drew ahead, he murmured, "It sounds like Hadley— or Jervis, if that's his real name—wanted the treasure, but he never intended to look for it himself. He appeared weeks after you arrived; it wouldn't have been hard to set up some arrangement so someone sent him word when you left your uncle's house. I take it Susan knew that was your plan—to leave as soon as you turned twenty-five?"

Em nodded. "Issy and I wrote frequently—it was an open secret between us and Susan."

"So Jervis knew all that, and guessed that sending the twins to you would increase the pressure on you to leave the instant your birthday came around."

"He was right in that," Em admitted. "Harold's attitude to them was the last straw."

They reached the mausoleum to find Thompson and Oscar perched on tombs, legs swinging as they waited. They slid back onto their large feet as the girls raced up to them, chattering about bad men and lanterns and knives.

Thompson cocked a brow at Jonas.

He tipped his head back down the passage. "Hadley's unconscious in a cavern further down. Both tunnels lead to the same place."

"Right then." Thompson lifted the lantern he'd left on a nearby tomb. "Me and Oscar'd best fetch him."

"Here." Jonas handed his lantern to Oscar. "One of you will need to go down each tunnel, or he could come up one while you're going down the other."

Thompson nodded, grinning with poorly concealed anticipation. "He won't get past us." Turning to Em, Thompson offered the canvas bag. "Think this is rightfully yours, miss."

"Thank you." Em took the sack, a smile softening what until then had been a serious expression.

"We'll go and fetch the villain, then." With a nod and a salute, Oscar headed for the further tunnel, leaving his older brother to lumber down the nearer one.

As the light from their lanterns faded, Jonas took the one Em still held. Ignoring the pain radiating from his shoulder, he raised the lantern high and ushered his charges up the winding steps to the crypt, and thence to the church.

There they found a gaggle of concerned supporters about to head down to help, Filing, Issy, and Henry in the lead. At the sounds of the twins' pattering footsteps everyone had fallen silent, waiting; erupting into an expectant quiet, the twins immediately set about occupying center stage. They happily told their tale, and Em's and Jonas's as well; exchanging a wry look with Jonas, Em left them to it—aside from all else, they were distracting everyone.

The same held true when, leaving Thompson and Oscar to their mission, the large group repaired to the inn. There an even greater number of village folk were waiting on tenterhooks to hear the outcome of the kidnapping and ransom demand. After Edgar had found Thompson, he'd returned to hold the bar; Em noted the inn was doing a roaring trade for what should have been a quiet Thursday evening.

Everyone was well primed, waiting to see Jervis-cum-Hadley when Thompson and Oscar brought him in, but all were disappointed.

"He'd gone," Thompson reported. "I reached the cavern first, but Oscar was only moments later. He didn't get past either of us, but he wasn't in the cavern—leastways not that we could see. We didn't hunt too far—figured he wouldn't try anything without even a lantern to guide him. So we came back up and locked the mausoleum door, and the crypt door, too." Thompson handed the big key to Filing. "Thought as you might want to keep this, Mr. Filing. Just in case anyone got any ideas about later going down to see whether he was waiting to be fetched."

"Best leave it 'til morning," Oscar put in. "After a whole night in the Colyton mausoleum, he should be ready to come peaceably."

All concurred, although some, Em noted, were more reluctant than others to leave Jervis stewing until morning. His attempts to gain the treasure—his attack on Jonas, then on the twins, and ultimately on her and then Jonas again—had stirred all the locals to anger, as if he'd attacked the village itself.

It felt both reassuring and uplifting to know she and her family were now included without thought among the "us" of village life.

One of the first people she sought out in the crowd was Gladys. Once Jonas's injury was pointed out, the housekeeper primmed her lips, then departed. Immediately the first furor had died, ignoring the constraint of their unfinished discussion and the consequent tension that hovered between them, Em gripped Jonas's arm. "Come into the kitchen so your shoulder can be cleaned."

He humphed, but allowed her to steer him through the door into the warm kitchen. She poked and prodded until he sat in a chair by the huge hearth, presently banked for the night. Hilda placed a basin of warm water and cloths on the table; Em wrung one out and set to work dampening his coat and shirt around the wound so he could remove both.

Eventually shirtless, Jonas sank back into the chair, squinting along the line of his shoulder at the torn flesh. Em peered, humphed, then started to gently wash the wound; despite all, he couldn't help feeling smug at her solicitousness, at the simple evidence of her caring.

He felt every gentle touch, every soothing press of her fingers against his abused flesh—felt the moment, and all it meant, all its connotations, softening his resolve, the determination he fully intended to bring to their postponed discussion.

Regardless of all else, she loved him. He knew it, could literally feel it in her touch as she patted his shoulder dry.

"Here." Hilda offered a pot of salve. "This'll help it heal."

Em dipped her fingers into the pot, then dabbed and smoothed the herbal salve over the angry flesh. Finally she set a gauze pad over the wound and bound it in place with strips of soft linen.

Just as he realized he no longer had a wearable shirt or coat, Gladys came through the back door carrying replacements for his ruined garments. Em had even thought of that.

He accepted the fresh clothes gratefully, stood and quickly donned them. Hilda and Gladys returned to the common room. He glanced at Em, caught her eye. "Thank you."

Clearing the cloths and basin, she shrugged. "It's the least I can do seeing you were wounded in my defense." She glanced at his shoulder. "Is it better?"

He shifted it, tested it. "Yes. Much less painful."

The tension of their unfinished discussion was like a wire stretched between them, taut and quivering. But now, and there, was neither the time nor the place to pursue it. He waited until she returned from the scullery, then followed her back into the fray.

Em remained supremely conscious of him; she could sense him in the same way one could sense an impending storm—a dark, forceful energy in the air, hovering close, waiting to sweep in. He was never far away as she played her role of innkeeper and circulated among the assembled crowd.

The rest of the evening passed swiftly. Although many questioned her about her ordeal, she turned aside all such queries with a smile and a lighthearted answer; her mind was much more deeply engaged with the discussion with Jonas yet to come.

Every instinct she possessed told her it would be, not just important, but critical if she were to accept him as her husband. Critical in exactly what way she didn't know, but when they finally closed the inn for the night and heard Edgar's footsteps retreating across the forecourt, she was more than ready to climb the stairs to her rooms—and have it out with the gentleman prowling at her heels.

Opening her parlor door, she led the way inside. She halted in the middle of the room, and was about to swing to face him when a large, hard palm made contact with the back of her waist and propelled her on—through the open doorway and into her bedchamber.

She stiffened, but acquiesced; the precise place in which they talked mattered very little, and she had no wish to become distracted by any physical tussle—she wanted her wits about her when they talked.

They both halted in the middle of the room. Facing him, she was grateful for the candle he'd brought in from her parlor. She waited while he set it on her dressing table; it burned brightly, casting sufficient light for them to see each other's faces clearly.

He straightened and turned to her. "Before you say anything, I want to make it clear that I don't dispute your actions in paying the ransom—I understand perfectly your reasons for doing what you did to save the twins. Of course I do." He slid his hands into his pockets, fixed his dark eyes on her face. "What I do dispute is you not discussing it with me beforehand—their disappearance, the ransom demand, and what you were planning to do."

His eyes seemed to burn as they held hers; she was sure it wasn't her imagination that made his face seem harder, the angles starker, more hard-edged.

"You *promised*. Promised to share any troubles you had, so I could help shoulder the burden. The reason I asked for that promise was simple—because you're important to me." Restlessly dragging his hands from his pockets, he hauled in a tight breath, let it out on the words, "*Not* just important— you're vital, crucial, *critical* to the rest of my life! I need you, I have to have you in my life, or it won't be worth living."

He didn't seem to know what to do with his hands; he clenched them into loose fists by his sides. "I love you. That's why I asked for your promise—that's why I needed you to honor it. But when that promise was put to the test, you broke it." His expression couldn't have been bleaker. "You didn't trust me."

"*Wait!*" She held up a hand. "Stop right there." She narrowed her eyes on his. "You think that because I didn't tell you, and seek your help to deal with Hadley, that I didn't trust you—that I didn't have faith in your love?"

His expression was shuttered, but when she waited—and waited—he gave a short, sharp—reluctant—nod.

Lowering her hand, she drew in a huge breath, let it out on an explosive "Well, you're *wrong*! The very reason I didn't tell you of the note, of the twins' disappearance, but instead left a note for you to find later, was because I *did* trust you." She glared at him. "I trusted that you *loved* me—I've grown very accustomed to how you react to any situation in which you perceive any potential danger to me." She jabbed a finger at herself, pleased to note the wary confusion that was seeping into his dark eyes.

"*Me!*" She pointed again. "That was what I felt confident about, what I felt I could place the most complete and absolute reliance and faith in—the fact you would try, and fight, and quite possibly succeed in protecting *me* at all costs! But this time, that couldn't be. This time, I had to risk myself to protect someone else—others whom I love and feel protective of—in precisely the same way *you* feel toward *me*.

"*And* incidentally, while we're on the subject of protecting those we love." She dragged in another huge breath, determined now she'd started to get the whole thorny problem into the open. "If *I* can accept, and acknowledge and embrace, the fact that you love me and therefore want to protect me, there's something you have to accept, acknowledge, and embrace in return."

His eyes were dark, fathomless pools; his face gave nothing away. "What?"

She waved her hands in the air. "That *I* love *you*! And that means *I* feel the same way about *you* as you feel about me. It means I won't stand meekly by, cowering like some helpless ninny, while some blackguard tries to harm you—that I'll act to protect you, just as you would me."

All her emotions seemed to be bubbling up and out of her. She stepped close and wagged a finger beneath his nose. "If our marriage is to work, I will not be a sleeping partner."

His lips twitched. He fought to still them, fought to hold her gaze. Failed.

She narrowed her eyes to slits. "Don't you dare laugh—that wasn't supposed to be a joke."

Jonas's smile broke free, irrepressibly. He reached for her as a rumbling laugh escaped. "I'm sorry." He drew her into his arms; she came, but stood stiffly. He wrapped his arms about her and held her close. "I . . ." He dragged in a breath, held it, fought to suppress his misplaced mirth; there was no small measure of relief mixed in with it.

If our marriage is to work. She loved him, trusted him. Regardless of all else, he'd won her.

"I understand." He did. "*But . . .*" He glanced down at her, waited until she looked up and met his eyes. "You were right." He grimaced. "I wouldn't have been easily persuaded to let you go into the mausoleum to hand the treasure to a villain—possibly wouldn't have been persuaded at all."

He felt his face harden at the thought of what she'd faced—might potentially have faced, the risk she'd knowingly courted—but he forced himself to admit, "I don't like it, not at all, but you were right, at least in going to rescue your sisters. However, I'm never, *ever* going to agree over you putting yourself at risk to save me."

She narrowed her eyes to lancing golden shards. "In that case . . . on that point we'll have to agree to disagree."

He hesitated; it took serious effort, but he forced himself to nod. "All right."

She eyed him suspiciously. "All right?" She gestured with one hand. "You don't mind that I'll act as I see fit if you're in danger?"

His lips thinned. "No. I'll mind. Every time, every minute. But if that's the price I have to pay to get you to marry me, then . . . all right. I'll manage."

Meaning he would do everything in his power to ensure she was never again placed in a position of defending or even assisting him in any dangerous situation.

From the look in her eyes, she understood that, too, but after a moment, she nodded. "Very well." The battle-ready tension thrumming through her faded. She studied his face, then, tilting her head, opened her eyes wide. "So—I believe you have a question you've been waiting to ask me?"

Her voice was soft, inviting.

The world seemed to still. He was suddenly acutely aware of the warm softness of her, supple and slender in his arms, acutely conscious of how much his life, and indeed his world, now depended and revolved about her. How precious she was to him, how vitally alive, how crucial to his future . . . and she truly was his.

The words came easily to his tongue. "Emily Colyton, will you do me the honor of becoming my wife?"

For an instant she simply held his gaze—as if all her faculties were focused on his words, on savoring them to the very last echo—then a soft smile spread across her features, bloomed in her bright eyes. "Yes, I will."

She pushed her arms up, wound them about his neck, stretched up on her toes, and touched her lips to his. "I'll marry you, Jonas Tallent—and I'll love you for the rest of my days."

He tightened his arms about her, set his lips to hers—kissed her with the same abandoned fervor with which she kissed him.

The night closed about them as, shedding clothes, they tumbled into her bed, as they dispensed with all barriers and naked came together, skin to skin, mouth to mouth, fingers linking as their bodies merged and danced to a rhythm as old as time.

As their souls touched, merged, separate yet entwined, as their heartbeats thundered and ecstasy caught them, shattered them, and broke them, then sent glory to spread through their veins.

As they clung, wrapped in each other's arms, and slowly drifted back to earth.

There was a promise embodied in such unfettered passion; as she settled her head on Jonas's undamaged shoulder and felt his arms close around her, Em thought that promise had never been so clear.

He and she stood hand in hand on the threshold of their future. Love had brought them together, welded them as one; love was now the cornerstone of their present, and the guarantee of what would come.

Love was at the heart of their world, the linchpin of their joint lives.

It was all so much more than she'd expected when she'd set her course for Colyton.

She'd been searching for treasure, and had discovered far more than she'd supposed. The treasure she'd secured for her very own was worth far more than jewels and gold.

Love had tempted; to love she'd surrendered, and now she was where she belonged.

Jonas shifted his head, pressed a kiss to her forehead.

She smiled, snuggled down, closed her eyes, and slept.

EPILOGUE

The Grange, Colyton
Four months later

Em fussed with her skirts, trying to settle the peach silk just so. She couldn't remember being so exercised on her own wedding day. Then again, on that day, now more than three months ago, she'd had so many others helping, there'd been next to nothing for her to do.

But today was Issy's wedding day, and Em was determined that everything—including the matron-of-honor's skirts—would be absolutely perfect.

The last four months, ever since she'd found the Colyton treasure, had seen many changes in her life, but those changes had all been for the better, to do with her new position as Mrs. Jonas Tallent of the Grange.

Along with Phyllida at the manor, and Jocasta at Ballyclose, she'd become the natural successor to old Lady Fortemain. She, Phyllida, and Jocasta were now bosombows; having close friends of the same status with whom to share her secrets was a boon she'd never before been granted—another part of her newfound wealth.

Her position at the Red Bells had, of necessity, changed, too, but she was still the innkeeper-manager, still oversaw the inn's workings, but from a distance. Edgar, Hilda, John Ostler, and Mary Miggins, who she'd hired as housekeeper, were now running the rejuvenated inn on a daily basis, and all was going well.

The village had swallowed her and her family up, incorporating the Colytons into the fabric of village life as if they'd never truly left; everyone seemed to think it only right that there were Colytons in Colyton once more.

Henry's studies were progressing well; they'd all agreed he'd wait until after his university years before looking for a house, but he'd already made it clear he wanted to return to Colyton, that he, too, felt most at home there.

With something akin to alacrity, the twins had made the Grange their new home; the house was large and could readily accommodate a multitude of children. Issy, too, had moved there, but from later today her home would be at the rectory, her marriage to Joshua Filing another, totally unlooked-for blessing.

The treasure itself, all the gold coins and jewels, had been converted to cash under Lucifer's careful direction, then Em herself had had to learn the ins and outs, at least the basics, of investment, something with which others in Lucifer's family, the Cynsters, had been wonderfully helpful.

There were times when, as now, she stood and looked into the cheval glass, in the large room she shared with Jonas at the Grange—not his previous bedroom but another, much larger, brighter room, one designed for a couple—and wondered at the changes in her life.

Looking at her reflection, looking into her own eyes, she could barely recall the life she'd lived before Colyton, with all its trials and tribulations, the worries and cares. She still had the occasional worry or care, but now those were always shared, and balanced by good things, exciting and uplifting things. Her life now was a far cry from that of her pre-Colyton days.

The only loose end from that earlier time was Jervis, Hadley as he'd called himself. Although a watch had been kept, and the mausoleum checked every morning for weeks, he'd never been found, never been sighted. It was ultimately decided that he'd either perished underground, or else found another way out of the cavern and disappeared for parts unknown.

Once the excitement over the treasure had died, Harold had retreated to Leicestershire, presumably to hire new household staff. Em hadn't invited him to her wedding, and Issy hadn't, either. Henry had proudly given Em away, and would do the same for Issy today, much to both sisters' satisfaction.

And then there was Jonas. Jonas, who had stood by her side throughout, who was now her husband in name as well as fact—as well as behavior, assumption, and presumption. What she felt when she thought of him could no longer be easily put into words. He was hers, her all, her everything.

Her ultimate treasure.

Along with, she hoped . . .

Turning sideways to the mirror, she smoothed the apricot silk over the slight bulge beneath her waist. The next generation, not of Colytons but Tallents, a merging of two of the oldest families in the village.

Yet another thing that seemed to be exactly as it ought.

A tap on the door preceded Jonas. He came in, his attention fixing immediately on her, his gaze traveling, openly possessive, from the top of her curls to the tips of her apricot satin slippers.

His slow smile warmed her; when his dark eyes rose to hers, love glowed in their depths. He arched a brow. "Are you ready?"

She glanced back at the mirror. "Yes." She turned to him. "Issy?"

"She's the epitome of calm impatience. She's sitting clutching her bouquet in the drawing room with Henry to keep her company. It's still too early to start for the church—the later-arriving guests would never forgive us."

"Indeed not. Some are traveling from quite a distance." The point held importance for both her and Issy; they'd both learned, by not having, to value what they now had. This was what they needed their future to hold—family, putting down new roots in the village that was theirs, growing new branches to their old family tree.

Lifting her own bouquet from the dressing table, Em smoothed the long ribbons, then turned and seized the moment to look at Jonas—to drink in the sight of him, her husband, her mate—then she smiled and went forward to join him.

His lips curved gently; he raised his brows. "What?"

She smiled up at him, let her own love show. "I was just thinking a thought I often have these days."

His brows rose higher. "Is this a thought I want to know?"

She chuckled. "I think so—I realized some time ago that the real treasure that waited for me in Colyton had nothing to do with gold and jewels."

His smile was triumphant. "I was waiting here—you came and found me."

She laughed and whirled to the door. "Indeed. I found you, I found love. I discovered I had a Tallent for loving."

He chuckled and followed her. "Talent and a Tallent—if I have any say in it, you'll have opportunity aplenty to exercise both for the rest of your life."

"I'll hold you to that," she promised. "I intend to make sure I do."

Jonas smiled and, agreeing entirely with her sentiment, let her have the last word.

The following is a preview of

The Untamed Bride

The first novel in

The Black Cobra Quartet

From *New York Times* bestselling author

STEPHANIE LAURENS

On sale in paperback

November 2009

From

Avon Books

Southampton Water, England
December 11, 1822

Del stood on the deck of the *Princess Louise*, the
twelve-hundred-ton East Indiaman on which he and his
small household had left Bombay, and watched the
Southampton docks draw steadily nearer.

The wind whipped his hair, sent chill fingers sliding
beneath his greatcoat collar. From horizon to horizon,
the sky was an unrelieved steel-gray, but at least it wasn't
raining; he was thankful for small mercies. After the
warmth of India, and the balmy days rounding Africa,
the change in temperature as they'd headed north over
the last week had been an uncomfortable reminder of the
reality of an English winter.

Artfully angled, the ship surged on the tide, aligning
with the dock, the distance between lessening with
every moment, the raucous cries of wheeling gulls a
strident counterpoint to the bellows of the bosun as he
directed the crew in the dicey business of bringing the
heavy ship alongside the timber dock.

Del scanned the dockside crowd waiting to greet those on board. He was under no illusions; the instant he stepped off the gangplank, the Black Cobra's game would be afoot again. He felt restless, impatient for action—the same compulsion he was accustomed to feeling in those moments on the battlefield when, with his horse skittish beneath him, held on a tight rein, he would wait with his men for the order to charge. The same anticipation rode him now, yet with sharpened spurs.

Contrary to his expectations, the trip had been anything but uneventful. They'd sailed from Bombay only to fall foul of a storm, which had left them limping down the African coast with one of their three masts crippled. Once they'd reached Cape Town, repairs had taken three full weeks. While there, his batman, Cobby, had ferreted out the information that Roderick Ferrar had passed through a week ahead of them, on the *Elizabeth*, a fast frigate, also bound for Southampton.

He'd taken note and so hadn't fallen victim to the knives of the two cult assassins left in Cape Town, who had subsequently joined the *Princess Louise* as crew and lain in wait for him on two separate moonless nights as they'd sailed up the west coast of Africa.

Luckily, the cultists had a superstitious aversion to firearms. Both assassins were now feeding the fishes, but Del suspected they'd merely been scouts, sent to do what they could if they could.

The Black Cobra itself lay ahead of him, coiled between him and his goal.

Wherever that proved to be.

He gripped the railing of the bridge deck, which, as a senior company officer—albeit resigned—he'd been given the freedom to frequent. He looked down at the main deck, to where his household staff—Mustaf, his general factotum, tall and thin; Amaya, Mustaf's short, rotund wife, who served as Del's housekeeper; and Alia, their niece and maid-of-all-work—sat on their piled bags, ready to disembark the instant Cobby gave the signal.

Cobby himself, the only Englishman in Del's employ, short of stature, wiry, quick and canny, and cocky as only a cockney lad could be, stood by the main railing at the point where the gangplank would be rolled out, chatting amiably with some sailors. Cobby would be first among the passengers to disembark. He would scout the immediate area, then, if all was clear, signal Mustaf to bring the women down.

Del would bring up the rear, then, once they'd assembled on the dock, lead the way directly up the High Street to the Dolphin Inn.

As luck would have it, Wolverstone had nominated the inn Del habitually used when passing through Southampton. He hadn't, however, been there for years, not since he'd set sail for India in late '15, just over seven years ago.

It felt like more.

He was quite certain he'd aged more than seven years, and the last nine months, while they'd been hunting the Black Cobra, had been the most draining. He almost felt old.

Every time he thought of James MacFarlane, he felt helpless.

Seeing more scurrying below, hearing the change in the bosun's orders, feeling the slight bump as the padding slung along the ship's side met the dock, Del shook off all thoughts of the past and determinedly fixed his mind on the immediate future.

Sailors leapt down to the dock, hauling thick ropes to the capstans to secure the ship. Hearing the heavy rattle and splash as the anchor went down, then the squealing scrape as the railing was opened and the gangplank angled out, Del headed for the companionway to the main deck.

He swung off it in time to see Cobby scamper down the gangplank.

Reconnaissance, in this instance, wasn't simply a matter of scanning for those with dark skins. Southampton was one of the busiest ports in the world, and there were countless Indians and men of other darkskinned races among the crews. But Cobby knew what to look for—the furtiveness, the attention locked on Del while attempting to remain inconspicuous. If there were cultists waiting to strike, Del was confident Cobby would spot them.

Yet it was more likely the cultists would watch and wait—they preferred to strike in less populated surrounds where escape after the event was more assured.

Del strolled to stand with Mustaf, Amaya and Alia. Mustaf nodded, then went back to scanning the crowd; he'd been a sowar—a cavalryman—until a knee injury had seen him pensioned off. The knee didn't discompose him in other ways; he was still a good man in a fight.

Alia bobbed her head, then resumed casting shy glances at the young sailors who rushed back and forth along the deck.

Amaya looked up at Del with liquid brown eyes. "It is very very cold here, Colonel-sahib. Colder than my cousin's house in Simla in the winter. I am being very very glad I was buying these shawls from Kashmir. They are just the thing."

Del smiled. Both Amaya and Alia were well wrapped in the thick woollen shawls. "When we stop at a big town, we'll have to get you some English coats. And gloves, too. They'll help keep out the wind."

"*Ai*, yes—the wind, it is like a knife. I am understanding that saying now." Amaya nodded, plump hands folded in her lap, thin gold bangles on her wrists peeking from beneath the edge of one shawl.

Despite her sweet face and matronly disposition, Amaya was quick-witted and observant. As for Alia, she would instantly obey any order from her uncle, aunt, Del or Cobby. When necessary, the small group operated as a unit; Del wasn't overly worried over having Amaya and Alia with them, even on the upcoming, more dangerous leg of their journey.

Regardless, knowing the Black Cobra cultists' vindictiveness, he wouldn't take the chance of leaving the women anywhere, even with Mustaf to guard them. To strike at him, the Black Cobra was perfectly capable of wiping out his household, simply to inspire fear and demonstrate his power.

Human life had long ago lost all meaning for the Black Cobra.

A shrill whistle pulled Del's attention back to the dock. Cobby caught his eye, snapped a jaunty salute. *All clear.*

"Come." Del took Amaya's arm and helped her to her feet. "Let's go down and head for our inn."

Cobby had commandeered a man with a wooden cart. Del waited with the women while their luggage was ferried down the gangplank and loaded in the cart, then he set off, leading the way off the dock and straight up High Street. The Dolphin wasn't far; Mustaf followed with the women close behind, with Cobby bringing up the rear, ambling alongside the carter, eyes constantly shifting this way and that as he chatted.

As Del walked up the street, he found his gaze drawn downward—to the cobbles that covered the ground, to the first steps he was taking on English soil after so many years away.

He wasn't sure what he felt. An odd sense of peace, perhaps because he knew this time his travels were over, a sense of anticipation over what his new and as yet unstructured future might hold, all tinged with a healthy dose of apprehension over what lay between this moment and being able to get started on shaping his new life.

Their mission to bring the Black Cobra to justice.

He was in it now. There was no going back, only

forward. Ahead, through whatever fire the opposition might send his way.

Raising his head, he filled his lungs, looked about. It felt exactly like the moment after the charge began.

The Dolphin was a town landmark. It had stood for centuries and been refurbished several times; it currently sported two wide bow windows fronting the street, the solid front door in between.

Del glanced back along the street. He couldn't see any likely cultists, but there were plenty of people, carts and the odd carriage thronging the cobbled thoroughfare—plenty of cover for anyone watching.

They would be watching.

Reaching the inn, he opened the door and went inside.

Securing suitable rooms was no difficulty; his years in India had left him very wealthy and he wasn't of a mind to stint either himself or his small household. The innkeeper, Bowden, a solidly built ex-sailor, responded appropriately, cheerily welcoming him to the town and summoning lads to help with the luggage as the others joined Del in the foyer.

With the rooms organized and their bags dispatched, and the women, Mustaf and Cobby following the luggage up the stairs, Bowden turned to Del. "Just remembered. I've two letters waiting for you."

Del turned back to the counter, brows rising.

Reaching beneath it, Bowden produced two missives. "The first—this one—came on the mail coach nearly four weeks ago. The other was left last evening by a gentleman. He and another gentleman have looked in every day for the last week or so, asking after you."

Wolverstone's escorts. "Thank you." Del accepted the letters. It was midafternoon, and the inn's public rooms were quiet. He sent an easy smile Bowden's way. "If anyone should ask for me, I'll be in the tap."

"Of course, sir. Nice and quiet it is in there at present. Just ring the bell on the bar if you need anything."

With a nod, Del sauntered into the dining room and through an archway into the tap, a cozy room toward the back of the inn. There were a few patrons, all older men, gathered about small tables. He went to a table in the corner where the light from the rear window would allow him to read.

Sitting, he examined the two missives, then opened the one from the mystery gentleman.

The lines within were few and to the point, informing him that Tony Blake, Viscount Torrington, and Gervase Tregarth, Earl of Crowhurst, were holding themselves ready to escort him further on his mission. They were quartered nearby and would continue to call at the inn every evening to check for his arrival.

Reassured that he would be moving forward, in action again soon, he refolded the letter, tucked it inside his coat, then, mildly intrigued, opened the second missive. He'd recognized the handwriting, and he assumed his aunts had written to welcome him home, and to ask and be reassured that he was, indeed, heading up to Humberside, to the house at Middleton on the Wolds. He'd inherited it from his father, and it remained their home.

As he unfolded the two pages, crossed and recrossed in his elder aunt's spidery script, he was already composing his reply—a brief note to let them know that he had landed and was on his way north, but that business dealings on the way might delay him for a week or so.

Reading his aunt's salutation, followed by an enthusiastic, even effusive, welcome, he smiled and read on.

He wasn't smiling by the time he reached the end of the first page. Laying it aside, he deciphered the rest, then tossed the second sheet on the first and quietly, but comprehensively, swore.

After staring at the sheets for several minutes, he gathered them up, rose and, stuffing the sheets in his pocket, made his way back to the inn's foyer.

Bowden heard his footsteps and came out from his office behind the counter. "Yes, Colonel?"

"I understand a young lady, a Miss Duncannon, was due to arrive here some weeks ago?"

Bowden smiled brightly. "Yes, indeed, sir. I'd forgotten—she asked after you, too."

"Indeed. I take it she's left and headed north?"

"Oh, no, sir. Her ship was delayed, too. She didn't get in until last week. Quite relieved, she was, to learn you'd been delayed, too. She's still here, waiting on your arrival."

"Ah. I see." Del suppressed a grimace and started making plans. "Perhaps if you could send word to her room that I've arrived, and would appreciate a moment of her time?"

Bowden shook his head. "No use at present—she's

out, and she's taken her maid with her. But I can tell her as soon as she comes in."

Del nodded. "Thank you." He hesitated, then asked, "Is there a private parlor I might hire?" Somewhere where he and his unexpected burden could discuss her onward journey.

"I'm sorry, sir, but all our parlors are presently taken." Bowden paused, then said, "But it's Miss Duncannon herself as has the front parlor—perhaps, seeing she's waiting to see you, you might wait for her in there?"

"An excellent notion," Del responded dryly. "And I'll need to hire a carriage."

But again Bowden shook his head. "I'd like to oblige, Colonel, but this close to Christmas all our carriages are spoken for. Miss Duncannon herself took the last of our post chaises."

"Fortuitous," Del murmured. "I was wanting the carriage for her."

"Well, then," Bowden grinned, "all's well."

"Indeed." Del pointed to the room to the right of the foyer. "The front parlor?"

"Aye, sir. Go right in."

Del did, shutting the door behind him.

With white plaster walls and heavy timber beams crossing the ceiling, the parlor was neither overlarge nor cramped, and boasted one of the wide bow windows looking out on the street. The furniture was heavy, but comfortable, the pair of chintz-covered armchairs well-supplied with plump cushions. A well-polished round table with four chairs stood in the middle of the room, a large lamp at its center, while a crackling fire sparked and flared in the grate, throwing welcome heat into the room.

Gravitating toward the hearth, Del noticed the three watercolors above the mantelpiece. They were landscapes depicting green pastures and meadows, lush fields and richly canopied trees beneath pastel blue skies with fluffy white clouds. The one in the middle, of rolling heathland, a vibrant patchwork of greens, caught his eye. He hadn't laid eyes on such landscapes for seven long years; it seemed odd to gain his first sense of home via pictures on a wall.

Glancing down, he drew out the letter from his aunts; standing before the fire, he scanned it anew, searching for some insight into why the devil they'd thought to saddle him with the duty of escorting a young gentlewoman, daughter of a neighboring landowner, home to Humberside.

His best guess was that his doting aunts had some idea of playing matchmaker.

They were going to be disappointed. There was no place for a young lady in his train, not while he was a decoy for the Black Cobra.

He'd been disappointed when he'd opened the scroll he'd selected and discovered he hadn't picked the original letter. Nevertheless, as Wolverstone had made clear, the missions of the three decoys would be vital in drawing out the Black Cobra's men, and ultimately the Black Cobra himself.

They needed to lure him into striking, and for that

they needed to reduce his cultists sufficiently to force him to act in person.

Not an easy task, yet by any reasonable estimation it should be within their collective ability. As a decoy, his role would be to deliberately make himself a target, and he didn't want any extraneous young lady hanging on his arm while he was so engaged.

A tap on the door had him hesitating, then he called, "Come."

It was Cobby.

"Thought you'd want to know." Hand on the knob, his batman hovered by the door he'd closed. "I ducked back down the docks and asked around. Ferrar arrived over a week ago. Interesting thing is he had no bevy of natives with him—seems there was no room left on the frigate for more than him and his man."

Del raised his brows. "Definitely interesting, but no doubt he'll have had cultists coming in on other ships."

Cobby nodded. "So you'd think. But it does mean he won't necessarily have all that many just at present. Might have to resort to doing his own dirty work." Cobby grinned malevolently. "Now wouldn't that be a shame?"

Del smiled. "We can but hope."

He nodded a dismissal and Cobby left, closing the door behind him.

Del glanced at the clock ticking on a sideboard. It was already after three, and what daylight there was would soon fade. He fell to pacing slowly before the fire, rehearsing suitable words with which to break the news to Miss Duncannon that, contrary to his aunts' arrangements, she would be heading north alone.

I t was well after four o'clock, and he'd grown increasingly impatient, before a feminine voice in the foyer, well modulated yet with an unmistakably haughty tone, heralded the return of Miss Duncannon.

Even as Del focused on the parlor door, the knob turned and the door swung inward. Bowden held it open to permit a lady—not so young, juggling a plethora of bandboxes and packages and dressed in a garnet red pelisse, with her dark auburn hair swept up and tucked under a jaunty hat—to enter.

She swept in, her face alight, a smile curving lush red lips, as Bowden hurriedly said, "I believe this is the gentleman you've been waiting for, miss."

Miss Duncannon abruptly halted. Animation leaching from her face, she looked across the room and saw him. After a moment, her gaze slowly meandered upward, until it reached his face.

Then she simply stared.

Clearing his throat, Bowden retreated, closing the door behind her. She blinked, stared again, then baldly asked, "*You're* Colonel Delborough?"

Del bit his tongue against an impulse to respond, "You're *Miss* Duncannon?" Just one look, and his vision of a biddable young miss had evaporated; the lady was in her late twenties if she was a day.

And given the vision filling his eyes, why she was still a miss was beyond his comprehension.

She was . . . *lush* was the word that sprang to his mind. Taller than the average, she was built on stately, even queenly, lines, ripely curvaceous in all the right places. Even from across the room, he could tell her eyes were green; large, faintly slanting up at the outer corners, they were vibrantly alive, awake and aware, alert to all that went on around her.

Her features were elegant, refined, her lips full and ripe, elementally tempting, but the firmness of her chin suggested determination, backbone and a forthrightness beyond the norm.

Duly noting that last, he bowed. "Indeed—Colonel Derek Delborough." *Sadly, not at your service.* Quashing the wayward thought, he smoothly continued, "I believe your parents made some arrangement with my aunts for me to act as escort on your journey north. Sadly, that's not possible—I have business to attend to before I can return to Humberside."

Deliah Duncannon blinked, dragged her senses from their preoccupation with shoulders and a wide chest that should by all rights have been encased in a uniform, replayed his words, then abruptly shook her head. "No."

Moving further into the room, she set her boxes and bags on the table, distractedly wondering whether a uniform would have increased his impact, or lessened it. There was something anomalous in his appearance, as if the elegant civilian garb was a disguise. If the intention had been to screen his innately vigorous, even dangerous, physique, the ploy had failed miserably.

Freeing her hands, she reached up to extract the long pin securing her hat. "I'm afraid, Colonel Delborough, that I must insist. I've been waiting for the better part of a week for you to arrive, and I really cannot journey on without a suitable escort." Setting her hat on the table, she swung to face the recalcitrant ex-colonel—significantly younger and immeasurably more virile than she'd envisioned him. Than she'd been led to expect. "It's quite unthinkable."

Regardless of his age, his virility, or his propensity to argue, for her, it was, but the last thing she intended to do was explain.

His lips—mobile and distractingly masculine—firmed. "Miss Duncannon—"

"I expect you're imagining that it will simply be a matter of bundling me into a carriage with my maid and household, and pointing north." Pausing in the act of removing her leather gloves, she glanced at him and caught a telltale twist of those disturbing lips; that had, indeed, been precisely what he'd planned. "I have to inform you that that's very definitely not the case."

Dropping her gloves on the table behind her, she lifted her chin and faced him squarely—staring down her nose as well as she could given he was more than half a head taller than she. "I must insist, sir, that you honor the obligation."

His lips were now a thin line—one she wanted to see relax and curve into a smile. . . . What was the matter with her? Her pulse thrummed in her throat, her skin prickled with unexpected awareness and he was still a good six feet away.

"Miss Duncannon, while regrettably my aunts overstepped their authority in seeking to oblige a neighbor, I would, in normal circumstances, do all in my power to, as you phrase it, honor the commitment they made. However, in this instance, it is entirely—"

"Colonel Delborough." She hauled her gaze from his lips and for the first time met his gaze directly, deliberately locking her eyes on his. "Permit me to inform you that there is no reason you could advance, none whatever, that will induce me to excuse you from escorting me north."

His eyes were dark brown, richly hued, unexpectedly intriguing, fringed with the longest, thickest lashes she'd ever seen. Those lashes were the same color as his burnished, lightly waving hair—a sable more black than brown.

"I regret, Miss Duncannon, that that is utterly impossible."

When she set her chin, retreating not an inch but keeping her gaze meshed unwaveringly with his, Del hesitated, then, far more aware than he wished to be of her sinfully sensual mouth, stiffly added, "I'm presently on a mission, one vital to the country, and must see it to its conclusion before I'll be free to indulge my aunts' wishes."

She frowned. "But you've resigned your commission." Her gaze slid to his shoulders, as if confirming the absence of epaulettes.

"My mission is civilian rather than military."

Her finely arched brows rose. Her gaze returning to his face, she considered him for an instant, then, in a deceptively mild—sarcastically challenging—tone, said, "So what do you suggest, sir? That I wait here, at your convenience, until you *are* free to escort me north?"

"No." He struggled not to clench his teeth; his jaw was already tight. "I would respectfully suggest that, in the circumstances, and at this present season with much less traffic on the highways, it would be perfectly acceptable for you to head north with your maid—and I believe you mentioned a household? As you've already ordered a carriage—"

Her green eyes flashed. "With all due respect, Colonel, you are talking through your hat!" Belligerent, determined, she stepped forward, face tipping up as if she intended to go nose-to-nose with him. "The notion of me traveling north, in this season or any other, with no suitable gentleman arranged and accepted by my parents as escort, is quite simply ineligible. Unacceptable. Absolutely 'not done.'"

She'd come so close that a wave of tempting warmth slid over the front of him, cascading down to heat his groin. So long had it been since he'd experienced such an explicit reaction that he was, for just an instant, distracted enough to simply stand and enjoy it, drink it in. . . .

Her gaze abruptly shifted to his left. She was tall enough to see over his shoulder. He saw her focus, saw her gorgeous jade-green eyes widen—then flare.

"Good God!"

She seized his lapels and dragged him, hauled him, tumbled him down to the floor.

For one crazed instant, his brain interpreted her actions as lust gone wild—then the reverberating explosion and the tinkle of shattered glass raining down upon them jerked his wits back to reality.

She had never left it. Trapped half beneath him, she wriggled and squirmed to get free, her horrified gaze locked on the shattered pane.

Slamming a mental door on the effect of her curvaceous form bucking beneath him, he gritted his teeth and pushed back to his knees. After a quick glance out of the window at the stunned crowd milling in the darkened street, he got to his feet and was assisting her to hers when the door slammed open.

Mustaf stood in the doorway, saber in his hand. Cobby stood beside him, a cocked pistol in his. Beyond them towered another Indian, swarthy and tall—Del stiffened instinctively. He started to step in front of Miss Duncannon, only to have her hand on his arm hold him back.

"I'm quite all right, Kumulay." Her small, warm hand still resting on Del's bicep, she looked up at him. "It wasn't me the man was trying to kill."

Del met her eyes. They were still wide, her pupils dilated, but she was utterly in control.

A hundred thoughts churned through his head. Every instinct screamed "*Chase!*" but this time that wasn't his role. He looked back at Cobby, who had lowered his gun. "Get ready to leave immediately."

Cobby nodded. "I'll get the others." He and Mustaf drew back.

The other man—Kumulay—remained in the open doorway, his impassive gaze locked on his mistress.

Del glanced at her. Met the green shards trained on his face.

"You are *not* leaving without me." Each word was carefully enunciated.

He hesitated, giving his mind one more chance to come up with an alternative, then, jaw set, nodded. "Very well. Be ready to leave within the hour."

Finally!" More than two hours later, Del shut the door of the post chaise Miss Duncannon had been farsighted enough to hire, and dropped onto the seat beside his unlooked-for charge.

Her maid, Bess, an Englishwoman, sat in the corner on her other side. Along the seat opposite, in a colorful array of saris and woollen shawls, sat Amaya, Alia and another older Indian woman and two young girls, the latter three all members of Miss Duncannon's household.

Why she had a largely Indian household he had yet to learn.

The carriage rocked into motion, rolling ponderously up the High Street. As the vehicle tacked around Bargate, then headed on toward the London road, Del wondered, not for the first time over the last two and more hours, what had possessed him to agree to Miss Duncannon's traveling on with him.

Unfortunately, he knew the answer, and it was one that left him with no other possible course. She'd seen the man who'd shot at him—which meant the man had almost certainly seen her.

Given the fact that cultists rarely, if ever, used fire-arms, that man was most likely Larkins, Ferrar's gentleman's gentleman and his master's most trusted aide, or Ferrar himself. Del's money was on Larkins.

Although Cobby had questioned all those who'd been standing in the street, still stunned and exclaiming over the shooting, no one had seen the man with the gun well enough to describe, let alone identify, him. All they'd learned was that, as expected, he'd been fair-skinned.

That the Black Cobra had struck so immediately and decisively had been a surprise, but on reflection, had he been in Ferrar's shoes, Del might have mounted a simi-lar preemptive gambit. If he'd been killed, the ensuing chaos might have proved sufficient for Ferrar to gain access to his room and baggage, and the scroll-holder. It wouldn't have played out that way, but Ferrar didn't know that. Regardless, Del was perfectly sure that if it hadn't been for Miss Duncannon's quick thinking— and actions—he would very likely be dead.

It was nearing seven o'clock. The night was dark, the moon cocooned in thick clouds. The carriage lamps beamed through the chill darkness as the four horses reached the macadam of the highway and lengthened their stride.

Del thought of the rest of their combined households, traveling with the bulk of their luggage in two open wagons, all Cobby had been able to hire at such short notice.

At least they were away, on the move.

And they knew that Larkins, and presumably therefore Ferrar, were close, and chasing him. The enemy had broken cover and engaged.

"I can't understand," Deliah said, "why you insisted nothing be said to the authorities." She spoke quietly, her voice sliding beneath the repetitive thud of the horses' hooves; she had no wish to communicate her dissatisfaction to anyone other than the man beside her. "Bowden said you paid for the windowpane but insisted nothing more be made of the incident." She waited an instant, then demanded, "Why?"

She didn't turn to look at him. The interior of the carriage was a sea of shifting shadows; she couldn't see well enough to read anything from his face—and she'd already realized that only showed what he wanted it to.

Silence stretched, but she waited.

Eventually, he murmured, "The attack was linked to my mission. Can you describe the man with the pistol? It would help."

The vision she'd seen through the window was etched in her mind. "He was somewhat above average height, wearing a dark coat—nothing all that fashionable, but decent quality. He had on a dark hat, but I could see his hair was close-cropped. Beyond that . . . I really didn't have time to note every detail." She let a moment tick past, then asked, "Do you know who he was?"

"He sounds like one of the men linked with my mission."

"Your 'mission,' whatever it might be, doesn't explain why you refused to alert the authorities to the action of a felon—any more than it explains why we're racing away in the dead of night, as if we'd taken fright." She didn't know much about Colonel Derek Delborough, but he didn't seem the sort to cut and run.

He answered in a bored, superior tone. "It was the right thing to do."

"Humph." She frowned, disinclined to let him stop talking. His voice was deep, assured, his accents—those of a man accustomed to command—strangely soothing, and after the excitement of the shooting, she was still on edge. Her nerves were still jangling. She grimaced. "Even if you didn't want to draw attention to yourself, you might at least—"

Del transferred his gaze to the unrelieved darkness outside. He'd glanced at her, seen her grimace, seen her lips pout . . . and felt a nearly overwhelming urge to shut her up.

By sealing those pouting lips with his.

And finding out how soft they were, and what she tasted like.

Tart, or sweet? Or both?

Quite aside from the audience lined up on the opposite seat, he felt reasonably certain any such action would result in him receiving at least one boxed ear. Probably two. Yet having her sitting beside him, her hip less than an inch from his, her shoulder lightly brushing his arm with every rocking motion of the carriage, the warmth of her bathing his side, was a temptation to which his body was shamelessly responding.

The search for the Black Cobra had consumed him for months; he hadn't spared the time to dally with any woman—and it had been far longer since he'd been with an Englishwoman, and never with a termagant of Miss Duncannon's ilk.

None of which explained why he was suddenly so attracted to a harridan with lips for which the most experienced courtesans would trade their souls.

He blotted out her voice, her insistent, persistent prodding, focused instead on the heavy rhythm of the horses' hooves. Leaving Southampton with all speed had been what he'd had to do, no matter how much it had gone against his grain. If he'd been carrying the original letter, then the necessity of keeping it out of Ferrar's clutches would have trumped any inclination to give chase.

If he'd stood and fought—tried to hunt down Larkins, even dallied to set the Watch on Ferrar's trail—Ferrar would have guessed that he wasn't all that concerned with the contents of the scroll-holder he carried. And then Ferrar would have shifted his attention, and that of his cultists, from Del to one of the others.

Were the others ahead of him, or were they yet to land in England?

With luck Torrington and Crowhurst would know. He'd left a short note for them with Bowden.

Given the hour, and the falling temperatures, and that more than half their number were traveling exposed, they couldn't go far. For tonight, Winchester was his goal.

He prayed he'd be able to resist the impulses provoked by the feminine muttering from beside him long enough for them to reach it.

The Swan Inn in Southgate Street proved sufficient for their needs.

Miss Duncannon predictably grumbled when he refused to stop at the larger Pelican Hotel. "There's so many of us to accommodate—they're more likely to have room."

"The Pelican is largely timber and lathe."

"So?"

"I have an unreasoning fear of waking to a house in flames." The Black Cobra's men had been known to use fire to flush out those they were chasing, without the slightest thought for any others who might get caught in the ensuing blaze. Climbing out of the carriage in the yard of the Swan, Del considered the inn, then turned to hand his burden down. "The Swan, however, is built of stone."

Taking his hand, she stepped down, paused to look at the inn, then, expressionless, looked at him. "Stone walls in winter."

He glanced up at the roof, where multiple chimneys chuffed smoke. "Fires."

She sniffed, lifted her skirts, climbed the steps to the porch and led the way through the door the innkeeper was holding wide, bobbing and bowing as they passed.

Before Del could take charge, she did, sweeping to the inn's counter and stripping off her gloves. "Good evening." The innkeeper scurried around the counter to attend her. "We need rooms for us all—one large chamber for me, another for the colonel, four smaller rooms for my staff and two more for his staff, and the colonel's parlor maid can room with my lady's maid—that's wiser, I think. Now, we'll all want dinner—I know it's late, but—"

Del halted just behind her—she knew he was there—and listened to her rattle off orders, directions and instructions, more or less without pause. He could have stepped in and taken over—he'd intended to—but as she was making such an excellent fist of organizing their combined party, there seemed little point.

By the time the luggage had been unloaded and ferried inside, the innkeeper had sorted out their rooms, arranged for a private parlor to be prepared for them, and sent orders to the kitchen for their meals. Del stood back and watched a round-eyed maid lead his charge upstairs to her chamber, then he turned to the innkeeper. "I need to hire two more carriages."

"Of course, sir. Dreadfully cold already, and they say there's worse to come. I don't have any carriages free myself, but I know the stableman at the Pelican—he'll oblige me, and I'm sure he'll have two he can let you have."

Del raised his eyes to the top of the stairs—and met Miss Duncannon's direct green gaze. She said nothing, however, but with a faint lift of her brows, continued on into the gallery. "Thank you." Returning his gaze to the innkeeper, he arranged for the members of his household and hers to be given whatever they wished from the tap, then left the now deserted foyer to climb the stairs to his room.

Half an hour later, washed and brushed, he was in the private parlor when Miss Duncannon entered. Two maids had just finished setting a small table for two before the fire; they retreated with bobbed curtsies. Del strolled to hold a chair for his charge.

She'd removed her pelisse, revealing a garnet-red gown trimmed with silk ribbon of the same hue, over which she'd draped a finely patterned silk shawl.

Sitting, she inclined her head. "Thank you, Colonel."

Strolling to his chair on the other side of the table, Del murmured, "Del." When she raised her brows, he explained, "Most people I know call me Del."

"I see." She considered him as he sat and shook out his napkin. "As we're apparently to be in each other's company for some time, it would be appropriate, I suppose, to make you free of my name. It's Deliah—*not* Delilah. Deliah."

He smiled, inclined his head. "Deliah."

Deliah struggled not to stare, struggled to keep her suddenly witless mind functioning. That was the first time he'd smiled at her—and she definitely didn't need the additional distraction. He was ridiculously handsome when serious and sober; when his lips softened and curved, he was seduction personified.

She, better than anyone, knew how dangerous such men were—especially to her.

The door opened and the maids reappeared, ferrying a soup tureen and a basket of bread.

She nodded her approval and the maids served. Deliah eyed the soup with something akin to gratitude, inwardly congratulating herself for having ordered it. One didn't need to converse while consuming soup. That would give her just a little more time to whip her unruly senses into line.

"Thank you." With a nod for the retreating maids, she picked up her spoon and supped.

He reached for the bread basket, offered it.

"No, thank you."

He smiled again—damn him!—and helped himself; she looked down at her soup and kept her gaze on her plate.

It had taken her all of the short journey, and most of the half hour she'd spent out of his sight, to untangle the skein of emotions besetting her. She'd initially attributed her skittering nerves and breathless state to the shock of finding herself looking down the barrel of a pistol, even if the gun hadn't been pointed at her.

The shot, the subsequent flurry, the rush to leave, the

unexpected journey during which he'd remained stubbornly uncommunicative over his mysterious mission—the mission that had led to him being shot at—were all circumstances that might naturally be considered to have contributed to her overwrought state.

Except she'd never been the sort to allow circumstances—no matter how dire or unexpected—to overset her.

In the quiet of her chamber, she'd finally unravelled her feelings sufficiently to lay the truth bare—it had been that moment when she'd found herself on the wooden floor with his hard body covering hers that was the root of her problem. The source of her skittishness.

If she thought of it, she could still feel the sensations—of his weight pinning her, hard muscles and heavy bones trapping her beneath him, his long legs tangling with hers, his heat—then the searing instant of . . . whatever it had been that had afflicted her. Hot, intense, enough to make her squirm.

Enough to make her treacherous body yearn.

But she didn't think he knew. She glanced at him as he laid down his spoon.

He caught her eye. "I should thank you for taking charge of the domestic organization."

She shrugged. "I'm accustomed to managing my uncle's household. It's what I've been doing in my years away."

"Jamaica, I believe my aunt wrote. What took you there?"

Setting down her spoon, she leaned her elbows on the table, lacing her fingers and viewing him over them. "Originally I went out to visit my uncle, Sir Harold Duncannon. He's the chief magistrate of Jamaica. I found the climate and the colony to my liking, so I stayed. As time passed, I took charge of his household."

"Your servants are Indian—are there many Indians in Jamaica?"

"These days, yes. After the slave ships stopped, many Indian and Chinese workers were brought in. All my staff were originally with my uncle's household, but over the years became more mine than his, so I gave them the choice of staying in Jamaica or coming to England with me."

"And they chose England." Del broke off as the maids reappeared. While they cleared the first course and laid out platters of succulent roast beef, roast potatoes and pumpkin, ham and a jug of rich gravy, he had time to consider what her staff's loyalty said of Miss Deliah— *not* Delilah—Duncannon.

"Thank you." She nodded graciously to the maids, and they departed. Before he could frame his next question, she fixed her gaze on him. "You, I gather, have been with the East India Company for some time."

He nodded, picking up the serving fork. "I've been in India for the past seven years. Before that, it was Waterloo, and before that, the Peninsula."

"Quite a lengthy service—am I to take it you're retiring permanently?"

"Yes." They served themselves and settled to eat.

Five minutes passed, then she said, "Tell me about India. Was the campaigning there the same as in Europe? Massed battles, army against army?"

"At first." When he glanced up and saw her plainly waiting for more, he elaborated, "Over the first years I was there, we were extending territory—annexing areas for trade, as the company describes it. More or less routine campaigning. Later, however, it became more a case of . . . I suppose you could say keeping the peace. Keeping the unruly elements in check to protect the trade routes—that sort of thing. Not really campaigning, no battles as such."

"And this mission of yours?"

"Is something that grew out of the peacekeeping, as it were."

"Being something more civilian than military?"

He held her gaze. "Indeed."

"I see. And will pursuing your mission necessitate you leaving me behind at some point well south of Humberside?"

He sat back. "No."

She arched her brows. "You seem to have experienced a quite dramatic change of heart regarding my presence consequent on you being shot at. I'm not sure I see the connection."

"Regardless, you see me resigned to your company— I'm waiting on confirmation of our exact route, but I believe we'll need to spend a few days, perhaps a week, in London."

"London?"

He'd hoped she'd be distracted with thoughts of shopping—she had been out of the country for years, after all—but from the calculation in her eyes, he could tell she was trying to see what going to London told her of his mission.

"Incidentally," he said, "why Jamaica?"

After a moment, she shrugged. "I was in need of new horizons and the connection was there."

"How long ago did you leave England?"

"In '15. As a colonel, were you in charge of a . . . what? Squadron of men?"

"No." Again she waited, open curiosity coloring her eyes and her expression, until he added, "In India, I commanded a group of elite officers, each of whom could take command of company troops and deal with the constant small insurrections and disturbances that are always blowing up in the subcontinent. But tell me, was there much of a social circle in . . . Kingston, isn't it?"

She nodded. "Yes, Kingston. And yes, there was the usual social circle of expatriates, much like any colony, I expect. How was India in that regard?"

"I was stationed mostly in Calcutta—the company headquarters are there. There were always balls and parties in the so-called season, but not so much of the matchmaking one finds at Almack's and the like."

"Indeed? I would have thought—"

They continued to trade question and answer as they progressed through the courses. Del tried to ascertain why she'd felt the need for "new horizons" while avoiding falling into the conversational pits she dug and revealing more than she needed to know about his mission.

He might have to take her with him to ensure her safety, but he intended to do all in his power to keep her ignorant and entirely separate from his mission, and as far as possible out of the Black Cobra's sight.

It was only after they'd risen from the table and together walked out of the parlor and up the stairs that he realized he'd spent an entire evening alone with an unmarried lady, doing nothing more than talking, and he hadn't even thought of being bored.

Which he usually was. Thus far in his life, women, even ladies, had fulfilled one and only one role; he'd had very little interest in them outside that sphere. Yet although he'd focused on Deliah's luscious lips far too often for his comfort, he'd been too engaged in their mutual interrogation—her quick wits had ensured he'd had to keep his own about him—to dwell on her sexual potential, much less act on an attraction that, he was surprised to discover, had not just survived the last hours but had, if anything, grown.

She paused outside the door of the chamber next to his and glanced up at him. Her lips curved lightly—a genuine smile tinged with a hint of appreciation and a soupçon of challenge. "Good night . . . Del."

He forced his lips into an easy smile. Inclined his head. "Deliah."

Her smile fractionally deepened, but her tone was entirely innocent when she added, "Sleep well."

Del stood in the shadowed corridor and watched the chamber door close behind her, then he slowly walked the few paces to his own, reasonably certain that her last wish was very unlikely to be granted.

HAVE YOU EVER WONDERED . . .

Where do Amanda and Amelia Cynster
fit on the Cynster family tree?

In which book did Demon Cynster first appear?

How did the Bastion Club begin?

**These questions—and many,
many more—are answered in**

THE WORLD OF
STEPHANIE LAURENS

Discover, at your fingertips, the information you want to know—
need to know—about the Bar Cynster and the Bastion Club,
including original material by Stephanie Laurens.

To view and download go to www.avonromance.com
or www.stephanielaurens.com

Once you enter the World of Stephanie Laurens
you'll never want to leave!

Wm WILLIAM MORROW

AVON

Imprints of HarperCollinsPublishers
www.harpercollins.com

ALL BOOKS ARE AVAILABLE FROM AVON BOOKS

LAUW 0509